THE BIRMINGHAM QUEAN

S.A.M. Trainor's

THE BIRMINGHAM QUEAN

by
Amrit Singh

restored, edited and annotated, with a bibliographic index,
by
Sam Trainor

Calé, P.O. Box 15737, Birmingham B13 3JS, UK

This edition published by Calé 2010

Copyright © Samuel Trainor 2006

Samuel Trainor asserts the moral right to
be identified as the author of this work

A catalogue record for this title is available from the British Library

ISBN 978-0-9538328-2-8

This is a work of fiction. Any references to real people, events, establishments, organizations or places are intended to give the fiction an ironic sense of authenticity. Other names, characters and incidents are either the product of the author's imagination or used fictitiously. Where a character shares a name with a real person, living or dead, it should be assumed that the character and the real person share nothing but a name; it is particularly to be stressed that this is the case for the name 'Sam Trainor'.

There are numerous parodies, pastiches, *détournements* and textual reproductions contained within this novel. A full source record for every quotation, paraphrase and conscious influence is provided in the Bibliographical Index on pages 553–580.

for all those who imagine
at some point in their lives

that they might never reach the end

Birmingham's what I think with.

It wasn't made for that sort of job,
but it's what they gave me.

    Roy Fisher 'Six Texts For a Film':
      '1. Talking to Cameras'
        (from *Birmingham River*, OUP 1994)

Acknowledgements

> Bruno Combertus *the High and Mightie Emperour of* Aethiopia, *and* Quoba Condona Pheodorwich *the puissant King of the large Territories of the invincible and invisible* Utopia, *it is said, that they are both in our Narrow Seas with a thousand shippes, gallies, sloopes, and other Vessels for the War, they have brought two thousand Tunnes of Gold, Silver, pretious stones, and some Hangings, they are come to aid us against the Rebels that obey the King, they have brought five thousand Pieces of wooden Ordnance, powder more than can be counted, or to be spoken of, and shot beyond reckoning, with all other necessaries for War or Peace, they were feasted bravely aboord our Admirall; and they will be ready to give Battail at* Brumingham, *as soon as ever the waters are high enough to bring the shippes thither.*
>
> (John Taylor [1643] *A preter-plvperfect spick and span new nocturnall, or Mercuries weekly night-newes wherein the publique faith is published and the banquet of Oxford mice described* [Thomason Collection, British Library; EEBO 1641-1700; 239:E.65, no. 1], p. 11)

Joking aside, a book like this writes itself. My involvement has been less a matter of invention than a heavy pregnancy culminating in a protracted labour. The metaphor is tired, almost postnatally so, but it's still fertile. We probably shouldn't think like this, but childbearing is a kind of metabolic civil war: a struggle for resources between mother and infant, even to the point at which the child siezes control of the adult's patterns of desire. A project of this sort is just the same. It swells inside the writer, oblivious to his hopes and fears for its future life: growing heavier by the day, craving strange nourishment, (the computer its placenta), until it forces its way out...

Fortunately, I haven't wanted for help. The project was originally undertaken as a doctoral thesis with the generous financial aid of a University of Glasgow 2001 Scholarship, for which I am very grateful. Where academic assistance is concerned, I should thank my PhD supervisors, Willy Maley and Adam Piette, for their unerring patience and wit, their faith and acuity. As a whole, Glasgow's Department of English Literature has provided quite undeserved levels of encouragement. All have offered kind and useful words, but special mention (for direct input) should go to Alex Benchimol, Richard Cronin, Bob Cummings, Rob Maslen, David Pascoe and particularly John Coyle. My thanks (and, in some cases, my apologies) go to those from elsewhere who have provided similar advice, reassurance, inspiration and/or references: Bernard Beatty, Alan Jamieson, Simon Kovesi, Luke Harding at *The Guardian*, the staffs of Glasgow University Library's Special Collection and Columbia University's Rare Book and Manuscript Library, and especially to John Gardner and Katie Murphy for (amongst many other things) indulging my numismatic and etymological obsessions. Any moments of lucidity are doubtless the result of these people's influences. The weaknesses, the wish-wash and the wild inaccuracies are all my own.

My most heartfelt thanks are reserved for family and friends (they know who they are; though some are also listed above, of course), in particular for Charlotte and for my parents. Without their practical, emotional and intellectual support, the over-ambitious workload would often have been too much to bear. Despite the protestations of a few, it is they who are most likely to understand it the way I do myself. Finally, my deepest gratitude and love go to Julie, in the absence of whose kindness, strength, tolerance, sensitivity, good humour and good sense this thing would certainly have finished *me* before I finished *it*.

Contents

	PAGE
A Note on Textual Restoration	13
The Birmingham Quean 'with Foreword and Commentary by R. H. Twigg'	15
Foreword by R. H. Twigg	17
Section 1(a) (stanzas 0-63: inc. stanza "½")	47
Section 1(b) (stanzas 64-144)	181
Section 2(a) (stanzas 145-196)	309
Section 2(b) (stanzas 197-240)	399
Section 3(a) (stanzas 241-247)	489
Section 3(b) (CODA)	523
Appendices	537
Appendix 1: 'The Manifesto of the Fiction Party'	539
Appendix 2: 'The Eight Types of Fiction'	541
Appendix 3: 'Unfencing Theory: A Defence of Fiction'	543
Appendix 4: 'Now Now: Holding on to the Present'	545
Appendix 5: Synoptic Manifesto Manuscript	547
Appendix 6: The Twigg Schema	549
Appendix 7: Original Manuscript Sample	551
Bibliography and Index	553
Reverse-Engineering Attribution	555
Bibliographic Index	559

Figures

A much larger number of drawings, diagrams and photocopied/scanned images were included in the original manuscript of *The Birmingham Quean* than appear in the present text. Many of these have been left out for rights reasons, others due to difficulties of reproduction and/or recollection. In any case, it was rarely clear how these images added anything to the text. An exception is the sequence of 'dartboard mutations' which, I think, neatly captures the psychological progression between Sections 2 and 3.

		PAGE
fig. 1:	mock up of cover page	15
fig. 2:	title page of *English* Vol. IX Summer 1953, no. 53	47
fig. 3:	diagram of the remnants of the Hubbard hopscotch court	269
fig. 4:	front cover of British *Vogue*, August 1953	275
fig. 5:	Queen's effigy as head of John Dee's alchemical *glyph*	310
fig. 6:	quantum equations	437
fig. 7:	the sovereign dartboard	476
fig. 8:	quantum dartboard with bullseye pentagram	479
fig. 9:	petagrammatic golden section dartboard	481
fig. 10:	demonic dartboard with radiating Baphomet	483
fig. 11:	fully demonised dartboard as sign of Baphomet	485
fig. 12:	'The Manifesto of the Fiction Party' p1 (facsimile)	540
fig. 13:	'The Eight Types of Fiction' (facsimile)	542
fig. 14:	'Unfencing Theory: A Defence of Fiction' p10-11 (facsimile)	544
fig. 15:	'Now Now: Holding on to the Present' p1 (facsimile)	546
fig. 16:	Synoptic Manifesto Manuscript p1 (facsimile)	548
fig. 17:	The Twigg Schema (facsimile)	550
fig. 18:	Original Manuscript Sample (facsimile)	552

A Note on Textual Restoration

Il restauro deve mirare al ristabilimento delle unità potenziale dell'opera d'arte, purché ciò sia possibile senza commettere un falso artistico o un falso storico, senza cancellare ogni traccia del passaggio dell'opera d'arte nel tempo

(Cesare Brandi: *Teoria del Restauro*, 1963. p6.)

The creation and fate of the original manuscript of *The Birmingham Quean* are important features of its narrative. It would be to do the text a serious disservice (in Hollywood terms, to open with a *spoiler*) if I were to pre-empt key plot elements at this early stage by specifying the details of their aftermath. However, a brief statement of restorational methodology might not go amiss.

It is a perfectly tractable argument that *The Birmingham Quean* was originally intended not as a *text* but as an *artefact*. Its physical attributes were such that it could as easily have been designed for display in a gallery or museum as for submission to a publisher. If a practical art historian like Cesare Brandi were to consider such a thing worthy of his attention (very unlikely) he would probably want to treat it with kid gloves and something analogous to *tratteggio*. That is to say he would seek to make it look, not *as it would have done* or *as one would like it to* but *as it should do, or would do, if it had survived intact*. For Brandi 'Restoration is the methodological moment of the recognition of a work of art in its physical consistency, and its dual aesthetic and historical polarity, with a view to its transmission into the future' (1963 p30: my translation).

It is a tractable argument, perhaps, but entirely wrong. Only could someone who had not read *The Birmingham Quean* treat it in such an anathemic way. Restoration of this kind would be a flagrant breach of its internal logic. *The Birmingham Quean* pulled few punches in this regard. The ideologically elitist notion of 'the recognition of a work of art' was roundly mocked. Universalising ideas like 'physical consistency' were persistently undermined. As for the 'dual aesthetic and historical polarity' of a work of art, it was an implicit contention of *The Birmingham Quean* that this dichotomy was false.

In preparing it for submission to publishers and examiners I have therefore committed two of the cardinal sins of restoration. I have completely altered the physical format and, where necessary, I have filled in gaps with imaginative and anachronistic detail. I have no doubt, however, that this was the only way to remain faithful to the letter and the spirit of the text.

There are one or two practical upshots worth noting. Firstly, use of different pens and colours of ink in the manuscript have not been reproduced but suggested analogically by means of typographic variation. Below is a table of basic correspondences (not exhaustive):

Pen, colour of ink, handwriting style, (use)	Font, size, (style)
Fountain pen, black, expansive (Foreword)	Garamond 14pt
Fountain pen, blue, cramped (Commentary)	Garamond 11pt
Ballpoint, red, erratic (Background/Biography)	*Times New Roman 10pt (italic)*
Gel ink rollerball, blue, neat ("Poet's notes")	Palatino 9pt

As for the tendency of notes in the manuscript to encroach upon both one another's respective stanzas and the opposite side of the physical document, I have chosen to suggest this effect by extending the usual academic practice of allowing protracted footnotes to run through to the next page by taking the relatively *un*usual step of allowing the text to encroach on the verso faces of the paper. (Hence the page numbering system.)

As a final point, it should be noted that certain of the (printed) stanzas that were definitely scored out in the original have not been left in *sous ratures* but have instead been inserted into the commentary text, accompanied by a clear indication (beside the stanza number of each) that they have been 'CUT'. A true rejection of the restoration ideology, in preference for a methodology of *creative editorship*, might require me to delete these stanzas and renumber those left accordingly. I confess to being somewhat analytically retentive: no doubt a symptom of my education. This should not, however, be construed as evidence of a hidebound adherence to memorialist culture. To apply Brandi's theories to a work like this would be to produce a real *'falso artistico'*.

The Birmingham Quean

fig. 1 Mock-up of cover design (pasted onto the brown roll).

> *Like the old phoenix which, the more it got*
> *Burnt up, (recycling its own stuff, no doubt,*
> *For it did not burn down) the more it grew,*
> *Although no fire consumes us, we burn with what*
> *Only the fire of doing can put out*
> *As part of me turns into part of you.*
>
> John Hollander 'The Mutual Flame'
> (*Paris Review* Spring 1999 p54)

NOTES

Sam Trainor
Dept. of English Literature
University of Glasgow

Dear Editor,

Please find enclosed a draft copy of *The Birmingham Quean*.

This book originally came to light as a 25m roll of brown parcel paper I discovered in the filing cabinet of a staff room at a major Russell Group University English department (not my own) whilst looking for the man I thought to be its author. I had no idea of its existence at the time & was interested in his whereabouts for different reasons. The text took the form of a narrative poem printed on A4 sheets & then glued onto the inner surface of the parcel paper, around which a large number of annotations had been handwritten in various colours of ink. The poem was a contemporary parody of Byron's *Don Juan*, narrated by the Queen's head on a counterfeit one-pound coin, concerning a drag-queen called *Britannia Spears*. The notes & foreword were fictionalised — just as they are in Nabokov's *Pale Fire*, for example — purporting to be written by a rather fusty old Oxford Don in 1953.

When I found the man I'd been looking for, he managed to convince me to destroy this document. Between us, I assumed, we had the right to take such a decision. I soon discovered I was wrong: we had the perfect justification, perhaps, but neither the license nor the capability. What you have in your hands, therefore (& I should thank you in advance for taking it out of mine), is a reproduction of the text I've made from memory & my notes, interspersed with an account of how I came to find it, trace its authorship &, finally, to reconstruct it.

I can really offer no more useful summary of its contents than that. It genuinely defies synopsis. Neither can I make an honest apology for its simultaneous submission to various publishers. This is not something I condone, but neither is it something over which I can any longer exercise control. You'll understand this soon enough. All I can add (more by way of warning than of recommendation) is that this text will not allow itself to stay obscure much longer. It has a will of its own & is struggling into existence. I have little doubt it will prove original & controversial enough to sell, despite its obvious strangeness. If it doesn't seem marketable at first, remember it has already demonstrated itself quite capable of mutating into whatever form is necessary to survive. It can (& will) do so again.

In short, this book will not allow you to stop reading it. You'll want to & you'll think you have, but you'll be wrong. If I thought it was 'fit for purpose' I would (as they say in Ireland) have 'put it beyond use' before now. You're welcome to attempt to prove me wrong. I don't, however, think that you'll succeed.

Yours faithfully,
Sam Trainor

P.S. If Hannah Arden contacts you, pretend you've never heard of her… or me.

Foreword

'Tis all in peeces, all cohaerence gone;
All just supply and all Relation:
Prince, Subject, Father, Sonne, are things forgot,
For every man alone thinkes he hath got
To be a Phoenix, and that then can bee
None of that kinde, of which he is, but hee.

John Donne *An Anatomie of the World*
(Grierson 1912, ll.213-218)

STRATFORD UPON AVON

The building didn't seem too threatening at first. I was relieved. You forget just how undemonstrative Midlands architecture can be. After ten years amongst Glasgow's looming spires, I'd been expecting something steepling & monumental. Our University Tower looks for all the world as if it were designed exclusively to attract fork lightning & vampire bats. Instead, this was the kind of place librarians & dentists might retire to. I was ushered hurriedly past the tea urn into the meeting hall, smoothing the back of my hair down, clutching freshly printed pages underneath a crumpled jacket sleeve, & glimpsed a gently terraced garden with neat lawns & raised flowerbeds beyond a bright Victorian conservatory where the mingling aromas of mint & coffee hung a bit too heavily to seem completely innocent. You could imagine Elgar writing overtures in it.

I bustled past the audience up to the lectern, rubber soles squeaking on the parquet, trying to look more busy than disorganised. I cleared my throat & began.

The date was June the 28th & this was my first ever conference: the Fourth Annual British Graduate Shakespeare Conference in Stratford. The paper was a rather haggard would-be article on the phallic/anti-phallic comedy of Lear's Fool, called: 'Cocking up King Lear'. As usual, I was claiming something 'serious' should be read as comedy: Robert Armin, the professional midget comedian in Shakespeare's company, so the argument went, doubled as Cordelia; when the King carries onto stage the body of his daughter, (& Burbage staggers on with little Robert Armin), howling, failing to revive her, it's a moment of acute black comedy that likens Lear (with his unresponsive *mini-me* grotesquely dragged up as his favourite daughter) to the impotent fool unable to make his limp *marotte* stand up & scare the ladies. Imagine, I suggested, Walter Matthau carrying Danny DeVito, or Barker cradling Corbett.

Despite a slightly tense exchange with one conference member (who had a pair of crutches leant authoritatively across her lap) about evidence that Robert Armin was genuinely a *little person*, the audience seemed by & large to be quite entertained. Afterwards, back in the conservatory, I was saved from a dickie-bowed old theatre critic (who had deftly segued from the usual stuff about Erasmus into a fruity anecdote concerning the compromising position in which two particular actors he could name had once been found during a closed rehearsal of the stocks scene) by a surprisingly forceful grip on my arm.

Someone had grabbed my right elbow. She pulled me round, mid-conversation. (A woman).

"Sam, can I just borrow you for a second? Sorry Derek, you can have him back in a minute, I just need to get some details."

She had a nice smile, dark lips, friendly-looking dimples, long brown curls. She was obviously trying to help me out. I'd only turned up that morning & had every intention of slipping away quietly again during coffee; I was about to make my own excuses (only a little earlier than I'd predicted) in order to rebut a very optimistic advance on the part of the man I now knew to call Derek. Despite this, I was immediately pleased she'd intervened.

Foreword

> *Bella, horrida bella,*
> *et Thygrim multo spumantem sanguine cerno.*

The supreme function of satire is to inveigh against preventable evils. In seeking to do so, it encounters obstacles which are deeply rooted in human nature. One is that by the very order of things such evils are not demonstrable until they have occurred: at each stage in their onset there is room for doubt and for dispute whether they be real or imaginary. By the same token, they attract little critical attention in comparison with current troubles, which are indisputable and pressing, and to which they are habitually imagined to be mere analogies: whence the besetting temptation of so much recent criticism to concern itself with the immediate present and the recent past at the expense of an encroaching future. Above all, we are disposed to mistake predicting troubles for causing troubles and even for desiring troubles: "If only," we seem to think, "if only people wouldn't write about it, it probably wouldn't happen."

Perhaps this habit goes back to the primitive desire of finding in literature the word and the thing, the name and the object, made identical again: a 'consummation devoutly to be wished' perhaps, but never entertained as a delusion. This is the cusp on which ironic satire in the Swiftian tradition stands. It is useless to blame the Houyhnhnms for driving Gulliver to a state of abject misanthropy with the moral certainty that stems from their idealistic culture and linguistics. Instead, it is an intellectual failing of Gulliver's that he can neither criticize the fantastic premises of their Utopia nor offer any more effective remedy on his return than to balk at the dissembling and degenerate 'yahoos'. Swift was never so unsophisticated as his travelling *ingenu*.

We got talking, at first (for Derek's benefit) on some concocted administrative theme about the registration fee. They had no record of my payment, she was saying, but that was almost certainly the institution's fault. Derek caught someone else's eye, not wanting to eavesdrop on a potentially embarrassing exchange. As soon as he'd gone, Hannah (she said she was called) confessed she had nothing to do with the organisation of the conference & was just trying to help a newcomer out of a tight corner:

"Apparently, he comes here every year & tries to pick up boys. It's quite sad really, but I feel more sorry for the poor guys he buttonholes. Don't know what's hit them, some of them. I could tell he'd go for you from the minute you breezed in. Just thought I'd keep an eye out."

"Well, thanks, yes: much appreciated." *Breezed* was nice: I felt more like I'd *scurried*.

"I suppose I shouldn't be too critical. Half the people at these things are here for sex."

I made an effort not to splutter my tea: "You think so?"

"Of course they are: it's the only time some of them get to see the light of day. There's a very fine line between postgraduate research & masturbation: the two go hand-in-glove, so to speak."

I laughed again. I really liked this girl already; she was funny, in a quiet sort of way: you sometimes had to strain to hear what she was saying as she moved around you smiling at people.

"Conferences are all about playing at having a career, & you know what that means..."

"Erm... sex?"

"Precisely. Graduating from fiddling with themselves to actual intercourse. The most attractive feature of an academic career for a large number of these people is the promise it gives them of access to two things the majority wouldn't have a hope in hell of finding in the real world..."

"Which are?" I prompted. It was obvious she'd practised this, but it was no less charming for being rehearsed. *She* certainly wouldn't have had much trouble in 'the real world." she blushed a little at her own studied forwardness & went on.

"... an almost endless stream of people in their formative years of sexual independence over whom they can exercise a nurturing influence, & a culture of relaxed sexual mores resulting from the relativistic philosophies (of one sort or another) they tend to circulate amongst each other for precisely the reason of justifying the sordid things they get up to in their bedrooms & their cosy little book-filled offices."

"I know. Some of the stuff that goes on at my place..."

"I'm sorry," she interrupted, nipping any ill-advised workplace gossip in the bud, "I'm Hannah, by the way. You've been dragged away from sweet old Derek only to get an earful from me. So, you're from Glasgow, then. You didn't come down this morning did you?"

Rejecting pompous veridiction and eutopian projection as methods of criticising the past and future directions of society, Swift knew that irony and parody (however ludicrous or unpalatable) were much more effective tools of political rhetoric.

The Birmingham Quean is a satire in this tradition.[1] My controversial admiration for a work of undeniable vulgarity, and my determination to embark upon the preparation of this edition, is born of a belief that *The Birmingham Quean* is a heavily ironic piece of visionary satire—a *dystopia*—no less visionary for being unpublishable. In contemporary terms, it is a devastating counterpart to Orwell's *Nineteen Eighty-Four*. It is designed to complement that author's warning of the privations that might beset humanity at the hands of an authoritarian regime with one that extrapolates the equally dehumanising effects American commercial liberalism might have on Britain in the next millennium.

It is only right for a poet, capable of such prescience, to denounce a possible threat to the foundations of British society of racial, sexual and economic anarchy concealed in the Trojan Horse of the almighty dollar. In turn, it is the responsibility of critics to highlight and support such revelations. In any event, the authors of *Hudibras*, *A Modest Proposal*, *Erewhon*, *Brave New World*, *Anthem*, *Nineteen Eighty-Four*, and (most recently) *Love Among the Ruins*, would certainly agree that the discussion of future grave but avoidable evils is the most necessary occupation for both the satirist and his commentator.

Those who knowingly shirk such responsibilities deserve the curses of those who come after. They are damning future generations with their silence.

---

[1] According to G. R. Negley and J. M. Patrick in *The Quest for Utopia* (1952: pp. xvii, 298), the tradition of English *dystopia* (a term they prefer to Bentham's *cacotopia*), begins with the *Mundus alter et idem sive Terra Australis antehac semper incognita* published in 1605 by an unidentified author under the sobriquet "Mercurius Britannicus". Just as More's *Utopia* is heavily influenced by the translation undertaken by himself and Erasmus in 1506 of Lucian's *Menippus Goes to Hell*, and just as Orwell's *Nineteen Eighty-Four* seems to have been instigated by his reading of a Bolshevik *dystopia* called *We* by the Russian author Evgenii Zamyatin, Swift's *Gulliver's Travels* owes a great deal to the *Mundus alter et idem*.

"No, no. My mom & dad live in Birmingham. I thought I'd kill two birds with one stone."

"That's nice. Do you get down to see them much?"

"Not really, no. Usually just Christmas. I agree with you though... these conferences." Not that I knew anything about it. I lowered my voice to her level none the less: "They're mostly about posturing — even the ones for students — & it *is* sometimes difficult to tell whether they're advertising what's in their heads or in their knickers." I was entirely failing to sound as pithy as her.

"Yes, or maybe they're saying what's in their heads is sexy enough that it doesn't matter about the disappointment in their knickers."

"Cunning linguists," I suggested.

She smiled wryly at the dry old joke.

"Would you like a biscuit?" she offered.

I took a custard cream. Only on polite occasions like this do I forgo the simple pleasure of prizing the top off a sandwich-type biscuit & using the filling as the medium for an impression of my crooked bottom teeth. I bit into it conventionally, in cross-section as it were, trying to hide my disappointment.

She watched in silence. She could have taken this opportunity to drift away, but she didn't. Perhaps she was taking a little pleasure in my crumby discomfort.

"So," it took what seemed an age to swallow the sweet pulp of the biscuit & busy my tongue about the residue between the upper molars, "what's your research?"

This is actually the worst question you can ask a budding academic. It tends to be interpreted amongst PhD students as a complete lack of interest: desperately significant of an absence of common ground beyond the University. If you want to get off with a PhD student, you can talk about anything — the more mundane the better — soap operas, shoes, children's TV, the crap jobs you've had (they're both particularly good subjects), Christ even the weather — whatever — but never your research. The ideal topic at this juncture would've been the custard cream. I was fully aware I'd potentially shifted the conversation from one of flirtatious cynicism to one of dreary self-justification. I don't think I did it deliberately. Though I may have been retaliating for the biscuit trick.

"I usually lie when people ask me that."

"Me too," I lied, "truth is I'm not that sure."

A month or two ago I fell into conversation with a student, a quite unexceptional young man educated at one of our minor public schools. After a sentence or two about the lecture I had just given, he suddenly said: "If I had the money, I'd go to college in America." I made some self-deprecatory reply to the effect that even my rambling introductory course on the Metaphysicals wouldn't last for ever; but he took no notice, and continued: "I have three friends there already, all of them went through film academy and two of them have found themselves jobs in Hollywood. I can't wait to get out there myself. In 15 or 20 years this country will be an American State, and we'll have colour TV.'

I can already hear the chorus of execration. How dare I repeat such an awful thing? How dare I stir up trouble and inflame relations with our closest ally by mentioning such a careless conversation?

In 1674 Thomas Hyde, the librarian of the Bodleian, identified this particular "Mercurius Britannicus" as Joseph Hall, who (as a student at Oxford) had been the author of the first true Horatian satires published in English: *Virgidemiarum* (1597). On the other hand, E. A. Petherick, in *The Gentleman's Magazine* (July 1896), suggested he was Alberico Gentili, the Regius Professor of Civil Law at Oxford from 1587 to 1608. It certainly would be curious to discover that Joseph Hall, the defender of the episcopacy and the future Bishop of Norwich—a leading figure on the side of the King in the process of Anglicanization of the Scottish Church which provoked the disastrous Bishops' Wars of 1639-40, and one of those imprisoned in the tower by the Long Parliament on New Year's Day 1642—used the same nom-de-plume as the Parliamentarian propaganda machine in the Civil War. If Hall was involved in any publishing at the time one would expect it to be under the auspices of "Mercurius Aulicus" (the newsbook of Royalist Oxford) rather than "Mercurius Britannicus". This has nothing to do with the name itself, however. The claim made by the puritan revolutionaries to be the messengers of Britain is entirely fraudulent if one recognizes the nation of 'Britain' to have been reasserted by the Stuart monarchy and reliant entirely on the King as the unifier of the ancient body-politic. I consider it quite likely, in fact, that 'Britannicus' is chosen by the revolutionaries specifically to attack this idea by subverting Hall's position as the most eloquent conciliatory voice of reason in the period, thereby mocking his perceived role in instigating the wars with Scotland. Hall was a Calvinist, we should remember, and therefore viewed by fanatical puritans as even more of a traitor, as an apologist, than those bishops they seriously suspected of 'popism'.

The chief fanatic of letters in the period is, of course, John Milton. Milton is the literary heavyweight of C17[th] revolution, conscripted explicitly to satirize this (former) satirist; I suspect his influence at work. Milton is the instigator of the luciferan revolutionary bent in English poetry and therefore a man well aware of the power of turning the language of the enemy against itself. I would not be surprised to discover evidence that he was responsible for this first violence against the name Britannia, carried to such an emetic extreme in this poem.

I tried to apologise with my eyebrows. Shifting the focus back to my own faltering research had been intended as an olive branch. In fact, I regularly confessed to my uncertainty. If you can really call it a confession, that is. I would later realise, thanks largely to Hannah's influence, that the appearance of disillusionment &/or desperate vagueness is actually a way of looking keen in certain British academic circles. Everyone assumes you're *making the best of a bad job* or *muddling through*. It's what they do in Oxbridge. It's almost patriotic.

"Well, actually I only lie to academics. Would you call yourself an academic, Sam?"

I appeared to think about this for a second. I only ever really lied about my research to people outside the University: friends & family. You could get away with it more easily. "No," I said.

"Good," she grinned conspiratorially, "do you fancy grabbing an early lunch?"

"Okay then, why not."

I took a last quick look around me for a reason not to go. Despite the possible professional advantages of hanging about for a bit, I'd never actually intended to do so in the first place & would certainly not normally be upset to leave a congregation of chinwagging oddballs in the company of a sexy girl. Without exchanging any more words, Hannah & I sloped away together through a narrow corridor that led to the foyer.

It was relatively difficult to see after facing the sunny patio full on. Hannah was nothing but the pencilled outline of a slim young woman in front of me. I felt an unaccountably guilty thrill as she emerged back into the light filtering through the window above the main door & reached up to take a cream-coloured jacket by the collar & whip it off the hatstand. She slung it over her shoulder, opened the door with her other hand & gestured with her eyes for me to lead the way.

We chose a respectable local pub & found a quiet corner snug, away from the bar. Not that there was anyone at it yet, apart from the landlady & two old blokes with glasses of wine at opposite corners picking over two different portions of the Times: a better class of drunk in these parts. It was only half eleven after all. We started to drink beer (which she bought) & then she let me in on her research.

"I'm studying academics themselves. That's why I lie to them;" she began, "they're like a cult I'm trying to infiltrate." She slid her eyes from side to side like a cartoon spy.

I smiled in response & leant forward, my chin on my hand.

"Seriously though, I'm studying academics in the Humanities in the same terms as Cultural Studies used to look at subcultures in the 70s & 80s. I'm particularly interested in how groups mimic & subvert one another's activities & behaviour in order to adaptively define themselves. Encounters between academic subgroups are fascinating — that's why I come to these conferences — but encounters between academics (with their academic hats on as it were) & other social groups — in sociological or psychological field research for example — are much more important. They're often these... *antagonistic moments of identity subversion*."

The answer is that I do not have the right not to do so. Here is an educated fellow Englishman, potentially a future statesman, who in broad daylight in one of the country's oldest and most sacred academic institutions says to me, his tutor, that he wishes his country to be subsumed by the trashy and deracinated culture of an ex-colony. I simply do not have the right to shrug my shoulders and think about something else. What he is saying, thousands and hundreds of thousands are saying and thinking in the sitting rooms and picture theatres of Britain. What is more, the words they are using to do so are increasingly those words released like a continual stream of spores into our fragile linguistic ecology by US culture since it descended on us in such massive numbers in the war. Most notably, these are the words that name the technological media by which their dissemination has been principally effected: 'the *radio*', 'the *TV*' and 'the *movies*'.

Herein lies the difficulty of The Birmingham Quean. Its strength as a work of Swiftian irony derives from its insistence on the unmediated employment of the language and ideology of the object of its satire. This is a rhetorical attack composed in the projected jargon of the enemy.[2] Where Edward Bellamy's Looking Backward is framed as the putative address of an apologetic representative of the old world (1888) to the inhabitants of a fantastic socialist utopia he has encountered in the year 2000, this poem is a vision of a *dys*topian future told as if *from* and (in some sense) *by* that future, rather than simply *about* it. To continue a previous analogy, imagine Orwell had written Nineteen Eighty-Four entirely in 'Newspeak' and from the narrative position of Big Brother speaking through the 'telescreen': give a man enough rope, this poem says (give an unconscionable speaker a platform) and he will hang himself.

---

[2] In this regard it is not dissimilar to the traditional ballad form so prolific in the C17th battles between puritans and the Crown. See esp. the 'Birmingham Broadsides' of 1681 and 1682. The sardonic pamphleteering that took place during the Exclusion Debates is the beginning of the tradition that finds its apotheosis in A Modest Proposal and The Drapier's Letters. The Broadside Ballads were simply the most populist form of publication in this pamphelteering tradition, appealing as they did to both the educated and the illiterate. It is consequently no surprise that Swift—the consummate comic pamphleteer—is such an important figure in the instigation of John Gay's The Beggar's Opera.

She chuckled likeably at her own jargon: "One of the ways counter-cultures (if you want to call them that) define themselves is by consistently undermining & mocking attempts by people like journalists & academics to define the group from outside the group. The upshot basically is that all the results are skewed. The process is entirely non-empirical.

Social scientists who study the behaviour of subcultural groups usually find what they look for precisely because these groups protect themselves by giving external commentators the performances they want to see. The conclusions & theories of social science are themselves very often just the stylistic signatures of academic group identities: as arbitrary as shaved heads or dreadlocks... or Charlotte Hornets caps on the back of the bus. They *mean* something, but only to other members of the group. Outside the group, they only say what group you're in."

I nodded in vague agreement. "Like all the different types of gowns, you mean... or PhDs for that matter: hardly seems any point in writing a thesis at all when only four or five people are ever going to read it... or care."

She frowned a little at my weak analogy.

"I'm not saying that you shouldn't bother," I continued, trying to appear a little more engaged in what at the time seemed a typically unimaginative bit of Political Correctness. "Maybe I'm saying *I* shouldn't bother. Yours seems much more... worthwhile: in itself." Platitudes, I thought, maybe I should argue with her instead: "It does seem like a slightly self-defeating thesis though. Aren't you just doing the same thing they are?"

"Well, no," she seemed pleased with the challenge, "the up-side is there's feedback in the process... a kind of *dialectic*', she added tentatively, "if you like."

At the mention of that word, I tried to pitch my smile somewhere between knowing superiority & enthusiastic encouragement. Whatever it looked like — a sufferer of Bell's palsy, I imagine — she carried on:

"... or there should be anyway. As pompous & self-deluding as this stuff usually is, it sometimes manages to stimulate the self-definition of the objectified groups, in defiance of the objectifying commentary. It's a whole different kettle of fish writing 'from' a culture rather than 'about' it. That's a good thing. It's what all the best cultural critics do. Just look at Stuart Hall."

I tried not to laugh as she took another swig of Burton Ale. The pint seemed immense in her slender fingers & the only Stuart Hall I could remember at this precise moment was the one who said *here come the Belgians!* in *It's a Knockout!* Maybe I was getting drunk already. I secretly wished Hannah was.

"If it takes some busybody to get the process going, then so be it. I hope I'm doing both."

This is a dangerous game. It relies on the eternal vigilance of the critical reader. To present a satire of a future society as if recounted by the physical embodiment of the very principle of decadence that has itself brought about that society's degeneration, and go so far as to allow that spirit of decadence to enunciate its own rabid satirical attack on a society it sees as not yet decadent enough, is to reach unprecedented levels of ironic immorality. The danger, of course, is that the irony will not be recognized.

This danger is covertly courted by the poet. His true satirical intentions are to be construed through not just one, but two levels of vocal masquerade. The first and closest level to the reader (in the sense that we hear from it most consistently) is the voice of the counterfeit-narrator: the Queen's head on a fake sovereign, stamped erroneously in reverse by an incompetent die-caster. As long as we remember who is speaking, it is very easy to doubt the value of any claims made by such a storyteller.

Much more perilous than forgetting the identity of the narrator is forgetting the identity of the poetic persona: that voice whose interjections form the guiding principle of the poem's explicit structure and politics. This is, as the pseudo-epigraphic Stanza 0 makes quite clear (see below), not the author's voice at all but that of a fictional 'continuity announcer': the mouthpiece of a commercial television station.

Even more than the ridiculous counterfeit, it is the logic and morality carried by this voice that the poet asks us to reject. Where it might be relatively easy to refuse, as Swift's *Drapier's Letters* demand, to pass debased currency (and thereby resist acquiescence to an Imperial monetary policy), this poem shows just how difficult it is to hold at bay the insidious colonising influence of the television on the psyche of the nation.

"So what do you actually do by way of research then?" I asked, "apart from hanging with the homies at conferences." I was getting into this. I didn't exactly know, or to be honest care, what she was going on about (I was still trying to replace the memory of *Jeux sans Frontières* with the Birmingham Centre for Contemporary Cultural Studies) but the way she spoke was so fluent & bright it bordered on a kind of midsummer delirium... Yeats's bee-loud glade. I couldn't have hoped to be so chirpy, even this late in the morning. But then I had been up all night finishing the paper in my old bedroom at my mom & dad's.

She paused for a second, as if about to change the subject — perhaps to take exception to my question — but thought better of it:

"I'm shadowing someone else's research." She looked me in the eye: from one eye to the other, in fact.

"Do they know?" I quipped, in order to break the tension.

She nodded my flippancy aside & continued: "He's doing primary research & I'm analysing it — his research — looking at the effects it has, the reasons behind it: the real reasons."

"God, he must be a good friend... to let you pull his work apart like that."

"He's interested in the same kinds of things as me. It's more *pulling together* than *pulling apart*, I hope. It wasn't really my idea at all. He as good as asked me."

"As *good* as?"

"Well, you know, there's a certain etiquette to these things. He wouldn't want to seem immodest. That's part of the research as well, I guess: a chapter maybe."

"So who is he?" Not a partner, I hoped, but not out loud. "Was he at the conference?"

"& there's a certain etiquette to this type of thing as well. That isn't something that you get to ask me."

"Oh, sorry," I muttered, but she didn't actually seem very serious "I'm... I guess I'm something of a neophyte."

"Better a neophyte than an epiphyte, though, huh?"

I laughed quickly, half getting the joke. Mistletoe was an epiphyte, I remembered: a kind of parasite. Anyway, my relief that she wasn't above a bit of crap University witticism herself was difficult to hide.

"Sorry, one of the dangers of studying academics is you end up talking like them... Besides, I couldn't tell you even if I wanted to. It'd influence the research & make the whole thing a lot more complicated if anyone else found out who the subject was."

"I suppose you're right. So, what? Do you follow him around then?"

"Not exactly, no." She paused, then, impenetrably: "I guess I do go where he's been though."

"To boldly go where one man has been before."

I am bound to point out that the word 'television'—which might, in some idyllic projection of society, have come to mean a technologically enhanced ability to peer into the furthest reaches of space and time (and the most obscure regions of human understanding)—is now irreversibly attached to the everyday *idiot-box*, from which we get a far more mindless depiction of the universe and the future reminiscent of the American 'B-feature.' *The Quatermass Experiment*, which seems to be quite literally *inveigling* its way into the nation's consciousness as I write, is no-doubt a particularly dismal example.

The consequences of the insidious influence television is already having on the national consciousness is dramatized by the poet more than it is explicitly denounced. The canto is easily read as a vitriolic satire on the kind of debasement of society and literature which this technological toy might instigate, depict and symbolically represent. 'Easily', that is, if it were always easy to remember. It is not. In a precise mirroring of the *process of forgetting* that characterizes our hypnotized response to the television itself—think of the 'soma' and the 'feelies' in Huxley's *Brave New World*—the poet allows us to lose sight of the influence this voice is having on our minds as we are lulled into a state of susceptibility by its mantra-like rhythms. As a response, he is demanding that we break the spell and perform, by a process of critical reading, precisely the kind of rejection of this voice that he would like us to enact in contemporary life.

Fortunately there are one or two moments, just as there tend to be in Swift, where this ironic masquerade cannot contain the poet's righteous indignation. The irony therefore becomes reversed and, rather like a double-negative, we catch a glimpse of what the poet really thinks. One such moment, perhaps the most important in the piece, is where this voice is allowed to express the poet's true belief that it is television which is turning us, metaphorically, into the debased coinage which is the spiritual voice of future decadence:

"That's right" she chuckled politely.

"The prime directive," I announced, milking the joke until it suddenly seemed to make a weird kind of sense.

She rolled her eyes by way of a playful dismissal of any such infantile analogies between her work & anything to do with science fiction. She clearly didn't know much about Star Trek, though. So I thought I'd work in the idea:

"Isn't there a danger your activities, your presence (however shadowy), might end up seriously affecting his work: making it into something else, something designed entirely for your consumption?" She winced at the word 'consumption'. "Or, on the other hand, maybe it could make him try too hard to produce something which confounds your interpretation?"

"I seriously hope so. That's the point." She beamed. There was some niggling uncertainty behind her confidence however.

"This dialectic effect you were talking about?"

"If you like." She seemed a little suspicious of the question, & suddenly rather fed up with the conversation.

"Interesting. So... on that thought: fancy another? Same again?"

I ordered two more pints, resisting the temptation to look back & check if anyone else could see just how pretty she was from this corner of the bar. She might be looking over here herself.

She changed her tone to gently ironise proceedings on my return, "Anyway, what about yours?"

I began a deliberately self-deprecating outline of my thoughts on comedy: how we should reread certain seemingly dead-pan sorts of writing as comic performances — especially criticism & theory, but also how I couldn't decide between following this idea up with a critical thesis on some delimited area of literature or criticism, or by actually coming up with my own new stuff: supporting the expansion of comic (rather than simple, truth-conditional) writing in the academy by actually doing it myself... blah.

It was a mess. I couldn't seem to make my ideas intersect as well as sometimes they miraculously had used to do all by themselves when I began to speak or write. (Hence my success as an undergraduate, & my funding.) I was groping around for a thesis like a man trying to scratch an itchy foot without taking off his shoe. She sat & watched me grope.

Somehow, though, with every garbled thought that struggled from my head, Hannah seemed to grow more pensive & less... happy. Eventually, as I trailed off into vapid speculation about writing a *fictional* thesis, something which might dovetail quite nicely with her own work (I was flirting very clumsily, I suppose) — a parody or something — she asked:

"Would you say it was... Creative Writing?"

36

TV's a stand-in for the British sun.
    We bronze our features in its beta rays.
And as it reaches its meridian,
    We're mad enough to keep it in our gaze
Until some lasting damage can be done:
    Our skin anneals; our eyes begin to glaze.
I sound like one of those self-righteous saddos,
But turn your telly round and watch the shadows

37

Reticulating round your furniture;
    Just give your own imagination sway
To picture its own mental signature.
    Perhaps you'll question what I can convey,
Redoing Plato's cave in miniature,
    But is it less insane the other way?
To contemplate a source of radiation
Was once a sign of mental aberration.)

The implication is clear: we should resist a surface reading of the poem (itself the voice of American-style commercial television) if we ourselves are not to become the counterfeit narrators of the dystopia it predicts. Television will stamp the fake values of a morally degenerative ideology in the substance of our psyches. We should look beyond this to the light outside Plato's cave and, in order to do so, we must constantly bring to mind the implicit distinction the epigraphic stanza draws between the ancient role of the poet-soothsayer and the modern role of the television station 'continuity announcer'. This first announcement—the only point at which the voice reveals whose it really is—both mocks and insinuates *television*'s shadowy connotations of supernatural prescience. The poem is thereby introduced as an appalling 'vision' poem (the pre-eminent mode of galvanising moral verse in the English tradition since Langland's *Piers the Plowan*; Skeat's seminal edition of which I can only hope to emulate here.)

She seemed upset. "Maybe," I concurred, if only in the hope it would cheer her up, "I don't actually like to call it that. I think of it..."

I stopped. Her head had dropped. A sound like someone winnowing grain or maybe gold-prospecting with a riffle tray, began to emerge as if through the top of her head, interspersed with little gasps whenever her lungs demanded oxygen. Her shoulders & the chocolate ringlets of her hair shuddered slightly with the effort.

I couldn't think of anything to do. A moment ago, she'd been as breezy as you like, & now... I'd certainly never had a reaction quite as bad as this one to an explanation of my academic work. Admittedly, my mom did fall asleep — & I mean, literally, she fell asleep — the first time I attempted to describe the thesis to her. She'd had a typically long day though, & was only asking out of kindness. This was different. Here was somebody who heard this kind of claptrap every day. She studied it. It couldn't possibly have been my incompetence that had upset her, could it? It must be something else.

I didn't think I knew her well enough to put an arm around her. I would have liked to. She had narrow shoulders that would've made my arm & hand seem unusually powerful & protective. I really would have liked to.

I searched my pockets for a tissue, knowing full well I didn't have one. Eventually, she wiped her eyes & cheeks with the red cotton of her long-sleeved T-shirt. Her nose wasn't running, thank God: the thought of snot dribbling over her top lip...

"I'm sorry," she said, "very embarrassing, I know."

"No it's fine... really."

"It's just..." she tried to form the shape with her mouth of the first vowel or consonant of the word she was about to say; it kept changing. Entirely inappropriately, my sleep-deprived imagination suddenly envisioned her breaking into some early fifties popular jazz number like a character in a Dennis Potter drama. I really hoped she didn't start to cry again; I didn't think I could bear any more of those little syncopated gasps: "you... what you said..." she finally cajoled the words out, "it reminded me of someone."

I waited. I wanted to know who. This was another 'someone' in her life: first the research-partner-cum-experimental-subject, now the one who I reminded her of & who made her cry. If I'd said anything I knew I wouldn't have found out. It's like one of those old text adventure games. Sometimes you have to just write 'wait' a few times to make the right things happen.

Wait.

Hannah lifts a ringlet of her hair away from her face & sighs.

Wait.

...

As such, it perhaps comes closer, both in terms of its form and its unsettling atmosphere of semantic and moral ambiguity, to Yeats's 'Sailing to Byzantium' (1927) than to the poem it explicitly burlesques. In other words, the tawdry parody of *Don Juan* is the surface sheen of the commercial television station: the poem's flimsy gilt-leaf. In truth the mettle of this poem is the ironic voice of a Yeatsian visionary.

The spirit of the piece might be understood as taking its 'bodily form' not

> … from any natural thing,
> But such a form as Grecian goldsmiths make
>   Of hammered gold and gold enamelling
> To keep a drowsy Emperor awake;
>   Or set upon a golden bough to sing
> To lords and ladies of Byzantium
> Of what is passed or passing or to come.

The 'Grecian goldsmiths' are identified by our poet not just as the artists who decorated the cathedral walls with 'gold enamelling' but also as the workers of the mint, the 'form… of hammered gold' being quite readily glossable as *a coin*.

Two facts of numismatic history are important to this reading. The first is that the foundation of Constantinople—the New Rome—and thereby the formation of the Christian Eastern Roman Empire we call 'Byzantium', was inseparable from the minting of the *solidus* (in terms of denomination, the ancestor of the English *shilling*; but in material, appearance and use, having much more in common with the gold *sovereign*). The pre-eminence of the Byzantine Empire over that of the Latin West throughout the Dark Ages was not merely *symbolized* by the new solid-gold coin of Emperor Constantine (introduced to halt the piecemeal debasements of the Augustan *aureus* over the previous two centuries) but quite literally *embodied* by it.

'You remind me of my favourite ever teacher,' she admits, at last,
'He was a lovely man: an English teacher, & a poet. He taught us
about the delicate power of words, how they actually changed the
way people thought — not just what they thought, but the way they
thought — & he taught us the physical beauty of words, how they
make the body change when you say them: the lips, the tongue, the
diaphragm, the expressions of the face. For him, poetry was something
you could taste & touch; it was a lover: it could make you laugh or cry;
sometimes you could argue with it, you could be furious; sometimes it
would baffle you with its enigmatic behaviour; but always you wanted
it to reach out & touch you, to comfort you or passionately tear your
clothes away. He made us learn whole poems off by heart & perform
them; which sounds fantastically dull, but it wasn't. It was fantastically sexy.'

Wait.

'All the girls had a crush on him. One Monday, we were all told in
assembly that he'd slid his motorbike on an icy road somewhere in the
Highlands of Scotland & plummeted over a cliff. He was trying to get
to a phonebox to call his fiancée. We all imagined we were his fiancée.
The girls were all so distraught they had to close the school for a week.'

Wait.

'To this day, every time I hear 'A Passionate Shepherd to his Love'
I tremble all over.'

Wait

'You don't know it do you?' she asks.

Say 'Come live with me & be my love...' etc.

What Hannah really told me that afternoon was the following, (to summarise): she had lived for two years with her ex-partner, a bright but unpredictable postgraduate student called Amrit Singh who was doing a PhD in literary theory with one of those ambitiously short titles: 'Plural Theories of Fiction Praxis' or something. In the third year of his research he had taken a decision similar to the one I was myself contemplating (one which, by the way, his supervisor considered to be academically suicidal): namely, to shift from simply expounding fiction praxis (as he called it) to actually employing it. He began a vast & seemingly interminable piece of self-conscious writing & research called *The Zomby Project*, which, because he was intellectually very obstinate, nobody (not even Hannah herself) could convince him to abandon. "This was before I'd really started my own research," she explained, "I didn't have the right air of authority..."

It is fair to say, I think, that 'Byzantium'—its cæsaropapism, its transcendental iconography, its use of Greek instead of Latin, its alchemical focus on gold as the perfect state of matter: the very epitome of the 'Unity of Being' summed up in the equivalence of form and content—*was* the Solidus; and the Solidus *was* 'Byzantium'.

The second fact is that W. B. Yeats, between 1926 and 1928, chaired the first coinage committee of the Irish Free State. In a speech to the Seanad Éireann on March 3rd 1926, he said: 'Designs in connection with postage stamps and coinage may be described, I think, as the silent ambassadors of national taste.' At the time of writing 'Sailing to Byzantium', the committee was engaged in a discussion as to whether the coins should carry (on the reverse) religious iconography (as had the Byzantine solidus) or mythographic animals like those depicted on the coins issued by the pagan city states of Ancient Greece. In the end it was decided that the 'wealth of Ireland', of which the coins were to be merely tokens, was 'natural'; and so the animal icons were chosen. To this day, the Irish threepenny piece appears to depict the hare of Messana, as does their shilling the bull of Thurii, and their half-crown the Carthaginian horse. 'Fish, flesh or fowl' were chosen over beatific 'monuments of their own *muni*ficence.' It was thought that if the coinage were to carry Christian iconography, there might be a serious impact made on the economy by the number turned into religious medals. Ireland always had a lot more God than it had gold.[3]

---

[3] There is some suggestion, though largely eradicated from *Coinage of Saorstát Éireann* (1928), that the eventual decision to commission the English artist Percy Metcalfe to design all 8 coins was a political one. It was taken, that is, in the knowledge that the chairman's own preferred solution—to use two or three designs from the best two or three artists—would have required the state to commission work from the Italian medallist, Publio Morbiducci. Five years earlier, Morbiducci had created the very first piece of Fascist art (and even provided the movement with its definitive icon) when he produced a *fasce* design (a bundle of rods rolled around an axe: originally a symbol of Roman Imperial power) for the reverse of the new 2 lira piece. The fasce had first appeared on a modern coin in the talons of the American Eagle on the reverse of the US 'Mercury' dime in 1916, but Morbiducci's design was the one to introduce a genuine 'fascist æsthetic' to the world. Yeats found it difficult to disguise his admiration for the new politics and new æsthetic of Mussolini's party. He described the muscular, threatening interpretation of the Bull of Thurii in Morbiducci's submission—with its heavy pistle and pawing right front hoof—as 'magnificent'.

His research seemed focused very heavily on envisioning the City of Birmingham from the point of view of its vagrants. He became obsessed with one old tramp in particular, a silent & almost entirely unresponsive old geezer who he would follow everywhere in order to observe. He virtually became a tramp himself, only returning home from his wanderings (& whatever else he got up to) every other day or so to eat; & only once a week, at erratic intervals, would he visit the office he shared at the University to transfer the jottings in his notebooks onto the computer or to photocopy things (often new editions or references he'd found to Luther's *Liber Vagatorum*, or something seemingly irrelevant about counterfeit coins).

This continued for about five months, during which time Amrit paid her no attention at all; he never even noticed that Hannah was becoming heavily pregnant. Her pregnancy was already well into its sixth month by the time she confronted him with the obvious truth to which he had somehow, up to that point, been studiously oblivious. "You have to understand," she said, "I was still somewhat in awe of him. Most people at the University seemed to think he was some kind of an eccentric genius. I didn't want to be the one who'd stifled his research. It sounds stupid, I know." Once she had convinced him to acknowledge the situation, though, he promised to stay at home & be more responsible. Over the last few months, he did stay at home, but spent most of his time in the little study, which he was supposed to be transforming into a bedroom for the baby, writing up the results of his stalled research. (God, I almost said *aborted*). Hannah didn't mind this too much because he seemed to be attempting to knock the thing on the head before the baby was born. So she let him get on with it. The baby could sleep in the same room as them for a couple of months, after all.

When Hannah finally went into labour, Amrit never left his study. She went to the hospital with her mother & a friend from University. The birth went okay. It wasn't as painful as she'd expected but it had taken longer: four hours, which isn't actually long at all but she'd just expected it to be quicker for some reason. Hannah was back in the house two days later & Amrit had never once been to visit her or their new baby boy at the QE. He was refusing to talk. He had fitted a bolt to the door. After a few hours of door banging & tears (the latter from both the baby & herself), she'd decided she was far too tired to care any more & that the best thing was to leave him to stew in his own juice for a while. This remained the situation for the next nine days — Hannah dealing with all the demands a new life makes upon the world & Amrit... doing whatever it was he was doing in his study & only sneaking out from time to time to piss or eat when they were both asleep, or occupied with something that distracted their attention.

Yeats' 'golden bough' alludes self-consciously to J. G. Frazer's eponymous 'Study of Magic and Religion'. Frazer's is an attempt to provide an account of the evolution of all religious thought by explaining, in anthropological terms, Virgil's symbol of the Golden Bough, on which the doves of Venus sit which sing the future to Æneas, who then—following the instructions of the Sybil of Cumæ—breaks it off and carries it with him in order to gain entry to (and have protection in) the underworld. Yeats is clearly drawing a comparison between his 'Vision' and that of Æneas witnessing the future glories of the empire he will found.

Considering Yeats's election to the senate of the newly formed Irish Free State, and his anti-Latinism, this comparison cannot fail to have its ironies. By turns, the poet of this Canto takes Yeats's debased comparison to its most grotesque extreme, presenting a vision of the future, not of a glorious Rome or a transcendent Byzantium, but of an all too earthbound and inglorious Great Britain: a society characterized by sexual and moral degradation, alcoholism, crime, violence and surreal reversals of logic, seen as if on Television. Just as Marlowe's Helen is a hideous succubus, Britannia has become a dark and towering *travesty* medusa in a Union Jack dress, against whom the fake gold sovereign is no defence precisely because it is itself the Mephistopheles that has brought forth the Sibylline harridan: it is a diabolical inversion of the *moly* which protects Odysseus from emasculation at the hands of Circe, the shields of Perseus and Æneas, the *ægis* of Athene and the Golden Bough itself.

It is worth quoting Yeats at length:

> I think that in early Byzantium, and maybe never before or since in recorded history, religious, aesthetic and practical life were one, that architects and artificers—though not, it may be, poets, for language had been the instrument of controversy and must have grown abstract—spoke to the multitude and the few alike. The painter and the mosaic worker, the worker in gold and silver, the illuminator of Sacred Books, were almost impersonal, almost perhaps without consciousness of individual design, absorbed in their subject-matter and that the vision of a whole people. They could copy out of old Gospel books those pictures that seemed as sacred as the text, and yet weave all into a vast design, the work of many that seemed the work of one, that made building, picture, pattern, metal-work of rail and lamp,

Hannah's mother would come round every day after work to help her out. On the eleventh day of the baby's life — he was still unnamed & officially unregistered (strangely, this was the thing that hurt her most, she said, perhaps because the comparison with the standard bureaucratic procedure had brought it home to her just how unusual & unfair her partner's actions had become) — Hannah got up to answer the door to her mother, as usual, leaving the baby asleep in the kitchen (for once). She couldn't have been gone for longer than a minute. They stood in the hall & chatted in hushed tones about the situation with Amrit, rehearsing the same old arguments, until they heard the baby crying in a strangely muffled way & hurried back into the kitchen to find Amrit slumped against the doorjamb with the baby in his arms, rocking backwards & forwards & repeating the word 'no.' Hannah screamed, worrying that he might do some damage, whether intentionally or not, & grabbed the bawling baby back off its father & handed him to her mom. She then approached Amrit, who was still rocking & saying simply, 'no... no... no' to the accompaniment of their wailing child, & reached out to touch his face. He flinched, then stood up & walked slowly down the hall & out of the house without closing the door behind him. She hadn't seen or heard from him since.

The baby was fourteen months old now & had never met his father. The CSA had turned up nothing in all that time. There were enough Amrit Singhs in Birmingham alone to make the job nigh on impossible. Anyway, he probably wouldn't use that name. He never did when he was 'undercover' doing his research. The baby's name was Sam: like mine. She confessed this was actually the main reason she'd come up & spoken to me in the first place... though she had been interested in my paper too: its similarities to Amrit's way of thinking. It was my abstract which had initially convinced her to attend the conference. She even thought I might've turned out to be him.

& also, if she was honest, her research was partly an excuse to go to places where she thought he might turn up. Or else to look for someone else who might... She wasn't so much angry with him. She had been to begin with, obviously, but not any more. She was worried. He must've had a nervous breakdown; maybe renewing contact with his son might help to bring him back.

I didn't know what I thought of that. I didn't have children of my own, & hadn't had a nervous breakdown... yet... touch wood. I wondered out loud whether men ever suffered from post-natal depression.

> seem but a single image, and this vision, this proclamation of their invisible master, had the Greek nobility, Satan always the still half divine Serpent, never the horned scarecrow of the didactic Middle Ages.
>
> (*A Vision*, 1925 p.191)[4]

The tempting Byronic flippancies are identified with the glib voice of commercial television and, like the cajoling words of Milton's Satan and the psychagogic incantations flirted with by Yeats, they are to be resisted. The linguistic and moral environments are both characterized by this dangerous Yeatsian antinomy; it is one in which 'the centre cannot hold'.

Words are 'counter words', not simply in the sense that their stems are severed from their roots and they become—like tokens in a game (or 'fiat money')—bandied about with little or no correspondence to their original meanings, but more uncannily as words which are 'contrary' to themselves. As Sigmund Freud contends, in the 'primal' semantic environment of dreams the only words that can exist are necessarily 'antithetical'.

There is a clear line of descent in this kind of thinking through the more tortured and tortuous meditations of German philosophy (Hegel, Schopenhauer, Nietzsche) and it is not at all irrelevant to a reading of this poem that this is the point at which Freudian Psychoanalysis is supposed by Lenin to intersect with Marxist Dialectics. This too, the poem says, is a tempting fiction to be shunned.

---

[4] This is a clear indication, if any were needed, of Yeats's gnosticism. Many gnostics of the Byzantine era, for example, believed the serpent in the Garden of Eden to have been sent as a messenger of *Sophia* (wisdom) to help humanity defy the *Demiurge* who had imprisoned them in his creation. There is also the Kabbalistic image to be borne in mind of the lightning strike of knowledge on the tree of life, which could just as easily represent a serpentine ascent as a thunderclap of revelation. The Kabbala, after all, is posited on the notion that the Bible does not mean what on the surface it appears to say. The final source from antiquity which might complete the trinity of the 'half divine serpent' is Pythia, the Sybil of Delphi, who is associated with the snake-goddess of Python—herself a version of the ancient snake-handling deities in the city-states of Assyria, Mesopotamia and Persia. This last example obviously bridges the imaginative gap back to the Golden Bough. The Sybil at Cumæ is, at the very least, the offspring of Pythia. She tells Æneas to search for a particular tree in the wood and to pull a golden branch off it. The story is patently similar to that of the Tree of Knowledge in Genesis. Who is to say the Golden Bough could not, in fact, have been a snake?

I don't really know why I was still playing the likeable dimwit; Hannah was obviously still in love with her ex & anyway, she had a kid to worry about. I'd also, however, never had an affair with a single mother before...

"I think I know how to find him," she said, returning from a trip to the toilet as if she'd made some kind of resolution in there, "but I just can't face the job myself."

"How?" I asked. I was about to say I didn't know what I was letting myself in for, but in a strange way I'm pretty certain that I did.

"There must be something in his papers that could hold the key to his whereabouts. He produced an absolute welter of writing in that little study in those last two months."

"You never cleared the study out? Or even read the stuff?"

"I couldn't face it. He was always very touchy with his papers. Or at least," she mustered a dark little chuckle to try & cheer things along a bit, "he never wanted *me* to be *touchy* with *them*. We once had a terrible row because I'd asked him to tidy up a bit. It was entirely for his benefit I was saying it. He could never find anything & it made him really angry with himself. To be fair, he never used to take it out on me, but he would punch himself on the jaw repeatedly & throw things about the place like a kid having a tantrum just because a reference to some obscure event in history from some even more obscure source had disappeared (even though he'd known *precisely* where it was before). I'd obviously moved things about, he would say. He had a very sophisticated system of piling things around his feet so that the layers of paper in his study corresponded directly to the way the memories of reading them were laid down in his mind. For this reason, my meddling attempts to rationalise his work like some kind of manic librarian (who could only put 'one thing in one place at a time': as if there were any other way of putting things in places) was actually more like a bull in a china shop than any rationalising influence. *You just want to take my brain & make it like yours*, he said. That really hurt."

"So I promised to leave his papers alone from that point on: not that I'd ever meddled with them much before, only fished out the occasional unpaid bill or thrown away a few plastic-wrapped sales brochures or whatever, but the point was that I wouldn't nag him about them either. When he left, I suppose I felt that tidying the room up would mean I didn't care about him any more; like I was going back on our agreement. That was his brain in there. I didn't want to make it look like mine."

She held back her tears — not for the first time that day — moistening her lips to control the tension in her face.

The example of this phenomenon most often cited in English is the verb 'to cleave'. The reason for its illustrative ubiquity is clear: the paradoxical action which the verb encapsulates (at once an impassioned combination and a forcible division—to cleave *together* and to cleave *in two*) is precisely the effect these words have upon their antithetical senses. It is therefore a word which slices through the thematic and semantic fabric of the poem.

It is the 'counter' however which is closest to this poem's core. 'Counter' is (amongst many other things) a colloquial term for a worthless coin. It is impossible to say whether this usage derives from the root *compter* (to count) or *contre* (against): both French. The former gives us *one who calculates* or *an object used in calculation*—and, thereby, *a symbolic token of value* and *an intrinsically valueless coin*; but the latter gives us precisely the same ultimate denotation via an abbreviation of 'counterfeit': *contrefait*—'made against' ('against', that is, the authority whose seal it falsely carries). A 'counter', in numismatic terms, is therefore something which stands both *for* and *against* the sovereignty which confers the value it claims for itself (in the absence of intrinsic worth) by inscribed denomination. A 'counter' is at once a *token* and a *fake*.

If 'cleave' is the verb that wields the semantic threat of the 'primal words' in this nightmarish premonition (from which we must force ourselves to awake), 'counter' is the noun that sums them up. *Cleave* is a *counter* and *counters cleave*.

To appoint a 'counter' as the narrator of a story that accosts the reader with a travesty (the *recounter* of an *encounter* with a *contradiction*), is implicitly (one hopes) to denounce the deregulated token monetarism forged in Birmingham, now returning to us from America, which debases all intrinsic value in our culture and society and therefore makes such debilitating and surreal artifices as this poem (such *brummagem toys*) possible. Instead, we should return to the ancient traditions of honesty, nobility and stable value embodied in the authoritative seal of the monarch.

I considered saying something jokey & complimentary about how cool her brain would probably look if it was a study — like a showroom in the Ideal Study exhibition, or something — luckily I thought better of it. I really *would* have to stop thinking about kissing her.

"But you'd never read any of it before?"

"No, never: I didn't want to jinx the thing. Some people can be superstitious."

"Yeh, I know."

"To be honest, the real reason is that I'm absolutely terrified of what I'll find. You know that moment in serial killer movies where they find the madman's secret cellar, or a shed or whatever, with bizarre cuttings & things in foreign languages all over the walls... it's a bit like that. You don't really want to look at it: just in case... not even when you know it's a fiction. It's hard to tell whether all that stuff is just a symptom of the madness, or whether looking at it all that time, & working on it, whether it's that strange, obsessive activity & all those crazy collages of information which have driven a previously sane man mad."

"Haven't you even been in there?" I asked, becoming genuinely worried I was being sucked into a gothic nightmare for a second.

"No, no, of course I have. I go in there almost every day, half expecting him to be hunched over the desk, asleep on his hands after working all night. I know full well it doesn't really look like some nutter's hideaway. It's a perfectly normal, messy little academic study with books & papers everywhere. There's a window. You can even see in from the garden. I've cleaned up all the coffee cups & ashtrays & stuff. It looks quite charming really. It's just that if I started reading, I'd be terrified of plunging into some twisted, mind-altering fantasy he was constructing. The things he used to talk about were sometimes very odd. I couldn't risk that, for Sam's sake."

"I'm sure it's perfectly normal... boring even."

"In some ways, it might be better if it actually *was* insane: completely impossible to fathom — d'you know what I mean? — that way it wouldn't pose a threat, I could just get rid of it all. Knowing Amrit though, it wouldn't be like that: he was usually very precise & persuasive in the way he expressed himself. He could say the most unlikely things, as I mentioned, but you always wanted to go with him, somehow."

"I think you should read it: some of it at least." By now, I thought we'd reached the stage of friendship, even though it had been less than a couple of hours, (or perhaps, at least, we'd reached the stage of drunkenness) at which I could offer my advice.

"*I* think *you* should read it," she replied.

I took a swig of beer to hide the shock. It was starting to taste a bit too warm & slightly acidic, but I wanted it all the same. I tried to laugh off her suggestion.

This can only happen if the monarch is allowed to 'tell the truth': if, that is, the value of the sovereign coinage is once again made to correspond directly to that of the gold and silver in which it is uttered. If we continue to allow Birminghamized American culture to force these debased coinages (semantic, monetary and pharmaceutical) to circulate in our mouths, our wallets and our arteries, the entire nation will be rendered shoddy, fake and barely conscious.

For these dangerous and degenerative elements commercial television is the very pabulum they need to flourish. Here is the means by which an *ersatz* ideology can consolidate its grip on the public imagination via the technological weapons which the ignorant and ill-informed have installed in their own sitting rooms. If we do not take heed of what this poem has to tell us, if we fail to reject the cunning rhetoric it satirically exemplifies, and which is already taking possession of our airwaves, soon it will be impossible to tell representation from reality, intoxication from sobriety, black from white and male from female; Britannia herself will be re-cast as a bibulous Creole homosexual dart-player; everything and everywhere, this poem cautions, will be *Brummagem TV*.

That tragic and intractable phenomenon of relativist anarchy which we watch with apprehension on the other side of the Atlantic but which there is interwoven with the history and existence of the States itself, is coming upon us here by our own volition and our own neglect. Indeed, it has all but come. It will be of American proportions long before the end of the century. Only resolute and urgent action will avert it even now. Whether there will ever be the public will to demand and obtain that action, and therefore to publish grievous warnings of this kind, I do not know. All I know... all this poem knows... is that to see, and not to speak, would be the great betrayal.

I hope my faith in its dreadful prescience will give me steel enough to bring the project to a point at which this preface might be fleshed out: to include, for instance, some discussion of the poem's authorship.

"No seriously," she said, "I'm sure you'd understand it more than I would. It's your field."

I didn't know precisely what my field was, but she was probably right about Amrit's work being the kind of thing I was a little more used to reading than a Sociologist would be.

"Do you really think it would help get your husband back?"

"My partner: we never married, for feminist reasons... his rather than mine."

"Shit, sorry," I said, through ironically gritted teeth "desperately old-fashioned thing to say." That really was a stupid mistake. The apology was even worse than the original gaffe. *Desperately old-fashioned*? I sounded like bloody Prince Charles. I was slightly mimicking her private-school accent, I suppose. I badly needed to eat something more substantial than a packet of salt & vinegar McCoys in order to soak up the booze. I was far too drunk already to make a rational decision on this subject. I couldn't even remember the basic details, for christsake.

She grinned, "I do;" she pressed, "there's got to be a clue in there of some kind."

"Yes," I nodded slowly, trying to use that few seconds to think up some way of wriggling out of this weird situation whilst simultaneously keeping open the possibility of seeing Hannah again; or, more to the point, of getting the opportunity to slowly take off her clothes. Nothing beyond sexual fantasies came to mind. There was nothing for it: I would have to change the subject.

"It must be hard looking after a kid on your own..." the words were like an instant cold shower; I usually have to think of my grandad pissing in a rusty metal bucket in the shed with nothing but a pair of wellies on, but this was just as good: "who's got him now?"

I bit into my gums to avoid literally kicking myself as she took the hint & checked her watch, "My dad: he's great with kids. I'd better give them a call though actually. He's driving us back to Brum."

"Yeh, sorry. I've been monopolising you."

She smiled in a semi-stoical sort of way & finished her drink. I really was fucking sorry: sorry that I wouldn't even get a chance to *share* her now.

She busied herself with her coat & phone & so on. She obviously had no intention of even leaving the pub at the same time as me after such a humiliating rejection of her plea for help. I took a quick sip of beer & put the glass back on the beermat with a gulp or two left in the bottom... like someone off Eastenders. I didn't want to prolong the awkwardness by making her wait for me.

"Erm..." I didn't know what to say. How the hell was I going to get her number now?

"Listen," she chirped, coming to my rescue — it was an act of extreme generosity & forgiveness, I think — "I want you to think about it. I really would be grateful if you could just take a quick look at Amrit's study one day... when you've got a bit of time."

I suspect however, by the time our tastes have been sufficiently inured to its indecent content for the piece to be deemed acceptable for publication, and therefore in need of a proper introduction, that its dire predictions (and those of my impetuous student) may already, necessarily, have come to pass.

        R. H. Twigg. Temple College, Oxford. October 1953.

I nodded as reassuringly, but also as non-committally, as possible. She took out a green pen & a pink rectangle of post-it notes & began to scribble something.

"I'll give you my email address;" she said, "send me a copy of your paper... I'd be interested to take another look."

She was about to hand it over — presenting it ceremoniously between her thumb & index finger like a priest with a fluorescent pink communion wafer — then thought better of it & leant over the altar of the pub table to press the sticky part gently against my forehead.

She smiled: more happily this time. "Bye bye," she said.

For some reason (perhaps it was an act of penitence) I didn't take the post-it off my head until the pub-door had shut behind her. I fully expected it to say *dickhead* or something of the sort, but it was genuinely an email address. It was obviously designed to let me know exactly where I stood though. Here it is:

> to find Amrit Singh
>
> gregorsamosa@hotmail.com

I can still feel her fingers dabbing it on my forehead like a kiss.

Section 1(a)

AT THE CORONATION

2 JUNE 1953

'I saw her youthful, saw her ardent brow
   For service and for sovereignty bent.'
'I heard the single music of her vow
   With great and ghostly voices in consent.'
'So young she looked for such vast enterprise.'
'Antiquity I saw in a young queen's eyes.'

'I saw her crowned.' 'I heard in solemn phrase
   The kingly God who crowned her called to bless.'
'Yet did I grieve that these ungentle days
   Should fall to one who looked all gentleness.'
'All gentle, yet she bore such royal mien
As when the first Elizabeth was queen.'

'If so it be, then may her reign inspire
   Men great with deeds and poets great with song.'
'Since so it was, may vision take new fire
   And ancient virtue through her youth be strong,
Till with her age's far horizon come
The second, a more true, millennium.'

G. ROSTREVOR HAMILTON

fig. 2: G. Rostrevor Hamilton 'At the Coronation', in *English*, Vol. IX, no. 53, Summer 1953 (title page) [facsimile]

From: "Sam Trainor" <invertedpodsnap@yahoo.co.uk>
To: "Amrit Singh" <gregorsamosa@hotmail.com>
Sent: Sunday, August 17, 2003 8:40 AM
Subject: Re: Re: to find Amrit Singh

Thanks for the tip. 2042 really would've been a long time to wait for me to get back in touch. I can't say I was any less surprised to find one from "Amrit Singh" in my Inbox though. That was really quite disconcerting. I have the preview thing switched off, in case of viruses, so I had one of those heart-fluttering moments when you don't want to open the message for fear of what's inside.

I guess you're just using an old email account of his. Do you have another one?
sam

-----Original Message-----
From: "Amrit Singh" <gregorsamosa@hotmail.com>
To: "Sam Trainor" <invertedpodsnap@yahoo.co.uk>
Sent: Saturday, August 16, 2003 8:21 AM
Subject: Re: to find Amrit Singh

>Thanks Sam, end of July sounds good. Drop me a line when you know travel
>plans and so on and we'll organise a day for you to come round.
>
>P.S. The time's way out on your PC. That's happened to me before. Remember to click
>Cancel rather than OK after you use the desktop calendar to look up dates.
>
>
>
>-----Original Message-----
>From: "Sam Trainor" <invertedpodsnap@yahoo.co.uk>
>To: "Amrit Singh" <gregorsamosa@hotmail.com>
>Sent: Thursday, August 14, 2042 3:34 PM
>Subject: to find Amrit Singh
>
>>Hi Hannah,
>>
>>Sorry this has taken so long. I've been pretty busy. I'm just writing... well, to
>>find out if this is the right address (like the name by the way) and to say that
>>I'd be happy to take a look through the papers in Amrit's study if you're still
>>interested. I finish teaching at summer school at the end of August, so I
>>might be able to make it back to Brum for the 27th or the 28th. Otherwise, it'd
>>have to be after Christmas.
>>Let me know what you think.
>>sam ;)

> 0
>
> *Next up on BTV — a counterfeiter*
>   *Takes on £e champion of drag-queen darts:*
> *Jeff Sloggy pits his wits against £e glitter*
>   *Of Tanya Spears in a bar-room farce*
> *Narrated by a one-pound coin. (It's shitter*
>   *£an Byron's, but it's got its so-so parts.)*
> *£is programme, from £e outset, uses slang which*
> *Some viewers might adjudge to be strong language.*

0.1 *Next up on BTV*: At first sight these initials seem to be an acronym for the new American-style commercial television station the government seems intent on franchising. Perhaps they stand for 'British Television' rather than 'Brummagem Television'; though it could just as easily be 'Beta Television' (the BBC's being 'Alpha Television'). The 'B' is uncertain, but 'TV' reproduces the habit of broadcasters on the other side of the Atlantic of abbreviating the word 'television' as if it were two hyphenated words. The predilection in the United States for firing hyphens into perfectly good words, like protons to split the linguistic atom, has proliferated so rapidly of late that the effect has gone thermonuclear: the superheated semantic atmosphere created by this morphemic fission has, that is, produced such a dreadful explosion of lexical 'fusion reactions' that it is perfectly easy to believe a sickening dialect of the kind portrayed in this poem could, if the effect were allowed to spread any further, be the ultimate fallout.

0.2 *drag-queen*: A homosexual who dresses professionally as a woman: usually a theatrical female impersonator or male prostitute who wears extravagant feminine attire and behaves in an exaggerated, lascivious manner for the comic and/or erotic entertainment of patrons. It is very important that there are notions implicit in the term 'drag' of advertisement, ostentation and transaction; it is therefore differentiated from 'transvestism'—which is a non-commercial private sexual behaviour, 'hermaphrodism'—which is an unfortunate genetic mutation, and 'transsexualism'—which is the delusional state of believing yourself (like Vita Sackville-West and her literary analogue, Virginia Woolf's *Orlando*), despite a total absence of biological corroboration, to have been born into the wrong sex.

    A drag-queen makes a simultaneous play (literally a *travesty*) of both an overstated femininity and an overstated masculinity. Drag deliberately undermines the fundamental dichotomy of sex, and it is this revolutionary æsthetic which has always appealed to the cackling perversions of those who seek to promote the forces of cultural decadence.

    It is a debasement of society resulting from the projected victory of these forces—and, like *The Beggar's Opera*, a debasement of that society's conception of the literary artform and *poetic justice*—with which this poem is concerned. It is entirely fitting that the state of antithetical vagary and debauched commerce should be overseen by a 'quean' (see below) whose stock-in-trade is the antithetical performance of sex.

0.5 *one-pound coin*: Another hyphenation. No self-respecting Englishman has ever referred to the sovereign in such a way. This clumsy phrase is used, rather than certain metrically much more balanced alternatives (such as 'sovereign coin'), in order to pile up the hyphenated Americanisms in this epigraphic stanza and thereby provide a foretaste of the artificially grafted neologisms (*cleavages*, in the Freudian sense) of which that country seems so fond (like The Duchess of Malfi, whose 'vulturous eating of the apricocks' from a grafted tree [II.i.2] belies her pregnancy with offspring of a dubious genetic heritage: 'a springal that cuts a caper in her belly') and which self-propagate in the futuristic dialect of this poet's dystopian vision. See *passim*.

(We should recall that the tree that bears the 'golden bough' in *The Æneid* is described as 'geminæ' *dual-natured* (Book VI li. 205). This is no doubt the source of the 'ympe tre' in the Middle English Romance *Sir Orfeo*, under which Heurodis falls asleep at noon and is captured by the Fairy King. Perhaps this 'imping' is more likely to be the result of a natural *epiphyte* than an artificial *graft* or *scion*. Virgil, after all, explicitly likens the Golden Bough to mistletoe, a fact which forms almost the entire premise for Frazer's study. The symbol of the epiphyte might turn out to be quite important to this work. The most famous example is, of course, the *banyan*, which begins as a small parasite (like mistletoe) and develops into a huge, encroaching tree that strangles and kills its host, leaving behind a hollow cylinder of knotted roots. The Britain in the poem is one which has disappeared, leaving only this ugly tangled structure of Brummagem Americanism.)

Then again, it might be better to think of these hyphenations as 'alloys' rather than as hybrids or banyans. The 'one-pound coin' itself—the narrator of the greater part of the canto—is made not of gold (in this future of British degradation in which one suspects all gold is paid in perpetual postwar tribute to Imperial America) but of a cheap mixture of copper, nickel and tin with a hyphenated name: nickel-brass. This reintroduction into circulation of a debased sovereign, in place of the one pound (promissory) note, seems to have been done—just as one suspects it may have been with the dodecagonal threepenny uttered in the same cheap metal—by way of a mocking depiction of some lack of intrinsic value in the currency and the constitution following the collapse of the Gold Standard.

The prosodic effect of these *alloys* in this and many other stanzas is to make a strophe of the ensuing iamb and therefore to force out the insistent rhythm of three consecutive stressed syllables:

> drág-queén dárts, bár-roóm fárce, óne-poúnd cóin, só-só párts.

The effort to reproduce these emphases makes the reader himself feel rather like a machine for stamping coins, the inexorable mechanical revolutions of which keep bashing out the poem's words. Or perhaps the poem is more like the piston driven machine and the reader the hero of a melodrama strapped to the conveyor belt, his head moving slowly closer and closer to the repetitively slamming stamp.

The sense of dangerous infection with everything that we call Birmingham (both the industrial city itself and, by extension, its industry of discounted mechanical reproduction) is a typical one. In Robert Southey's *Letters from England*, for example, the poet's fictional Iberian alter-ego *Don Manuel Alvarez Espriella* is left reeling after the briefest of encounters:

> I am still giddy, dizzied with the hammering of presses, the clatter of engines, and the whirling of wheels; my head aches with the multiplicity of infernal noises, and my eyes with the light of infernal fires,— I may add, my heart also, at the sight of so many human beings employed in infernal occupations, and looking as if they were never destined for any thing better. Our earth was designed to be a seminary for young angels, but the devil has certainly fixed upon this spot for his own nursery-garden and hot-house... Every man whom I meet stinks of train-oil and emery. Some I have seen with red eyes and green hair; the eyes effected by the fires to which they are exposed, and the hair turned green by the brass works. You would not, however, discover any other resemblance to a triton in them for water is an element with the use of which, except to supply steam engines, they seem to be unacquainted...

½

(This poem's going out to Andrew Motion,
    Who couldn't tackle 'Johnny Wilkinson'.
Perhaps I haven't any right to question
    What England's rhyming Rumplestiltskin's done,
But, Andy, couldn't you best serve the nation
    By sticking poems of that ilk in some
Recycling bin for use as royal bogroll?
Then you could really lick arse with your doggerel.)

> The noise of Birmingham is beyond description; the hammers seem never to be at rest. The filth is sickening… it is active and moving, a living principle of mischief, which fills the whole atmosphere and penetrates every where, spotting and staining every thing, and getting into the pores and nostrils. I feel as if my throat wanted sweeping like an English chimney. [Letter 36, pp.196-8]

0.6 *sh*tter than Byron's*: If it were not for the scatological inarticulacy of the comparative I would certainly concur. But this is a typical effect: good taste precludes my seconding of the sentiment and, by default, I feel implicated in condoning what is in fact a much more disturbing visionary canto than any in *Don Juan*, despite (in fact *because* of) its trashy inferiority of style.

0.6 *so-so parts*: Perhaps we are meant, beneath the creak of this see-sawing expression of mediocrity, to hear a homophonic version—'sew-sew parts'—the 'stitching and unstitching' of Yeats's Penelopean lines: fragments of an unfinished and unfinishable tapestry, embroidered by day and unpicked by night to delay the consummation of an appalling future it must never be allowed to depict, commemorate or instigate.

0.7 *slang*: As well as the definitions under the first sense: 'language of a low and vulgar type' etc., the OED also provides the following senses for *slang*: 2. 'Humbug, nonsense.'; 4. 'A license, *esp.* that of a hawker.'; 5. a. 'A travelling show.', b. 'A performance', c. '*attrib.* As **slang cove**, **cull**, a showman.'; 6. 'A short weight or measure.'

The word manages polysemously to connect the 'short measure' of the counterfeit coin and the world of the dubious hawker of 'humbug' verse to the 'slang cove' *drag-queen*. The OED fails to provide any etymology for this word (perhaps one of the few serious failings of a nevertheless seminal work of reference if you consider its integrity as a categorical heading in so many of the dictionary's entries) and adds a note to the effect that all senses other than 1. are themselves 'only in slang or canting use.'

The connection here, and also elsewhere one suspects, is the language of Gypsies. Vagrants, carnival folk and tinkers have always dissembled with their tall tales and their fraudulent performances, hawked their counterfeit objects and their counterfeit coins, and baffled the credulous with their shabby diversions of *legerdemain* and *legerdemot* (the hand is quicker than the eye; the tongue is quicker than the ear). The trinity of senses that interlock like the brass rings of a fairground conjurer in 'slang'—*cant*, *con-man* and *counterfeit*—are first demystified by Luther's *Liber Vagatorum*. The father of Protestantism, who has a natural predilection for denouncing the supposed chicaneries of certain mendicant orders of monks (and indeed implicitly to liken the activities of all profiteering tricksters to the clergy), provides not only a typology of peripatetic fraudsters, but also an itinerary of the counterfeits they pass and a glossary of their argot. This book is therefore probably the progenitor of the modern 'Dictionaries of Slang', whose regularity of publication in recent times (at the hands of idle lexicographers too unimaginative to innovate other than by listing the transient contemporary idioms that thankfully remain too marginal to warrant inclusion in a genuine dictionary) seems only to have encouraged a proliferation of slack usages and the development of countless arcane jargons. Luther's design is far more ambitious and holistic however; for him, all three aspects (the vagabonds, the counterfeits and the words), are part and parcel of the same circulating infection of society for which he prescribed his assiduous schema as the pedagogic cure.

Crucial to this poem's omnipresent implication of self-criticism, is the idea of poetry's complicity in the progress of this infection: the idea that the degeneration of poetry itself has created this *vagrant* slang, a symptom of the material changes brought about by capitalism and the profound damage relativist economics has inflicted on our understanding of the value of words. As Schreiber puts it:

> poetry had estranged herself from the Nobility; knights no longer went out on adventures to seek giants or dragons, or to liberate the Holy Sepulchre; she had likewise become more and more alien to the citizen, since he considered it unwise to brood over verses and rhymes, when he was called upon to calculate his profits in hard cash. Even the "Sons of the Muses," the Scholars, had become more prosaic, since there was so much to learn and so many universities to visit, and the masters could no longer wander from one country to another with thousands of pupils. Then poetry (as everything in human life gradually descends) began to ally herself with beggars and vagrants. That which formerly had been misfortune and misery became soon a sort of free art… Mendicity became a distinct institution, was divided into various branches, and was provided with a language of its own.
>
> Doubtless… it was the gypsies—appearing… in larger swarms than ever—who contributed greatly to this state of things. They formed entire tribes of wanderers, as free as birds in the air, now dispersing themselves, now reuniting, resting wherever forests or moors pleased, or stupidity or superstition allured them, possessing nothing, but appropriating to themselves the property of everybody, by stratagem or rude force.
>
> [*Taschenbuch fuer Geschichte und Altherthum in Sud-Deutschland*, I, 330. trans. D. B. Thomas *The Book of Vagabonds and Beggars* London: Penguin, 1932, pp.7-8]

As a piece of pure speculation, I would add that the probable reason 'slang' is the word for the way these people speak (deliberately to trick the decent) is that it is their own word for these linguistic tricks. D. B. Thomas continues his introduction to Luther's glossary of *Rotwelsche Sprache* thus:

> [It] was a strange conglomeration of hybrid, misbegotten phrases… As in all lingos of the kind, Beggar Welsh, with its twisted allegory and bastard metaphor luxuriates in the heterogeneity of its associations, and glories unashamed in its unacknowledgable larcenies from other tongues… Much that seems obscure comes from another language, but occasionally it would seem that by some twist of fate a root meaning, forgotten and unused elsewhere for many centuries, lingers on in the undergrowth far from the high road of progress. Latin and Hebrew supply most of the strange outlandish words…

£e Birmingham Quean

clerks in Minor Orders had been tramping the hedgerows for three centuries: from Prague to Bologna, from Oxford to Paris generations of wan-dering scholars had begged a crust and a glass of wine to further them on their way. Nor do the beggars spurn the Pandemian Goddess—those hungry mendicants pretending to be followers of St Jacob or St Michael, the Abram Men, and the 'Scholastics' whom the vulgar call *vagantes* who deceive innumerable simple men with their artful tricks. And so the Latin. [1932: 53-55]

The word *slang*, amongst such people, could be a shibboleth: a mystifying variant of 'lang' which shifts that Latin word away from its perfect integration of physical and semantic properties. 'Lang', that is, traces the semantic and phonetic length of the 'tongue' perfectly. The addition of the initial sibilant would seem to transform both the name and the organ of speech that provides its etymological root, and its vehicle of articulation, into the forked tongue of the snake: the perfect tool with which to form the baffling, antithetical conceits that trick the simple-minded. *Slang* is the *tongue* of the serpent.

Quean: From Old English *cwene* (weak feminine), as opposed to the cognate form *cwēn* (strong feminine) which gives us 'Queen'. The word, having returned to a position of homophony, became a sardonic counterpart of its homonym, meaning *slut* or *hussy*. By this process it has retained only the variant spelling as an orthographic reminder of a previously much more tangible bifurcation of the stem based upon what might be called 'etymological irony'. It has always therefore been implicated in Republican carping. A sneering example appears in an epigram Byron sent to John Murray from Ravenna on August 17th 1820 (Letter 817. Prothero [ed.] 1904: p65):

> Mr. Hoby the Bootmaker's soft heart is sore,
> For seizing the Queen makes him think of Jane Shore,
> And, in fact, such a likeness should always be seen –
> Why should Queen's [sic.] not be whores?
> Every *whore* is a Quean.

The word has now unfortunately come to mean an effeminate homosexual or, indeed, a 'drag-queen'. As if the <a> had been imported from the word 'drag' and concealed beneath the fabric of a feminine homonym like the male member underneath the pervert's lingerie. This ongoing semantic deviation from the upright progress of its sister-word is expounded by the deviant persona responsible for the Byronic parody.

In fact, I would argue, it is made even more acute via an obversive reassertion of the old phonetic difference. That is to say, he intends this word to be pronounced differently from *Queen*. It is a *Birmingham* Queen not only in the sense of *counterfeit* or *shoddy*, but also in having a Birmingham accent. The word is to be rendered something like 'quayn' and therefore comes perilously close to homophony with *coin*, usually uttered in that dreary part of the country as 'quoyn'. This transformation of the mouth into a zone of semantic (and moral) ambiguity by yawning slides of vowel pitch is one of the most devastating weapons in the poet's satirical arsenal. He is flirting with the metamorphic power of poetry to change us physically and mentally by recruiting us to the performance of its sound and sense. He is daring the reader to *become* the object of the satire, for a while at least. Rejection of this trashily alluring culture is to happen as an exorcism of the evil influence that has quite literally taken possession of our muscles and our minds.

1

   I want a heroine, a common one:
     Not quite as trailer-tra$ as Bonnie Tyler,
   And no€ing crass, like a Mancunian,
     But not a princess ei£er. I'll compile a
   Quick list, I €ink, like Byron in *Don Juan*.
     (£at's 'ɒwan' not 'Ju-an', which is even viler,
   And might permit a foreign audience
   To €ink all Engli$men are stupid cunts.

1.1 Byron's line is 'I want a hero, an uncommon want': the effect being of a *semantic flip* from 'desire' to 'lack'. Here there is a similar *flip* of the entire line achieved by means of an elongated pun. This 'sex-reversal' is mirrored by the *prosodic flip* of feminine to masculine rhyme in the pronunciation of 'Juan'. See below.

1.2 *as trailer-trash as Bonnie Tyler*: A recent addendum to the OED reads, 'TRAILER, *n.* **9.** *Cinema*. A set of short extracts from a film advertising it in advance' (something not dissimilar to the 'programme introduction' of the previous stanza.) Its combination with 'trash' is another of the hyphenated Americanisms in the poem.

 'Bonnie Tyler' is a feminized version of 'Bonny' Wat Tyler the leader of the peasants' revolt in 1381. The poet is alluding to the preface in Byron's parody of Southey's 'A Vision of Judgment.' Byron taunts the poet laureate, who had previously been a fellow Jacobin and written a play called 'Wat Tyler' with obvious allusions to contemporary politics (of which he was now trying to suppress all evidence), for producing an apotheosis of George III. This persona's parody of Byron's parody is perhaps intended by the satirist to reassert Southey's identification of Byron as 'Satanic'. This is probably more of a compliment than Byron assumes. Southey is likening him to Milton's Satan and therefore celebrating his erudition and prowess whilst also denouncing his regicidal politics.

 This poet, however, is taking up Southey's cause by comparing Byron's 'Vision' to those sensationalist advertisements for 'future presentations' with which Hollywood bombards our cinema audiences. He 'counters' and 'Birminghamizes' Byron's octaves in order both to flatter and indict. The implication is, I think, that we treat the entire poem as 'trailer-trash'.

1.3 *Mancunian*: An inhabitant of Manchester. This was, alongside Birmingham, the other major English city created by the rapid expansion of industrial capitalism during the Industrial Revolution. Both conurbations pose a serious problem for the Saxon shire system in England: Manchester spreading into both Cheshire and Lancashire, and Birmingham making a mockery of the boundaries of Staffordshire, Worcestershire and Warwickshire. 'Mockery' is the right word. Birmingham especially seems to owe its existence to a bloody-minded capitalist and industrialist rejection of the ancient authority of both the shire towns (like Warwick and Worcester) and the diocesan seats (like Lichfield and Coventry) which surround it. As such, both cities stand as particularly unbecoming monuments to the defiance of the ancient institutions of English culture which has led inexorably to this nation's moral decline. The petty rivalry implied in this line between two such remarkably similar revolutionary cities is revealed by this satire as part and parcel of the small mindedness which is the result of the proletarian mindset they have conspired to spawn.

1.5 *like Byron in <u>Don Juan</u>*: The reversal of the anglicized and metrically *feminine* bisyllabic 'Ju-an' (to rhyme with 'new one') back to the Castillion and metrically *masculine* monosyllable 'Hwon' is the opposite of the process (see *passim*) of introducing, by means of metrical implication, a diæresis into Birmingham diphthongs. 'The metrical gender' of words (in this semi-technical sense) is never allowed to remain stable.

1.6 ₤wan: The reader will have noticed the unusual orthography throughout this poem. There are two versions of the sterling *livre* symbol £ and ₤ (one single barred, the other double barred for emphasis) which are used to correspond directly to the runic edh (ð) and thorn (þ) letters of Old English. It is pleasing to reassert the distinction of these two phonemes. For this reason, I would personally be in favour of their reintroduction into English orthography. The currency symbols used here serve to remind us, however, that the words belong to the commercial television station (which introduces their use in the epigraphic stanza), intent on commodifying the language rather than returning it to an old phonemic writing system.

There is some evidence the poet initially intended to include the American cent (¢) symbol to replace <ch>, and thereby emphasise the US reverse colonisation suggested by the use of the dollar sign for <sh>. Such a decision might have been particularly effective if we consider the echoic connection between the words containing this phoneme and the sounds that coins themselves make when coming into contact with one another. (See 'chink' &c.) Perhaps the decision not to use the cent was based on the impact this would have on overall readability, in combination, that is, with a desire to emphasize a direct connection between the dental fricative articulation (so characteristic of both English and the Castillion Spanish of this example) and the insidious commercialism he wants to reveal. Perhaps this has to do with it being (when unvoiced) the sound made by a snake. A French colleague once confessed to me that he was instructed as a child that the trick to these alien lisps was to imagine he was *un serpent perfide comme tous les Anglais*.

I assume this particular example therefore to be some kind of futuristic symbol of currency used to represent the uvular fricative phoneme for which there is no equivalent in English: perhaps (God forfend) it is the symbol of the 'metric pound'.

1.8 *c*nts*: Its paradoxical detachment from the proper sex makes this squalid usage of the most profane of words much more offensive even than its precise, earthy employment in Lawrence and Joyce. The synecdochic derogation of women is bad enough, but only the worst educated men use it in reference to the stupidity of one another. This process of collapse from 'cunning/quaint' femininity to the index of plebeian imbecility is co-relative to that via which currency descends from inherent value to 'fiat-money'. Thus the word is emblematic: the epitome of the *counter*. This society is one in which exposure to the sexual organs and the words denoting them is so quotidian that both are a debased currency. This poem, however, warns of an imminent threat to language and culture. It would not be justifiable, I think, to use this word's appearance in the poem as a pretext for its expurgation, as has been the case with both *Ulysses* and *Lady Chatterley's Lover*.

2

>   We are, of course. Ask anyone from Spain
>   Who's seen £e lager-lads descend on El
>   Candado: football fans fucked out £eir brain —
>   All pulling moonies in £e Don's Hotel
>   And puking calimari down £e drain:
>   Ano£er Helicon becomes ano£er Hell.
>   I sound all $ocked-and-stunned but £en I'm pissed
>   Myself… I €ink I'll get back to £at list.)

2.1 *Spain*: The dichotomy of England and Spain is as archetypal as that of England and France. The choice of a Spaniard, *Don Manuel Alvarez Espriella*, to provide Southey's critical vision of England in 1807 (when the countries were on the verge of a new alliance against France) must have come quite naturally. Spain is the familiar 'other.' As the two great Atlantic naval empires of the reformation and counter-reformation, for example, England and Spain were, in the C16th and C17th, two sides of the same American coin.

This relationship is as crucial to this poem as it is to *Don Juan*. Spanish is the source of some of the most important words in its thematic substratum: *tobacco*, *cigar*(ette), *real* ('royal', as a sarcastic pun on the sense 'authentic'), and (most importantly, I suspect) *flamingo*. There is another word, however, which is of great importance here in terms of its iconic status and its dubious etymology. That word is: *America*.

The two most cogent derivations of this word play out the battle for the continent itself. The 'Spanish' version claims America was named after Amerigo Vespucci, the Florentine navigator in the pay of Ferdinand and Isabella who had accompanied Columbus on his initial voyage of discovery and was the source of the view that this was a new continent and not East India. Supposedly, the reason for 'America' and not 'Columba' was that a German mapmaker, Waldseemüller, had made this choice explicit in his 1507 map of the world (this error being repeated by Mercator). This ur-document was only unearthed mysteriously in a German castle in 1901 however; all other maps by the same cartographer labelled the continent 'Terra Incognita' and Vespucci's Christian name was usually printed 'Albericus' and not 'Amerigo'.

If we dismiss the typical French fiction of Jules Marcou—who suggested in 1875 that 'Amerrique' was the Carib word for the mainland—we find the only perfectly competitive account in the 'English' theory of scientist Alfred E. Hudd. Hudd simply pointed out, in a paper for the Antiquarian Society of Bristol in 1910, that the Venetian Giovanni Capoti landed in Newfoundland in 1497 (two years before Columbus) on a voyage out of Bristol, and the records of that city showed the project had been funded by the Custom's Collector: Richard Amerycke (whose odd name derived from Welsh). The explicit statement, on an official calendar of the year, that the place discovered would therefore be called 'Amerycka', has unfortunately been destroyed in a fire, but other documents making the link between the two men apparently still exist.

The point here is that it is impossible to disentangle these etymologies, and to tell history from fiction, one language from another. One suspects the whole issue to be a trail of forged documents, seaman's tales and cabbages and kings. 'America'—the word, the idea and the nation—is rootless, fake, and treacherously ambiguous. America is a *counter*. America is, this poem urges, Brummagem.

2.2 *lager lads*: One might expect drunkards of this name to be German rather than English. If the persona were more committed to his attack on the English, a more apt coinage might have been 'the bitter boys.' This would, however, preclude the implicit comparison of this unwanted plague of locusts with the Spanish Gitanos, whose dialect Thomas and Borrow both reveal to be called *Germania*.

2.2-3 *El Candado*: Spanish for 'padlock'. Perhaps this is intended as an infamous jail in Madrid in which drunk and disorderly English football supporters (the new 'Zincali') are to be imprisoned in large numbers.

2.3 *football fans*: Needless to say, this abbreviation of 'fanatic' is American.

2.3 *brain*: The intoxicated football supporters are being satirized for having (literally) the single-mindedness of a gang or crowd. Of course, the pressure of the rhyme here might be the only reason for the singular form, but I think the implication of individualist rationalism as an alternative mentality to be mourned in an English culture which has been entirely taken over by the *lumpenproletariat* is strongly intended.

2.4 *pulling moonies*: the slang sense for *moony* in the OED is 4. b. 'slightly intoxicated'. In the broadest semantic way, this does at least suit the context of drunkenness. The vulgar description of the level of inebriation which precedes it, however, suggests the 'fans' are much further gone; why, in any case, pleonastically add to such a powerful indictment with a phrase one might gloss merely as 'behaving tipsy.' A much more fitting explanation might be that *a moony* (a count noun in this sentence rather than an adjective, you'll notice) is supposed to be a futuristic slang term for a drink. A pint of stout or porter does, after all, have a smooth white head of foam when first 'pulled' which, when viewed from above by the addled drinker at the point of taking his first quaff, might just resemble the full moon.

2.5 *calimari*: Spanish for 'squid'. One of the most beautiful sights available to the Mediterranean traveller is of the hundreds of lambent squid and cuttlefish that bob to the surface of the calm night sea attracted by the moonlike lantern of a fisherman. One sincerely hopes this timeless image of civility and intelligence is slowly returning as the waters around Gibraltar are cleared of their mines and oil-slicks. For this poet to imaginatively compare such a simple miracle to fish-suppers regurgitated in a torrent of beer from the œsophagi of drunks is truly sickening.

To add insult to injury, the persona is also playing (one assumes) on the brainless application of the word 'squid' in the dialect from which his work supposedly originates as a canting plural (by Spoonerism, as it were) of 'quid' meaning 'a Sovereign'. The vomitus ejected is therefore metonymically reduced to the money paid to fill the guts of these neanderthal with alcohol and battered fish. (Just as it was by a philosophical dipsomaniac I once overheard aphorising as he addressed himself erratically to the urinal: 'You earn your money then you p*** it up the wall.') Not only is one of the wonders of nature reduced to a scatological eruption in these lines, but the Sovereign (money and monarch) also undergoes an ignominious metamorphosis in 'the belly of a beggar' into vomitus.

These effects allow the poet to provoke an almost literal physical rejection of the future his poem forces us imaginatively to ingest. This is *emetic* satire.

> Dame Edna, Lily Savage, Danny LaRue,
>   The Lady Chablis, Rupaul and Divine:
> £ey had £e fifteen minutes £ey were due.
>   And if £at's your €ing… well, it isn't mine.
> Don't get me wrong, I'm into drag, £at's true,
>   But £ese celebrities can wait in line
> Wi£ all £e Beaux-Belles of *Les Travestis*,
> £e Monsieur-Mariannes of Gay Paris,

2.6 *Another Helicon becomes another Hell*. The first of what I will refer to throughout as 'Birmingham Alexandrines'. There are quite a large number of these hexameters in the poem; the vast majority occurring on the sixth line of the stanza. I intend to provide further illumination of this effect at a more appropriate juncture below. The important thing to notice here is how the line pivots on a rather unnecessary repetition of the word 'another.' Why not 'A Helicon becomes another Hell'? The indefinite article does quite enough to suggest the idea (itself a debilitating one, even without reference to the infernal regions) that there is more than one *Parnassus*.

The answer is that the poet is again drawing our attention to the process of dehumanising and sacrilegious mechanical reproduction which characterizes the Birmingham æsthetic of the poem. To repeat 'another' is to repeat a repetition; and to flip 'Helicon' to 'Hell' is to suggest both places are rendered (by this diabolical counterfeit environment) 'two sides of the same coin.' Compared to Jamesian 'elegant variation' there is always something ominous about any such witless reproduction. Yeats in particular makes ample play of this kind of incantatory rhetoric.

Again, I am brought back to the juxtaposition of the debased Byronic wit of the persona (Byron was self-confessedly the most Popean of the Romantics) and the visionary æsthetic of W. B. Yeats. Evidently, this line is a parody of the witty turns and nuanced repetitions, so elegant in *Shakespeare*'s Sonnets and the Verse-Essays of Alexander Pope. The word 'becomes' is crucial to this effect. In a reversal of logic, this Helicon (one amongst many) might *become* this particular Hell, not only in the sense of metamorphosis, but also in the way a mincing tailor assures his customer the suit he has stitched *becomes* its wearer.

The difference, though, lies in the deliberate weakness of style, the threateningly bulging metre, the gratuitous repetition of 'another' (so suggestive of inexorable doom): all of which is the work of the Yeatsian visionary. In all senses of the phrase, even the most nihilistic, this poem is the vision of Great Britain 'becoming unbecoming'.

2.7 *I'm pissed*: Such a crass claim of intoxication, rather than a genuine confession on the part of the poet, is probably more likely to be a parodic reference to the following contemporaneously unpublished stanza which appears on the back of one of the pages of Byron's manuscript of the first Canto of *Don Juan*:

> I would to Heaven I were so much Clay—
>   As I am blood—bone—marrow, passion—feeling—
> Because at least the past were past away—
>   And for the future—(but I write this reeling
> Having got drunk exceedingly to day
>   So that I seem to stand upon the ceiling)
> I say—the future is a serious matter—
> And so—for Godsake—Hock and Soda water.

The reader will note here the fixation on the future, the sense of insidious intoxication and the reversal of perception ('I seem to stand upon the ceiling'), all of which are characteristic of the present work. I don't think we are seriously to understand that Byron is actually drunk when he writes this. Much more likely is the explanation that he begins the stanza under the influence, reaches the word 'future' in the fourth line and abandons it only to complete the octave in the morning, tinged with the guilt of a hangover, in such a way that it both confesses and captures the drunkenness which embarrassingly disabled him the night before. The Scotch rhyme of the final couplet is picturesque self-admonishment. One can almost smell the pickled breath of the belligerent Glaswegian alcoholic and feel the spray of spittle off his recalcitrant lips.

'Pissed', of course, could also literally mean *micturated*. In this case the persona could be allying itself not so much to the 'fans' (the drunken vomiters) as to the 'calimari' (that which is expelled). 'Pissed', in this reading, is an action rather than a state; the idea being that we see the voice of the poem not as the 'psyche' of the poet (his *breath* and *soul*) but as the persona's *urine*: a waste product rather than an essence.

3.1 *Danny LaRue*: A professional 'drag artist'. One imagines the other personalities to be cut from the same cloth.

3.8 *Marieannes*: Marie-Anne is a French pastiche of Britannia. She is often conflated with a personified 'Liberty' because her first appearance—bare-breasted in that typically rustic French manner—is in Delacroix's 'Liberty leading the people'. Contrary to popular belief, this painting was produced to commemorate not the Jacobin revolution of the C18th, but the revolution of July 1830 in which the legitimate Bourbon monarchy (re-instated after the defeat of Napoleon by Great Britain) was replaced with the 'Orleanist' monarch Louis-Phillipe. This depressing event was actually very similar to the so-called 'Glorious Revolution' in England in 1688. It was carried out by Bourgeois politicians in order to create exactly the kind of faux constitutional monarchy which they had identified as the only power capable of defeating their own Revolutionary Imperialism at Trafalgar and Waterloo. Another of the iconic national artworks created to commemorate what was, therefore, actually a short-lived Whigist coup in 1830, was Berlioz's arrangement of *La Marseillaise*: to this day the official version of the national anthem. So much for *vive la différence*. What followed was anarchist insanity in the Paris Commune, The *Internationale* and *Les Folies Pigales*.

> And all £ose queens who stretched £e frontier
>   Of queer politics, like Charlotte Von
> Mahlsdorf and Marsha Johnson, Sylvia
>   Rivera, Charlotte Bach and Ray Bourbonne,
> Whose feats relived £e *aristeia*
>   Of Charles Chevalier d'Eon de Beaumont.
> My work can do wi£out a famous name;
>   Not even some old hasbeen panto-dame:

4.2 *queer*. This is the first of innumerable examples in which this poem's drawling Birmingham diphthongs are stretched across two syllables by means of an implicit diæresis: a particularly unpleasant form of phonetic prevarication which nevertheless serves, by means of a kind of phonic mimesis, quite helpfully to mark the key concepts in the poem's dealings with the moral and cultural prevarications which are its theme.

    'Queer' is an obvious choice. In Standard British English it originally meant *skewed* or *non-perpendicular*, and carried not entirely unfavourable connotations when used metaphorically. In criminal cant, however, the OED shows there to have been a simultaneous homonym used by thieves and low-lives to castigate (or perhaps to flatter) those who were even more disreputable than themselves. It was also, therefore, used in reference to counterfeits. Perhaps it is from this form that we get the American sense intended here: *sexually deviant* or *homosexual*. The uncanny combination in this word, of the debased sense and the debased sound, suggests to me that these instances of dialectal diæresis in the poem might be labelled *queers*; perhaps it would be even more accurate to say that words treated in this fashion have been *queered* (not just 'made strange' but 'quizzed', 'ridiculed', 'puzzled', 'imposed upon', 'cheated', 'swindled', 'despoiled'. This is not to mentioned 'queried' and 'made querelous'.

4.4 *Rivera*: era 1

4.5 *aristeia*: A rare example of a genuinely justifiable diæresis (such as the one in the word 'diæresis' itself).

    This poem is itself a debased *aristeia*, of course, at least from the point in stanza 64 where it begins to ape 'The Rape of the Lock'. The standard pattern—the arming scene, the evocation of the brilliance of the armoured hero, the exhortation of followers, the first exploit, the wounding, the divine intervention, the renewed exploits, the double simile, the kill, the taunt—is identifiable. It undergoes, however, a fission-like disintegration across tawdry characters and scenes. Some of this is the result of following the Wasp of Twickenham, but where Pope is gently mocking Society by comparison with a stable heroic matrix, the poet of this Canto is presenting a nightmare vision of a world in which heroism is entirely exploded. Pope uses ancient heroism to mock the unheroic modern world; this poet summons up a world in which heroism is itself mocked by its counterfeit embodiments. The result is a terrifying evocation of an utterly deracinated culture. We should only, suggests the poet, venture into this poetic Ææa if protected by the *moly* (from Sanskrit *mūla*, 'root') of literary, linguistic and historical knowledge which can avert our moral emasculation: our transformation into unthinking swine after drinking from the cup of the grotesque transsexual Circe who is its anti-heroine. I will venture, in these annotations, to provide the reader with his *moly*.

4.2-6 The rhyme 'Von', 'Bourbonne', 'Beaumont' is off. 'Ray Bourbonne' is a feminized and Frenchified version of 'Ray Bourbon' (an American female impersonator with links to the Communist Party) designed to insist on both the iambic stress and the correct vowel sound to rhyme with Von. Presumably, 'Beaumont' is intended to be pronounced with a silent <t>, as in French. It can only be a half-rhyme if it is: the final consonant being a velar, rather than an alveolar, nasal. It is characteristic of an uneducated anglophone pronunciation to stress the last syllable of all French names. This bourgeois overcorrection marks the speaker out as Birmingham *nouveau riche* in comparison with the aristocratic anglicisms of Byron, who rhymes 'Ribaupierre's' with 'grenadiers' and 'appears' (DJ VIII.71) and 'Gulf of Lyons' with 'only die once' (DJ II.39), as might any unpretentious artisan.

'Frontier… / Sylvia… / *aristeia*' is a mite less forced, but no less unpleasant on the ear.

4.8 *panto-dame*: This is typical of the debased amphibious hyphenations in the poem. The Greek prefix *panto-* which elevates the term to which it is attached to a superlative, unique or all-encompassing status, has become a decrepit slang abbreviation of the infantile theatrical form *pantomime*. A term which might have meant *the quintessence of noble womanhood* is therefore rendered, quite literally, as a *travesty*: an ageing thespian of dubious sexual morality playing a risible old battleaxe to glut the basest comic appetites of the crowd.

5

> £e Great Suprendo as £e Widow Twanky,
> > Or Hinge and Brackett, Joe Grimaldi, Dick
> 'I like you' Emery, or Jimmy Krankie
> > (I'm not £at fussy which way round — a chick
> In drag's as capable of hanky panky
> > As any two-bit Mrs Shufflewick.)
> But stars don't get a look-in in £is ditty.
> My unsung diva's from an unsung city.

5.6 *two-bit*: another Americanism with a vulgar pun. The phrase means 'worthless' and derives from a jocular American name for the 'quarter', the coin worth 25 cents. The name suggests the existence of an entirely fictional coin, the 'bit', worth one eighth of a dollar. I say fictional, but crucial to the distinction between decimal and Imperial coinage is the idea— still carried as an idealistic hope in the latter—that coins of intrinsic value can be physically divided in order to create 'change'. This is the reason for the Base-12 system of calculation in the shilling, for example. As a way of partitioning the circle, twelve is a much more useful number than 10. This is something the Greeks and Romans learned from the inventors of the measurement of Time in ancient Babylon. And this astronomical, geometrical system was applied to money in order to mirror on Earth the way the gods revolved the heavens. Before the rot set in, the silver penny could literally be divided ('cleaved' you might say) into the ha'penny and the farthing; similarly a groat could be divided into four pennies, a shilling into four threepenny 'bits' and a sovereign into four crowns; and the reverse impressions on the coins were divided into four sectors by means of a symmetrical Christian cross for precisely this reason. Of course, this is only possible if coins are worth what they claim to be worth.

The 'quarter' is a hangover of this sensible way of doing things in the world's first decimalized monetary system. To call a quarter 'two bits' is to reassert (however ironically) the value of precious metal over the arbitrary signification of value. If a dollar were a pound, 'a quarter' would be 'a crown'. It is not, though. Whatever the exchange rate now—since Bretton-Woods—a dollar was originally four shillings. It was a Spanish coin otherwise known as a 'piece of eight' (being worth eight *reals*). It is the *real* that was the 'bit' therefore: a silver coin similar in size and weight to the sixpence. To this day, the Irish call a sixpence a *reul*.

It is characteristic of the violence done against the stable values of nobility by capitalist American revolutionaries that 'two-bit' (a sum of money now laying claim to be equivalent with the 'crown') has become synonymous with 'penny-pinching'. Decimalization was (and still is) the consolidation of a decadent shift of currency from intrinsic value, via promissory money, to arbitrary tokens of exchange, with all the logical and moral abstractions this entails. The conspiracy behind the metrical measurement of space and mass, the digital representation of time, and so-called 'relativity' (which this arbitrary thinking has inevitably spawned) is one that seeks to bring all our transactions and even our models of the universe down to the level of an Arab market-trader counting on his fingers for the venal purposes of haggling.

'A bit': *a morsel* is etymologically derived from *the result of a bite*. I cannot help but note how ironic the memory is that this evokes of Arab stallholders 'testing the mettle' of suspect coins with their teeth. The vulgar pun also has its part to play. A polysemous strand of the noun 'bit' is the sense: *the part of something that bites*; hence *drill bit* and *the bit of a key*. The crudest synonym in French for the phallus is 'la bite', and there seems no reason why a similar slang term could not be prevalent in this future dialect. The amphibious threat of this decimal/Imperial coin—the definitively worthless US version of the Crown—is conflated (next to 'Dick… chick… and Shufflewick') with the drag-queen's hidden phallus

5.6 *Mrs Shufflewick*: A crude penile pun: a bowdlerized version of 'shuttlecock'. There are overtones of the role of Industry in the masculinisation of women here too: the *shuttle* being the weaver's tool and the mechanisation of the shuttle—in one of the earliest developments of the Industrial Revolution—making it possible for women (whose arms were shorter) to operate the looms. Thus the industrial working class was feminized and the conflation of bolshevism and so-called *women's rights* was begun. The Spinning Jenny is the true ancestor of Celia Pankhurst; the bawdy proletarian hermaphrodite, *Mrs Shufflewick* is the imagined offspring.

5.7 *Stars don't get a look-in*: 'Look-in' is seemingly used here as in the OED sense 2. '*Sporting slang*. A chance of success' and 'stars' as in *celebrated performers*. These early hints of a reversal in the transitivity of gaze and its relation to the night sky cannot however be ignored. Celestial bodies are made out to be the eyes of readers in the poem's heavens from which the voice seeks (paradoxically perhaps) to hide. Think again of Einstein's 'relativity'. See: 118:8, 144:2

5.7 *ditty*: A quid-dit(t)y [Poet's note]

The atmosphere of decadence the poet is attempting to evoke reaches (even at this early stage) deep into semantic roots. 'Quiddity', which was once a scholarly term for *the definitive essence or nature of a thing* has undergone—via sneering parodic use—a deterioration which has left it meaning *a pedantic quibble*. This poem itself stands as an epitome of this process of decay. Quiddity has become so derelict in this future that it has been cleaved with a hyphen (to resemble the innumerable American slang pairings) so as to mean *a nonsense rhyme sung by a debased sovereign*: a 'quid-ditty'—the quiddity of this poem (in the old sense) is truly expressed by such a quidditative epithet (in the modern sense).

5.8 *unsung city*: The last line of this stanza originally read 'My real Queen comes from a real city', expressly recalling Eliot's 'unreal city.' Clearly Eliot means both 'spectral' and 'ersatz.' I think the cinema must play a role here. These are not just (un)*real* but also (un)*reel* cities. Eliot sees cities 'superimposed' on one another: Dante's Inferno, London, Troy, Baudelaire's Paris and so on. And it is this last which I think provides the key. Eliot spent 1911 in Paris at the time when Lumiere's crowd scenes and the 'fantastic realist' work of the Gaumont's artistic director, Louis Feuillade, were the newest and strangest way of envisioning the urban scenery of the undisputed world capital of cinema. When Eliot returns to London (after the war), he can see these ghostly monochrome moving-images of Paris 'unreeling' through the City's streets, mingled with memories of the 'filmreels' of marching soldiers and the European walking wounded.

The punning repetition of 'real' here, with the usual Brummagem diæresis, emphasizes the bitter irony of a semantic flip from 'authentic' to 'cinematic'. Another, very disturbing, layer of homophony suggests there might also be a play on the Spanish bisyllabic form *real*, (mentioned above) cognate with 'Royal.' Clearly, this 'Queen' is to be neither *real* nor *royal*. Like both Byron and Southey, this all leaves me (royally) 'reeling.' (cf. 0.5 and 2.7)

> Most writers would concede a sense of place
> > Is vital to a narrative's success.
> £e tru€ is — even if it's set in space,
> > Cloudcuckooland, or ancient Thrace — unless
> It's got some kind of geographic base
> > We recognise, a story won't address
> Our needs. Our minds will find £e *pleasure dome*
> Of Kubla Khan a less fantastic home

6.4 *Cloudcuckooland*: Aristophanes' *The Birds* is a very important source in this work. Despite the clear analogy of the role of the pub 'The Black Swan' (and indeed of Birmingham itself) as a place of pivotal revolutionary possibility—the headquarters of a 'counter-society', the reason for this may be as dubious as the fact that 'bird' is a slang term for a woman in contemporary English: a fact which reverses wholesale the definitively phallic/masculine sexual overtones of the birds in Aristophanes. It is adult male birds, and not the females, who are the preening, gaudy, screeching characters of erotic display, as Aristophanes was well aware. Colloquial urban English therefore turns the word into another 'counter.' The many references to birds (especially in the deleted 'dawn' stanzas, 68-78, and in reference to the heroine's entourage) therefore carry symbolic overtones of the wider instability of sex in the poem. It is the symbol of the flamingo, however: the upside-down pink bird, the leader of the Aristophanic chorus, the phoney phoenix, a pan-cultural emblem of sexual deviance with a name that has one of the language's most dubious foreign etymologies (see 175.2) which carries the greatest force in the poem. Given time, I shall explore this topic further.

6.7 *pleasure dome*: Coleridge's ethereal 'pleasure dome' of 'Kubla Khan' (1797) was in Xanadu: or *Xuang-du*, the summer capital of the Mongol Empire in China. This place has echoes in Yeats' imaginary *Byzantium*. (In 'Sailing to Byzantium' he originally intended to include the words: 'Saint Sophia's sacred dome... Mirrored in water.') Nowhere could sound more dissimilar than that most unromantically named English village, Porlock. One suspects Coleridge of inventing the whole anecdote of 'the man on business from Porlock' in order to assert this geographical juxtaposition.

We cannot ignore the history though. In 1797 rumours abounded of French Revolutionary forces plotting to stage an invasion of England. The North Somerset coast was singled out for particular attention when the government was asked by locals to investigate mysterious figures who had been heard speaking a foreign language and roaming the moors around the coast, near to Porlock, taking notes. These suspected French spies turned out to be the poets Wordsworth and Coleridge who were just rambling on Exmoor and writing poetry, as was their wont. They had, of course, been outspoken supporters of the revolution of 1789 but had become sufficiently disillusioned by the *reign of terror* no longer to be taken seriously as a revolutionary fifth-column. The suspicion was quashed.

A crucial upshot of the environment of national paranoia that led to this misunderstanding, however, had been (earlier in the year) a run on the Bank of England. Such a large number of people had demanded the redemption of their bank-notes for bullion that the Government was forced on February 26th to suspend the principle of redeemability and enforce a 'fiat' money system. Naturally enough, it was this event which led to the great Bullion debates of the period, which set British monetary policy for a century. This cannot have been far from Coleridge's mind when he wrote his famous fragment. The legend of the Kubla Khan was, of course, originally brought to the West by

Marco Polo. Immediately after describing the opulence of the tyrant's summer palace in Xuang-du, the Venetian explorer includes the following chapter (ed. H. Yule 1871. pp. 378-80)

> *How the Great Kaan Causes the Bark of Trees, Made into Something Like Paper, to Pass for Money...*
>
> Now that I have told you in detail of the splendour of this City of the Emperor's, I shall proceed to tell you of the Mint which he hath in the same city, in the which he hath his money coined and struck, as I shall relate to you. And in doing so I shall make manifest to you how it is that the Great Lord may well be able to accomplish even much more than I have told you, or am going to tell you in this Book...the way [the Emperor's mint] is wrought is such that you might say he hath the Secret of Alchemy in perfection, and you would be right. For he makes his money after this fashion.
>
> He makes them take of the bark of a certain tree... What they take is a certain fine white bast or skin which lies between the wood of the tree and the thick outer bark, and this they make into something resembling sheets of paper, but black. When these sheets have been prepared they are cut up into pieces of different sizes... All these pieces of paper are issued with as much solemnity and authority as if they were of pure gold or silver; and on every piece a variety of officials, whose duty it is, have to write their names, and to put their seals. And when all is prepared duly, the chief officer deputed by the Kaan smears the Seal entrusted to him with vermilion, and impresses it on the paper, so that the form of the Seal remains imprinted upon it in red; the Money is then authentic. Anyone forging it would be punished with death. And the Kaan causes every year to be made such a vast quantity of this money, which costs him nothing, that it must equal in amount all the treasure of the world.
>
> With these pieces of paper, made as I have described, he causes all payments on his own account to be made; and he makes them to pass current universally over all his kingdoms and provinces and territories, and whithersoever his power and sovereignty extends. And nobody, however important he may think himself, dares to refuse them on pain of death. And indeed everybody takes them readily, for wheresoever a person may go throughout the Great Kaan's dominions he shall find these pieces of paper current, and shall be able to transact all sales and purchases of goods by means of them just as well as if they were coins of pure gold...
>
> When any of those pieces of paper are spoilt—not that they are so very flimsy neither—the owner carries them to the mint, and by paying 3 per cent. on the value he gets new pieces in exchange. And if any baron, or any one else soever, hath need of gold or silver or gems or pearls, in order to make plate, or girdles, or the like, he goes to the Mint and buys as much as he list, paying in this paper money.

The image of a palace of unsurpassed opulence created entirely out of air by the quasi-divine process of 'decree' finds neat analogues in the idea of the Khan's invention of the great economic fiction: 'promissory' money. The fact that England was in the throes of a national debate about precisely the same monetary system at the time of writing should not go unnoticed by critics, however 'new' they think themselves to be.

Xanadu seems, quite wrongly, to have become conflated in the popular imagination with the oriental idyll of *Shangri-La*. The latter derives from James Hilton's *Lost Horizon* (1933). Quite unlike the magnificent but ironic epitome of imaginative human ambition in Coleridge's vision-fragment, it is a rather more homely centenarian's paradise, supposedly in the mountains of Tibet, which reminds the hero "very slightly of Oxford" (page 212): a resemblance which I find it difficult to imagine today, despite the view through my window of the neatly tended quad.

<pre>
                             7
             For instance, in (say) Rome or Jodrell Bank,
                 Or round £e corner from £e Cutty Sark,
             Or where Titanic or £e Bismark sank,
                 Or perched on Ararat like Noah's ark.
             It may as well just be a Sea-Life tank,
                 £e Eden Project, or a Centerparc.
             You're welcome to your own New Xanadu,
                 I'm gunna do £e place I wanna do.
</pre>

7.1 *Jodrell Bank*: By a rather staggering coincidence this place was mentioned in a copy of a popular scientific journal I recently came across in the neighbouring classroom. If I remember rightly, it is a botanical research site owned by the University of Manchester, 20 or so miles to the south of the city, on which an astronomer called Lovell (the Kubla Khan of the piece) is planning to construct the world's largest 'radio-telescope': which is not a wireless set through which one can see the *Jolly Roger* of an approaching pirate ship, but an enormous rotating dish with the surface area of a football pitch that looks for all the world as if it were designed as a docking-place for one of the 'flying saucers' piloted by extra-terrestrial aliens about which the scaremongers have recently found it impossible to hold their peace.

7.2 P. Y. Gerbeau: *ze tent*. [Poet's note]

One assumes the above to be an incomplete bibliographic citation. The *Cutty Sark* is, of course, the old tea clipper moored at Greenwich quay. The name comes from Burns's 'Tam O Shanter' where it is used to refer to the revealingly short-cut dress worn by one of the witches who accost Tam on his drunken ride home. Quite what the title of the book might be is hard to make out: it looks like '*ze tent*', but that makes no sense in any language of which I am aware. 'Zee' (with two <e>s rather than one) is Dutch for *sea*—which would seem, on the surface at least, to have a direct connection with the sailing vessel—but that is about as far as my knowledge of that language stretches and it might just as easily be read as the American rendering of the last letter of the alphabet; besides, it seems much more in keeping with the poem's thematic focus on cheap, flashy temptation and resistance of the demonic fake feminine that the poet would choose to cite a reference to the Burns rather than the ship.

7.5-6 *Sea Life tank, The Eden Project… centerparc*: Dreary Science-Fiction jargon for futuristic public buildings. One imagines the glass-sided edifices so beloved of modern visions of the city. It is the most memorable architectural characteristic of Zamyatin's 'dystopia' *We*, for example, that all buildings are transparent, thus banishing privacy entirely. The most memorable narrative characteristic is its opening (like this poem) in a heavily ironic vein, narrated by an ardent supporter of the society it depicts. This man, who is called simply D-503, tellingly refers to 'One-State' as a 'Golden Eden.' Titles like 'The Eden Project' and 'Centerparc' (with its amphibious combination of American and French misspellings) would not be at all out of place in Zamyatin's innovative work. 'Sea Life tank' one presumes to be a massive aquarium of aquatic animals bred in captivity; the actual sea being so polluted or built-over in this era that it can no longer support life.

8.6 As the following stanza explains, the word 'Birmingham' (meaning *counterfeit*) was introduced into the language in the 1670s when the number of fake groats brought into circulation from the workshops of that town became so large that it seriously threatened the national economy. The word very quickly became transferred to the Whigs in Parliament, ostensibly via an abbreviation of 'Birmingham Protestant' as a denunciation of their claims to the religious high-ground. In my opinion, however, this epithet stands much more tellingly as an affirmation of the genetic connection between the radical side of the political divide and the non-conformist capitalism lingering in the dingy midlands since the Civil War: bitterly resentful of the Restoration and now intent on revolution via these insidious means.

It is quite fitting that the second of the poem's 'Birmingham Alexandrines' is chosen as the line in which to introduce this usage of the word. The Alexandrine is generally denounced by English poets:

> A needless *Alexandrine* ends the song,
> That like a wounded snake, drags its slow length along
> (Pope *Essay on Criticism* 358-359)

Pope is caricaturing the pompous habit of finishing a poem of pentameters with a gratuitous six-foot line. He is almost certainly thinking of the imitators of Spenser, whose stanzas routinely end in a hexameter. In particular, this example recalls the last line of the following stanza in *The Faerie Queene* (XXX.xi.28. Smith, 1909: p.498):

> For round about the wals yclothed were
>   With goodly arras of great maiesty,
>   Wouen with gold and silke so close and nere,
>   That the rich metall lurked priuily,
>   As faining to be hid from enuious eye;
>   Yet here, and there, and euery where vnwares
>   It shewd it selfe, and shone vnwillingly;
>   Like a discolourd Snake, whose hidden snares
> Through the greene gras his long bright burnisht backe declares.

This is an erotic tapestry seen by Britomart in the hallway of the burning house of the tyrannical Busyrane, and by Scudamore beyond the flames through which (unlike his virtuous female counterpart) he cannot pass. Britomart—both a version of the Minoan goddess of chastity, Britomartis, whom Spenser would have read about in Virgil's epyllion *Ciris*, and a chivalric elision of Britain and Mars—was self-evidently a literary model for the revival of the figure of Britannia in the C17th. Spenser likens the violent lust depicted in the tapestry, and the treacherous lustre lent to it by the use of gold thread, to the fire burning around the house and the 'hidden snares' of the snake in the grass. The phrase 'faining to be hid from envious eye' is crucial to Spenser's examination in Book 3 of the perils of the dissembling æsthetics of seduction. Just like our poet, Spenser uses his Alexandrine to mimic the enemy. The multiple alliterative stresses of 'long bright burnisht back declares' serve to 'wound' the iambic flow of the line so that it 'drags its slow length along'. The effect on the reader is one of suddenly discovering the snake crawling in his mouth. Britomart is the embodiment of resistance to such insidious influences. Her travesty in *The Birmingham Quean* is quite the opposite, of course.

It is important to remember that the Mediæval French 'Alexandrin' was originally not a hexameter at all, but a line consisting of two hemistichs of two trisyllabic feet. The *Roman d'Alexandre* of Alexandre de Paris—from which the form gets its name—has a rhythm much more akin to the triplets of Byron's 'The Destruction of Sennacherib' than to anything consonant with the stately tread of iambic pentameter.

> 8
>
> Our scene is set in Birmingham: a town
>   Whose expertise in manufacturing
> Attracted ra£er dubious reknown
>   In 1680-odd when, fracturing
> £e House of Lords to bring £e Tories down,
>   Shaftesbury's Whigs – or £e *Birminghams* – backed £e King
> Into a corner wi£ a 'counterfeit':
> A plot to get £eir man a crown to fit.

It was Ronsard who first identified the Alexandrin with the resonant hexameter of classical epic. He was at great pains to keep his six feet in line. Spenser, at the highpoint of this Renascence hybridisation of medieval romance and classical epic, quite naturally incorporates these newly classicized Alexandrines into his verse. He understood very well, however, that the medieval metre 'lurkèd privily' in the rhythmic weave and that its 'discolourd' stresses could 'shine unwillingly' at moments of this kind.

Pope was aware of precisely the same thing. The second hemistich of his 'needless Alexandrine':

drágs its slów léngth alóng   but also   drags its slów length alóng   and even   drágs its slow léngth along

(*Shedding its skin of iambic pentameter*)

The Alexandrine is therefore correctly used, in my opinion, not to refer to unproblematic hexameter, but only to those instances of dodecasyllabic lines which carry this threat of metrical disturbance. Clearly, this line is an example. The possibility of a triplet rhythm is overtured by the trisyllabic rhyme (manu)facturing / fracturing in lines 2 and 4 and is consolidated in line 6 by the central dactyl '*Birminghams*'. Consequently, it is difficult not to read this line as dactylic; something which emphasizes the irony of 'backed the King' (to be undercut by 'Into a corner') by tempting the reader to skip blithely over the normal emphasis on 'King'.

Despite considerable evidence that the poem was begun with the intention of ending each stanza on a disruptive *Birmingham* Alexandrine of this kind, the extant 'hexameters' appear almost exclusively (as here) in the sixth line of the octave. The effect is a bathetic one. A kind of *rubato* sensation is created—or perhaps its opposite: an acceleration, like the pattering steps of a long-jumper approaching the take-off board—before the stanza tumbles headlong into the comic couplet. It is a rhythmic effect similar to the semantic one via which Tamburlaine's most transcendent speech collapses (like Phæton pranging the chariot of the sun, and Icarus splashing down in the Ægean) into 'The sweet fruition of an earthly crowne.' (1590: II.vi.69)

For a discussion of how this effect brings together the bathos of comic doggerel with the sense of a vulgar poetics of prescience we need to turn to De Quincey:

> as Grecian taste expanded, the disagreeable criticisms whispered about in Athens as to the coarse quality of the verses that proceeded from Delphi. It was like bad Latin from Oxford. Apollo himself to turn out of his own temple, in the very age of Sophocles, such <u>Birmingham hexameters</u> as sometimes astonished Greece, was like our English court keeping a Stephen Duck, the thresher, for the national poet-laureate, at a time when Pope was fixing an era in the literature. Metre fell to a discount in such learned times.
>
>   ('Style' Part II: D. Masson [ed.] 1890, Vol X., p.171. My emphasis.)

He resists using the word *Alexandrine* for the obvious reason of avoiding an anachronism, but the ironic attachment of this idea of 'discounted' hexameter to the figure of Alexander the Great is crucial to the hermeneutic reading this poem demands. It was Alexander the Great, we should remember, who first understood the importance of a bimetallic standard to the stability of empire. He did not hoard the gold he won from Darius; instead, he minted the first truly abundant gold *stater*, whose value he fixed in relation to that of the Attic standard of the silver *drachma*. Alexander it was who also took the fateful step beyond the innovation of his Great Grandfather, Alexander I of Macedonia (of inscribing his name on his coins) by posing himself for the portrait of Herakles. He was therefore legendarily the first ruler whose image appeared on his own coinage. After his death, those who sought to capitalize on his supposed divinity transposed the portrait from the drachma to the stater. Thus was Alexander reified.

The bitterest intellectual opponent of Alexander's reign was the Cynic philosopher Diogenes:

> the son of a disreputable money-changer who had been sent to prison for defacing the coinage... His aim in life was to do as his father had done, to 'deface the coinage', but on a much larger scale. He would deface all the coinage current in the world. Every conventional stamp was false. The men stamped as generals and kings; the things stamped as honour and wisdom and happiness and riches; all were base metal with lying superscription.
>
> (Gilbert Murray, *Five Stages of Greek Religion*, Oxford: Clarendon Press 1925, p.117)

Every schoolboy knows the story of Diogenes replying, when asked what the emperor could do for him, simply 'stand out of my light': a particularly caustic remark when one considers Alexander's traditional identification with Apollo, not just on the disc of the gold stater but also on the face of the sun whose light it reflected. Never was envy of inherent nobility so loathingly expressed. Diogenes, the presumptuous son of a coiner, is truly the progenitor of the sneering hypocrisies of the Puritans and the Birmingham non-conformists who eventually came to see themselves as the future leaders of a Capitalist Empire of America.

Like Diogenes, the persona of this piece seeks to 'deface the coinage' with its Birmingham Alexandrines: to 'back the Queen into a corner with a counterfeit'.

9.1 *something cheap and fake*: Southey demonstrates neatly just how and why the name of this city continues to be synonymous with the blasé illegality and infernal ingenuity in the cheap replication of valuable objects (in this case, objects of literary art and the symbols of nation and civilisation) which define both the mimetic method and the thematic nub of the poem (*op. cit.*: Letter 36, p.198):

> In some parts of Italy, the criminal who can prove himself to be the best workman in any business is pardoned *in favorem artis*, unless his crime has been coining; a useful sort of benefit of clergy. If ingenuity were admitted as an excuse for guilt in this country, Birmingham rogues might defy the gallows. Even as it is, they set justice at defiance, and carry on the most illegal practices almost with impunity... The officers of justice had received intelligence of a gang of coiners; the building to which they were directed stood within a court-yard, and when they reached it they found that the only door was on the upper storey, and could not be reached without a ladder: a ladder was procured: it was then some time before the door

A *Birmingham*, you see, was some€ing fake,
    Because £ere'd been a ra$ of dodgy groats
From £ere when Brummies worked out how to make
    A decent replica of all £e coats
Of arms and heads of kings £ey'd need to take
    £e taxes back £ey'd lost to royal boats
And wars: no need to axe £e monarch's head
When you can stamp it on some tin instead.

---

could be forced, and they heard the people within mocking them all this while.When at last they had effected their entrance, the coiners pointed to a furnace in which all the dies and whatever else could incriminate them, had been consumed during this delay… An inexhaustible supply of halfpence was made for home consumption, till the new coinage put a stop to this manufactory: it was the common practice of the dealers in this article, to fry a pan-full every night after supper for the next day's delivery, thus darkening them, to make them look as if they had been in circulation.

9.2 *rash of dodgy groats*: The image of coins as plague-sores is a gruesome favourite of Thomas Dekker's (*News From Gravesend* 1604, in Wilson [ed.] 1925: p.37, ll. 17-30):

For then the Vsurer must behold
His pestilent flesh, whilst all his gold
Turns into Tokens, and the chest
(They lie in,) his infectious brest:
How well heele play the Misers part
When all his coyne sticks at his heart?
Hees worth so many farthings then,
That was a golden God mongst men.

And tis the aptest death (so please
Him that breath heauen, earth, and Seas)
For euery couetous rooting Mowle
That heaues his drosse aboue his soule,
And doth in coyne all hopes repose,
To die with corps, stampt full of those.

9.6 *taxes*: Specifically, the Hearth-Money of 1662-1689. This was a property tax levied by Charles II. According to popular belief—in thrall to puritans who likened it to his father's infamous 'Ship Money'—this tax was used exclusively to fund the complex naval wars between England, Holland and France (through which Dryden steers a steady course in *Annus Mirabilis*.) It was actually a fair and simple tax, at least in its drafting: a fine example of legislative success during the early Restoration. The charge was biannual, collected on Lady's Day and Michaelmas, at 2 shillings per chimney in each dwelling. All households with 2 chimneys or less, and all hearths used as forges or what have you, were to be exempt. Thus the tax would not affect the poor, and neither could anyone say the King was avenging himself against the Parliamentarian armourers.

    The tax's only fault lay in the decision to farm collection out to profiteers. These private bailiffs were often unscrupulous and tended to ignore the exemptions. The people hardest hit were the small metal-workers in towns like Birmingham and Sheffield. In a broadside petition of 1680 made by the Hallamshire Company of Cutlers to Parliament, Birmingham is the only town mentioned by name:

> At *Brimmingham* are Sword-Smiths, Cutlers, Spurriers, Bridle-Bit-Makers, Naylers, and divers other Handicrafts Men who live by Manufacturing of Iron and Steel, are very Poor, have numerous Families, moſt of them Working at *6 d. or 8 d.* a day Wages, cannot make any Work without Blowing, and therefore muſt have Blowing-Forges in their Houſes… ſome of them (though the pooreſt Men of all) have Two or Three…
>
> For ſeveral years after the Act, and Additional and Explanatory Acts, and Votes and Reſolves aforeſaid concerning the Duty of Hearth-Money paſſed, there was no demand made of theſe poor People of any duty for their Forges.
>
> But ſince the Collectors of the Chimney-Money have made Demands upon all thoſe poor People of *2 s.* a Forge, (which is expreſly againſt the Letter of the Acts and Votes aforeſaid) and for non-payment have made Diſtreſſes, taken away their Goods, to their great prejudice, whereby they are diſcouraged from continuing to work any longer. And which is moſt ſevere, they commonly deſtrain upon their Working-Tools, which for want of Money they cannot ſometimes redeem in four or five days; all which time ſtand ſtill, and muſt loſe the getting much more than might have paid the Duty.
>
> ('The Case of the Company of Cutlers… etc.' Parliamentary Archives HC/PO/JO/1680)

This is, I think, the first document to be produced by a revolutionary industrial 'Trades Union' movement. Do not be fooled by the apparent humility of the plea. There is a thinly veiled threat here. These men-not-working, because of the tax they refuse to pay, are men who can (and have) made swords and guns when organized together. The appeal to Parliament, and Parliament alone, is telling. There is no mention of the King, which serves only to imply some collusion between The Crown and those who defy their 'Votes and Reſolves'. (The King had recently dissolved Parliament; an exclusive appeal like this was quite provocative.)

It is easy to see how the Whigs might use a seething underbelly of Parliamentarian discontent in the heartland of industrial non-conformism as a threat to wave under the noses of Court during the Exclusion. Many still carried scars from brummagem blades and balls. The 'divers Handicrafts Men' of that town might find it just as obvious a choice to exact revenge with a bit of coining.

9.7-8 *axe the Monarch's head… some tin instead*: The thoroughgoing ironies of this piece are of course reliant upon the 'dissociation of sensibility' which T. S. Eliot discovers in the work of all English poets after Milton ('The Metaphysical Poets'). This is perfectly fitting however; the 'dissociation of sensibility' is the central theme of the entire piece and Mr Eliot is himself a progenitor of the kind of irony employed to dramatize this theme. It is an irony that may be called historical: the ignoble present is suddenly thrust into contrast with the noble past.

The poet is identifying Byron as the epitome of the genetic heritage of this Miltonic, regicidal poetics and Birmingham as the epitome of the same violent dissociation of value in the country's economics. To elucidate, I think the poet (quite rightly) conflates the severance of face value and intrinsic value in the coinage with the severance of sense and sensation in the national language and poetry. He dates the moment of this severance (as does Eliot) to the execution of the King in 1649. It would not be a surprise to learn that the axe-head used to carry out this awful deed was made in Birmingham. What is certain is that the Non-Conformist weapons manufacturers in that place resorted, at the Restoration, to coining as a way of ensuring that the King's head (as a stamp of value) was kept apart from the economic body-politic and that the words of their burgeoning industrial dialect contained precisely the same dissociation of value. In the long-run this slower and more insidious axe-swing has been much more devastating.

10

  And Brum is still £e place for $ady coins.
   £ere's always been an unofficial mint
  Or two to profit from pastiche designs:
   Ca$-forges £at do pretty well by dint
  Of negligible overheads and lines
   Of dunderheads who're sucked in by £e glint
  Of gold. And since £e sovereign's still £e prize,
  £ey won't need to replace £e Royal dies.

10.1 *Brum*: short for 'Brummagem' of course. The minor variations on the names of this definitively treacherous, unstable and dissembling location are of much greater numbers than any other town in England. They include (and this is by no means an exhaustive list) (Hamper 1868: Vol 1., p.502) [I recommend the use of a magnifying lens to read them]:

Baemegum,	Bermingheam	Birmygham	Bremisham	Brinnicham	Brumidgum	Bryingham	Brymscham	Burmyngcham
Barmegam,	Bermyncham	Birmyncham	Bremmencham	Brinningham	Brumigam	Bryminham	Brymysham	Burmyngeham
Beringham	Bemynehelham	Birmyngeham	Bremygiam	Bromedgham	Brumigham	Brymmyngeham	Byringham	Burmyngham
Berkmyngham	Bermyngam	Birmyngehame	Bremyngham	Bromicham	Brumingham	Brymmyngham	Byrmyngham	Burmyngham
Bermechagm	Bermyngham	Birymincham	Brennyngeham	Bromichum	Brummagem	Brymmyngiam	Burmegam	Byrmegham
Bermengeham	Bemingham	Bormingham	Brimcham	Bromidgham	Brummejam	Brymycham	Burmegam	Byrmicham
Bermengham	Bemynghem	Bormyngeham	Bremiechame	Bromidgome	Brummigham	Brymychcam	Burmegum	Byrmingcham
Bermgham	Beringham	Brammingham	Brimcham	Bromincham	Brummingham	Brymycham	Burmicham	Byrmincham
Bermicham	Birmincham	Breemejam	Brimingeham	Bromingham	Brummingsham	Brymyham	Burmigam	Byrmingeham
Bermicheham	Birminghcham	Bremecham	Brimingham	Bromisham	Brumwicham	Brymymcham	Burmingham	Byrmingham
Bermigham	Birmingecham	Bremicham	Brimisham	Bromycham	Brunningham	Brymyncham	Burmucham	Byrmyncham
Bermmgaham	Birmingeham	Bremichem	Brimmidgham	Brumageum	Brymecham	Brymyngam	Burmycham	Byrmyncham
Bermincham	Birminghame	Bremingham	Brimmigham	Brumegume	Brymedgham	Brymyngiam	Burmycheham	Byrmyngcham
Bermingeham	Birmingingham	Bremingham	Brimmingham	Brumicham	Brymicham	Brymynham	Burmygham	Byrmyngham
Bermingham	Birmingyhame	Bremiseham	Brimyncham	Brumidgham	Brymingecham	Brymycham	Burmyncham	Byrmyngyhame

The illiteracy of the inhabitants has no-doubt played a role in this, but one suspects the reason to be more disturbing and deliberate. Disguise, resistance of authority, and the shoddy mass reproduction of decorative goods are the hallmarks of the place. The city seems, to this day, to churn out lazy, metathesized versions of its name just as it always churned out cheap variations of the sovereign coinage, in absolute contempt of all who try to regulate its anarchic dialects and forges. Hence its aptitude to the Exclusion debates:

> *Flaſh.* Gentlemen, ſhall not I come in for a ſnack among ye? I have a *Puppet-ſhow* of Religion in me too. Gentlemen, let me know what it is you'll be at? I'm for any thing in the world to pleaſe ye: wold you have me a Papiſt? Gentlemen, your humble Servant: would you have me a Mahometan? Gentlemen, I'm yours. A Jew, a Heathen, a *No-Religion-man*, one that ſhall Fear God, and Honour the King, and do neither? Gentlemen I am for who bids moſt; I love to be Complaiſant.
>
> *Fly-blow.* Thou put'ſt me to a little kind of a puzzle: what art thou call'd? haſt thou got never a Name as well as we?
>
> *Flaſh.* Yes, yes, they tell me I am a thin braſs Proteſtant ſilver'd over; but for brevity ſake though, they call me a *Brummegeum*, which is my Chriſtian name, but my Sirname is *Flaſh*. At preſent my Religion is built moſtly upon Intereſt; if that can but make me *Rich* and *Great*, I have as much as I deſire in this world, without putting my ſelf to the trouble of a thought for the next. I'm juſt like a piece of ſoft wax, and can (as a Conſcientious man ſhould do) receive any impreſſion of Religion that takes well with the Times.
>
> (*Popish Fables etc.* [anonymous broadside] London: John Spicer, 1682)

Brummegeum Flash could easily be the name of the persona of this poem.

10.2 *mint*: I mint what I said. I made an absolute meant. [Poet's note]

It is fundamental to this poem that *money*, *meaning* and *moaning* are cognate forms, and that the dialect used forces them back into a single vulgar 'utterance' of Brummagem coinage. I will return to this point.

10.4 *Cash-forges*: This play on 'forge' reminds us that the usage 'make in fraudulent imitation' derives from the older sense (from Latin *fabricare*) 'to manufacture', most often used in English to refer to precisely the trades of smithying and metalworking which led to Birmingham becoming the spiritual heartland of coining. The rather nice distinction made in contemporary English between 'counterfeit' and 'forgery' in reference to the illegitimate reproduction of money (the former being reserved for coin and the latter for bank-notes) is therefore rendered meaningless by etymology. Unfortunately, this appears to be a self-fulfilling prophecy embedded in the language; this differentiation, which required such a distinction to be made by legislators, between intrinsically valuable coinage and the promissory bank-note has all but disappeared. It is 'forgery' (of capital and power) which has made this happen.

Like so much else to be regretted about the breakdown of stable values of nobility, the *forges* of Birmingham can be identified as the infernal source:

> Assignats were forged here during the late war... The forgery of their own bank notes is carried on with systematic precautions which will surprise you. Information of a set of forgers had been obtained, and the officers entered the house: they found no person on any of the lower floors; but when they reached the garret, one man was at work upon the plates in the farthest room, who could see them as soon as they had ascended the stairs. Immediately he opened a trap door, and descended to the floor below; before they could reach the spot to follow him, he had opened a second, and the descent was impracticable for them on account of its depth: there they stood and beheld him drop floor to floor till he reached the cellar, and effected his escape by a subterranean passage.

(Southey *Letters from England*, Letter 36. 1951: p.199)

10.4 *by dint (of)*: The word 'dint' (it is another version of 'dent') has progressed from meaning *the action of striking* through *the force of a blow* to *the impression left by a stroke*. i.e. *an indentation*. It is only in the construction 'by dint of', used here, that it retains an older sense of *force* or *power*. The poet is playing on the contradictory ideas of the impression stamped on a 'blank' to make a coin and the idiom glossable as 'as a result of' in a way which calls into question the processes of transitivity involved in the poem. We should ask ourselves whether the voice of the poem is the thing impressed (the blank) or the thing that impresses (the stamp)? Is the poet? Is the reader?

This is another example of a 'counter': it is impossible to say which way the 'dint' is to be administered (and even—as we shall see—which way the effigy itself is therefore supposed to look) because (like Janus) the word (the world) faces in both directions. This is not, one suspects, merely a matter of 'quiddity'. The power to act (and to 'impress') and the moral responsibility for actions (which create these 'impressions') are at stake. The poet is presenting us with a dreadful future in which free-will and moral accountability have been eroded (as has the sense of stable transitivity in—and even *of*—semantics) by a collapse of the stable dichotomies of civilisation into a monstrous amphibology: black and white, good and evil, male and female, self and other, adulthood and childhood, the watcher and the watched, the subject and the object...

                            11
                Because we'll *never* join £e Eurozone.
                    We'll never be prepared to scrap £e pound;
                It seems to glitter like St Edward's €rone,
                    Reflecting all £e glory of £e Crown
                And State: a figurehead £at stands alone —
                    A royal sun to cast its glow around
                £e realm. We love our sovereign coin despite
                £e fact it's less Shinola £an cheap $ite.

11.1 *never join the Eurozone*: This refers, presumably, to the proposed alignment of sterling with the decimal systems of European currency: tantamount to a surrender to Napoleon or Adolf Hitler.

11.3 *St Edward's Throne*: This is usually called 'St Edward's *Chair*'. It is the throne built around the Stone of Scone for Edward I after he had captured it from the Scots. It is housed in Westminster Abbey and has been used in every coronation ceremony since Edward II (except that of Mary I, who provocatively had another throne blessed by the Pope) as the chair on which the Sovereign sits for the physical act of crowning. The recent coronation of Queen Elizabeth II was no exception, I presume. (I have yet to see the film of this occasion of national pride.) Crucially, it does not 'glitter' much at all. There was a time when it was intricately decorated with gilded gesso and pounced, but this detail has long since disappeared. No doubt this has something to do with its muscular removal from the Abbey (the only time this has ever happened) for use in Westminster Hall during the installation of Cromwell as Lord Protector in 1653. One cannot imagine Oliver Cromwell resting his warts-and-all buttocks on a seat embossed with birds and foliage and the image of a seated king. Unlike the other two St Edward pieces used in the coronation—the crown and the staff—the chair was not refurbished in 1661 for the return of the King. Notwithstanding the gilded lions which support it, the chair is therefore puritanically drab. A typical piece of republican Americanized sarcasm on the part of the 'voice of BTV.'

11.6 *A royal sun*: 'Now is the winter of our discontent/Made glorious summer by this sun of York.'
     Aside from the usual complex connotations of Christ in the pun on 'sun'—the pagan resurrection of the *sun* at the equinox with, superimposed upon it (as Frazer implies), the resurrected *son* at Easter—there is also a very strong numismatic thread to Gloucester's opening speech. The personal heraldic symbol of Edward IV, which had appeared on his standard at the decisive Battle of Barnet against *The Kingmaker* (the Earl of Warwick) on Easter Day 1471, was the 'white rose en soleil'; and this had also been chosen as the image for the reverse of the new standard gold coin, the *ryal* (from the Spanish; it was known in the vernacular as the 'rose-noble') in Edward's fundamental reformation of the coinage in 1465.
     Edward's strong, stable and fair economic policy was part and parcel of his success as a King and a military commander; the new Ryals and Angels of the 1465 recoinage stand as the most lasting icon of his legacy. By contrast, coins from the short Protectorate and reign of Richard III are notoriously dubious and poor in quality. (C. Blunt, 1935: 'Some notes on the coinage of Edward IV...', in *British Numismatic Journal* 22.) 'I that am rudely stamped' continues Shakespeare's Gloucester (16) '... I that am curtail'd of this fair Proportion,/Cheated of Feature by dissembling Nature,/Deform'd, vn-finish'd, sent before my time/Into this breathing World, scarse halfe made vp...' (18-21) 'Haue no delight to

passe away the time,/Vnlesse to see my Shadow in the Sunne/And descant on mine owne Deformity.' (25-27).

This carries quite uncontroversial numismatic overtones. Where I read Yeats as holding one of the new Irish coins when (in the original draft) he begins 'Sailing to Byzantium' with '*This* is no country for old men', I think a film adaptation of *Richard III* might find it quite effective to have Richard holding up a Ryal to the light when he says 'this sun of York'.

To play Richard as a hunchback is, I think, rather over-literal. This is a moral deformity expressed in terms which liken him as much to a counterfeit as to a cripple. Surely Richard (like the boar that is his own symbol on the coinage) is simply ugly: more 'nasty, brutish and short' than he is physically disabled. One might argue that, like Yeats, he is implying impotence and the consequent rejection of 'such sensual music' as 'the lascivious pleasing of a lute', but his later scenes with Anne suggest the opposite.

It was Henry Tudor, Richard III's successor, who introduced the Gold Sovereign in 1489; and, in the great recoinage of 1560, which once again restabilized the national economy after the incremental debasements that had been the result of the upheavals of the Reformation, Elizabeth I took the crucial step of differentiating the Sovereign (worth 30s) from the smaller 'one pound coin' (worth 20s) and thereby dealt with the relatively high gold value as compared to silver at the time. Shakespeare would therefore have been well aware of how the links between tyranny and debased coinage, and between usurpation and counterfeiting, are not simply metaphorical. The two plays written at the time of the uncertainty surrounding the succession of James I, *Hamlet* and *Measure for Measure*, are shot through with this same metaphoric quality, like a seam of gold that the delving critic can mine.

The relatively high value of Elizabethan coins—their purity, mass and fine striking—is a given in English numismatics. It is, for example, the basis for the plot in Addison's 'Adventures of a Shilling' (cf. 14.6). This is a direct result of the introduction, in the great 1561 recoinage, of England's first 'milled' coins. In fact, these coins were 'pressed' rather than 'struck' using technology first described by Leonardo Da Vinci (who was no doubt influenced by Gutenberg's printing press) and built by the French moneyer Eloye Mestrelle, which employed mill-horses to turn the wheel: hence 'milled'. The Company of Moneyers was extremely suspicious of this alien technology and their influence was behind Mestrelle's sacking in 1572. Six years later he was hanged for counterfeiting.

The fact that this poet travesties the 'pound coin' of Elizabeth II makes this very biting numismatic satire. The use of 'royal sun', with the glinting pun on *ryal* and *real*, is every bit as sarcastic as Gloucester's.

11.8 *Shinola*: A proprietary name for a brand of boot polish in the United States. An American colleague once colourfully demonstrated to me that *not to know sh*t from Shinola* is that country's equivalent of the idiom *not to know one's arse from one's elbow.*

In England, we say *sugar* instead of *sh*t*, where the French say *merle* ('blackbird') rather than *merde*, when we (and they) would rather avoid profanity. 'Shinola' is also an American equivalent; the idiom having a second meaning—not to know the difference between *saying* 'sh*t' or 'Shinola'. It is a shame, perhaps, that this poem could not employ a few more of these controlled expressions in place of the vulgar epithets. This would no doubt weaken the excremental effect of the satire, however. All that is gold does not glitter.

12

The Swan in Hurst Street is our bird's back-yard.
    I'll warn you now, $e doesn't spread her wings
Just yet. So if you €ink you'll find it hard
    To hold at bay £at snobbi$ sniggering
Whose Cavalier prejudice has marred
    Our image since Bob Porter fought £e King,
£en hide out in *The Oak* (£e 'sovereign tree')
Like Charles £e First, or get to Coventry.

12.1 *The Swan*: The name of the pub is poetically apt. The OED has:

> The name was app. applied orig. to the 'musical' swan, having the form of an agent-noun f. Teut. *swan-*:—Idg. *swon-*: *swen-*, represented by Skr. *svánati* (it) sounds, L. *sonit* (it) sounds, (*sonĕre*, later *sonāre*), Ir. *sennaim* I make music, OE. *geswin* melody, song, *swinsian* to make melody.

Cynewulf plays on this idea in 'The Phoenix'—Shakespeare's 'bird of loudest lay' whose song in the Old English poem marks the hours like a magnificent cuckoo clock: think of the peacock timepiece of James Coxe in the Winter Palace at St. Petersburg, so reminiscent of Yeats's clockwork bird, (he may well have recently seen it depicted in Eisenstein's Bolshevik film *October*, 1927). For Cynewulf, it is as if the feather of the swan were the very substance of transcendent birdsong:

> ne magon þam breahtme byman ne hornas,
> ne hearpan hlyn, ne hæleþa stefn
> ænges on eorþan, ne organan,
> swegleoþres geswin, ne swanes feðre
> ne ænig þara dreama þe Dryhten gescop
> gumum to gliwe in þas geomran woruld.

('The Phoenix' from *The Exeter Book*, li 134-9. Krapp & Dobbie 1936: pp.97-8)

In Riddle 7 of the *Exeter Book* the swan says 'Frætwe mine/swogað hlude ond swinsiað', but only in flight.

Cynewulf is, however, paraphrasing the Latin 'Carmen de ave phoenice' which has *olor moriens* 'the dying swan' rather than any reference to the West Wind in the *sygnet*'s wings. The fact that the *swan-song* (which turns out to be a pleonasm in English) is heard only on the point of death is disconcerting:

'So on *Meander's* banks when death is nigh / The mournful *Swan* sings her own Elegie' (Dryden, *Dido to Æneas* ll. 3-4): a typically polished piece of Augustan translation which perfectly summarizes this archetype of the Ovidian Heroïdes. Pope wittily incorporates the suggestion of a melodramatic alternative into the 'battle scene' of the 'Rape of the Lock': 'Thus on *Meander's* flow'ry Margin lies / Th'expiring Swan, and as he sings he dies' (canto V 61-2).

Perhaps the poet intends some hidden warning. We are to be taken *inside* the 'Th'expiring Swan'—not the melodious White Swan, but the dissonant Black Swan: an obvious symbol of death and chaos—and we are not just to hear, but to participate in its grating song.

77

12.1 *back-yard*: This is presumably a territorial epithet used by the kind of people likely to have such an uncultivated patch of waste-ground at the rear of their homes (properties they are actually quite unlikely to own themselves) to refer to areas that come (as it were) under their jurisdiction. In the jargon of the police force in metropolitan areas I believe this is sometimes referred to as a 'manor.' Traditionally, of course, the public house has always been the focus of territorial influence amongst the criminal classes, who—in the dreadful vision of this poem—seem to have inherited the Earth.

12.4 *snobbish*: Like so many crucial theme-words in this poem, 'snob' has undergone a semantic reversal. Originally it meant a cobbler's apprentice, and (by figurative extension) any honest hard-working person of the lower classes free of vulgar pretensions to status: like Willie Mossop in *Hobson's Choice* [Harold Brighouse, 1916].

('Hobson's choice' as an idiom derives from the Cambridge carrier, Tobias Hobson who Milton tells us allowed his clients to choose from amongst his horses but only as long as their choice concurred with his own. The contemporary version of this is Henry Ford's infamous statement that customers of his new Model T: 'can have any colour you like, as long as it's black.' Three things occur to me: firstly, this idea reveals the hegemonic, imperialist desires embedded in the fiction of industrial/capitalist 'choice'—it is no coincidence that Henry Ford, the inventor of the 'production line', is as much a hero in the Soviet Union as he is in The United States; secondly, a surface level reading of this poem would seem to present the reader with a *Hobson's Choice* between two sides of the same ideological dialect—the cynicism of Diogenes and the dictatorship of Alexander; thirdly, *Hobson's Choice* is, I think, cockney rhyming slang for 'voice'—especially in reference to someone with a particularly *brazen* one—and might therefore be quite apt if used to signify the utterances of this persona.)

In Cambridge, the word 'snob' was used until very recently (and not without a certain connotation of respect) to refer to men of the town, rather than the gown. These days—I suspect under the influence of insidious Bolshevism which has sought to recast the honest hardworking Englishman with no desire to upset the social hierarchy as an apologist for the bourgeoisie and hence used the word as a synonym for 'blackleg' (originally a *turf swindler*)—it has come to mean precisely the opposite: a person displaying overt and sneering pretensions of nobility, education or rank. This progressive degradation of semantics and society towards the increasingly indelicate, ostentatious and dishonest is the fundamental characteristic of a malignant revolutionary process of history capable of creating the kind of future this dystopia depicts.

12.6 *Bob Porter*: Robert Porter was the most infamous of the Parliamentarian armourers at Birmingham in the Civil War. When Prince Rupert fired the town in 1643—the event which led to the city's first great flurry of publications (uniformly vehement anti-royalist propaganda), one of which was authored by Porter himself—it was specifically in order to put a halt to this man's operations. Before the Battle of Birmingham, it was estimated that he had produced over 15,000 swords for Cromwell's army. It was very difficult to stop the activities of the cutlers and gunsmiths, however. The loss of Porter's factory was only a temporary setback in the town's weapons manufacture. We should not snigger at Birmingham; we should shudder at its irrepressibility. (Wise and Johnson 'The Changing Regional Pattern During the Eighteenth Century', in *Birmingham and its Regional Setting* 1950 p.175)

12.7 *The Oak*: One imagines this to be another (rival) public house in the area, with a rather less unpatriotic and amoral clientele: definitively *not* 'our bird's back yard'.

13

So anyway, I mustn't lose my drift,
  I €ink I'll need to travel forward in time.
(It's not £e last occasion £at I'll $ift
  £e temporal framework to produce a rhyme.
I'd ra£er put up wi£ some tensual rift
  £an sound like Sondheim doing pantomime.)
Okay, so now it's two €ousand and eight,
  ('It is' just makes it nicer to narrate);

13.1 *drift*: This is another 'counter': one that carries a typical ambiguity of direction. 'Drift' can mean, in the idiom in which it used here, *progress along the proper course* (and metaphorically therefore *meaning, tenor, scope* and even *plot*). In the marine sense, however, (as most commonly seen in the adjectival form 'adrift') it suggests precisely the opposite: i.e. *deviation from the proper course* or *aimless movement*. There might be an amphibolous multiple negative at play here: 'I must not deviate from my *proper deviation*.' It is impossible to ignore the moral implications of this ironic refusal to semantically identify a correct path (through the narrative, through politics, through life). In fact, it is vital that we do not ignore such implications. The anachronisms that follow in its wake are more than frivolous.

13.2 *Forward*: A monosyllable; to rhyme with 'bored'. This is the flip-side of the Birminghamized prosody that produces so many yawning diæreses. There is also a punning desire, I think, to remind us of Henry Ford and, more disturbingly, of a *ford* in a stream: disturbing because it suggests the idea not of travelling (as it were) 'downstream' in time, but of wading across the river (The *Scamander/Meander*?) to look at it from the other bank so that the direction of the flow of time appears to be reversed.

13.5 *rift*: As regards the previous note, the OED has a fourth homonym:

  RIFT, *sb.*[4] U.S. [? Alteration of *riff*, obs. var. of REEF *sb.*[1]] **1.** A rapid, a cataract.

13.6 *Sondheim*: Obviously an invented name. It means *sound-home* in German, I think.

13.6 *Pantomime*: This word originally referred not to the idiotic Christmas show—with its two-man horses, its old thespians in drag, and its 'he's behind you' nonsense—but to a much more graceful and edifying type of non-verbal 'mime' as exemplified by the film *Les Enfants du Paradis*. The 'sound' of a pantomime might therefore be analogous to the proverbial song of the swan.
  The traditional denouement of the pantomime (of the lovers Harlequin and Columbine) is the ennobling transformation scene. The 'toilet' passage in this poem can be read (amongst other things) as a debased and misplaced version of such a metamorphosis: one that insists upon the modern low-brow figure of the panto-dame, rather than the beautiful and pure Columbine, as its heroine. Instead of a transcendent romantic encounter with Harlequin, she will later have a much more threatening, dishonest and tawdry clash with a criminal: Jeff Sloggy.

13.7 *okay*: The numerous occurrences of this word in *BQ* do as much to suggest American cultural colonisation as any other quality of the text. It is noticeable how regularly it introduces temporal paradoxes or explicit switches in the direction of, or position within, time. (See esp. 63.1 and 144.1). These moments are the most overt interjections of the TV announcer-persona and it is quite clear the poet intends 'okay' to be a totemic word of this disruptive voice's insidious influence. Later in the piece it regularly finds its way into the mouths of the characters (see 175.8, 177.7, 206.8, 216.8).

The multiple possible etymologies of this definitively mindless Americanism are notoriously impossible to disentangle. Some contend it comes from Scots *och aye*; others that it is from French *au quai*, yet more that it is a patois word derived from an American Indian or West African (slave) word for 'yes', 'it is' or 'I agree'. Most sensible commentators admit that it has come to be understood (at least) as a jocular abbreviation of some misspelled affirmation; though precisely what this might be is just as unclear: perhaps *orl konfirmed* or *orl korrect*. If the latter theory is the most likely, we can see how intrinsically paradoxical and dangerously ambiguous this seemingly innocent bit of American flippancy is. There is nothing in the least *correct* about abbreviating 'all correct' as O.K; not unless they are to suggest an even more heinous restructuring of English orthography than the one already carried out by Webster. The archetypal use for this word would seem to be the mimicking of a semi-literate worker in that immigrant society (perhaps a speaker of one of the languages from which the word is supposed to be derived) who is reporting on the completion of a (no doubt) botched job. *Okay* might therefore be called a *brummagem* abbreviation: a perfect word to be attached to this persona's insecure treatment of narrative time; and yet another example of the connection between Birmingham—and all it stands for (and stands against)—and America, and all *it* stands for (and against).

It is important, I think, that the poet is blaming this *OK time* on the logic and stylistics of television. It strikes me that this medium is capable of dissembling and distorting time in a way that cinema is not. It must be difficult, perhaps impossible, to distinguish between live broadcasts and recorded pictures and therefore between fact and fiction. This is, of course, just as true where wireless is concerned, but the lack of visual content seems to make this infinitely less dangerous. What hysteria might have been created if Orson Welles' infamous version of *War of the Worlds* had been 'seen' instead of simply 'heard' does not bear thinking about.

14

  Our character's Tiberius Mercator:
    (I didn't make him up, I nicked him from
  A book called *The Invisible Spectator*
    Or else: *The Counterfeit of Birmingham*.
  £e novelist tries to impersonate a
    Distinguished writer, but can only plumb
  £e dep€s of *badder-£an-bad* narrative:
  Much *badder* still £an £at comparative.

14.2 *nicked*: 'Tallied', 'resembled', 'stole', 'tricked', 'hazarded', 'guessed correctly' etc.

14.6 *Distinguished writer*. Perhaps Sterne is the most likely candidate. C18th 'romances' with unusual narratives are often homages to *Tristram Shandy*, and the beginning of the coin's narration in this poem (stanzas 27-29) is indisputably a parody of the first chapter of that novel.

 Unlike Thomas Bridges' 1770 *Adventures of a Bank Note* however, the book cited here as the source of the narrative frame—*The Birmingham Counterfeit, or The Invisible Spectator*: a novel/romance anonymously published in 1772—makes no specific reference or allusion to Sterne's infinitely superior work. *The Birmingham Counterfeit* is no doubt influenced by *Adventures of a Bank Note*, but Bridges hardly qualifies as a 'distinguished writer.'

 The history of these fancifully covert first-person narrations seems to be as old as narrative itself. The earliest surviving text that might be loosely called a 'novel', for example, is the *Metamorphoses* of Lucius Apuleius: a major source for both Boccaccio and Cervantes. Also known as *The Golden Ass*, this book (recently subject to a fine new translation by Robert Graves) is narrated almost entirely from the point of view of a man who has been transformed into an ass and can therefore observe human behaviour unseen. To all intents and purposes, Lucius (the ass) is an 'Invisible Spectator.' This narrative is a curious mix of the moral satire and prurient pornography: the two main uses of this technique. The former being exemplified by Anna Sewell's *Black Beauty* and the majority of 'money talks' narratives (of which more below), and the latter by the erotic cliché of the 'Ovidian flea' ('Carmen de Pulice': *Dr Faustus* v.285), which finds its most sophisticated embodiment in Donne's 'The Flea' and its crassest in the anonymous salacious novel of 1887: *Autobiography of a Flea*.

 The *Metamorphoses* of Apuleius is an important antecedent of this text. Robert Graves, despite the clarity of his translation, is capable only of a dark introductory hint at the work's most important feature where the current study is concerned. He explains the name, *asinus aureus* like this: 'Professional storytellers, as Pliny mentions…, used to preface their street-corner entertainments with: "Give me a copper and I'll tell you a golden story". So "golden" conveys an indulgent smile…' (1950: p7) What Graves's 'indulgent smile' occludes is the fact that *aureus* is also the name of the Augustan gold coin, which was undergoing a serious decline during the period. The name therefore implies *asininus aureus* 'the assinine aureus', a fact which ties in neatly with the pun in English *The Golden Æs*. (The *æs* 'brass' being the least valuable of Roman coins.) Lucius, whose only means of progressing from one episode to another is (like Black Beauty) to be the subject of continual barter transactions that never allow him to lose sight of the ongoing diminishment of his exchange value, is very similar to a circulating coin, clipped by each of its exploitative owners (and carrying the scars as proof). So, 'give me an *aes* and I'll give you an *asin(in)us aureus*' is punningly and (heavily ironically) equivalent to 'give me a penny and I'll give you (back) a counterfeit sovereign… a fictional profit…'

 All 'invisible spectators' (not all as literal as Wells' *The Invisible Man*) can trace their origins to the legend of Gyges—the mythical inventor of money, and the owner of the 'ring of invisibility'—a discussion of which (along with some analysis of its ongoing use in the fiction of Professor Tolkien) will have to wait.

The earliest narrative explicitly delivered by a coin that I can find is 'Adventures of a Shilling' by Joseph Addison (*Tatler* no. 249 November 11, 1710). Addison says the idea was suggested to him by an unnamed friend. A reference in the December 10th entry of *Journal to Stella* reveals this friend (unsurprisingly) to have been Jonathan Swift. Addison certainly is a 'distinguished writer':

> "I lay undiscovered and useless, during the usurpation of Oliver Cromwell.
>
> "About a Year after the King's return, a poor Cavalier… fortunately cast his Eye upon me, and, to the great Joy of us both, carried me to a Cook's-Shop, where he dined upon me, and drank the King's Health… I found that I had been happier in my Retirement than I thought, having probably, by that Means, escaped wearing a monstrous Pair of Breeches.
>
> "Being now of great Credit and Antiquity, [this is a Queen Elizabeth shilling] I was rather looked upon as a Medal than an ordinary Moin; for which Reason a Gamester laid hold of me, and converted me to a Counter, having got together some Dozens of us for that Use. We led a melancholy Life in his Possession, being busy at those Hours wherein Current Coin is at Rest, and partaking the Fate of our Master, being in a few Moments valued at a Crown, a Pound, or a Sixpence, according to the Situation in which the Fortune of the Cards placed us. I had at length the good Luck to see my Master break, by which Means I was again sent abroad under my primitive Denomination of a Shilling.
>
> "… I fell into the Hands of an Artist, who conveyed me under Ground, and with an unmerciful Pair of Shears, cut off my Titles, clipped my Brims, retrenched my Shape, rubbed me to my inmost Ring, and, in short, so spoiled and pillaged me, that he did not leave me worth a Groat. You may think what a Confusion I was in, to see myself thus curtailed and disfigured. I should have been ashamed to have shown my head, had not all my old Acquaintance been reduced to the same shameful Figure, excepting some few that were punched through the Belly. In the midst of this general Calamity, when every Body thought our Misfortune irretrievable, and our Case desperate, we were thrown into the Furnace together, and (as it often happens with Cities rising out of a Fire) appeared with greater Beauty and Lustre than we could ever boast of before. What has happened to me since this Change of Sex which you now see, I shall take some other Opportunity to relate.

The '*monstrous pair of breeches*' references John Philips' 'The Splendid Shilling: an Imitation of Milton' which, at the end of the essay, the coin jocularly claims to have directly inspired, calling it 'the finest burlesque poem in the British language.' 'The Splendid Shilling' is itself burlesqued by James Bramton in 1743, the coin and the poem being rendered even more ironically grotesque and devalued as 'The Crooked Sixpence'. It is along the same satirical lines that one supposes the author of *The Birmingham Counterfeit* to have copied Addison's influential little piece: the 'splendid' shilling having become definitively 'crooked'. It is rather formulaic and laborious, however, and has none of the verve of Addison's short piece.

> But *bad* is good £ese days, and *wicked*'s ace.
>   *Kickass* is great, magnificent is *dope*,
> And *hectic*'s doper; *dark* is glorious
>   And *phat* is *fit*, *dead nasty*'s what we hope
> A *biatch* is; *chilled out*'s a state of grace;
>   And even £e *dog's bollocks* is a trope
> For some€ing unexceptionably fine:
> It's all about £e flip-side of £e coin.

This sketch manages, in the space of just a page, to cast its eye over much of the territory of *The Birmingham Quean*: America, royalty, republicanism, Civil War, defacing of coinage, gambling, the phoenix, transsexualism, blindness, beggars and burlesque poetry.

Other examples of this oeuvre include: 'The Adventures of a Halfpenny' by John Hawkesworth in *The Adventurer* no. 43 (1753)—very much derivative of Addison's; *The Adventures of a halfpenny: commonly called a Birmingham halfpenny or Counterfeit: as related by itself* (J.G. Rusher, Banbury 1820)—an illustrated children's book; and Hans Christian Andersen's 'Sølvskillingen' (1861).

15.2 *Kickass*: Perhaps a term of derision like 'Jackass' but intensified by *portmanteau* to suggest that the he-ass in question is so stubborn and uncooperative as to require regular kicking. By what process of grammatical laxity it comes to be used as an adjective—let alone by what diabolical process of semantic revolution it, and the other words and phrases like it in this stanza, come to be synonymous with positive exclamations—I hate to think.

The overtones of *asinus aureus* are obvious.

15.2 *dope*: Further to the equine connotations of the previous reference to an ass, 'dope' is most commonly used to refer to a preparation of opium employed in doctoring horses before racing in order to fix a result. According to one of the 1933 OED addenda, *dope* has also come in the U.S. to mean information regarding the condition of a racehorse, and thereby any form of more or less fraudulent 'insider' information ('straight from the horse's mouth' as it were). The entire point of this narrative, however, is that we take great care to look this particular 'gift horse' (this 'golden æs') in the mouth.

15.3 *hectic's doper*: The effect of 'dope' is usually taken to be the opposite of the excited and disturbed condition of the 'hectic' (traditionally equivalent to a sufferer from consumptive fever). This difference is more than simply analogous to the ancient division of *ecstasy* (delirium) into *melancholy* and *phrenesis*. Traditionally, the diagnosis is made by observations of the complexion, temperature and pulse: the melancholic (or 'doped') patient having an unchanged pulse and temperature and a pallid complexion; and the frenetic (or 'hectic') having a raised pulse and temperature, and dark flushed skin. Melancholy and madness are in fact defined by Hippocrates (and all who followed him) specifically as delirium *without* the usual febrile symptoms. Robert Burton makes this quite explicit at the outset of his study: 'Phrenitis… differs from melancholy and madness, because their dotage is without an ague' (*The Anatomy of Melancholy*: Section I, subsection iv.) So, in expressing her fear of Hamlet's madness when he sees the ghost in her bedchamber by saying 'This is the very coynage of your Braine,/This bodilesse Creation extasie is very cunning in' the Queen is diagnosing delirium as a result of *melancholy* not *frenzy*. Her son completely misunderstands her concern (which is excellent proof of just how right she is): 'Extasie?/My Pulse as yours doth temperately keepe time,/And makes as healthfull Musicke.' (Folio II.ii.1442-7)

Similarly, there is nothing 'dope(d)' about the '*hectic*': just like the 'bronzed' complexion of the 'brazen' hussies who are the heroines of this piece (the coin and the West Indian drag-Queen), and the blushing reader on discovering he has been *duped*, the hectic is characteristically *red-faced*.

15.7 *unexceptionably*: This is not the correct word. The intention of the phrase 'unexceptionably fine' is to denote 'of unequalled value' or, as a numismatist would say, 'proof quality'. As a piece of generous conjecture, one might speculate that the correct word 'unexceptionally'—which is currently a perfectly uncontroversial falling hexasyllable—might have deteriorated into a rising pentasyllable in the future of the poem; the poet could therefore deliberately be misemploying the subtly different concept of exceptionability in order, not to make any kind of nice distinction, but simply to maintain the prosody and thereby emphasize the couplet. Where the merit of artificial rhyme and scansion is concerned, however, one is sorely tempted to concur with the proposed resemblance of the phrase to the æsthetic qualities of canine gonads.

15.8 *the flip-side of the coin*: Indeed this rhyme is, in the original King's (or should I say *Queen's*) English sense of the word, *bad*. The simplest gloss of the quasi-Americanism *flip-side* is 'the reverse'. Such a reading could just as easily be obtained from 'back-side', however, and one has to assume that the decision to go with a neologism in place of such an obvious alternative (one whose sniggering prurience surely would recommend it to the context) is significant. There is a moment toward the end of the canto, (stanzas 215-216) when the coin expresses its deep desire to hang in the air, perpetually spinning. In this state, the coin would in fact look like a sphere, as described by the revolutions of its edge. One often forgets that the coin has not two, but three sides. Every time a coin is tossed there is a tiny, but genuine, theoretical chance that it will land on its edge. The *flip-side* might therefore be 'that side of the coin visible when the coin is tossed or (in the American) *flipped*': the edge—the *liminus* between *heads* and *tails*; the (revolutionary) surface of the coin that carries the threat of undermining the definitive game of binary probability.

We are talking about *counters* again: not simply words that stand both *against* and *for* themselves (as they spin perpetually in the air, as it were), but also words (and sexes, morals, politics, natures) which threaten to 'stand on their edge', refusing to come down on one side or the other so as to insist on the existence of this third (sublunar) dimension through which each of the 'sides' extends. It is this third edge which gives a coin its material substance, and its value, thus making it both *more* and *less* than the Platonic *idea* of a binary unit.

Which is quite apt, considering £e fact
    £at $ady coins are what I'm on about:
Specifically, £e way £ey counteract
    Our ideology to cast in doubt
£e single-minded way we all transact
    Our lives by stamping one-eyed logic out.
£at sounds far-fetched and dull as any€in,
But look at all £e places coins have bin,

16.3 *counteract*: era 2

16.5 *single-minded*: Another of the terms undergoing semantic deterioration towards negative connotations which seem so popular in the construction of this decadent dystopia. The OED says this originally meant: 'Sincere in mind or spirit; honest, straightforward; simple-minded, ingenuous.' Clearly, the positive nature of single-mindedness is lost in an environment of such threatening ambiguity and equivocation.

16.6 *stamping one-eyed logic out*: 'To stamp out', as well as *to extinguish* or *eradicate*, could also mean *to emboss* or (in the numismatic sense) *to strike*. Furthermore, the effigy of the monarch ('single-rule'—the embodiment of the *single-minded* nation, in the original sense, and the defender of the monotheistic faith) on a coin is traditionally in profile and therefore—while cubism is kept out of the Royal Mint—only has one eye. This phrase therefore encapsulates the thematic and stylistic duplicities of the stanza by being simultaneously glossable as 'eradicating single-mindedness' and 'counterfeiting the effigy of the monarch.'

It is worth noting the similarly ambiguous (and near antithetical) nature of the phrases with which this line rhymes. 'On about' is obviously a colloquial idiom meaning *talking about* (short for 'going on about'), but in the clause 'shady coins are what I'm on about' there is an insistence upon the words 'on' and 'about' as prepositions rather than an abbreviation of a participle. If we literalize the clause, therefore, we might read it as: 'counterfeit coins are what I am on [and] about'—i.e.: 'I am the Queen [and] edge inscription'.

Similarly, 'cast in doubt' is a shoddily inverted version of the phrasal verb *to cast doubt upon* (itself a whimsical coinage that plays upon a reversal of the metaphorical idiom *to cast light on [a mystery]*) which manages to suggest that counterfeit coins are literally 'cast' in an alloy so dubious it is actually *called* 'doubt'.

16.8 *bin*: Despite what we hear from the proliferation of reproductions by lazy actors, there are a number of diphthongs which, rather than being protracted or interpolated by Industrial urban accents are often nullified: 'seen' can become 'sin', 'been'—'bin', 'take'—'tek' and so on. Other diphthongs are flattened; it is often an error to pronounce (as the poorly schooled at sounding poorly schooled habitually do) the word 'go' as 'gow' when it is far more often 'goo'. The point is that these are flexible variations. At the end of a clause, these kinds of words will often broaden into the diphthong; *within* a clause however they are more likely to be monothongs. There are grammatical tendencies too: diphthongs being more often used for common nouns than common verbs, (which is an intriguing analogue to the grammatical stress-flip in certain noun and verb pairs in English: such as '*con*script' and 'con*script*'). When all is said and done, however, one would rather actors set an elocutionary example to the slack of vowels rather than attempt half-hearted emulations of their mumblings.

MOSELEY

Moseley is probably the kind of area of Birmingham you want to live in if you're not from Birmingham. It has listed buildings — proper old ones — an eighteenth century pub & a street of big detached Edwardian townhouses that were the first ever to include built-in garages. Not that it's actually genteel or anything. It's also the suburb of Birmingham in which you want to hang your belly out in the sun if you're a snoring old wino or where you go to be schooled in the ancient wisdom of illegal horticulture by a frazzled acid-head picking her feet on a flaky bench.

This is because the people of Moseley pride themselves on their unusual liberalism: there's a Jewish primary school, for example, with a majority of Muslim pupils. & they take their local-colour just as seriously. A man once wandered stark naked round Kwik Save four days in a row, filling his basket with washing powder & fabric conditioner & walking out again, before anyone decided it was strange enough for them to consider alerting the authorities.

They say a ley line runs straight across the High Street, which might explain the endurance of indigestible health-food shops & the lingering aroma of sandalwood, emanating from those emporia of vaguely eastern smells & bells, that drifts around almost every corner. Where precisely the lay-line goes from Moseley into the surrounding area, no-one else in Birmingham has ever bothered to find out. Imagine Glastonbury with Balti Houses. In neighbouring Kings Heath, we invariably refer to it as *Muesli*.

It should have come as no surprise that this was where Hannah lived. I was strangely ill at ease however, arriving on foot, passing through such blithe, familiar surroundings with the autumn sun making little effort to heat my back. Her drive was hedged with hawthorn rather than the usual privet. That was classy. A careworn fuchsia sat hunched over the bonnet of an Austin Se7en with a flat front tyre. Tired blooms snivelled at the dew clinging to their stamens as the breeze went by.

It was one of those 'imposing late Victorian villas' that had been converted into flats for a better class of students & young professionals. I stepped into the porch. She opened the door before I'd had time to decide which one might be her buzzer.

"Sorry... I was up half the night..." She looked endearingly rumpled. She was wearing white cotton pyjama bottoms, a plain green T-shirt & leather flip-flops, & was in the middle of the laborious process of wrapping a bulky camel-hair overcoat around her as if she was about to go out like that & fetch the Sunday papers. There was a crease in her cheek. She rubbed the mucus from her eyes, "heating's packed in... been here long?"

"No. I never even got to ringing the bell."

"Doesn't work anyway," she said.

She smiled weakly rather than plumping for a handshake or a kiss & turned away, thrusting her arms almost up to the elbows into the deep, clownish pockets of the overcoat. I followed her towards the hall. Her front door was at the bottom of the stairs. There was no window in it. No way could she could have seen me in the doorway from inside the flat.

£e heady tales of fortune £ey could spin.
    If all £e queens on one-pound coins could speak
£ey'd have an inkling of £e state we're in.
    £ey've got a vantage point from which to peek
At certain fantasies £at underpin
    £is blinkered monarchy, to see how weak
It is, despite its pompous institutions.
Perhaps £ey could suggest a few solutions…

17.1 *tales they could spin*: Another reference to the revolutionary liminality of the spinning coin. The pun on *heady tales* and *heads & tails* here is as close to a definitive exposition of its own technique of acute and unnerving narrative irony as the poem ever comes.

17.3 *inkling*: Professor Tolkien runs a literary club here called The Inklings, the meetings of which I have once or twice had the honour of being invited to. Tolkien's astute philological play on *inkle*-ings (insights) and *ink*-lings (the children of ink) is typical of the man. If I am right in saying of this poet's politics and artistic vision that he is maintaining a strong position of traditional royalism, antidis-establishmentarianism, ennobling anti-capitalism (as opposed to the Marxian version), and a poetics of strong imagination coupled with plain speech—specifically by satirising the poetics and morals of the antithesis—then he could easily be a member of Professor Tolkien's admirable group.

There are many thematic overtones shared by this poem and Tolkien's own work in progress, *The Lord of the Rings*. Most obviously, I think, the resurrection of Plato's myth of Gyges, and the recognition of its true allegorical import, is crucial to both texts. Both are aware of the golden ring of invisibility as the symbol of the invention of monetary tokenism to fuel the tyrannical ambitions, and both play on it in subtle ways. The entire motivational framework of Tolkien's text is posited on the insidious influence of 'The Ring', and the quest is for the discovery of strength enough to overcome temptation and destroy it. If we replace 'The Ring' with 'The Quean' this drama might be understood as one very similar to Tolkien's, but played out on the level of *mimesis* rather than of *diegesis*. Tolkien too, it should be remembered, comes from Birmingham.

To compare this poem to that of the Inklings might be to suggest, however, that Tolkien's group are something like the Scriblerus Club. They most certainly are not. I hope they will not consider it reductive if I infer their outlook to be led, for the most part, by the writings of Owen Barfield, who suggests that the project of human literature should be to heal the *linguistic fall* by reconstructing a 'mythopoetics' which transcends rhetoric and speaks directly to the ancient wisdoms embedded in the collective unconscious. I find Mr Barfield's arguments very cogent and refreshing in the main, but would not want to dismiss out of hand all 'rhetorical' devices, especially not in satires on the 'fallen' world. Like myself, the poet of this canto might be someone on the periphery of this group: admiring but in a position of fundamental disagreement; not a member, or even a regular attender, but someone who has glimpsed their work. If I were looking for him, this might be just the place to start.

17.3 *the state we're in*: A very commonplace pun.

She padded in. She was smaller than I remembered, softer, less beautiful perhaps but somehow prettier for it (it was the lack of makeup, probably, I've still never got used to that): "shut it behind you, will you... fancy a coffee? I can't show you the study just now, Sambo's asleep under the desk. I sometimes wheel him in there in the buggy when I can't get him off. He seems to like it."

It really was quite cold in the kitchen. I accepted the coffee. I normally don't drink the stuff — it makes me jittery — but I needed something to warm my fingers. "Would you like me to take a look at the boiler?" I offered.

"Goodness gracious, are you a plumber too?"

"No, nothing so prestigious. I could take a look though anyway." There's nothing like fixing things to get you in a woman's good books. I had a boiler in Glasgow that sometimes overheated. You just had to stick your finger up it to get it working again. Besides, a bit of strategically-placed facial grime never went amiss. I sat down without being asked. She was spooning coffee into a stovetop cafetiere.

"Can't, I'm afraid." She snapped the pot shut & put it on the hob. "It's upstairs in a locked cupboard. I'll have to get the landlord out. Anyway, we should get down to business. I can fill you in on the background while we're waiting for his majesty to let us have the study back. Have you got a pen & paper?"

I did. They were already on the kitchen table. I'd actually forgotten to bring anything with me when I left my mom & dad's, but I'd stopped at a newsagent on the way & bought a fibre-tipped signature pen, an A to Z & what at the time I'd thought was a rather cool-looking large black notebook. As I opened it for the first time & leafed through its pages, I realised it was a 2004 day-to-a-page diary. It was September. They couldn't possibly be selling diaries for next year already. I turned as nonchalantly as possible to the 'Notes' section at the end & unlidded the pen.

"Amrit was never going to take to fatherhood that easily," she began, rather too professionally, I thought, "I knew that from the start. His own upbringing was far too strange. When he found out I was pregnant it must've brought it all back to him. Not that he wasn't already obsessed by the whole question. But if I'd known just *how* obsessed... well, what *would* I have done exactly?"

"Until he was twelve, Amrit thought his name was Martin, the son of a bus driver from Druids Heath called Leon Higgs & his rather more middle-class wife, Carla. But then Leon Higgs died & Martin's whole life-view was given a sudden smack in the teeth."

"How did he die?" I wanted to knock her off the prepared spiel. She took it in her stride.

"He had an asthma attack during a thunderstorm... never had one before. It happens more often than you'd assume, apparently. I think he was trying to fix a leak in the garden shed & fell off the roof... Don't laugh."

18

Some people €ink a sexual scandal could
    Destroy £e country's royal lineage,
But scandal doesn't do us any good.
    £e rumour-mill's a kind of patronage,
Promoting rich celebrities who $ould
    Be stripped of power, property and privilege.
You don't bring down £e crown by dropping hints
About a butler fingering a prince.

18.4 *rumour-mill*: Yet another hyphenated neologism suggestive of the linguistic environment of the future.

18.8 *fingering a prince*: Aside from its bawdy connotations (played out in the following stanza), the verb *to finger* is used, one assumes, in the American slang sense 'incriminate' or 'inform', as in 'to point the finger at'. This is heightened by the undertones of 'steal' and 'handle covetously', and the prestidigitative pun on *fingerprints*.

"Anyway, what's important is that the legal processes surrounding the death — the reading of the Will & so on — revealed to Amrit not only that Leon had never been married to his mother, but wasn't even his father. In fact, Amrit had never even been adopted because of objections on Carla's part. Seemingly, she wanted to keep all knowledge of Amrit's real father from her child & she was prepared to go as far as defying her partner's wishes to do it. Leon had wanted her to tell him anyway but had respected her decisions about how to raise her own son.

"But then, one day, precocious little Martin suddenly reads the headline on the front of his mother's Guardian out loud — **Nixon to call OPEC's bluff**, or something."

The coffee pot began to make that gargling sound that struggles out of Jabba the Hutt when he gets throttled with his bondage gear by Carrie Fisher in a bronze bikini. She got up & took it off the heat, then poured the thick black stuff into two mugs & brought them over.

"His mother was so shocked that she went round collecting up all the documents in the house that had anything to do with Amrit's father: his letters, photographs & so on, & even documents that revealed Amrit's name (including his Birth Certificate) & she threw them in the leaf-burner in the garden. Leon, on the other hand, reacted by rescuing a photograph of the man as a teenager in Uganda. He put it in a wooden box that contained his own childhood toys — dinky cars & a draughts set & so on — with a short letter explaining who the man was in the picture. Most importantly, when he came to make a Will a few years later, he specified that the box should be left to "Amrit, the son of Carla McGrath & Sanjit Singh.""

"But surely she would have checked the contents of the box before she gave it to him."

"She may have done, or it might have slipped her mind. Maybe she couldn't bring herself to take it out; maybe it was Leon's dying wish that she let her son know the truth. Besides, she'd also have to keep the Will secret too. & you simply can't do that. Whatever happened, Amrit ended up with the box containing the letter & the photograph. But it took him years to fill the gaps in; his mother refused to have the subject mentioned. There were plenty of details he would never be able to recover."

"She wouldn't talk to him about it, even when he knew the truth?"

"No. Well... no, she lied to him at first. Unfortunately the letter gave away very few details & failed to say how Carla had also managed to keep most of the story from Leon. It just said something like: "I'll always be your dad, Marty, but the man in the photo was your dad too, before I ever was. You should ask your mother to explain." I suppose he thought she wouldn't have a choice if Amrit confronted her with the picture. Anyway, it was *her* story, not his."

> Who cares for christsake? Let £em have £eir plea$ure.
>   If Charlie Windsor gets £e plumber in
> To fix a leaky tap, and maybe mea$ure
>   His standpipe, and move on to tinkering
> Around £e riser to relieve £e pre$ure
>   Wi£in £e royal hose, is £at a sin?
> £e crime we $ould indict £ese people for
> Is claiming sovereignty above £e law.

19.4 *standpipe*: An all-too malleable and all-too ductile example of smutty tradesman's cant.

19.5 *tinkering*: 'Mending or working metal in a clumsy, ineffective way.' Many of the activities of the characters in this poem, not to mention the bungling octaves of the (shoddily worked) counterfeit narrator, might be described as 'tinkering'. The *double-entendres* running through the plumbing of this stanza ring particularly hollow. If I dared risk such a tinny pun myself, I might say they plumbed the depths of taste.

There is also a potential allusion to the revolutionary republican 'Tinker' Fox here. (See 56.2 *copper*)

19.5 *riser*: See 19.4 *standpipe*

19.6 *sin*: This is a very carefully worded rhetorical question. Crucial to the proliferation of coining amongst C17th political dissidents and non-conformists in the new Industrial areas of England was the notion of the *sinless crime*. That is to say, a crime which is arbitrarily identified by a tyrannical power and has no basis in scripture. There is nothing in the Decalogue which forbids anything like it; the injunction against the creation of 'graven images' being, in the popular imagination, a stronger argument for the sinfulness of the Crown in minting a quasi-divine image of the sovereign than of those who defy the monopoly it exercises. Coining, outside of London especially, seems to have been regarded by those who rejected the divine right of the monarch as a 'social crime' rather than a sin; like rioting or poaching, it was transgressive behaviour, subject to punishment by those in power, but justifiable as righteous action if the victims had themselves been identified as sinfully abusing power.

Complex attempts were made by educated people of the capital to justify the heavy punishments meted out on coiners; lawyers and clerics suggested that defacing or imitating the image of God's chosen sovereign was a sinful form of High Treason. John Evelyn even went so far as to call coining 'a wicked and devilish Fraud, for which no Punishment seems too great… one of the most wicked, injurious and diabolical Villanies Men can be guilty of.' For Evelyn the coiner makes the King seem 'as great a Cheat and Imposter as himself' and pointed out (quite accurately) that adulteration of the coinage had been the first step in the decline of the Roman Empire. (*Numismata*, 1697, p.225)

It is quite obvious that such arguments, when received by the skewed ideology of capitalist non-conformism, were likely to exacerbate the situation. The last thing likely to convince the Birmingham coiners to halt their operations is a scholarly reference to the divinity of the Stuart monarchy as embodied in the commonwealth or the faded glory of Rome. Crucial to their thinking is the egalitarianism of all men—made in God's image—subject only to Christ himself. The great moment of the Gospels in this regard—the crux for Lutheran fanatics of a rejection of all learned arguments over blind faith—is Matthew 22:15-22: the 'quibbling' Pharisees hand Christ the coin and he says:

> Whose is this image and superscription?

> They say unto him, Cæsar's. Then saith he unto them,
> Render therefore unto Cæsar the things which are Cæsars;
> and unto God the things that are God's.

Taken far too literally and tendentiously, we can see how this might be seen to combine the following two glosses: firstly 'we, being stamped with God's image, all belong to God; Cæsar is no exception'; and secondly 'if this coin were melted down and restruck with the image of the Jewish king you desire it would no longer belong to Cæsar; your acquiescence to the authority of Cæsar's money is a defeat whereas my rejection of it is the ultimate victory.' The fatal weakness of moving from these glosses to an argument condoning coining in C17th England is patent: Christ pointedly avoids suggesting any criminal or revolutionary activity in preference for a transcendent vision which sees the coin as a symbol of man's relationship to God, rather than the worldly token of exchange that the Pharisees, for all their political and philosophical finesse, completely fail to see beyond. It is crucial to my understanding of this passage that Christ does not make any reference to all of God's 'coins' being of equal value. The fact that an analogy can be made between God's and Cæsar's coinages suggests that, just as in all currencies, the relative values of different pieces of differing intrinsic worth is not *nullified* by the sovereign stamp but *asserted* by it. A hierarchy of nobility amongst those who bear God's image is therefore scripturally condoned.

I reckon £ey $ould be a docu-soap:
   We let £em keep £e palace, but we rig
£e joint wi£ mikes and cameras in £e hope
   £ey'll entertain us; we could earwig
And put £eir lives under £e microscope
   As often as we want — like Royal Big
Bro£er: £at'd kick up a furore.
But anyway, I'll get back to my story.)

20.1 *docu-soap*: Perhaps a sort of amphibolous television programme (see 20.4 *earwig*). There is also the possibility however of glossing this *alloy* as 'didactic cash' or 'browbeating money' (from Latin *documentum* 'lesson' and the American slang sense for *soap* 'money').

20.3 *rig the joint*: 'Rig' here is used in the sense of 'rigging a ship': *to ready the ropes and sails*. 'Joint' is an American slang term meaning a place for illicit entertainment, drinking or drug-taking. Specifically, in this case, it might be intended to denote a *fairground tent*, the 'fitting out' of which would not be unlike rigging a ship. This would achieve two effects: firstly to perpetuate the tawdry environment of carnival slang, and secondly to reduce the substantial centrepiece of Britain's constitutional monarchy to the status of a flimsy tarpaulin tent in which one hurls wooden balls at coconuts or peeks at gruesome biological oddities preserved in thick glass jars of yellowing formaldehyde.

20.3 *cameras*: era 3

20.4 *earwig*: The insect *Forficula auricularia* which is supposed to creep into the ear at night.
   The phrase 'fly on the wall', referring to a privileged position from which to spy on somebody else's activities, has become fashionable. The metaphor comes from the jargon of the American intelligence services who call hidden sound-recording devices 'bugs', presumably because the small microphones involved are sometimes disguised as domestic insects. At first sight 'earwig' seems to be used here as a verb meaning to take up this position of the 'fly on the wall', the *bug*, and to 'eavesdrop'. (See notes to stanzas 14 and 15 on the 'Invisible Spectator', the Ovidian flea and *asinus aureus*.) The word 'earwig', however, does not mean to *deliberately overhear*—which would be inconsistent with the mythical ear-burrowing activities of the insect—but to *insinuate* or *covertly influence*. A *docu-soap*, in the purgatorial future envisioned in this poem, would therefore seem to be a 'counterfeit documentary', a television serial which presents itself as a 'documentary film' (an objective, observational form) but is actually a *soap opera*: a scripted 'realistic' quotidian drama designed (in the United States, of course) to influence housewives to buy certain brands of domestic products by interlacing advertisements with a recognisable portrayal of lives like their own. The idea is not only to debase the future status of our new Queen to one which is indistinguishable from a normal housewife, in furry slippers, but also to represent the monarch and her household as mere puppets of the scriptwriters of popular, commercial entertainment. The nightmare scenario is evoked of a Royal household whose sole function is to advertise the brands currently marked 'by appointment...', slavishly repeating words given to them by scriptwriters and therefore playing out artificial lives designed to be recognisable to the public in a seat of regal power which is nothing but a studio-set.

20.6-7 *Big Brother*: A clear indication of the influence of Orwell's novel on this poem; one that extends the reversal of televisual transitivity mentioned above by insinuating the haunting symbol of the 'telescreen', through which 'Big Brother is watching you'.

"Leon couldn't have been more wrong. She just told Amrit the man was a very close friend of his dad's from the buses who'd come over during the expulsions. She said the man had lost contact with his family in the move (they had Ugandan citizenship) & had killed himself when they didn't follow on because he was very unhappy in England without them. During his final depression, she said, Leon had promised to name any children he had after the man's estranged family. It wasn't till two years after Sanjit's death that she met his father. Carla was quite insistent on that point... It was actually the other way round, of course."

I glanced around for sugar as she spoke. There wasn't any.

"Eventually, one of Amrit's aunts told him what had really happened. It was a couple of years after Carla had left Sanjit in Uganda at the height of the civil war that she met Leon. He could never be sure, but Amrit always said he thought his mother & Sanjit had been very much in love & Carla, when she found out she was pregnant, had tried to get them both out of the country at the same time, via the British Embassy. But for some reason they got separated — maybe he had other things to deal with, maybe he really did have another family — whatever the case, she left without him, hoping he would follow on. He never did. After the expulsions, she spent weeks searching vainly for him in the relocation camps."

"I suppose it goes to show you should always tell your children everything."

"You obviously don't have children, Sam. You couldn't be more wrong. You've got to lie to them sometimes; there's no way of bringing them up otherwise. She probably thought she was doing the right thing. It's strange: you get into the habit of not quite saying everything you could & then... anyway, the point is that you need to know where to draw the line... when to stop..."

"& *she* didn't."

"Obviously not. It wasn't until he was a young adult that he started using his given name. The incredible thing was that Carla had never known what Sanjit's family-name was. It was hardly surprising that she couldn't find him in 1972. All she knew was... 'Sanjit Singh', so that's all that was entered on the register."

"It must have been a pretty short affair... if she didn't know his name."

"I suppose so, but I bet it was exciting."

I tried to work out whether this was meant to be flirtatious. Hannah was looking just to the right of me as if I were slightly blocking her view of something she'd misplaced. She seemed more reminiscent than keen, I had to say... unfortunately.

"All that ducking & diving," I offered, "secret assignations in the middle of a crisis." Obviously the thought had occurred to me that this was still something of a crisis for Hannah: even this long after Singh had left. In the circumstances I might convince her it could be quite exciting to get up to a bit of ducking & diving of our own.

21

  Tiberius Mercator, £en, he's like
   £is bankrupt businessman who's just… too nice.
  When two competitors ganged up to psych
   Him out by undercutting him on price
  And bribing all his contractors to hike
   £eir charges, he rejected £e advice
  To pay £em back in kind: his probity
  Was being compromised for nobody.

21.1 *he's like* [etc]: It is difficult to tell whether this is a simile or a sloppily expressed statement of fact. In any event 'like / psych / hike' is an extremely overworked rhyme. If I am to continue with the argument that this poetry is deliberately, satirically bad, however, I might do so by inferring that the future world it attempts to portray is so acutely ersatz that it is no longer necessary (or even *possible*) to differentiate between a truth-conditional statement and a simile.

21.3 *psyche*: As a monosyllabic verb, this is a term used in Bridge to refer, I think, to bluffs in the bidding process whereby one attempts to make the opposition believe a partner's genuine bid is phoney, or vice versa. It strikes me that the poet might be a card player; but I have neither the expertise nor the patience with the tedious reference material to back this notion up with any serious analysis. Suffice to say, it is a matter of common knowledge that the vagrant confidence trickster begins his education by learning *Find the Lady*, in which the card you think is the Queen invariably turns out to be a lowly number card.

  Presumably, we are to understand that Mercator's unscrupulous business competitors are attempting to force him out of business with a 'price war' or 'bidding war' in which they combine their knowledge and resources and thereby give a false impression of their economic position in relation to his own. The occasional intimations of extra-sensory perception in the poem—which suggest *psych* might carry some rather more fantastic sense of telepathic attack using magical powers (such as those supposedly possessed by Aleister Crowley)—are, I trust, insufficient to support such a reading. It is not so difficult to imagine a businessman driven to suicide by economic failure that one would require a psychic explanation for the severity of his melancholy, I hope.

21.5 *hike*: American slang, meaning to drastically raise the price of something.

21.7-8 *probity… nobody*: This rhyme relies on a lazy American pronunciation of the first word with a voiced, rather than an unvoiced, alveolar plosive as the penultimate consonant. The ongoing Brummagem/American deterioration of the pronunciation of the Queen's English is not, it seems, exclusive to the vowels.

She ignored me & took a sip of coffee: "By the time he had enough evidence to challenge her with it, Amrit had left home & Carla simply refused point blank even to have the subject broached around her. She would usually say 'Marty, it took me a long time to get over your father's death & I don't want to dredge it all up again now.' if he attempted to suggest, perhaps, that his real father wasn't dead, she'd just silently busy herself with something else or walk straight out of the room. He stopped going to see her in the end."

"I suppose you would."

Hannah didn't say anything. I tried the coffee. It tasted just the way it looked: like diluted bitumen. I decided I would have to bring her up to date as soon as possible. We were getting bogged down in the past: "So you think, when he found out he was to be a dad himself, he might have decided to track down his own father maybe, & tell the old man he was to become a grandad? Maybe we should think about Uganda as a place to look."

I was thinking of that exciting affair against an exotic Ugandan backdrop — something like *The English Patient* meets *Gorillas in the Mist*.

Hannah turned her head very slightly from side to side through the vapour rising from her mug: too slow & deliberate to call it 'shaking'. There was emotion in her expression, but of what sort I couldn't really tell: "But he didn't, did he? He stayed & he worked on his PhD. Amrit had long since sunk all his life & thoughts into that thing. If he was looking for his father, it wasn't the real man, Sanjit Singh, but the idea of a missing fatherhood, a missing history that wandered the streets of the city like the tramps he followed into bushes in parks, up alleys behind the shops, down dank canal tunnels &... I shudder to think where else."

She actually did shudder. It was very sexy.

"If only he'd just asked me for help, or at least tried to find what he was looking for in the world of flesh & blood instead of chasing it around like a bit of scrap paper blown by the wind through the screwed-up streets of a screwed-up fucking paper city."

She looked like she might begin to cry, then chuckled at her own spontaneous melodrama.

"So I guess that's why you need me, doll," I chimed in, doing an awful Bogart, "if you wanna find a man lost in a screwed-up paper city, you need a screwed-up paper kinda Private Dick who thinks he knows his way around."

She grinned... rather desperately it has to be admitted. This would have been a good moment for the kid to start blarting. *He* didn't, but Hannah did: only one or two tears, & she didn't cover her face or let it twitch. This was the second time she'd done this to me. Our conversations seemed to be developing a pattern. The cloudy drops clung to her chin as she continued to smile, like rain on an unpainted garden gnome. I couldn't decide whether this was a good sign or not: her willingness — half willingness at least — to show me her emotions. I tried to touch her fingers. They were laced around the yellow coffee cup. She pulled her hands away slightly, the mug inside them, very subtly, so as not to offend.

> His business went into receiver$ip,
>> £e mortgage-lender €reatened to foreclose
> — Which obviously wasn't brinkman$ip —
>> His creditors immediately froze
> His bank accounts, and cards, and moved to strip
>> His assets, leaving him wi£ just £e clo£es
> He stood in and a pocket full of change.
>> And now we find him wi£ some coins arranged

22.3 *brinkmanship*: Perhaps *Brinkman* is supposed to be the name of some paper tiger of a future money-lender: one whose bark is much worse than his bite. *Brinkmanship* could therefore mean something like *Faux-Shylockism*. The poem contains many of these unexplained bits of jargon, something which actually makes it quite superior to humdrum Science Fiction, avoiding as it does that dreary tendency to give laboriously precise explanations of every new bit of futuristic terminology.

22.5 *cards*: One can only guess this to be a reference to some system of keeping accounts of debit and credit using something analogous to today's 'index cards' which can (in this almost entirely unregulated market) be used as a kind of currency: a chaotic system of transferable IOUs that allow everybody to behave as if they were a bank. To 'freeze' an individual's ability to carry out such transactions might therefore be the definitive act of bankruptcy.

(This idea—that, eventually, every man will be his own bank—is no doubt the ultimate dream of puritan capitalism. Birmingham was the birthplace of many of the modern financial institutions of Great Britain: most notably Lloyds Bank. Wise and Johnson (1950: p.176) are explicit about the origins of these activities in C17th forges: 'Many ironmongers acted as moneylenders and from this practice emerged… the importance of Birmingham as an early centre of banking.' We can safely read *ironmongers* as a euphemism for 'coiners.')

It is impossible to ignore the continuing implications made of a possible reading of this poem as an encoded game of cards, however. It is not as obvious here as in Lewis Carroll, but one cannot fail to notice how the poem seems to follow a pattern similar to that of a hand of whist: the final scene being the final *trick* in which the Queen (Britannia) *trumps* the King of a lesser suit (Sloggy) to win the pot.

"Sorry," she said "bit tired. I'd better go & get him out of there now anyway. If I let him sleep all day he'll only keep me up again. Then you can get cracking."

The boy was older than I'd expected. Bigger than a toddler: 2 or 3. Not the kind of child you'd expect to keep his mother up at night much any more. He was slumped forward like an old drunk in his pushchair. Loose brown curls, almost indistinguishable from his mother's, were stuck to his forehead. His lips glistened luridly. His bare legs were smooth & buttery, the knees beginning to lose that chubby expression of the crawler. He pulled a gargoylish face as his mother began to tickle his nose with her dry lips.

I decided to avoid any awkward introductions & sidled off into the study straight away. Children of that age invariably run screaming when they see me, or else accuse me of being their *dada*. Besides, I secretly suspected my namesake would be able to see right through me; he would know instinctively that I wanted nothing more than to be able to wake his mommy up tomorrow morning the way she'd just done to him today. Hannah let me go, suspecting something similar. I shut the door behind me.

For the rest of that week, I spent my daylight hours hiding in that little room, going through Amrit's papers. If I'm honest, it was more as a way of killing time whilst trying to get Hannah on her own than out of any real interest in the work. I soon realised she didn't need to socialise with me though & only really wanted to talk when I had something to report. So I got on with the work. She offered me lunch that first day, & I declined, wanting to avoid the child. From then on, I would turn up in the morning after breakfast & bring a packed lunch with me, & I'd go home around 5 before they ate their tea. No-one else came round.

The room was unusually bright & cheerful. It was difficult to fathom how anyone could hide in there. It was almost entirely taken up with a large south facing bay window that looked out onto a strip of overrun garden with a laurel bush enveloping the fence at the end. It did, however, have a heavy set of velvet curtains you could close, but which, for some reason, I never dared to touch. There was a slight smell of damp & old books... most of which were arranged in rather useless vertical stacks on either side of the door. Besides that, there was nothing much else except for a swivel chair & an old desk that had been given a few too many coats of beeswax over the years so that any wood still left exposed amongst the valleys of a small mountain range of A4 paper was slightly tacky to the touch.

Notwithstanding the volume of stuff, the task turned out not to be as daunting as it seemed at first. An awful lot of the bulk was provided by multiple printouts of the same files with very minor variations: updates & edits. I spent an hour or so on the first Sunday trying to work out in what order one of the most common files (called 'Unfencing Theory') had been produced, but realised this was a futile exercise. I should focus on the content, I decided. I simply collected together the versions of each document that contained the most important information.

                    Around his feet, and pots of sleeping pills
                        And letters littering £e kitchen floor:
                    Diazepam and several unpaid bills,
                        £e invoices he'd chosen to ignore,
                    His will — wi£ all its pointless codicils
                        To outline who his long-gone €ings were for.
                    He squats amongst £e remnants of his life
                    And struggles wi£ a trembling Stanley knife.

23.3 *Diazepam*. These 'sleeping pills' which Mercator takes seem to be illicit narcotics rather than prescription drugs; or perhaps the distinction no longer exists in this lawless world of unregulated marketeering. 'Diazepam' would appear to be a slang name derived from bastardized Turkish: *azap* meaning 'pain' and *amme* meaning 'all'; the whole coinage (*di-azap-amme*) meaning 'against all pain.' Turkey is notoriously the source of much of the illegal trade in opium in Europe, the strongest preparation of which in contemporary chemistry is called 'heroin'. This word, according to the OED addenda, is 'said to be so derived [from **hero**] because of the inflation of the personality consequent upon taking the drug.' Perhaps this is the source of the alternative (quasi scientific) name here: 'Valium.' In Turkish a 'Vali' is a petty potentate whose title can no doubt trace its etymology to the Latin *valēre* 'to be strong'. The possibility exists, of course, that this root of strength (*validus*) simply reveals the name to be a coinage which makes reference to the potency of the preparation of opium rather than any bolstering effect upon the user. Mercator, at least, is in no way empowered by its effect; quite the opposite.

Crucially, this recalls a possible pun on 'heroine' in stanza 1. To gloss the opening clause as 'I want a dose of heroin' would certainly be consistent with the poet's reversal of Byron's witty flip from *desire* to *lack*. It is certainly structurally worthwhile for the poet to remind the reader of this opening craving just before the appearance, in a drug-induced hallucination, of the anti-heroine narrator whose depraved influence is to be resisted just like that of the homophonic opiate.

For my part, I would remind the reader of Canto V of *Don Juan* where Byron's hero is dressed as a concubine in a Turkish harem at the orders of the Sultana. Despite the opening parody of Canto I, it is this fifth Canto which the poet is most influenced by here. Byron directly alludes to Milton's Satan when describing the Sultana. The poet hints that the reader should struggle against the influence of his counterfeit heroine just as Byron has Juan (himself reluctantly dressed in *drag*) resist the Circean charms of the Sultana:

> Her charms had all the softness of her sex,
>   Her features all the sweetness of the devil,
> When he put on the cherub to perplex
>   Eve, and paved (God knows how) the road to evil;
> The Sun himself was scarce more free from specks
>   Than she from aught at which the eye could cavil;
> Yet, somehow, there was something somewhere wanting,
> As if she rather *order'd* than was *granting*.—

The widest variety was to be found amongst the photocopies: academic articles & extracts from monographs. Obviously he only had one each of those. But they were remarkably diverse — a bit of pretty average history & criticism, a smattering of theory (most of it predictable enough), & quite a lot of stuff in foreign languages (both Modern & Classical) but there was also a good deal of mathematics & biology & some serious linguistics — despite the variety, though, you could still easily have stored it all in one drawer of a standard filing cabinet. As for his own work, there were numerous versions — he had a habit of changing titles of things without altering the content much — but very few genuinely discrete documents: a parody of the Communist Party Manifesto, a few derivative poems, the embryonic first chapter of his thesis 'Unfencing Theory', a chapter breakdown of the project in the style of an eighteenth century contents page, a pastiche of Joyce's *Ulysses*, a short story called 'Mustard Oil', & a number of unfinished essays. Singh's stock-in-trade appeared to have been a very *close* form of parody: he made perverted copies of famous (infamous) texts in which he would change only certain key words & phrases. It was a kind of creative criticism. Strictly speaking, he managed to avoid veering into plagiarism by surrounding his texts with large amounts of ingenious annotation that was explicit & thorough in citation & insistent that the minor damage inflicted on source-texts was a useful form of post-deconstructive intervention.

A few things quickly became apparent: firstly, it was about as likely that I would find anything in this (so-called) academic work to help Hannah find her missing boyfriend as it was that Amrit himself would have found anything amongst the tangled mass of ideas to form a proper thesis.

Secondly, Hannah's idea that the work was all about looking for a missing father-figure, or at least recovering a lost idea of fatherhood in the labyrinths of theory & Birmingham *geo-poetics* was pretty wide of the mark. Amrit's approach was based almost entirely on debunking the search for origins. He was a rather typical neo-Marxist, neo-Feminist, neo-poststructuralist theorist influenced by Bakhtin, Adorno, Derrida, Kristeva, Foucault, Deleuze & so on. His big idea was *dividualism*, the opposite of *in*dividualism. He saw the 'zomby' human being that was the potential product of the patriarchal capitalist society as the victim of a reduction (a near annihilation) of its mind & its identity to a material singular whose very epitome was the idea of the legacy of *fatherhood*: capital, cultural, genetic. If his upbringing influenced his work at all it was to make him argue that people should be more like him: they should develop multiple identities & break free of the one that society insists is their inheritance. What he had got by accident, he wanted to deliberately pass on to others: multiculturalism, polyvalent imagination, & so on. Fiction he saw as a way of doing it, both for himself & for readers; the dramatic activities of reading & writing were both a way of accessing some higher (*musical* or *contrapuntal*) truth & the route eventually to something like a socialist utopia. You could, I supposed, craft the argument that this was evidence of an obsession expressed as a fantasy of its absolute rejection — theoretical Oedipalism. The practical upshot was, however, that I wasn't going to find Amrit's dad — or any explicit evidence of a search for him — amongst his academic writings.

24

Despondent £at he can't extend £e blade
    Because £e Valium has dulled his brain,
He drops it, and collapses backwards, splayed
    And weak, and begs £e ceiling to explain
How it can calmly watch a man be flayed
    And not do any€ing to ease £e pain.
He plonks his cheek against £e lino tile.
He drools and sinks into £e Queen's profile,

Something imperial, or imperious, threw
    A chain o'er all she did; that is, a chain
Was thrown as 'twere about the neck of you,—
    And rapture's self will seem almost a pain
With aught which looks like despotism in view:
    Our souls at least are free, and 'tis in vain
We would against them make the flesh obey—
The spirit in the end will have its way.

        (*Don Juan* Canto V, stanzas 109-110)

23.3 several: era 4

24.2 Valium: See 23.3 *Diazepam*.

24.7 *plonks*: An onomatopoeic verb. We are, I think, intended to hear the sound as if *inside* (as well as *from*) Mercator's own skull as his face hits the floor. This is therefore the moment at which we pass from watching him as if standing 'upon the ceiling' to inhabiting his perspective as the 'doped' narratee (see 15.2 *dope*) of the rest of the canto.

24.7 *lino-tile*: 'Lino', according to the OED addenda, is an abbreviation of 'linoleum' '[f. L. *linum* flax + *oleum* oil.] A kind of floor-cloth made by coating canvas with a preparation of oxidized linseed-oil.' It is possible the linoleum is itself cut into tiles which are stuck to the floor with an adhesive. Considering the theme of tawdry imitation which pervades the poem, however, it seems much more likely to be that type of rolled linoleum printed with a design that (entirely unconvincingly) mimics marble tiles. That this should also tend to leave an impression of the word *linotype* on the imagination (see OED Supplement Lino³) is very telling: 'A machine for producing stereotyped lines or bars of words, etc. as a substitute for type-setting.'

The third & most obvious thing I realised was that Amrit Singh had probably run away because he was weak. He simply wasn't a man 'ready for commitment' as they say. If his work was evidence of anything it was evidence of that. The only *thesis* he would commit to was that truth was always plural & could only be reduced by an act of cultural violence even to a *dialectic* thesis. His most obviously heartfelt piece of work was a reversal of the 'Penelope' chapter of *Ulysses* which replaced the repeated *yes* with a repeated *no*. Little wonder he couldn't commit to family life. Toward the end, he was probably suffering in a dutiful attempt to make all these chaotic imaginings come together into something presentable for a degree... in time to become a proper father: one like Leon, who went to work every day & earned just about enough money doing something quietly worthwhile to keep his family in mince & dungarees & caravaning holidays. As the deadline loomed, however, & he knew he was no closer to achieving even this, he probably came to the dull, but still quite dreadful realisation that he simply couldn't hack it: neither as an academic nor as a dad. It wasn't rocket science. He didn't have some romantic nervous breakdown because he'd delved too deep into the human psyche, or capitalist culture, or the nature of the universe. He wasn't Faust. He wasn't even Moses Herzog. He probably just legged it the first time he heard the kid screaming or cast a desperate eye over his latest bank statement.

Most importantly, it became rapidly evident that I couldn't tell Hannah anything: not if I wanted to carry on coming to her house, not (being brutally honest) if I wanted to get her into bed. I couldn't tell her why I thought he'd run away. I couldn't tell her how disorganised & flimsy his research had been. I couldn't tell her there was going to be nothing in it to help her trace him, that her best chance would be to find a diary or a postcard (something unrelated to the work) hidden in a drawer or underneath a pile of photocopies. I couldn't even explain that her theory about Amrit's father was probably a red herring. I needed her to think that she'd been right: in part, at least. How else could I convince her it was worthwhile me continuing to look for him?

For five evenings in a row I fended off her enquiries, telling her it was coming together & I'd let her know when I had a clearer picture. Stuff like that. She tried to hide it, but I could see the desire brimming in her as the days went by: a desire for anything, the smallest titbit, some clue about her lover's inner life. It was that eagerness of hers that made me keep delaying her. I wanted to watch it grow. Every afternoon she would appear even closer to the brink of some magnificent, mind-altering discovery. & I was the key to it. Once her knowledge & my own, newly enriched, were brought together, some kind of critical mass would be reached. There would be bright reaction & the generation of a considerable amount of heat.

> Which grins maniacally beside his nose,
>   A ripple on £e surface of a coin,
> Becoming larger as his eyelids close
>   And brighter round £e forehead and £e line
> £at marks £e boundary of her jowl and $ows
>   Her age — her curlered hair begins to $ine
> Like her tiara's fairy lights and tinsel —
> To call it just a *crown* would be an insult.

25.6 *shows her age*: I am reminded of one of the numerous portraits from the long reign of Queen Victoria: not the so-called 'old head' with the *chaperon* demurely veiling the widow's shoulders, and certainly none of the 'young heads' or the ravishing 'gothic' portrait of the 1847 crown and the 'godless' florin of 1849, but the peculiarly unflattering effigy of the Jubilee coinage of 1887: on which the Queen seems to be standing to military attention, with heavy bags under her eyes and sagging cheeks, like some kind of weary old soldier on the parade ground. The 'line that marks the boundary of her jowl' is quite prominent in this portrait. I can hardly imagine the charming young woman just crowned Queen becoming old enough to have such an unpleasant feature appear upon her profile.

25.7 *fairy lights and tinsel*: Cheap Christmas decorations, but *tinsel* also refers to all sorts of low-quality gilt jewellery: precisely the kind of thing Birmingham—the city Edmund Burke baptized 'the great toyshop of Europe' (in the House of Commons: March 26, 1777)—is famous for producing. I am surprised the poet could not find a place in the canto for the word *bauble*. It is often used by Shakespeare as a shorthand for this kind of thing, and might have been particularly fitting.

The *Birmingham Counterfeit* has the following. The debt is incontestable:

> Overwhelmed with defpair, giving up every thing for loft, [Mercator] determined to put in execution the refolution he had long fince formed. Taking one of the piftols out of his bureau... feating himfelf on a couch, he placed the muzzle to his forehead, and was that moment going to pull the trigger, when, lo! A deep fleep fuddenly feized him, the piftol dropped from his hand, and he fell backwards on the couch.
>
> It was in this fituation he fancied his eyes fixed upon his laft piece of cafh, the Birmingham fhilling; and, to his great furfprife, imagined he beheld it fwelling to a prodigious bulk, and then burfted with a report louder than that of a cannon.
>
> A figure, difficult to be defcribed, immediately ftood before him. On his head was placed a crown of tinfel imitating gold, from every part of which the curious eye might obferve the moft venomous poifon exuding: his perfon was tall, and feemingly majeftic; his robe was of yellow, ftriped with gold and filver, which the wind fometimes waving to and fro, difcovering a body covered with an inner filthy garment; in his left hand he carried a looking-glafs, with which he ufed to amufe the rafh and credulous, by flattering them with the refemblance of a face not their own, while he ftabbed them to the heart with a dagger, which he bore in his right hand, and which he concealed in his bofom. On his face was a mafk reprefenting the features of a moft beautiful virgin; but this dropping off, a moft hideous and frightful countenance was difcovered.
>
>   [*The Birmingham Counterfeit*. 1772, vol I. 36-38]

I began to convince myself, I suppose, that her desire for Amrit was as good as a desire for me. I would compliment the work as vaguely (but as convincingly) as possible: it was fascinating, bizarre, original, I'd say, I'd never read anything like it. The implication was obvious. I was becoming acquainted with some exquisitely unstable secret that she wanted to know, that she needed to reach out & touch somehow, to bring her life back together, & open her up to the world again. I wasn't going to disabuse her of a fantasy like that.

I was obviously becoming a replacement for the man. I must have realised, instinctively, it was the only way I'd have a chance of loving her. She began to treat me like him in the subtlest of ways. She would shush the child & make sure he didn't come into the study, as if to say *don't disturb your father while he's working*. She would stand in the doorway & look at me as I pretended to pore over something new, not saying anything, the way you do only when you know somebody so well you recognise every movement their body makes, better than they might themselves. Despite the pain it probably caused her, I think she secretly enjoyed the whole experience. I would stay in the study all day long & she could pretend that it was Amrit in that little room, refusing to come out, the way he always had when she was pregnant.

By Friday, I'd been through most of the stuff on the desk. I hadn't actually read most of it but I had made sure I was pretty certain what it was, what kind of thing it said. I realised I'd have to tell her something by the weekend. I was becoming confident enough, however, to think I could spin a tale sufficiently alluring to start the process of shading Hannah's desire for Amrit into a genuine desire for me. I didn't care how long this took. I just knew I couldn't pass up the opportunity.

There was something genuinely troubling me, though. There was no computer in the study, not even any sign of one: no floppy discs, or cables, or CD-ROMs, not even a printer that might have produced all that inkjet paperwork strewn around the place. I didn't really want to entertain the possibility that there might be a PC somewhere with another morass of Amrit's research on it, but I couldn't ignore the fact that Hannah might not take me seriously if I didn't bring the question up. It might have been a test. I had to ask.

I left on Friday at about 4 or 5ish, as normal, but made arrangements to come back in the evening & tell her what I'd found. I brought a bottle of brandy & a packet of dates. I had to stand outside in the drizzle, tapping the neck of the bottle on the living-room window for a while before she let me in. She was in the back & there was a locked gate on the alley. She didn't apologise when she finally came. She didn't need to. She looked stunning.

She swung the door open. An eager breeze from the drive vacillated over which lush curtain of inviting fluidity to riffle first: her long patchwork skirt or the glossy, herb-scented curls, tumbling reluctantly over one of her shoulders, left pink & bare by the material negligence of an army-surplus vest. The heating was obviously back on again then. She grabbed my wrist & tugged me inside, grinning & kicking the door shut as I entered. Her lips were already dark with wine. Everything about her seemed incredibly unfashionable & incredibly beautiful. I thought for a second she might take me straight into the bedroom.

26

$e grows and fills his vision like £e flame
   £at fills an oil lamp; her arms unfold
Imperiously, burning wi£ £e same
   Warm glow, £e colour of a marigold,
But bright enough to put £e sun to $ame:
   $e's quite resplendent, painful to behold.
(In case you €ink £ese descants overrate her,
   I warn you, $e's £e story's main narrator.)

26.2 *oil-lamp*: I am old enough to remember the domestic oil-lamp. The truly wonderful thing about these objects, lost in this age of electric lighting, was their portability: not like a battery operated torch, that weapon of anonymous accusation the policeman or the air-raid warden wields like an extended finger of approbation; but as an almost magical illumination that would first make the bearer glow himself before spreading out to light up his surroundings. The energy seemed somehow to radiate directly from within. I can still hear the dull pop with which the flame lit up the gas mantle… the clatter of the tube in its casing, the clink of the glass globe on its metal ring when the lamp is carried from one room to another.

26.4 *marigold*: The orange blooms produced by plants of the genus *Calendula*, associated with the Virgin Mary. It is also perhaps important that the word was Restoration slang for the gold sovereign.

26.5 *shame*: To pick up the C17[th] overtones once more, there is a possible play here on 'put the sun to *sham*' ie *shoddily imitate the sun*: something which carries precisely the opposite connotations to those of 'surpassing' or 'outshining' suggested by a surface reading. 'Sham' is commonly supposed to be derived from a dialectal form of *shame*. The OED quotes the following by way of explanation:

> *a*1734 NORTH *Exam*. II. iv. §1 (1740) 231 The word *Sham* is true Cant of the Newmarket Breed. It is contracted of *ashamed*. The native Signification is a Town Lady of Diversion, in Country Maid's Cloaths, who to make good her Disguise, pretends to be so *sham'd!*

The simulation of shame—perhaps the ultimate act of immorality if one considers the quintessential shamelessness required—is therefore captured in this word by mimicking its use by prostitutes who thinly disguise their tell-tale urban argot with a gilt of rural vowels, associated in the public imagination with naivety. There is a distinct similarity here with both the origins of 'drag' and the stylistic techniques employed in this poem. The idea is not one of genuine disguise, but of titillation (or in the case of the poem, satire) by means of an ironically poor veneer which reveals that which is supposedly hidden.

It is, of course, during the period of invented plots and dissembling politicking of the late 1670s and early 1680s (the period that gives us 'Whig' and 'Brummagem') that the word becomes current. ''Tis my Resolve to quit the nauseous Town' says John Oldham in his 1682 'Satyr, in imitation of the third of *Juvenal*', thereby coining the traditional moral divide between town and country, 'Let the Plot-mongers stay behind, whose Art/Can Truth to Sham, and Sham to Truth convert' (li. 38-9).

26.6 *Don Juan* Canto XII.12:

> How beauteous are rouleaus! how charming chests,
>   Containing ingots, bags of dollars, coins
> (Not of old Victors, all whose heads and crests
>   Weigh not the thin ore where their visage shines,
> But) of fine unclipt gold, where dully rests
>   Some likeness, which the glittering cirque confines,
> Of modern, reigning, sterling, stupid stamp:—
> Yes! ready money *is* Aladdin's lamp.

26.1: *the flame*.

> Hic focus et taedae pingues, hic plurimus ignis
> semper, et adsidua postes fuligine nigri.
>
> Virgil, Eclogue VII

My room is on fire. I can see very little any more besides the desperate shapes of these words scrabbling out from underneath my pen: to swarm into the vacant gutters of the manuscript like fleeing rats. I do catch the odd glimpse of the flames from time to time — their naked colours, their ecstatic sacrificial dance — but only as the oily reflections in my pen-nib and the trembling shadows of my hand. I can hear it though, all around me: a choir of hot, bright tongues swelling to a crescendo of unbearable polyphony. 'Flames are wood turning itself back into music', *somebody once said, it is not important who: they are the souls of trees escaping from imprisonment amongst a building's eaves (or the pages of a book perhaps), trumpeting the fanfares of liberty they were once content to weave into the whispers passing through their living foliage.*

There is no smoke. At least, no smoke except these words; sometimes the letters seem to curl like incense fumes. The smell is not entirely unpleasant. It is mostly burning wood and paper, but there are sometimes overtones of cinnamon or nutmeg, or... perhaps... angelica. Maybe this is the effect of burning ink. The slight bitterness it leaves at the back of the tongue is very similar in taste. 'God changes the way fire does when mixed with spices' *Heraclitus riddles*, 'and is named according to each spice.' *He also says:* 'all things can be exchanged for fire, and fire for all things: as goods for gold and gold for goods.'

He is right. I am on fire too.

*   *   *

27

$e goes, "I wi$ my dads had took £e time
                To concentrate and do a decent job
When £ey were making us. It's such a crime,
        £e half-arsed cock-up of a woman's gob
£ey gave me, for example. Just no rhyme
            Or reason to it. Picture £is: Fat Bob
Picks up a brand-new little golden pound
And says, 'you sure £e head's £e right way round?'

27.1 *"I wish…*: *Tristram Shandy*, Chapter 1:

> I Wish either my father or my mother, or indeed both of them, as they were in duty both equally bound to it, had minded what they were about when they begot me; had they duly consider'd how much depended upon what they were then doing… I am verily persuaded I should have made a quite different figure in the world.

She goes: 'She says'—a slang reporting clause which betrays a certain lack of education on the part of the speaker. Perhaps the vocal distinction between the more sophisticated poetic persona and the 'common' coin-narrator is deliberately inconsistent. The environment of this poem is one in which no such logical distinctions can be allowed to hold; not even the structure of the narrative is immune from the encroachment of a debilitating ambiguity.

27.1 *took*: The use of the preterite form in place of the past participle 'taken' is intended to set up the 'common' voice of the coin mentioned in the previous note.

27.4 *half-arsed cock-up of a woman's gob*: The counterfeit queen is complaining that her mouth has been so poorly rendered by the die-casters that—in a very unfeminine way—it resembles a buttock with a distinct turn up (cock-up) at the end; or perhaps even a filleted (*half-arsed*) Indian fish: the Cockup (*Lates calcarifer*).

27.8 *the right way round?*: The reversed layout of this stanza—the lines being justified to the right rather than the left margin—is a typical mimetic gimmick. It is genuinely important to the hermeneutics of this piece that the coin is mis-struck as a mirror image, though. Apart from the fact it makes the object seem less like a coin and more like a 'plate' for printing bank notes, this detail also allows the poet to include yet another encoded reference to the thematic importance of C17th and C18th coining.

    The direction in which the monarch's portrait faces is traditionally consistent throughout the reign, and only alternates from one reign to the next. This pattern was first significantly interrupted in 1672, at the apex of Hearth-Tax counterfeiting, when the first ever regal copper coinage was issued by Charles II. Private copper tokens had circulated for some time—especially in the new metalworking areas; when the King introduced his own it was as another token currency not an intrinsically valuable one. The law at the time did not make copper tokens the monopoly of the Crown as they were not considered part of the nation's wealth, not being re-exchangeable for gold and silver. Two decisions were taken, however, that are crucial to this poem: the first was to reverse the direction of the King's profile, and the second was to show Britannia on the reverse (for the first time since the Roman era). Like the edge inscription DECUS ET TUTAMEN, introduced in the same period to deter clipping, these measures were deemed necessary because of the likelihood coiners would silver over ambiguous halfpennies to make them look like shillings.

The next important reversal of direction took place in 1821 when Britannia was turned to face right (permanently as it turned out) in the first copper minting by the Crown since the 'cartwheel' coinage of Boulton and Watt's Soho Manufactory had revolutionized the milling process with steam power. The first cartwheel set of 1797 is the only copper coinage in history to have had an equivalent intrinsic value. I think it no coincidence that the creation of this heroically valuable coinage was simultaneous with the suspension of bullion convertibility (see 6.4). Boulton was attempting a practical intervention on the Bullionist side of the debate: one which involved him in an expensive and courageous private war against the coiners of the city in which he operated, whose machines and rings of distribution he paid personally to have broken.

Perhaps the decision to make Britannia drop her olive branch and turn (as it were) away from the West (in which pose she had resembled the island of Great Britain itself), is significant of a hardening in the C19th of the Empire's attitude to America after the 1812 war, and a change of focus towards Asia.

*   *   *

My room had seven sides. It was heptagonal. I miss it already. Four of its sides were walls (my four walls), the other three formed an oriel of leaded glass set directly in the bare, honey-coloured stone jutting into the quad. Before the fire, I could sit and watch the starlings scavenging amongst the rosebushes at dawn, loose-haired students breezing past the borders at the chimes — I might do even now if it were possible to tear my eyes away from this flickering scrawl — but the first time I opened its door (the door I can no longer turn to see behind me) the daylight world was banished from this room by stacks of yellowed paperwork.

It was a kind of oratory once I think, but long abandoned. By the time of the blitz, it had become a repository for unnecessary flammable material (the irony of it) — drafts of essays, working assessment documents, disciplinary records, excess paperwork from the bursars' offices, society records, posters advertising social events, messages from notice-boards, informal or unwanted letters, minor internal memoranda, minutes of unofficial meetings, newspapers and journals, albums and loose collections of photographs, even common room menus — all of which was meant to be destroyed but had been unpredictably preserved by a lazy porter or a sentimental college secretary who simply couldn't bring herself to do it... or perhaps by some bright spark who realized Hitler would never allow the Luftwaffe to bomb this city.

*   *   *

'Fuck me' moans Sloggy, crouching next to Bob's
    Gigantic oily machinery,
Which buzzes like a Sabbath gig and €robs,
    Lending £e grimy Hurst Street scenery
A nice satanic flavour; £en he sobs,
    Ironically, of course (but £at Ribena he
Mixed wi£ £e gin *had* made him feel sick),
'I can't believe you Bob, you're fucking €ick.

28.2 *oily*: Another diæresis. These broadly arcing slippages of vowel pitch make the mouth and mind seem as full of lubricating engine oil as the chambers of the machine-parts produced in the grimy city they derive from. The incessant pistons of this chugging Midland verse are driven inexorably in and out of them.

28.3 *Sabbath gig*: Rather than a small horse-drawn carriage, I assume this 'gig' is a *whirligig*: either a small wind-driven wheel of feathers designed as a children's toy (or as a trap with which to catch small birds), or else a different toy made from a hammered coin, or some other form of flat disc, through which is threaded a string or lace at four different points so that pulling the ends apart causes the disc to spin and create a whirring sound and a multi-coloured visual animation. Toys of this latter kind have been found at various archæological sites around the world and were used in primitive shamanic rituals to create hypnotic effects in the participants. This 'gig' for use in a demonic 'Sabbath' ceremony is likened to the poem itself whose 'buzzing', whirling, hypnotising octaves are to be resisted, encapsulating as they do its awful vision of the future, in which dire birdtrap a flighty, unsuspecting reader might otherwise find himself entangled.

28.6 *Ribena he*: This is one of the least convincing rhymes in the poem; the enjambment is almost unspeakable. The trashy quality of the verse is no doubt intended to reflect the trashy quality of Sloggy's work and language though. 'Ironically, of course' might therefore be read as appositive to the ensuing parenthesis, something like a stage direction or line reading in a theatre script:

READER AS SLOGGY: [*ironically, of course*] That Ribena I... etc.

The brand of blackcurrant syrup mixed with his gin (a product issued to children throughout the war as a desperately needed source of vitamins) is intended to imply Sloggy's combination of alcoholic degeneracy and childishness. This is a characteristic of his which the poem later reveals to be not at all unusual. The vision is truly Hogarthian.

Instead, she led me the same old way down the long book-lined Victorian hall towards the back of the flat & the kitchen. Sitting at the table as we entered, already pouring a third glass of wine for whoever was about to walk in, there was a very tall black woman with a broad metallic ribbon wrapped around the base of her unkempt afro like an over-risen chocolate cake. A bright red leather biker's jacket was slung over the shoulders of her chair. She widened her eyes in mock astonishment when she saw me. It struck me that she probably did that whenever she met a person for the first time. It was probably a way of pre-empting the same reaction in her new acquaintance. I was certainly taken aback by her. She was really quite enormous: long-limbed & angular. The fingers on her right hand almost fit completely round the wine bottle. I should have been upset to find someone else in the room — especially when I'd been envisioning candlelight & hushed excitement with Hannah — but the sheer size & colour-definition of this figure against the drab wood-grain of the kitchen units stunned any inward objections I might have had to silence.

"Oh, this is Lynne," said Hannah, "we used to work together... she just dropped round." She didn't tell Lynne my name. It didn't occur to me that they'd already been discussing me before I came. I just assumed that Lynne didn't need to know, or (more likely) didn't need to be told. She slid the wine over to me with the faintest of smiles, saying nothing. Her movements were slow & careful... like a delicately powerful insect under a magnifying glass: one that has evolved specifically to be magnified to such unnervingly beautiful proportions in order to teach human entomologists an intricate lesson in design. She turned back to Hannah, who was asking:

"So it's a proper tenure-track post & everything?"

"Yeh, the works."

"& she's never published a thing? Just goes to show you should use whatever you've got."

"Whether it's between your ears or between your hips."

"I reckon they all want to get her into bed just to shut her up. She asks those interminable bloody questions, without even a modicum of relevance, just so as everybody in the room gets to see her lips in action & to hear that charming little accent as she works her tongue around the jargon. If I was a bloke, & I had to choose between listening to her wittering on about *stratified methodology* or trying to make her grunt like a sunbathing walrus up against a hotel bedboard, I'm not so sure I wouldn't shag her too. It's just incredible that afterwards they always want to give her jobs as well."

"Oh she knows what she's doing. It's just like the music business, honey: if you wanna get ahead, you gotta give a little."

> 'I worry about you sometimes, mate. I doubt
>   Ano£er bugger's ever had to stop
> A run and pull £e fucking blanks all out
>   For such a trivial mistake. £e top
> Is meant to go £e o£er way about,
>   Besides, £e bleedin artwork int much cop:
> It looks like some old bag out on £e piss.
> I ask ye. Jesus. At a time like £is!'

29.3 *blanks*: The plain, unstruck discs, also known as *flans*, that are milled or hammered in the striking process. The word has a number of other senses in both numismatics and printing however which might be informative here. *Blanks* are: 'French 5-denier pieces of the early Renascence', 'the smallest subdivisions in the system of measurement of precious metals used in minting', 'unprinted pages in a proof' (see missing stanza 180), 'profane or potentially libellous words replaced with a dash in a published text', and 'the empty spaces inside individual letters of a typeface.' The last of these are also called *counters* by typographers: the largest and best example being the 'hole' in the upper-case O (though the matrices for movable type are obviously made in relief, so it would actually be the opposite of a *hole* in production).

I am quite certain the poet intends us to think of the printing process as much as coin-milling in this scene. The 'gigantic, oily machinery' could just as easily be a large printing press as a mint. The difference is not large. Gutenberg was a goldsmith and his invention of movable type was self-evidently an adaptation of techniques used in the production of dies for coins. We should remind ourselves that mass dissemination of the printed word in metal predates its mass dissemination on paper by some two thousand years.

If they were minted as mirror images, coins themselves could act as 'type': coat a very fine example in ink, press it onto paper and you would get a pretty decent image. This is no surprise; the origin of numismatic stamps is probably to be found in the 'seals' on noblemen's *signet rings*, which were specifically designed to make a recognisable impression in a soft medium like clay or wax.

Coins, however, should carry more than significant value. The printed word (or the impression in a wax seal) is simply the trace of a 'type' which the reader cannot touch. In this system, the typographic *counter* is a strange zone of absence—an enclave of lost tangibility which seems to crave the impossible: to be filled with disambiguated meaning. On a sovereign coin of precious metal, on the other hand, the form, the value and the substance are not divorced. Its worth is both embodied and signified by its presence and its form.

Obviously this is no longer true if coins are token or counterfeit. In this case, their form takes over from their content. They are reduced to the status of texts—hardly any more valuable than the mark they could make on a piece of paper—unstable, revolutionary texts which carry all the ambiguities of significance that Gutenberg's *counters* seem to have introduced into the Bible.

29.6 *int much cop*: Perhaps this means 'is not very good' from 'is not much *copper*' (an important word in this poem). This suggests an æsthetic judgement on the design expressed exclusively as a sardonic reference to the paucity of intrinsic value of the material in which it is struck. A typical bit of Brummagem nonsense.

29.8 *I ask ye…*: *Tristram Shandy* Chapter 1:

> *Pray, my dear*, quoth my mother, *have you not forgot to wind up the clock?* — Good G—! cried my father, making an exclamation, but taking care to moderate his voice at the same time, —*Did ever woman, since the creation of the world, interrupt a man with such a silly question?*

*　　　*　　　*

I had known for years of the existence of the door without ever having tried its handle. There were two ways to approach it. The first involved climbing a narrow spiral staircase made of brass: the only continuation of Stair Six between the second and third floors. The soles of students' shoes would sound the steps off one by one, the resonances spiralling back through the metal as they went—tank, tank, tank, tank—*like Navy-issue boots descending into a submarine. At the top there was another door that opened out into a small, unlit hallway containing three further, similarly broad oak doors. Mine was on the left. Straight ahead, it was an old Victorian toilet that was neither used nor cleaned by anybody else these days. The last led to a disused teaching room: Room 666.*

I realize this sounds unlikely. You must believe me though: the only element I have invented in the entire manuscript to which these marginal memoirs are just the final signature, and which will soon curl up in the flourishing heat and wrinkle into ash, is you... the reader. You of course can never have existed, but every word used — every name and incident besides this one fictional (functional) exception— is accurate and true.

The second route to the door was via 666, itself most commonly entered through Room 667 at the end of corridor H. Being at one time a rather vexatiously overused thoroughfare, 667 had traditionally been appointed as a small meeting room to Faculty Assistants: temporary junior tutors employed by University rather than College who were occasionally invaded *(as we say) to cater to a fashion for one subject or another. Somebody had once pinned a sign beneath the copper number disc (to think I could ever have dismissed it as a waggish undergraduate):* '667' *it read,* 'The Neighbour of the Beast'

*　　　*　　　*

                30

            A time like what? You ask. And so you $ould.
                I can't stand stories where you haven't got
            A clue what time of day it is. I could
                Have said a word about £e Muse and what
            £e £eme is too, to make it understood
                £is is an epic poem. But it's not.
            £e only 'mews' £at's ever touched £is bard
            Was up £e back end of a vicar's yard."

30.7 *mews*: This pun on *muse* is typically unamusing; the tawdry double-entendre designed to undermine both Parnassus and the royal stablery with its insidious suggestion of sexual impropriety amongst the Anglican clergy, does not deserve a second look.

30.8 *yard*: See 12.1 *back-yard*

          *   *   *

The flames hold fast to the rough skin of my knuckles like seaweed and waft gently in the breezes from the window as I write. The skin is slowly bubbling. My surface fat has begun to melt and simmer. It is seeping through the crisping epidermal layer to lard my hair and the fabric of my clothes: a kind of beeswax engorging the tissues of cotton and wool so that I feel I have become the wick of the candle in the centre of the room. I am burning very slowly... and entirely painlessly. My room has become the furnace of Babylon.

The first time I opened the door to this room it was out of a desire for change. I had arrived at one of those periods in life when anything new, however dreary or unpleasant, seems like a boon. I had recently been granted a premature sabbatical on 'compassionate grounds'. The Provost envied me, he said. If he were me, he would roam the Shropshire countryside in the footsteps of Housman: 'to replenish our reservoirs of poetry from the bright, fresh springs of the living landscape that inspired it'. The Provost is a geographer and shares a predilection with many of the better schooled of his empiricist colleagues for a rather dewy-eyed nostalgia when it comes to the literary education they regretted having to abandon. 'It might *produce an article or two' he added, his gaze fluttering above the bookcases as if the thought had suddenly arrived from that direction like an unexpected Cabbage-White descending ash-like from its camouflaged position in the cornicing. His real motive was to expedite the secondment to my post of a fierce-browed young linguist from Montreal: a vigorous mountain climber, and an equally vigorous publisher of quasi-learned articles, to whom he had taken something of a shine.*

It is quite impossible to underestimate the strength with which the Rhodes conspiracy has taken a grip on the administration of this University. Preferment has become its virtual monopoly. Slack-voweled, corn-fed American graduate students are arriving under its auspices in greater numbers every year. It grieves me to think that an admirable thinker like John Ruskin could have been involved in instigating such a dubious Masonic project to marginalize the careful, episcopalian tradition of learning that has been this institution's mainstay for an era, only to replace it with tasteless Internationalist ambition in the guise of 'Humanism'.

          *   *   *

They carried on gossiping about ex-colleagues like this for a good hour before Lynne made her excuses. I attempted to chip in from time to time with observations, but I could tell I would be much better appreciated as an audience than a participant.

My presence actually seemed quite important. They were being pointedly indiscreet & carping about members of their old department, whose surnames I could easily have traced by looking up the staff list on the internet, but rather than pretending I wasn't there or modifying their references the way you do when talking about hidden Easter Eggs in the presence of a child, they would glance over at me every now & then to see if I was enjoying the performance. I would shake my head in disbelief or laugh & they'd take visible encouragement from my responses. Those looks also made it clear, however, that I was not supposed to use any of the privileged information I was being given. In fact, I was not being given the information at all. The content was not the focus of the exercise. I was supposed to enjoy the fact of the conversation's intimacy rather than being allowed any lasting access to it. I was supposed to disengage my memory, sit back & enjoy the ride.

The conversation followed a pattern that was becoming familiar to me: Hannah would do most of the talking, with Lynne feeding lines to her — even when it was actually Lynne who was revealing information or telling a story. That was the way Hannah spoke to me as well. Once she'd heard enough of your idea or your anecdote to take up the reins, she would begin to speculate about what you were about to tell her, often extremely accurately, so that any new material you contributed seemed to be a minor ornamentation of a theme she'd already introduced. Perhaps this was one of the reasons I'd been avoiding giving her reports on my discoveries in the study. I couldn't tell her the truth, but her uncanny ability to pre-empt your words always made me feel rather anxious about spinning her a yarn.

Unlike me, however, Lynne seemed totally at ease with this way of doing things. She would wind Hannah up & then occupy herself with the zen-like performance of some simple task: the rolling of a cigarette, the pouring of wine, the changing of a record. She got out of her chair as Hannah spoke, unrumpling the vertiginous length of her body, & carefully organised her surroundings. She behaved very much as if it were her own house & Hannah an unexpected & slightly over-talkative visitor — she straightened picture frames & wiped down the working surfaces — without ever once appearing fidgety. Perhaps the muscles responsible for animating such an impressive skeleton find it difficult to fidget.

The elaborate performance of these two women had something like the same effect on me. I was engrossed. I quickly lost any sense of nervous apprehension & began to take real pleasure in observing their complex dance. It was almost as if I had stopped existing as anything but an integral function in their show. I had become a voyeur, & nothing else. My body seemed entirely autonomous & self-aware, which made my movements all completely unselfconscious. There was no question of my taking a wilful decision to move an arm or turn my head an inch or two; everything around me, including even the smallest of my own physical motions, was to be experienced rather than controlled.

31

>   (I've heard of poets talking to £e dead
>   And getting verses from '£e o£er side',
>   To pass on what £eir predecessors said
>   In seances where, conjured to confide
>   £e low-down on £e afterlife, instead
>   £ey spell out villanelles. I've never tried
>   Myself: I've no need of a ouija board
>   To plead for ghostly help… and be ignored.)

31.1 *poets talking to the dead*: This is clearly an allusion to Yeats' *A Vision*.

31.2 *The other side*: The afterlife of Spiritualists; one from which the dead are supposed to be able to make contact. It is sometimes identified (by the most acutely unscientific of occultists) with the 'dark side of the moon'. Consider this, from the most pretentiously harrowed of second-rate romantic poets, Charlotte Smith:

> And oft I think, fair planet of the night,
>   That in thy orb the wretched may have rest.
> The sufferers of the earth perhaps may go,
>   Released by death, to thy benignant sphere,
> And the sad children of despair and woe
>   Forget in thee their cup of sorrow here.
>   (Sonnet IV 'To the Moon')

There is, of course, no *dark* side of the moon, only a *far* side: which gets plenty of sun, but which human beings have never seen because the moon takes precisely the same amount of time to rotate on its axis as it does to rotate around the Earth. This seems a remarkable coincidence to the weak minded, but is in fact quite a predictable feature of the gravitational interactions of the Earth and its satellite. The big coincidence, where the moon is concerned, is its objective appearance in the sky, which makes it seem precisely the same size as the sun and therefore allows for the 'ring' effect of a total lunar eclipse: something which must have influenced the myth of 'The Ring of Gyges'.

31.5 *low-down*: Yet another sleazy hyphenated Americanism. British journalistic slang would render it 'the dirty truth'. Here it carries connotations of the underworld: the spirits are perhaps to be understood as quite literally speaking from 'low down' (i.e. *hell*)… and/or with deep bass voices. At least they are being 'conjured' to do so. (It is a silly commonplace of Jacobean Tragedy for ghosts of the buried to speak in comically booming voices from beneath the stage: see Marston's *Antonio's Revenge*, for example.) Instead, these particular spirits behave like effeminate troubadours.

31.6 *villanelles*: I can not for the life of me find any Villanelle for which the poet claims a ghostly agency. The most recent I have read however—'Do not Go Gentle into that Good Night' by Dylan Thomas (from *In Country Sleep*, New York, James Laughlin 1952)—does deal directly with the subject of death. Mr Thomas is himself a somewhat dense and dark poet with a penchant for both the public house and the depiction in his poetry of certain less wholesome sections of society. I would not put it past him to be acquainted (if not actually in contact) with the author of the present work.

31.6 *Ouija*: This proprietary brand name for the 'supernatural' board-game (registered as a US trademark from July 1st 1890 by the Kennard Novelty Company, Baltimore) is formed from the French and German affirmatives: 'oui' and 'ja': the implication being that when the séance-leader intones 'is there anybody… *out there*?' the answer is invariably 'yes'. There must have been an element of irony at play. It is a surprising act of restraint that the poet declined to use 'ouija' as a feminine rhyme in this couplet; it would be in keeping with the general flippancy, ambiguity and laxity of articulation to round the stanza off with something like: 'There's no point trying to contact ghosts by ouija: / You try to talk to them, they'll never heed ya.'

I find it disquieting that I have succumbed so quickly to an internalisation of this dreadful persona's style that I should already be producing more of it. This weird allure is testament to the poem's satirical prowess.

*   *   *

I have no hesitation in identifying myself as a victim of this process. My gradual sidelining in college, the thinly veiled aspersions cast against my focus of research and the 'archaism' of my prose, the rejection of my article on Edward Benlowes' Altars *by the P—————— Society, even the disintegration of my marriage, all of these things can be traced directly to men connected to the group who dine together at the G—————— Club on every second Monday of the month. Needless to say, the Provost (and now, no doubt, the Canadian) are invariably amongst them. One can only hope that they have been consumed by flames by now.*

Instead of pointing out to the Provost that Housman had spent most of the period in which he wrote The Shropshire Lad *squinting at the Clee Hills through the window of a bungalow in Bromsgrove, I agreed and thanked him for his refreshing idea. I then set about secreting myself within the College: somewhere genuinely secluded where I could continue work on* Poetry and Prophesy *undisturbed.*

For reasons that should remain obscure for the moment, I had developed something of a habit – an expertise, in fact – for clandestinity. Nevertheless, my own decision soon became unfathomable to me. Why subject myself to such unnecessary duress? Why pretend I had gone down instead of coming clean about my project? Why continue with this never-ending piece of work, whose instigation had been an intellectual response to the final breakdown – ten years previously – of my long-doomed marriage? This sabbatical was, after all, my own to do with as I pleased. I adhered to it nonetheless; I understand now that such decisions were never mine to take.

Having somehow been conjured into magnanimously offering a year's occupation of my (old) room to the Canadian, my first thought was to find a storage space or cupboard in which to keep my books and papers while I was supposedly away. It took no time at all for my mind to turn to the numberless door opposite Room 666. It seemed uncannily appropriate.

*   *   *

> *"Of counterfeits and of £e woman/man:*
>
> *£e Quean, I sing.* How's £at? Derivative,
>
> I know. I've tried too hard to make it scan,
>
> It's just a $am. But frankly I don't give
>
> A damn. I've done about £e best I can.
>
> No muse, you see: I'm just a karaoke div.
>
> A time like what? you ask me: was it late?
>
> Dunno, £e clock had stopped at ten past eight,

32.2 *Derivative*: Of Dryden's translation of the *Ænied*: 'Of arms and of the man, I sing…' (*Arma virumque canō*). It is from Virgil that poets seem to get this habit of beginning in a measured tone with 'of', and then the topic. Homer starts with much more gusto, immediately and emotionally invoking the muse. Milton opens with: 'Of Man's First Disobedience, and the Fruit/Of that Forbidden Tree'; Ariosto has a rather rambling list to match his rambling tome: 'Le donne, i cavalier, l'arme, gli amori,/Le cortesie, l'audaci impresi, io canto'.

32.4 *sham*: (See 26.5 *shame*.) Macaulay says it was during the 1680s that 'sham' and 'mob' entered the language; as did both 'Birmingham' meaning a fake (a 'sham') and a Whig exclusionist and 'anti-Birmingham' meaning a Tory (as did the words 'Tory' and 'Whig' themselves. Paradoxically, 'Whig' came from the nickname of a radical Scottish Presbyterian group defeated at the battle of Bothwell Bridge by the Duke of Monmouth, who the Whigs definitively supported.) (*History of England*, Vol I., ch. II.)

32.4-5 *give a damn*: It was the censors who insisted on Clark Gable's infamous anapæstic rendering of 'give a damn' in *Gone With the Wind*. I recall being bored to distraction by the grimacing American melodrama and wishing the film-reels had been destroyed in the climactic fire.

32.6 *karaoke div*: 'Karaoke' appears twice in this poem. The second instance in stanza 130 is in the phrase 'TV karaoke bar'. 'Bar' is in the American sense of 'public house', which suggests that 'karaoke' is a kind of intoxicating drink which one can imbibe at such an establishment, presumably whilst watching Television. 'Karaoke' might therefore be a narcotic made from 'karaya', a gum extracted from the Indian tree *Sterculia urens* and used, like *gum tragacanth*, (see note to 'gum') as the basis for liquid medicinal preparations. There are certain cough medicines which use this gum as a viscous medium and contain opiates like codine and morphine. (*Oke* was a unit of measurement in the Ottoman Empire, roughly equivalent to the metric litre.) Perhaps, in this bleak future, we are to understand that 'karaoke' is a product like this, served in large quantities as a stupefying drink in sleazy 'television bars'.

As for concerns of prosody, the other occurrence of this word (at 133.7) suggests it to be a tetrasyllable rather than *ka-ra-yoke* or *kar-yoke*. This line is therefore another Birmingham Alexandrine. Perhaps this has to do with the gormless Americanism worming its way into our urban dialects: 'okey-dokey'. (see 13.7 *okay*.)

div, (to follow the thread of Asian/Islamic influence) is an ancient Persian demon or evil spirit, so named because of a negative transformation in that culture's early religions of the Indian gods into devils (Sanskrit *dēva*, 'god', from which root both Italian and therefore English get their *diva*: 'goddess' or 'prima donna'). A 'karaoke div' is therefore a *karaya-drug demon*: an addict of this gum-based narcotic.

32.8 *ten past eight*: The hands form a straight oblique line (at an angle of about 40° from the horizontal) across the face of a clock at ten past eight. This has the effect of 'crossing it out'. The clock has not only stopped, to recall Sterne's joke about the pause of narrative time at Tristram Shandy's conception, but is also *sous rature*.

& yet they were *all* experienced. It was no more true that I could ignore the tiny physical changes in the shape or state of my body than that I could predict them. Every movement became like the beat of my heart: a precursor to, rather than the subject of, any mental act of will.

I'd experienced something similar, from time to time, when playing musical instruments. If you're lucky enough, you can reach a stage where it seems that you are no longer playing a piece of music, but that *it* is playing *you*. The music exists as a complex organising principle that has come to inhabit your mind through multiple exposure to its organic structures. It brings together items of your imagination & functions of your body that normally remain detached & employs them to bring itself into existence, driving your limbs, your lungs, your mouth, your fingers to reproduce its multiplicitous vibrations by interacting with the objects they can touch or the breath they can control. This is like the music flourishing: attempting to breed by bursting out of the silent compost of the brain in which it has been germinating & mingling with the other, libidinous musics that are troubling the air, reaching out to clash or harmonise with them. When that happens, you graduate from being just a *player* to being a *musician*: no longer the reproducer of the music but a member of a special audience whose minds & bodies are co-opted by it to take part in an erotic ritual of contrapuntal sonic interaction.

This was how I felt when Lynne & Hannah spoke. My neck & eye muscles were entirely at the whim of their speech patterns. My gaze wafted back & forth like a blade of kelp in the ebb & flow of a coastal swell. It was not always clear which was which, or indeed if I was really in the room at all. What is certain, is that I'd forgotten about Amrit Singh.

When Lynne suddenly announced she had 'a dinner date' (at a quarter past eleven on a Friday night), flipped her heavy jacket off the chair & reached inside it one arm at a time, it came as a real shock: like an unexpected teaspoon full of mustard. She zipped it right up to just beneath her chin then took my hand & shook it extremely gently, but without seeming in the least dismissive or insincere.

"Nice to meet you, Sam... sure we'll catch up again sometime. Don't bother getting up Han," she turned to her friend & bent down to the unlikely depth necessary to kiss her on the top of the head. Whispering assurance that she knew the way out, she allowed her long thumbs to meet across the half-exposed skin of Hannah's shoulder-blades, the fingers exploring the brinks of her pale arms like the tentacles of an octopus. She straightened up again, but dipped slightly to get her hair under the doorframe as she loped into the hall.

We heard the flat-door close... neither of us said a word... then the front-door of the building. I considered leaning forward & kissing Hannah there & then. There was a click & a hum as the fridge came on.

>   But June £e second, two €ousand and €ree,
>   £at was £e date: I know £at; I could see
>   Some program on a portable TV
>   About £e news of Edmund Hillary
>   On Everest, and $erpa €ingummy,
>   And how it dovetailed wi£ £e Jubilee,
>   Or some€ing. Was it Coronation Day?
>   Whatever…" (just some way to make us pay

33.3 *portable TV*: One of the fantastic contraptions typical of (and perhaps ultimately definitive of) so-called Science Fiction; presumably we are to understand this to be a miniature, battery operated version of a television set one can hold in one's hand: being, to the *mains* television set, what the torch is to the standard lamp. There are other, seemingly, *portable* gadgets in this vision of the future, most prominently the telephone. Both of these fictional inventions are fundamentally illogical and, worse, extremely disturbing. Why anyone would want to watch television whilst on the move, ignoring their native environment in preference for the mind numbing propaganda of American commerce, or use a telephone whilst out of the house, I cannot imagine. The ludicrous image suggests itself of two men sitting with their backs to one another on a park bench discussing the *inveigling* television programme they are both watching on their personal, hand-held televisions by speaking into their personal, hand-held telephones. Something akin to this nonsensical tableau happens (in 229-230) when Sloggy—whilst still in the same bar-room—attempts to telephone Perry pretending to be someone else, in order to cheat on a wager: a fundamentally deceitful act which seems to encapsulate the distorted morality carried by the distorted logic of such an 'innovation'.

33.5 *Everest*: The ever-(r)est mountain (for) ever. [Poet's note]

These short interjections are very useful as a demonstration of the poem's thematic drive. This one clearly demonstrates the dystopian concern with time. Everest is the highest mountain in the world. At the time the poem was written, it was yet to be successfully climbed. This scribbled note equates a symbol (therefore) of geographical insurmountability with the concept of temporal permanence by suggesting a folk-etymology based upon an illogically hypersuperlative transcendence of time and history: rather like the infantile solecism, 'bestest'.

In fact the mountain was named after Sir George Everest (1790-1866), Surveyor General of India, whose name is one of the variations of 'Everard'—derived from the Mercian Saxon *Eoforheard* ('sturdy boar')—of which 'Everett' is the most common alternative. The parenthetical insertions serve a morbid desire to evert this sense of ultimate unconquerability by implying 'Everest' could also be synonymous with *requiescat in perpetuitatem*. The Earth's highest mountain is also one of its most lasting monuments to death; it is quite literally the tomb of dead climbers, clinging petrified to the permafrost on its slopes like the leopard on Hemingway's Kilimanjaro, whose frozen grimaces serve (like the gargoyles on Christminster Cathedral) as warning to all who aspire to conquer the seemingly unconquerable. The man named here (as *obscure* as Hardy's Jude in the poet's vision), Edmund Hillary, is predicted to become one of its sepulchral statuettes.

In this sense, the mountain is not dissimilar to the gorgon in the poem's symbolic stratum.

Sherpa Thingummy: 'Sherpa' is a job-title given to the Tibetan mountain porters in Nepal and India. *Thingummy* is a typically vague algebraic formula used to stand for an abstruse oriental name. It is amusing to note that I was initially taken in by it, not being able to recall the correct name of Tenzing Norgay; there is a certain phonetic proximity of the word to a name one might expect from an inhabitant of the area. This is black comedy, however; we should not forget that the porter's own frozen body is envisaged in this bleak prediction to be the only monument left to mark his grave, and anonymity would make his death in the service of a tragic adventurer all the more poignant when one considers the numerous unmarked graves of soldiers in the recent war—many of them Gurkhas.

Of course, what the poet could not possibly have known as he wrote this dire premonition was that the 'news of Edmund Hillary' was in fact not of tragic failure, but of a transcendent success. The event actually predated the Coronation by several days but the news was only released in London on June 2nd after a sturdy young reporter for the Times, James Morris, who had manfully gone more than half way up with Hillary and Sherpa Tenzing, had, trudged back down from Camp IV at 20,000 feet through extremely inclement conditions and concocted a sophisticated plan involving a relay of local message-runners in order to bring the news back home.

In order to avoid the theft of this scoop by reporters lacking Morris's undoubted spunk, the decision was taken to relay the message in code: *Snow conditions bad* was to mean 'Everest climbed' and the climbers were given code names—Sherpa Tenzing was *awaiting improvement*, and *advanced base abandoned* referred to Edmund Hillary. So when, on May 31st, Morris sent the message: *Snow condition bad hence expedition abandoned advance base on 29th and awaiting improvement being all well*, the newsdesk understood it to mean 'Everest climbed on 29th of May by Hillary and Tenzing; both are well.'

The news was more than good: not a foreboding shadow of mortal failure looming over the crowning of the new defender of the empire and faith, as this poet warns, but as much a beacon of hope in dreary times for the commonwealth as was the ceremony with which it coincided.

This serious error of judgement on the poet's part proves the poem to have been written very recently indeed: lately enough to have heard of the mission but not of its success. One can only hope that more of the dire predictions it contains turn out to be similarly false.

33.6 *dovetailed*: No appearance of a bird in this charged environment is ever purely innocent. It is the dove who first returns with news of land after the flood: the source of its identification with peace (with the olive branch as evidence) and with the Holy Spirit. It is for this reason that *Columbus* is such an apt name for the discoverer of America—he is the bird sent from the European ark who returns with the olive branch of the 'West Indies', a little like Æneas with the golden bough. (All the more reason to suggest a rejection of America might lie behind Britannia's turn from West to East, discarding her totemic sprig of olives).

This stanza is (wrongly) concerned, however, with the reportage of glowering *bad* news sent back from the top of the world via television. Where the dove is traditionally the bringer of good tidings and blue skies after the storm, this poet has transformed its active principle of combination, in the (Christian) carpentry term *dovetail*, into an insidious harbinger of doom: from pure white dove to sooty storm-crow. In Russian, I believe, the words for 'dove' and 'sky-blue' are cognate: *golub* and *goluboy* and an alternative name for 'television' (supposedly more patriotic than one derived from English) is *goluboy ekran* (the azure screen).

Imagine a dove killed instantly, impacting on a television screen, fooled by a depiction of the sky.

                                       34
                    Our TV license fees and our respects
                       To all £at telegenic speciousness:
                £e stately, gilt-edged pomp £at intersects
                    £e nation's gaze, till it's as meaningless
                 To ask, as any play of Bertolt Brecht's,
                    Who's really in £e spotlight — £em or us?
                 Like loyal, statuesque domestic grooms,
                 We hold our sofa-cades in living rooms,

34.1 *license fees*: The means by which BBC television is funded. It is surely much more desirable to run the system this way than to succumb to American style commercial television. At this point, though, we are directly inside the anti-royal, capitalist propaganda voice of BTV. This mask slips a little over the next few stanzas however. This is not, I think, a weakness. It may be slightly illogical that the voice of BTV would inveigh against television itself (rather than simply *the state television of a constitutional monarchy*, as here) but a little respite from the otherwise relentless adoption of the voice of the enemy is very welcome. This way we catch a glimpse of what the poet really thinks.

34.5 *Bertolt Brecht*: A Marxist German playwright famous for opposing realism in the theatre. Brecht's stylistics appears to be based entirely upon a rejection of the credulous, pleasurable response to drama in preference for one in which the audience is never allowed to forget that performances are artificial; they should therefore respond to them as artistic constructs whose import is to be intellectually extrapolated. He is also (consequently) famous for encouraging the use of harsh lighting effects that are physically unpleasant to endure, and also for refusing to allow the house-lights to be dimmed during performance. His version of John Gay's *The Beggar's Opera*, called *The Threepenny Opera*, therefore considerably weakens the original, failing to recognize the dramatic necessity of balancing these 'alienation effects' with the lulled, pleasurable responses he tries entirely to disallow: typical of his dour socialist piety, not to mention his non-existent German sense of humour. Hopefully, this kind of pretentious nonsense will never seep into the English theatre. The idea that an obscure Joycean like Samuel Beckett, whose apparently plotless 'pièce de theatre' *En Attendant Godot* is currently showing in Paris, might decide to produce something similar in his mother tongue is truly horrifying. If Cromwell had tolerated theatre, perhaps it would have been like this.

34.8 *sofa-cades*: A fanciful neologism of the persona's, made by analogy with the American portmanteau of 'motor-car' and 'cavalcade': the *motorcade*. Virginia Woolf would never have used a word as crass as this, but perhaps the first appearance of such a thing in literature might be the moment in *Mrs Dalloway* where the laborious and ludicrous Viceroy's cavalcade scene in the 'Wandering Rocks' chapter of Joyce's *Ulysses* is elegantly pastiched as a very English stir of various reactions caused when the prime-minister's car backfires on Bond Street. *Sofa-cades* is self-consciously silly. It is a surreal comic image of all the viewers sitting down in their living room furniture to watch the procession to the Abbey for the Coronation, being somehow transported into Westminster to glide down Horse Guards' Parade on their sofas. Unlike most of the other jargon in the piece it is therefore to be understood as a sneering invention of the persona's rather than a piece of current *newspeak*.

"So, Sam, what have you come to tell me?" she asked.

I couldn't remember exactly. I'd been practising on the way here, but now... "Fancy a date?" I said, it was a stupid joke, "they're the perfect accompaniment to a cognac." I tried to sound like Noel Coward as I said that last bit but my tongue, tapping about amongst all those enamelled consonants, was less a linguistic Fred Astaire than a demented moth trapped in an upturned tumbler.

She took one anyway, which was a great relief, & accepted the generous glass of brandy I poured out.

"Have you any idea..." she teased the long, woody date-stone around in her mouth as she spoke, "where he might be?"

"Perhaps," I exaggerated, "but we'll come to that. First, I should tell you how I've managed to arrive at my conclusions." (& perhaps I could think of something as I did.)

"Amrit's theories are fascinating. The principal text, I think, is his parody of the Communist Party Manifesto."

A glimmer of a smile started in the corner of her eyelids. Maybe she was remembering something. She pouted rather than broadening her lips though, & the date-stone half ejected like a bank-card from an ATM. She pulled it out & dropped it next to her glass: "Tinker", she whispered. She didn't take another. She was encouragingly tipsy.

I considered commenting on this, but found myself just carrying on.

"It seems a pretty cheap trick at first: he just changes a few words here & there & makes it into a manifesto of the 'Fiction Party'. But then you realise just how hard it is to keep this effect up & how cunningly he's done it. It's not so much a parody as a kind of fruitful mistranslation. It owes a lot to deconstruction, I suppose, but it's a lot more positive. I mean, it *is* a deconstruction in the sense that it deliberately mishears the first sentence of the Manifesto: 'Ein Gespenst geht um in Europa: der Gespenst des Kommunismus' as 'Ein Ge*spinst* geht um in Europa...: not 'A spectre haunts the land of Europe...' but 'A *yarn* (the result of spinning)...' or 'A *tall tale* haunts the land of Europe: the tall tale of Communism'.

"But from there he moves on to imply that not only Communism, but also the manifesto itself, is a self-conscious fiction which is designed to reveal the truth of a Socialist Utopia that haunts the Capitalist present like a ghost of the future: one that can only be brought about by such acts of fiction."

This was utter crap, but Hannah's smile was encouraging, &, to be fair, it was precisely Amrit Singh's kind of utter crap.

"He sees the manifesto, & even *Das Kapital*, as something like gothic Science Fiction: closer to *Frankenstein* than any genuine history or economics. That's why Karl Popper gets it so wrong. In order to tell her story, Mary Shelley needs to invent a world in which the creature's reanimation is scientifically possible. The same goes for Marxist historicism...

35

> £eir weal€ electroplated on our faces
> As we spark our B&H cigarettes.
> £at's what £e light in Tarantino's case is,
> Nostalgia for a golden-age £at $eds
> A homely glow on us, like £e fireplaces
> We 'upgraded' wi£ television sets,
> And filtertips, American sitcoms,
> Positive economics, and atomic bombs.

35.1 *electroplated*: Unsurprisingly, electroplating was invented in 1840 by a Birmingham doctor called John Wright (a follower of the city's pre-eminent republican scientist, Joseph Priestley, no doubt) who used Potassium Cyanide as an electrolyte for suspensions of gold and silver. He sold his invention to local jewellers Henry and George Richard Elkington who used their monopoly on the technology (which was much less costly to use in terms of materials, time and effort than traditional plating methods) to turn out cheap gilt rubbish at enormous profits. The legal protection given by the Crown to such insincere processes is, in my opinion, tantamount to a license to print money. The idea that royal 'wealth' can be 'electroplated' on the faces of the common people by the radiation of the television or the glow of a cigarette is obviously sarcastic.

35.3 *Tarantino*: I imagine this to be the name of a supposedly exotic conjurer who makes use of a luminous box or 'case' of some sort in his televized performances. The name suggests a connection to the Tarantula spider, and therefore also the dance, *The Tarantella* and the archaic illness, *Tarantism*: both of which are characterized by jerky, erratic movement thought to be the (*phrenetic*) result of a bite from this arachnid. Perhaps the magician uses spiders in his act, or else behaves like a *tarantato*.

Another possible connection is to the word *taratantara*: which is an (originally Italian) echoic imitation of a brassy fanfare: a sound made when introducing something trashily impressive (like a magic trick) within the suggested idiom of showbusiness. An equivalent in more regular English usage might be *ta-daa!* This would certainly suit the connotations of cheap showiness here, not to mention those (*passim*) of 'brass' and 'brazen'.

A strange usage of this word in Italian identifies it with a winnowing tray or a sieve used in gold-prospecting. This reminds me of a theory I once heard mooted around the peripheries of a conference by an eccentric young Strabo scholar that 'the golden fleece' brought back to Greece by Jason, in the first great story of foreign trade in the Classical tradition, was actually a technology (of *placer* mining) using sheepskin to filter the silt of gold-rich rivers in Colchis. I seem to remember the argument went that the *golden fleece* was therefore simply a synecdochic representation of the legendary wealth of the place and not a magical object at all. This might be persuasive if it were less self-contradictory: a place of great wealth would surely not need to go to the desperate lengths of slopping about in mud with the soggy pelt of a sheep looking for one or two grains of precious metal. This would turn a story of great heroism into one in which a pastoral scene of unambitious and contented shepherds was transformed, by alien greed, into one full of filthy, desperate *forty-niners*.

35.6 *'upgraded'*: This is a veiled barb directed at the Grade brothers, Lew and Leslie, who are the 'theatrical agents' behind the Independent Television Company seeking a franchise to bring American commercial Television to Great Britain. (See note to 0.1.) The inverted commas clearly make an irony of the prepositional prefix (another of the typical reversals of direction in the poem). The prefix that best captures the projected effect on the nation's hearth and home of the Grades is not *up* but *down*-Graded, and ultimately *de*-Graded.

35.7 *filtertips*: Futuristic slang for cigarettes with a filter mouthpiece designed to reduce the tar content of the smoke. These already exist of course, and are more popular in the United States than Britain. The first brand to be introduced were, however, British, and heavily marketed as such: Benson and Hedges *Parliaments*. This brand are sold in gold-coloured packs which carry the coat of arms of the British Sovereign; the firm being "tobacconists by appointment" to the monarch. They turn up *passim* (B&H in 35.2 is an abbreviation), presumably because of their royal connection and the gold appearance of the pack.

    I do not think the poet (who has begun to speak directly at this point) is actually attacking the filter technology, however. It seems quite a sensible invention. There is a new version on the market in America, the Lorillard *Kent* brand, which has a patented filter made from a substance called 'Micronite'. This is in fact a tightly textured fibre derived from *amiantus*: a fire-resistant mineral whose other name, 'asbestos', is paradoxically misapplied, meaning as it does *unquenchable* rather than *undefilable*. (A similar folk-etymology is spreading like wild-fire which derives from the increasingly common solecism of using 'inflammable' as an antonym, rather than a synonym, of 'flammable'.) According to their advertising "Kent and only Kent has the Micronite filter, made of a pure, dust-free, completely harmless material that is not only effective but so safe that it actually is used to help filter the air in operating rooms of leading hospitals." This does not seem like the sort of thing the poet would disapprove of, rather he is probably satirising cigarette smoking in general (as opposed to the more genteel and considered English habit of the pipe) with all its attendant notions of packaged, prefabricated convenience so characteristic of US culture.

    Crucially, the poet seems particularly scathing of the advertising jargon involved in selling these 'convenience items', particularly on commercial television. The most successful programme in America is, I am told, a supposedly 'comic' everyday drama series called 'I Love Lucy.' This series is sponsored by the tobacconist Philip Morris, who has recently taken over Benson and Hedges, and each broadcast begins with an advertisement for this brand of cigarettes.

35.7 *sitcoms*: These invented compound terms are the stock-in-trade of the science fiction writer. Infuriatingly, however, (though infuriation is a perfectly justified intention in the circumstances) this poet often fails to explain, or even make illustrative reference to, the technological innovations he names. I can only hazard a guess, though knowing the clichés of the oeuvre I am fairly confident of my guess, that the items in question are communication devices. Just as 'telegenic' in the previous stanza has recently been newly fangled from 'television' and 'photogenic', this word seems most likely to be an *alloy* of 'sitting' and 'intercom', and therefore used to denote some contrivance which allows the user to communicate with others over long distances without getting up from his seat. Like the *filter-tip*, this seems on the surface to be something beneficial rather than unpleasant. No doubt it is the laziness implied in the need for such a thing that is the subject of the poet's ire.

> TV's a stand-in for £e Briti$ sun.
>> We bronze our features in its beta rays.
> And as it reaches its meridian,
>> We're mad enough to keep it in our gaze
> Until some lasting damage can be done:
>> Our skin anneals; our eyes begin to glaze.
> I sound like one of £ose self-righteous saddos,
>> But turn your telly round and watch £e $adows

35.8 *Positive economics*: A book, and an ultra-capitalist theory, published this year by American economist, Milton Friedman. It argues, or so I am led to believe, for absolute deregulation of international currency markets, and the abandonment of material wealth standards for an absolute assertion of relative exchange values. It is the cornerstone of my politics that this should be identified as the thin end of the wedge of revolutionary Marxism. His name would be almost laughable if it were not *quite* so apt.

36.1 *stand-in for the British sun*: 'Stand-in' is another of the hyphenated *alloys*—a current slang term meaning an actor or actress engaged literally to stand in the place of a principal player of a film during the preparations for shooting so that the 'star' can avoid all the tedious business of arranging the lighting and camera angles. In the circumstances, all the connotations of illumination, 'stardom' and the manipulation of the moving image are heavily ironic.

It is curious to note that the moon might be seen as the perfect object to carry this epithet. For the Lunar Society of Birmingham (Boulton, Watt, Wedgewood, Darwin, Priestley et al.: the self-styled great figures of the 'English Enlightenment'), the moon stood quite literally in the place of the sun as the means to light their journeys home after their clandestine meetings. The revolutionary implications of this should not go unnoticed. Many of the group, (the ironically named) Priestley in particular, were more than sympathetic to the anti-royalist revolutions in America and France. Moreover, to continue the discussion of the total solar eclipse as the model for the Ring of Gyges (see 31.2), we should recall that it was Newton's fascination with this event in his childhood which inspired him to the work on optics without which the television would probably never have been invented. The television, as 'a stand-in for the British sun', could therefore easily be seen to have the revolutionary (ecliptic) aspirations of a Cromwell or Napoleon.

There is a reference, which I take to be an ecliptic image, in Shakespeare to the theft (to paraphrase) of the moon's *'dusky fame'* at the hands of the Sun's *'gilt orb'*, but I cannot find it for the life of me.

36.2 *bronze our features*: This is an extension of the idea of 'electroplating' in the previous stanza. *Bronze* is also used in this narcissistic age to mean 'deliberately get a *sun-tan*'. Why anybody should want to make themselves look like an Arab or an Irish navvy heaven only knows, but more and more of us seem to be obsessed with doing precisely that. I cannot help but think it has something to do with Technicolor images of Americans. Clearly the radiation emitted by a television set is not sufficient to brown the skin (see next note) but the connection between atomic technology (which self-evidently mimics the sun) and the technology of television is not illogical. To look into the faces of those transfixed by television is very similar to watching people 'sunbathing'; their skin changes colour and seems to wither and age before your eyes. At some level, all the implications of Æneas and the 'brazen', must suggest this poem hints that television is somehow taking us back in time; it is not just 'burnishing' our faces, but also 'taking us back to the bronze age.'

36.2 *beta rays*: Despite the perfectly justifiable paranoia expressed here, I am assured that the beta radiation in the cathode ray oscilloscope (television set) actually impacts on the opposite surface of the screen, rather than literally radiating from the objective side. This is another of the poet's reversal (*counter*) effects. In order to conflate the television with the nuclear bomb he turns its scientific properties inside out and makes the viewer's face into the 'screen.'

Screen is another crucial linguistic *counter*: as a verb and as a noun it can both obscure and/or display. The basic point made here about the television set being a source of (electromagnetic) radiation is nonetheless entirely valid. The poet finds complex analogues of colonisation in the difference between the reflected light of the cinema screen and the radiated light of the television which turns our faces into *screens*.

36.5 *Our skin anneals*: In minting, the *annealing* process involves re-heating and slowly cooling cast coins in order to eradicate tiny fissures and flaws in the metal. The word derives from Old English *ǽlan* 'to burn' (transitively, i.e. 'to set on fire'). It is also used in reference to 'glazing' ceramics.

36.7 *saddos*: presumably a putative dialectal form of *saddhus*—ascetic Indian holy men who eschew modern technology and society and profess a transcendental gnostic ideology with a number of relevant similarities to that of Plato. Though the poet could just be spelling it like this to make it rhyme with 'shadows'.

*   *   *

Late one Saturday afternoon, two weeks before the ingress of the new college, I climbed the spiral staircase and entered the lobby. It had been a particularly balmy day and a parallelogram of worm-eaten floorboards was still illuminated by the dwindling September sun, which had gained a temporary access through the open door and frosted skylight of the neighbouring classroom. For reasons I could not articulate at the time, I wanted to avoid any bodily contact between myself and this ochre light as I stretched to try the door handle. This proved an arduous task. Before I could even bring myself to extend an arm, I had to judge the angle at which the sunbeam fell towards the floor.

*   *   *

> Reticulating round your furniture;
>   Just give your own imagination sway
> To picture its own mental signature.
>   Perhaps you'll question what I can convey,
> Redoing Plato's cave in miniature,
>   But is it less insane £e o£er way?
> To contemplate a source of radiation
> Was once a sign of mental aberration.)

37.1 *Reticulating*: Forming a web. I am not sure the poet actually means to use this word. Perhaps he means 'articulating' as in 'moving strangely'. Whether or not he intends it though, the word suggests something rather more uncanny than the *flickering* or *dancing* fire-light evoked in Plato's cave: if we remember 'the light in Tarantino's case' perhaps there is some sense in which the poet means to combine the radiation emitted by the television with image of a monstrous spider's web in which we have been trapped.

37.3 *signature*: Rather than a handwritten name, this word originally referred to the impression of a signet ring on the wax seal of a document. It is therefore very closely related to the authenticating stamp of a coin and carries many of the same connotations—both literal and metaphorical—of the word 'impression.' I think, in fact, the poet is employing the same analogies of coinage and utterance that Bacon uses to capture the chimerical notion of imaginative reproduction in *The Advancement of Learning*:

> there is impressed upon all things a triple desire or appetite proceeding from love to themselves; one of preserving and continuing their form; another of advancing and perfecting their form; and a third of multiplying and extending their form upon other things; whereof the multiplying, or signature of it upon other things, is that which we handled by the name of active good.
>
> (*The Advancement of Learning*, 1605: Book II, XXI)

This metaphor of the King's effigy on an utterance of coin is made most clearly in his dedication:

> This propriety inherent (the logical PROPRIUM QUOD CONSEQUITOR ESSENTIAM REI) and individual attribute in your Majesty [i.e. learning] deserveth to be expressed not only in the fame and admiration of the present time, nor in the history or tradition of the ages succeeding, but also in some solid work, fixed memorial, and immortal monument, bearing a character or signature both of the power of a King, and the difference and perfection of such a King.

Bacon would be well aware that the longest lasting 'monuments' of past kings are their coins. He is using the metaphor of the 'multiplication' of the monarch's abstract power and value—as represented and effected by the literal 'multiplication' of his 'signature' by the coin-press—to talk about a universal desire for self-propagation in all concrete and abstract 'forms'. This metaphor is only possible because there is, in the coin of Bacon's day, a near perfect correspondence between the value of the substance of the coin and the value of the form imparted on that substance by the King's stamp, which allows this transference from the concrete to the abstract to take place.

The honorific prose of Bacon's dedication is typically as self-congratulatory as it is loyal. He extends his metaphor of the 'solid work' from the coin-press to the printing press, and the 'signature' from the King's seal to his own verbal composition. He is, to coin a phrase, extending the 'signature' of his own form upon the King. The bumptious overtones of Bacon are, however, infinitely more tasteful than the tinny indelicacies meted out by the persona of *BQ*.

37.5 *redoing*: There is a combination here of the senses: 'doing again' or 'making over' and (more colloquially) 'redecorating'. The two senses can sit logically beside each other only if the poet is offering what you might call a 'doll's house version' of Plato's cave (from the Republic, see next note) as an analogy for his imaginary *mise-en-scène* in the reader's living room. This is obviously meant to deflate the philosopher's original metaphor to a derisive degree and (just as the society the poet is attempting to represent has done to Byron's *Don Juan*, as his counterfeiter has to the sovereign coin, and his heroine to womankind) to show how the world he is predicting undermines all stable values of truth, replacing them with flimsy caricatures of even the most profound intellectual concepts.

37.5 *Plato's cave in miniature*: Against my better judgement perhaps, I am going to assume the education in the English speaking world at the time this work is eventually deemed publishable to contain sufficient remnants of the Classics that I need not explicitly refer the reader to the pertinent passage in *The Republic*.

37.6 *other way*: Again, you'll notice this is a 'flip-side of the coin' effect: another *counter*.

"£e television and £e coronation,
　　£e B&H and chinking nickel-brass,
Half-wittedly embossed in imitation
　　Of Albion's *materfamilias*,
£ese €ings were ga£ered like a congregation,
　　All winking as £ey welcomed me to mass.
On Bob's palm I was £e communion wafer
But Sloggy grabbed me like a cheesy quaver.

38.2 *chinking*:

Too much you mint me that cheating counterfeit
Of gaiety: too often pay me thus.
I know, I know you are winsome so, but you cheat
Me out of my proper dues with your chinking jests…
Ah coin me speech of your heart's gold furnace heat.

Mint me beautiful medals, and hand them me hot
From the fiery hammering of your heart: I cast
My all into your flux, you melting pot
Of my old, white metal of meaning, you fine
Crucible where new blossoms of shape are begot.

　　　　　　　　　　(D. H. Lawrence 'Aloof in Gaiety' 1910)

Lawrence's poem is a gamut of Birmingham Alexandrines. The fact that its 'chinking' 'cheating' 'speech' is so vulgarly echoic of coins rubbing together is, I suppose, not entirely unjustified considering its theme.

　　This sound is crucial to *BQ* and there are numerous examples of alliterative repetition of the dental fricative articulations, for which the poet originally intended the orthography of the two American currency symbols. The decision to get rid of the logograph for the cent (¢), presumably taken for reasons of textual clarity, was particularly regrettable when you consider it might have found its way into key words like 'speech', 'rich', and 'chime'.

　　The standard metonymic connection between these kinds of sounds and the confidence trickster was most famously asserted by Charles Dickens when he gave the name Jingle to the vagrant 'gold-digger' and philanderer whose wanderings form the active principle behind the initial plot of *The Pickwick Papers*.

38.2 *nickel-brass*: *Nickel* is an abbreviation of German *kupfernickel* which means 'coppersprite' or 'copperdwarf'. At first sight this seems to carry a meaning like 'false' or 'dissembling' copper (as in the English *fool's gold*), but in fact refers quite serendipitously to a naturally occurring alloy of copper and nickel (niccolite) which is not dissimilar to cupronickel, the metal now used in what were previously the definitive 'silver' coins of sterling (see note on the 'commemorative crown'), and was so named because of the infuriating difficulty of extracting pure copper from it.

　　The OED points out that 'cobalt' has a similar Germanic derivation:

> the same word as *kobold*, etc., goblin or demon of the mines; the ore of cobalt having been so called by the miners on account of the trouble which it gave them, not only from its worthlessness (as then supposed), but from its mischievous effects upon their own health

and upon silver ores in which it occurred, effects due mainly to the arsenic and sulphur with which it was combined.

It is this kind of thing that informs what is actually a fairly commonplace Spenserian metaphor of (Elizabethan) virginity as equivalent to the purity of precious metal in Milton's *Comus* (436-7): 'No goblin, or swart Faërie of the mine/Has hurtfull power ore true virginity.' (That *ore* instead of *o'er* is not an error.) The fact that Milton co-opts this idea of virginal nobility (not to mention the Platonic doctrine of invincible virtue) in order to justify a prototypically anti-nomian position is quite in keeping with his puritanical perversion of Spenser's legacy.

Of course, the *Nibelungen* in the German literary tradition which finds its apotheosis in Wagner's *Der Ring des Nibelungen* are the dwarves: the spirits of the mines and the holders of esoteric knowledge which they encapsulate in a Ring of Power. This is obviously the other major source (alongside Plato's account of Gyges) for Professor Tolkien's current work. Considering the prehistory of coinage in the (signet) rings of kings, it is impossible to extract these myths from the story of the invention of money.

Conventionally we differentiate between *ring* 'circlet' and *ring* 'resonance' as if they were clear homonyms. They are actually not so easily disentangled. The sound *ring* is prototypically the one made by the hammer on the anvil, and the prototypical circlet *ring* is the metal type we exchange at weddings. These ideas converge in the oldest *assay* of objects made from precious metals, (especially those which, like the ring, historically conferred authority on the rightful owner) is a simple test to see if they 'ring true'. And it is obviously in coinage—the offspring of the signet ring—that we can see this idea has survived. It is encoded in English in the word *shilling*, for example, which derives from Teutonic **skell-* 'to resound' 'to ring'.

The alloy mentioned here as the one from which the pound-coin is said to be made, *nickel-brass*, is notable for producing a very dull sound when struck. Notwithstanding its ability to be mixed so as to have a colour not entirely dissimilar to dirty gold, it is therefore avoided by all but the most dimwitted counterfeiters. It is used in genuine British coinage only for the dodecagonal threepence, first issued in 1937 just after the reign of Edward VIII. The ill-fated abdicant appeared in portrait only on the usual coronation proof-set; his effigy was never circulated except on a short experimental run of these odd coins which carried a much more elegant reverse design and depiction of the Thrift plant than any subsequent version. Despite obviously representing a cost-cutting innovation in its replacement of the silver threepenny bit (hence the Thrift plant), these 1937 Edward VIII threepences are extremely rare and therefore much more valuable than their sterling forbears in numismatic circles. Curiously, Edward VIII's portrait faced left on these coins, like Edward VII before him and George V after him (and also, one assumes, the mirror-image effigy on this bungled counterfeit). He is therefore the only monarch since Charles II was himself *flipped* over for the first copper coinage not to follow the traditional pattern of alternating profiles.

Thus the *counter* effect is backed up with the steady encroachment of token money into sterling. In 1937, the silver coinage had already become only 50% pure, and the steady inflation paper money had caused over the preceding two centuries meant that the distinction between the (token) copper coinage and the (intrinsically valuable) silver and gold coinage was being gradually eroded. Basically what happened was that the threepenny was made into a *copper*. The natural resistance people would have to this was mitigated by a moneyer's sleight of hand; instead of copper, an even cheaper alloy was used so that the threepenny could still be *passed off* as a type of genuine sterling. This was tantamount to state-sponsored counterfeiting.

> 'Righd-o,' he sighed, '£ey'll have to be restruck…
>   Set up £e run and use £ese as £e flans;
> £e old Gibraltan dies in Chris's truck
>   Are all we've got as backup, as it stands:
> £ey'll have to do. I just don't give a fuck.
>   We'll palm em off in change to Villa fans,
> Or some€ing.' £en he put me in his pocket.
>   '£e keys,' he said, 'remember to relock it!

Only recently, in 1951, however, the greatest crime against the coinage was perpetrated by the government. Realising that the public would not accept the transformation of the entirety of sterling into copper tokens—a move necessitated by the payment of all the nation's gold and silver reserves to the United States as remuneration for the debts of war—they instructed the mint to produce debased counterfeits of the extant silver coins using cupronickel. The idea is to fool enough of the public with the shiny new issues (in American *nickel*) that Gresham's law might be defied, and thereby that mass withdrawal from circulation of the much more valuable Victorian and Edwardian silver coins can be avoided. How they could think we might not notice, I cannot imagine.

I have no hesitation in identifying the initial inspiration for this satire as that single, monstrously disloyal act of government. It has surrendered *sterling* Britain to *brazen* Birmingham and *nickel* America.

> It seems to us this city's often done
> The same thing with its best and brightest sons
> As ancient money and the newest gold.
> These coins: not clipped or fake, but to behold,
> We think, quite lovely; they're the only things
> Struck with the proper stamp in gold that rings…
> Amongst the Greeks and the Barbarian states,
> It's not these but cheap brass that circulates,
> Just hammered yesterday with shoddy dies.
> So too with men we know are just and wise:
> The noble citizens of circumstance,
> Well trained in music, wrestling and dance,
> We hate them; yet bronzed slaves and copper-nobs,*   *πυρριας : 'fire-serpent',
> All worthless bastards, take up all our jobs.   'redhead', 'slave'
> Before, we didn't search for antidotes,**
> We just picked immigrants as our scapegoats.**   **φαρμακόν / φαρμακός

(Aristophanes *The Frogs* li 718-733: my translation)

38.4 <u>materfamilias</u>: One can almost taste the rodentine sneer of the sardonic Birmingham Latin in this ironic identification of the Queen with a tribal matriarch. We should not gloss over the implication of radical republicanism, though. If the Queen is literally, rather than metaphorically, to be *the mother of the nation*, then her *subjects* become her *children* and therefore assume, *en masse*, a claim to the throne.

38.6 *winking*: Achieves a distant internal rhyme with *chinking*. The word brings up all the usual ambiguities of vision, reversals of gaze and communications of the eyes that pepper the coin's view of things. The wink is obviously the most important of these. It is the conventional indicator of secret collusion, the expression of clandestine intimacy, the indicator of encoded or ironic speech, the signal by which those 'in the know' are differentiated from the credulous. (See, for example, esp. 147.2, but also 118.7, 126.7, 204.6 and 222.6). It is also, in French critical parlance (*clin d'œil*), used to mean 'a comic allusion'. The significance of all this is patent.

Alongside literal nictitation, there is perhaps also an obscure reference to *tiddlywinks*: a bar-room game whose name probably derives from slang for 'a little drink'; players attempt to propel four small wooden or plastic discs into a *tiddle*-cup by pressing down on the edges with a larger disc, causing them to skip. Like many of the more idiotic bar-games designed for gambling purposes, the tokens used were no doubt originally coins, the cup being a beer glass. I cannot imagine the paralytic state of indolence necessary for the mindless drinker to focus the entirety of his thought on winking his last few farthings into a tiddle-cup.

38.6 *mass*: The play on 'substance' and 'Eucharist' is acutely venal. The coin is offering an interpretation of her creation as a sub-Einstinian progress from *energy* to *mass* in terms of *the word made flesh*. There are layers and layers of irony here, almost too many to contain with any sanity. A coin is obviously *not* mass derived from energy—however disruptive such radical scientific ideas might be of the metaphysics implied in the Mass—but an extant chunk of metal which is simply reshaped. If the form it receives means that it now carries more value than it otherwise would as *mass*, then this moment of reshaping might be interpreted as supernaturally transformative. Sloggy is therefore compared to a priest who, with Fat Bob as his bumbling altar boy, transforms the (circular) communion wafer into the body of Christ.

The fact that this pun posits a connection between transubstantiation—to this day the touchiest subject of Anglican theology—and the minting of a token coinage bearing the image of the *head* of the Anglican church, the Defender of the Faith, makes it one of the most important tropes (for all its throwaway flippancy) in the entire piece. I am only scratching the surface of its implications when I say there might be a thesis here of a direct causal link (rather than a coincidental or analogous one) between puritan theology and the deregulated monetarism of Birmingham / America.

One can imagine cabals of these budding, calvin/capitalists literally winking as they shook one another's hands during the ceremonies they despised, as if they had their sooty fingers crossed.

38.8 *cheesy Quaver*: I hesitate to gloss this as 'malodorous pudendum', but I think it is correct to do so. *Quaver* and *quiver* are onomatopœic words prototypically represented by the sound of a 'thrill' through a spear or arrow shaft. I find it hard to believe there is no etymological connection between this *quaver/quiver* and the homonym meaning the receptacle that holds arrows. It is not hard to believe the latter could be used as a crude vaginal image however, especially when one considers the figure of Cupid and the possibility of the arousal his evidently phallic arrows are supposed to instigate in previously still womanhood: the *quavering quaint* is the *quiver* of his arrows. I hardly need to point out that this poem turns out later to be quite literally *picaresque*, in that it concerns a *darts* match; the implications of sexual deviance cannot be overstressed.

The diabolical mixture of desire and disgust with which Sloggy is seen to grab the coin/queen is therefore representative of its satanic fall from grace: from the body of the King of Heaven (*communion wafer*) to the stinking genitals (*cheesy Quaver*) of a prostitute *quean*. This demonising transformation can also be quasi-philologically mapped: *king… cunning…quaint… cunt.*

I'm goin down £e pub.' I'm not sure why
   He didn't €row me back. Perhaps I willed
Him not to. I'm convinced he caught my eye,
   For maybe half a second, and was filled
Wi£ £e desire to protect me by
   Pretending to forget I'd just been milled.
He took me wi£ him. £ere's no question he
Was cast to carry out my destiny.

39.1 *righd-o*: It is noticeable how the letter O, appearing on its own like this, looks like a coin. There is also a hint that we are actually to see the shape of Sloggy's lips as he sighs (such is, after all, the probable derivation of the character O: your mouth should look like it in order to create the sound it signifies). The prurience of the surrounding metaphoric environment suggests his mouth might also be envisaged as an anus, and the sigh a 'silent' fart. Thus, after the *Quaver* immediately preceding it, the *counter* (that gaping absence in the middle of the character) becomes even more disturbingly associated with *the other hole, the back-side*, the uncanny and infertile orifice of sodomy.

39.2 *flans*: A synonym for *blanks* (See 29.3); the word derives from *flawns* 'round custard pies.'

39.6 *palm em off*: In Britain 'palm' is used alone (without the preposition) in the sense: 'to pass off fraudulently'. The metaphor is from the literal prestidigitative manipulations of gambling cheats who use the palm as an arena of exchange and concealment in order to switch cards or dice. Counterfeiters traditionally employ precisely the same techniques to show legitimate coin and then pass a Birmingham. The phrasal usage here is another of the encroachments of copulative American English into the poet's future dialect. We are constantly having these Americanisms palmed (off) on us.

39.6 *Villa fans*: Supporters of Aston Villa Football Club, founded in 1874 by members of the Bible Class of Villa Cross Wesleyan Chapel in the Lozells area of the Borough of Aston in Birmingham. It was the director of this club, William McGregor, who organized the foundation of the Football League in 1888, a competition they won in 1894, 1896 and 1897; their biggest success, however, has been in the FA Cup, which they have won more often than any other club (six times: in 1887, 1895, 1897, 1899, 1900 and 1910). The decline of the club's fortunes since the First World War has matched the decline of the city in which it is based: from the world's leading centre of technological manufacture at the turn of the century (at which time the club also had a strong claim to the title of best in the world) to the bombscarred wasteland we know today, swarming with immigrants from the countries to which it once exported its mechanical prowess. (See 2.3)

Perhaps they could have seen this coming though. The club's history is marred by such invasions and disturbances. As well as the Football League, Aston Villa was also infamously the club responsible for the creation of the 'pitch invasion' when, during an FA Cup match against Preston North End, the supporters occupied the playing area on two separate occasions when displeased with how the match was progressing.

Ultimately, one can not help but relate this back to the eponymous 'Villa' of the club's name. This is a familiar way of referring to Aston Hall, the Jacobean mansion built by Sir Thomas Holte between 1618 and 1635, which was (of course) the site of one of the most ruthless and spiteful sieges of the English Civil War, in which a minuscule garrison of Royalist soldiers to whom the Baronet was good enough to provide shelter were massacred by invading Parliamentarians who had been tipped off by vengeful local smiths.

40.8 *cast*: This is a highly polysemous word. The pun here makes a rather nice distinction—when one considers the antithetical senses which thrive in this linguistic environment—between 'given a role or part to play' and 'cast from molten metal'. The underlying deterministic idiom is 'the die is cast' which actually derives not from the sense suggested by the situation of the narrator's own creation (a falsely cast 'die' which cannot be remade), but from the sense of a (single) 'dice' which has already been thrown, the result of which can therefore not be altered. This sense of *cast*—basically 'to throw' or 'to throw away'—is in fact the oldest, and is the predicative suffix of another word crucial to this poem: 'broadcast'. The verb might therefore be employed almost paradoxically here to remind us of precisely what Sloggy *fails* to do: discard the counterfeit which will bring about his downfall.

So we can see how another eversion is achieved: rather than vice-versa, it is obviously the *coin* who has been 'cast' to carry out *Sloggy's* destiny.

*   *   *

Light (it is one of God's most whimsical paradoxes) is entirely invisible beyond the source of radiation unless it has something off which to reflect. This creates a serious problem when attempting to extrapolate its shape into a third dimension. Unfortunately the light which fell across the hallway had nothing like the necessary luminosity to make the dust particles in the dry air appear, as they sometimes miraculously do, like floating stars in a miniature domestic galaxy: the most beautiful of natural phenomena, I think; more transcendent than any waterfall or mountain vista.

Resinous wood creates a similar effect when burning, as John Evelyn demonstrated in the Fire of London. Those eddying particles he saw above the Thames were the bright seeds of the future, imprisoned in the dead wood of the past, ecstatically released by the fire's blooming present. As I read this back, I can feel the hot, red sparks swarming around me intently like bees exploring the fertile possibilities of a garden.

If I had the ability to reach out and consult the book, I might elucidate this comment with a small passage from Elysium Britannicum *on Wilkins's transparent hive. Although, that too is probably on fire.*

*   *   *

>   He left £e work$op, headed for £e pub.
>   I jockeyed for position wi£ his keys;
>   A nail file had begun to rub
>   £e $ield on my back, which didn't please
>   Me much. I $uffled round, and some fat Chubb,
>   Who wasn't very keen to let me squeeze
>   Between his chunky barrel and £e file,
>   Turned round and sla$ed me: hence £e Chelsea Smile.

41.2 *jockeyed for position*: Rather than trying to gain a racing advantage by legitimate means, 'jockey for position'—like so many other idioms in the piece (see for example 'dope', 'punter', etc.)—suggests fraudulent trickery in the world of gambling. The noun 'jockey' derives from a Scots and Northern English diminutive form of 'Jack' which carries particularly apt connotations of criminal artifice and mischievous ingenuity. It was originally used of strolling minstrels and vagabonds (like Dickens' Jingle) and came to be applied to untrustworthy horse traders before shifting to the slightly more respectable—but no less mischievous—practitioners of the equine arts. The verb has never mounted even to that minuscule level of respectability.

41.3 *nail-file*: The consecutive diæreses here, whilst not unique (see 138.3 *steer clear*), are very unusual and therefore serve to emphasize the oddity of the item. A nail file seems a rather effeminate grooming tool for Sloggy to be carrying. The idea of him checking his manicure and absent-mindedly filing away the odd rough edge is not at all in keeping with his hard-man image. Perhaps the poet is insinuating something about Sloggy's overt machismo. In any event, the grooming tool chosen combines this effeminate symbolism with two linguistic components that both in fact sound very hard and masculine: 'nail' and 'file.' The overtones of metalworking and jailbreaks actually make me think of this, not as an emery board, but a small pointed steel implement: the kind of thing that doubles as the lever on a pair of nail clippers, (or a weapon… at a snip).

41.4 *shield*: On the surface, this suggests the reverse of this *pound-coin* literally depicts a shield: not at all unusual. There were many gold sovereigns minted between 1825 and 1874 with a heraldic shield, rather than St. George, on the reverse. This was done specifically to cater to those parts of the Empire (principally India) with large Muslim populations who objected to the supposedly idolatrous depiction of religious figures in any medium, but especially in gold. Mercifully the more assertive late Victorian Empire, The *Pax Britannica*, put a stop to such superstitious nonsense.

Another reading, however, might interpret the shield as the coin itself. This reading relies upon extrapolating from the missing motto the connection between the coin and the shield of Æneas. This is a relatively complex connection. *DECUS ET TUTAMEN*, 'an ornament and a safeguard' was first introduced on the edges of the milled re-coinage of Charles II, specifically to deter the clippers. It was included at the suggestion of John Evelyn and is taken from the Æneid, Book V where it refers not to the famous shield on which the future glories of Rome were depicted, but to a suit of golden armour, taken by Æneas from Demoleus in battle and presented as a gift to Mnestheus as a demonstration of the hero's generosity. Two things are obvious: firstly, this is meant as an imitation of the armour of Achilles in the *Iliad*, itself explicitly associated with the Ægis of Athene (in turn associated with the severed head of the Gorgon, Medusa); secondly, it prefigures (and perhaps justifies) Venus's gift to Æneas of the shield which carries (as tableau) the future history of Rome up to triumph of Augustus at the Battle of Actium: an object which might therefore completely independently echo the armour of Achilles and the Ægis of Minerva and so on. Moreover, crucial to this reading is the identification, always present in both Roman and British thinking, of Britannia as a version (an *avatar* if you like) of Minerva (just as she is a version of Athena).

So we come full circle: this counterfeit is not just a travesty of the sovereign coin, but also of the shield of Britannia, the armour of Achilles, the Ægis of Athena, and the shield of Æneas. Instead of carrying a glorious Augustan future engraved into its golden surface, it speaks a dreadful future of a degenerative Britain in its cheap alloy of a Birmingham accent.

41.5 *chubb*. The OED has:

> In full *Chubb's lock*, *Chubb-lock*: a patent lock with tumblers and, in addition, a lever called a detector, which fixes the bolt immovably when one of the tumblers is raised a little too high in an attempt to pick the lock. So *Chubb-key*.

The ironic implication of security is typical, the threat obvious.

41.8 *hence the Chelsea Smile*. The gash in the effigy of the Queen caused by this encounter with the key in Sloggy's pocket has left it with the kind of fixed smile one might expect to see on the face of an inhabitant of the genteel squares and gardens of the Royal Borough of Kensington and Chelsea, photographed beside their townhouses—something entirely undignified in the monarch's seal.

It is a matter of deep regret that, regardless of one's mood, we are universally required these days to *smile please!* whenever we have our photographs taken. Even the Queen herself cannot escape this tyranny of expression. I know they were laboriously artificial, but I find the earlier, more dignified, statuesque photographs a good deal more honest nonetheless. It is as if photographs—once a treasured gift or family heirloom like a painted portrait—have become a replacement for memory: the idea being that we manufacture a much more pleasant past for ourselves and our families than the one we actually experienced so that, by meditating on the smiling images produced throughout our lives, we might hypnotically become party to some infinitely happier existence. This tendency has got to be American. The analogues with counterfeits and token currency are unavoidable.

As Sloggy made his way across £e street,
    Closed-circuit cameras focused in on him.
His tracksuit and his tennis $oes, complete
    Wi£ just £e logo and a subtle trim,
Were Sergio Tacchini, white and neat;
    He $one out like one of £e seraphim,
Immaculate against £e sooty brick,
£e gum marks on £e kerb, £e spla$ of sick.

42.2 *cameras*: era 5

42.2 *Closed-circuit cameras*: If *closed circuit* is not some abstruse electrical jargon, it might mean 'unbroadcast', 'for private viewing only'. If so, the fact that we are privy to the pictures is obviously ironic. Unlike the authoritarian dystopia of Orwell—in which the state carries out perpetual surveillance on its citizens—we can imagine something closer to Zamyatin's *universally transparent* environment in which everybody is capable of watching what everybody else is doing, the right to use technology to spy on neighbours being entirely deregulated and condoned by a prurient anarcho-capitalist ideology completely devoid of any inclination to protect privacy, or indeed to institute decorum.

42.3 *tracksuit*: Another characteristically dystopian invention. It is presumably a suit designed to allow the wearer to be 'tracked' or his position identified at any time. In an Orwellian vision this might have been a technological innovation introduced to the uniforms of party members to allow Big Brother even greater knowledge of their movements. Here though, one assumes the garment to have been willingly bought by the wearer specifically to make a spectacle of himself: a logical extension beyond the visual spectrum of electro-magnetic radiation of the wearing of ostentatious colours. Again, this tends to feminize Sloggy and make a nonsense of his dialectic opposition to Britannia.

42.4 *logo*: Notwithstanding the riddling tendency of this poem (a perfectly respectable form in English poetry if we are to take the *Essex Book* as the matriarch to *Beowulf*'s patriarch), I doubt this is short for *logogriph*: a kind of lexicographic puzzle in verse. Much more likely are *logograph*—a letter-word or single word-character such as hieroglyphs and currency symbols like £ for *pound*—or else it could be short for *logotype*: a combination of letters into a single character in typography, such as Æ and Œ. Perhaps we are therefore to understand the *logo* to be the symbol of the brand (Sergio Tacchini) designed to act as an abbreviation of the name. In this case it might be both a logo*graph* and a logo*type*. Something like: **$**

    This is curiously similar to the dollar sign: **$** which itself certainly began life as a *logo*(graph-type). Whilst the possibility exists that this may simply have been a representation of the initials of the new nation: **$** I think it much more likely that the inspiration was the logograph of the infamous Renascence Italian tyrant, Sigismondo Malatesta: **$** which appears on the façade and the interior design of the temple of San Francesco in Rimini: a purportedly Christian church designed by Leon Battista Alberti, at the behest of this petty dictator (who fancifully considered himself to be in direct competition with the Vatican), as a pagan shrine to his own Imperial pretensions and the very earthly love of his mistress, Isotta degli Atti. Malatesta was probably the most important early patron of so-called 'Humanism' in Renascence Italy. It is widely suspected that he was actually a Satanist, and murdered his first two wives. The logograph on his personal seal was, on the surface, a simple logotype in which his own initial (**S**igismondo) winds lasciviously around that of his mistress (**I**sotta). There is a deeper, more troubling, reading of this symbol however—one entangled in the implications of original sin self-evidently present in the thing: the image of an **S** spiralling around the upright stem of an upper-case **I** quite deliberately, I think, insinuates a vision of the serpent (*Sàtana*) coiled around the tree of forbidden knowledge in Eden. What is quite undeniable is the influence Malatesta's hubristic legacy had upon the Borgias, the Medici and Machiavelli. And it is certainly not beyond the bounds of possibility that there is a direct line of descent through influential esoteric groups analogous to the Freemasons and Rosecrucians which could have carried Malatesta's ideology to lead directly to the revolutions of the C18th in America and France. One need only examine the reverse of the 'Great Seal' of the United States to discover how occultist were the nation's founders. It is a thirteen stepped pyramid with the eye of providence in a triangle at its zenith; the motto is *NOVUS ORDO SECLORUM* 'A New Order of the Ages'. Or perhaps that should be 'a new order of the secular oligarchy': the Masonic epigraph *par excellence*; it is an allusion to Virgil's Fourth Eclogue:

> *Ultima Cumæi venit iam carminis ætas;*   The final prophecy has come to the Sibyl of Cumæ;
> *magnus ab integro sæclorum nascitur ordo.*   the great revolutionary order of the ages is born.

My translation is intended not to be perfectly accurate, but to reflect the insidious revolutionary possibilities of its typical Virgilian ambiguity in the mind of a republican *plotter* (in Hebrew a *sātān*). Dryden sticks much closer to the probable Augustan spirit than he does the actual words when he assumes *ab integro ordo seaclorum* to refer to cyclical history, something like the Platonic Year (or one of its analogues) beginning afresh to usher in a new Golden Age:

> Now the last age by Cumæ's Sibyl sung
> Has come and gone, and the majestic roll
> Of circling centuries begins anew

In order to do so he needs to assert a disassociation of the Cumæan Sibyl from the vision. In Dryden's version this is definitively *not* the prophecy of the Sibyl but a future (implicitly Christian) beyond her ken that the poet can see but she (as the epitome of the bygone pagan æra) cannot. I am reminded of Yeats's *gyres*; but when one considers the satanic implications of the logo of the US currency, one can not help wondering: *what foul beast…*

42.6 'se**ra**phim': era 6

42.7 *sooty brick*: Despite being famous for its red brick (hence the epithet used for the new C19th universities of which Birmingham's was a prototype) virtually all buildings in the city are black with layers of soot deposited like palimpsests of mechanical reproduction on the surface of their frontages. This is how 'The Black Country' gets its name (the area that spreads like eczema out of west Birmingham over Worcestershire, Staffordshire and Shropshire). It is curious to note, however, that the Commonwealth immigrants currently flooding into the country on the Government's behest seem therefore to have identified the Birmingham area as the place set aside for Blacks.

Sometimes Birmingham buildings appear to be as heavily made-up as Olivier playing Othello. One can almost imagine St Martin's in the Bull Ring tap-dancing on its foundations and singing 'Mammy'. No wonder the duskier inhabitants of the Empire find the city so inviting.

> He $oved £e door, and in £e pub he strode.
>   Before we watch him get into a scrape
> However, £ere's ano£er episode
>   I $ould relate. So let's rewind £e tape…
> As Sloggy foxtrots back into £e road,
>   He moves like Harold Lloyd, whose latest jape
> Involves him in a counterfeiting ring
> Which (obviously) he'll wind up toppling.

More seriously though, we should bear in mind Birmingham's history as the capital of non-conformism. Many of the West Indians are Evangelicals, Methodists and Baptists and consequently feel more at home in Birmingham and Manchester than the shire towns or the Episcopal seats. That Muslims, Hindus, Sikhs, Janists, Buddhists, Zoroastrians and so on, from the Indian sub-continent and the Middle East (equally as intent on thumbing their noses at the established church and English tradition) should find these cities just as tempting comes as no surprise to an historically informed commentator.

What the effect on evolution might be one shudders to think. There is already a local moth—previously brown and speckled as camouflage against tree-bark—which has mutated to become almost entirely black so that it can disguise itself on the filthy surfaces of the industrial midlands.

42.8 *gum-marks on the kerb*: Where soot might be a palimpsestal trace of industry, this 'gum' covering the pavement is more like the dirt agglomerated on a coin: the trace of human physicality. If we are to understand this particular gum (amongst the other sorts: *karaya*, *laser*, *viscum* etc.) to be American 'chewing gum', spat directly onto the paving stones by the uncouth, then we can see this 'trace' as both the orally deposited genetic material ('DNA' as we are now to call it; see 143.3) and the masticatory impression of the spitter's teeth. These misshapen discs of hardened gum, which we first began to see encrusting our pavements ('sidewalks' they called them) when American 'GI's were stationed here, bear an eerie resemblance to ancient coins (Offa's Pennies perhaps), the impressions of overdeveloped molars in the viscous medium mimicking the coiner's stamp.

I believe the poet sees chewing gum as one of a cluster of reverse-colonising American products in his anarcho-capitalist dystopia. The rash of 'gum-marks' is spreading across the city streets like sores on the skin of a syphilitic prostitute, and this is just the surface symptom of a much deeper infection intent on taking over the entire body politic. Many of the putative technological innovations are given distinctly Americanized names (like *tracksuit* and so on) but the extant products in this cluster that spring immediately to mind are *lager*, *television* and *cigarettes*. The last is obviously important. Tobacco is the iconic product bought back to the Old World from the New by Walter Raleigh. It is an obvious choice as the symbolic thin end of a wedge of reverse-colonialism. As mentioned above, the cigarette is characteristically a feminine, foreign or American way with tobacco; an Englishman prefers a pipe. The *most* American thing to do with tobacco, though, is to chew it. It is no coincidence that chewing-*gum* acts basically as a substitute for chewing-*tobacco*. Nor is it a mere coincidence that a single pinch of tobacco deemed an ample sufficiency is called a *quid*. This derives not, as in the English slang for a pound, from the Latin for 'something', but from the word 'cud'. The implication being that the *quid pro quo* of American involvement in the war has been to turn these future British people into a herd of ruminating cattle, hypnotized by their television sets and the drone of washing machines to such an extent they are no longer capable of seeing the decay their perpetually unnourishing pseudo-consumption is causing.

43.4 *rewind*: Another portmanteau, I think, short for *reverse-wind* ('reel backwards' rather than 'headwind', I think, though the ambiguity of the homonym persists). The effect that follows is as if a film-reel is fed through the projector upside down and backwards so that the action appears to take place in reverse: an absurdly literal *countering* effect which nevertheless suggests two very important things. Firstly, the action of the plot is to be understood as extant and 'recorded' (i.e. not happening 'live'). This is actually very unusual on television, where even fictional dramas are 'repeated' by means of a literal repeat performance. It does exist however, and—alongside the fact this renders the empirical 'liveness' of all 'live' broadcasts dubious (see 13.7 *okay*)—it also suggests a fundamental distortion of the geography of time. Just as film-characters often take impossible routes through towns and cities in order to prejudice the æsthetics of locations over geographical accuracy, a recorded drama on television (a predominantly 'live' medium) can pass off all the anachronisms of fiction as genuinely temporally possible. Secondly, the insidious influence of the persona/film-editor is made all the more acute. Not only is he capable of cogently disturbing the order of temporal events, he can also change the very direction of time, the logic of cause and effect, and therefore, ultimately, morality itself. Hence a scene climaxing in a brutal act of wife-beating can be described as 'a therapeutic tryst'.

43.5 *foxtrots*: The *Foxtrot* is a dance invented in America by vaudeville performer Harry Fox. It was created during World War I as an adaptation of the *two-step* to the new Negro-inspired syncopations of *ragtime*. (The extent of this dusky, loose-rhythmed and loose-moraled influence can be seen very clearly in the latest of these 'foxtrots' to have swept across the Atlantic leaving all musical refinement in its wake: 'Rock Around the Clock' by Sunny Dæ and the Knights.)

Almost definitively, the leading partner in the couple never goes backwards. Now that the direction of our interpretations are to be reversed, it is difficult to say whether this is meant to enforce the latent effeminacy of Sloggy's portrait (with the nail-file and the colourful clothing) or to deny it. One might argue either. Perhaps his perpetually front-facing machismo has been 'translated' into quintessentially feminine behaviour by this reversal of direction; all his overtly masculine gestures becoming mincing ones, and so on. If so, this would prefigure his emasculation at the hands of the demonic drag-queen rather more subtly than it does the fox scene immediately following it.

43.6 *Harold Lloyd*: An acrobatic American slapstick star. Unlike Buster Keaton or Charlie Chaplin, who explored much greater depths of pathos and complexity, Harold Lloyd's shorts invariably conclude with complete (and completely unlikely) romantic success and victory over the 'bad guys'. The *inevitable* success implied in the formula is obviously employed ironically here and, considering the reversal of logic, tends to inculcate a feeling of impending doom rather than a sure and certain hope in the fragile 'little guy' triumphing over the looming threat of a powerful criminal underworld or a terrifying patriarch. We should not forget, in this temporally subversive moment, that the most famous stunt of Harold Lloyd's involved him hanging from the clock-face of a skyscraper above the teeming streets of the American metropolis.

>   Hot-footing it towards £e die-cast $op,
>   He doesn't seem to heed £e green cross code:
>   He doesn't look each way, or €ink, or stop
>   Before reversing out into £e road
>   At pace, and swerving round a dark soft-top
>   Mercedes which had left a space and slowed,
>   Before reversing off itself. £en Sloggy
>   Recedes from view; £e focus goes all foggy.

43.6 *jape*: This is one of those words that seems almost definitive of the poem itself. The OED suggests it derives from Old French *japer* 'to yelp' (like a small dog), though there may also have been influence from *gaber* 'to mock': the noun forms being *jap, jape, japerie* and *gab, gabe, gaberie*. It is, I surmise, the figure of the fox which combines these forms; its characteristic yelping bark can sometimes sound so much like mocking laughter that one can imagine our streets and gardens to contain nocturnal hyena. The fox is obviously the iconic trickster, and from this connection we might get the meaning 'trick' or 'deception'. Usage in this sense died out in the C16th when the word became vulgarly associated with sexual intercourse (though its use by Walter Scott suggests it persisted untainted in Scotland). The modern sense of 'joke', 'shaggy dog story', or 'burlesque' was revived in literary usage by Charles Lamb. The other, obsolete, sense was 'trinket' or 'toy'. The capacity of the word to summarize this piece is therefore multiple. It is a cheap *Brummagem trinket*, a *burlesque*, an *act of frivolous sexuality* and a *deception*, in a broken whining voice like the yelp of a coupling fox.

44.2 *Green Cross Code*: *Green Cross* was the name (from the denotative symbol they carried) of the phosgene gas shells and canisters used by the Germans in the First World War. Obviously, in the context, it is much more likely to have something to do with 'crossing' the road. Perhaps there is a convoluted system of cryptography which allows people to know when and where to cross in this future of competitive technology. There may be tolls charged for the use of more or less effective, privately-owned pedestrian crossing points, recognized by codes of coloured shapes. Sloggy is presumably defying the code he has been given: analogous to jumping a queue, perhaps, or riding a bus or tram beyond the value of one's ticket. The threat of the subliminal 'gas' metaphor suggests that the exhaust fumes created by the use of futuristic fuels designed to increase performance might be so poisonous as to be like actual chemical weapons.

44.4 *road*: The previous stanza contains the rhyme triplet *strode, episode, road*. Here we have: *code, road, slowed*. The phonetic repetition emphasizes the reversal of movement by focusing attention on the rhythmic tread of Sloggy's soles on the tarmac. We are not allowed to lose sight of his physical movement (*strode* and *slowed*), nor of the cryptic temporality of the passage (*episode* and *code*), nor of the strange direction he is taking (*road* and *road*). The fact that the street-crossing has previously been associated with fording a swollen river of rapid currents (the flow of a river itself being a standard metaphor for time), suggests to me a deeper homophonic repetition not of *road* but of 'rowed'. One rows backwards, of course, and Sloggy has 'rowed, rowed, rowed his boat' not 'gently down the stream' of time so much as *forcefully across* it.

44.5 *soft-top*: Presumably a 'convertible': a type of car so named (in the United States, where the climate makes this most ostentatious of designs a possibility) because of its retractable leather roof: another amphibology.

44.6 *Mercedes*: An old German car company, now defunct after being taken into state ownership by the Nazis. It is the explicit intention of the Marshall Money to revitalize Germany's industries by instigating American business models. The *Mercedes* car mentioned here is presumably the projected result: a much more American car (with its *soft top*) than a German one. Perhaps, by this time, the German 'federal states', which are already overrun with US troops, have actually become states of the Union.

In philological terms, the choice of manufacturer is telling. Despite looking like an Ancient Greek hero, *Mercedes* comes from *Maria de las Mercedes* 'Mary of the Mercies' in Spanish: precisely the kind of name you might expect a car manufacturer in a town like 'Los Angeles' or 'San Diego' to have. This is a far remove from the overtly Germanic *Volkswagen* or the brands of Britain's foremost manufacturing city—through whose streets the vehicle is driving like a gilded Roman chariot through a village of Britannic Celts—*Morris*, *Austin*, *Lucas* et al.

There is also a kind of *logogriph* here. *Mercedes* contains a 'visual rhyme' with the first word in the last line of the stanza: *recedes*, which itself 'recedes from view' simultaneously with the car. The past, traditionally, is understood to recede from view as we move further away from it—hence the need for history—but here we are talking about the future, not the past. The effect is therefore one of feeling ourselves *receding*, as our vision becomes blurred and history moves off away from us carried by a reversing apparition of the merciful Virgin as a gaudy American automobile with its leather veil rolled back.

However, we can pick him up again
>   On Fat Bob's own surveillance videos,
(Which Birmingham Police discovered when
>   £ey searched £e place). £is footage clearly $ows
An unexpected little mise-en-scène:
>   He hands £e suspect coin to Bob, who knows
A phoney sovereign when he sees one, so
He puts it wi£ £e o£ers, presses go

45.2 *Fat Bob's own surveillance videos*: *Videos* is no doubt projected US and/or Birmingham jargon for 'films'. The phrase provides as good evidence as one could ask for in support of my theory, outlined above (see 42.2 *Closed-circuit cameras*), that this is supposed to be a society in which private individuals (even ones as common as Fat Bob) have the technological means, the inclination and the license to carry out intimate surveillance of each another.

45.4 *footage*: An indeterminate short sequence of cinematic images (usually a single scene or event) couched metonymically in terms of the literal, physical length of film (in feet) on which they are printed. The pun on 'metric footage' (as it were), combining the same synecdoche of metrical units standing for the scene they contain, is obviously intended.

45.5 *mise-en-scène*: If the colon which follows this term is supposed to mark the next clause as appositive, then it is misapplied. The *mise-en-scène* is the background or setting of a scene, not its events. If we bear in mind the previous metonymic play on *footage*, however, we might assume this is intended to suggest a blurring of the distinction between the 'backdrop' and the 'action', serving either to flatten the scene into a shoddy two-dimensional tableau, or else to insinuate a demonic animation of the background and the props. Either (or, indeed, both) would be perfectly in keeping with the mimetic qualities of the satire (and, in fact, the whole concept of the moving image.)

45.7 *phoney*: Another Americanism meaning 'fake'. A possible etymological link to *phone* and *phonic* seems to imply the word has something to do with the *dud* sound of a counterfeit. The fact that Fat Bob (actually a complete dullard) 'knows [one] when he *sees* one' is therefore a typically ironic switch of the senses.

*   *   *

The obvious solution to the problem was to light my pipe. It is one of the immutable pleasures of the cinema, invariably more enjoyable than the dreary features themselves these days, to watch unfurling fronds of smoke emerging from the undergrowth of heads to describe the animated cone of light that beams out of the projector. I had been to see a film called The Man in the White Suit *the previous Wednesday and had noted how the play of brightness and dark in the photography had mimicked the experience of the cinema itself: the luminescent suit like the 'silver screen'; the dingy railway arches and back lanes through which its doomed designer was pursued by crowds like the darkened hall full of fidgeting spectators; there was even a scene in which Alec Guinness hid in a blacked-out booth of his laboratory, underlit by a single bulb like a demonic projectionist changing the reel.*

My fascination with this correspondence led me, inevitably perhaps, to spend a lot more time watching the illuminated faces of my neighbours than looking at the screen. I distinctly remember my gaze travelling down from the thick-lipped husband nibbling his untrimmed moustache for the want of rationed humbugs, to his daughter's thighs squeezing together under her woollen skirt like gristly sausages sweating beneath their thick, brown butcher's paper, and then quickly back aloft to watch the smoke from my pipe fleshing out the flickering two-dimensional image of a fluorescent liquid in a large round-bottomed flask. If I had not remembered this moment of idle pleasure as I pondered my next move, I think I would have tentatively beaten a retreat. I might never, that is, have made it to this room.

I did remember though. I turned and sat in the doorway with my feet on the top brass step, my back towards the pool of light, and stuffed my pipe with St Bruno. When I was finished, I dropped the tobacco pouch back in the sagging inside pocket of my sports jacket and lit the pipe with a match that needed some persuasion to ignite against the pinkened strip of sand paper on the side of a tatty box of England's Glory. I puffed at the mouthpiece to get it going properly, then twisted back, blowing sweet cheekfuls through pursed lips to fill the space with smoke.

The skewed hexahedron of light protruding into the hall from 666 appeared in the fug. I took my jacket off and rolled up my shirtsleeves. On my side of the light there was little enough room to reach over its top plane at anything like the necessary angle to get purchase on the door-handle: not even on tiptoes. So instead of trying to reach over I pressed my back flat against the adjacent wall, biting hard on the nozzle of my pipe so that it stuck out purposefully like a tug boat captain's in the Solent, and stretched my left arm out parallel to the door. I ran the back of my hand down the wooden panels, horripilation spreading in the direction of my elbow, and grabbed the broad round door handle. I attempted to twist it back towards myself. I could not turn to look at what I was doing for fear the bowl of my pipe might break the swirling surface of the sunbeam. There was very little give. Often these old doors can warp if regularly exposed to sunlight; consequently the mechanism of the latch can become rather rigidly ensconced. I was used to this. I changed to an overhand grip, the proud hairs on my forearm trying to dip themselves in the glow.

The smell of burning hair has always held a fascination for me.

I turned my wrist. This time the handle's mechanism sprang. I had not really expected it to be unlocked; it was something of a surprise to hear the door extract itself with juddering relief from the narrow frame and swing out into the room. I unpocketed my pipe and turned my face to examine the results. The door was half open, mirroring the one to 666. It had stopped against a stack of foolscap suspension files. The darkness it revealed was coolly inviting. Wielding my pipe behind me for balance like a scorpion's sting, I sidled along the wall until my shoulder touched the flat edge of the jamb. In order to negotiate this obstacle I would have to risk the illumination of the rim of my rather prominent right ear. Alternatively, if I were to turn my head back, the end of my nose might be exposed. I was convinced this would carry the direst of consequences. I still am.

* * *

And up £ey're sucked into his big machine
  To wipe £e soapy smiles off £eir faces
And Sloggy visibly cheers up; his keen
  Expression reappears; he embraces
His colleague like a friend, and £en he's seen
  To take a few steps back, untie his laces
And moonwalk over to £e loading bay.
He clambers in £e van, and drives away.

46.2 *soapy*: The texture of counterfeit coins is sometimes described by numismatists as 'soapy.' One can often feel a fake before one sees it. Whether this is to do with a slight difference in the metals used or some inconsistency of the annealing process I can not be sure, but the effect is quite noticeable.

46.7 *moonwalk*: Perhaps this is supposed, via an adaptation of 'mooning about', to suggest the slow and transfixed movement of someone mesmerized. We must not forget he is moving backwards, though: something which, if done for any protracted period in the normal world, would appear a watertight case for a diagnosis of lunacy. This reminds me of a mime artist I once saw beneath the Eiffel Tower, walking on the spot, sliding his feet backwards on the park's yellow gravel, whilst holding out a cardboard moon on a stick in front of him and gazing longingly towards it, as if he were strolling in the evening and ruing with each step his inability to get any closer to the moon. It struck me that anyone displaying such disturbingly deluded behaviour in England would probably (quite justifiably) be escorted politely to a hospital by a policeman.

   *   *   *

I paused, wishing I could suck my pipe again as I contemplated my dilemma. I certainly had nowhere near the kind of patience required to wait for the rotation of the Earth to change the angle at which the sunlight fell across the hall. Besides, I was rather disoriented in this Hawksmoorish annexe of the college and could not be sure in which direction the sun would move. I decided to risk it. I pressed my cheek hard against the jamb and slipped around it. I have no idea whether the sunlight touched my ear. I felt no increase in its temperature so, in my more fantastically optimistic moments, I still like to pretend I managed it.

Squeezing through the space between the door and the stack of files, I was forced to climb on a precarious hillock of the paperwork to close the door. It would require a firm push to force its relaxing shape back inside the frame. Teetering, I gave it an exaggerated shove. The overstuffed card folders planed against one another underneath my shoes. I adjusted my weight backwards to compensate, but too quickly and too far. My feet shot forwards with startling rapidity. I grabbed the pipe with both hands as if it were the banister of a loosely carpeted staircase in a miserly widow's guest house. Obviously this achieved nothing. My body creased and I crumpled back against the papers, causing two or three folders to slide off the summit and thud contemptuously into my lap.

   *   *   *

"The reason why Popper gets Marx so wrong is that he tries something similar to attacking Mary Shelley's *Frankenstein* on the grounds that it is not scientifically accurate. Dialectical Materialism in Marx is like the Alchemy in *Frankenstein*: it's simply the premise on which an important fiction is posited. & for Singh the *fact* of fiction & the encouragement of fiction as a way of thinking are more important than the content of any one fiction. Singh believes..."

I paused. I pretended to need a sip of brandy. I noticed that I'd somehow switched to calling Amrit by his surname: 'Singh'. The trouble was, I thought, if I switched back again I think I'd have to start using the past tense. That'd be even trickier. Anyway, Hannah seemed fine with it. As far as I was concerned, though, I may as well have been providing her with a sophisticated display of tonal flatulence.

"... he believes that post-protestant, capitalist individualism is the real barrier to Socialism, that we need to create 'dividuals' capable of 'contrapuntal', 'dramatic' modes of thinking as opposed to surrendering to the capitalist idea of the 'unit' & the dead hand of the balance-sheet equation. He sees Enlightenment rationalism, if we are to understand it as being entirely free of irony, as the work of men who thought like cartographers & accountants: men who wanted (& still want) to see everything at a single glance & are prepared to kill all that is lively & in flux in order to tame into comprehension a fertile & multifarious world that continues to resist their efforts to understand it."

"Which makes him sound like a typical Nietszchean Post-Structuralist, but he isn't that at all. He has particular affinities with a lot of German theorists: Ernst Bloch & the Frankfurt School. He even supports Habermas's call for a return to the Enlightenment project & the idea of an 'ideal speech situation.' it's just that where Habermas insists, in a rather Blochian way, on talking up the possibility of a utopian ultra-rationalism of discourse, Singh insists that the 'ideal speech situation' must be dramatic, or (more to the point) 'musical'. Not *irrational* but *super*rational. He says that the contrapuntal sophistications of fiction (by which he also means poetry & drama) are the only linguistic mode that can allow people to be genuinely, psychologically plural & therefore to achieve consensus without compromise."

"That's all Bakhtin, really: the *dialogic imagination* & all that. & it also reveals just how anti-Marxist Bakhtin really is; or, at least, how deconstructive of any surface-level interpretation of Marx. At core, what we're talking about is using the superstructure to alter the base, rather than the other way around: it's carnival, not the shop-floor or the battlefield that is the real revolutionary forum. This is because Singh & Bakhtin are both much more like followers of Bakunin than of Marx. They're both First Internationalists at heart: 'no socialism without freedom & no freedom without socialism'. But what Singh is capable of making explicit, something that Bakhtin (because of his precarious position in the Soviet Union) can only hint at, is that Marx actually thought pretty much exactly the same way: you have to change minds before you can change society; there is no external socialism (of culture) without internal socialism (of the mind); or, putting it another way, you can't break the grip of capital on society until you break its grip on our imaginations."

His whereabouts between eight twenty-four
   And two o'clock have yet to be establi$ed.
We do, however, know — some time before
   He gets back home — his van becomes 'undamaged'
In an accident. So if you saw
   A Transit in an incident £at managed
To somehow perfectly repair its wing,
£en give Bellevue Police Station a ring.

---

47   The idiom graduates here into that of a Police press conference about the movements of a missing suspect. The appeal for information at the end is clearly ironic. It makes the gaping fictional divide between the world of the reader and that of the parodied voice seem all the more unbridgeable. Or perhaps it does the opposite; perhaps it actually holds out the possibility of telephone communication between one generation and another, and thereby shows just how close to this dreadful future we have come.

47.6   *Transit*: Intended, I think, as a futuristic generic term for a motor vehicle.

47.7   *To somehow perfectly repair*: The infinitive is split, not just once, but twice in this phrase. This is very ugly. When we consider what it means (even outside its pointedly illogical context), we can see just how self-conscious the *bad* writing in this poem has become. *Repair* means not only 'fix' but also 'revert' and 'go back'. To do this *somehow perfectly* (or should I say: 'to *somehow perfectly* do this') is to damage the phrase in a quite deliberate 'accident' of *reparation* ('making over' and 'going back'). *To somehow perfectly repair* might therefore be cast as a semi-permanent ironic new coinage: a convoluted phrasal verb meaning something like 'to damage a thing by attempting to fix it with one blow of a *Birmingham screwdriver*' (ie. 'a hammer').

47.8   *ring*. 'A telephone call'. This derives from the 'resonance' sense of the word rather than 'circlet'. There is a clear possibility, however, that the telephone network could be referred to as a *ring* in the circular sense. The two meanings seem to coalesce within a phrase from American business jargon *ring round*, which means to call a number of connected people on the telephone in order to organize an event. We can also add to the senses of *ring* already discussed above *passim* (see esp. 38.2 *nickel-brass*) the phrasal versions which crop up as important in this poem: *ring-road, ring of spies*, etc.

47.8   There is a deliberate attempt made here to hint that readers are not only capable of acting as witnesses to this event (pictures of which we are paradoxically being told we can not see because the persona has *lost track* of Sloggy at this point, despite his *tracksuit*), but also that we might ourselves be *seen*, and therefore (as they say) be *placed at the scene*.

"That's what brings him closer to the Frankfurt stuff, & even the Birmingham School, I suppose."

I looked to her for confirmation. She nodded wearily, drunkenly.

"That's why Lukács talks about the novel rather than the factory; that's why Benjamin champions *mimesis* rather than armed struggle: not because they're middle-class dilettantes (thought they are, of course, but then so was pretty much every other major thinker in the history of Communism) but because they believe these things will turn out to be more effective in the long-run. They just don't think the dictatorship of the proletariat will work because it won't change minds the way capitalist individualism has. & they're dead right."

"But it's probably Bloch & Bakhtin who are the most important. They offer a sense of hope & of direction. Most of the others are pretty dismal, only really capable of saying what's wrong with our culture: with its commercialised artefacts & its modes of imaginative circumscription. Most of the French post-structuralists & their followers are the same, as far as Singh's concerned: cynical & defeatist, for all their sly wit."

Fart, fart, fart, fa-fart, fa-fart. This was a Souza marching band of le petomaine clones playing variations on a meaningless soundbite about political literary theory with their arses... but I needed to keep the hot air coming to keep Hannah drinking. I drank too: a lot.

"So what Singh does, basically, is to say that *fiction* is the answer: fiction is a kind of philosophical practice that is the path towards the contrapuntal psychology necessary to dramatise a socialist utopia. As far as Singh is concerned, the material dramatisation of a Socialist utopia is the ultimate goal of both fiction & communism. Hence his approach. What is crucial to remember, is that Singh doesn't mean just 'novels & short stories' when he says *fiction*. It wouldn't make any sense if he did. He doesn't even mean 'all imaginative literature & drama'. His *fiction* is something with a much wider philosophical remit. He takes Roy Bhaskar's four-stage rejigging of Adorno's *negative dialectic* (with its final phase of residual, continually energised, non-synthesis) & fuses it with (amongst other things) Bakhtin's *heteroglossia*, Bergson's *durée*, Benjamin's *mimesis*, Derrida's *différance*, Habermas's *ideal speech situation* & John Austin's *performativity* to create something he calls *fiction*. This he sees as a 'musical' form of linguistic mental activity which is capable of 'performing' psychological revolutions on its performers following its own dialectic pattern: i.e. not *thesis — antithesis — synthesis* (which he calls 'Hegel's balance-sheet equation': something of a misattribution) but *thesis — antithesis — fission — polyphony*. Fiction is therefore a contrapuntal *process* rather than a homogenous *product*, a process which (unlike both 'cultural criticism' & 'deconstruction') is capable not just of revealing & undermining a perceived 'false consciousness' but also of providing a positive 'alternative consciousness'. It's this switch from product to process which is at the heart of fiction's role in moving the defining interactions of a culture from the (unethical) product-focused capitalist transaction to the (ethical) process-focused co-operative transaction."

> At two O seven, a surveillance crew
>> (A special team £e fraud-squad had in place)
> Picked up £e van on Benmore Avenue:
>> We hear its tyres screeching like a drag-race
> As, skidding round £e corner off Bellevue,
>> It brakes, wheel-spins, and fills a parking space,
> £en shudders. Sloggy leaves £e van, turns round
> And stumbles forwards; his toes scrape on £e ground

48.4 *drag-race*: Obviously, this pre-empts the 'screeching' appearance of the 'racial drag-queen'. Cinema is a self-conscious influence upon this scene. Perhaps we are to take it that the medium has become so degraded in the future that the only films available to view are in the mode of those awful American 'B-Movies' about illegal *hot-rodding* and races between criminal gangs of motorcyclists, with names like *Hot Rod Gang*, *Thunder Road* and *Devil on Wheels*.

48.5 *Bellevue*: An obviously invented street name with a typically American feel: note how pretentious is the absence of a descriptive headword like *road*, *street*, *lane*, *close*, or *crescent*. Considering how dreary the city is, the name (from French 'beautiful view') is almost certainly a joke.

48.8 *stumbles forwards*: Sloggy is therefore obviously going backwards at this point, just as he is in the following stanza where he 'faces front and trudges to the door.' Note the habitual monosyllabic rendition of *forwards*, to pun on 'fords', as Sloggy once more crosses a stream as he crosses the street.

*   *   *

I sat and breathed steadily until my heartrate slowed again. The darkness in the room appeared to banish not only the light of the outside world but also its noise and atmosphere. I could barely hear or feel even the workings of my own body. I struck a match — as much for the reassuring scratch and whiff of phosphorous as anything — and relit my pipe. I had just enough time in its faint glow to see there was still a bulb in a brass fitting hanging from a plaited brown electric cable next to an access hatch in the middle of the ceiling. It was only from the ceiling in fact that the hectagonal shape of the room was at all discernible. I counted the sides: **one two d d d d...** *seven. Apart from that I knew only that I was sitting at the bottom of a bank of dusty papers. I could see no light-switch. Instinctively, I shook out the match as it began to burn my fingers.*

Considering my present predicament this childlike reflex playing itself over in my memory seems touchingly irrelevant. As I write, my body is beginning to curl down towards the paper like the stamens of an amaryllis, the pungent corolla of fiery petals opening out around me.

*   *   *

"The payback for those involved is the inherent *pleasure* of fiction: not Barthes' *plaisir*, not even his *jouissance*, but something more akin to the pleasure of musical participation. He calls this 'the pleasure of becoming human'. When it boils down to it, Singh's vision is sentimental socialism of the most benign sort. He basically thinks that people become increasingly unhappy the more they are scared by the results of inequality into hoarding, fighting & barricading themselves off; when they would actually be much happier sharing, co-operating & pulling down the barricades. He thinks this needs to happen in the head & in the heart before it can survive in society, & that the type of discourse he calls *fiction* is the way to do it. He literally believes that constative social-scientific & historical discourses are just another form of ideological self-expression on the parts of the bourgeois capitalist societies that produce them; that the sheer attempt to 'sum up' any set of human interactions (even in a communist analysis) is a way of trying to profit (to 'maximise knowledge-capital') by forcing naturally plural processes to become singular products (of research): ones that can then be hoarded, defended & fenced off. That's why he calls it *unfencing theory*: not just 'taking down the fences of theory' (like the Berlin Wall) but also 'the theory of *unfencing*' — collapsing barriers & calling off the fighting."

"So then comes the tramp. Like Ernst Bloch, Singh wants to see things that most left-wing critics portray as the worst symptoms of failure & ugliness in a capitalist society & reveal how they can also contain utopian visions of hope. This tramp, who entirely neglects society & its laws, who treats everybody else around him as if they were not there, who never speaks until he's drunk & then sings & chatters incomprehensibly with the voices in his head, seems at first to be the 'Zomby' of the piece — the human being without consciousness. He seems a hollow shell of a defeated man: the remnant of some broken marriage or closed factory discarded like a husk. But you soon realise that Singh intends him to stand as a beacon of hope: not just a symbol of the arbitrary exercise of social control over those considered to be psychologically deviant, as Foucault might have it, but a figure of revolutionary anarchy, symbolic of society's complete failure to do what Foucault says it must. This tramp lives in a happier world than everybody else: one in which all efforts of material sequestration fail to deny his ability to conceive of a utopia."

"But he's not an angel, or even some sort of mystic ascetic, instead he's just a natural man living as a natural man should in his situation. He is more like a permanent Lord of Misrule, a Shakespearean Fool whose foil isn't an old, mad, blind, despised & dying king but the kind of bourgeois individualism Harold Bloom claims Shakespeare virtually invented. It is those who are not capable of imagining what he imagines who are the real *zombies*. For Singh, the tramp is both the *Gespenst* & the *Gespinst* of a utopian future that haunts the wasteland of the capitalist past."

"Yes," Hannah finally butted in, putting me out of my misery, "& that's deliberately just like Derrida saying Marx haunts the Elsinore of his philosophy as the ghost of Hamlet Senior. Which is precisely why the whole thing's obviously just about Amrit looking for his dad."

As he decelerates to some€ing close
    To normal walking speed. He faces front
For once, uncharacteristically morose,
    And trudges to £e door, which bears £e brunt
Of his despair; becoming bellicose,
    His movements are abrupt and violent:
His right hand penetrates £e letterbox
And, juddering wi£ effort, £e door unlocks

49.1 *decelerates*: era 7

                *   *   *

Over the next few days I took up the task of reorganising the room. I began by shifting the papers away from the window and piling them in the shallow triangle formed by the two walls to the left of the door as one entered. I wanted to get the job finished before the new intake arrived and the more adventurous amongst them took it upon themselves to investigate the college passageways. It required a considerable effort of will to resist reading any of the documents. I had to think of it all as so much paper, rather than an archive. In order to fit it into the space available I built tall stacks all the way up to the ceiling. I found it necessary to take one of the stepladders from the college library: a theft for which I am suddenly, strangely, very ashamed.

The paperwork was now arranged in such a way that the door was able to open fully perpendicularly to the frame. This provided just enough space to manoeuvre furniture. From 666 I took a small writing table that would not be missed and placed it in front of the window; and from my old room I took the only item I really cared about: a rotating, high-backed wooden armchair, cushioned in green leather, which my ex-wife had given me as a ploy to keep me out of her hair by improving the comfort of my workplace. The joints in my previous chair, you see, had taken to producing a particularly irritating creak every time I changed position and I had become so exasperated one morning that I returned home at an unexpected hour only to hear, as I unlatched the garden gate, precisely the same sound coming from our bedroom window... accompanied by my wife's unmistakably unconvincing rhythmic whinnying.

Her response, as practical as ever, was to have a new chair made by the local master carpenter (one of the area's gratuitous air-raid wardens) so that I was not reminded of that archetypal little tableau every time I sat down to work. (Our son, Phillip had yet to leave for London.) She also oiled the bedsprings.

                *   *   *

"Listen, Sam," she pushed herself up out of her chair & moved towards the back window of the kitchen, hugging herself & rubbing her upper arms, "I've heard all this before. It's nothing Amrit hasn't said to me himself after a few too many on a Friday night. & it's total rubbish: we both know it is."

I supposed I had to agree with her there. I didn't let her know though.

"I'm not saying it isn't clever or anything. *I* couldn't have thought of it..."

"Me neither."

"He probably did read all those interminable German books. I wouldn't have had the patience for it. & he certainly *is* very smart. It's just that... he was also completely wrong, & he knew it. There's nothing in the least bit admirable about a man who can't even be trusted to watch a child for five minutes, let alone bring one up. It's escapist, weak-minded male claptrap. He was obviously mentally ill, or at the very least a chronic alcoholic, & in serious need of medical intervention."

"Who, Amrit?"

"No, you clot, the tramp... well, maybe... I don't know: you tell me. That's exactly the kind of thing I thought you might find out."

"Well... it's hard to say."

"No, you see... Amrit knew that utopian stuff was just a fantasy; he told me so himself."

I got up & walked towards her. I reached out from behind her with both hands to touch the gooseflesh that had started to appear just below the banister-like smoothness of her shoulders. She let me do it. I moved slowly enough that the soft hairs, standing up, tickled my fingers. I shivered slightly as they did.

"He was going to move towards a focus on *place*, on Birmingham, with the tramp as a more traditional remnant of a lost age of manufacture & innovation & so on: inhabiting the past rather than the future. His supervisor wanted him to do that anyway. It made a lot more sense. But I think he became obsessed with this thing about his father when he found out I was pregnant..."

We were both looking out into the darkened garden through the silhouettes our own shapes made in the reflection of the kitchen. I began to rub her arms a little — like she'd been doing herself a few moments ago — to warm them. Her hands moved up to cover mine. She seemed to be reciprocating, but also saying "don't polish me like that, a genie isn't going to pop out of my mouth & offer you three wishes." I let her still the movement of my palms, but planned my wishes anyway.

"Sam... I need to know where he is? I need some kind of lead. I know the theory already; what I need are the specifics."

And flings itself wide open wi£ a wham.
　　He $outs some garbled words, £en in he stumps,
Turns back, and $uts £e door; he doesn't slam
　　£e €ing £is time, he clicks it to and clumps
Upstairs. A special streetlamp digi-cam
　　Gets clear pictures of him as he dumps
His tracksuit top beside £e bedroom door.
His girlfriend (Crystal)'s head slides off £e floor

50.5 *streetlamp digi-cam*: I take this to refer to a tiny film camera the size of a finger (*digi(t)*) which is concealed inside the streetlamp somewhere: presumably not at the point of radiation because this would surely pose a rather severe technological challenge. None the less, the idea of the thing which is supposed to *give* light becoming something which is supposed to *receive* light as images is another reversal of the transitivity of gaze of which this poem seems so fond. I am reminded of T. S. Eliot's 'Rhapsody on a Windy Night': 'Half-past one, / The streetlamp sputtered, / The streetlamp muttered,…'

50.7 *tracksuit top*: See 42.3 *tracksuit*. The rather vague monosyllable *top* may be used instead of 'jacket' simply for reasons of prosody. There is a possibility however, if we revive the theory that this is an encoded hand of cards—recalling games in 'The Rape of the Lock', *Eugene Onegin*, *Alice in Wonderland*—it could be something like 'the ace of trumps': *top* being 'the card of highest value' and *tracksuit* 'the suit you need to follow.'

　　　　*　　　　　　　*　　　　　　　*

The next job on my list would have to be the rehousing of my own books and papers. I had already come to the conclusion that this was an important historical archive and in order to extinguish my curiosity I would have to take the time to catalogue and reorganize the contents of the room before even contemplating a return to Poetry and Prophesy. *I therefore took the decision to explore the access hatch in the ceiling to see if it concealed a possible alternative storage space for my books.*

It did. There was an attic approximately a third of the volume of the room in the form of a domical vault. Needless to say, there was no such feature visible from the exterior. Instead the oriel window seemed to be topped with a tiled semi-dome. At the time I could conceive of no reason why an architect would want to build a complex turret beneath the roof of a building and yet disguise it from the outside world. I realize now that it was meant to form a focus for the flames.

　　　　*　　　　　　　*　　　　　　　*

"I think he's out *there*." I said. I knew this was what she wanted to hear.

She didn't reply.

"I think he's still in Birmingham. Maybe he's looking for his father or maybe... he's just... watching... waiting for the right moment to come back."

Her breath deepened almost imperceptibly, in range & tone.

"He could even be in Moseley Bog, in those bushes where his tramp was supposed to sleep during the summer: the bushes he could see from the window of the study. He could be watching us looking out at him right now from his own kitchen."

I was whispering, by now, as if he could also hear us. Hannah pulled my right hand gently over her breasts with her left & my left hand down towards her crotch with her right, so that her arms uncrossed to reveal her sapling body to the garden, my arms wrapping around her trunk like two stalks of aspiring ivy.

"Have you seen him?" she asked.

She bent her head back. I tried to kiss her throat but she pushed my lips away with her cheek so that they brushed against her ear.

"Can you see him now?"

She pushed my left hand under her skirt towards her... *sex*. That's the word Anaïs Nin would use. Nin would have my middle finger snaking into the clump of wiry hair that covers it — like that tuft of dewy *hay* above the hot, soft heart of a steamed artichoke, in search of the *sauce Hollandaise*.

I was obviously supposed to talk, however, & not to quote Anaïs Nin. "No, I don't think I can, but I'm sure he's there... somewhere..." my finger sank up to the first knuckle in the cup of melting butter, "sneaking around in the dark."

What the hell was I saying? If my finger was an eager little snake in Hannah's grass then the snake in *my* bit of turf wasn't having any of it. This was really screwed up. Hannah was already humming & curling her thorax like a hornet dying of an overdose of sugary drinks at the thought that her ex-boyfriend might be out there watching me fiddling around in her knickers — which is an outcome I would have snatched up in a second before I got here — but it was suddenly making *me* feel nauseous. I could feel the colour drain from my cheeks & a cold sweat prickling my forehead. Large amounts of saliva began to drip over the sides of my tongue. It was a gruesome imitation of the lubrication coating my finger.

I pulled my hand sharply away from her grip beneath the skirt to cover my lips as I began to retch. For some reason, I realised at that moment — no matter how indisposed it might be at the time — I'd always used my left hand for this job. I wondered why. The smell of her on my fingers was enough. I rushed to the sink & did my own impression of a dying insect.

> And up £e wall to wipe an inky smear
>> Away from skirting board and woodchip paper.
> He reaches slowly out to cup an ear
>> As up $e rises, £en begins to $ape
> Her nose again, remoulding it wi£ $eer
>> Brute force against £e wall. His nails scrape
> A few more scratches off, and £en his fist
> Brings closure to £is £erapeutic tryst

51.4 *As up she rises*: This swells rather sickeningly with nautical undertones, recalling the Royal Yacht Britannia which has just been launched. It comes from the bawdy sea-shanty about so-called *brewer's droop*: 'What shall we do with the drunken sailor?' The finest drunken sailor in modern poetry is perhaps Wallace Stevens's from 'Disillusionment of 10 o'clock' who 'Drunk and asleep in his boots, / Catches tigers / In red weather.' It seems hard to say those last two lines without slurring your words and retching.

There is a comparable effect here. Though the underlying tone is almost the opposite. The bitter ironies involved in the reversal of direction hit home more forcefully than anything we have previously been witness to. Sloggy's girlfriend slides up (to use the prurient terms thinly veiled in the song) from limp to erect: a cruelly sardonic effect which serves both to emphasize the acute belittling of this poor girl in the mind of her abuser and the terrible image one is forced to reconstruct in one's own mind of her sliding *down* the wall like Stevens's drunken sailor after a vicious attack has left her badly wounded.

51.5 *Her nose again, remoulding it*: This reconstruction of the nose, couched in terms of therapeutic *plastic* surgery, is obviously the opposite. Sloggy's aggression towards the protrusion in the middle of the woman's face prefigures his desire to castrate the drag-queen (or perhaps it is an echo, one can never be quite certain of the order of events). The nose is an obvious phallic symbol. Rostand's *Cyrano de Bergerac* makes extensive use of the commonplace correspondence. He is unusual in making his hero have a long nose, however; it is usually shorthand in the lower forms of theatre for villainy. Though perhaps these pantomime villains need also to appear Semitic in order to access those wells of racial memory that hold the key to frightening the uneducated.

51.6 *His nails*: Another insinuation of Sloggy's private effeminacy, marked by a carving diæresis. If Sloggy is capable of using his fingernails as weapons, we have to assume them to be unusually long. Scratching (along with hair-pulling) is the characteristic effeminate attack: something homosexuals might threaten in order to appear particularly womanly.

As discussed above (See 41.3 *nail-file*), this word also reminds us of Sloggy's ideological (and perhaps genetic) ancestry amongst the unregulated Birmingham nailers whose sideline was in weapons manufacture.

A further crucial dimension is to be found in the avian overtones of the scene. The references to Aristophanes's *The Birds* flock around the poem; the portrayal of Sloggy here recalls a cockatoo clawing at a victim and threatening a deadly bite. The poet is perhaps more likely to be thinking, however, of Epops: the hoopoe—the incarnation of Tereus—which fouls its own nest. In this schema, Sloggy's girlfriend might either be seen as Procne or Philomel (who are traditionally often mistaken for one another after Ovid's confusion of the nightingale and swallow): a kind of sister to the drag-queen. (The fragility of her name, Crystal, is obviously pointed.) Sloggy is (in reverse) breaking and flattening his girlfriend's nose, rather than cutting out her tongue. His apparent intention is, nevertheless, to stop her 'singing'. The similarities between cutting out the tongue, clipping the beak (as it were) and Sloggy's later castration fantasies are obvious.

51.8 *closure*: The poet is playing on two senses: one derived from a piece of jargon in Gestalt psychology, introduced into New Criticism by I. A. Richards, meaning the completion of an incomplete process specifically via the subjective input of a viewer (or reader); the other being the literal formation of a fist by closing the fingers into a ball of knuckles. Obviously this event, rather like the canto as a whole, is actually quite the opposite of a *closure*: it is the *overture* of an unfinished fragment of action. Its closure, in Richards's sense, can only be brought about via a clear understanding of the ironic antinomy of this usage of the word.

51.8 *therapeutic*: era 8

* * *

The night I first ventured into the roof, a persistent rainstorm was drumming its fingers on the windowpanes. Somehow the vague impatience of the weather had begun to infect me and I felt the need to do something callisthenic to alleviate the boredom. This whole scene of bizarre confinement in which I had found myself began to feel portentously contrived. It was one of those occasions on which you stop believing in the random flux of events which turns the millwheel of mental liberty and feel yourself coerced by some invisible presence to perform in a more or less predictable fashion in response to stimuli: like a rat in a behaviourist's maze... or more like Eve in Milton's Eden. On these pivotal moments in life (one example in particular sticks in the memory from childhood in which I inflicted a crippling illness on a cabhorse by feeding it a jar of mustard piccalilli) one sees oneself as in a vivid memory, as if the act of playing out the unfolding scene is merely one of physically remembering what one has already (spiritually) done

It was the fear of recapitulations of this effect in my life which kept me from working on Poetry and Prophesy. *This book, of course, will never now be written. Its content might however have been quite relevant to the present work. It was intended to explore attempts by poets – the Metaphysicals primarily, but also their more recent imitators like Manley Hopkins, Eliot and Pound – to invoke this very feeling in their readers: to remind them of their own futures, not so much by transmitting personal visions of the poets', but by recreating the prophetic experience in the reader with their incantatory words.*

* * *

                    52
>   By glancing off her cheek as if to say,
>   '£at's you all fixed.' $e seems to find her zest
>   For life. $e skips towards him to display
>   Her gratitude. $e's clearly impressed.
> $e whoops and wags a finger to convey
>   Her jubilation, like a bowler in a test
>   Who's just clean-bowled £e innings' final wicket,
>   Affirming £at $e certainly *can* kick it…"

52.8 *kick it*: The poet probably decided not just to employ the conventional rhyme of *wicket* with *cricket* so as to recall the deterioration in both the game and the language used to describe it that seems to have been heralded by the series defeat suffered by England at the hands of The West Indies three years ago. The awful triumphalist *calypsos* that followed have precisely the same kinds of shoddy rhymes employed here (and indeed throughout the poem). A fact which insinuates a creolization of British culture in this dystopia under the influence of the Guyanese Britannia of the piece, and everything for which she stands. England recently took their revenge on tour in the Caribbean, and it seems unlikely that they will ever lose to such inelegant cricketers as those spawned in the Americas again. We shall probably never be allowed to forget this defeat of 1950, however; unashamedly Marxist journalists from the region like C. L. R. James have latched onto the bastardization of this quintessential English sport (born in the rituals of the Ancient Druids, I believe) as a way of undermining everything their parent country stands for.

*   *   *

It was not my intention to hawk a version of Pythagorean metempsychosis—certainly not to dally at the margins of theosophy like Yeats—instead I wanted to explore the nature of that Socratic stroke of genius that casts learning as a process of reminding oneself of latent truths: provable truths specifically because they are provably latent in the mind. My desire had been to take this notion beyond the fields of pure reason and social ethics into the deeper psychological and spiritual remit of great literature.

Just as the logic of Socrates cannot be denied, and the reason for the impossibility of denial lies in the impact of his measured words upon a human reason that exists solely as the ability to receive such an impact, the spiritual salience of certain forms of metaphysical poetry is unavoidable precisely because its musical and semantic qualities are those that both pre-empt and result from the activities of mind capable of revealing to us the spiritual (rather than the logical or physical) truths of our existence.

We are not 'reincarnated', neither need we aspire to the cheap gypsy fairground trick of 'predicting the future', but each human child is born containing the entire temporal, logical and spiritual 'truth' of their nature: truth that can be accessed via certain activities of mind and body—logic, reasoning, mathematics; athletic exercise and dance; the most important of which, I would go on to contend, was poetry.

'Prophesy', in this vision, becomes not the prescience of things to come so much as that kind of speech which derives from and brings about the apprehension of a reality beyond such quotidian notions as the present and the future. In such a state, a man discovers the innocence of a new-born child on his death-bed and the wisdom of a dying man inside the womb. It is in order to give to

others such an apprehension that he works, and this is why he works in strange, beguiling metaphors and the spiralling music of his words. One cannot bring on states of mind in those to whom they have become alien by reporting what one have discovered for oneself, or simply by saying 'you should think like this' or 'go forth and see the truth.' Instead one must use one's materials in such a way as to instigate the effect in one's participating audience.

Such minor forms as meditative lyric, the pastoral and even love poetry become, in this way of thinking, much more important than the longer dramatic or narrative forms to which they are traditionally believed to be the mere apprentice-pieces. It is via these distilled forms, these atemporal whisperings, rather than the professional outpourings of the tradesman writer, that the eternal verities are glimpsed. Of course, no-one seriously believes Murder in the Cathedral *to be more important than* The Four Quartets, *but who to date has called 'The Phoenix and the Turtle' the greatest of the works ascribed to Shakespeare?*

The crux of this project was a single curious, disturbing thought. I could not believe the book did not exist already. I spent years—it is no exaggeration—it was literally a number of years, during which I should have been occupying myself with something more practical, looking for this book amongst library catalogues and notebooks and the commentaries of the great works of literature. I asked colleagues for their help. They invariably suggested something fascinating to peruse, but it was never the book that I was trying to remember. The point was, I was sure that I had read it before. It had been amongst a large pile of monographs I had borrowed as an undergraduate when writing an essay on a subject I could no longer recall. Eventually I submitted to the inevitable fact that if it did not exist already then I would have to be the one to bring it to the world. Perhaps, I mused, this was the way a good idea always struck: as something one finds it inconceivable that nobody has ever done before.

I was consequently quite terrified of this book before it had even been written. By the time I climbed into the attic and set in motion the train of events which would prove to me that I could never avoid the truth, I had been working on it for more than fourteen years and had put into finished prose only the first sentence of what I conceived nevertheless to be a work secure in imaginative completion:

"Poetry reminds us we have lived our lives before," it read. Whenever venturing to write a second sentence, I could do nothing but inwardly pronounce the echoes of the first… until the reading of it became itself a prophetic incantation of the kind I wanted to describe:

‖: *"Poetry reminds us we have lived our lives before."* :‖

*   *   *

(I must apologise for £at last stanza.
  My final couplets $ouldn't be so crap.
£ese octaves can become a c/rhyme bonanza
  I must admit, I've half a mind to scrap
£e lot, but £en... £e reader understands a
  More elegant approach could handicap
£e comic verse, I guess. And blinkinell,
  At least it's better £an a villanelle.)

53.3 *c/rhyme*: Usually when one employs this oblique line within a compound word it is simply to offer two alternative first letters in a pair of interchangeable near homonyms. This would, however, make the pair in this instance *rhyme* and *chyme*: the latter being the name, from archaic medicine, for the substance produced by the stomach from food which is in turn transformed by the liver into blood. This is very unlikely. Instead the intention is quite obviously to pair up *rhyme* and *crime* and thereby conflate a phrase along the lines of 'a bonanza of criminal rhymes' (a very accurate description of 'these octaves'). It is worth noting however, how formal verse of this kind does sometimes come across as a *distillation* or *concentration* of the narrative: something not dissimilar to *chyme*. The form *c/rhyme* itself is rather like a 'digest' of the longer phrase. We should perhaps take the hint that we should not *swallow* such 'crap'.

53.8 *villanelle*: A play on *she-villain* perhaps. Other than that, I fail to see what the persona might have against the Villanelle. It is really not a comparable form. I suspect he is supposed to get some irreverent gratification from the Brummagem rhyme with 'blinkinell'.

I slept on the sofa that night, the washing up bowl beside me on the floor. Well, actually, I lay there motionless between the clenching gastric expulsions, mulling over every move of the thirty or forty disastrous seconds of physical intimacy with Hannah, which I knew to be the first & last. When the slice of dim light that cut a gap in the velvet curtains drifted towards me, brightening a little, to reveal the dappled surface of the slush inside the green basin, I struggled to a sitting position, & then, teeteringly, to my feet. I took the bowl to the kitchen to wash it, trying not to hear the liquid slapping gently against its plastic sides. I was still drunk, thank god. It was only about 5 in the morning. After emptying the bowl & sluicing bleachy water around it in the sink, I plodded into the study to collect a folder I'd put together, containing one or two things I wanted to hang on to: a set of keys I'd found in an encrusted old mug at the back of the desk drawer, a few papers — the Marx-Engels parody, 'Unfencing Theory' & the Penelope reversal. The kid was in there, asleep under the desk in his pushchair, breathing heavily through a snotty nose. I was sure he couldn't have been there all night. The study comes off the kitchen. We would have made far too much noise for him to sleep. Hannah must have put him in there while I was unconscious... for some reason. Though I didn't remember being unconscious at all. Perhaps you never do.

I crept round the pushchair, trying not to look at him, like it might cause him to wake up. I reached out to lift the folder by its flap. The papers around crackled louder than a spitting bonfire. The cardboard bent & made a dull *thunk* like an axe biting deep into a treetrunk. I froze. Not daring even to turn my eye muscles to glance at the slumbering little tyrant. I was Tom. I had Jerry, the folder, by the ear. The child was the lazy bulldog. I held the folder to my chest without closing it. Then I crept backwards out of the study, turned as soon as I passed the threshold of the door (again, not closing it) & scurried straight out of the flat. I did close the two front doors though, clicking their mechanisms open & shut as quietly as possible. Success.

I needn't have bothered. It was extremely noisy in the street. There is apparently enough green territory in this part of Birmingham to support the level of avian claimants necessary to make a dawn chorus more of a dawn cacophony. What elsewhere might have sounded like the cheery whistling of a few early-rising gardeners competing in the music-hall vibrato stakes, in this part of Moseley seemed like the various alarms you'd imagine to be produced by a nuclear reactor going into meltdown... with all its squealing descants of expanding metal & escaping steam. Or, then again, it might only have been the overture to a hangover. Wodehouse captured this effect quite brilliantly (somewhere): 'A cat stamped into the room', he wrote. I understood precisely what he meant. I felt a little like a seismograph.

A little further down the street, two seagulls were swashbuckling over which one deserved the right to perch on the side of a yellow city council bin, attached part-way up a lamppost, & dip its bill into a pot of pink pakora sauce. Despite the fact I'd never worked out how a single seagull ever found its way to Birmingham, let alone enough of them to cause a run on pink pakora sauce, this made me feel suddenly much more at home than I ever did in Hannah's typical Muesli flat, with its Organic handicrafts & Fair-trade bongo drums.

> "£en, mirroring his movements in a kind
>   Of practised celebration dance, $e hops
> From foot to foot, £en wheels round behind
>   His back triumphantly and hoots. He flops
> Exhausted on £e futon to unwind.
>   £ere's more of her applause, and £en $e stops
> To close £e blinds and let him sleep. $e leaves
> £e house at two wi£ $opping, which $e heaves

54.4 *flops*: Sloggy's body is usually erect. This moment of *flopping* is the moment we leave him and follow first his girlfriend, her car, and then the fox towards Britannia's bedroom. It is almost as if he is no longer Sloggy when, like the 'drunken sailor', he slumps—in the way a phallus is no longer a phallus when not engorged—and his character literally 'unwinds': *unravels* and *runs out of wind* (like a sail going limp.) Later his physical body will become dissipated in a different way by the coin's gaze through the mock crystal-cut ashtray (see 229.3).

                  *   *   *

A continued effort to avoid the implications of this smouldering discovery lay behind my decision to go exploring. But even as I did, I could feel the very experience I was trying to evade consuming me. Not only was I failing to distract myself from the truth, I was enacting a pivotal moment in an existence which I knew to be hurtling unstoppably towards the fatal realisation of its own predestination. When caught in this lemniscate loop however, one must continue to act in order to continue to exist; just as the reader must continue reading for the story to take place.

Having shifted most of the possessions I still kept in college away from the centre of the room, I positioned the stepladder directly beneath the access hatch: or as close as all the papers would allow. Mechanically, I climbed up past the lightbulb (which I had switched off for fear of electrocution, preferring—apparently—to conform to the parlous gothic cliché of carrying out this kind of clandestine exploration entirely by candlelight).

I tried the hatch-cover with the fingertips of one hand: no movement. It was sealed with at least one layer of heavy, leaded paint. I hesitated. The rain continued drumming, the candles on the desk glaring back at me expectantly. What else could I do? With a single sharp thud of the heel of my hand, I struck the centre of the flimsy hatch. It jumped up a few inches into the roof-cavity releasing a shower of paint flecks, some of which fell directly into my eyes and mouth. I spluttered and blinked repetitively, wondering why I had not looked down.

Edging the cover away from the access hatch, I felt around the immediate surrounding area with my two hands. If there were any rodents or insects lurking on the brink, I theorized, it would be preferable to be bitten on the finger than the nose or ear. Besides, the hatch looked barely wide enough to take the full breadth of a grown man's shoulders. I might get stuck up there with the offending creature fastened to one of the tenderer of my facial extremities, and no way to pull my arms into the space to fight it off.

At first I felt nothing but a few small lumps of plaster and a rough beam. When I allowed my hands to pat tentatively around the opposite side of the opening, however, (hoping to find another sturdy wooden feature which might allow me to spread my weight and haul myself into the cavity) I came across what I assumed to be a roll of wallpaper.

What I pulled out of the loft was in fact a peculiarly thick and heavy roll of brown parcel paper. This I took down the ladder. Without brushing it clean, I leant it in the corner of the room next to the door. For months it stood there in a ring of dark red brick-dust. It is now the only thing I am capable of looking at, but that evening, and for the intervening period, I thought only that I might keep hold of it in case I wanted eventually to pack up the material and send it to an appropriate library for continued maintenance.

Other than this, the attic seemed entirely empty. In a matter of two or three hours I managed to haul the boxes up there one by one and stack them in the space above the window. I took great care to organize them so that all the weight was distributed evenly. Lifting in such a confined space was also taking a rather heavy toll on my back, but I might have done the job in half the time had I avoided hunkering down occasionally, or sitting on the beam with my legs dangling through the access hatch, trying (pointlessly, of course) to visualize where I was in relation to the outside of the building.

Once the necessary space had been cleared, I spent the next few days making the room passably comfortable. It was really very cosy by the end. I could sit facing the window with the door behind me to the right and the stack of papers behind me to the left, the folded step ladder propped against it. On the only bare wall I hung a brass-rubbing my father had made of a monument to a Medieval knight in his Parish church. I had a sheepskin rug in the middle of the floor on which I would sometimes get a little sleep during the day. On the desk, apart from the large accounting book (a 'triple cash book') in which I had decided to catalogue the contents of the archive, there was a strictly rationed single row of essential reference works between two white ceramic book-ends, an empty Players tin containing pencils and a slide-rule, a cheap but heavy cut-glass ashtray, a pair of opera glasses I would use at idle moments to identify the species of a distant tit or thrush, and, vice-clamped to the right side of the desktop, was my dented but largely still co-operative anglepoise task lamp. I had everything I needed. I felt absolutely at home.

You must forgive these protracted banalities: I have to explain all of this now and in the kind of detail to convince myself, when reading back each paragraph, that any of it really happened. It is the only way I can remember what the room actually looked like. You see, not just this marginalia but in fact this entire work is simply a prologue to the annihilation of all three of us: myself, the past (as I may as well call it now) and you: the reader. My peripheral field of vision over the past few months has gradually been dominated by the greedy progress of the fire that has now finally engulfed us all.

*   *   *

>   Into a silver BMW
>   And drives away. And £at's about your lot.
>   I €ink, at £is point, I $ould muddle €rough
>   £is segue to £e next bit of my plot;
>   £e action's over. I won't trouble you
>   Wi£ every passer-by £at comes in $ot.
>   Except to say, at one point £ere's a fox
>   Regurgitating in a pizza box.

55.6 *comes in shot*: Hair in the gate. [Poet's note]

    The fact that you 'shoot' with a camera has always lent it a far more aggressive attitude than other ways of recording what is seeable. The perfect combination of lens and gun is to be found in the *sniper's rifle*. There is, I think, the threat of the sniper's lens to be felt in all telescopic, observational photography. The snap of the shutter being obviously analogous (though, typically for this poem, in reverse) to the firing of the gun: it cannot kill but nevertheless, in some sense, captures the life photographed. The instant of capture never happens where moving pictures are concerned of course. The exposures are motorized and occur continuously. Even so, the sense pervades when watching such 'footage', of the quasi-divine ability on the part of the viewer to snatch away at any moment the fragile life it is observing. The fact that everybody seems capable of seeing everybody else in such a way in this *panopticon* city of the future makes the existence of individual creatures seem infinitely delicate. The future city resembles a besieged Stalingrad.

    The fox, as well as being the animal symbol of cunning and deception, is also the definitive object of the hunt. The paradoxical calm and self-assurance of this particular fox is not, I think, to be interpreted as the opposite. The fox stands as the perfect counter to the sniper's-eye view. It absolutely defies the threat by bringing calm to the *mise-en-scène*, and does so specifically because of its permanent assumption of the threatening viewer. The fox, unlike all the humans in the piece except for the demonic Britannia, never labours under the delusion it can be invisible.

    For more reasons than this, the first appearance of the fox is a breathtaking moment of poetic distraction. The burlesque is suddenly thrown into relief. The scene's effectiveness comes from the creature's temporal ambidexterity, achieved by a metaphoric transformation of the cityscape through which it moves. The fox is just as natural as ever when its actions are reversed. It therefore trumps the stylistic gimmick and denies the irony. It is portrayed not simply as a responsive and sensitive creature which comes out when the street is deserted, but also as the dramatist of the scene, entirely in control of its environment. The problem of the bubble of quietness surrounding the appearance of the urban fox is perfectly evoked: one can never be quite sure which is cause and which effect. We like to think the fox only shows itself when the coast is clear, but we suspect it has a hushed exclusion zone magically projected around it as it goes, as if the deluded people and their delusional technologies are dumbstruck by its passing. It is not to be trusted though; its *jape* is never far away.

    This moment is very different to the poem by the current laureate, John Masefield 'Reynard the Fox or the Ghost Heath Run', and yet it must have been an influence.

55.8 *pizza*: Italian for 'pie'. The word is used in ironic pretension; the box is probably just one of those flimsy folded card affairs in which bakers put cakes for transportation. The moral environment of gluttony and careless littering ('wrapped up' in Italianate language by way of a sarcastic mock-dignification) is therefore driven home: this is a society in which people routinely eat sugary cakes or pies in the street and toss away the packaging. One cannot avoid being reminded of nursery rhymes: 'A Song of Sixpence' for example, 'Simple Simon', and (perhaps especially) 'The Queen of Hearts'.

The second occurrence of this word—in stanza 148, in a prurient pun: '*12 inch pizza boy*'—forces us to acknowledge the proximity of this foreign word to the English 'pizzle' (originally the member of a bull used as a flogging instrument, but now the penis of any large mammal). Perhaps there is a deliberate employment of these phallic undertones to raise the 'pizza box' to the level of a *totem*: both a site of disruption and a shamanistic gateway between two worlds—that of Sloggy and that of the fox. It is also possible, therefore, that the word is to be pronounced not /ˈpiːtsa/ but /ˈpɪzə/ or even /ˈpiːzə/ in this Birminghamized dialect (the latter being homonymous with the town containing Italy's most infamously crooked phallic symbol).

It turns and $ambles off towards its bru$.
　　£e tufts of dirty copper in its dorsal
Fur stand stiff against £e breeze. A hu$
　　Descends along £e carriageways of Balsall
Hea€ as if it's paid to stop £e ru$
　　Of traffic wi£ an offering: a morsel
Of kebab meat spewed into £e street.
　　Down Per$ore Road, it lollops its retreat

56.2 *copper.* (See 26.8 *the right way round?* for a discussion of copper tokens as opposed to gold and silver money.) The association of the fox with copper is a natural poetic commonplace when one considers its colour. The question we should ask, however, as with any well-thumbed copper coin, is not what is its natural worth, but what precisely does it stand for? A certain cunning in defiance of the noble hunter, no doubt; a disregard for estate and property; an ability to breach the frontiers of the proverbial henhouse; the mentality of the disobedient scavenger: these things are salient but tend to miss the importance of the creature's name beyond its beastly nature. Four men shared the name with the creature through the period of history that formed this city into the icon of the new dissenting revolutionary movement: Charles Fox, the leader of the Whigs in Parliament in the C18[th], who supported the French Revolution; George Fox, the founder of The (Quaker) Society of Friends, whose ideas and followers laid the crucial foundation stones for the capitalist industrial revolution in the English midlands; John Foxe, whose *Acts and Monuments* (better known as *The Book of Martyrs*) was perhaps the most important text in the birth of Puritanism and later the fomenting of the Civil War; and Colonel 'Tinker' Fox, a Birmingham metalworker who became the leader of an extremely cunning, unruly and effective band of Parliamentarian guerrillas who used Edgbaston Hall in the town as their headquarters during the period of the 1640s (between its infamous sacking and the creation of the New Model Army.)

　　This last figure is without doubt the most likely to be referenced. 'Tinker' Fox's virtual single-handed disruption of Royalist control of the Midlands (always the main battleground of the war) provided not just the impetus but also the logistic model for the Parliamentarian regrouping and Cromwell's ultimately successful new army. Fox's was a troop of full-time professional soldiers who were drawn almost exclusively from amongst the metalworkers and new tradesmen of the area and they shared a zealous and radical non-conformist faith extreme enough to label the enemy 'Amalekites'. He was eventually sidelined towards the end of the war because of his persistent refusals to compromise in terms of theological politics and the (quite unsurprising) prevalence of support for the Levellers amongst his followers.

　　It cannot be emphasized strongly enough how important was the Civil War in cementing the symbolic relationship between Birmingham and the libertarian anti-royalism emphasized in this poem. Before the war the town was just a sapling of the dominance of commerce and industry over the ancient values of order and nobility that would characterize the next three centuries. It was little known beyond its immediate environs. The arming of the Parliamentary forces by Robert Porter, the ubiquity of the pamphlet *Birmingham's Flames* with its satirical woodcut of Prince Rupert firing the town (plus another, equally biased, on the same subject by Porter himself), and the 'heroic' tales of Tinker Fox's exploits which subsequently circulated in the dissenting underground all changed that. Birmingham became genuinely famous. Clarendon was moved to single the town out as 'notorious' for 'hearty, wiful, affected disloyalty to the King'. Never again would anyone have to wonder which town in England stood purely for radicalism, industry, unfettered commerce, and defiance of the church and crown. Birmingham had *foxed* the monarchy.

56.2-3 *dorsal / Fur.* There is a good deal of evidence that the poem was originally intended to be even more prosaic than it is. The 'unstuttered' enjambments that characterize this stanza—in which lines ending with a falling multisyllable are followed by trochees, so as to avoid interrupting the regular alternations of stress—are very common in the erased stanzas (see 68-78 for example). The result is to prejudice the continuity of prose rhythm over the purity of the poetic line. Obviously, the 'purity of the poetic line' is hardly a great concern in this intentionally sub-Byronic idiom, but it is interesting that the poet should choose this moment in particular to legitimize these otherwise rigorously eradicated, prosaic enjambments. One might expect the fox's linguistic environment to be more, not less, poetic; and in lexical and metaphoric terms, at least, I think it is.

The prosaic rhythm may just derive from a desire not to abandon the rhyme on *Balsall (Heath)* which cannot be achieved in any other way. There is a sense, however, in which this rhythmic suppleness mirrors, in the prosody, the transformative effect the fox has upon the viewer and the whole environment. There seems to be an inability on the part of the verse-form to *contain* the fox. Just as, in the following stanzas, the fox's image appears to distort its televisual representation (as if it emits some form of *jamming signal*), here its casual/causal movement effects a metamorphosis on the shoddy burlesque: it trots between the stationary rhymes like treetrunks, turning Ottava Rima into what, these days, we might want to call *prose-poetry*.

And tentatively backs into þe park,
    Where huddled silver birches let it hide
Amongst þeir shadows, merging wiþ its dark
    Extremities. Its paler underside
Gets lost between þeir curls of sallow bark:
    Like bandages embalmed wiþ sap and dried
By tomb air þrough þe ages till þey look
As browned as pages of a dog-eared book.

57.6-8 *bandages embalmed with sap… dog-eared book*: The poet is playing on the idea of 'foxing' (the build up of mineral and fungal deposits, similar to certain varieties of lichen, creating a mottled orange/brown effect) in old manuscripts. 'Dog-eared' obviously adds, metonymically, to the effect. The likening of this deterioration of old books to the flaky bandages on Egyptian mummies is very worrying…

embalmed with sap: In a cloyingly solecistic contribution to the latest Philological Quarterly (XXXII, III, July 1953: 344-6), Robert A. Day from Dartmouth College supports Grierson's tacky suggestion that 'glew' in 'To His Coy Mistress' by Andrew Marvell ("Now therefore, while the youthful hew / Sits on thy skin like morning glew,") refers to "the glistening gum found on the bark of certain trees" on the startling grounds that Marvell could have read Gavin Douglas's Middle Scots mistranslation—'gum or glew'—of *viscum* ('mistletoe') in the description of the Golden Bough from the *Æneid*. Not only does Day countenance Grierson's reading (can we really accept that Marvell, despite his love of the unsettling image, is suggesting this young woman appears to be covered in something resembling Lyle's Golden Syrup?) but he also excuses Douglas's translation for the reason that *viscum* can also refer to myrrh or birdlime.

This is patently absurd. Marvell means 'glow', nothing more unpleasant. He is likening the girl's blushing skin to the approaching sun—the first pink light of morning—and therefore intensifying the paradox of his seductive appeal that she join him in escaping it. The standard emendation to 'dew' is wrong, but perfectly understandable in the context; and much less ridiculous than 'glue'.

Day has stumbled blindly upon something vital in this Virgilian thicket, however. The 'glew' in question (though neither 'gum' nor 'mistletoe') nevertheless might bear arboreal overtones: 'thy willing soul transpires / At every pore with instant fires.' A surface gloss might be something like: *So, while you are still in the pink, like the first light of dawn, and while the burning blush in your skin betrays your concealed arousal* ['willing soul' as opposed to resisting body]… A deeper reading, however—one that approached a little closer to the Marvellian idiom—would suggest the contradictory images of biological mortality and spiritual immortality which co-exist as a transcendental paradox in the phallic icon of the Golden Bough. To return to the arboreal overtones, perhaps 'instant fires' might therefore be glossed as *fox-fires*.

Fox-fire, to elucidate, is an unearthly phosphorescence emitted by naturally decaying wood. A perfect metaphor for Marvell and also, I would have the temerity to suggest, a much more likely explanation of the Golden Bough phenomenon than Frazer's: that the mistletoe itself is what makes the bough 'golden' (led by a desire to literalize the connection he sees between the Druids and the ancestors of the Romans). Virgil simply uses *viscum* as a metaphor, perhaps (out of a desire to draw the same universalising analogies as Frazer) in the knowledge of Druidic ritual use of the winter-fruiting epiphyte. It certainly seems much more natural to me that the glowing branch should be literally (and very practically) incandescent (Virgil is at great pains to emphasize the gloominess and deathliness of the grove) and that the ease with which Æneas can detach it from the trunk can be explained by its rottenness. The important connection Frazer draws with lightning need not be lost. The tree could easily be one that had been struck by lightning (hence the dead bough) and understood therefore somehow literally to contain the power of the thunder god (Jove).

All of which brings me back to this strange, foxing moment in the copse of silver birches. The fungal deterioration of a book, the bandages around a mummy (usually encased in figurative golden sarcophagi), the strange glow emitting from dead wood: all these things seem to be disturbing portents of the 'first glimpse of our heroine'. We are about to watch as, like the *morning* (or 'mourning') *glew* that sits on the skin of Marvell's Coy Mistress, the 'sun leaks bright lines on... the landscape of [Britannia's] skin like grapefruit rind.' Unlike Marvell, though, there is nothing in the least bit 'coy' about this Sibylline hag.

The fact that *fox-fire* also (once again) connotes George Fox's *inner light* of Quakerism should not go unnoted.

book: The etymological roots of this word are traditionally traced to *bók*, Old Norse for 'beech', with the explanation that runic writings were thought to have been originally cut into the bark of these trees. Our poet appears to have found some deeper common origin however. The most primeval forms of writing in forested countries—analogues of which can still be found in English woods—might easily have been short messages of love, warning, belonging and self-assertion carved into the trunks of trees. So, a hypothesis: 'beech', 'birch', 'bark' and 'book' are all cognate. I do not have the resources to check this properly at the moment, but I suspect I am right.

Furthermore, if I were to choose from amongst the indigenous species a type of bark which might be easily taken off and used in a similar way to modern paper, I would choose not the beech, but the silver birch.

> þe fox moves calmly þrough þe trunks. It lopes,
>   Half-formed, like someþing drawn by Francis Bacon
> To torture one of þose Velazquez Popes
>   Behind a curtain in some godforsaken
> Bastille of streaks: þey look like zoetropes
>   To animate bleak horrors, and awaken
> Ghosts… except þe fox strolls past and calms
> þe histrionic scene, and all our qualms

58.2 *drawn*: A wincing play on 'sketched' and 'dragged' or 'gutted' (as a corporal/capital punishment).

58.5 Notice that the camera 'shot' has become like paint on canvas. The fox has also become 'half-formed' (*quasimodo*). The suggestion is, I think, that the fox's influence on the scenery has extended to the lens through which it is supposedly seen. Its nature cannot be contained by the technology and is disrupting the reception. In literal terms, I see this as a moment in which the 'screen' on which the fox is being watched suffers *noise* and problems with its *horizontal hold* creating a distorted and disturbing appearance similar to one of the grotesque and apparently vandalized parodies of the portrait of Pope Innocent X by Velazquez with which the *enfant terrible* of the British artworld, Francis Bacon, has been trying (more than a little phantasmagorically) to terrorize the critical establishment this year. The effect is only temporary though, and, of course, it is the fox that fixes it.

*   *   *

I started this fire. Or, to be more accurate, it started inside me. I suppose I can be no more to blame for this tragic turn of events than can a building made with faulty wiring…

It began with an itch. Before I even registered any sensation, I would find myself scratching vigorously at the skin between the crease of my thighs and my buttocks. It seems impossible that my hand could creep past the waistband of my trousers and start to rake unceremoniously through my underpants without the slightest conscious knowledge on my part of the discomfort it was attempting to relieve, but that is precisely how it happened. Soon enough, a hard, brown crust began to form on that part of my body, not dissimilar to the surface of a crème brulée, which spread first to my inner thighs and then my abdomen and round into the small of my back.

By this time, I was so in thrall to the poem I was attempting to stop working on that the following couplet forced itself into my mind:

> The eczema spread across his perinæum
> Like dry-rot in a crypt or a museum.

*   *   *

Directly in front of me, on the other side of the road, a figure hunched beneath a dirty orange Wolverhampton Wanderers benny hat shuffled into view, making little progress in the direction of an equally dirty orange sunrise. The reflections of the sky in the dewy surface of the kerb made the pavement look a bit like a fairy-lit catwalk. The figure — a beardless leathery-cheeked man — trudged down it, also sporting a torn tweed jacket with PVC elbow patches over a blue nylon parka, chocolate brown three-stripe joggers (from the 1978 Salvation Army summer/autumn collection) & a pair of filthy silver-shadow trainers, one of which had not been 'laced up' so much as tied directly onto the foot with a good length of that green garden string that stains your hands when it gets wet.

I found myself following him. I really don't know why. To be honest, I was feeling sorry for myself & I didn't know what else to do. I couldn't go back to my mom & dad's at this time of the morning... even if I *was* leaving today. I didn't have my key. I think I felt a bit like an old tramp myself: just another of the urban dispossessed.

He passed the bottom of Springfield Road & turned left into Green Road. I kept pace with him about twenty steps behind as he approached the concrete bridge across the ford. It was actually quite difficult to keep my distance inconspicuously at first. He really wasn't moving very quickly. I soon realised I had no real need to be inconspicuous.

Instead of using the bridge, he stepped down into the road & crossed over to the cracked footpath beside the river. I thought for a second he might ford the Cole in his trainers, instead he went off up Millstream Way, managing somehow not to dislodge a single drop of milky dew on the taller clumps of grass or disturb the magpie strutting round the fringes of the path.

I had no idea where he was taking me. He didn't seem like a man *going* to Small Heath, just one that happened to be heading in that direction. He never stopped to look through a bin or to collar someone for the price of cup of tea — a jogger, say — I would have been the obvious choice myself. He just carried on walking along like he was killing time by going for a constitutional along the river. Maybe he was. *I* was killing time, why couldn't a tramp do the same? It really did feel as if he was leading me on though. More than that... it felt as if he wanted to encourage me to be like him. I quickly lost all curiosity about the purpose of this little journey & lulled myself into its plodding rhythm.

As I followed him downstream along the leafy footpath, veering around the occasional overhanging willow, trailing its tentacles like a colony of polyps, then trying not to let my footsteps echo in the bridge under the Stratford Road, I found myself imitating the way he walked: eyes down to the space a yard in front of me, only glancing up occasionally to check his steady progress & the river's snaking route; my back hunched beneath my rucksack to maximise the amount of coat material insulating my torso; each foot lifting only just enough to clear the obstacles — a bit of root-cracked concrete, an uneven cobble, a grey spatter of Canada goose shit — & planting itself back down little more than a heel's width from the standing foot; my fists unclenched but withdrawn deep into my sleeves as my arms hung loosely from my sides, as if there were no arms inside the sleeves at all.

> Wiþ its portrayal of instinctive ease.
>   It pricks its ears as a water vole
> Dives — *plop* — out of þe river when it sees
>   Þe fox, and scurries off towards a hole.
> But þen our fox just saunters þrough þe trees
>   As if it knows it can't become a stole
> Þese days. It clambers headfirst in its den
> To join its vixen and its cubs again…"

59.6 *stole*: A play on 'fox-fur' and 'stolen goods' presupposing the wrongfulness of 'thieving' the life of a fox. This pun therefore pre-empts the discussion on putative legislation forbidding fox hunting. (See stanza 61).

59.8 *vixen*: The word vixen sounds plural to me. The extra syllable, *–en*, is a pluralising suffix in words like *children*, *oxen* and *brethren*. This seems to go along with a multiple sense of femininity, compared to singular masculinity. The genitals must have something to do with it. A phallus is a one; it stands up to be counted. The pussy is… more complex: not a pussy at all… *a vixen's den*.
[Poet's note]

This is by far the longest of the poet's own marginal interjections. The handwriting is strangely childlike and inconsistent. I hold little store with graphology however and refuse to draw any conclusions from this. I shall also resist speculating as to whether these brief annotations are not, in fact, the work of the original poet, but of some interfering editor. The free license taken in erasing and altering the text, the flippancy and brevity of the comments, the similarities in turn of phrase to those which appear in print all suggest a writer editing his own work. It is this entry in particular which serves to justify the philological-hermeneutics of my approach. The poet is revealed to be an explorer amongst the linguistic undergrowth, intent on unearthing the hidden, tangled roots of words.

That said, however, there is a seriously tendentious and narrow account of the *–en* suffix given here. This ending carries its own complexities and ambiguities as a morpheme. It can form diminutives like *kitten* and *maiden*, feminines like *vixen*, plurals like *oxen*, adjectives from nouns as in *golden*, verbs from adjectives as in *darken* and *fasten*, and past participles (and therefore adjectives) from strong verbs as in *sunken* and *broken*. It is a multiplicitous and metamorphic suffix which is given its only surviving 'feminine' aspect by the word *vixen*. The poet is perfectly aware of this, I think. He perhaps sees these marginalia as part and parcel of the ironic effect, and therefore by no means as exegesis. The idea is probably to bring us back to the dangerous ambiguities and multiplicities of language which surround the anti-heroine to whom we are imminently to be introduced.

I felt old. My tongue lolled thickly against unwashed teeth, which were aching to drop out. My skin hung heavy from my face, reminding me of Hannah's velvet curtains: the sunlight on my right cheek only penetrating through the slight gap of my mouth, which tired facial muscles seemed incapable of keeping shut. My joints stiffened & my lungs rasped.

There were moves afoot at the time (there probably still are) to cash in on the film adaptations of the Lord of the Rings by getting this walkway from Solihull Lodge to the Ackers renamed 'The Shire Country Park'. Something that soon appears ridiculous as you approach the brickworks at Sparkhill with a hangover. Try getting kids from Dorset or Herefordshire to think of all that celtic-twilight incidental music & the uber-teletubbies film-set as they trudge past the backs of the grey prefab hangars at Tyesley Industrial Estate. What the good folk of Hall Green seem to be ignoring — if their forgotten little corner of Middle Earth is supposed to be the Shire: the idyllic 'tiny hamlet of Sarehole' the Tolkien Society keep going on about, (with Moseley Bog as the Old Forest) whilst Mordor is to be found in the furnaces of the sooty industrial heartland of Birmingham — is that it only takes a gentle ten minute shuffle for an old rough-sleeper to get from one place to the other, & it always has done. Not much of a quest that. The 'tiny hamlet of Sarehole' was part of Birmingham well before that Jacobite South African rolled up like a peripatetic wizard with a head full of fantasy fireworks. Every willow, waterway & 'bit of garden' belonging to a local Gaffer Gamgees owes its very existence to the infernal forges of Birmingham Industry.

Nevertheless, as we approached the embankment of the Grand Union Canal, & climbed steadily up towards the towpath, I couldn't shake the thought of the old tramp skipping about in an amdram puck outfit as Tom Bombadil, reciting that godawful Tolkien doggerel in some not-so-rare deleted scene on a special edition DVD. He reached the top, with me halfway up the bank, & shuffled on past the dry ski-slope towards town.

It seems hard to believe now, but it wasn't until we got to the top of the Camp Hill locks & I watched him scuffing along the cobbles of the narrow-walled walkway up to the black & white cast iron bridge at Bordesley Junction that I remembered Amrit Singh. I was still amusing myself with the idea of this old tramp as Tom Bombadil traipsing blithely on against the backdrop of a redbrick factory wall almost entirely covered with three or four generations of multilingual graffiti, when it dawned on me... This was Singh's Zomby.

I stopped in my tracks, trying to shake off my own dullness.

He had come from the direction of Moseley Bog & was walking silently around the Birmingham Canal Navigations, just like Singh's tramp. What's more, the ironic image of Tom Bombadil was Singh's. I hadn't thought it up myself, I must have read it a couple of days ago in one of the versions of 'Unfencing Theory' I'd unearthed.

I'd always assumed Singh made up his tramp. I never thought he was a real person, just a symbol of something. Or a ghost, perhaps. I genuinely shivered as I said that to myself.

A ghost.

(Apologies for waxwing lyrical.
    I really don't know what came over me.
I promise to be more satirical
    From here on in. £at's how it's meant to be.
Don't worry, it'd take a miracle
    To make me stick to writing 'poetry.'
I won't conform to prim poetic taste
If all £at means is being po(et)-faced.

60.1 *waxwing lyrical*: 'Waxing lyrical'. Anyone who has spent time in archives of manuscripts, examining the work of C16th and C17th scribes (or even reading the increasingly shoddy work of modern students) will recognize the syllabic repetition of the first letter of a word as one of the most common orthographic errors. The phrase is still rather dubious however. I assume it to be used by analogy to the growing moon and in reference to a blooming or strengthening of intense poetic diction. There is also a simultaneous strand of the usual negative, tawdry symbolism. Employing a painterly metaphor, one can refer to *purple prose* as 'laying it on thick' or 'with a trowel', an action which seems very similar to another denotation for *waxing*: the daubing of depilatory wax on the hirsute limbs of a female impersonator.

    The bird, *Bombycilla garrulous* is famous for being a pretentious chatterer and also a herald of cold weather and bad tidings. In French it is *jaseur*, which also means 'a pompous, verbose critic', after its incessant and over-elaborate chirruping. In Dutch it is *pestvoegel* 'the plague-bird' being the leader of the migrators from Siberia which fly before the blizzards like the flagships of an invading Slavic winter. For once, however, despite the obvious preoccupation with Aristophanes, I think it might be a little far-fetched to argue that the poet intends this error. Allusions to Icarus are certainly beyond the realms of possibility.

    *   *   *

Over the next few days the spread of this lichen, *this* vagabond-flesh, *over the entire surface of my limbs and torso was accompanied by a burgeoning unrest in my alimentary canal. As my skin became hard and rough and almost entirely senseless, my guts growled and rumbled. My diet had not changed. I still ate the same kinds of leftovers from the common room as I had done throughout the preceding six or seven months: cold beef and potatoes, the bonier flakes of cod set in congealed lumps of parsley sauce, dry scraps of roly-poly left because they had never come into contact with the jam, the odd stale muffin or two, sometimes a bit of shredded lettuce and slice of semi-ripe tomato. Nevertheless, my intestines now seemed to have turned into an orgiastic nest of dragons.*

I began to fart. It was not just the usual increase in sporadic releases of trapped wind that everybody suffers now and then, but a seemingly interminable exodus of angry flatulence that struggled out of me with all the force of a vast litter of pigs fighting to be born, filling this little room with noxious, brooding gases.

    *   *   *

I was spelling the word 'horripilation' out to myself (probably wrongly — I suppose as a way of stopping it from happening) when a cyclist in bright red lycra & yellow wraparounds dismounted on the other side of the bridge & waited for the tramp to cross, acknowledging the older man politely between deep gulps of air before he wheeled his racer up & over it. He hadn't noticed me cowering in the dim corridor of sooty brick beyond the bridge's hump, but had, quite obviously, seen the tramp. He didn't seem at all disturbed by this.

So not a ghost then... or not a ghost except in Singh's imagination. & for Singh this tramp was no average ghost, not a remnant of the past floating in the suddenly becalmed river of the present, but a beacon of hope sent back to lead the people of a frozen time (frozen in fantasies of the lost glory of a past that never existed) downstream towards the delta of a truly glorious future. This derelict old man, with his desperately unfashionable trainers tied up with garden string & his ironic Wolverhampton Wanderers woolly hat, was Marx's *Gespenst des Kommunismus*: troubling only to those who resist the fate it represents.

I set off again, almost scuttling the cyclist over the side, as he swung his left leg up above the saddle & I loomed out of the shadow beside the entrance to the bridge. The tramp went down the Saltley Cut, carefully placing his soles down on the sloping cobbles so the string around his left foot fit in between them as he went.

If Singh's idea was ingenious it was only because it *was* so utterly absurd. It took more than a simple leap of the imagination to cast this broken figure, shambling in & out of the chilly shade of the bridges that strap down the Birmingham & Warwick Canal, as the spirit of human progress & potential. He was patently a man whose life was behind him & who was resigned to spending what remained of it going nowhere in particular, achieving nothing whatsoever. This was no utopian *flaneur*. The fact that Singh was capable of walking the way I was (both in the footsteps of the tramp & very probably in this same rhythmic, imitative fashion) & hypnotising himself into the opposite of melancholic nostalgia — a dream of what Walter Benjamin would call *messianic time* (the ongoing progress of the irresistible & infinite perfectibility of humanity) — was proof either of Singh's genius or his utter madness.

It was ridiculous, of course, like Hannah said it was: offensive even. To watch this poor old sod wandering aimlessly past the sunbleached beer-cans behind the aluminium fence rammed deep amongst the roots of the shrub-grass along the sidings & to think of the generalisms of social democracy & the human mind — rather than (say) where is his next meal coming from? or how does he stay warm at night? or what can I do to stop this happening to anyone I know? — was precisely what was wrong with arty-farty left-wing theorists like Amrit Singh... like me. Even Beckett had realised that.

It was strangely compelling though. You had to hand it to him. I replayed Hannah's words in my mind — *there's nothing in the least bit admirable about a man who can't even be trusted to watch a child for five minutes*. I wanted her to be wrong, but I was also thinking this meant I should offer to babysit some time. A thought that was at least as terrifying as anything to do with ghosts. I couldn't be sure *I* could be trusted to watch a child for five minutes either.

                    61

>   And as regards £is €ing about £e fox,
>   I €ink I $ould point out I'm not obsessed
>   Wi£ hunting. If our 'noble' chamber blocks
>   £e bill to stop po$ bugle-blowers dressed
>   As redcoats chasing animals across
>   £eir territory, so what? £ey're just a pest.
>   Fox-hunters make us €ink £e 'countryside'
>   Is just where tally-ho-ing cunts reside,

---

61 We are, I think, to take it that fox hunting has been made illegal by Act of Parliament. When so many other, infinitely more bestial, activities seem not only to be quite legal but also societally condoned, one must assume this to have been an act of pure class-hatred on the part of the market traders and mechanics who no doubt make up the majority of MPs in this brummagem future, and who (having nothing better to do because they are, in all other respects, anarchists and eschew all moral and societal intervention by governments) are attempting to take even the simplest pastimes away from the traditional, rural folk who they despise. Think of the Rump Parliament…

There is also a hint of metropolitan sexual deviancy in this sentiment. Effeminacy has inculcated itself amongst a certain type of 'artistic' male in London since the days of Oscar Wilde and Conan Doyle. These sensitive types have always been squeamish when it comes to killing animals: a sensitivity which they seem perfectly capable of circumnavigating when it comes to wearing fur. Wilde himself, having nothing like the knowledge of ancient English traditions that he flamboyantly displayed in his clothing, described fox hunting as 'The unspeakable in pursuit of the uneatable.'

The idea has just struck me that London need not have anything to do with it. There is no reason to assume Britain has the same legislative or executive constitution in this future as it has today. Westminster may have no jurisdiction here. Perhaps Birmingham has long since declared itself an independent republic or an anarchist commune; perhaps the 'war' for independence from Great Britain is continuing as the events unfold; the characters' actions being much more easily understood if only we could interpolate their attitudes to this situation and their potential roles in the conflict. There are no direct references to any war or alternative political establishment, but the underlying echoes of battles between Birmingham and the Crown, and of the unfettered anarchism of the city, cannot be ignored. I shall certainly need to give this hypothesis some thought.

VAUXHALL

I gave up watching the tramp as I considered this. I sighed hungover sighs. I suppose I assumed he would carry on to Spaghetti Junction the way Singh's tramp always had. When I finally dredged my gaze out of the glassy green canal water & my thoughts from the overfamiliar embraces of self-loathing, it was to see nobody at all in front of me. I turned & looked behind. I'd just emerged from a dank, wide road-bridge: no. 107, said an iron plaque. The tramp was nowhere to be seen: either in the shade of the bridge or beyond. Half-way up a set of locks, which I had no memory of passing, the only humanity visible was the top half of a middle-aged woman in a rather keen looking Gore-Tex anorak & a red silk scarf who was fitting a windlass in the paddle spindle of the gate.

A large truck trundled over the bridge. I ran up the steps towards the road & looked along the pavement. There was nobody on foot, just cars & lorries. I squinted through the traffic, still only half above the level of the street myself, desperately scanning the other side of the road from right to left like Luke Skywalker searching the Tatooine horizon with his binoculars for the two missing droids. What a prat. How could I lose an old man with a top speed less than half what C3P0 could muster with a Jawa on his (camp brass) tail?

I climbed all the way up to the street & finally caught sight of him again, emerging from behind a bus beyond the bridge over the Rea. I hovered on the edge of the kerb, waiting for a break in the persistent, pungent rumble of delivery vans, & watched him disappear slowly down the staircase into Duddeston Station. I could see there was a train coming, so I ran.

By the time I'd drum-rolled down the steps & rallentandoed onto the platform, the train was pulling off towards Curzon Street. I slumped into a plastic bench, breathing heavily & throwing back my head. I was desperately unfit. As the back end of the train chugged off & my chin lolled back towards my chest, I saw the tramp on the opposite platform staring straight back at me.

I looked away again. Danielle Steele had a new one out, I read (or someone of the sort). It had one of those pseudo-handwritten title-headers that are so effusively calligraphic that they're virtually impossible to read. I remember thinking it was a shame they didn't put the contents in that kind of font. Or maybe they did. I wouldn't have known.

I glanced back. I've never been able to look a person in the eye for long. Not properly. I was actually unbeatable at those staring competitions you have as a little kid because I used to make my eyes go out of focus — not cross-eyed or anything, just totally relaxed, so that I only saw the blurry outline of a human being there in front of me — something that presumably made me look so gormless that the stoniest opponent couldn't help but crack. But then I wasn't looking.

He was staring straight at me. Or... maybe... he was staring at where I would have been if anybody else was ever visible to him. Maybe they weren't. Maybe Singh was right: this tramp inhabited some other, better world that didn't have me in it. If he did, it was a world in which you could sit on a railway station platform & piss yourself.

But, frankly, how could tally-ho defiance
  Of Parliament be €ought of as a top
Priority? Except, I guess, compliance
  Could motivate us all to put a stop
To landlords and £e Countryside Alliance
  Who try to cream us wi£ £e riding crop.
Because we'll never manage while we're smitten
By all £e feudal trappings of 'Great Britain'.)

62.7 *smitten*: The reliteralisation of this metaphor makes me flinch. The verb *to smite* could have come straight out of the King James Old Testament, but the tendency in contemporary English is to restrict the word's use to the past-participle metaphor meaning 'love-struck'. The persona insists, however, on the *riding crop* as the most salient of the *feudal trappings* and therefore brings us back from *smitten* to *smite*. This is the anti-Episcopalian hatred of the TV-voice infecting the metaphoric undertow of the stanza. As a rather Miltonic gesture, it is championing the proto-communist egalitarianism of industrial capitalism and likening the traditional deference to (or *smittenness with*) aristocracy and sovereignty amongst the unpoliticized peasantry to idolatry. Within this ideology, the only figure allowed to *smite* is God, between whom and the puritan individualist no man shall come. The *riding crop* is therefore depicted as a cheap, idolatrous imitation of the holy thunderbolt.

Crop also carries obvious agricultural overtones which allow it to reap an allegorical harvest from the traditional political divide between town and country. Remember, for example, the importance of the Corn Laws in the creation of the modern Conservative Party. Further evidence of this castigation of the putatively feudal aristocracy and its proponents, is the word *trapping*, which, (before it was generalized to mean any surface adornment denoting status) was originally a decorative *caparison* covering a horse's saddle, and therefore a natural partner to the *crop*. It also has its own obvious hunting connotations.

*   *   *

Then, inevitably perhaps (it seems inevitable now), one afternoon as the sun began to sink over the gatehouse, I burped: not a loud, rasping belch; it was more like an isolated little hiccough, and yet a long, bright yellow tongue of flame flickered out from between my lips to dab a disc of soot onto the window-pane. It happened again: more forcefully this time, more like vomiting a hot, purple cone of fire. Next my nose and ears began to act like Bunsen burners and, eventually, the fire grew up through all the cracks in my desiccated skin like dandelions in a pavement.

This is not only a fire in my *room, and* my *fire; this fire is* me. *If I thought it would do us any good, I might apologize for this. It could make no difference though. I no longer have a will. I have become nothing but the performative function of a diabolical future which speaks itself into existence in a fiery voice...*

*   *   *

The tramp stared at the place I should have occupied, like a newly elected Pope practising his beatific gaze, & a patch on the left leg of his acrylic trousers began to darken. The opening that stood out slightly from his yellow ankle — despite elastication — dribbled liquid into his trainer... an exposed gutter pipe in a summer shower. Without making the slightest adjustment of his expression, or to the angle of his head, or shoulders, or revealing any other indication of a change in physical state beyond the puddle of urine spreading out from his left foot, he began to sing: *Marta! Marta! tu sparisti...* An operatic aria in misheard Italian belting out from the near motionless diaphragm of a ventriloquist Caruso.

This isn't something you can look at for too long in real life. If it'd been a Dennis Potter drama, I'd have found it entertaining, but in the cold light of a summer morning, on the platform of a Centro railway station, it was embarrassing in the extreme. Hannah was quite right. This was a mad old alcoholic, waiting to die. I looked anywhere but at my micturating tormentor, praying some station master would emerge through one of the unmarked doors & shoo him off.

No-one came. I counted the pillars holding up the station roof, entirely numberlessly. His voice toppled over the cadences, fleeing before the onrush of incomprehensible Italian in exactly the same way I wished his body would collapse onto the tracks before an oncoming train. For his own sake as much as mine, I thought... but that just wasn't true.

I read everything I could: adverts for broadband, bathroom suites, Sunny D, the Territorials. This was degrading. Even more degrading for me in my inability to witness it — plunging into any kind of text I could find, however mindless, just so as I didn't have to wrench my eyes back there — than it ever could have been for him... even if I'd filmed him doing it & put it on the internet. I resorted to the graffiti on the sidings. Perhaps this was the real reason people read so much. It was just a way of avoiding looking at those around us for fear of what we might discover: something terrible lurking inside them — a bladder full of urine dying to burst out; a mind struggling to contain volumes of meaningless music... one glance & we might prick its distended surface, open up the floodgates.

That's why commuters always read on the tube; it's how the tabloids keep their sales up. You convince your readers the world is full of disgusting, predatory, stupid & dishonest people they wouldn't want to look them in the eye & you give them something disgusting, predatory, stupid & dishonest to read as an excuse to look away. Gaze too deeply in a stranger's eyes & you'll uncover the desires of a paedophile or a fraudster.

It's obviously all about death. What the eyes of every human being contain *in the flesh* (so to speak), which no photograph or cinematic close-up or television broadcast ever could, is that single thing: the mutual awareness of one other's inevitable deaths. Even these words here, forming in our heads, are saying: *keep on reading me & you won't have to look.*

I was desperate. This was the worst thing imaginable. I would have babysat Hannah's drooling lump of pudge for weeks to get away from this. My gaze leapt on to the graffiti further up the tracks... & there it was: a single word in angular metallic spraypaint — bizarre & terrible...

ZOMBY   the tramp's piss may as well have shot out
         & hit me in the face

                    63
            "Okay, let's stop rewinding now; £e sting
                Has gone from £e effect. Let's just press play
            And pull back from £e foxes' den to swing
                £e camera up across £e River Rea.
            Let's zoom-in €rough £at window £ere and bring
                £e bedroom into $ot. £e light of day
            Is breaking €rough, so I can let you in
            To catch your first glimpse of our heroine…

63.1 *sting*: The crop has left its mark.

63.2 *press play*: One can only surmise the hyphen to have been accidentally left out of this particular American scion. There is a typical pattern involving two apparently contradictory complex verbs here: the compound *press-play* and the phrasal *pull back*. The latter, via an analogy with retreat, probably denotes the action of reducing the magnification of the scene by mechanically reducing the distance between the two lenses in the camera whilst the film is still running. This is also, I believe, 'to pan out', the opposite of the action that follows: *to zoom in*. *Press-play*, is perhaps an American sporting or military metaphor, literally meaning to push forward quickly into opposition territory (the opposite of a retreat) and thereby put them under *pressure*. In Britain we might say *press forward* or *press on*. In cinematic/televisual terms this could refer to winding the 'tape' forwards at a faster than normal speed to skip over unessential material or else create a comic effect. Obviously, however, if one wanted to create this effect in filming (rather than in projection or editing) one would have to do precisely the opposite; namely, slow the revolution of the film spool in the camera. The apparently oxymoronic action of *press-playing* and *pulling back*, is therefore revealed to be a *counter* effect: a vulgarly rapid change of scene in which the camera angle and focus are suddenly changed without filming being stopped. The poet is clearly tempting us to call out 'cut!'

63.4 *camera*: era 9

63.4 *The River Rea*: The Rea is one of the three main rivers in Birmingham; the others being The Tame and The Cole (all three of which flow North and East to join The Trent). The city's name most probably derives (though more on this below) from the Toll bridge across the Rea at Deritend which was controlled by the De Bermingham family, who diverted the river to create a moat around their estate. The standard story of Birmingham's strange rise as a new commercial and industrial city can be summarized as follows. Conrad Gill in his recent first volume *Manor and Borough to 1865* in the large two-volume *History of Birmingham* published last year by the OUP suggests the city's birth was:

> curious and unexpected, for it was an obstacle rather than an advantage to transport that brought trade to this village… In the middle ages there was traffic between Wolverhampton, West Bromwich, Walsall, Sutton, Lichfield, and Tamworth on the north side; Coleshill and Coventry on the east; Warwick, Stratford and Henley, Alcester and Droitwich, ranging from south-east to south-west; and on the west side Halesowen and Dudley. The routes between these places would keep to high ground as far as possible, but every traveller on them, in the middle of his journey, would be bound to cross the marshy valley of the River Rea… In this way the routes from all the country round converged… and most of the traffic passed through Birmingham itself, up or down the slope of Dibgeth and through the Bull Ring. So Birmingham became a 'nodal point' on these roads, a natural centre of exchange for all the district within a radius of two dozen miles.

Thus, even in the late Anglo-Saxon period, an inauspicious bog came to rival (for example) the Episcopal seats of Coventry and Lichfield as a place of exchange simply because most traders travelling between these two established cities had to meet there and queue up with many others just to ford the River Rea. When the Norman Peter De Bermingham quickly grasped the new opportunity in 1154 to buy a Market Charter for the place, and soon after (around 1166) to declare its legal transformation from a feudal village to a manorial borough, things really took off. Birmingham began to germinate into one of the new Bourgeois capitalist towns, about whose revolutionary potential Marx has such thinly veiled admiration in the *Manifesto*, that were springing up like weeds all over Europe to throttle the noble cathedral towns that still overshadowed them.

It is no coincidence that these new towns were the hotbeds both of non-conformism and new industrial technologies. Both things involve the desires of men to contain, unmediated by authority, the fires of creation in their own homes: to each man his own kingdom, and that the kingdom of (a) god. Even before Abraham Darby's invention of the coke smelting process—a curious literalisation of the 'inner light' of Quakerism—the industrial revolution was well under way in Birmingham. The first description of the town not made for tax purposes appears in John Leland's (1538) *Itinerary of Britain* (Toulmin Smith [ed.] 1908: Vol. II, pp. 96-7):

> I came through a pretty street as ever I entred, into Bermingham towne. This street... is called Dirtey. In it dwell smithes and cutlers, and there is a brooke that divideth this street from Bermingham... The beauty of Bermingham, a good markett towne in the extreame parts of Warwikshire, is one street goinge up alonge, almost from the left ripe of the brooke, up a meane hill, by the length of a quarter of a mile. I saw but one Parroch Churche in the towne. There be many smiths in the towne that use to make knives and all mannour of cuttinge tooles, and many lorimers that make bittes, and a great many naylors. Soe that a great part of the towne is maintained by smithes, who have their iron and sea-cole out of Staffordshire.

In the next century the town was to stand to the fore of an avant garde of new Puritan, industrial, commercial centres: places where the absence of any mediating authority became both an (anarchistic) end and the (anarchic) means to achieving that end, especially when it meant the inhabitants could manufacture their own swords, guns and coins. In a section on 'Birmingham Groats' from his *The Making of Birmingham* (J. L. Allday 1894, p.49), Robert K. Dent descants in typically unapologetic style on this theme:

> [Birmingham] awarded almost perfect freedom to all who chose to come. Dissenters and Quakers and heretics of all sorts were welcomed and undisturbed, so far as their religious observances were concerned. No trades unions, no trade gilds, no companies existed, and every man was free to come and go, to found or to follow or to leave a trade just as he chose. The system of apprenticeship was only partially known, and Birmingham became emphatically the town of 'free trade,' where practically no restrictions, commercial or municipal, were known.

Indeed, but the unwary traveller must remember, just like the unwary reader, that it always costs to cross the Rea. In order to enter this infernal utopia, this Brummagem Commune, this prototype America kindling in the heart of Old England like the coal at the centre of a blast furnace, you have (as it were) to pay the ferryman... the Styx, the Rea, and the Atlantic.

Section 1(b)

That tiny golden figurine was the point of light under a vast burning-glass; the vision of an uncounted multitude was narrowed down to this.

Margaret Lane, 'The Queen is Crowned',
New Statesman *Coronation Issue*, June 1953

NOTES

<pre style="text-align:center">64</pre>

£e sun leaks bright lines on £e carpet €rough
    £e tilted slats of her venetian blind;
£ey climb £e bed, approach her side, and queue
    Politely up £e slope of her behind.
Her naked contours are revealed to view—
    £e landscape of her skin like grapefruit rind;
$e'd cover up if $e was lucider,
But pin-stripes always ra£er suited her.

---

64 I can no longer belay the suspicion, which has been forming in my mind over the past few days, that everything I have written about this poem up to now has been entirely wrong. This is no satire. The distinction I have assiduously drawn between the ironic *persona* of the poem—the television continuity announcer—and the moralist poet is simply not sustainable. The tone throughout the following expository segment in the heroine's house, reveals her to be just that: a *heroine*. The poet cannot conceal his erotic addiction to this creolized and travestied Britannia, and therefore all the decadence she stands for. The relationship is somewhat analogous to that between the *Will* of Shakespeare's Sonnets 127-152 and his *dark lady*: the distillation in a complex proper noun of the poet's self-consciously tortuous desire, and the shadowy object of this desire. It is one of self-destructive lust for someone and some*thing* he knows he should not want, but also that he cannot *help* but want: in this case, as political a lust as it is sexual.

    Rather than a *dystopia*, this poem is a *libidinous* fiction: a vision of the future that intends to come into existence by convincing readers to believe it to be a genuine or desirable prediction; provoking them to act (however involuntarily) to make it come about. There is no better example of this kind of thing than Marx and Engels' *Communist Party Manifesto*. That most blood-stained of documents is framed as if it were a gothic drama: 'A spectre haunts the land of Europe,' they begin, 'the spectre of Communism'. Like necromancers, they attempt to conjure up a spirit from the past to talk into being something which, as yet, does not exist: they invoke the ghost of a Socialist future which supposedly haunts the industrialized nations as a dismal threat of revolution. It is only by convincing their readers that this shadowy presence of the *proletariat* actually exists that it can ever really be embodied. They want the *bourgeoisie* to run scared... to believe in the bogey man and engage in a 'holy witch-hunt' to root it out; in turn, they want the working-class to re-make itself into the unvanquishable hydra of the piece. Only by persuasive fiction can their demonic vision of class-hatred and class-war come to ultimate fruition.

    Something similar is at play in this poem. In place of the ghost of Socialism (in the strictest Marxist sense), the spectral vision that stalks the streets of this poetic manifesto—the Birmingham Quean—is the ghost of Anarchy. The ideology is closer to that of Proudhon than of Lenin, the Birmingham depicted more a Paris Commune than a Kremlin. This *Britannia* is a Lord of Misrule in drag, the enemy of all property and all propriety, the perverter of sex and religion, the icon of demonic amphibology; and the poet wants us to believe in her, to be enraptured by her luciferan glamour, so that we can lend her an imaginative existence and thereby sow the seed of all she stands for in the furrows she ploughs through our brains.

    I have neither the inclination nor the energy to revise my entries at present... maybe in the future. Meanwhile, I shall do my best to help the reader keep this insidious anarchism at arm's length.

64.7 *lucider*: Since childhood, unusual comparatives like this have never failed to remind me of Alice's 'curiouser and curiouser'. This one is included not only as a jocularly spooneristic rhyme with *suited her*, but also as a pun on 'Lucida'. The *Camera Lucida* is an invention which employs a lens to project a scale image of a scene onto a screen; it is therefore the ancestor of photography, cinema and television. It is alleged by the iconoclastic whisperers in certain of the more dubious Art Historical circles (homosexual and communist, no doubt) that Renascence artists used these things to create their wonderfully accurate paintings. The story goes that they simply projected the tableaux already set up in their studios directly onto canvas and then traced them. Similarly, I have heard it suggested that Giotto, who famously won the richest commission on offer to an artist in his day by providing the Pope with a perfect freehand circle he had drawn, was also a technologically assisted cheat. He had, they have attempted to insinuate, a double-hinged contraption, similar to the one now marketed to children as a toy, which allows a shape to be traced and enlarged. The idea being that he had simply drawn round a coin and the machine had done the rest.

Envy lies behind most of this disparaging rubbish. There is a clear motive to deny all gifts of God, all inherited nobility and skill. The Giotto anecdote is telling. The artist knew the pontiff would appreciate the import of this purest of submissions. This was the age of European Neo-Platonism. Giotto's ability to draw a near-perfect circle was a physical extension of his inward ability to come close to the Platonic Idea, and therefore to approach the ultimate creativity of God. The deity could offer no more precious gift to the artist, nor the artist to his patron. 'He will understand' Giotto said; and so he did. Those who seek to debunk such patent genius do so out of a desire to assert a blindly egalitarian ideology. Those who see concealed technological trickery behind all that is fine and beautifully wrought, those who can tell no difference between great craftsmanship and cheap mechanical reproduction, see Brummagem everywhere and everywhere as Brummagem.

The poet is therefore insinuating that his own *nude* is (as it were) just *painting by numbers*, but that there is no difference between this cheap imitation and the supposed *masterpieces* that it apes. In fact, he goes as far as to suggest his portrait is somehow even more authentic and more *naked* than the 'covered up' old masters, despite the fact its ugly monochrome streakiness (created by the light penetrating through the slats of the *venetian blind*—notice the overtones of Renascence manipulations of vision) makes her look as though she has a pin-striped suit painted directly onto her skin: more paradoxes, more strange transitivities of vision and more transvestism. This is the kind of anarchistic vandalism of high art that we are up against.

> About £is time, £e tits and blackbirds cheep
>> Like car-alarms and SOS ring-tones;
> £e magpies rat-a-tat and seagulls keep
>> £eir peckers up wi£ fake-orgasmic moans,
> As limp commuters groan to hear £e bleep
>> Of chirpy melodies from mobile phones.
> Like most of us, $e misses £e dawn-chorus.
> We hear £e call, but €ink it isn't for us…

65.1 It is the case, I believe, that since the Blitz a number of common birds surviving in the bombed-out areas of major cities—which include most notably Great Tits and Blackbirds—have been heard to mimic air-raid sirens in their songs. Birds known as mimics (counterfeiters, as it were) have therefore taken over the role of harbingers of doom from the traditional screech owl (barn owl) and the crow. These avian echoes of 'car-alarms and SOS ring-tones' are presumably the futuristic equivalent. The idea is to liken the poet's own voice to those of these mocking-birds. No longer is the harbinger of doom a coarse, inarticulate screecher; now it is a fake: a mechanical copier of mechanical songs.

65.3 *magpies rat-a-tat*: As well as a portentous knock at the door (like the ghost of Christmas Future), this is intended to liken the call of the magpie (something I have always thought resembled the sound made by those primitive children's toys which consist of two small wooden balls strung to a handle that describe two mirrored, ricocheting semi-circles as one clacks them up and down) to the characteristic rattle of an American *sub-machinegun*. One might surmise that *magpie*, in this anarchist *Cloudcuckooland*, has become (after the birds' colouring and their traditional association with theft) a canting word for mulatto criminals, or else *the magpies* might be the specific nickname of a multiracial gang for whom these typically indiscriminate American firearms are the weapons of choice.

Seagulls (if we are to follow this thought through) might be slang for male prostitutes (or 'rent boys'), based upon the resemblance of their dress, behaviour, sound or (one quails at the thought) their piscine stink to those ubiquitous coastal scavengers. Perhaps there is also a traditional association with sailors to be born in mind.

Tits and *blackbirds* both also come with obvious sexual and racial double-entendres. I am not suggesting all of these species are not still, simply, the birds likely to be involved in the dawn chorus of an industrial city, merely that (just as they always are in Aristophanes) their names and traditional folkloric identities act simultaneously as allegories or nicknames for the unsavoury types intent on living outside the law. Wild birds have long been symbolic of freedom; and the caged bird of unjust incarceration. It sometimes seems as if the ability to defy gravity and the ability to defy authority are more than just analogous. In this anarchist enclave of the West Midlands, as in the London of *The Beggar's Opera*, the *ladies of the night* and *the gentlemen of the road* are *as free as birds*; the incessant chatter of their guns and the repeated moans of their furtive liaisons up dank alleys are part and parcel of the early morning *birdsong*. Unlike *The Beggar's Opera*, though, this is not satire. The poet has a diabolical lust for this dark and immoral anarchist metropolis, and seeks to bring it into being.

65.4 *peckers*: Ostrich Seagull [Poet's note] The word is vulgar American slang for 'phalluses'. (See above) The comic association of bird and phallus is as old as comedy itself. *Cloudcuckooland*, as well as a toll-gate between heaven and earth, is also a kind of Sodom—a city of unfettered amoral sexuality in which the play of libidinous linguistic associations in the myriad puns is as much a mimesis in itself of the orgiastic nature of the place (so attractive to the two escapists) as it is the means by which this sexual metaphor can be revealed. It is, to be crude, a land of *cocks*.

The idiom *to keep one's pecker up*, in British English, obviously likens the nose rather than the penis to the *pecker* ('beak'), and therefore provides a simple alternative version of *to keep one's chin up*. The euphemism *beak* to mean 'phallus' is not unknown in English, though, and it is presumably this (plus a typically coarse switch to an agent-noun) which lies behind the vulgar use of *pecker* in the United States. It is probably the *woodpecker*, whose beak is definitively long and penetrative, which is the model. The insistence here on the American interpretation of the word therefore transforms a phrase which originally captured a definitive British virtue (*to keep one's pecker up* is almost synonymous with keeping *a stiff upper lip*) into something very grubby indeed: 'to maintain an erection'. This is precisely the kind of effect the entire poem is intent on pulling off. It takes the tradition of English narrative verse and gives it a Brummagem spin with the aim of completely undermining British values with a trashy, bastardized American prurience.

Peckerwood, a morphemic metathesis of *woodpecker*, is also a black American racial epithet for a white man. Whether this came before or after the phallic usage, is hard to tell. Normally I might hypothesize it was the source—phrases usually being abbreviated over time, rather than elongating—but there seems no other reason, beyond the obvious genital crudity, why the blacks would want to liken Caucasians to a kind of spoonerism *picus*.

A joke (of an entirely unfathomable sort) amongst these former slaves—a classic example of the American *one-liner*, apparently—is purported to be the following: 'A peckerwood mosies into a speakeasy and says, *Where's the bar-tender?*' What this signifies and why anyone might find it funny, I have no idea. It is probably blue and certainly couched in an obscure argot.

65.5 *limp*: Clearly emphasizes the phallic interpretation of *keep their peckers up*. 'Wood' is also, I think, Negro *jive* slang for the state of penile engorgement. As in the (barely sentient) idiom 'He got wood'.

65.6 *mobile phones*: The word *phone* is used as an abbreviation of *telephone* throughout the poem. These 'mobile phones' are, however, probably a different technological contraption to the *portable telephone*, which is so crucial to the climactic scene in the pub. Perhaps they are small *musical headphones* one can wear outside one's house to listen to 'chirpy melodies' as one walks around the city or rides in on the train. Commuters are well known for their desire to hide behind a newspaper in order to avoid interacting with anyone so early in the morning. These inventions might therefore be specifically designed to drown the sound of the city out.

In the United States this kind of 'piped' background music is apparently common in their *supermarkets* and *elevators*. So common, in fact, that they have a name for it: *muzak*. This is supposedly a hybrid (yet another) of 'music' and 'Kodak', the latter being the company responsible for providing the initial technology for its introduction into use. The idea that something as universal as music can be synthesized by (and with) a particular brand of gadgetry is very disturbing. The poem seeks to condone the encroachment of this American technology into its Brummagem society in order to destabilize traditional hierarchies and even the natural state of humanity. Presumably we are to see these *mobile phones* as individual *muzak* sets. The fact that the 'commuters' are listening to 'chirpy' sounds, in order to avoid hearing the real birds and the sounds of urban degeneration that surround them, is intended not as dystopian satire but as a demonic vision of a near *robotic* future which the poet takes a luciferan pleasure in creating.

> Like Beckham in Sam Taylor-Wood's portrait,
>   We might just stay and watch her toss and turn:
> £e sleeping body in its natural state—
>   As 'still unravished' as £e Grecian Urn.
> (£is kind of €ing is what makes Britain 'Great':
>   €ank God £e National Gallery can turn
> £e world's (self-styled) best dresser and best crosser
> Into a would-be Turner-nominated tosser.)

66.1 *Beckham... portrait* Some of the fanciful cultural references in the poem have, by this point, become entirely impenetrable. A certain alienation of the reader is no doubt deliberate on the poet's part; the desire being to mimic the dislocated response of the viewer to the culture that produced the 'Grecian Urn' (see next.) The names 'Beckham' and 'Taylor Wood' have probably been chosen for their unlikeliness as those of celebrities, recalling as they do two of the more unprepossessing and quite unremarkable Boroughs of South London. The former is particularly banal; nobody with such a name is ever likely to be famous, especially not (as seems to be the implication here) as some kind of an outré couturier.

66.4 *'still unravished'*: Notwithstanding the ambiguating tendency of the (so-called) New Criticism (about which I am decidedly equivocal), a standard reading of Keats 'Ode on a Grecian Urn', which—perhaps for reasons of decorum—ignores some of its more unpleasant ironies, still holds sway. It runs like this: the poem is, as befits an ode, an animating apostrophe, or rather a series of animating apostrophes, which allows the reader to share in the apprehension of some eternal truth garnered in reaction to this object by the hypersensitive imagination of a Romantic poet schooled in English adaptations of German philosophy and the Burkean *sublime*. Just as the object itself is somewhat paradoxical—a symbol of both fertility and death—the 'animation' is similarly paradoxical: life is breathed into a dead object by the vision of a poet, but the pastoral scene depicted on the urn does not move; the experience is not one of joyful, teeming, fecund entertainment like a Disney cartoon; instead it is conceived as an image of nature permanently frozen on the verge of consummating a ritual of fertility. Thus the immortality the urn and its pictorial inhabitants achieve comes at the necessary price of eternally 'winning near the goal'. This is as petrifying as it is diverting. And so, by becoming entangled in the complexities of address (which scholars have already spilled far too much ink in an attempt to disentangle) the reader is supposed to come to understand the poet's sudden, overwhelming apprehension of an eternal truth (of life and death) beyond the prettiness of the urn, in the same way he perceives such things beyond the surface prettiness of Keats's own neatly ornamented stanzas.

I do not mean to suggest this reading is wrong. It is perfectly adequate as a basis for further comment and has been the result of a century's careful study. What also genuinely lies beneath Keats's stanzas though is something more destructive and disturbing. As William Empson has notoriously commented, 'his desire for death and his mother has become a byword among the learned.' (*Seven Types of Ambiguity* p.20) Rather than a choric spectacle of the sensitive imagination receiving an intimation of the eternal and sublime, this poem can just as easily be read as a self-conscious expression of penetrative *thanatos* and lust. The (virginal) object which knows nothing of sex or death (having been frozen in time at a point of Edenic adolescence just before the fall) is being deliberately, satanically injected with such temporal concerns by the violating Keats: the serpent in the garden. It is particularly the phrase used by the poet here that opens up such a reading. 'Still unravished', when applied (presumably) to an urn depicting what is patently a ritual 'rape', could mean not simply *well preserved* but also *as yet inviolate*. The threat is tangible. It crosses, as it were, the bedchamber of our slumbering imaginations 'with Tarquin's *ravishing* strides'. The ambiguities of apostrophic address are designed specifically to make this possible. Can we be sure, by the end, who or what is speaking to whom? It is always possible in lyrics of this sort to imagine oneself, the reader, to be adopting both the role of the persona speaking and the object of address. Out leaks the threat. Like Milton's Satan, Keats is trying to fill us with a lust for sex and death as couched in terms of knowledge of eternal truth. More than any other of the Romantics, Keats desires to pass on (like a psychological infection) his penchant for indulging in persistent foreplay with the thought of dying. Keats wants us to take the knowledge of our own mortality like a philtre, in shuddering drafts of his concoction.

Nothing could be more Satanic. The desire of the poet of *BQ* is absolutely similar. This *libidinous* fiction of an anarchic future requires just such an arousal of existential futility in order to provoke the amorality which is its obvious prerequisite. The drag-queen is sarcastically likened to the urn, of course—s/he is a profoundly non-virginal figure. (The difficulty I am having with a choice of pronoun to attach to... *it* is symptomatic of this diabolical libido). But there is something more profound at work than irony. Keats is recalled precisely to enlist a lust to *ravish* and *be ravished* with ultimate abandon. However ironically, the naked *quean* in such a vulnerable pose is made a sacrificial offering to the empowered reader, who need only violate this fragile receptacle with his aroused imagination—bite into the forbidden fruit—to be penetrated himself with that shuddering remembrance of death.

The next stanza (67) is clearly designed to imply the reader is a lover slipping away from a clandestine sexual tryst after the ironic (anti-)climax; and the image is bound up with that of eyes turning prematurely from the sight of a corpse and the mind from the thought of animal mortality.

£e tru€'s not *written* on £e sleeping face
    But £en we can say more if we don't speak
£an we might like: each morning £ere's a trace
    Of cares, like pillow creases, on £e cheek.
We slip away from lovers to replace
    Such tender revelations wi£... mystique.
Some €ings a trespasser $ould never see;
Perhaps we should respect her privacy...

---

68 CUT But even so, the radio-alarm,
    Whose tinny chant had deejayed restless dreams
Since five when it went off, disturbs her calm
    From time to time with gospel jingle themes,
A reggae setting of the hundredth psalm
    And then Diana Ross and The Supremes,
Whilst Tannia, in her snoring psycho-drama,
Is wrapped in bindweed singing like Bananarama.

69 CUT 'You're my Venus,' mime its pouting petals,
    Dancing, 'You're my Fire, my Desire.'
Then the soft voice of the DJ settles
    In her ear, like the butterfly a
Heady scent has tempted through the nettles;
    And, to swelling harmonies of some church-choir,
Reads today's romantic song request:
A love poem, anonymous and unaddressed.

70 CUT (I must confess, I'm not sure which——*est* rhyme was best.
    So, in the interest of confession, here's the rest:
'A heartfelt plea some heartthrob's getting of his chest';
    'A blushing birthday message, gushingly expressed';
'A boyish gesture made at loverboy's behest';
    'A note to the obsession from the one obsessed';
'The kind of thing to make a single girl depressed',
'... To make you feel underdressed.' Are you impressed?)

71 CUT 'Dis one is far...', (he reads like John Agard),
    '... "De sweetest girl dat Inglan's ever known"...
"First time I saw you darlin, at the bar,
    I thought an angel had come down and flown
Me to Guyana. It was like a star
    Was shinin on you far me, and you were alone
Wid me on Gargetown beach, wid sandy feet
And all dese hummingbirds and parakeets

72 CUT "Dat hovered round and nested in your hair,
    And caught the starlight wid dem wings and lick
De nectar from your lips, without a care
    For all de jealous guys dat watch you, sick
As parrots, cause not one of dem would dare
    To kiss your mouth in case they died on your lipstick
Like gnats on flypaper. Darlin, you are
The true West Indian goddess of Great Barr."'

73 CUT In Tannia's dream, the voice came from a swan
                With paper feathers stained by nicotine
        From all the weed it smoked to keep it floating on
                The cosmos and the boating lake, between
        The water-lilies, where the moonlight shone
                Like a blancmange in soup; it drifted up, serene
        And stoned, as Jimmy Cliff began, and made her
        Listen to some crap like Carlos Castañeda:

74 CUT 'Women have these fuckin flocks of birds
                Protecting them,' it blabbered on, 'it's dark.
        They make this halo round their heads; I've heard
                Them man, its like that cage in Kings Heath Park
        With all the fuckin budgies. There's a verse
                That proves it in the Bible, man, the Gospel of St. Mark.
        "Behold! The angels spread their wings in prayer
        With all the birds of heaven as they take the air."

75 CUT 'Which means a woman's spirit is transformed
                By so-called 'death' into a bird that suits
        Her character, and off she fucks to swarm
                Around some new-born girl. She just reboots
        Her sofware and returns to her true form
                And joins the spirit-kingdom's RAF recruits.
        I tell you man, for every bird you see,
        There's thousands more in case of an emergency.

76 CUT 'A real flygirl turns into a swift,
                And if she's sweet and chirrupy, a tit
        Or something. City pigeons come from if
                She's like this skanky bitch who's mad for it,
        And picks up loads of randy cunts who sniff
                Around her constantly like fuckin flies on shit.
        A snooty cow'll come back as an owl;
        And if she's thick, a chicken or a guinea-fowl.'

77 CUT The swan went on about 'a woman's borders'
                Next, how birds protect them from attack,
        Repelling any migrants or marauders,
                Sending all the bogus claimants back,
        And putting weaker rivals to the sword as
                Quick as lightning, in accordance with the 'fact'
        That victory flows from swift decisive orders,
        And nothing wins a war like *shock and awe* does.

78 CUT 'And that's where I come in' the swan went on,
                'I'm like the mole in their intelligence;
        I'm *deep throat*, man, I'm your informant on
                The birds' manoeuvres, all the shady stunts
        They pull. I'm busy at the moment on
                This latest shit about asylum applicants,
        And I should warn you man, they're on to yer;
        They'll never let you past their fuckin frontier.'

> £e birds had long since given up £eir song
>> When Tanya's body $ivered and woke up.
> Her radio-alarm was going strong
>> However. Groping fingers found a cup
> Wi£ liquid in beside £e bed and flung
>> It at £e clock, which happily soaked up
> Its unexpected $ot of morning booze,
>> 'Can't put me off,' it said, 'or onto *snooze.*'

79.3 *radio-alarm*: In 1928 the Bulova company in the United States released the first 'clock-radio.' This was simply an alarm clock which, instead of ringing a bell at the set time, tripped a switch which in turn activated the wireless to which the clock was attached. Bulova, established by a Czech of the same name, was previously the first company in the world to advertise on the wireless and did so in the form of sponsorship of 'the time.' The announcer would say something like 'At the tone, it is 8 AM, B-U-L-O-V-A Bulova watch time.' This sponsorship continued into the early life of the 'clock-radio' and so, because the majority of owners would set the alarm to go off on the hour, Americans in the 1920s awoke increasingly often to the sound of a time announcement sponsored by the maker of the wireless set on which it was suddenly being announced. The 'clock-radio' therefore represents, for this poet, the encroachment of an Ouroborean American commerce into the metaphysics of his putative future Britain: time itself, the only constant of Einstein's physics, has become a medium for the voice of autoconsumptive American advertising and, thereby, the bulwark of anarchism.

(The inarticulacy and lexical impecunity which necessitates this particular spliced coinage is reflected in the dubious 'ingenuity' of the conjugative innovation it denotes. I will never fail to be amazed by the grotesquely amphibious environment of this poem, the generative cause of which is undoubtedly the sexual perversion of the *hermaphrodite*, employed by the anarchist poet as a revolutionary figurehead: an embodiment perhaps of dialectical materialism. This example is indicative of how important the American free market is for this poem's anarchism as a revolutionary avant-garde. It is on the back of American commercialism and media that the republicanism it propounds is to be insinuated into British culture.)

The replacement of 'clock' with 'alarm' has two effects. The first is to emphasize 'radio': a totemic Americanism, the victory of which over the British word 'wireless' the poet supports as yet another example of the deleterious effect of that culture on the intellectual territory of its (now old and frail) mother nation. The second effect is to imply the 'alarming' anachronism of the piece as a whole. The poem is a dream full of evil omens for the future. This scene, in which Britannia fails to silence the Americanized voice which regulates the hours of the day, calls to mind Julius Cæsar in his nightgown on the tempestuous morning of the ides of March. Shakespeare's infamously anachronistic penultimate exchange between Cæsar and Brutus itself recalls the prediction of Christ that Peter will deny him three times at the crowing of the cock: 'CÆSAR: What is't a Clocke? BRUTUS: *Cæsar*, 'tis strucken eight.' (II.ii.474-5)

Brutus's 'strucken' is quite rightly revealed as an anachronism. The practice of striking bells a number of times to indicate the hour of the day was not introduced until the Medieval period. The critic should beware anachronies in his own reading however. Time on the 'clock' in Shakespeare's own day carries much less of the contemporary meaning— 'the way the hands are pointing on the dial of a timepiece', and much more of the older meaning—'the last number of bells to have rung from the tower'. As such, it is a useful theatrical sound effect to indicate the passage of fictional time and orient the audience temporally in the action, and also an obvious shorthand for mortal fate with the vertiginous dimensions of the Gothic cathedral: 'Ask not for whom the bell tolls…' The point being, of course, that a single bell is repetitively sounded to represent both the hour of the day and the death of a congregation member. Something Eliot understands quite well (and probably alludes to) when he writes 'With a dead sound on the final stroke of nine' (*The Waste Land* li.68) I suggest, therefore, that the bell might actually have sounded throughout this speech heralding the entrance of the conspirators. Cæsar hears a bell striking but has been distracted by the storm and the new arrivals and wishes someone else to provide him with a count.

Brutus's response serves to remind the contemporary audience of the original meaning of 'clock'—*bell* (related to French *cloche*). It also presages the eight strikes of the conspirators' swords as, one by one, they murder Cæsar in the Capitol (at nine o'clock): the ninth of which is obviously Brutus's. The iterative striking of the bell, representing the inescapable approach of doom, also manages to mimic the iterative strokes of mortality which will end Cæsar's rule. Shakespeare is quite deliberately couching this in terms of an anachronism. This is not a joke (though an anachronistic reference to a clock might elicit knowing laughter) but rather *Shakespeare*'s intention is to make the portent of this scene, and of the play as a whole, relevant to Elizabethan society. The audience are to hear, like Eliot, Cæsar's death in the bells of London.

The allegories could therefore be allowed to resonate. Might Shakespeare be predicting the downfall of the Earl of Essex? A little far-fetched perhaps, for the actor from Warwickshire, but not so unlikely coming from an agent in Walsingham's ring of spies. Who knows what a living Christopher Marlowe, a Marlowe whose death was not *ordered* but *faked* by the head of Her Majesty's Secret Service in ~~1953~~ 1593, might have known about the plot to punish the audacity of Robert Devereux? Who better to depict the tragic censure of ambition whilst simultaneously celebrating its doomed embodiment?

It was Archie Webster whose essay in *The National Review* (Vol. 82, September 1923, pp.81-86) first propounded the theory (two years before Hotson's discovery of the dubious coroner's report into the playwright's death) that Marlowe wrote what are called *Shakespeare's Sonnets*. He concludes by hinting he has evidence that Marlowe also wrote *Othello*, *Lear* and *Hamlet*, and therefore (one presumes) much else besides. (*Richard III* and *Macbeth* I consider strong candidates.) If we are to assume these pieces (either individually or as a corpus) to be the work of just one man—something of which I do not think we can be certain—then I find this a convincing argument: much more so than the official explanation of Marlowe's 'death' or the idea that 'Shakespeare' was the work of one rather poorly educated actor from the Midlands.

My personal addition to the debate would be to suggest a focus of attention on the (real) deaths of both Marlowe and Shakespeare. The former, I suspect, actually died around 1611, having recently contributed (perhaps in a state of terminal ill health) to a reconciliatory reworking of the play that had made his name as a brash young playwright (*Dr Faustus*). The play was called *The Tempest*. This would explain, I think the oddly untimely retirement from 'writing' of the actor from Stratford. I have no concrete evidence to support this though. Yet, following his death in 1616, somebody unknown erected an enigmatic monument of a very concrete sort to "William Shakespeare":

> There is serious plagiarism on pages 193-4.
> See Bibliography, Internet Websites Cited:
> 'Farey, Peter (1999)' for full citation &
> www2.prestel.co.uk/rey/epitaph.htm
> [S.A.M.T.]

Comprising a bust and an odd piece of doggerel, the monument stands directly above the unnamed tomb of the local squire—which carries the rather dreadful epitaph: 'GOOD FREND FOR IESVS SAKE FORBEARE, / TO DIGG THE DVST ENCLOASED HEARE: / BLESTE BE Y^E MAN Y^T SPARES THES STONES, / AND CVRST BE HE Y^T MOVES MY BONES.'—in the Church of the Holy Trinity at Stratford. Despite not being quite so reminiscent of bad vaudeville, the inscription on the monument is also very strange indeed. It reads:

> STAY PASSENGER, WHY GOEST THOV BY SO FAST?
> READ IF THOV CANST, WHOM ENVIOVS DEATH HATH PLAST
> WITH IN THIS MONVMENT SHAKSPEARE: WITH WHOME,
> QUICK NATVRE DIDE: WHOSE NAME, DOTH DECK Y^S TOMBE,
> FAR MORE, THEN COST: SIEH ALL, Y^T HE HATH WRITT,
> LEAVES LIVING ART, BVT PAGE, TO SERVE HIS WITT.

The standard interpretation, achieved by a good deal of rejigging of spelling and syntax it must be said, is something like the following: 'Wait, passer-by, why do you move on so quickly? Read, if you can, [the name of he] whom envious Death has placed within this monument… Shakespeare: with whom [*for/in* whom] natural life has died, [but] whose name gives greater ornament to this tomb than any costly decoration [could] since everything he has written leaves behind a living art, which is nevertheless only this: the page, to pay testament to [or 'to keep alive'] his wit.'

The most obvious weakness of this reading is the freedom it takes in interpolating its own punctuation. A typical passage of Marlowe's own should provide some illustration as to why this is not at all a negligible interference:

> This letter, written by a friend of ours,
> Contains his death, yet bids them save his life.
> *Edwardum occidere nolite timere, bonum est*;
> Fear not to kill the king, 'tis good he die.
> But read it thus, and that's another sense:
> *Edwardum occidere nolite, timere bonum est*;
> Kill not the king, 'tis good to fear the worst.
> Unpointed as it is, thus shall it go
>
> *Edward II* (V.iv.6-16)

Similarly, there are two places where the orthography has to be substantially altered to make this reading possible: the two separate words 'with' and 'in' in the third line need to be elided to 'within' and the seemingly nonsensical word 'Sieh' in the fifth needs to be amended to 'sith'. Most importantly, however, this gloss fails entirely to explain the bizarre clause 'read if thou canst.' Surely this cannot be glossed over. It would be a very strange joke indeed that doubted the eyesight or the literacy of someone already reading it.

Something else is afoot. To be brief, I believe the epigraph contains a cipher: one that proves Marlowe to have been the most important figure behind the works attributed to (his partner) Shakespeare. It is this first pair of sentences which marks the thing out as a riddle: 'Stay passenger, why goest thov by so fast? read if thov canst, whom envivos Death hast plast with in this monvment Shakspeare' might no more synthetically be understood to mean *Wait hasty reader, why do you pass on so fast? decipher if you can whom it is that envious Death has placed in this monument alongside Shakespeare...* Only this, I believe, can readily explain 'read if thov canst'.

Here, then, is the cipher as I have decoded it... 'whose name doth deck this tomb', means not the name on the monument but the one inscribed on the grave ('tomb') beneath it, of which there is only one: Iesus, or else *Christ*; 'cost' is a synonym for the contemporary word *ley* or *lay*; and 'Sieh all' is not a spelling mistake at all but a *rebus* decodable as *he is [returned] [with] all* (or *withal*). So the answer to the riddle (*decipher if you can who it is that Death has placed in this monument alongside Shakespeare*) is *Christ + far more + ley + he is returned withal*. Which is patently: *Christofer Marley: he is returned withal.*

This is not even a very difficult riddle to disentangle. Any regular solver of the Times crossword would turn up something like the same solution as my own in minutes if only they were told they were to be encountering a puzzle. I need only quote one more passage of Marlowe's in support of my interpretation. It is, I contend, an encoded reference to the ambitious actor from the Midlands with whom Marlowe had recently agreed to form a professional relationship that would endure from the time of his own imminent (faked) death until the moment in 1611 when the pair would be forced by the death of one of the partners to quit... On hearing of Zenocrate's death, Marlowe has Tamburlaine say this to his absent wife:

> Until I die thou shalt not be interred.
> Then in as rich a tomb as Mausolus'
> We both will rest and have one epitaph
> Writ in as many several languages
> As I have conquered kingdoms with my sword.
>
> (*Tamburlaine the Great, Part 2*. II.iv)

(For 'sword' read 'pen'.) It is entirely uncontroversial, of course, to say that *Shakespeare*'s plays are haunted by the ghost of Marlowe. Most put this down to influence, but I consider his shadowy presence to be much closer at hand. The scene from *Julius Cæsar* is a good example. It is explicitly reminiscent of the final scene of *Dr Faustus*: the striking clock, the blood in the fountain, the thunder and lightning, the demonic appearance of the conspirators out of the storm. Such things are not Shakespeare alluding to, or parodying Marlowe (as might be the case in the playlet within *Hamlet*), instead they are the result of Marlowe's characteristic habit of recycling material both from the Classics and his own previous work. Marlowe—perhaps quite naturally considering his clandestine profession and his own experience of 'death'—is the consummate dramatist of foreshadowed and impending doom. His reuse of half-familiar material achieves a dreamlike poetic *déjà vu* that can provoke a genuinely uncanny response in audiences.

$e struggled to her feet, her eyes still closed,
   And slipped into a white silk dressing gown.
$e left a little $oulder-skin exposed
   On purpose as $e tied £e belt around
Her waist, light-headed as $e almost dozed
   And floated to £e ceiling-rose like down
Above a pillow-fight (or like a bird
At dawn, in fact, but Tanya hadn't heard).

Crucially, this is often given an erotic charge. The line of poetry that Marlowe has Faustus cry just before he is dragged down to hell is from Ovid's *Amores*: '*lente, lente currite noctis equi*'. 'Run slowly, slowly, you horses of the night!' This captures the idea (a romantic cliché even then one assumes) of a secret lover wanting to delay the dawn. If it were just this, Marlowe's use of it would be evidence only of his acerbic wit. Ovid is also dramatising, however, as a much more explicitly erotic metaphor, the failed attempt by Phæton to control the two horses that pulled the chariot of his father, Apollo, which carried the sun across the sky. The trope is intended to imply the tempering of sexual excitement and, thereby, delay of climax: something already present, I suggest, in the legend of an adolescent boy attempting prematurely to take on the adult, fertilising role of (universal) fatherhood. Clearly, this is a legend in the world of the gods whose analogue in the world of men is that of Icarus. As such it is a much more poignant thing for Faustus to cry out: evidence of an awareness gained through the genuine education of experience of his own *overreaching ambition* and his inability to control not just the revolutions of the orbs, but also *himself*.

It is quite typical of Marlowe that this carries with it a reflexive quality. Just like Lear booming 'blow winds, crack your cheeks', Faustus is not only *apostrophising* but literally *addressing* the horses pulling Apollo's chariot that were depicted as part of the permanent stage 'machinery' at the Globe Theatre. Thus Marlowe's consummate mimetic technique of likening the overwrought experience of the drama itself to the spiritual events depicted is extended to the very building in which the events are supposed to take place, and an almost magical equivalence takes hold between the theatre and Faustus's metaphysical and moral universe.

The number of times this thematic leitmotif recurs in *Shakespeare* is staggering. I will limit myself to two notable examples; but there are many more. The first occurs in the first act of *Romeo and Juliet*: 'Gallop apace, you fiery footed steedes, / Towards *Phoebus*' lodging,' Juliet implores in her first soliloquy, 'such a Wagoner / As *Phæton* would whip you to the west, / And bring in Cloudie night immediately' (I.i.1584-7). This is a brilliant piece of typical Marlovianism which manages, with a reversal of Ovid's worldly epigram, both to capture the naïve impatience of young love and to foreshadow the catastrophe that must (in the tragic matrix) be its inevitable result. Juliet is literally wishing away the daylight of her life.

The second is from the most overtly Marlovian of the so-called (Blackfriars) 'Romances', *Cymbeline*. The most disruptive element in this play is the character Jachimo, a stereotypical Marlowe-Machiavellian, who acts entirely anachronistically as a Renascence Italian trickster (a republican) in the court of an ancient British king who is fighting a war of independence against the Roman Empire. Like Iago, whom he implicitly recalls, Jachimo is intent on faking the infidelity of an innocent wife whose husband will be all too quick to accept the veracity of his shoddy evidence. Using the same method by which the Jew of Malta smuggled himself back behind the city walls, he hides in a trunk and emerges into Imogen's bedchamber when everyone else has gone to sleep, then delivers a characteristic soliloquy of self-conscious self-narration as he takes what he needs to evidence her putative adultery. The speech involves the usual Marlovian reflexiveness; he apostrophizes the stage-scenery and provides the lush literary ornamentation of an erotically-charged scene so characteristic of the three great epyllia: *Venus and Adonis*, *Hero and Leander*, and *The Rape of Lucrece*, as he not only speaks but actually *writes* what he sees. The speech (Act II, scene ii.) winds up as threateningly as it had begun (alluding to Tarquin) with references to Tereus and Philomel and then, as he lowers himself back in the trunk, concludes like this:

> To'th'Trunke againe, and shut the spring of it.
> Swift, swift, you Dragons of the night, that dawning
> May beare the Rauens eye: I lodge in fear,
> Though this a heauenlly Angell: ell is heere   *Clocke strikes*
> One, two, three: time, time.
>   *Exit*

This may be comic stuff, but it is ripe with foreboding of mortality and damnation, and it trails off (as does the Doctor who sold his soul for secret knowledge) into the mutterings of a semi-conscious dreamer descending into the inferno. Jachimo is Faustus (*SIEH ALL*).

   This play is at once sarcastic and disturbing in the extreme: a deliberately shaky and risible 'celebration' of the ancient history of a newly reunited nation which also makes it seem, deep in its very roots, a gruesome and uncanny place. This is the Britain of *Gorboduc*. It includes, for instance, a joke based upon the mistaken identity of a headless corpse and a phantasmogorical (anti-)masque that seems specifically designed to make a laughing-stock of James I. Zeus, an obvious regal analogue, is winched down in the middle of the demonic action as a *deus ex machina* to provide the story with its grievously unconvincing comic denouement, couched as a thinly veiled parody (in the style of oracular doggerel) of one of James's proclamations on the Union of the Crowns.

   As Swinburne's somewhat naïve label for him, 'the father of English blank verse' can only hint, Marlowe it is that lies behind the 'Satanic' (republican) tradition which stalks English poetry, coming down to us through Milton and then (as Southey knows, despite his penchant for stanzaic forms) through Byron.

   The clearest modern source for its sardonic employment in this passage of our poem is the second part of Eliot's *The Waste Land*: 'A Game of Chess.' Recent work by Dr. G. Melchiori has pointed out (*English Studies*, February 1951) that the opening 'paragraph' of quasi-Jacobean blank pentameter recalls not only (as Eliot himself explains) *Antony and Cleopatra*, Dido's banquet for Æneas in the *Æneid*, Philomel in Ovid's *Metamorphoses*, Satan's first view of Eden in *Paradise Lost*, and Middleton's *Women Beware Women*, but also (much more thoroughly, in fact, than any of these previous examples) the scene in Imogen's bedchamber. The threat of violation hangs as heavy in Eliot's opulent scene as does the awkward parody of a 'sevenbranched candelabra' suspended from the 'laquearia'. To this I would add only the very humdrum observation that this section of *The Waste Land*, just like (therefore) the ensuing passage of *BQ*, is also a parody of Belinda's toilet scene in the *Rape of the Lock*. We are straying, as have Eliot, Byron, Pope and Milton before us, into the most dangerous of poetic environments: that of *Cristofer Marley*.

$e slid £e door back on her brand-new toilet,
    Still blinking as £e dazzle of £e light
Reflected in its $een made her recoil at
    Its luminosity. It was a sight:
£e kind of bog £at makes you want to spoil it
    Wi£ a really sticky, satisfying $ite:
It had a poli$ed marble-effect bowl,
A hardwood seat, and hinges made of gold.

82.1-8 *toilet… gold*: 'The chair she sat in, like a burnished throne,' etc. (T. S. Eliot *The Waste Land* ll.77-110)

         *   *   *

It was not until I had spent three blissful terms slowly working my way through the prodigious pile of college documents that it contained, and keeping what I hoped would be an equally worthwhile diary of avian activity in the quadrant, that I was reminded of the cylinder of packing paper in the corner of my room.

This was the happiest year of my life. I had managed to annex, for my sole use, a small rarely visited corner of the college building. It had been remarkably easy to secure my privacy. Two sturdy sliding bolts fitted to the inside of the door to 666 and the one at the top of the spiral staircase meant this area was, with some ease, rendered inaccessible. To the front of each of these doors I had also screwed an enamelled tin plaque on which was embossed the word 'Maintenance'. I found these signs hanging up amongst the bootlaces and keyrings in the little cobbler's booth outside the railway station. 'Maintenance', I surmised—rather than 'No Entry', 'Ladies', 'General Office', or (to think I even considered this one) 'Fire Exit'—was the only choice available as similarly unlikely to appeal to the curiosities of students as it was to raise suspicions in the staff.

Except for once or twice when the door at the top of the staircase was tentatively rapped, and an isolated occasion on which an overimaginative student slipped an index card under the door of 666 on which was scribbled "Are you in touch with Moscow?", throughout the first three terms this simple ploy was impressively successful. I soon felt as though I were literally living in the period from which the documents all came. I could find little around me to recall contemporary society: even through the window, the gardener having the manners, the healthy vigour and the good taste, for example, not to resort to the use of a motorized lawnmower.

         *   *   *

I climbed out of my seat & wandered as casually as I could along the platform to get a better look, opening my rucksack as I went. I felt like a hunter who's just happened upon some kind of prize game in an unexpected clearing. The tramp had begun again: *Marta! tu sparisti*. He only knew one bit. I was doing my best to ignore him whilst looking as if I wasn't occupying myself with this little task purely for the reason of ignoring him.

I pulled the diary I'd been using as a notebook out of the rucksack: the diary I'm writing in now in fact. As I did, I heard a soft metallic gallop along the line. Looking to my left I saw the snub-nose of an approaching locomotive. I didn't have much time. 30 seconds maybe. I took the pen out of the inside pocket of my jacket. The thought did cross my mind that I might tear a page out of the diary, jump down onto the tracks & try to trace the tag before the train arrived, leaping out at the last minute like a silent movie hero with the love-interest swooning in my arms. I dismissed it though & set about sketching the thing.

I've never been good at drawing; the first attempt I made was useless. The second I did slightly more carefully though & it was going pretty well as the squeal of the breaking train grew closer & began to compete with the tramp's high notes. I'd reached the letter B when the train passed in front of the tag & screeched to a halt. I did the extended Y from memory, the train releasing a pneumatic hiss as its doors slid open.

I was about to finish off the tag with the swirl above the word, but my pen stopped on the page.

Silence.

I couldn't hear anything at all. The tramp had stopped singing. I glanced up without moving my neck to see him drifting slowly along the aisle inside the train on his way, presumably, to some favoured seat. I stuffed the diary back in my bag & legged it up the steps & onto the footbridge over the lines. The sound of my pounding feet slapped backwards & forwards off the stressed plastic windowpanes of the covered walkway, which had been scratched to almost total opacity, like a flurry of moths trying to escape from an aquarium... like my heart inside my chest. I felt the muscles cramp along my neck & my left shoulder. I stopped running & leant against the side. The train was already leaving. I was never going to make it. I was really *not going to make it.*

I imagined somebody from Casualty saying it. *He's not going to make it*. I crumpled against the metal wall & sucked in air. For a minute or two, I honestly thought I was going to die right there. It was a particularly insalubrious spot to choose. It was almost funny.

I actually recovered pretty quickly. It was probably just cramp down my left side. I hadn't eaten or drunk anything since the previous night's alcoholic over-exertions & I'd certainly lost a lot of minerals when I threw up. It was no great surprise I couldn't run that fast without a bit of pain & disorientation. I made my way gingerly back into the unmanned station to look for a payphone.

$e tottered in towards £e edifice,
   Unscrewed a pot of pills, picked up £e lid,
And took a seat, two aspirin and a piss.
   $e'd been afraid of toilets as a kid:
Who knew what might have lurked in £e abyss?
   £e Lampton Worm? £e Kraken? Giant squid?
£ere might be some€ing under Birmingham
£at swims up U-bends and £en up your bum.

83.6 *The Kraken*: it is Tennyson's juvenile poem of the same name which introduces this sea-monster to the English literary tradition. Floating to the surface of the poem as it does just here, it is indicative of the poet's contemporary concerns, however. The stanza is one that drifts off into a scatological version of the tendency in contemporary English 'Science Fiction' to project its vague paranoia about world politics, atomic science and space exploration onto monstrous alien beings. One writer in particular, who coincidentally also comes from Birmingham, is exemplary of this kind of thing. His name is John Wyndham and his latest book, released only this month, is called *The Kraken Wakes*. No doubt it is similar in most respects to his debut effort *The Day of the Triffids* (1951), which apparently distinguished itself only in being able to elicit, from a young female reviewer in *The Observer* (Marghanita Laski), a notice which initially deceives with its girlish enthusiasm only to display considerable brevity and wit in managing, in the space of three sentences, to turn subtly from an ingenious play on the word 'stalk' to a very serious warning indeed:

> *The Day of the Triffids* is such a very jolly and exciting piece of – I suppose one should call it science-fiction, that it recalls the great days of H. G. Wells. Mr Wyndham pictures an England in which nearly everyone has been blinded by a single act and giant vegetables of infinite malevolence stalk the land. The hero's private story is quite as good and thrilling as the broader ingenuity, and a good time can be had by any reader who likes this kind of phantasmagorical catastrophe, including those who may care to speculate on the reason for the recent appearance of so many novels based on the end of our civilisation.
>
> *The Observer* 26th August 1951

*   *   *

The autumn and winter of 1952 and the spring of 1953 hardly occurred. For me, it was 1928: the Kellogg-Briand pact was being signed, Hoover being elected US President, Zog crowned King of Albania, and Hirohito Emperor of Japan; 'The Singing Fool' was the talk of the town; women were getting the vote and competing in the Olympics; the gold standard was being maintained; and I was beginning my second, relatively untrammelled year as a Fellow of Temple. I became so submerged in the period that I would catch myself, as I worked through another wonderfully uncomplicated undergraduate summation of the Peace of Nicias or the theories of Malthus and Ricardo, unconsciously humming 'The melody lingers on' or 'We all scream for ice cream'.

*   *   *

The thing was, as I'd sat against the riveted panelling of the bridge, imagining myself into the first stages of cardiac infarction, limbs in spasmodic freefall, all I could think of was Hannah's phone number. I kept repeating it myself. I'm not so sure I could've remembered my own name if a member of the Emergency Services had asked me for it; but I still remembered that. I seemed determined to make that featureless set of digits my last words. As I got a grip of myself again, I made a mental note to buy a mobile phone. I'd always resisted them before, considering any form of telephone an invasion of my privacy, let alone one I was meant to carry round with me all the time. But if I'd had one that day, with a built in camera, I could've photographed the Zomby tag & sent it straight to her. If I'd genuinely been on the brink of death I could have dialled 999. &, most importantly, if I'd had her number in my phone, I would never have needed to commit it to memory in the first place.

Hannah wasn't in... or wasn't answering. *Hi* her voice said on the tape, *you're through to Hannah's* — she sounded slightly weary like she was fed up of repeating this unimaginative greeting to all & sundry — *leave us a message, thanks.*

"Hi..." *beep beep.* I put my twenty pee in the slot: "Hi, Hannah... sorry... I'm still in Birmingham. Well, of course I am... but I'm leaving today. My train's about 2 o'clock. Listen, we need to talk. Are you there?... I'm really sorry about last night; that was embarrassing. The thing is... well, there's something else. I've found something I think you'd be interested in... Shit, what time is it? You're probably still in bed. It isn't eight o'clock yet. I hope I haven't woken Sammy up... I'll try again later. Or I'll email you from Glasgow. Sorry, Hannah..." *click.*

I caught the next train into town & then the bus back to my mom & dad's. The front door was already open when I got there. I went straight upstairs & got into bed without letting anybody know I was there. (Though they never realised I hadn't come back late the night before. I don't normally forget my keys.) After an hour or so of lying sleeplessly on my back, listening out for stamping cats, with the image of that tag in Duddeston Station burning a headache into the back of my eyes, I swung my legs out of the bed & began to stuff my things into the rucksack. There was no way I could sleep. There was something I would have to do before I went back up to Glasgow.

I had a shower then skipped downstairs with my rucksack on as airily as possible & said my goodbyes to my parents. They were already in the garden. It had turned into a lovely morning. I told them I didn't have time for breakfast because my train was at 10 but I *did* still have time to catch the bus, so there was no need to offer me a lift. I'd just get a glass of water on the way out. They were busy weeding or pruning or whatever anyway.

Instead of going straight to New Street I took a detour via the University. My train was actually not until 13:57; there was a good 4 hours before it left. Until this morning I'd only been interested in doing the minimum necessary to look for Singh. I'd really had no interest in him. Now things were different. Looking for his computer (or at least some files or disks) had mutated from being something I might never get around to, into something I couldn't even imagine putting off until the next time I came down to Birmingham.

$e dabbed herself wi£ lilac toilet roll,
   Stood up, and $ivered as $e pulled £e chain.
$e ambled over to £e sink and stole
   A quick look in £e mirror. Once £e pain
Had eased of finding such a sorry soul
   Inspecting her, $e managed to regain
A smidgen of composure and imagine
£e kind of face whose features are all matching.

84.1 *lilac toilet roll*: One presumes this to refer to toilet paper which has been impregnated with lilac perfume: an iconic extravagance which is rumoured to have been supplied by the landowners of the Languedoc to the court of Louis XIV. It seems a particularly sensitive insertion in the context; ours is a country emerging only now from postwar rationing and habituated to barely absorbent grey rolls of institutional grease-proof paper. The poet also intends to keep up the scatological literalisation of the word 'toilet' in his version of the *toilet scenes* from *The Waste Land* and *The Rape of the Lock* by bringing the fragrant opulence of the Elizabethan epyllion, with which these poems have been doused, into direct proximity with the paper used to wipe away our faecal remnants. Here, of course, the 'heroine' has simply urinated and is using the paper (not so much out of necessity, but as a feminine adornment) to 'dab herself'. This is an ironically coy reference to what amounts, in allusive terms, to this drag-queen Britannia wiping the end of its tainted penis on the canon of English poetry. In turn, this poet seems happy to be likened to a fox spraying his stink up the side of the Bodleian in the belief that this is somehow marking out his territory.

*   *   *

The work was methodical and repetitive. After examining and reading a new document I would record it at the front of my large triple cash book in a numbered index. This was a simple list of documents in the order they were read and then re-piled (with numerical dividers between every ten documents) in the space between the desk and windowsill. Each line of the index was split under the following column headings: index number, author, title, addressee and/or brief description of content, format *(that is: paper size, printed or handwritten etc.), and* date *(if known). I would then turn the book over and enter the record in the appropriate generic category list: 'Correspondence', 'Academic Writing', 'Administrative Documents', 'Society Ephemera', 'Publications', 'Posted Messages', 'Photographs', 'General Miscellany'; and it was in these sections that I would cross-reference any salient features. The organisational principle involved could not initially be alphabetical or chronological but was instead based on the order of the newly indexed piles. A perfectly normal cross reference in the Correspondence section might therefore be 'reply to 58 further to 177': 177 being the letter initiating correspondence but having been entered in the index after the response (being 58) because that was the order in which the two documents were read.*

*   *   *

EDGBASTON

I had everything I needed: in my pocket were the keys I'd found in Singh's desk drawer (I was sure they were for his room at University), I had some ideas already jotted down about what his network password might have been, & I had my cover-story sorted just in case — if anybody asked me, I was a close friend of Amrit Singh who used to work here & who had asked me to fetch some files & personal belongings he'd left in his old room & send them over to Uganda where he was looking for his missing father (so that he could tell him he'd become a grandfather). As tall tales went, it seemed a pretty convincing one to me. It might even (almost) have been true.

No-one stopped me though. The largest of the three keys worked on the main entrance to the building that contained the English Department. The place was deserted: not even a janitor in sight. I locked the double doors again behind me. The second key had a number stamped on it: 426. I examined the board at the bottom of the stairs & found that 426, rather unsurprisingly, was on the fourth floor. It was labelled 'English Staff Room: Teaching Assistants'. I climbed up the flights of stairs that wound around an old lift until I reached the fourth floor. Behind the fire-door that led to 426 there was a very dark narrow corridor. I hesitated before switching on the lights but decided to trust to my story. The neon tubes blinked into brilliant action a couple of seconds after my finger touched the switch, revealing a rather sterile refurbishment job with an institutional blue carpet & matching numbered doors, which various junior academics had tried to cheer up with colourful calls for papers, a Vermeer print, a photograph of W. H. Auden & a screenshot from Cousteau's *Orphée*. At the end of the corridor was room 426. No-one had tried to cheer that up with anything. The door & the notice-board beside it were covered in various class-lists, tutorial plans, bibliographies & so on. There seemed to be at least 7 or 8 members of staff who used this room during term-time. Amrit Singh wasn't one of them.

I didn't need to use the key. The door was unlocked. To the right of it, on the other side, there was a sort of corner kitchen: a sink & draining board with a kettle & cups, a fridge, a microwave... To the left was a small bookcase with nothing much in it: a few obsolete old volumes the library had discarded, back issues of the *TLS* & *The London Review of Books*, that sort of thing. The desks were at the other end of the windowless room. Three creaky looking old PCs (two of which were not properly set up) sat on laminated tables on the left hand wall. Opposite them were filing cabinets & a row of low fabric-covered sponge & metal coffee chairs. It was an airless atmosphere.

I put my bag on the chairs, not bothering with the lightswitch (there was enough light coming in from the corridor) & sat at the connected PC. It whirred slowly into life, emitting the kinds of noises you expect from a newfangled contraption in an Ealing comedy.

The blue network security box finally appeared. It was more complicated than I'd expected. It required a username as well as a password & didn't give any clue as to what this might be. I tried logging on as a guest, but it didn't work. I wasn't going to spend hours working out how they formed their IDs here. I decided to see if the third key fit any of the cabinets.

> $e raised an eyebrow like a virtuoso,
>   And pressed £e nozzle on £e foam (Gillette
> 'Cool Blue')—*kllchhhhhl*—like steaming cappuccino
>   Behind £e counter where $e sometimes ate
> When $e was tired of $opping—Café Prego.
>   £e white stuff gu$ed into her palm and set,
> Expanding in £e cupped heat of her hand
> And stiffening into a soft meringue.

85.1 *virtuoso*: This word carries etymologically encoded undertones of masculinity that lurk beneath its surface like the drag-queen's elicit member beneath the soft sheen of its silk peignoir. It is obviously an Italian nominalisation of *virtuos* from the Latin *virtus* 'virtue' 'manliness', which derives ultimately from *vir* 'man'.

    I am reminded, I think consciously, of *La Zambinella*: the castrato *virtuoso* who becomes the curious obsession of Balzac's 'Sarrasine'… 'C'était la femme avec ses peurs soudaines, ses caprices sans raison, ses troubles instinctifs, ses audaces sans causes, ses bravades et sa délicieuse finesse de sentiment.'

85.2 *nozzle*: It is beyond my comprehension why shaving soap should have a 'nozzle'—originally a jocular version of *nose* which is used these days to signify an applicator valve on a hose or pressurized container for dispensing fluids (like the Gaggia coffee machine: see below). Perhaps we are to understand the soap to be encased in some form of 'aerosol' canister capable of producing an instant lather as the gas is released. To my knowledge, this technology has only ever been employed to date by the US military in the Far East in the form of the 'bug-bomb': a portable tin of insecticide which is a convenient (if rather gratuitous) method of fumigating temporary camps during jungle warfare. A friend of newly elected Vice-President Richard Nixon, Robert H. Abplanal has, The New Scientist informs me, just invented a thing called the 'crimp-on valve' which might make it possible in the future to dispense more viscous substances in this fashion. Why one might want to force a tin to contain something as benign as soap, however, the mind boggles to imagine. Perhaps everyone has become so frightened of an imminent nuclear catastrophe that all daily necessities (though shaving soap hardly qualifies as a 'necessity') have to be kept in military-style containers to protect them from radioactive contamination.

    I assume it to be no more necessary for me to engage in the distasteful task of highlighting how masculine this linguistic environment is, considering the persistent use of the feminine pronoun in the narration, than to grapple with the phallic connotations of the word 'nozzle'.

85.2 *Gillette*: In the 1890s a travelling salesman from Chicago called King Camp Gillette, invented both the 'stamped' steel replaceable blade for the safety razor and, much more significantly, the business model known today (variously) as *the bait and hook model, the tied products model, the loss-leader* and (in honour of its original application) *the razor and blades model*. The idea exploited the entirely non-utilitarian qualities of sophistication that could be brought to products by innovative technology in order massively to increase the profit margins of its patent-holder. It was also very simple: the razors themselves were well made and sold at a loss, thus acutely undercutting the competition, but the blades were mass-produced by means of a 'stamping' process (using machines precisely equivalent to those employed in coining) and were given a series of elaborately patterned holes (each the subject of specific patents) by which they (and only they) could be attached to Gillette's razors. They were very cheaply made and designed to lose their edge quickly and therefore require extremely regular replacement. This business, in my opinion, was little more than ingenious (though sadly typical) combination of usury and coining. Gillette was simultaneously passing a kind of shoddy 'milled' currency with little intrinsic value and swindling those of modest incomes into taking out what were (in effect) very high-interest loans. Nevertheless, as a result of the prodigious financial success of this shady enterprise, Gillette is today the world leader in the sale of safety razors.

The reader will not be surprised to learn that this kind of sharp practice originated in Birmingham:

> My maſter ſoon found an opportunity of repaying himſelf for the loſs he had ſuſtained by my coming into his ſervice, and for his trouble and trifling expence in making my new dreſs. [Lacker is a publican who used to be a goldsmith and has gilded the counterfeit shilling he has been passed (the narrator) to look like a guinea.] One Chriſtian Todamite, a methodiſt, returning from Dudley to London, called at Birmingham in his way home, deſigning to lay out a ſmall ſum of money in the manufactures of that place. He put up at my maſter's houſe, who, accoring to the cuſtom of the Birmingham publicans, acquainted the tradeſmen in his intereſt of the arrival of a ſtranger: ſo that Todamite had no ſooner expreſſed his intentions of purchaſing goods, than there was a variety of all ſorts laid beofre him. He choſe what beſt pleaſed him, and among them were ſome dozens of razors.
>
> At night, taking the goods up into his chamber, in order to examine them, he approved of every thing but the razors, of which, out of ſix dozen, after having ſoaped his face, he could not find a ſingle one that would ſhave him, and was at laſt obliged to ſend for a barber, to finiſh what he hemſelf had begun. The owner of the goods, who had heard from the landlord what had paſſed, the next morning paid his compliments to Todamite: "But what am I to do with theſe razors?" continued he. "Sell them, Sir" (replied the cutler:) "theſe goods are made for ſale, not for uſe." Todamite took the hint, and bating the man one fourth of his price, deſired Lacker to give him caſh for a bank note. He took me for a guinea among the change, paid for his goods, and I and my new maſter very contentedly ſet off for London.
>
> [*The Birmingham Counterfeit* Anon. 1772: p.46-47].

The return of this Brummagem trickery and double-talk to these shores, amplified by American ambition in the form of Gillette, is the kind of thing this poet's republican hubris would support.

85.3 *steaming cappuccino*: This is probably some sort of Italian foodstuff but the poet seems to take an almost luciferan pleasure in the connotations it might carry with it of the ritual burning of a Franciscan monk.

85.5 *Café Prego*: The Italian film actress, Gina Lollabrigida opened *The Moka Espresso Bar* in Soho this year and a rash of them, with similarly ersatz Mediterranean names like *Arabica* and *Mocamba*, have sprung up like fungi downwind of its pungently 'exotic' perfume. They attract, I am led to believe, the worst kind of pseudo-intellectual jazz enthusiasts, wittering political radicals, second-rate poets, hashish nibblers and thumbers of slim volumes of Jean-Paul Sartre. (I am reminded of the Whig coffee houses.) If one were genuinely interested in coming face to face with whatever goateed zealot was the author of this piece, such places might be the natural starting point of an inquiry. He certainly supports their propagation in the provinces.

£e artwork on £e canister was dull.
  It $owed a whip of fluff just like £e one
$e'd made. £ey bo€ looked faintly comical.
  £e essence of man—odd-smelling, €ick, and, on
£e whole, unnecessary. Quizzical,
  $e tried to read £e Scandinavian
Translations: *Partavaahto*, $e pronounced it
Just like a cryptic epigram in Sanskrit,

---

86 CUT The coffee bar… The stainless steel counter:
         Streaky ghosts of spotlights glowing in it,
       Following your head. She'd shuffle round to
         Catch a glimpse of him for just a minute
       In the mirror, trying to surmount a
         Fear of revealing how embarrassing it
       Was for her to see the waitresses,
       Reflected in the stylish, glassy surfaces,

87 CUT Discussing her around the Gaggia.
         She'd sit up on a windowstool and heat
       The polished metal of its tubular
         Footrest between her flip-flops and her feet
       And tell herself she was *spectacular*.
         He'd carry on regardless, sketching on a sheet
       Of paper, pulling at a tuft of hair
       Like he was milking it, completely unaware.

88 CUT He sat there with a single can of pop
         —San Pellegrino—so he'd never need
       To buy fresh coffee when it cooled, and stop
         Whatever he was scribbling. It freed
       His cash up too; he rarely touched a drop,
         Which meant a cut-price 'day at work' was guaranteed.
       He'd also never have to choose between
       A latte and a mocha, or a range of beans.

89 CUT The woman with the second-hand fur stall
         In Oasis called things 'cappuchino' when
       She meant 'pretentious.' Like that shopping mall
         With Harvey Nichols in where businessmen
       Do lunch—*The Mailbox*—it's what she'd call
         'A bit too cowin cappuchino.' Then again
       There's no£ing much more cowin cappuchino
       Than a can of Orange Pellegrino.

90 CUT A certain captivating diligence
         Controlled the way he took his little sips.
       It lent the task a weird elegance.
         He'd hold the can with just his fingertips
       And tilt his head with it. She tried it once.
         It's sweet and bitty and it gives you sticky lips.
       It's really no£ing special, but the can's a
       Kind of gorgeous firework extravaganza.

- *stainless steel counter*. Obviously this phrase could be interpreted as meaning a fake coin, a major drawback being that stainless steel is a considerably more valuable metal than the one already used (cupronickel) to mint the (previously silver) coins it might have been used to counterfeit.

- *sketching… scribbling*. It is unclear who this character might be that Britannia sees in the mirror during her expurgated flashback to the coffee bar. He is 'sketching on a sheet of paper' (stanza 84), whatever he is 'scribbling', she cannot see it. 'Sketching' suggests figurative drawing, but 'scribbling' is a much less conscious and responsive activity: the impatient trace of internal mental activity interpolated into movements of the hand gripping the pencil, rather than any objective attempt to represent the outside world, and (crucially) a term much more often used in reference to writing.

   The reason for the lack of clarity is the graduation that occurs across this scene (as the 'heroine' comes into psychological focus) to an interior monologue or stream of consciousness style of narration. To my knowledge, this is unprecedented in extended narrative verse. There are one or two examples of this kind of mixed voice writing in Don Juan—a symptom of Byron's explicit desire to create a 'verse Tristram Shandy'—but nothing so fluid as to be so reminiscent of the writing of Virginia Woolf as this, nor fragmentary enough to read so much like a pastiche of Joyce.

   The scribbling of the 'artist' I take to be the inscription in the work of the poet's own fantastic version of himself. This is, after all, a particularly 'sketchy' scene. It is like El Greco including himself in *The Adoration of the Shepherds*. Or, rather, it is like the artistic self-obsession of the bohemian French flaneur of the C19th which finds its most lasting visual depiction in the work of Edouard Manet. The shift from 'sketching' to 'scribbling' is like the movement across that century amongst this French bohemian class from objective to impressionist and expressionist art; something closely mirrored in the burgeoning self-consciousness and introversion of writers in this culture (Balzac, Baudelaire, Flaubert, Proust, André Gide—whom one always imagines inhabiting the libertine world of Manet) which is the philosophical source of the *stream of consciousness* in English modernism.

   The poet clearly likes to think of himself as a bohemian *caféiste*, a left-wing existentialist, overtly the inheritor of this francophone tradition, and therefore wrote himself into the piece as a figure of desire for his own abhorrent creation as an act of blatant exhibitionism and self-aggrandisement.

- *Gaggia*: The 'espresso' coffee machine was invented by Italian, Achilles Gaggia in 1946 and is the ubiquitous 'futuristic' altarpiece of these new chapels of rebellious gossip. It is designed to look as much as possible like an industrial machine, but one from an age before the internal combustion engine; as if it were a Victorian's dream of how coffee would be made in the future: the kind of thing you might find aboard the Nautilus or one of the flying machines of Wells's *aviators*. As such, it is being used here specifically to recall that most famous of Birmingham inventions, the steam engine: the machine that drove the Industrial Revolution, pumping water out of mines, automating factories, driving ships and trains, and minting coins. The home of the Newcomen/Watt steam engine was, of course, the other English 'Soho': the place where Handsworth (what an ironic name) gives way to 'The Black Country'. Thus the poet manages to superimpose one Soho on another and suggest the hissing music that once accompanied the drive for progress now accompanies a slide into inevitable societal degeneration: something which he supports and it had always heralded.

> Er... *Baberskum, Raklödder*... ¿*Baberskum*?
> How was a nice-girl meant to get her gob
> Round £at? $e plonked it down and used her €umb
> To try £e texture of £e wrinkled blob.
> It bulged and split its surface. Scooping some
> $e muzzled slightly and began to daub
> Her cheeks and upper neck, her €roat and chin;
> It spread like fondant icing on her skin.

- *it freed his cash up too; he rarely touched a drop*: To continue the atmosphere of pseudo *rive gauche* café culture, this is, I think, a joke based on the French for 'cash': *le liquide*.
- *weird*: Another of the *queer* diæreses.

91.4-5 *The essence of man... unnecessary*: Obviously a distilled reversal of the previously mentioned quotation from Balzac's 'Sarrasine'. (See 85.1 *virtuoso*.) Balzac's eponymous sculptor, an explicit analogue of Pygmalion, is in search of the perfect female form and the quintessence of natural femininity. The irony being (typically French in its understated poise between shock and titillation) that he only manages to find what he is looking for in the caricaturally feminized persona of a famous castrato. Balzac's story is a bit of risqué bohemian deviance dressed up as an enquiry into the nature of art (and the art of nature), undoubtedly influenced by Byron and therefore an obvious source of interest to this poet. What he does with it here is to turn Sarrasine's moment of revelation on its head so that an even more monstrous version of *La Zambinella* expresses an everyday realisation of the 'nature' of masculinity (an entirely pejorative caricature of it) as a soft amorphous substance (rather than an elegant form in marble). This is also a direct reversal of the Aristotelian theory of human generation which states (at a time before microscopy and the discovery of ova and spermatozoa) that the female provides the substance of a new infant, as menstrual blood, and the male the form, distilled as both a blueprint and a shaping principle in semen. As the witless homoerotic sniggering in the next stanza attests, it is obviously this last substance which is the focus of the sarcastic misandry of this passage. I suppose the poet thinks it terribly dry to liken male 'sexual essence' to a substance used to lubricate the process of removing the external signs of adult masculinity.

91.8 *cryptic epigram*: (See 79.3 *radio-alarm* and missing stanza 80)

92.3 *plonked*: (See 24.7 *plonks*)

92.6 *muzzled slightly*: 'To muzzle' is presumably something like *to pull a face like a bulldog* in this context, but is obviously much more often used to mean *to put a muzzle on* i.e. *to orally restrain* or *to gag*. In this second sense there can be no gradation: a dog cannot be *slightly* muzzled. One suspects this particular canine to have a bite at least as bad as its bark.

The normal filing cabinets were having none of it, but when I tried it on the big grey one with double doors beside the bookcase, the key turned easily in the lock. There was a dull thud. The right hand door swung open. On the second shelf from the top were a couple of empty shoeboxes, a broken red desklamp, a used jiffy bag addressed to somebody other than Amrit Singh & a grimy cream-coloured telephone. There was nothing else inside the cabinet except, at the bottom — where a rectangle of the blue carpet was surrounded by the base of the plastic-coated metal frame — a bulky roll of laid parcel paper, the colour of demerera sugar, lay slightly unravelled, face down on the floor. There were no papers or computer disks. I didn't want to leave any indication of my presence & assumed the thud I'd heard when I unlocked the door had been the roll of parcel paper falling over, so I bent down to pick it up. As I did, I felt something stuck to the other side of the unrolled flap.

I lifted the whole thing out of the cabinet to get a better look. I held it in my hands & unrolled it a bit further. This was actually quite tricky. My left hand was nowhere near big enough to fit around the circumference of the roll. There was a wrinkled sheet of A4 paper stuck to the inside with a stanza of poetry printed on it, numbered 257. All around it there was a scrawl of bizarre notes & doodles in red, black & blue ink: a picture of a naked man mutating into a mandrake root, for example, & short list of words in English that contain the embedded three-letter word *era*.

I thought I recognised the handwriting. It was much messier & more frantic than I was used to, but it was very similar to Amrit Singh's. I dropped the thing instinctively like it was charged. Probably another effect of the hangover. I shook my head sharply then prodded at it with my feet to open it again, the way you might with the wing of a bird you're not quite sure is dead. I stood on the end with my left foot & kicked the roll firmly across the room with my right. It unrolled smoothly, like a red carpet with Cleopatra hiding in it, until it was stopped by a chair-leg, still much less than a tenth unravelled.

I got down on my hands & knees to get a better look. I didn't dare put the light on though, not now. This was the last moment at which I wanted anyone to find me. There was more verse on A4 sheets — four stanzas to a page — & a lot more of the barely legible, barely recognisable annotations & illustrations. The pulse was wood-blocking faster & faster in my head. I tried to calm myself down. I hadn't had a heart attack in Duddeston Station but that didn't mean I couldn't have one now. The stanzas were numbered from the early two hundred & twenties onwards. I'd obviously opened it at the end. I looked underneath & discovered that the handwriting often carried over to the other side. In fact, the only area of brown paper not covered in the rash of Singh's scribbled notes was the last two feet or so, which he'd left clean to act as camouflage when it was rolled up.

Camouflage... Without examining my decision too much — this was obviously the kind of thing a friend of Amrit Singh's had a perfect right to take — I rolled the thing back up again so that it reverted to a tight cylinder of plain brown paper, & I made room for it in my bag.

I locked the cabinet, put the wheezing computer out of its near pre-electric misery, & left.

Her fingertips left imprints in £e foam;
   £ey dabbed £eir craters in £e crescent moon
Benea€ her nose. $e grimaced like a gnome.
   Her face reminded her of some cartoon
$e'd seen on telly by Max Beerbohm:
   Half Lady, half Victorian buffoon.
$e smeared £e knobs wi£ whitestuff as $e turned
£e handle of £e tap. $e never learned.

93.3 *gnome*: It was the C16th Swiss alchemist, Phillipus Aureolus Theophrastus Bombastus von Hohenheim, who (no less ludicrously perhaps) also called himself 'Paracelsus', who introduced this fantastic creature to the world. Through some quite unfathomable blunder, he gave *gnome* as an alternative name for the *dwarves* or *pygmæi*—the spirit of the Earth (self-evidently related to the *goblins* and *nickels* of the Germanic mining tradition. See 38.2 *nickel-brass*)—in his bizarre system of elemental beings, expostulated in *Liber de nymphis, sylphis, pygmæis et salamandris et cæteribus spiritibus*. These creatures were certainly no more *gnomon*-like than any of the others (either in the vaguer sense of containing knowledge, or in either of the more specific senses of indicating a trustworthy time or a perpendicular angle as, respectively, the centrepiece of a sun-dial or a carpenter's set-square): probably much less so, as they lived underground and were supposed to be definitively mischievous.

This sense for the word was introduced relatively recently into English, however, and has been consolidated only in the last few years on the back of a proliferation of those dreadful little plaster statuettes one sees springing up like the symptoms of a surreal virus of Teutonic bad taste in the gardens of suburban England. Originally *gnome* was used to mean a sort of maxim, or aphorism: something that contains a distillation of 'knowledge'. It was Alexander Pope, of course, in the poem so crudely burlesqued here, who introduced its usage to denote the nasty German creature to the English canon—as part of the employment of a Paracelsian 'machinery' in ironic imitation of the gods of classical epic. The gnome, Umbriel, is the spirit of mischief who provides the driving principle behind the 'catastrophe' of *The Rape of the Lock*. Here is his plea to the Queen of the Nymphs:

   Hail wayward Queen! [etc…]
A Nymph there is, that all thy Pow'r disdains,
And thousands more in equal Mirth maintains.
But oh! if e'er thy *Gnome* could spoil a Grace,
Or raise a Pimple on a beauteous Face,
Like Citron-Waters Matron's Cheeks inflame,
Or change Complexions at a losing Game;
If e'er with airy Horns I planted Heads,
Or rumpled Petticoats, or tumbled Beds,
Or caus'd Suspicion when no Soul was rude,
Or discompos'd the Head-dress of a Prude,
Or e'er to costive Lap-Dog gave Disease,
Which not the Tears of brightest Eyes could ease:
Hear me, and touch *Belinda* with Chagrin;
That single Act gives half the World the Spleen.

                                  [IV.57-78]

It is quite clear that, in this poem, it the gnome itself who is putting on the guise of a grotesque Belinda.

It has not escaped my notice that a usage of this word within my own University—one that plays neatly on the false etymology—could provide some clue to the proximity of the poem's authorship. At Balliol, I'm told, they refer to anyone considered to be an outsider, especially somebody unpatriotic or *unBritish*, as a *gnome*. The standard waggish explanation of the term being 'you wouldn't gnow'm if you saw him'.

93.5 *telly*: Before it transformed into a phonetic rendering of 'Tele'—a childish and uneducated abbreviation of *Television* (see 0.1 *BTV*) which reminds me somewhat of that most numbskulled of Americanisms, *burger*—this term (particularly in the plural: *tellies*) had a brief currency in the pre-war period as an alternative to 'talkies' (cinematographic films with sound). The link was obviously the verb *to tell*. This fact is crucial to the identification of this poem's overarching *narrator* or *persona* with the continuity announcer of a commercial television station. *Telly* might also be short for *teller*: both the recounter of a story and (in the American sense) the cashier who works behind the counter of a bank—he who keeps a *tally*.

93.5 *Max Beerbohm*: This Victorian 'wit' has been enlisted to bring to the scene the following kind of 'æsthetic' double-talk as a disruption of the search for truth and honesty beneath a surface sheen of artificially applied extra value. Especially if taken without irony, as I think it has been here, this is Brummagem æsthetics at its worst: its logical extrapolation the perversions of Balzac's 'Sarrasine' and its natural bedfellow Oscar Wilde:

> And now that the use of pigments is becoming general, and most women are not so young as they are painted, it may be asked curiously how the prejudice ever came into being. Indeed, it is hard to trace folly, for that it is inconsequent, to its start; and perhaps it savours too much of reason to suggest that the prejudice was due to the trustful confusion man has made of soul and surface. Through trusting so keenly to the detection of the one by keeping watch upon the other, and by force of the thousand errors following, he has come to think of surface even as the reverse of soul. He seems to suppose that every clown beneath his paint and lip salve is moribund and knows it (though in verity, I am told, clowns are as cheerful a class of men as any other), that the fairer the fruit's rind and the more delectable its bloom, the closer are packed the ashes within it. The very jargon of the hunting-field connects cunning with a mask. And so perhaps came man's anger at the embellishment of women -- that lovely mask of enamel with its shadows of pink and tiny-penciled veins, what must lurk behind it? Of what treacherous mysteries may it not be the screen? Does not the heathen lacquer her dark face, and the harlots paint her cheeks, because sorrow has made them pale?
>
> ('A Defence of Cosmetics', in *The Works of Max Beerbohm*, 1896 pp. 110-11)

$e $ould've put it on before £e soap.
    $e often did €ings in an Irish order.
$e always *was* an out-of-sequence dope.
    $e'd switch £e kettle on, £en put cold water
On £e teabag in her favourite cup, or grope
    Around her laundry basket, where $e stored her
Damp wa$ing and her ironing toge£er,
And try (by sense of touch) to work out whe£er

94.1-4 *She should... She often did... She always* was... *She'd switch*: The phonetic effect of these repetitive lateral and dental fricatives, interspersed with the odd syncopated alveolar tap, is designed, I think, to mimic the sound of a jazz drummer using 'brushes' on a 'snare-drum'. This is commonly understood as the basis of music to accompany the exaggerated movements of a sexually attractive woman in American 'movies': perhaps a *femme fatale* in one of those inferior simulacra of *The Maltese Falcon* that have become so popular. We are to understand this particular *femme fatale* to be so mannered as to behave in this sexualized way even when doing tasks as mundane and domestic as those listed here. Her caricatural and perverted performance of femaleness continues round the clock (as if she can always be seen... perhaps she can) and her laxity in matters of domestic organisation and hygiene (which goes so far, apparently, as to mean she omits even to wash before applying cosmetics) is all part of the performance. She permanently plays the role of a shameless slattern and has the verbal music to go with it.

It is our mouths that are being enlisted to recreate these noises. I feel mine is becoming like the interior of a seedy after-hours drinking den where 'jazz-men' drawl in a smoky transatlantic argot between protracted periods of drug-induced extemporisation that always manage, like the ramblings of De Quincey, to sound the same as one another.

West Midlands University Library is open on Saturdays in the summer vacation. Of course, it's not just the 'library' nowadays. Now it's a branch of 'Information Services'. Which sounds like the official governmental title of a fascist torture squad.

I spent the rest of the day in a quiet corner behind a shelf of old Russian newspapers & Slavic periodicals, where I was pretty confident nobody would see me, pouring manically over the poem like it was one of the dead sea scrolls. I didn't bother with the handwritten stuff just yet, unless it actually appeared on the white pages of A4, assuming it all just to be Singh's elaborate working notes mixed with a bit of tasteless self-congratulatory exegesis.

The original plan was to take a look at the poem in the library, then put it back where I found it. Then I'd post the keys to Hannah from New Street with a note about where it was & what I thought she ought to do with it. But by the time I'd read the whole thing through the first time & checked my watch, it was already half past one. I'd never make my train. I didn't even want to try. I resigned myself to the obvious fact this was a day on which my train would always have just left. I was secretly quite pleased I wouldn't have to take the poem back. I started scribbling a few notes in my diary. Things like:

Amrit gay? Mixed up in something dodgy?

Saddam the Zomby? Would they know him in the pubs?

Obviously reading Butler & Queer stuff into fiction-theory... fiction & non-fiction as genders?

Nairn & republicanism somehow.

Can we call this counter theory? From Bhaskar's Critical Realism to Singh's Counter Realism: the fourth phase of dialectic as counterpoint.

Also Vonnegut, Martin Amis, Auden & Macneice, Douglas Oliver, Roy Fisher, Geoffrey Hill, John Wyndham, Nigel Kneale, Alain Robbe-Grillet, Georges Perec, Dennis Potter, Deleuze & Guattari, Marc Shell, Angela Carter, Dorris Lessing, Barthes, Derrida, Bakhtin (obviously), Nabokov (obviously), Joyce (obviously), Byron (obviously) Pope, Gay, Swift, Sterne, (all obviously), Addison, Dryden, Richardson, The Earl of Rochester, Marston, Dekker, Yeats, Pushkin, Vikram Seth, blah blah, Langland, Chaucer, Shakespeare, Marlowe, Milton, Pound, Eliot, Basil Bunting, Pablo Neruda, Fernando Pessoa, Borges, Cervantes, Donne, Marvell, Robert Tressell, Derek Wallcot, John Agard, Fred D'Aguair, Jean Binta Breeze, Al Alvarez, Simon Armitage, Webster, Germaine Greer, R. D. Laing, the (other) Romantics, Balzac, Hughes, Heaney, the Brontës, Tolkien, Muriel Spark, F. H. Bradley... etc...

Check around Hurst Street.

At ten-to two an announcement in one of those ultra-calm *countdown-to-self-destruction* voices informed me that the library would be closing in ten minutes. Not wanting to cross the cardiganed enforcers of Information Services, I rolled the poem up & shoved it down the side of my rucksack, scooping out some space for it next to a rumpled T-shirt & a plastic bag stuffed full of dirty socks. Then I wandered out.

>   £e pants were clean or not. And £is despite
>   £e fact $e didn't iron underwear,
>   (Who does?) so fre$ ones didn't have £e right
>   To even *be* £ere. Once $e found a pair
>   Of brand-new camiknickers, out of sight
>   Benea€ a ba€-towel and a Marie-Claire.
> $e'd never had a chance to wear £e €ings.
>   £ey'd langui$ed £ere for mon£s. Her earrings

95.6 *Marie Claire*: Perhaps the kind of flimsy object of silk lingerie a woman with a name like this might wear.

*   *   *

There were obviously clusters within folders which were internally organized. In this case folders carried their own index number and individual documents within a file were given a split designation: like 286:4, 286:5. The eventual intention was to hand the numbered documents and the record over to librarians who would use the index and information to reorganize the archive however they saw fit. Crucially, of course, I would insist if they were to update the index in accordance with a new system of categorisation, that they include a key of correspondences between the two systems.

It seems unlikely, I admit, but I found this whole process eminently satisfying. A moment of pure joy might be provoked merely by discovering on a list of students a name I recognized as the addressee of a letter from a tailor politely reminding his client of an unpaid bill for a three piece suit.

After a few months, my knowledge of the interweaving references in all these documents was thorough enough to give the impression I actually knew some of the characters involved. I introduced a section in the middle of the book which I simply gave the title 'people'. Here I listed, with the relevant cross references, anybody named in more than two or three different documents. Most commonly and most frequently these were members of staff: the Bursar, the Chaplain, the Provost's secretary. But it was the students I really felt I knew. I could examine their clothes and their haircuts on the photographs, but I could also imagine where they ate lunch, which of them would picnic expensively on a gingham tablecloth by the river and which would frequent a town pub to drink brown ale and mingle with undeferential locals. I knew which tapped cigarettes on cases and which sliced the ends off their cigars, which joined in with politics and which with theatre or sport, which were in love (or at least perpetual state of fickle lust) and which were only here to study. In short, I felt like one of them.

The truth is that I had been. This was not my undergraduate college (I was at St Anthony's), and my period of study was slightly earlier than the vast majority of references, so I had little expectation of finding an uncanny reference to myself, but I had been a student at the same time as a number of these bright young things and I discovered close to the termination of this period of carefree cataloguing that one of them was a rather unfortunate acquaintance about whom I had long forgotten.

*   *   *

I soon found myself trudging along the Bristol Road towards town. I hadn't eaten all day & it was after 2. I felt weak. Loaf-shaped buses — sixty-twos & sixty-threes — were swishing by so frequently, each one slapping me in the face with a baking slipstream of eddying grit, that I began to feel this might be decent training for a solo desert-crossing.

At Belgrave Middleway, I avoided using the pelican crossing at the drive-thru McDonalds for fear of being tempted by the aroma of those griddled discs of reconstituted bullock-gristle, stuck between two pads of orange wheat-foam by the adhesive properties of various shades of sweet acidic goo. In my weakened state I suspected I'd be forced to abandon a long-term militant refusal to accept that the landmark at this crossroads was anything other than the ABC cinema. Instead I scuttled over to the forecourt of Bristol Street Motors, crossing seven lanes of traffic, their roasting bumpers pawing at the tarmac like Pamplona bulls, feeling light-headed enough to imagine my skull as a cardboard take-out cup sloshing full of icy *root-beer*. I almost wished the big King Kong was still there, thirsty enough for something on the rocks to cool his sun-beaten savage breast that he'd snatch me off the central reservation with his huge black fingers & carry me to the summit of the hi-ball Rotunda, where he'd suck my fizzy brains out through a straw... sightseers buzzing round his own hot head in chartered helicopters like mosquitos, their zooming camcorders guzzling up the view.

At the synagogue I turned downhill towards Digbeth. As the concrete & the galvanised railings of the Bristol Road gave way to Victorian red brick, it dawned on me that this was precisely the area in which Singh's poem had been set — Birmingham's pink triangle; also the crucible of the city's stubbornly still-existent metalworking industry. If I carried on this way I'd come to *The White Swan* on Sherlock Street. *The White Swan* was a well-known gay pub I thought very likely to be the one on which the venue of the poem's climax had been based. I reckoned I could kill two birds with one stone: get a pint & a pub lunch & ask around a bit. I considered myself to be sufficiently grimy & harrowing in my malnourished state to be in little danger of getting cruised: not on a Saturday afternoon. My mind turned back to Derek in his dickie bow at the Shakespeare Institute for a second... Hannah grabbing my elbow from behind. Besides, I thought, any potential Dereks would soon be turned off by a lot of irritating questions about a missing poet.

It turned out to be an odd little place. As much a local boozer as a gay bar: a gay local boozer, if such a thing exists. I didn't feel comfortable enough to order any food though. It wasn't so much that I felt like an outsider, more that I thought I'd look like a particularly desperate kind of insider if I sat at a lounge table on my own with a pint of stout & plate of sausage & mash. I ordered a packet of cheese puffs & an orange juice — a combination I can't recommend weakly enough — & told the barmaid why I was there.

She wasn't at all how I imagined a barmaid in a gay pub to be. I don't think I expected a bar*maid* at all. She was *blousy*, that was the only word for it. Well what did I know about it. This was a lesbian pub too. Maybe there are some lesbians who really like a blousy barmaid.

> Would wind up snagging on a poloneck,
>> Between £e collar and a tangled sleeve,
> Because it always slipped her mind to check
>> If £ey were in before $e went to heave
> It off. $e managed frequently to wreck
>> Her tops like £at. And you would not believe
> How many pairs of trousers $e'd abused
> By wrangling £em off before her $oes.

96.1 *wind up*: This phrasal verb is a very important one that recurs on multiple occasions throughout the canto. (See: 42.8 *wind up toppling*, 165.3 *wind up in the clink*, 189.6 [cut] *wind up on her own*, 227.7 *wind up doin time*, 256.8 *wind up comforting a suicide*.) In every case it is being used primarily in the colloquial sense to refer (by means of a prediction) to a determined eventual outcome: a picturesque synonym for 'to end up' which captures the idea of the three fates *winding* the yarn of a man's life onto a spool. There are also always complex connotations, however. Here it carries a play on 'end up' and 'become entangled', which might seem benign if one were not so sensitive to the unnerving revolutionary undertones of the piece. There is a persistent desire at work to self-consciously disrupt simple denotation and, as it were, to make the senses of the words *end up entangled… they wind up winding up*. If we take 'ear-rings' as possibly punning on 'hearings' then the sentence could become a revelation of the fateful entanglements of meaning that the many occurrences of this phrase in the aural pattern of the poem could be intended, like a demonic mantra, to provoke.

Most tellingly, the phrase connotes the idea of clockwork. Where 'wind up snagging' is like a tautological pun on entanglement, 'wind up doin(g) time' (227.7) is similarly pleonastic in its play on winding a clock (an image well understood as a symbolic joke on the notion of narrative time since its use in the opening chapter of *Tristram Shandy*: see note to 29.8 *I ask ye*). The phrase occurs at such regular intervals through the canto that it seems like a reminder to the reader to wind the poem's own clockwork mechanism. Its whirring stanzas certainly seem at times to have a very stiff and mechanistic form of operation that might indeed require some winding up. The fact that the work is based on the premise of a kind of time-travel obviously makes this into a childish joke: the time machine is clockwork. But, as usual, it is a joke with very disturbing overtones; something Yeats understood quite well when he made his uncanny mechanistic bird capable of singing of things 'to come'.

Outside my office there is a small cast-iron box the size and shape of an electric plug-socket with a keyhole at its centre. The words embossed above the opening read: *NATIONAL TIME Recorder*; and below it: *St Mary Kray. Kent.* (There are some letters after 'Recorder' that I can not make out.) When I enquired as to the nature of the object a few years ago, one of the surlier youths on the Bursar's staff informed me (rather laconically it must be said) that it was probably just a thing called *a wind-up*. What it was for, and what awful fate might befall the individual in question (or indeed the nation) if one were to discover the key and turn it in the lock, he declined to say.

DIGBETH

She'd never heard of Amrit Singh, or anyone who called himself Zomby, or a dart-playing drag-queen. I felt very stupid indeed, but I had to persist. She asked a couple of the regulars at the bar, who repeated the questions in whimsical shouts to others who weren't anywhere near the bar. There were various positive results on the name Amrit Singh but these turned out to be irrelevant people: a bloke who ran a garage in Handsworth Wood, a kid someone went to school with in 1967 who used to hide sherbet lemons in his topknot.

"Zomby, with a Y" did meet with glimmers of recognition but no-one could agree on which of the several theories regarding who it might refer to was the most believable: a band, a graffiti artist, a punk from Hay Mills who carried a hamster around in his pocket, & so on. As for the dart-playing drag-queen, one trio of wags at a table by the fruit machine were so taken by the idea that they began planning a tournament there & then. No-one knew a real Britannia Spears though. Stupidly, I mentioned how the poem had been pasted on a roll of parcel paper I was carrying in my bag. That opened up the flood-gates. All the regulars wanted to take a look. The prospect of a verse novel set in their own pub (& in which they may very well have appeared themselves) was a sore temptation. I was forced to make excuses, down my orange juice & leave.

This pattern of false leads was repeated up & down Hurst Street, along Kent Street, Wrentham Street, The Horsefair & Gooch Street North. No matter the kind of establishment — traditional pubs, style bars, cafés, sleazy dives (ok, there were some I didn't have the guts to try) — the results were pretty much the same. I soon gave up asking for Amrit Singh. All the irrelevant possibilities were a distraction. I was pretty sure he wouldn't have used his real name around here anyway. I also made sure not to reveal that I was carrying the poem any more. By the time I was about an hour into my research, & fending off hypoglycaemia with constant hits of peanuts & tomato juice, people would already know I was coming. Pretty much every time I entered somewhere new I'd have to explain that, unfortunately, I didn't have the poem with me. I had to make a few promises to come back & show the infamous thing to people. Though I don't suppose anyone seriously expected me to keep them. The only thing to elicit any recognition was the name *Zomby*.

I also tried asking around at the back doors of a few die-casters & brassworks — with more of an emphasis on counterfeiting than drag or poetry though, obviously — but the fellars in those old brown shop-coats were all either too busy or too puzzled by my questions to be of any real use. I don't suppose, if they'd known anything about local counterfeiting, they'd have been likely to tell somebody like me. One old bloke with a precisely measured old-school Brummie accent did extol the educational virtues of taking your grandchildren to the Birmingham Mint, but that was it. I switched to asking if anyone else like me had come round recently asking weird questions. Aside from a few teachers cajoling teenagers into career-research, & journalists wanting information about the possible impact on them of a closure of Longbridge, no-one could remember anybody unofficial or unconnected with the industry taking more than a passing interest in their work for years.

$e spla$ed away £e soapy residue
    From skin and metal. Gingerly, $e trailed
Her fingers in £e tapwater, which grew
    Opaque and hot; it twisted as it paled.
Like waltzing in £e dark, she €ought… $e knew
    A woman down £e market who regaled
£e pub wi£ stories of her $ags; some chauffeur
Had once beguined her naked round £e sofa,

97.6 *regaled*: This is a commonplace hyperbole. The metaphorical idea of *regaling* with stories is based on the Spanish 'regalo': a banquet in somebody's honour or a gift of expensive and exotic food and drink. There seems to be some vagueness (especially in the OED) as to the etymology of the word but its use in this context enforces what seems to me a rather obvious likelihood: that it has to do with being *royally entertained* (also a standard piece of English idiomatic hyperbole). That is, despite its pronunciation, the word is less *re-galed* and more *regal-ed*. Thus sarcasm is heaped upon sarcasm by this republican anarchist poet.

97.7 *shags*: Presumably by synecdochic extension of a synonym for *beard*, this appears to be a cant term meaning 'men': the chauffeur mentioned being an example.

97.8 *sofa*: A 'lounge', from an Arabic import via Spanish. It is a better word, all things considered, than *couch* or (god forbid) *settee*. The rhyme with *chauffeur* insists on that word being an unpretentious English trochée: more the language of the 'woman down the market' than the Brummagem transatlanticism of the poet or Britannia; both of whom would be more likely to pronounce it as a pseudo-francophone iamb… and, indeed, to say *settee*.

After exhausting those two avenues, I moved on to the rag-market. It had not long-since reopened in a brand new building which matched the rest of the redeveloped Birmingham markets. No more the draughty hangar that looked as if it should have had spitfires trundling in & out of it. (*Contact!*) The place was now all frosted zinc & firedoors. Not that it made any difference. The rag market isn't a building, it's a community. You could put it in an igloo & it'd still be the rag. They say you miss a lot of a city if you don't look up. That's cobblers. You'd have to be some kind of masochistic archictecture junky to spend all your time looking up in Birmingham. You'd miss a hell of a lot more of the place if you went round examining joists & glasswork when you could be talking to people. The council are trying hard, which is nice of them. Better they spend money on this than some pretentious landmark. But it makes no real difference. The rag is the rag is the rag. At the end of the day, your non-stick frying pans are still 2.99, ladies & gents – no matter what the inflation rate (that & the price of draw), & you can still see dried pigs' ears selling cheek by jowl with Eastern European army surplus gear, rolls of sari silk, Boer war bayonets, dried hibiscus, two-tone nylon underpants & a spectrum of hand-stitched Jamaican leather hats.

I jostled my way up & down the aisles meekly interrogating stall-holders & receiving useless advice from all quarters. Nobody knew anything I hadn't already heard, & none of that more than vague speculation.

Two things became clear: there was no Britannia Spears or anyone sufficiently like her to constitute a proper lead; on the other hand, people did think they remembered seeing the name Zomby (with a Y) on billposters & flyers & considered it not beyond the realms of possibility the person referred to was a performance poet, or at the very least the vocalist in a cabaret band of the same name (or possibly both). The two venues that kept cropping up in speculative connection with this name were *The Custard Factory* & *The Pussy Club* in Hockley. If anybody was going to know, it would be at one of these.

I knew the *Custard Factory* well. I even had a friend who put shows on there from time to time. What's more, in the course of going through Amrit's files, I'd stumbled across something I remembered as an extraordinarily odd couple of pages in which he envisioned, in the form of a silent film seen on one of those early coin-operated *mutoscopes*, the history of Bird's Custard & the eventual transformation of its factory into a trendy 'arts venue' as the emblematic history of both the city of Birmingham & the entire British Empire.

I'd already planned to ask my friend about *Zomby*, & didn't need to go to the place to do it. Anyway, I was exhausted. Maybe I could check out the Pussy Club later that evening, but right now my feet hurt & I wanted to catch up on some sleep. So, instead of making the psychological leap of crossing the High Street at Deritend, by Sparky's pianos (a shop still claiming to be owned by the only living relative of William Shakespeare), I went back down the hill to a hotel I'd seen opposite the back end of the brassworks on Alcester Street, & checked myself into a room for the night.

Or so $e said. £e plug went in; a cloud
    Of steaming water filled £e sink, £e mist
Descending like a water-vapour $roud
    Across £e glass. Reluctant plumbing hissed
And spat as pipes eventually allowed
    £eir joints to swell, unable to resist.
$e stopped £e tap and used a dried-up flannel
To wipe £e drizzle off £e mirror-panel.

98.3 *shroud*: An allusion to the *Sudario* of Turin is absolutely clear. This object, supposedly the winding-sheet in which Joseph of Arimathea wrapped the body of Jesus, has been conclusively shown by French bibliographer, Ulysse Chevalier, to be (despite its superiority in terms of a certain artistic cunning) another Medieval fake (*Le St Suaire de Lirey-Chambéry-Turin et les défenseurs de son authenticité*, 1902). Its metaphoric use here is designed to suggest the clouding of the mirror to have added an extra layer of irreverent masquerade to this counterfeit Britannia by combining her image with that of a counterfeit Christ. The 'dried-up flannel' used to wipe away the 'drizzle' is a reference to the real meaning of *sudarium*: a napkin or handkerchief used to wipe sweat or tears from the face; from *sūdor* 'sweat'. This word is used to refer to the Turin/Chambéry relic by the Italians and the French (who call the thing *Le Saint Suaire*) in erroneous identification of the object with the cloth St Veronica legendarily used to wipe the sweat from the face of Christ on the road to Calvary. The mirror-image of a mirror-image of the fake Son of God is therefore supposedly imprinted on a desiccated rag. The depths to which this Brummagem blasphemy will sink apparently know no bounds.

      *   *   *

His name was Lionel Hubbard, known quite unaffectionately as 'Mother'. He was a grammar school boy from one of the sootier industrial towns of South Yorkshire: a small, ginger-headed fellow with mottled complexion (not unlike a blue cheese) which was capable of revealing every tiny variation in the bloodflow to the capillaries which his untameable emotions could provoke. His other most noticeable feature was a hunched back developed in wilful defiance of the straight-spined non-conformist posture of his education. A slight fricative lisp in his deliberately standardized pronunciation of the English language was, I think, both the result of and the cause of long, awkward pauses in his speech which made all subsequent utterances eject from the mouth with a kind of malign urgency accompanied by canine snarls of effort and an almost literal sprinkling of liquid vitriol. Mother's unaskedfor interjections into conversations were like rainclouds at an April picnic.

      *   *   *

It was a relatively posh old-fashioned kind of a hotel to occupy a block in this down-at-heel no-mans-land between the inner ring road & the Middleway. It had a brass bell on the hardwood counter, patterned carpets held in place by copper rods on all its staircases, a carvery staffed by men in tall white hats who smelled of boiled swede & vinegar, that kind of thing. The price, thankfully, was more of a reflection on the surroundings than the décor. Though perhaps a tariff in shillings & pence would have been more fitting, & still better value. I worried for a moment, as I signed the register, that they might not let me go up to my room until some ancient porter could be roused from the steamy haze of a perpetual teabreak to stagger up the stairs beneath the meagre weight of my mud-spattered rucksack.

They let me carry it myself, thank god. The room was small & bland, & quite a way *off-suite*. I immediately wrenched the sheets away from the mattress to allow enough space between them for the slimmest of human beings, then took off my coat, bag & shoes, & squeezed my socked feet & linen trousered legs into the bed. I covered my head with the blankets, rather than get up again to shut the curtains, & quickly twitched my way into unconsciousness.

I must have slept for a good four hours. It was after half past ten by the time the bright red clock on the television sharpened its gaussian blur enough to render its digits readable. I lay still, my cheek beside a patch of my own drool for a minute or two, then clambered out. I unwrapped the complimentary disc of soap & washed my face & armpits in the little corner sink, then took the rolled up poem out of my rucksack & arranged them both beneath the covers of the bed. It was like a bolster to fake a sleeping man in one of those prison-camp films that always seem to feature Richard Attenborough. Once I was happy with my work, I put on fresh (but not clean) clothes & went out on the town.

It was a warm night. The air smelled of paraffin & donuts... perhaps quite literally of paraffin-filled donuts. I made my way up into town, past the wholesale markets & the new Bull Ring. (Or, simply, 'Bull Ring' as it's known these days. They paid someone thousands just to drop the article.) The new Selfridges was slumped against the exposed structure of the shopping centre, a bellyful of churning alcopops bulging out from under its tight, glittery blue party top. The sandblasted facade of St Martin's looked naked & vulnerable, it stonework cringing at the lurid glamour of its neighbour. I moved through the High Street crowds & up on past the back of Rackhams, then across the yard of the cathedral. There was a silent order of goths congregated around the gravestone of the smallest woman in England, drinking snakebite. It's a shame for goths these days. They used to shock old ladies. Now old ladies just embarrass their forty year old daughters by saying to their grandchildren "look dear, isn't it sweet, that's what your mother looked like in the nineteen eighties."

I took the footbridge to the Jewellery Quarter & turned back uphill towards the railway arches that slouch off past the bottom of the Post Office tower behind Snow Hill Station. I knew the club was here somewhere. I'd just have to walk along beside the tracks & check each bridge. It didn't take me long to find it. The 2nd road off Livery Street descended from an old Victorian pissoir built directly in the arch towards Summer Lane & Old Snow Hill.

> And £ere $e was. At least $e would be once
> $e'd got £e decorating over: strip
> £e anaglypta (and £e evidence),
> A lick of paint, a bit of craftsman$ip
> Wi£ polyfilla and emollients,
> A steady pencil to define her lip.
> If only $e could stop her belly $owing.
> ($e needed Laurence Llewellyn Bowen.)

99.3 *anaglypta*: Embossed wallpaper of a rather tasteless sort: the kind of thing one might find behind an obtusely angled flight of three ceramic ducks on the walls of those more likely to possess a 'garden gnome' than a shotgun and the skill to use it. The word is a trade-name derived from *anaglyph*, meaning any low-relief image. The effigy of the Queen's head on a coin is a perfect example. *Anaglyph* also refers to those 3-Dimensional stereoscopic photographs one views through double coloured spectacles. There is perhaps a self-congratulatory little reference here to what one might call the *stereosemantics* of this nasty little *stereotype*.

99.5 *polyfilla*: Doubtless intended, by way of a supposedly humorous metaphor for *foundation* make-up, as a trade-name for some sort of plaster, or similar builder's material, capable of 'filling' multiple cracks. There are other, cruder sexual connotations, obviously.

There is therefore also a probable allusion to *Mr Eliot's Sunday Morning Service*: 'Polyphilo-progenitive / The sapient sutlers of the Lord / Drift across the window-panes. etc.' Eliot's is an intelligent, witty and profound effort to employ his theory of *the objective correlative* to bring together Christian theology and the modern (post-Darwinian) biology of generation. The insects drifting across the window-panes become the focus for an uncanny fecundity that creates 'superfetation of τὸ εˋ ν': a reference both to the Trinity and to biological theories of multiple fertilisation and parthenogenesis. The poet of *BQ* is extending the wilful blasphemy of the previous stanza's allusion to the Turin shroud into a vision of the 'quean' as a gruesome combination of the virgin, the child, and the sacred artist: 'A painter of the Umbrian school / Designed upon a gesso ground / The nimbus of the Baptized God' says Eliot; the absurdly-named *polyfilla* being both a version of the 'gesso' and a degenerately crude reversion of the principle of the word made flesh in Eliot's tour de force of a poetic gambit; whilst the clouded image of the transvestite in the bathroom mirror (previously envisaged as an analogue of the *Saint Suaire*) is therefore simultaneously the 'The nimbus of the Baptized God', holder (obviously) of the 'blest office of the epicene', and (*apeneck*) Sweeney who 'shifts from ham to ham.'

It is usually assumed that the 'sapient sutlers of the Lord'—aside from a possible ironic reference to angels or saints depicted in a stained-glass window—are the same creatures as 'the bees with hairy bellies.' I suppose it is perfectly sensible to suggest that bees, as 'traders' (as it were) in pollen, are like *sutlers* of war… and perhaps the implication is that, as befits 'the blest office of the epicene', they sell to both sides. This poem is clearly a list of observations though, and 'sutlers' just do not sound to me like bees. It is a word too suggestive of dirtiness, drudgery and ignobility—none of which characteristics seem at all apian—and is related to the modern German *sudeln* 'to sully'. Furthermore, I have little doubt that Eliot stumbled across the word having already decided to write about (and perhaps to cast himself as a representative of) 'The masters of the subtle schools'. If we are to imagine the word as a neologism or a nonsense agent noun—by analogy with 'scuttlers', a perfect synonym for crabs or spiders, I think—then I suggest it implies creatures that 'move subtly'. *Sutlers* are, that is, as well as 'base' and 'unclean', also 'insidious'.

I have recently come to envisage them as woodlice. One justification for this lies in the Latin name: *Oniscus asellus*. As often happens in Linnæus, this is something of a tautology; both words are diminutive forms of *ass*: the former Hellenistic Greek, the latter Latin. The ass is, of course, the traditional beast of burden of the trader: something that would have been equally as true in the C16th when the word 'sutler' was introduced into English from the Dutch as it was at the time of the Apostles (and also, obviously, *Asinus Aureus*: see 14.6 *distinguished writer*).

My room is periodically infested with these ugly, ancient little beings: the result of the encroaching damp and the piles of cardboard and filing paper in the loft above my head. I have consequently become something of an expert in their behaviour. Their movement is the apotheosis of subtlty. They 'drift' (it is the perfect word) across new unexplored surfaces dabbing with their long articulating antennæ at every inch over which their several legs are about to ripple. More tellingly, their fecundity seems to know no bounds; populations multiply in days: from straggling scouts to sheer carpets of creeping grey crustacea. They seem to have developed a particular taste for the roll of brown parcel paper on which the manuscript I am currently annotating is glued. Its surface has become pock-marked with the traces of their small, ovate corpses.

I feel no guilt at this. I regret killing most creatures, even flies and spiders, and always silently apologize as if, as the Hindus believe, they were the reincarnated souls of sinful men. For woodlice I can feel no compassion: they are pointless and unpleasant. The anarchist ideas contained within this poem have a strange affinity with these things. Where a hive of bees is an ordered, efficient and noble hierarchy that fertilizes plants and produces honey and wax—more like the angels, or at least the gardeners, than the *sutlers* of the Lord—an agglomerate mass of woodlice is more like an anarcho-syndicalist commune. They are gruesomely homogeneous; they hide beneath objects in the dark and come crawling slowly, ineluctably out of the woodwork at night to feed on only what is dead or rotten; they are seemingly ineradicable: no matter how many you crush—and they are easy to crush—there are thousands more of their mindless progeny clinging to some word that has lain like a log in the garden, accumulating generations on its rotten underbelly. Nevertheless, I am rapidly reaching the point of wanting to carry out some act of genocide against them both.

99.8 *Lawrence Llewelyn Bowen*: Perhaps a Welsh cosmetic surgeon, or else a retailer of cummerbunds or corsetry.

$e took £e razor and began to $ave.
    $e did it seriously, evenly.
From £e impression hunks on adverts gave,
    You'd €ink £eir jaws were unbelievably
Robust: £ey'd scy£e £e foam away wi£ brave
    Expansive sweeps, to $ow £e seemingly
Veneered skin: £e perfect satin $een,
As if £eir chins were made of plasticine.

100.2 *shave… seriously, evenly*: This is how 'stately, plump Buck Mulligan' shaves at the beginning of *Ulysses*. Joyce's 'stately' is typically double-edged; Mulligan is not just ironically statesmanlike, but also a sardonic symbol (deluded and dependent, to Joyce's radical eye) of the entire Irish 'state': a foolish version of a John Bull or an Uncle Sam. Britannia, in this poem, is obviously an even more sneering embodiment of a degraded nation.

It is absolutely crucial to an understanding of the insidious revolutionary approach to language taken by James Joyce—and by his imitators (amongst whom the poet of this piece should clearly be numbered)—that one should read this 'seriously' as being applied to suggest almost entirely the opposite. The seriousness and evenness of Mulligan's shaving is pointed and exaggerated for his ever-present audience like the gestural performance of a mime: otherwise it would warrant no mention; it is one of the 'turns' of a buffoon mock-statesman who has nothing to offer, even to his own fragmented reflection, beyond such empty comedy.

100.8 *hunks on adverts*: In the United States they have the equivalent of printed advertisements on their commercial television stations. These, with typical ingenuity, they call *teevee commercials*. The fact that these *hunks* can be seen carrying out an action suggests that the moving image, rather than printed artwork, is the medium of advertisement.

Hunk is either a pejorative American term for a white immigrant or Scots for a sluttish woman. The usage here is typically confusing. I can see no reason, at least, why it should have anything to do with roughly hewn or torn-off lump of bread or cheese.

HOCKLEY

Halfway along the tunnel to the left, beyond a couple of lock-ups, the blue fluorescent outline of a cat glared back at me. "A real rathole..." I thought as I approached it "... But there's one thing you've got to admit. [Full stop.] A rat always knows where his tail is. [Full stop]. But when Mark Binny went down into Skinscapes he might just as well never have learned the difference between his tail & his elbow. [Full stop.] [New paragraph.]"

The door was closed & windowless. I almost turned back, but a bouncer — who presumably had seen me on some form of CCTV as I climbed down the two or three black steps that led to it — pulled the door open as I approached. I never got a chance to break my stride. Acknowledging the perfunctory frisking of his eyes with a smile, I passed on to the ticket office, the rare-groove bass beginning to pummel at my sternum. They had one of those old-school mechanised ticket-desks behind a window. A middle-aged woman in a leather jacket & a pearl choker, formed a whimsical expression as she took my money off me & turned the handles that made the coloured slips of paper poke out of their slots. It was quite expensive. I needed two tickets: one for the club & one for the cabaret bar, the first of which was immediately taken off me again by a rather incongruous gum-chewing skinhead who held back a curtain to let me into the main dance-hall. I considered asking him about *Zomby* — or the woman at the desk, or the doorman — but none of them had the air of people who wanted to be asked a question.

"The doorman of a nightclub can always say it's lipstick & not blood on his collar."

The noise & humidity hit me like a chloroform-soaked pad, applied aggressively from behind by mobsters. That was always happening to Tintin. I swooned a little as my eyes adjusted to the dark. The club's design appeared to be based on the erotic nightmare of a Seventies' housewife. Caged pogo dancers of indeterminate gender, in body-paint & PVC & thigh-high boots took up five strategic positions around the dancefloor similar to those the snipers might adopt around the exercise yard of a Texan jail. Each one was developing his/her own idioms of suggestive contortion in almost perfect non-correspondence with the rhythms & dynamics of the DJ's nerdish electronic disco repertoire. The seating was all animal prints & sparkly plastic. There were glitter-balls. You get the idea.

It was a pretty mixed crowd, quite studenty: not really a fetish club, nor strictly gay, but there was quite a lot of risqué fancy dress — if any such thing as 'fancy dress' exists these days. A good deal of reflective makeup had been applied & there was an absolute absence of self-consciousness on the dancefloor, which thankfully did not revolve. In fact, the dancefloor was irrelevant. These people hadn't paid their money for a sit down & a chat. They were not going to let the arbitrary boundaries of a designated area restrict their freedom of gyration. Any desire they might have to test the lubrication of their pistons in the company of other pumping limbs was to be entertained wherever it occurred. There was writhing around banisters & jogging up & down the steps. There was pirouetting over tabletops & sliding in between the legs. Every surface was being danced on, every fitting used as an accessory. It was like a party in the County Jail.

£at isn't how you $ave. A proper man
    Takes care and time. $e used to watch her dad.
$e'd perch behind his arm as he began,
    And crane her neck, and fidget, till $e had
A decent view. He did it slower £an
    £e waxwork beefcakes on a $aving ad.
Each razor-stroke was like a fre$ decision;
He used it wi£ a toolmaker's precision.

101.4 *crane*: The use of *crane* as a verb probably owes more to the machine used in construction than the bird after which it was named. This simple metaphoric transference would seem to be based simply upon the similarity of appearance of the contraption and the bird. This does not explain, however, how species of the family *Gruidæ* should be chosen over other grallatorial birds with similar physical characteristics. The stork in particular is taller and has a longer beak and therefore much more closely resembles the piece of lifting apparatus. The answer lies in the attic belief that cranes—particularly weak fliers who are easily upset by even the lightest of breezes—carried rocks in their beaks as ballast when migrating across the Mediterranean to Libya. For this reason, Aristophanes cast them as the carriers and movers of the rock that made the walls of Cloudcuckooland in *The Birds*, and I would suggest it is directly from this most anarchic and profane of Ancient Greek plays (See 65.4 *peckers*) that the metaphor is taken. This is by no means the last time this influential work will make an appearance in these annotations. The notion of a separatist, anarchist Birmingham with a burlesque monarch—a utopia for all that is financially, intellectually and morally bankrupt—is an obvious analogue of Aristophanes's creation.

    This is not the end to the classical resonances though. In *Metamorphoses* VI, Ovid explains the Greek word for crane, γέρανος, (from which we get the name of the 'geranium') with the story of Gerana, the Queen of the Pygmioi in Egypt, whose hubristic vanity led Artemis and Hera to transform her into a crane as punishment. It is this legend that Homer is alluding to when he has the Trojans, in the third book of *The Iliad*, as cranes attacking the 'pygmy' Greeks; a mythological association of almost symbiotic antagonism that leads Pliny the Elder to pass on the following tittle-tattle:

> fama est insidentes arietum caprarumque dorsis armatos sagittis veris tempore universo agmine ad mare descendere et ova pullosque earum alitum consumere; ternis expeditionem eam mensibus confici; aliter futuris gregibus non resisti. casas eorum luto pinnisque et ovorum putaminibus construi.
>
> (*Natural History* VII.26)

There is a final genetic implication at work, I think. Aside from the physical reality of a child (a pygmy of sorts) stretching to approach the line of vision of someone much taller, the fact that Britannia 'cranes her neck' to watch her father at this moment of intimacy is also (metaphorically) a disturbing intimation of the perverted, possibly incestuous, masculine sexuality of this act of libidinous voyeurism. There are always, as the Aristophanic overtones of this poem never let us forget, phallic implications lurking beneath the analogical surface of such tall marsh birds. This act of 'craning' is obviously being likened to a Freudian sexual awakening and quite literally to a *debut* erection. This child is, of course, a boy. Taken in this context, the scene must become representative of a kind of anarchically imploded Oedipal vision: a desire *for* the father and a desire *to be* the father which becomes a desire to usurp both father *and* mother—to 'know' and to become both King and Queen at once.

The English word *pedigree* comes from the French *le pied de grue* 'the crane's foot' after a curved triple line, resembling the claw of a crane, used to denote succession in royal or aristocratic genealogical charts. The act of craning in this poem might therefore not only be seen as an aggressive act of Oedipal usurpation, on Britannia's part, but also (via the connotations of incest) expressive of a desire to confound the normal tree-like structure of 'descent' and form anarchic, perverted links across generations that completely undermine the moral pattern of genetic nobility. This is a desire the poet shares. This 'craning' vision is also a reference to the imaginative effort made by the 'heroine' to recall the visual impression of a scene from her past, and by analogy an effort on the poet's part to co-opt readers empathetically into a similarly destructive sexual fantasy. We are asked not only to extend the memory of some early experience of our own of a dubious sexual awakening, but to cross-fertilize it with the poetry to which it clearly alludes: think of the 'spots of time' from Wordsworth's *Prelude*.) It is a desire both to bastardize and, by means of an incestuous generation of the artistic imagination, to subvert the internal logic of the canon and of our constitutional monarchy.

101.6 *beefcakes*: Seemingly another tasteless synonym for the previous *hunks* (see 100.5). You can also, I suppose, have 'hunks' of meat. A *beefcake* is probably something like a 'meatloaf': a stereotypical American family dish which involves mincing meat, mixing it with eggs and onions, plastering it into a bread-tin and baking it in the oven. The synthetic nature of these things, along with their unappetising, amphibious names, are further representative of the American/Brummagem perversion of society and sexuality this poem ostentatiously supports.

£e woman in £e mirror stretched her €roat
   And $aved across £e contours of her jaw.
£e lubrication meant £e blades could float
   Quite smoo£ly. Once an inch of foam (no more)
Accumulated gradually to coat
   £e razorhead, $e'd rinse it off before
Resuming. Bit by bit, her skin appeared
As, bit by bit, $e poli$ed off her beard.

102.3 *blades*: Presumably a misspelling of the singular 'blade', though perhaps the poet intends to imply that the Gillette *bait and hook* business model (see 85.2 *Gillette*) has become so pernicious by this stage in the Americanisation of the British economy that one is required to insert multiple blades in the safety razor before it will work. It seems obligatory, furthermore, to use the proprietary shaving soap in order to provide sufficient lubrication for a shave: the bluntness of the edges and the multiple blade design being deliberately inefficacious so as to necessitate further purchases.

*   *   *

Hubbard had two obsessions. The first was D. H. Lawrence, about whom I knew very little at the time—I suspect my reluctance to read him was due in no small part to the influence of my irksome new acquaintance—but now I realize he must have recognized in Lawrence something of a kindred spirit. (Perhaps that is to be just a little unkind to Lawrence.) The second obsession was for games: specifically their histories and their anthropological roots. It was this latter quality which brought us together. Hubbard (I did not know to call him 'Mother' until well after our acquaintance had been ended) had placed a scruffy notice on the message board at the entrance to the University Library. I was thinking of buying a second-hand bicycle and I discovered his note next to one advertising cello lessons which had caught my eye with its rather comical sketch of a stick-man attempting to play the instrument as if it were a banjo. Typically of Hubbard, he had not brought his own piece of paper but (extremely rudely, I thought) had written on the back of somebody else's: an old don looking for a student to organize his home library in return for a year's free bed and board. Hubbard's pencilled scrawl read as follows:

PARALUDIC SOCIETY

Abstract games were designed as training for war and commerce, as metaphors for reproduction and death, as routes to wisdom and enlightenment, as ceremonies of reification and sacrifice.

Are you interested in discovering, discussing, recreating and playing games from the world's ancient civilisations? Why not try your hand at one of our weekly meetings?

Saturdays 6pm: door 12, Chapterhouse, Temple.

*   *   *

The only place that seemed immune from this attack of automedicated tarantism was the bar. More important things were happening there. I sidled over to it trying to look like a disgruntled employee. I decided this was not the kind of place you went about making enquiries about missing persons. Not unless you were genuinely a detective. (What a ridiculous word that is. *Detective*. It sounds less like a job-title than a property a chemist might ascribe to a radioactive molecule.) You'd need that world-weary scowl they develop to deter the constant sarcasm. Anyway, it was the cabaret I was after, not the dance-club.

I noticed a doorway to the right of the bar labelled 'Toilets' & 'Cocktail Bar'. I shimmied round the frotting mass of would-be drinkers, all attending to their orders of various shades of things to sweat, & made my way into the corridor. The smell from the toilets was like purple play-dough drizzled with acid-drops. I couldn't decide whether it was really better than the more natural fish-cakes & ammonia. Further down, beyond one of those glittering crystal-cut bead curtains, the same incongruous skinhead from the foyer was leaning at the entrance to the Cocktail Bar. They were either twins — which is how magicians do it — or there was some quicker way of getting here than squeezing through the heaving dance-hall & he'd taken it in order to bring a modicum of variety to his otherwise joyless working life: a bit of David Lynch-like entertainment at the expense of a befuddled newcomer. He took my second ticket & pushed aside one of the frosted double doors.

This was more like it. It was a smaller room than the last. Though it still managed to occupy an entire railway arch. The clientele had a very Los Angeles late 1940s look. Almost half of them were cross-dressed. There were women in fedoras & button-down braces smoking slim cigars, or short leather bomber jackets, tight wife-beaters & tattoos on their hands. Men wore strapless dresses with diaphanous silk scarves sliding off their shoulders, Rita Hayworth or Lauren Bacall wigs, smudgable lipstick & flamenco-heeled shoes with thongs that tied above the ankle.

The music was sub-Duke Ellington big-band (not live). There was a roulette wheel on the far side of the room around which people were gathered: more to swap wisecracks as they watched the numbers spin than to gamble away their quota of free plastic chips. The most important thing about the place, however, seemed to be the smoke. Everybody smoked. & everybody tapped their cigarettes on something flat before they lit them up. Then they would use the little glowing sticks to animate the conversation: butch-types leaving them stuck to a bottom lip as they screwed their eyes & drawled one-liners — the butcher the type, the closer to the centre of the mouth — sultry *femmes* held theirs at eye-level delicately punctuating anecdotes with inverted commas of smoke; a short, sharp puff for each full stop. Sluttier, heavier-lidded *dames* said nothing, taking long drags & keeping up the pout as they exhaled & tapped their ash. One of the most elegant by the bar wore a glove on her smoking hand. She held the cigarette perfectly perpendicular to her front two fingers & pushed it slowly to arms-length beside her hip as if the thing resisted being taken from her lips, then blew the used contents of her lungs down towards the other side with a slight embrasure, a twine of blue-grey smoke constantly climbing up her from below.

If $e was honest, $e was fond of £is.
   $e didn't want to chuck away her razor
For (say) a course of electrolysis
   Or regular appointments wi£ a laser.
Some women suffered from psoriasis
   When treated wrong. £at didn't really faze her.
But no€ing $ort of $aving could replace
£is sense of intimacy wi£ her face.

103.4 *laser*: The OED has 'a gum-resin mentioned by Roman writers; obtained from an umbelliferous plant called *lāserpĭcium* or *silphium* (σίλφιον).' Dealing as it does with the removal of unwanted hair, one can only assume that the application of this word in the stanza must be by way of reference to some form of futuristic herbal species of depilatory wax.

The only other gloss available, considering the syntactic context, might be that 'laser' is intended to denote *one who *lases* (hence the ability to take 'regular appointments'.) Perhaps the poet would like us to imagine the word derives from 'glazer'; that is: one who *burnishes* the skin.

*   *   *

I was intrigued by this notice. At the age of eleven, during a period spent living at my mother's parents while my father was posted to the Falkland Islands, the estate gardener, Arthur, had taught me chess. I remembered mysterious autumn evenings spent with him as the sun cast lengthy shadows of his hefty handcarved pieces across the board from the cobwebbed window of the outhouse, his brow furrowing with frustration as he tried vainly to impart the understanding which would make it slightly less easy for him, despite his meagre education, to check me in a trice.

There was always a smell of creosote and paraffin from the heater which mingled with the salty tang of soil from the fork-tines and his massive, yellow fingers... I can still catch the whiff of smoke from the perpetual bonfire of fallen leaves that smouldered at the bottom of the garden, clinging to his undied woollen cardigan and badger-coloured hair. I was useless at the game precisely because I could not think of it as abstract. For me, the pawns were real footsoldiers like Arthur (who had been a private in the colonial army in Ceylon); the bishops were real bishops, the King a king, and the rooks were the walls of a castle that could magically move about the countryside.

Chess was a deliciously poignant fairy tale. I imagined myself as the spectator of an ancient and dignified field of battle and that my role was to play the part of the losing king. Every game was a glorious tragedy in which I was both dramatist and sacrificial hero. I would give my pieces names (like Bishop Turneval and Sir Edmund Chevalier) and they would deliver little speeches befitting their characters and actions as they fought and died.

*   *   *

I bought a whisky & sat at an empty table in a shady corner of the room. I didn't drink it. I swilled it around a bit & waited for the show to start. This seemed perfectly ok. Nobody came up to talk to me or offered me another drink. I liked the place, I have to say: just as long as I didn't have to get involved; just as long as I could sit there soaking up the cigarette smoke & the low lighting, my ears taking a jacuzzi in the constant babble of the crowd.

The first two acts were nothing remarkable: a female Bing Crosby who also did Alison Moyet numbers (with a vocal range that wasn't really up... or rather *down*... to either job) & a *comedienne* (her term) with a Zsa Zsa Gabor accent whose act consisted almost entirely of insulting non-existent members of the audience.

But the headline act was something else. She was billed simply as *Meta*. She'd changed her clothes, but as soon as she walked out on stage I recognised the unusually elegant figure I'd seen at the bar with the elbow-length smoking glove. Now she was dressed like Kitty Collins in *The Killers*. In fact, she wasn't just got up like her, she looked incredibly similar to Ava Gardner. Dark back-combed hair wafted just above the level of a single cross-strap over her left shoulder. It was obviously her own. Just as it was obviously Gardner's natural colour. She was incredibly womanly, much more curvaceous than a modern movie star, (which in this case was probably all padding) but also with a distinct masculine quality: strong hands, broad shoulders, a slightly lantern jaw & dimpled chin. Crisp, quiet piano chords began to slice sharp edges in the hazy spotlighting as she moved beneath it: a brilliant cut applied to a smoky diamond. The audience settled down. Then gradually, as if warming to its task... her voice: fragile, vulnerable, but also husky & delicately predatory.

The more I know of love, the less I know it... the more I give... the more I owe it...

This was a drag-act who knew her business & her talents. She had none of the crude banter you expect. In fact, she never spoke at all. There was a reverent hush whenever that skimpy, fraying voice drifted out of her; a burst of whoops & whistles, out of keeping with the studious cool of the occasion, whenever she sighed off the final cadence of a song.

Her repertoire was all late night Blues standards & cool-jazz ballads: her accompaniment only ever the soft tinkling of a piano. One or two numbers she sang *a capella*. There was no reverb on her microphone & she left lingering, breathless pauses between each phrase. The effect produced was of an almost embarrassing intimacy with the movements of her vocal organs. Her lips & tongue felt as if within touching distance of the eardrum, the warm vibrations of her throat & diaphragm passed into your own by some mysterious means of sonic radiation.

As she sang, her definition blurred. As far as my imagination was concerned (what Singh would rather call my *dramatination*), she was no longer a specific woman, or even the impersonation of one. Instead she had become an emblem: a quintessential embodiment of the masculine idea of a woman. & she was somehow all the womanlier for the sad streak of manly longing that ran through her voice like a seam of some unminable ore: a longing for the fathomless nature of womanhood, a longing for impossible salvation at the hands of a departed goddess. If you'd closed your eyes, you might have though it was Chet Baker.

It's easier to do your legs. £ey're flat,
    Which makes your movements lazier, but much
Less comfortable, like when you stroke a cat
    Who barely seems to tolerate your touch.
Her skin, against £e la£er's egg$ell matt,
    Was glossy. When $e'd fini$ed, inasmuch
As cheeks and chin were done, $e changed her grip
And nipped £e last few remnants off her lip.

104.4 *tolerate*: era 10

    *   *   *

Arthur's exasperation with my refusal to think strategically eventually provoked him to upturn the table in the middle of another Shakespearean death-speech and slap me violently around the head. He burst my left eardrum with a single stroke of his huge, rough palm. His refusal to apologize for this to my mother, exacerbated by what I realize now were some rather inadvisable insinuations about her husband, resulted in his dismissal. I did not want him to go but mother was insistent. Arthur left and I managed not to play another game of any sort (besides the ones involved in the compulsory physical exercise at school) until I met Hubbard.

When I saw his notice in the library it struck me as the perfect opportunity to reacquaint myself with that forgotten pleasure. Its author seemed to feel the same way that I had as a child: games were not competitions but stories… ceremonies even.

That Saturday I paid a visit to Temple. It rapidly became apparent that Door 12 was not a well known location. Neither the chaplain, the bursar's secretary nor the butler of the junior common room could offer any viable theory as to what it might denote. The porter patiently explained that the numerical room codes in the college always consisted of a letter and three digits: the letter referring to the quadrant (A for the first and B for the second) the first digit of the number indicating the staircase via which the room was most easily accessed, and the other two digits the number of the room. All numbers ending –01 to –19 being on the ground floor, –20 to –39 on the first floor, –40 to –59 on the second floor and –60 to –72 in the 'attic'. He then asked me with whimsical politeness why I was looking merely for a door, rather than, as most people might, the room behind it.

    *   *   *

What I thought of next was Hannah. Not my drink-fat fingers groping round her nipples & her clitoris last night, but something else: something I could never put my finger on. Something behind every turn of phrase, every giggle & quick sidelong glance, which were the only things about her I could call to mind just then. There was a property of hers, a quality of instinctive knowledge or of physical awareness of a hidden thing a man like me could never have. Perhaps no man ever could. I couldn't even name it, or describe it, but I wanted it. I wanted to taste it & touch it. & it was this I heard in every one of Meta's songs. Not Hannah's *great whatsit*, but a craving that was even deeper than my own smouldering desire to open her Pandora's heart & take a look at this impossibly elusive thing that she'd been hiding. Even if it killed me.

But there was something else in Meta's voice too. It was something I was only now beginning to appreciate: a quietly reverberating resignation to the impossibility of it all. This was a quality that could only come from long experience of being the public expression of such an exquisitely melancholic craving. Meta's voice was dripping with a knowledge I could only catch in passing droplets as I listened. Meta, like perhaps nobody else, knew the one thing both of us were looking for — she to *be* it; I to have it in my hands — did not exist at all. Open up a woman's heart & you'll find engraved there just the same insatiable desire as a man's. It was this knowledge that was the real sad music of love, I realised.

This knowledge came & went with Meta's set. The words that tell it still remain behind, like sand between the toes after a picnic on the beach, but are little help in making myself understand the way I felt that night. Perhaps the effort to extract a conclusion from such an intense cluster of experiences will always kill their memory. Nevertheless, that's precisely what I did. I wrote them on a napkin. It took three goes to get the list just right:

CONCLUSIONS
1. I'm in love with Hannah.
2. I don't want to be. She's not in love with me.
3. She's still in love with Amrit Singh.
4. If I want to change this situation, I'm going to have to find her ex.
5. The Quean's the key to everything.
6. This is a really fucked up state of affairs.
7. Ask Meta for her help.

The last thing on the list was obviously the first I had to do. As I pocketed the napkin I saw the skinhead & the doorman had begun asking people to gather up their things & go. They were politely breaking the concentration of a snogging couple when the main lights came on. Everybody seemed to freeze for a second. It was a snapshot of the kind of wreckage you might associate with the petrified aftermath of a small pyroplastic Vesuvian eruption...

Out popped £e plug. £e sink slurped down its soup.
    $e towelled her neck, too languid now to spla$
Herself. Her raw skin needed to recoup
    Its ceramides, $e €ought. (No $aving ra$
Just yet, €ank God.) $e squeezed a generous gloop
    Of moisturizer out; and where moustache
Had been, $e dabbed it on; £en, down her cheeks
And €roat, $e ran her fingers, leaving streaks

105.2 *languid*: A deliberately sexualized word which forces the readers tongue to engage in the kind of *articulatory mimesis* referred to above (see 0.7 *slang*). Like *slang*, it traces the length of the tongue definitively slowly, pushing out the lips into a fleeting pout in order to make the morphemic transition twice from back to front in order to produce its final syllable. The effect is supposed to be, I assume, one of making the reader feel the same feline combination of lethargy and arousal that has overcome Britannia as a result of the reverie she has deliberately (almost ritually) used the razor and the shaving mirror to provoke.

105.4 ceramides: era 11

105.4 *ceramides*: This is a very odd neologism indeed. It seems to have something to do with *ceramics*. It is not beyond the realms of possibility that the poet is recalling his previous likening of the gruesome heroine to the 'Grecian Urn'. There might also be uncanny undertones of the *Rubaiyat* of Omar Khayyám: 'What part the pot? What part the potmaker?'. This would at least tie in with the idea of Britannia 'making up' her face as being like a self-creating artist/artefact, in that Wildean sense. Baudelaire is thinking of something of this sort in 'L'amour du Mensonge'. He is probably recalling Keats's odes when the object of his supposed adoration is rhetorically asked:

> Es-tu le fruit d'automne au saveurs souveraines?
> Es-tu vase funèbres attedant quelque pleurs…?

What *ceramides* might literally be in this context, however, one can only guess. The OED Supplement has only *ceramidium*, which it explains is (I think) the outer-coating of a specific family of algæ (a 'cystocarp'; the name being derived from its urn-like shape). Perhaps the drag-queen intends to rub some ghastly preparation of this stuff into her skin.

105.6 *moisturizer*: Another American neologism quite unproblematically denoting *cold-cream*. F. Scott Fitzgerald has a telling sentence in the short story 'The Bowl': 'The face of young Ellen Mortmain regarded him with the same contagious enthusiasm that would launch a famous cold-cream.' Fitzgerald is niftily playing on the infamous Marlowe line that captures Faustus's incredulous rhetorical response to the appearance before him of Helen of Troy as a hideous succubus (it is one we would do very well to remember here): 'is this the face that launched a thousand ships?'

Everything looked rather sordid covered in its light sprinkling of ash. People were caught in the most unflattering of poses. Some had narrowed eyes & open mouths. Others' tongues were hanging out or they had glasses half-raised to their lips. Various isolated individuals appeared to be standing in as models for the monuments to various historical world leaders: their index fingers pointing to the future or their palms imperiously resting on their chests. There were couples petrified in hilarious seaside postcard positions of sneaky mutual groping; even what appeared to be a same-sex threesome in the middle of the floor (though you can never be sure about these things.) Everywhere, for just a second, was the Elgin marbles or the theatre at Herculaneum. But I wasn't an Elgin or Alcubierre. I was more like Lurkio in *Up Pompeii*... "infamy! infamy!... they've all got it in for me."

& then... everyone just drifted off. Couples wandered away from one another without a word, or made a joke of it & shook hands, or stayed together interlacing fingers. Previously languid loungers, sanguine storytellers & sultry tangoers were left scurrying off to blink & cringe as their arms tunnelled under piles of coats & bags in various corners of the room like cellar rats evading discovery by a roving torch. "Yes sir, the way those creatures gnaw & nibble at your soft underbelly can do a lot of damage to your nerves. [Full stop. New paragraph.]"

I had to act quickly. Without asking for permission, I sneaked round the side of the stage to the entrance where the performers had come in. A surprisingly long corridor stretched off beyond another pair of meaninglessly gendered toilets. How big could this place be, I wondered. I tried one or two of the closest unmarked doors without success: one was a broom-cupboard full of empty wineboxes & packing crates, the other was locked. I moved a little further down the corridor, through a fire door, treading warily. The flooring from this point on was old fake-floorboard lino that was curling round the areas that had been ripped by a heavy piece of stage equipment or melted by an unattended cigarette. It was obviously not supposed to entertain the public.

There was another door immediately to my left. It was ajar & there was a bright light inside the room. I knocked on the frame then pushed it gently open, just in time to see Meta swivel back round on a leather business chair & confront herself once again in the dressing-table mirror with a look of ironic inscrutability. She had a plain white hand-towel wrapped around her torso, a corner of it tucked back underneath itself beside her left armpit. But she still appeared to be wearing her dress. To see her like that made me feel uncomfortable. If I'd caught a glimpse of shaved male chest beneath that towel just then, I would have felt much more embarrassed than if I'd happened on a woman with bare breasts.

She continued teasing away at the false lash that was hanging off her eyelid when I knocked.

"Come in," she winced. She moved onto the other eyelid, the first lash still in her fingers. She tore it off considerably more bravely than the first, presumably for my benefit, the skin stretching to at least an inch proud of her eyeball, "I've been expecting you."

106

  Like camouflage: a zebra in reverse.
    $e closed her eyes and rubbed £e streaks away,
  £e twitching in her eyelids getting worse
    As fingers massaged £em like lumps of clay.
  $e waited for £e feeling to disperse
    £en turned her gaze towards £e vast array
  Of quality cosmetics on £e $elf.
  To €ink… £ese days $e bought it all herself…

106.4 *lumps of clay*: Again the drag-queen's face is being likened to the various urns and vases of the poetic canon, which tend to stand for death and fragile beauty. The self-creating/creature is once more both the pottery and the potter.

    *   *   *

College porters, in the olden days at least, behaved towards all but the most influential undergraduates with either brusque irritation or world-weary amusement. I was, I supposed, pleased to be dealing with the latter rather than the former. I ignored his sarcasm and told him about the notice for the meeting of the Paraludic society. He scratched his forehead underneath his cap:

'Don't exist.'

'Well they did have an advertisement.'

'The door I mean; it probly don't exist… Lud*icrous* Society, you say?'

'Forgive me, but why would they… Para*ludic*, but… I suppose… now you come to mention it…'

'I think they played you for a fass one, son… There's only one place springs to mind.'

'… *the notice itself* could *be some kind of a false lead… if I find door twelve there'll be another sign directing me to some new equally obscure location in the college, and so on and so on. Probably some sort of test. Maybe a riddle. I should really have brought the notice with me… or a copy of it anyway…*'

'It's on third floor: stair six.'

' "*Why not* try your hand *at one of our meetings*" it said. That sounds rather like a challenge don't you think.'

'Third floor, stair six.'

'I'm sorry?'

'There's an extra door into B666. It's blocked by a bookcase on the other side but you can still see it from the hallway. I'd say that was the most lud*icrous* door in the college. God only knows why they put it there. Begging your pardon, son, you're not Theology are you?'

'No, no… intriguing… thank you, porter.'

    *   *   *

"Er... have you? Sorry, I suppose you must think I'm somebody else." She looked slightly irritated, "... I suddenly feel a bit like William Holden in *Sunset Boulevard*," I added

"Shall I take that as a compliment?" she asked. She was still in character. If you can call it that. She used that sassy, breathy accent women from 1940s gangster movies seem to have learned directly from the saxophone. Maybe that's where 'sassy' came from. She was nothing like as authentic sounding as when she sang. Presumably that's why she never spoke on stage. I was disappointed. I'd been expecting something more... or something less...

She dropped the lashes into a small plastic cup, reached down under the table & pulled out a bottle of whisky.

"Well no, not *Sunset Boulevard*... um, something else. Sorry. Great show, by the way." I was back-pedalling hopelessly, "I thought it was... charming." it smelled of damp & butane.

"Really?... would you like a Gin & Tonic?"

She screwed the lid off the bottle of Teachers with a single flick of the left hand. It span up off its transparent thread & skipped along the surface of the dressing table, coming to rest at the third attempt in a small basket of plastic jewellery. A masculine gesture, I thought.

"No, no you're fine thanks."

"You may have whisky if you like."

"Ok, please, that'd be nice."

She emptied the false lashes out of the plastic cup onto her open makeup bag like they were salt in a chip-shop shaker, then blew into it, fluttering her eyelids as if all kinds of imaginary stardust & iron filings had puffed out to sprinkle her magnetic aura into an instant of miraculous visibility. She glugged a large dose of whisky into it & held it out.

"Miserable weather we're having isn't it," she said, crossing her legs beneath the rumple-free black material. I didn't actually know. It was dark outside. Anyway there were no windows backstage. I approached her & took the cup, then sat on a long PVC brown sofa with tubular stainless-steel armrests that had been pushed against the wall. It squeaked as I sat down. I couldn't tell if it was the metal or the PVC. The noise of people leaving the club was diminishing in the background.

"Are you acquainted with this city?" She asked.

"Yes, we grew up together."

She grinned, obviously pleased I was prepared to play along, "Indeed?"

"We were pretty much inseparable for the first 18 years of my life. Haven't lived here for years though. I'm out of touch. I certainly didn't know they'd done up any of the arches around here."

$e used to steal her makeup off her friends.
　　It isn't hard. You lock £e ba€room door
An hour or so before a party ends
　　And take one €ing—mascara, say—you're sure
£ey'll €ink £ey've lost it somewhere, (makeup tends
　　To disappear), £ey'll never see you, or
Surprise you in £e act, because it's locked.
$e always did it; $e was never clocked.

107.4 *mascara*: There are four instances of this word in the ensuing section of the poem. The other three all occur as the first words of the first sentences in the first lines of their respective stanzas. It is obviously a word of primary importance.

　　In etymological terms, it is cognate (unsurprisingly) with 'mask'. Both words derive from the root that gives us: Catalan *mascara* 'soot'; Portuguese *mascarra* 'stain' or 'smut' and *mascarrar* 'to smear'; French *mâchurer* 'to daub' or 'to blacken the face'; Spanish *máscara* and Italian *maschera* both 'mask'. The oldest denotation in English of *mask* is actually 'net' or 'noose', via a non-palatalized dialectal remnant of the Scandinavian etymon of the Standard English *mesh*. The common denotation came into English in the C16th from the courtly French *masque*. The object is therefore indistinguishable in our language from its function in the semi-theatrical form that finds its apotheosis in the work of Ben Johnson. Johnson, of course, famously invented the *anti-masque*, which tended to involve demonic creatures and personified sins. In doing so he seems to have stumbled upon the original sense and style of the *masque*: a carnivalesque array of mischievous or phantasmagorical ghosts, skeletons and devils, whose name comes from the post-classical Latin *masca* 'demon' or 'evil spirit', which is probably the common root of all these words (but more on this below). The most ancient forms of such rituals, which still survive in Europe and America (as cultural imports), involve men painting their faces black and causing licensed havoc on religious feast days. In Britain these are called *mummers' plays* but the name is neither as authentic nor as apt as the older *masks*.

　　The history of this lexical cluster clearly shows how the courtly and noble tradition of the *masquerade*, which is supposedly counterpoised by *anti-masque* and the common *carnival*, has its roots in precisely the same disturbing pagan rituals of sex and death. One might like to go as far as to assert that the apparent *racial drag* implicit in its linguistic history reveals the *masque* to be a European interpolation of African *voodoo* ceremonies in which disguised participators literally believe themselves to have been transformed into the spirits of the dead, or into demons, and to carry the power of death at their touch.

　　But what is the link? There is a word from Midlands dialect that seems at least to support a connection between the older and newer versions of *mask*: 'trap' and 'facial disguise', respectively. The verb *to masker* means 'to bewilder' or 'to trick' and, despite probably being cognate with *mesh* rather than *masque*, nevertheless gains natural folk-etymological support from the latter. A much more convincing nodal point, however, (and one the OED seems to have missed) is the Arabic word *maskhara* 'jester' or 'fool'. This character from traditional folk theatre has many of the characteristics of the European *fool*: satirical license, caricatural mimicry, defiance of authority, riddling double-talk and so on, but also displays an overtly demonic and uncanny relationship with magic and death.

　　The obsession of this drag-queen and her poet with *mascara* is therefore an emblematic one. In putting on *mascara*, the unnamed actor who becomes 'Britannia' is actually transforming himself (with a cosmetic *wand*) into a *maskhara*: a jester, the spirit of mocking laughter, an icon of social and moral indeterminacy, and therefore (potentially) a *witch*. The most disturbing aspect, as per usual, is how the poet tempts the reader to take on precisely the same sort of theatrical transformation by (as it were) simultaneously 'putting on the drag-queen's mask'. He seems constantly to be asking us to treat his poem as a score for our performance: one that (in performance) will make us into something we would rather not become. It is we who can bring his words to life, but in doing so it is we ourselves who come to embody precisely that spirit of *brummagem* degeneration depicted. The poet is using the word *mascara* (with all its unsettling undertones) like a marker of musical notation that signifies the tempo or the style of articulation at the beginning of an orchestrated passage; 'mascara, say' could be an imperative: *mascara, speak!*. He is not just telling us what to say and when to say it, but also *how* we should say it in order for the spell to work. Just as *andante* means 'walking pace' and *vivace* means 'lively', *mascara* could mean 'mockingly', 'demonically' or 'pretentiously'. In the final analysis, the closest synonym is *brummagem*: we are to *black-up* as the cackling spirit of anti-monarchism, iconically embodied as both the drawling, sarcastic, grimy-faced coiners of the 'Black Country' *and* the gruesome drag-queens of the *carnival*.

Just how this bubbling crucible of lexical ore might trickle its molten implications into our understanding of '*masc*ulinity', one prefers not to think.

107.8 *clocked*: 'Noticed'—yet another of the supposed American slang items in the poem. This one has important undertones of temporal paranoia designed, one presumes, to generate a frisson in the reader encountering a text putatively from the future. If the clock (the machine that records time) has idiomatically (if not literally) become an instrument of surveillance, then the atmosphere of constantly being 'watched' which is so characteristic of this dreadful future becomes (risibly enough) directly focused on the *watch*. Essentially this involves a re-fusion of the bifurcated noun *watch* so that the personal timepiece (originally the 'face' of a *clock*) is made the tool with which some sentinel or other can 'keep a watch': in this case, one assumes, upon its owner. In fact, rather than an authoritarian 'telescreen', it seems more likely that the wristwatch has become a contraption with which anybody can watch anybody else at any time: the object strapped to the arm having an extra function as a selective transmitter and receiver of images. Hence the surveillance is anarchic.

It is a modern commonplace of course, since Henri Bergsen and Einstein, for writers and artists to exploit the frailties of an Enlightenment trust in 'time on the clock'. Nevertheless, the *clock* or *watch* is an object of ingenuity that has been so important to the power of this nation (since Harrison's success in the race to measure longitude), and stands for so many notions of scientific accuracy and trustworthiness, that to make it such a bizarrely literal object of paranoia in this way—based entirely on a cheap conceit—is actually to pass on a kind of linguistic dysfunction that might not merely be a symptom of a moral, political and psychological insanity, but also its contagious germ.

$he wasn't brave enough to buy £e stuff.
  £e way £ey looked at her, £e orange chicks
In uniform—$he felt a total scruff:
  A haggard junkie begging for a fix.
£ese days $he was decidedly more tough.
  Eventually, her friends found €ree lipsticks
Inside her handbag at a bir£day do.
$he had a good excuse, but £ey all knew.

---

    *   *   *

You will know by now the way I got to 666. I have yet to tell you about door 12, however. There are in fact not three but four doors leading from the hallway at the top of the spiral continuation of stair 6. I failed to mention this before because... well, to be honest, because I had forgotten it. It lies just beyond the door behind my back, long obscured, I admit, by the burgeoning encroachment of papers and rubbish that began to emerge from this room the moment I unleashed the brown roll as nourishment for the resulting fire, but I find it impossible to believe in its existence any longer. Perhaps the fact I forgot it means it has already disappeared. I cannot decide how I feel about this....

Unlike the other doors in the hallway, and in fact the entire college, it was partially glass. The top half contained a window into which was negatively etched the number 12 inside an opaque bordered box: like the office of a private detective in a tawdry American film. I think it particularly telling that none of the college staff to whom I spoke remembered this. Door 12 had no apparent function. It was right next to the other door into the teaching room and neither 666 nor the hallway showed any signs of having been partitioned in the past. The first time I saw the door there was a sign pinned to it, written in the same impatient scrawl I had seen on the notice board in the University Library. It simply read:

    PARALUDIC SOCIETY
    Please do not use the other door.

Bizarre, I thought. I could hear voices though, so I knocked. There was no response. I tried the handle, just in case. It was locked... or blocked... or both. I checked my wristwatch without actually taking any notice of the time of day and knocked again. The voices in the room went quiet. My heart was racing. There is something primeval about standing on the threshold like this. I felt an unaccountable blush spreading from my collar like the shadow of a strangler's grip. There was a somewhat protracted scuffling and scraping of chairs. The door beside me opened and Hubbard's Reynardish scowl emerged from behind it at a lower position than one might normally have expected.

'Oh, hello, afternoon.' I offered, 'Twigg. Sorry to disturb you but...'

'Come in' he snapped, without taking my hand... or even showing me one of his. I followed him in.

    *   *   *

"Yes, these old places can be amusing when they're remodelled, can't they?"

"Hmm mm," I swallowed, "have you seen *Hear my Song?* I always fantasised about running a place like that. There's an old building in Glasgow I've had my eye on. Looks like something out of nineteenth century New York. I couldn't get the cash together though..." I don't know why I said that. I suppose I hoped this was the kind of thing she'd like someone to say.

"I've never been to New York."

"No, neither have I. Listen, I should tell you why I'm here, really. I know it sounds ridiculous, but I'm looking for someone: a man called Amrit Singh..." *blah blah*. She regarded me with a quizzical expression as I rambled through the same old details. "You might know him as a slam poet called *Zomby*. Some people round here seem to have heard of him; & I've been told you're the person to ask about the cabaret scene." That was a lie, nobody had even mentioned her to me before.

"Maybe he bills himself as a comedian. If not, perhaps there's another drag performer you've come across who calls herself Britannia Spears... plays darts..."

She just chortled & carried on smiling at me with exaggerated bedroom eyes. I suddenly felt very tired: as if they were literally bedroom eyes; as if she'd taken those big false eyelashes off her own lids & put them onto mine, & now I was struggling to hold them up with my desperately untrained facial muscles.

She's drugged me, I thought. But then, it was just as likely I was suffering from fatigue. It was two in the morning. I'd been asking these same questions all day & getting nowhere. I hadn't slept properly or eaten properly & it was very warm in the dressing room. A small calor gas heater in the middle of the floor filled the area directly between the two of us with a slightly pungent heat that was seeping rapidly through the gaps between the buttons of my shirt & creeping up my trouserlegs like bindweed on a timelapse nature video. It was probably just the whisky going to my head. That's why I hadn't drunk the one I bought before. The sweat on my back had made my clothes adhere to the skin several hours before. I was in a state. No wonder I felt dizzy.

"Listen, Meta," I said, "or should I call you something else?... I'm sorry. I come barging in here unannounced, asking stupid questions & accusing you of being a dried-up movie star like Norma Desmond & then I say your show is *charming*, which seems like an even more ridiculous thing to do. Who the hell says 'charming' any more?"

"You know," she said, "you're really rather charming yourself, but I'm afraid I don't *quite* understand you."

Was £at not hers? It really looked like hers;
    $e had one just £e same; $e used it €inking
It was, and £en just put it in her purse.
    £e tru€ was £at $e'd nicked it wi£out blinking,
Assuming £at £e owner'd have to nurse
    A hangover before $e saw a €ing.
($e'd knocked back loads of vintage Armagnac.)
£ey €ought $e might be kleptomaniac,

---

             *   *   *

That evening I joined the Paraludic Society. I remained a member for the rest of the year. Its meetings initially consisted almost entirely of providing Hubbard with the vocal acquiescence he required to continue his projects (which needless to say never came to fruition) of organising University-wide tournaments and exhibitions of games he had discovered and was in the process of recodifying.

In later weeks however—I flatter myself this may have been a direct result of my own influence—one or two of us would begin each meeting by introducing a new game we had found or invented ourselves, or a historical reference we had come across, or some other small contribution to the Society's research which reflected our personal interests.

My own interest was not in playing these new games or providing them with written rules—most were either much too complex and difficult or much too childish and simple to provide any real engagement—but in drawing out the origins and anthropological functions of already common examples. This was, I confess, very much inspired by Hubbard's way of thinking. Despite our obvious differences of character and upbringing, we discovered we shared, for example, an interest in W. G. Frazer's The Golden Bough *and I found myself agreeing with him that most games encoded sacred rituals analogous to those described in Frazer's great work. Furthermore we agreed that games were largely meaningless when extracted from their historical contexts and that the real interest lay not in winning but in understanding. We needed, we decided, an etymology of games.*

My mind, part of it at least, was still in Arthur's shed; I focused mostly on board games with heterogeneous 'character' pieces—especially those with a 'King' or 'Queen' piece such as chess and its homologues—and their connections to sacrificial rituals.

Hubbard on the other hand was fascinated by the games children play in the streets: particularly the family of games called 'hopscotch.' These, he claimed, were not merely derived from the training routines of Roman footsoldiers in Ancient Britain (as a middle school teacher of mine had once explained) but had been extant on this island long before the Romans had arrived. They were, he would insist, the basis for transcendental Druidic ceremonies which the Romans had quite typically subsumed and put to materialistic use. According to Hubbard, hopscotch was the key to many of the Neolithic sites in Britain; it was a route to perfection and immortality; it was the core of what he called the 'Mystery of Brigantia.' Hubbard's conviction was unfaltering. He clearly believed his own theories. It was not until later, however, that I discovered Hubbard also believed in *them.*

             *   *   *

"No, no, I'm probably not making any kind of sense. It's been a long day. I ought to go. Thanks for the drink." I gulped the rest of it & grimaced slightly to stop myself from shuddering like Muhammad Ali as it went down.

"Are you worried about something?" she asked.

"No... I don't know. Should I be?"

"Not if you do what you're told."

"What? are you saying you can help me?"

"Just as far as I *have* to... can you find your way to one hundred & fourteen Fulmer Street?"

"Probably, yeh. I've got an A to Z. Why, is that where he is? When?"

"Tomorrow. I'll be there... in the flat of a dope-dealer called Eels. You can call for me at 12 & look around. I can depend on that. We'll leave together. In a day or so, he'll take some papers home with him. I'll let you know; then you get them. He won't be there."

"What, *Eels*? Where will he be?"

"With me: I'm his... secretary."

"Let me get this straight. Is what you're telling me that a drug-dealer you work for called *Eels* can get hold of papers of some sort that reveal where Zomby is & that you think I should case the joint with you & then go back when he's not there to steal the stuff."

"It is."

"What for? Why don't we just ask him? What's in this for you?" I hauled myself out of the deep crater my bum had managed to impress into the sofa & dropped the cup back on her dressing table. It blew over in the tiny slipstream of my arm making a strange hollow sound that reminded me of a ping-pong ball I used to bounce on the tiles in the hall at my mom & dad's place when I couldn't sleep. The whisky dregs trickled out into the dusty remnants of a powder I hoped was just foundation makeup. "I only need to trace this Zomby character if he's really Amrit Singh. I can think of a number of good reasons why he might be, but I don't want to run headlong into breaking..." my vision began to darken... "& entering..." I grabbed her shoulder to steady my teetering, deciding this was a slightly less embarrassing option than any of the alternatives: the most likely of which seemed to be keeling over like the plastic cup to lie there drooling whisky at her stilettoed feet.

"Do you always go around leaving your fingerprints on a girl's shoulders?" She teased. The last thing I saw as the black frame growing around my eyesight spread quickly inwards to blot out the entire picture were Meta's eyes narrowing in amused imitation of my own. "Not that I mind particularly. You've got nice strong hands."

£e partner acted all compassionate
   And asked her quietly. $e was abrupt;
$e flounced out histrionically and $ut
   £e porch-door in his face, £ey'd best break up,
$e choked, €rough half-au£entic whimpers. But
   $e texted him £e morning after: LETS MAKE UP.
£e next few weeks, $e snuck round and replaced
£e €ings $e'd lifted. $e was SO barefaced.

110.6 *texted*: no doubt 'texting' is some form of instant orthographic communication. One imagines an inkless pen which, when used on a specially transmissive pad can cause the message to appear like a temporary tattoo on the skin of the recipient, perhaps most logically on the back of the hand. The brevity of the message and the thematic context of cosmetics and flirtatious, duplicitous private communication would seem to make this reading quite appropriate.

110.6 <u>MAKE UP</u>: The infantile play on words here is not simply an unapologetic gibe based on the confusion of the senses 'to re-establish friendly relations' and 'to apply cosmetics'. We should take notice of its emphatic orthography and its position at the end of yet another *alexandrine* and take courage in applying it more globally. In so doing we discover complex and debilitating ambiguities.

The first thing to note is how truly antagonistic are the two contextually most obvious (predicating) denotations. One concerns conciliation and carries connotations of confession and honesty; the other connotes disguise, flirtation, pretension and a fundamental *dis*honesty. This goes further than the surface specifics however. At root, these applications are only symptoms of a much more unstable paradox inherent in this polysemous phrasal idiom. On the one hand we have the idea of *make-up* as the fundamental or total structure of a concrete or (much more often, metaphorically) an abstract thing. The uses of the verb *to make up* which mean 'to be reconciled', 'to compensate' and 'to add the requisite amount of something to overcome a deficit' are all focused upon stabilising the *make-up* (the 'total construction') of a thing of value. However, from a degrading ironic usage of the verb that plays on the central/neutral denotation—'to construct'—we derive the senses 'to invent', 'to lie' and 'to synthesize appearance by means of the application of cosmetic *paints*'.

The drag-queen's message—however it might be sent in technological terms, the implication is clear that it is intimate rather than public (if any such distinction can any longer be made, of course)—is obviously designed to be a shamelessly immoral temptation: a predatory sexual advance thinly veiled beneath a kind of colloquial diplomacy. *Let's construct a fiction (together)*, it says; *let's put on cosmetics (together)*; *let's lie (together)*; and ultimately (with all the prurient connotations she can muster) *let's erect something (together)*.

In doing so, the drag-queen expresses precisely the desire to enlist the initiating role of the reader in an effort to bring about a morally and socially degraded future that drips from the pages of this *libidinous fiction*.

I came-to in almost total darkness. I had never really *come-to* before. *Coming-to* necessarily follows *passing out* & I wasn't sure I'd ever done that before either.

I had no idea where I was. All I could see was the dull glimmer of an Emergency Exit sign depicting a yellowing man escaping through a yellowing door against a yellowing green background. Imagine that page in *Tristram Shandy* that's entirely black, but with a little picture in the far left corner of Michael Jackson moonwalking away from the pitch of a badly irrigated Pakistani cricket ground.

There was a woman in the education service at University who would ask me every time I went to see her for a metaphor to describe my current feelings about my PhD; I made a mental note to use that last sentence in my next consultation. It made me chuckle, which made my head hurt rather badly.

I groped around a bit & recognised the textured tackiness of the PVC sofa. Meta had obviously dragged me up onto it last night & left me there to sleep. Or was it still tonight? I rolled off onto the floor & felt for my jacket like a man searching for a makeshift raft amongst the flotsam of a shipwreck. It was underneath the armrest, thank god. I stood up, much more carefully this time, & put it on, checking it still contained my wallet & so on, & made my way towards the little Michael Jackson, who I hoped was just above the door. My right hand brushed against the heater as I passed it. It was cold. I must have been out for hours.

In the corridor there was another Emergency Exit to the left. I knew the cabaret club, then the main hall & then the lobby & the entrance were all to the right, beyond the toilets, but I wanted to get out, rather than to venture deeper into this tobacco-fumigated warren underneath the Hockley railway arches. I headed left, keeping my finger at the right page of the Fighting Fantasy book that seemed to have taken the place of my recent memory... just in case I'd need to double back. There was a fire-door at the end of the corridor with a push-bar mechanism. I prayed (to nobody in particular) that it wouldn't set off an alarm & gave it a weak shove.

The door swung open easily enough to reveal painfully bright sunlight gleaming along the polished metallic edges of a commercial carpark. I staggered under the luminescent impact of it. The front door to the Pussy Club had been underneath the railway. It was dank & blackened with small stalactites of Victorian mortar growing from the gaps between its upper tiles. You could never imagine even a Saharan sun making much headway in its dinginess. This side of the building was quite different though. You certainly wouldn't have guessed something like a nineteen-forties fantasy club could lie behind the anonymous double doors that closed themselves behind me. I trudged out into the painful world. I felt like an alpinist with snow-blindness.

From £en on, $e was blasé: even spotlit
    And dazzled by £e ultra-gloss Clinique
Or Clarins stands in Boots, $e wouldn't bottle it.
    $e had a newly minted daring streak.
$e'd bare her wrist to test a perfume droplet
    And $ock £e women wi£ her brazen cheek
By asking, wi£ affected inhibition,
For stuff £at doesn't smell like a beautician.

111.2-3 *Clinique… Clarins… bottle it*: Sometimes the jargon in this poem descends almost to the level of nonsense poetry. I can hardly decipher most of this stuff and cannot begin to guess at what all the polysemous conceits in which it is no doubt steeped are meant to signify. Perhaps there are alchemical overtones. We certainly appear to be confronted with something akin to an array of apothecary's vials. Pope's use of Paracelsus should not be overlooked. I refuse to delve, however. I will not be conjured into conjuring. If the tiniest possibility exists of inadvertently causing something terrible to come about, I would rather not find out the meaning of such silly hocus pocus.

    *   *   *

After the theory and history, the meeting would usually move onto Hubbard's much more practical, though no more realistic, agenda for advertising and promoting games within the University and beyond. As the evenings wore on, these discussions very often descended—or perhaps it might be more accurate to say ascended—*into lofty, near Utopian discussions of a future enlightened and unified by the playing of universally engrossing games. This wild optimism was fuelled by the large volumes of wine and cheese which was our only sustenance on Saturday evenings and of which Hubbard seemed to have an inexhaustible supply. I noticed—though I believe myself to be the only one who did—that as soon as Hubbard had instigated both the topic of discussion and the alcohol-warmed atmosphere which made these fantastic sessions possible, he very often disengaged himself gradually and seemingly quite deliberately from conversation and slipped away. I could not say how late or early he would leave; he was never polite enough to excuse himself or say goodbye and I must confess I was usually quite engrossed. All I can say is that by the end of the night he was never anywhere to be seen.*

As much out of a desire to observe the internecine squabbles and thinly veiled flirtations of my fellow members as any genuine attachment to the society's idealistic mission, I continued to attend these meetings well into my second term of University. Hubbard though was becoming more and more erratic, zealous and mysterious. He seemed to be using the group simply as a sounding board for the development of an occultish metaphysics. His interruptions in meetings became more frequent, more vehement and more irrelevant. As an implicit admonishment of us irritating neophytes, for example, he would suddenly launch into a completely non-sequitorial meditation on gnosticism or alchemy in the middle of some cheerily light-hearted conjecture about prehistoric tiddlywinks.

Many of us began to suspect his sanity. The group dwindled.

    *   *   *

As I negotiated the labyrinth of subways & pedestrian flyovers that always seem to come back to the Kennedy mosaic at St Chad's Circus, feeling very sorry for myself, I thought about asking for a refund when I got back to the Hotel. I considered the fact I hadn't actually stayed there overnight perfectly good grounds on which to ask them for at least a major discount. How I might explain my actual whereabouts though, & why I'd booked into a hotel room when I didn't mean to sleep in it, I didn't know. I spent a while worrying around at a few ingenuitive excuses — like a variety of things on my dinnerplate I didn't want to eat — then graduated to the much more pressing matter of the previous night's antics.

What the hell had happened? Not only had my mind started playing tricks on me — making me see kicking-out time at a nightclub as Vesuvius erupting on Pompeii, causing me to arrive at the frankly ludicrous conclusion that I'd discovered the sad secret of true love in the crooning of a female impersonator — but I'd also keeled over with exhaustion (or something much more serious) & nobody had seen fit even to call a taxi for me, let alone an ambulance. For all I knew, & for all Meta knew, I could have had some kind of narcoleptic episode. I could have been suffering convulsions in the night. I could have had a brain tumour. I could have died. How could she just go off & leave me on the sofa like a homeless drunk?

Behind this all was Amrit Singh. A week spent going through his stuff, a morning following his tramp from Moseley up to Vauxhall, an hour or two in the weird company of his Don Juan parody, an evening ferreting around for him in the seedier parts of Birmingham's inner ring & I was already beginning to lose my marbles. Amrit Singh was making me go mad. The rest of my life might very well be spent in paroxysms of incomprehensible regret that I'd ever heard of him, or read his poetry, or (more to the point) that I'd ever fallen in love with the mother of his child.

My anger gave way to irritation at the newspaper headlines that seemed intent on spinning up to slap me in the silver-screen of the imagination: Body Found in Drag-Queen's Dressing Room. Sex-Change Slasher Strikes Again. Boffin Carried Off In Coffin! that kind of thing. I was relieved to turn the corner onto Alcester Street. It was already half past nine. I wouldn't get a chance to get back into bed.

I was far too self-conscious to talk to anyone when I followed the revolving door into the hotel foyer. Instead, I tried to cultivate the air of a healthy city gent who'd just returned from a quick digestive Sunday morning turn around the town post-breakfast by skipping lightly up the stairs. The reception staff were quietly unconcerned.

I had a sudden whim, back in the room, to revenge myself on them & their punitively early check-out time by stealing all the bedding. It was very easily done. There was still quite a bit of room inside my rucksack, even with the rolled up poem. I simply stuffed in everything I could: a pillow & a couple of blankets. Ok it looked a good deal plumper than when I'd first arrived, but who remembers things like that: there wasn't ever any porter. I couldn't really afford to get another room for the night, so I guess I thought these things might come in handy... just in case. They did.

Unzipping her maroon eye-makeup bag,
    $e grinned defiantly and rummaged round
Amongst its innards, trying not to snag
    A fingernail on £e zip. $e found
£e liner pencil; stuck it, like a fag,
    Behind her ear, where curly sidelocks wound
£emselves around its stem: half white, half black.
$e flexed her hand and plunged it quickly back

---

        *   *   *

I had always considered myself a sympathetic character and, though tolerably popular, had prided myself at school for at least avoiding (if not actually standing up to) the cruel marginalisation and bullying of those who were perceived to be a little different. There was, for instance, a Jewish boy with rather severe halitosis: a problem that was unfortunately exacerbated by the stress of the ostracism to which it inevitably led. The other boys, almost without exception, had taken to pronouncing his surname (which I will refrain from repeating) in a ghostly whisper as if the very annunciation of it was enough to release a noxious gas. (I cannot fail to recognize, with a good deal of shame, how the bitterest of ironies can be found today in what was then a commonplace example of childish anti-Semitism.) His name, said in this fashion, became a warning signal for his odorous approach: a kind of anti-shibboleth. Not only had I refused to join in with this fashion, but I tried quite often to accompany him when walking through a corridor in which he might be humiliated in order to distract his attention with talk of something about Chemistry—in which class we shared a bench and a Bunsen burner.

After a few of these occasions however, he erupted into a sudden violent attack, pinning me to the wall, his fists full of my shirt and blazer, muttering guttural obscenities I imagined to be in Hebrew. At the time I was indignant, but after some reflection I came to the magnanimous conclusion that he must have imagined me to be involved in his humiliation: I was, after all, regularly present when he heard his name spoken as if it were a necromantic spell. He had simply mistaken my intentions. Seen in this light his actions appeared restrained and admirable. From the evidence of his tight grasp on my lapels and the sinuous grind of his substantial metacarpals, he was quite capable of knocking the stuffing out of me.

It was for this reason I refused to laugh when Dawkins mixed iron sulphide and sulphuric acid in the ceramic jar in the middle of our bench during a particularly dull Chemistry lesson and began a sotto voce *chorus of his victim's name, which reached an aspirant crescendo as the pong of hydrogen sulphide filled the lab. The science master was obliged to evacuate the spluttering students. I felt strongly enough to take the quite uncharacteristic step of informing the headmaster of what I had seen. Dawkins was expelled.*

        *   *   *

DIGBETH

I didn't leave immediately. I sat on the edge of the bare mattress with my A to Z & looked up Fulmer Street. It didn't exist. There was a Fulmer Walk near Spring Hill but no Fulmer *Street*. I supposed Meta had just made a slight mistake with Eels' address. This Fulmer Walk didn't seem too likely to have a number 140 though. It wasn't very long. It didn't even look like the type of street that had addresses on it.

Anyway, I had an appointment at 12. I was going to try & keep it. I hoped that she'd meant noon not midnight. Apart from anything else, I wanted to find out why she'd abandoned an unconscious stranger in the Pussy Club.

I left the hotel, dutifully handing in my key without a word, then made my way through what was soon to be called *East Side* (by nobody except the Council) towards what they already referred to as *The Chinese Quarter*. I decided to avoid the main drag of the City Centre. Lately, Sundays could be as bad as Saturdays as far as herds of shoppers were concerned. I went up past the Hippodrome, which was still the Hippodrome, & The Futurist Cinema, which had obviously not been deemed quite futuristic enough & was now called *Spearmint Rhino Extreme* & claimed to be 'Europe's biggest lap-dancing superclub'. I crossed the Ring Road via the subway opposite the old Royal Mail Sorting Office... which was now a swanky shopping centre called *The Mailbox*.

I suppose all this redesign should have come as no surprise. This is what Birmingham does. It changes. It changes quickly & it changes drastically. It's done precisely this at regular intervals of forty or fifty years throughout its history. The Georgians flattened the muddle of the North part of the old town to bring some kind of sense to it; the early Victorians did away with the Old Georgian Square for precisely the opposite reason; then Chamberlain pulled down half of what his predecessors had done to start afresh. & so it goes on: Manzoni puts up his 'concrete collar' round the inner city in the sixties; then the 'Highbury Project' sets about folding that respectably back down again & donning something equally impractical & modish. Sometimes they make a pig's ear of it; sometimes not. It doesn't really matter. Birmingham treats itself as worked in metal rather than set in stone. You can always bend it around a bit if isn't the right shape. Or simply melt it down & start again. The point is that the city just gets on with constantly counterstamping its own effigy in the knowledge that if it doesn't work out, there'll always be a next time.

They say Corbusier invented 'Continual Revolution'. & it was Corbusier's fault that Birmingham ended up with the old Bull Ring & the inverted ziggurat Prince Charles said ought to be for burning books rather than preserving them. Two ideas occurred to me as I skirted round the Mailbox. Firstly, the Central Library, with the sun on its gravity-defying terraces, looked a good deal better than Charlie grinning & bearing it in gold epaulettes next to Lady Di on a collector's item Wedgewood Plate. Secondly, if 'Continual Revolution' was Corbusier's conception before Mao adopted it, then it was Birmingham's idea well before Corbusier was a twinkle in his old designer's eye.

Inside £e pouch. Mascara, copper blu$,
    Metallic eye$adow—a single pot,
Like a commemorative crown—a bru$
    Wi£ bronzing pearls, and lipgloss, *apricot*.
$e plonked £em down: £ere wasn't any ru$.
    $e used to regiment £em so $e got
It all in order, like a TV cook:
$e wanted it laid out so $e could look

113.3 *commemorative crown*: From the time of its initial debasement at the end of the first war, until the end of the last, all 'silver' coinage in Britain still had a genuine silver content of 50%. Since 1947 though, bullion debts owed to the United States have required all the nation's silver stocks for their repayment. Every 'silver' coin, with one exception, has been drastically debased and minted entirely from cupro-nickel. Until very recently, the one exception had been the Crown—self-evidently a symbol of the Commonwealth's pride. But Canute could only hold the tide back for so long. In 1951—the year of the Festival of Britain, and the last full year of the reign of the late King—the first commemorative cupro-nickel crown was issued, carrying (at the ideological behest of the Labour government which had been so insistent on debasing it) the tasteless socialist edge inscription: CIVIUM INDUSTRIA FLORET CIVITAS. Now a second cupronickel crown has appeared in the Coronation utterance. One can only pray that next time the royal title DEI·GRATIA·BRITT·OMN·REGINA·FIDEI·DEFENSOR appears on a British Crown it will be impressed upon genuine Sterling and Mr Churchill will have succeeded in extracting the Commonwealth's economy from its subordinate exchange relations with the US dollar and will have returned us to the Imperial Gold Standard.

    If it serves any worthwhile purpose at all, this poem is certainly a useful warning of the possible social and moral consequences of surrendering to the aggressive free-market monetary policies of the United States. What worries me, however, is the likelihood it is designed, instead, to be a self-fulfilling prophecy.

113.4 *bronzing*: Another allusion to *Æneas*.

113.7 *TV cook*: Doubtless this is a reference to Marguerite Patten whose valiant attempts practically to liven up and expand the cuisine of ration-book England have been one of the only genuine social benefits of BBC television. Her latest creation is 'Coronation Chicken': an ingenious party dish employing spices, mayonnaise and dried fruit to miraculously transform the less desirable parts of a cold chicken into an exotic treat which has recently graced celebratory tables from Buckingham Palace to the narrowest and most soot-blackened terraces of Orwell's Wigan. The anarchist poet could hardly fail to take a pot-shot across the bows of such an optimistic flagship of good old-fashioned English pragmatism.

ROTTEN PARK

There was nowhere to live on Fulmer Walk. These were the backs of houses not the fronts. If this was Surrey, & the building in whose shadow they were built was not a generic 1960s tower-block but a country house by Lutyens, it would almost certainly have been called a *mews*. I strolled as nonchalantly as possible over to the block of flats & took a look at the buzzers. They had no names on them. There was a flat 14/0 however. If anything in Birmingham came close to the address 140 Fulmer Street, this might've been it.

I pressed the buzzer. The only response was a reciprocal buzzing sound from the front doors. I wasn't going to go in there without finding out where I was going. I pressed it again.

Ye-es? Just push the door.

"Oh, hello, I'm sorry to disturb you... erm... is Meta there?"

Meeta? Yeh, ok mate, come on up.

"Sorry about this, it's just she said to meet her at 12."

Are you accompanied by members of the local constabulary by any chance?

"Er... no."

Only kidding, come up. The lifts are being fixed, so you're going to have to use the stairs.

The doors buzzed again. I went in. The tiled stairwell smelled of disinfectant & various flavours of Sunday lunch as I climbed. I saw nobody on the stairs, which was strange, but also a relief. I began to wish I didn't have a rucksack though. I seriously considered dropping it off in one of the flats & asking them to hold it till I picked it up on my way down.

Eels met me at his doorway on the fourteenth floor. He was a big man with a greasy brown pony-tail & a moustache. He was leaning against his doorjamb in a garish red & orange Italian football jersey, Roma I think, though I'm no expert.

"I'm sorry about this," I said, "it's just..."

"No, it's me who should apologise, mate. The meters are all on the ground floor. It's you who's just walked up fourteen flights for nothing. I forgot, man, sorry. You can get the readings off the warden. Mind you, I would've thought you'd know that shit yourself."

"I've obviously got the wrong address. I knew I had."

"Don't think so, mate, I've been expecting you. I never pay my bills, you see. It's a matter of principal. I thought there might be a bit of official bother. That's why I put my slippers on."

That was a weird thing to say. "I think there's been some misunderstanding." I explained, "I met this woman called Meta. Well, actually, it was a... a female impersonator, a cabaret singer, & she told me to go to 140 Fulmer Street at noon today & she'd be there."

"A fellar called *Meeta* told you to *meet her*?"

I shook my head. "She said this was the flat of someone called *Eels*. It's ridiculous."

  And see £e process in a single go.
    Her make-up, £ough, was always lacklustre—
£e loss of spontaneity would $ow.
  $e'd had a darts-match up in Manchester
One time—it was a gay-club called *BarPeggio*—
    Her fussy make-up job embarrassed her;
$e lost all her compo$ure, and her eye;
Her wig and her direction went awry.

114.5 *gay-club*: The employment of *gay* to mean 'homosexual' is an iconically degrading American usage (of what was previously a word of almost unparalleled positivity) currently sweeping its way like a plague of locusts into the heartlands of Standard English. It is a euphemism, of course, but that is not a mitigating factor. *Merry* meaning 'slightly intoxicated' is a similar, if not as disturbing, twentieth century innovation. Both words used to mean 'blithe' and 'carefree': the most desirable and summery of the attributes of unburdened youth. Furthermore they were particularly characteristic, we used to think, of our own country; so much so that *Merry England* was a Tudor cliché.

 One hates to think what effect on the understanding of poetry this kind of semantic dereliction might have on the students (if any such rare creatures still survive) in the awful future this poem seems to want to bring about. One already finds it difficult to stop their infantile tittering at Coleridge's 'thick, fast pants' and Eliot's 'An old man on a windy nob'.

     *   *   *

From that point on I had developed something of a penchant (whether or not it was conscious I can no longer say) for attracting unfortunate marginal characters. I had soon realized that Hubbard was one of these, and initially had relished the challenge of bringing him to his senses (as it were) by engaging him in his own interests. I confess, however, that I slowly began to realize how far beyond my abilities of rehabilitation his strange mind was, and I became afraid of allowing myself to be sucked into what I believed at the time to be his paranoid fantasies and delusions of grandeur. By the sixth week of the Trinity Term therefore, like all the other members of the group, I was finding the meetings too uncomfortable and Hubbard's behaviour too bizarre and unpredictable to tolerate. That night, after his usual sly exit, the conversation turned rapidly to anything but games and tournaments and ancient history, and soon dried up. I distinctly remember feeling as if, as a group, we had come abruptly to the simultaneous realisation that we really had very little in common except for Hubbard, and we no longer wanted anything to do with him. We tacitly agreed never to meet again.

Occasionally, of course, I would bump into an ex-member who would swap anecdotes with me about what 'Old Mother' was up to now. It was Dudley Polsworth, a jovial badminton blue from Rugby with a slightly irritating habit of coughing and winking simultaneously as if failing to suppress the symptoms of a fashionably decadent lifestyle he obviously did not have, who I first heard refer to Hubbard in this way.

     *   *   *

He grinned at me for a second or two. Then just: "Yep, come in."

"No, listen, I'm sorry for bothering you. I'd better go."

"The least I can do is offer you a cup of tea after your exertions. Come on in."

It didn't sound like a request. & I really did fancy a cuppa. I followed him into his flat.

"Meta told me you were coming. She's not here yet I'm afraid."

"Are you taking the piss?"

"I deal drugs, mate, I've got to have some kind of firewall. Some people go for reinforced steel doors & spyholes & a replica shooter by the intercom. But that's strictly for your headbangers. You may as well put a sign up saying Crack House... My way's better."

I had to agree there. I'd never have guessed.

"Meta does a bit of work for me from time to time. The way I operate requires a very complex system of accounting. I need somebody who's good with figures. & Meta's *very* good with figures. She comes round every Sunday & looks through my books. It's pretty rare for her to come this early though. She works on Saturday nights."

He pointed me to a seat on a sofabed in a sparsely decorated living room. There was only one poster on the wall: a black & white nineteenth century litho of some sort of large public demonstration. People were waving Union Jacks & also what appeared to be French Tricolores. That struck me as rather odd. There was no sound-system, no books or even a TV, just a computer on a wheel-around desk with a shelf you pulled out to get at the keyboard. The floor around it was covered in CD-R & DVD-R disks & empty jewel-cases. Presumably he used his computer to listen to music, play games, watch TV... everything.

On an armchair beside the PC, a pale teenager in a baseball cap & an improbable number of coats was arranging a few small lumps of something brown — I hoped it was just hash — on top of an old brick. When he'd finished, he patted himself down in search of some forgotten accoutrement. Eels went into the kitchen to put the kettle on. "She'll be here later though," he continued, "make yourself comfortable... here!" A piece of cutlery flew out of the kitchen, skimmed along the carpet & clanked against the brick. It was a small butterknife with a plastic handle. The teenager picked it up & examined its charred end with some approval.

I took my bag off & put it at the end of the sofa furthest from the teenager, then sat next to it, jamming it against the armrest. The sofa was very soft. I sank into it, my legs angled upwards. It felt difficult to get up, which made me rather anxious. I dragged myself forward again & perched on the edge of the sofa as the teenager began to heat the butterknife with a red candle his skinny body had previously managed to obscure.

"You're a friend of Meta's then?" Eels voice asked from the kitchen, accompanied by clinking.

"Well... to be honest, I only met her yesterday."

$e told herself from £en-on $e'd relax
> And put her face on wi£ a bit more flair.
A slow me€odical approach detracts
> From £at vivacious look. $e still took care,
But now $e'd leave £e stuff in jumbled stacks
> And do it as an improvised affair.
£ese days, when Tanya went out on £e raz,
Her make-up job had genuine pizazz.

115.7 *went out on the raz*: That is *made up [her] face after shaving*, 'raz' deriving from French—*rasure*

115.8 *pizazz*: Yet another American slang term. It is echoic of *jazz* (both the word and the music) and refers to that glittering ostentatious glamour emanating unavoidably from Hollywood and Las Vegas. Other coinages, like *razzle-dazzle* and *razzmatazz*, carry similar meanings and similarly extravagant profusions of what they will insist on calling 'zees', and which they use to garishly embellish their new synthetic version of our language the way they do their signs with neon and their frocks with sequins.

*   *   *

Polsworth broadsided me one day coming out of the buttery.

'Say, Twiggs, [squink] have you heard what Old Mother's up to now?'

'Old Who?'

'Old Mother Hubbard. He's evidently experimenting with timetravel. [squink] What a hoot!'

'Yes.' I said, not wanting to prolong my discomfort any longer than absolutely necessary, 'yes, I know.'

'Oh you do? [squink] What's his plan? I'd love to hear the juicy details.'

'Well no, I don't know but I'm not surprised.'

'Nor me, old man, not a bit... [squink] saw it coming.'

It was painfully obvious to all but the most insensitive of former members (Dudley being unfortunately a fine example) that these furtive snippets of gossip concerning our mutual acquaintance were simply a method of averting the acute awkwardness of mutual uninterest we felt when encountering one another in the street. The myth of Old Mother Hubbard was spread by us merely as a way of avoiding the admission we had nothing else in common and nothing whatever to say to one another. I am ashamed to admit that more than once I found myself inventing things about him just to make these moments of social infelicity a little less unbearable.

*   *   *

"& she invited you here today. Yeh, that's Meta all over."

"The thing is..." I didn't know whether to tell him the truth or not. Meta seemed to imply that we were going to lie to him. I decided I had no more reason to trust her than him: "The thing is that I'm looking for someone & she thought you might be able to help."

"Oh yeh?"

"He's called Amrit Singh..."

"A paki?"

"Well... no." At the time, I was trying to develop a new tolerance for this word where it was applied to actual Pakistanis, along with a complete intolerance of its misapplication in reference to Punjabis & Bangladeshis & so on. I'd heard a perfectly convincing argument from a student at a conference who described himself as a *Paki Firebrand*, that it was far preferable to the term 'Asian'. But this was not the kind of man you lectured about political correctness. "He's a poet. Bit of a weirdo. You probably know him as *Zomby*."

There was no reply. The roar of the kettle peaked & it clicked off. The teenager applied his hot knife to the hash & held a pintglass above the brick. It quickly filled with blue-grey smoke. Careful not to let any of the precious stuff curl out from under the lip, he put down the knife, picked up a yellow & white striped bendy straw, inserted it upside down in the pintglass & sucked out all the contents in a single breath. As Eels came in with three cups of tea in one hand, the teenager replaced the glass & the straw on top of the brick, threw back his head & blew what remained unextracted by his young efficient respiratory system up to splash all over the ceiling. He stayed in that position as the tea was doled out.

"Tell me about him." Eels said.

So I did. I spent a hot cup of tea's worth of time explaining everything to him. I told him about meeting Hannah at the conference, about my week spent going through Amrit's things, about my failed attempt to get off with her, about following the tramp, about the graffiti, about finding the poem, about the hotel, about Meta & the Pussy Club, everything. When I came to a pause or took a sip of tea, Eels offered the simplest prompts: 'what happened next?' or 'go on'. He never asked me why, or questioned any of the information or appeared in the least doubtful of events, some of which seemed frankly quite incredible even to me. As I spoke, the teenager continued with his hotknifing ritual. He became much less adept & accurate as he got stoned & a lot of the smoke was escaping from the glass, finding its way into my own lungs. The smell of it was overwhelming. As a result of Eels subtlety & the effect of the stray cannabis, I found myself going into more & more detail. It was as if I needed to explain it all to myself. I seemed incapable of holding back any of the salient facts.

All, that is, except one. I never let Eels know I had the poem with me in my bag. I don't know why, but I told him I'd put it back in Room 426 the previous afternoon when I'd left the library & gone into town. Maybe I didn't want to admit I'd stolen it. I couldn't say.

> $e slid £e liner pencil from its groove,
>   Took off £e black end's metal cap and licked
>   £e point. (Mechanics do £at, men who move
>   Your furniture around in vans.) $e flicked,
>   A line across each eyelid to improve
>   £e definition of its edge, £en ticked
>   Away from where her eyelids met: to lift
>   £e corners up and make £em less skew-whiff.

---

*   *   *

The process of forgetting about Hubbard began by making him a legend. It soon became quite easy to believe that he did not exist. I had long forgotten him when I found the letter:

> Dear DG
>
> We should proceed cautiously on this matter. It would be inadvisable to allow the news to spread. At the very least, correspondence with the University should be avoided at all costs. If you have not already seen to this, it should go without saying that the papers and so on are to be immediately destroyed.
>
> If there are, as you imply, no records of a home address for Hubbard, or even next of kin, my advice would be not to enter him on the register as withdrawn but simply to remove him from the list altogether. As far as teaching staff are concerned, his attendance has simply tailed off in the second year. There is nothing very unusual about that. I do not know what your experience has been elsewhere, but in delicate cases of rustication there has always been a tradition here of striking students' details from the list and behaving officially as if they left at the end of the previous year. This is as much for their own sakes as the college's. The preferred route on this occasion might be simply to extend this erasure to include his first year of attendance and therefore eradicate him entirely from college records. It is something which staff, students and authorities alike will understand and is not at all unprecedented.
>
> My only additional suggestion is that a rumour might be instigated to explain this course of action. (The most effective method is to instruct the butler of the Junior Common Room in strictest confidence to scotch any such idle talk should it arise). Perhaps socialism or sodomy.
>
>   yours, NHT

This letter was my Madeleine. I was not three sentences into reading it when I began to tremble uncontrollably. I had often indulged in Proustian fantasies about the other documents I had read, imagining the past flooding back at the instigation of an evocative sentence or a moving photograph, but as soon as I read the word 'Hubbard' in that second paragraph, I became aware that previous to this instant I had only been going through the gestural motions of nostalgia: as if the rapturous intake of breath, the wide-eyed gaze into the middle distance, the flicker of a smile, the slow shake of the head might somehow combine to bring about that sudden saturation of memory I secretly acknowledged would probably have to precede these outward symptoms.

*   *   *

When I finished, Eels said simply: "Yep, I can tell you what you need to know."

"You can? So Zomby *is* Amrit Singh?"

"Fucked if I know, mate, but I can tell you where to find him."

"That's great."

"Before I do though, I'm going to have to explain something to you."

"What's that?"

"I don't deal in money."

"You don't?"

"Money is shit. Money, as the man says, is the root of all evil. I have lived for the past fourteen years without handling a single penny of any official currency."

"Really?"

"Yeh, really. I said I had a complex way of doing business & that's it. That's why I need Meta. I'll deal drugs, but I won't touch any form of state-backed token of exchange."

"Ok."

"You see, you probably think I'm some sort of low-life scum..."

"No, not at all." I laid a hand on my bag & glanced at the teenager. Thankfully, he seemed to have drifted off into oblivion. I reckoned I could get away from Eels if I needed to. He didn't look that fit.

"... but I don't do this for profit, man. What the fuck d'you think I'd be living here for if I did? & I'm not a junky. I never touch any of the stuff I sell. I don't even drink. I wouldn't do this shit if I didn't think it was making a difference. But it is. I'm bringing a new economics to the street. Everybody knows they can come to me for anything they want, but if they bring cash into my flat, they don't get squat... & they don't get to come back."

"So, what? you barter?"

"No I don't fuckin barter. I give people what they need for free. Then they have to do something for me. It doesn't have to be a material exchange at all. They can offer me a service... advice or whatever. As soon as they can offer me something I want, I'll give them something else for free. I decide what. I decide when. & I decide how much. & when they're giving stuff to me, or doing me a favour, they get to behave in exactly the same way. You always can when you're doing favours. That's the beauty of it."

"That sounds cool." I was wondering what the hell they gave him. He didn't seem to have anything worth mentioning around in his flat.

"*Cool* is a stupid word, man. It isn't in the least bit *cool*. Its fuckin radical. The idea is to make the state entirely irrelevant in the daily lives of the people on the street. & to break them out of the cycle of authoritarian dependency."

($e still looked like $e'd just got out of bed.)
    $e turned it round and licked £e o£er tip.
At £is rate, all £e waxy two-tone lead
    Would make her tongue look like a barcode slip.
£e mirror-woman tilted back her head
    And folded down her left eye's bottom lip,
Exhibiting £e socket's $ocking pink,
An outline round its edge in wet red ink.

117.4 *barcode slip*: I am sure this line contains encrypted information. As in a crossword puzzle, 'slip' prompts a rearrangement of the previous word. It seems, on the surface, to explain the mysterious 'barcode' appearance of the tongue (perhaps a word one might alternatively interpret as 'excluding the cryptic', like in 'bar-none') as an elision of 'barrocoed', meaning *made Barroco* (i.e. *decorated with Baroque ornamentation*). The 'slip' would therefore be a simple *coup d'oueil* to the reversal of prosodic emphasis from the less unusual, but iambic, 'Baroque(d)'.

There is, however, (unsurprisingly) another much more disturbing meaning hidden here. If 'Baroco(ed)' only has a single <r> it reproduces a mnemonic of scholastic philosophers, first used in Medieval Latin, in which A indicates a universal affirmative proposition and O a particular negative proposition. It denotes the fourth mood of the second syllogistic figure (AOO-2), in which a particular negative conclusion is drawn from a universal affirmative major premise and a particular negative minor: *all futures come to pass, but certain visions never come to pass, so certain visions are not futures*.

I am increasingly of the opinion that simply scanning my eyes across each line of this encrypted future might in some way be contributing to its initiation at the expense of other more benign possibilities. I have recently curtailed all attempts to reproduce its tasteless Birmingham articulations vocally out of a growing worry that the thing might be some kind of spell: a vision of the future whose annunciation could become its own enactment.

117.6-8 *left eye's bottom lip… wet red ink*: The implication is that the eye can speak, both as a mouth and as a 'bloody letter' like the one that flutters down from the balcony in Thomas Kyd's *The Spanish Tragedy* or the contract for the soul of *Dr Faustus*. The ludicrous fashion in which Christopher Marlowe is claimed by the Queen's coroner to have died (he was, of course, acting well outside his jurisdiction) recalls that most apocryphal of English deaths: Harold Godwinson on the battlefield of Hastings. Both men are supposed to have met their end as the result of a violent penetration of the left eye: in Harold's case by a fatefully stray Norman arrow and in Marlowe's by a dagger in a quite unlikely thrust during a common brawl. There are obvious Masonic overtones to all of this.

"I want to get the local dropouts using their natural ingenuity & talents rather than just robbing credit cards & cashing giros. I'm not doing this for fuckin style points. & if I can shift their perceptions at the same time... get a bit of overdue medical intervention in to fuck about with their artificially constructed psyches, all the better."

"This has got something to do with Zomby hasn't it?" I thought I recognised this stuff.

"Well, I'll tell you what it really has to do with him. It means you're going to have to do something for me if you want to find out where he is. I don't normally divulge any information about my trusted clients to anyone except my other trusted clients. Get my meaning? In my line of business that's a given."

"Of course. That makes sense."

"So what can you offer me?"

I thought about this for a second. I didn't know. I wasn't much good at practical things & what the hell would he want with anything I owned. He didn't seem to have a bike, though. I had a bike in Glasgow he could have. He was some kind of anarchist. Anarchists like pushbikes. There's something pugnacious & defiant about them. The trouble was, I liked my bike too & couldn't really afford to get another one. & Eels didn't seem like a man built for collecting objects... or for cardio-vascular exercise for that matter.

"Why don't you ask me what I want?" he said.

"Ok, what do you want?"

He smiled & folded his arms, "I want the poem."

A wave of panic ran through me. What would a man like him want with a poem. This was serious, though. I really shouldn't have had the thing at all. I couldn't even be sure it was actually Amrit Singh who'd written it. Well, ok, I probably could, but what I'd told him about putting it back in the cupboard yesterday absolutely should have been the truth. As I sat there, the poem less than an inch under my palm, I wished it was true.

"Well, you see, I can't be sure it was actually written by... Zomby. I mean I don't know yet if Zomby really is Amrit Singh. Not unless..." I fished desperately, "you can tell me that he is..."

"The poem's all I want. That's it. Or... I suppose you could just give me the keys & I could pick it up myself..."

"mmm... I don't think that'd be very wise."

"I'm not a thief you know. Whatever. I want that roll of parcel paper with the poem on it. Then I'll tell you where to find the Zomby. I'll even take you to him myself."

I squirmed. It's not a metaphor. I literally squirmed in my clothes. The one thing in the world I wanted most right now was to get out of there. I wanted to throw my bag out of the window & run. I think I'd have promised him anything. Just as long as I didn't actually have to surrender that document to him.

£e sight of it was always a surprise.
    It isn't some€ing £at you're meant to see:
Your eyeball swivelling away... £e size
    Of it. Imagine if it just popped free:
A gaping tunnel to £e brain. Do eyes
    Still function dangling down? £ere used to be
A glass-eyed barman down £e Swan; he'd wink
And say 'aye-aye,' and £en he'd get your drink.

---

*   *   *

A Madeleine is wrong. It was more blunt—more violent and shocking—like the detonation of an unexploded bomb. The whole story of Hubbard's disappearance spattered my imagination as this fragment of historical shrapnel flew up from the explosion site and struck me in the face. I quite literally reeled from the impact, the images trickling before my eyes like blood from the wound. Most vividly of all, I witnessed Hubbard hunched over in the quad, muttering something to himself, his lips and eyeballs bulging as he dug maniacally into the gravel path with a dessert spoon. I watched him framed by the window of this room as if that was how I had originally seen him: in the moonlight, replacing the gravel in each circle with a different powder from a case of small glass jars with heavy stoppers.

I had not seen him at all, of course; nobody had. All that was found the next morning by the students of Temple were ten round scorch marks in the gravel, the size of saucers. There was no sign of Hubbard ever again, but it took a while for anyone to notice he had gone and consequently nobody put two and two together. There seemed little reason for the Temple students to doubt the groundsman's theory of a prank involving Chinese fireworks, especially when two notoriously louche postgraduates were reprimanded for damaging college property and (despite the fact nobody had even noticed at the time) for causing a disturbance. Beyond the college, however, (strangely, besides Old Mother himself, no other Temple student ever came to the PS) there were those of us who had heard Hubbard speak of 'Dancing Bridget's Flowers'.

This marginal anecdote is already bulging well beyond the proportions I initially intended for it, so I will avoid a full rendition of Hubbard's game: strange perhaps when one considers that it was in order to find whatever I could about Hubbard's performance of this ceremony on the night of his disappearance in 1922—to recapture that addictive coup de memoir *which had left me tingling with desire for more as if my skin were alive with hungry ants—that I abandoned my previous work and spent the next fifty or sixty hours burrowing physically without rest amongst the documents, screwing up irrelevant papers, even tearing them with my teeth in painful frustration and scattering them about me like a nesting gerbil. Exhausted and exasperated I took the unprecedented decision to go out into the quad to see if the pattern was still there.*

It was as I staggered out into the dark of March that I must have knocked the roll of parcel paper onto my sheepskin rug.

*   *   *

"Ok," I said, "how about I photocopy it?"

"You can do what you like with it, pal, but I want the original."

I was sure he was eyeing my bag. I was shivering slightly. It was a very warm day, I shouldn't have been shivering. I moved even further forward on my perch & tried to enter into the negotiations a little. I needed to do something quick. He was walking all over me. He had been ever since I'd pressed his buzzer.

"That seems a strange request for a man who doesn't believe in material property," I countered, "what difference does the format make? I've never been able to understand book collectors & all that myself. Surely, if you don't believe in commodification you should believe the text is its verbal content, not some physical object that's been mystically imbued with value because it's been touched by a historical figure... or, worse still, just because it's rare. As far as I'm concerned it's madness to pay a thousand pounds for a first edition of a 'classic' you can pick up for a quid in the local W. H. Smith's. You should read 'The Work of Art in the Age of Mechanical Reproduction.' I'll make sure it's a good copy. It'll all be readable. Well, as readable as it is in the original, at least."

"That's good... because it's you who's going to have to read it. & if that's really what you think, that's gunna be just fine with you." He put his empty mug down for subtle emphasis.

I had no answer for that. I was trembling with adrenaline. Eels seemed as calm as ever.

"But listen," he relented, "I realise making a photocopy is an extra hassle. I should repay your for it. I'm going to give you something." He got up & made his way across the room.

"No, really, that's not necessary. I agree. You might as well have the original." As things stood, I realised, I could promise Eels the world & then just disappear. I didn't owe him anything just yet. All I'd accepted off him so far was a rather weak & nasty cup of tea. If he gave me something else though, something he considered valuable...

For all his talk of anticapitalist economics, Eels could quite easily have been just another kind of loan-shark. He gives you something when you're really in need. He seems very generous about it. But then he owns you. Then you have to keep on offering him favours until he decides you've earned the right to get a bit more of what you need: just enough & just in time to keep you coming back.

Maybe he wasn't like that. Maybe he really was a tracksuit-trousered philanthropist, but I wasn't taking any chances. I tried to catch him by the arm as he went past. He shrugged me off, politely enough to make it seem a threat rather than a reflex.

"I insist," he murmured.

As soon as he'd shut the living-room door behind him & padded off down the hall, the teenager's head snapped back upright. He turned to me. His eyes were yellow & bloodshot.

"Get out!" he hissed, "Get up out of that seat & get out of here now!"

$e delicately whitened £e soft ridge
    Towards £e tear-duct: a trick $e learned
Under a makeup artist's tutelage:
    A must where blood$ot eyeballs were concerned.
In Italy, women of privilege,
    To get £e bright eyes courtesans all yearned,
Had deadly night$ade eyedrops—*belladonna*—
One swig of £at and Romeo's a goner.

119.7 *deadly nightshade*: Despite beginning his 'Ode to Melancholy' thus:

> No, no! go not to Lethe, neither twist
>   Wolf's bane, tight-rooted, for its poisonous wine;
> Nor suffer thy pale forehead to be kissed
>   By nightshade, ruby grape of Proserpine;

John Keats, who seems to have had a taste rather above his meagre means and social station for exotic fruit, slips all too predictably into the implied combination of feminine sexuality and death that is the quintessence of *belladonna*:

> Ay, in the very temple of delight
>   Veiled Melancholy has her sovran shrine,
>   Though seen of none save him whose strenuous tongue
> Can burst Joy's grape against his palate fine;
>   His soul shall taste the sadness of her might,
>   And be among her cloudy trophies hung.

It is no coincidence that it is by bursting 'Joy's *grape* against his palate fine' that the epicure in question is to find the *sovereign shrine* of Melancholy, and that these lines rhyme with both *wine* (the result of its fermentation, cognate with *vine*) and the previous occurrence of the name of the same fruit: 'nightshade, ruby grape of Proserpine.' This reference completely flouts the traditional association of Persephone with the pomegranate, of course, and does so in order to assert precisely the metaphorical graft that Keats finds in a cluster of rhymes. It hardly requires me to point out that the connotations of royal sequestration in 'veiled Melancholy in her sovran shrine' are specifically designed to recall Persephone, and therefore, one assumes, Keats' own mother: the perpetual figure in his mind who combines an aggressive sexual desire with death.

Keats, as the Freudians cannot stop telling us lately, is probably suckling at the metaphoric breast. It is a cliché of the bacchanalian poetic image that the grape is symbolic of the nipple. Book II of *Endymion* tells us that the hero had 'commun'd / With Melancholy thought: O he had swooned / Drunken from pleasure's nipple' (870-872) and making a quite clear allusion to the cosmetic use of *belladonna* refers to the following: 'Those lips, O slippery blisses, twinkling eyes… these tenderest milky sovereignties… the nectar-wine' (758-60).

This last term puns on another fruit which takes its place in this cluster of intoxicating rhymes and for Keats seems to embody pleasure itself:

Talking of Pleasure, this moment I was writing with one hand, and with the other holding to my Mouth a Nectarine--good god how fine--It went down soft pulpy, slushy, oozy--all its delicious embonpoint melted down my throat like a large beatified strawberry. I shall certainly breed.

(Letter of the 22nd Sept. 1819)

In the 'Ode on Melancholy', as in *Endymion*, the lips, the eyes, the nipples and *the ruby grapes of Proserpine* are crushed together into a exotic oozing *sépage* of metaphoric sexual-mortality beneath the poet's squelching iambic feet:

And feed deep, deep upon her peerless eyes.

She dwells with Beauty—Beauty that must die;
  And Joy, whose hand is ever at his lips
Bidding adieu; and aching Pleasure nigh,
  Turning to poison while the bee-mouth sips;

This passage of *The Birmingham Queen* is ripe with the same *slushy* implications of *thanatos* in the libidinous highlighting of the features of feminine sexual attraction that find such a perfect metaphoric *embonpoint* in the ironic employment of a pretentious, ornamental word like *belladonna*.

*   *   *

On second thoughts, I might permit myself a paragraph of explanation...

'Dancing Bridget's Flowers' was a version of hopscotch. (Hubbard's obsession with this game had become so all encompassing that, by the time of the society's collapse, he was expressing a troubling desire to infiltrate his adaptations into schoolyards.) In this particular variation the court was a homologue of the Kabbalist Tree of Life. Each of the 'squares' was actually a small circular pile of an unstable substance with a direct alchemical correspondence to the 'sephira' it occupied. The ultimate goal was to reflect one's spirit off the dark side of the moon, or some such thing, by accurately reproducing the astrological alignments at the time of the ceremony with the correct numerical and geometric patterns of play. The paths one took also allowed words to be spelled out in Hebrew which made it possible, via some mysterious interaction of the semantic and the geometric, for the player to move through time. If I recall correctly, the phase of the moon was supposed to determine the direction of travel: full moon towards the future, new moon towards the past, and everything in between. The marker used was, predictably enough, a copper coin; other than that, the rules were the same as your common-or-garden hopscotch. If the ceremony was perfectly enacted the sephira would ignite spontaneously one by one during the final pattern as the powders mixed beneath the soles of one's bare feet (it was quite typical for Hubbard's later games to require players to be naked). 'Bridget's Fire' would be projected from the moon into the centre of the abyss (the invisible Da'ath sephira; Hubbard gave this mystical emanation a welter of alternative names: 'The Tree of Knowledge', 'The Universal Hearth', 'The Cosmic Focus', 'The Vagina of the Goddess', and that kind of thing), then in you hopped and off (into the mists of time, presumably) you popped.

*   *   *

$e did £e o£er side. Eye$adow next—
　　$e flipped its lid and set it down to dab
Her middle finger in £e deep convex
　　Erosion mark. £e silver had gone drab
And brown around £e edges where £e flecks
　　Of different makeup formed a dirty scab.
But in £e centre it was soft and bright.
　　$e smudged it on her lids: left hand for right

120.4-6 *The silver had gone drab… a dirty scab.* The silver 'Eyeshadow' has previously (113.3) been likened to a 'commemorative crown' in order to make the point that in the cases both of the cosmetic paint and of the new cupronickle coinage (which includes the Coronation Crown depicting the new Queen on horseback) the 'silver' in question is an imitation. Here the degradation of the silver coinage (the embodiment of Anglo-Saxon wealth and unity since Offa's penny) is extended to include the dirt it has picked up from countless thumbs and fingertips in circulation. There is a clear implication that the 'flecks of different makeup' that form 'a dirty scab' are a comment on the debilitating effects on English society and industry of the current flood of immigration into our major cities and their workplaces (the so-called *windrush*). This might seem like a timely warning—the kind of sensible artistic contribution to the debate on immigration that is all too easily dismissed as *racialism*—it might, that is, if it were not that the poet clearly relishes this muddying of Britain's cultural waters.

Birmingham, quite unsurprisingly, is currently at the epicentre of this reverse-colonisation from the old Empire. This poet's choice of that shady place as his dire utopia—with its huge, dusky Guyanese travesty of Britannia—is clear evidence of his desire to pursue a bloody-minded *multicultural* agenda. There is the typical combination of perverse lustfulness, *thanatos* and virulent anti-Englishness in this image of the big Negroid thumb sinking into the little pot of dirty silver grease like a bruised exotic fruit and then smearing the resulting warpaint on its heavy eyelids. Sterling has become just a colorant accessory to a performance of creolized sexual abandon that simultaneously recalls the Classical image of the two staters placed on the closed eyes of a corpse to pay Charon for his passage across the Styx. The Britannia of this poem is not just black, male and monstrous but also, seemingly, the walking dead: a *zombie*.

121 CUT
And right hand for the left. *His* eyes were green
　　And wet. Not beautiful exactly, but
You kind of sank in them. She'd never seen
　　them focus on her, they were always shut
Or staring through her, and beyond—their sheen,
　　their sense of depth—they seemed immaculate.
She'd think she was dissolving in his gaze,
As if his focus was enough to phase

122 CUT
Her body out of all existence; or
   She'd sink in bogs between their tangled ferns
—The squelchy pitfalls of the forest floor—
   A brave, pith-helmeted Victorian who earns
A slow death for presuming to explore
   Their sacred jungle, suffocating as he learns,
Too late, that he can never own this rich land
Because his body's a possession of the quicksand.

- *phase*: A misapplication of the homophone for 'faze' under pressure from the imaginative context of a hypnotic gaze. The poet's (literally *lunatic*) mind is subconsciously orbiting the image of the moon from which we get the word. It is a poetic commonplace to liken the romantically enhanced gaze to lunar light, and the poet has succumbed to the temptation unconsciously to invent the phrasal verb *to phase/faze out* meaning, one presumes, to disturb (*faze*) to such an extent that the effect is similar to the waning of the moon (ie. *moving to a weaker phase*).

    It is possible that 'fade-out' also plays a part in the psychological pressure behind this lexical error. This is a term of jargon from the world of cinema and television photography, and is an effect (of a slow diminution in the definition of the picture until the image disappears) which has become a cliché in the portrayal of romantic scenes.

    Rather than a mistake, therefore, we might speculate that this is an intentional neologism on the part of the poet, who wishes to combine the semantic fields of *faze*, *phase*, and *fade* in order to represent a clichéd romantic moment of the meeting of eyes across a room in terms which cause us to accept the much more insidious messages extant in his characteristic layering of romantic clichés from bad poetry and worse cinema and television.

    Unlike this caricatured Britannia, who disappears into fictional oblivion like a romantic lead as the picture *fades* (or the moon as it approaches its last *phase*), we need, despite the poet, to remain *unfazed*.

And right for left. Mascara next: you pump
    It like a piston for a bit. God knows
What £at accompli$es... it stops a lump
    From forming on £e bristles, $e supposed.
Of course, it wasn't likely it would clump
    Toge£er; it was dear. Tanya chose
£e product for its 'smoo£ness on £e la$es'.
(Which made her €ink of when £e Captain €ra$es

123.1-2 *pump / It like a piston*: This is an obvious likening of the *mascara* tube to the Newcomen/Watt/Murdock steam engine. The fool (the *maskhara*: See 107.4) in both formal and folk theatre always has a *marotte* or truncheon that he uses variously as a puppet *altar ego*, a *slapstick* weapon and a bawdy phallic symbol. The tube of mascara definitively fulfils something akin to this cluster of functions for the fool-transvestite in this scene; its similarity to the working core of the steam engine, the piston (obviously a piece of machinery with sexual connotations; its name is cognate with *pestle* and *pistil*), is designed to make this association much more global. In the ensuing stanzas the unsheathed brush is to be likened to a sado-masochistic 'bullwhip' (originally a *pizzle*), a sword (perhaps a *pistolese*) and a conductor's baton.

123.4 *she supposed*: At first sight this sudden intrusion into what had apparently become the character's unmediated thoughts seems to be a simple reporting clause. There is a typical confusion of multiple voices at work, however: one that ambiguates the relationship between private thought and enunciated speech to such an extent that the difference between these things is almost nullified. This sentence could just as easily be understood as an ironically indirect version of reported direct speech: ' "I suppose it stops a lump from forming on the bristles", she said' as it could a genuine direct *quotation* of an internal statement which only the external narrator (the coin) adjudges to be a *supposition*, or even a report (a *translation*) of a non-linguistic psychological event. Thus, just at the point where we are suddenly made aware again of the multiple levels of narration we had been deliberately lulled into forgetting, the voices are actually being mischievously confused via the employment of a narrative technique (so common amongst the libertine Bloomsbury set) whereby consciousness and speech are represented as vaguely and fluidly as possible. This effect demonstrates how the poem's continually anarchic and prurient breaches of privacy—designed to propound an acute anti-individualism: an uncontrolled hedonistic orgy of societal agglomeration—go far enough as to completely undermine any clear distinction between psychological interiority and public speech.

I frowned & mouthed the word *why?*

"If you're lucky, he's gone to weigh you some draw. It'll take him a few minutes. Get the fuck out of here while you still can. You don't know how much danger you're in, man..."

The kid was obviously getting paranoid. It wasn't a threat. He actually thought he was warning me of some impending doom. He was obviously off his tree. He looked truly terrified & truly terrifying though. His eyes were wide & his pupils were entirely dilated. It was almost as if his gaze was contagious. I was breathing it right into me.

"You don't know who this guy is, man. You've walked into the fuckin lion's den. This is the quartermaster, man, he's fuckin dark. I'm tellin ye. You've got to get yer arse out of this flat, pronto."

I put my bag on, but I didn't get up. The teenager leant forward, extending his long torso out over the brick like the front end of a python.

"You never heard of ABRA, man?" I shook my head, "The Associated Birmingham Republican Army. You're a fuckin liability, you are: you're so fuckin ignorant. You've really never heard of them?" I shook my head again. "They're made up of all sorts of badass fuckin terrorist rejects & drug-dealers & political nutcases & stuff: dropouts from the IRA, the Red Brigades, Anarchists & Trotskyists & fuckin Maoists, & now there's Gypsies & Eastern Europeans involved & Islamicists & every other hairbrained fuckin maniac you can name. They've even got magicians & witches & stuff who are supposed to do magic. People say they can time-travel & shit like that. You remember that vampire in Ward End. That was one of them, man, they're fuckin everywhere. But they're no new thing. They've been around for ever, man."

"Eels is the Quartermaster. He gets hold of things for them. He's the procurer. That fuckin ladyboy's high up as well. The one who sent you here. Her & Eels work together. They're supply & recruitment. They must've thought their fuckin boat had come in when you turned up with that stupid fuckin look on your face, asking questions about the Zomby. Jesus. The Zomby is their fuckin leader man. The Zomby is like the fuckin messiah to these people. I should just chib you now & put you out yer misery, ye stupid cunt."

"The thing is," he backed off a bit & laughed nervously as I stood up, worrying he might've been mistaken about my wimpish appearance, "there's a legend that some document exists that was the original basis of the organisation. It was the Zomby who looked after it. It was supposed to have come back from the future to some period in the past — maybe the nineteenth century, maybe even earlier — to predict the formation of a separatist republic in Birmingham in the third millennium: a kind of anarchist city-state that would eventually lead the rest of the world into a massive revolution to overthrow capitalist America. In the seventies man, they thought it was about to come true. The Zomby was active. It was gunna be the new *Free Derry*. Some shit like that. Anyway, the Zomby lost it somehow. That's what led to the pub bombings. & he's been hiding out, waiting for it to turn up again. & now they think it has... They call it *The Scroll*."

£e sailors on a $ip: like Fletcher Christian
   In *Mutiny on The Bounty*—sauerkraut
And whips. $e'd always harboured a suspicion
   £at £ere was some€ing prurient about
£ose scenes: £e manly backs, £e bullwhip swi$ing,
   £e muscles… *crack!* £e stripe, £e stifled $out:
£e discipline! £ose sailors were as scarred
As any slave of £e Marquis de Sade.)

124.2 *sauerkraut*: This putrid German cabbage pickle was carried by the British Navy as a reserve source of essential vitamines (not that the word for these essential nutrients was known to them) to protect sailors from beriberi and scurvy. The word itself is a good example of the differing attitudes to foreign terms in different languages. The English version is simply a reproduction of the High German. In French, however, the Alsatian dialect form *sacrote* has been naturalized via a typical folk-etymology into *choucroute*: from 'chou' *cabbage* and 'croûte' *crust* (a word which, by colloquial extension, has come to mean *food in general*). The propagation of words across the continent has always been a game of *cabbages and kings*. It is in the rotting mulch of fecund ambiguities this process inevitably creates that this poet's linguistic, political and moral ideas have been allowed to multiply like the writhing larvæ of a pestilential revolution.

124.5-8 *the bullwhip swishing… the Marquis de Sade*: This is based, no doubt, upon a quotation commonly (and entirely apocryphally) attributed to the current Prime Minister, Winston Churchill, during his time as First Lord of the Admiralty. When accused of flouting the ancient traditions of the Royal Navy, he supposedly remarked: 'The traditions of the Navy, what are they? just rum, sodomy and the lash.'

This was obvious bullshit — sub-Buffy The Vampire Slayer bullshit — & I didn't need this kid's ranting to put the frighteners on me in such a delicate situation, but it was scaring the shit out of me nonetheless. It wasn't the fantastic content of it so much as the sudden bizarre fluency of ideas. After the first quarter of an hour I'd spent in his company, I wouldn't have been surprised to discover he was mute. Now an endless stream of paranoia, laced together from the conversations he'd overheard, was pouring out of this kid's racing mouth with all the abundance & fluidity of the used cannabis smoke that had previously been fountained through its lips. I was obviously a bit stoned myself, & you know what they say: *out of the mouths of babes.* I started edging towards the door.

"They think you've got it. They'll stop at fuckin nothing to get it back. Your life is worthless to them, man. All they want is the scroll. Tolkien knew all about it, man. So did John Wyndham. Read the fuckin Birmingham writers, man."

The kid was right about one thing, at least. I needed to get out of there.

"Listen, Eels," I called out as I hurried to the front door, "forget it, mate. The photocopying's on me. I don't smoke weed any more myself, these days anyway. I'll bring the poem round tomorrow, shall I?... See ya."

I didn't wait for a reply. I closed the door behind me & ran. My blood raced round my body as I scuttled down the steps, carrying the drug I'd inhaled faster & faster to every part of my metabolism as it went. I helter-skeltered down the flights. Approaching the ground floor, I slipped on my heels & slid down on my rucksack & my hands. The lift engineer, who'd been working just below me, popped his bearded head round the lift door:

"You alright, mate?"

"Yeh, yeh, it's ok." I clambered up & hurried on out as he continued.

"You could've used the other lift you know. I never knock them both down if I can help it. I only work one shaft at a time... as the actress said to the bishops."

I didn't know what to do with myself. I walked quickly back the way I'd come... at least I think it was the way I'd come. I couldn't be sure any more. My body had become like an off-road motorbike with a child on board. It was far too heavy & far too powerful. All I could do was hang on to the handlebars & maintain the revs up just enough to keep the thing upright, hoping it didn't slide away beneath me on a patch of mud. My chest roared & spluttered, my feet seemed to keep slipping off whatever footrests they were supposed to be on, my right side grew a stitch like an over-taut chain, the fingers of my left hand kept feeling for the brake & my right clenched desperately around the throttle. Everything about me throbbed.

I was on the canals. I stayed on the canals. When I got to the deep cuttings junction I didn't want to cross any footbridges so I continued North towards Aston. The canals seemed safer than the roads. Somehow, I didn't think...

$e drew £e spiral bru$ out like a sword.
    £e tube went: *pwup*. $e used it as a baton,
Conducting for a second, leaning forward
    To bring £e cellos in (and leave a pattern
Bespeckling £e sink.) $e soon got bored
    However; blinking, $e began to fatten
Her fea£ery black eyela$es wi£ deft
Bru$-strokes. £e right side's easy, but £e left

---

*   *   *

The porter had been right all along: it was absolutely ludicrous. The fact remained however that Old Mother disappeared leaving Temple College with nothing but a few scorch-marks in the path at the South East corner of the second quadrant.

The marks were hastily concealed by the groundsman but when I turned up one quiet afternoon to see for myself—the word of this remarkable coincidence having reached me via a fellow ex-Paraludican—I found it not at all difficult to rediscover the shape of the marks by scuffing aside the gravel with the outside of a casual shoe whilst pretending to pace up and down as I memorized a bit of Shakespeare. The pattern I revealed was obviously sephirotic. It was also very accurately measured out. A large pair of dividers or compasses (or perhaps just a cord and peg) appeared to have been used to score a vesica pisces *of three circles with a radius of two feet onto which the sephiroth were plotted as a tree of ten touching circles, two feet in diameter. In the centre of each of these there was a scorch mark.*

This was not the work of drunks. It was clearly a Hubbard hopscotch court:

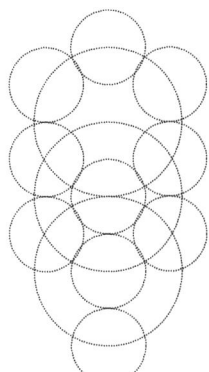 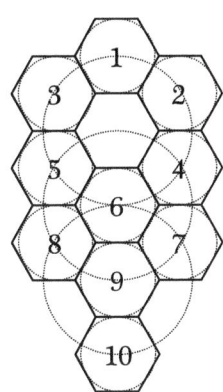 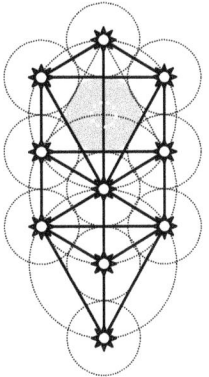

fig. 3: remnants of the Hubbard hopscotch court (as a kabbalist *tree of life*)

It was in this same geometric form that the memory of Hubbard's disappearance struck me on the night I read the letter. Each of the sephira on Hubbard's Kabbala hopscotch court seemed to strike a point on my face as the impact overwhelmed me: the tenth the chin, the ninth the bottom lip, the seventh and eighth the corners of the mouth, the sixth the nose, the fourth and fifth the cheek-bones, the second and third the eyes, and the first the middle of the brow. The image of the tree of life, which I had neither needed nor tried to visualize since my student days, was burned into my imagination once again. I knew immediately I would have to see if it was still there.

*   *   *

HOCKLEY

I didn't think what? That ABRA agents wouldn't come looking for me? That I could hide down here? That was fucking ludicrous. I was stoned. I had to get a grip on myself. I sat on a bench & felt my face. It was like an animated waxwork. What the hell was going on? It can't just have been the passive smoke from the kid's hotknife marathon. It must've been something else they gave me...

The tea! Of course. It had tasted very strange. Magic mushrooms maybe. That was probably the kind of thing a slimy bastard like Eels would do. He looked the type. But who was this Eels anyway? Was he even called Eels? I tried to reason the thing out. Socrates claimed that wine had no effect on his ability to reason. So hemlock was no challenge either. Liberty caps he would have taken in his stride.

Number one: it was only Meta who told me about Eels. & she gave me a different address altogether. It was similar, but not similar enough to have much chance of being the right place. No, there was the teenager too. That's number two. But he only mentioned Eels' name after he'd heard me tell the story... number three... during which time I'd thought he'd been asleep. So he was obviously capable of lying. Number four. As was Eels. Number five. Even if he was the person Meta had referred to, & even if all that cobblers about not letting silver cross his palm was true, that still meant he'd given me a load of crap about a meter reading when I'd first encountered him.

But that meter reading stuff was more believable than any of the rest of it. What was more likely was this Eels & his mate were just a couple of bored stoners looking for a passing stranger they could headfuck on a lazy Sunday morning. Er... number six. When I'd pushed the buzzer, they'd really thought I was the meter-reader & had planned to give me mushroom tea as a gag. That was fucking underhand that was: plotting to spike the cuppa of an innocent house-caller. It wasn't that strong though, thank god. I could still... number seven... well just about... From that point on they'd simply gone along with me until the drug began to work & then... stuck the knife in. They were probably still giggling uncontrollably about it, the cunts.

I was at the Farmer's Bridge locks. Right beneath the roots of the Telecom Tower. I daren't look up to see the spiky bloom of dishes & aerials at the summit of its long grey stem. Who knew what kind of psychoactive nectar such a monumental triffid might contain? If I climbed up to the street at the next bridge though, I realised I'd be virtually right outside the Pussy Club. That was weird. It seemed very odd that Eels's flat should only be five minutes from the place I'd learned about it. Things are rarely so close together in this Jackson Pollock of a city. But obviously they weren't. I couldn't even be sure that Eels existed. I'd have to go & see if I could find Meta again. I had to try & work out what the hell was going on.

Actually Birmingham is more like a thin growth of mould on a week-old cottage loaf.

> Is trickier. You ought to do it first,
>   But if it slips your mind, you have to lean
> Your head in a peculiar reversed
>   Approach to keep your o₤er eye pristine—
> Your elbow up. But $e was well rehearsed.
>   It had become a part of her routine.
> Her slender lashes curled, $e winked and felt
> ₤e lick of dominance her eyewhips dealt.

126.3-4 *Your head in a peculiar reversed approach*: A reminder of the coin's mis-struck effigy. The *coin* and the *quean* are becoming as indistinguishable as their names and their voices under the influence of the *maskhara*'s wand.

*   *   *

The night was cold and the temperature appeared to drop a little further as I struggled blindly down each flight of the stone staircase. The steps were worn into deep convexes by the millions of students who had trodden them across the years. It was treacherous under foot. I had to shuffle forward until I felt each bevelled ledge through the leather sole of my left shoe. I then stepped down with my right and repeated the process until I reached a landing where I could feel my way round to the next banister and start again. Having finally arrived at the entrance—it must have taken me ten minutes—I released the top and bottom latches which drove up and down directly into the bare stone from the left hand door and slid back the heavy bolt that fastened it to the right.

The metal was cold and rough. The fresh air rushed in through the opening as I pulled the handle back towards myself, a violent shiver coursing through my body. Every muscle seemed to tense in a way I had not experienced since my first gulp of Gin and Lime as a young boy. The night genuinely had a taste of alcohol and juniper. I retched like a cat expelling a fur-ball and screwed my eyelids up.

And there I stood, unable to go further, my hand fastened to the bolt. I had not set foot outside this building more than once or twice since my meeting with the Provost almost a year earlier. The ten-foot patch of gravel path I wanted to examine was clearly visible from my window. I had spent a good deal of the preceding months gazing intently at it: quietly spectating as a yellow wagtail bobbed the length and breadth of it or a blackbird scrabbled in its fringes. When it actually came to approaching it as a tangible reality however, I was petrified. I no longer felt any more capable of escaping the confines of this edifice of stone and wood than its own shadow was of drifting up into the clouds, or its reflection of floating down the river and out to sea. I was disgusted with myself. I could not even brave the relative shelter of a college quadrant any more.

I can not be sure how long I stood there: long enough, at least, for the tang in the air and the icy glimmer of the moonlight to give me vertigo. With each cool gust of the spring breeze I experienced—I can not even say it now without my frozen breath juddering in my lungs—I experienced... a primeval surge of terror more debilitating than the last.

*   *   *

There was no-one at the Pussy Club. The door was locked & there was no reply when I pressed the doorbell. I banged on the door. Nothing. That was hardly a surprise. It was a Sunday afternoon. I stepped out of the doorway back into the dingy arch of the railway bridge & tried waving at their CCTV camera to get the attention of some Security Guard.

Cooooeeey

I turned to see nothing but a pale flash of forehead splash itself dark red into the crunching give of my nose. My eyes filled with tears & my throat with blood. I choked & spat. I staggered. I saw nothing else for a good five minutes.

I hadn't gone down under the headbutt. But I crumpled as a trainer hit my gut from the other side. I slumped back against the wall & slipped down so my rucksack was in the join between the pavement & the tiled wall. I lay like an upturned tortoise as two men gobbed on me & kicked my sides.

I won't repeat the words they used. I can't. It was a stream of clichés. As their kicks & punches struck my body, various patches of me became strangely numb. There was no pain at all, just a spattering of insensibility, bursting & dissolving like falls of huge, heavy raindrops in the sea, rushing & waning on the gusts of wind. I began to giggle. I'm not sure why. I think there was a great feeling of relief. Like I'd been waiting to have the shit kicked out of me for years. Each dull blow seemed to carry with it a sense of purposeful release. It was a brutal variety of massage.

& there was something else. The reason they were doing this to me: it was obvious & it was stupid & it was bizarrely unthreatening. They thought I was gay. This was a gay club after all. & I'd been waving at the camera, probably looking as camp as Christmas. But there was no way the ideas of people like this could hurt me. Even if they kicked me to death, I wouldn't have been in the least bit worried about the way they thought. What they wanted more than anything was to see me broken. & they had no idea how to go about doing it. This wouldn't work. They were like a pair of conjoined twins who'd discovered their own penis was homosexual & were manically beating it to make sure it stayed down: to make sure it didn't stand to attention when it saw the bare arse of a seventeen year old boy. There was only one thing for it. They'd just have to cut it off.

I laughed & laughed as they pummelled me. They were probably enjoying this a lot less than I was. I'm no masochist. It's just that to find your enemies so ineffectual is always gratifying. Maybe if I'd actually been gay I would've been much more hurt by this: much more offended, much more indignant... maybe I'd even have been ashamed. I'm not so sure though. I think I'd still have felt like a man whose opponent in a duel has just pulled the trigger of his pistol to reveal a small red flag that pops out of the barrel to say "Bang!".

I heard the sound of doors unlocking. My attackers ran. The echoes of their footfalls skeetered around the tiles as they went. I began to hurt all over.

127

> Mascara done, $e slid £e bronzing pearls
>   From underneac€ her old cosmetic glue.
> $e screwed £e lid off, and wi£ gentle swirls,
> $e ga£ered colour on £e bru$. $e blew
> £e end and gave £e €ing a quick few twirls
>   To get £e excess off. And £en, wi£ two
> Neat bru$strokes—lighter £an a fea£er duster,
> $e lent her cheeks a touch of extra lustre.

---

127 There has previously (111.6) been a reference to Britannia's *brazen cheek*. Here, as the drag-queen applies bronze colour to highlight her cheekbones (and her appearance thereby comes more and more to resemble that of the narrating coin), we witness the metaphorical idiom undergoing a ludicrous literalization. As previously mentioned, *bronzing* is usually understood to mean the action of the sun in darkening the skin. In this case, however, it is important to notice the reversal of the process. This is more like pig-iron being given a bright bronze plate. The cosmetics applied to the upper regions of the face are certainly lighter than the skin onto which it is daubed or brushed. The result is no doubt garish and synthetic in appearance. One imagines the aspiration is to the extreme artificiality and metallic rigidity of a Nephertiti.

The more relevant antecedent in linguistic terms, however, is Æneas. Again we see Britannia likened to the man of Bronze whose descendants are to become the founders of New Troy in Rome. We should not forget that similar legends inform our understanding of the origins of the nation for whom this travesty so sarcastically means to stand: Great Britain. Geoffrey of Monmouth and Holinshed leave to the canon a tradition that asserts the founder of British civilisation (out of the wilderness of Albion, overrun with giants) to have been one Brutus, the Great Grandson of Æneas. The fact that this name is the one emblematically associated with Roman republicanism is not to be overlooked. The Brutus that supposedly gives Britain its name, is not just a king but is *the* original King of the Britons. His name however cannot fail to remind those secretly republican and atheist (like Christopher Marlowe) of the man who founded the republic at the death of the last Tarquin (*The Rape of Lucrece*) or who was the most important of the assassins of Julius Cæsar.

Strong hands forced their way under my armpits. I helped them help me up, wincing.

"Come on, let's get you inside." A woman's voice, but hard-bitten & unsurprised.

She helped me limp along. I wiped the tears from my eyes with a sleeve & recognised the lobby of the Pussy Club. I was still giggling a little, but now it hurt my ribs. She didn't seem in the least perturbed by this odd behaviour. Maybe it wasn't odd behaviour at all. Maybe people often laugh when they get beaten up.

She led me past the ticket desk into a little office. There was a small TV screen on the desk.

"Do you want me to call the Police?" She lowered me into a big wooden Queen Anne armchair with patterns carved into the arms. It seemed very out of place in there.

I shook my head a little, trying not to extend my aching neck muscles "Didn't get a look at them."

"We might have them on video."

"No, no, I'd rather not." I didn't want anybody seeing that. I'd look like a loony: laughing all the way through a case of GBH. Anyway, what was I doing here in the first place?

She nodded. This came as no surprise to her. "You know, if more people prosecuted..." She poured me a cup of water from a bottle & sat on the edge of the desk & handed it to me. She was a woman in her fifties. Quite small, with bleach-blonde hair tied back in a very tight pony-tail. She was wearing shorts. The tanned skin sagged slightly around the backs of her knees like she'd recently lost weight. She had intelligent-looking eyes: kind but also tough & realistic.

I shrugged & took a sip. Both things hurt. I swilled the metallic taste in my mouth & forced myself to swallow it. A drop of blood began to fledge tiny terracotta feathers on the surface of the water.

"So... you've got my attention, bab." She said

"I'm Sorry?"

"You were waving at the camera."

"So you saw that?"

"Yeh, I came as quickly as I could. I was on the other side of the building. It was obvious what was going to happen."

"Thanks."

"No problem. Sorry I couldn't get there any sooner. Are you going to be alright? I think you can breathe ok. Any bones broken?"

I tried moving things & prodding at my ribs. I felt bruised & cut but not injured.

"No... no I don't think so."

"So why were you looking for me?"

£e lipgloss was £e last €ing to be done.
    $e had uneven lips—$e'd bite £e skin
When $e was stressed. $e always had to run
    A fingernail on £em to begin
By scraping off all dead or alien
    Material. £e sleazy origin
Of which did not bear wondering about.
    $e did a sideways, off-£e-$oulder pout,

128.3 *stressed*: This is an archaic abbreviation of *distressed*. There is something very worrying about the implications for temporal continuity of this resurrection of an obsolescent item in the poet's futuristic dialect.

Spenser, in the *Faerie Queene*, provides a good example of this archaism (in a context which adds a little to our discussion of the legendary history of the nation) when introducing Dunwallo Molmutius (II.x.37-9):

> Then vp arose a man of matchlesse might,
> And wondrous wit to menage high affaires,
> Who stird with pitty of the stressed plight
> Of this sad Realme, cut into sundry shaires
> By such, as claymd themselues Brutes rightfull haires,
> Gathered the Princes of the people loose,
> To taken counsell of their common cares;
> Who with his wisedom won, him streight did choose
> Their king, and swore him fealty to win or loose.
>
> Then made he head against his enimies,
> And Ymner slew, or Logris miscreate;
> Then Ruddoc and proud Stater, both allyes,
> This of Albanie newly nominate,
> And that of Cambry king confirmed late,
> He ouerthrew through his owne valiaunce;
> Whose countreis he redus'd to quiet state,
> And shortly brought to ciuill gouernaunce,
> Now one, which earst were many, made through variaunce.
>
> Then made he sacred lawes, which some men say
> Were vnto him reueald in vision,
> By which he freed the Traueilers high way,
> The Churches part, and Ploughmans portion,
> Restraining stealth, and strong extortion;
> The gracious Numa of great Britanie:
> For till his dayes, the chiefe dominion
> By strength was wielded without pollicie;
> Therefore he first wore crowne of gold for dignitie.

fig. 4: front cover of British Vogue, August 1953

It is the 'dignity' of the Molmutine Law which gives Dunwallo the right to wear the golden crown. It is quite clear to me that such a correspondence is the antecedent of a stable gold-standard. This poem is making a mockery of such just and pragmatic ancient notions.

128.8 *off-the-shoulder*. This latest example of a hyphenated neologism denotes the pose much favoured on current feminine magazine covers where the model looks back over her shoulder at the camera as if the viewer is seeing her merely *en passant*. This is the epitome of the flirtatious 'sidewards glance'. On the cover of the most recent edition of *Vogue* (Aug 1953), for example, (see fig. 4) the model has her face pointed straight at the camera, whereas her shoulders are directed almost at a right-angle. She appears to be delicately curling the lashes of her left eye with the index finger of her bare left hand and holds a small compact mirror in the silk glove of her right. Her mouth is suggestively open, baring a row of bright, white teeth against the blood-red of her painted lips; her tongue is visibly arched as if she were *la-ing* a contented little tune. Her gaze is directed not at us but at the mirror: the reflective surface of which we need not imagine as we know already what it shows. This has the effect of revealing the pure whites of her eyes to the viewer. It is as though we have voyeuristically caught her in the act of some intensely private and intimate ritual, but that she is nonetheless so alluringly pleased to have been spied that we suspect her of being the kind of girl who might put on that kind of a performance entirely for our benefit. She is, after all, only looking at the same thing we are and seems permanently on the verge of shifting her eyes from the mirror to return this acutely intimate gaze. The multiple directions of her pupils, her shoulders and her nostrils suggest promiscuity and faithlessness, like a wife turning her torso towards her husband in a public place while her face and gaze flit invitingly in the direction of other passing men.

    I seem to remember reading an article in the literary periodical *Cosmopolitan* a few years ago decrying the bastardization of classical images (particularly the depictions of femininity in the Elgin marbles) on the covers of fashion magazines. We should thank God such erudite publications survive to counter these peddlers of woolly thinking and low-cut morals.

    It is this kind of complex and ambiguous pose the drag-queen strikes: one side of her body hidden, the other knowingly revealed (remember she allowed the dressing gown to slide off her shoulder 'deliberately') relishing the knowledge that she is always being watched. If the Queen's head on the obverse of a coin were to turn from its profile and look directly at us, it might look like this.

128.8 *pout*: The etymology of this word is obscure. The OED conjectures an agent noun *púta* from the putative verbal stem *put-* 'to swell'. To this I would add the observation that in an environment of such vague speculation the effect of possible folk-etymologies on the semantic development of these kinds of words cannot be ignored, especially not when deciphering a text so steeped in slang. There are a two here that might be influential. The Spanish for 'whore', for example, is *la puta* (something Swift plays on brilliantly in his page of reported discussions from the linguists of Laputa as to the origin of their floating island's name). The 'pout', remember, is not only the characteristic expression of feminine sullenness but also (therefore) a sign of sexual arousal and overt receptiveness (like the swollen hind quarters of a baboon on heat). A French borrowing in English reveals the traditional link between these things: a *boudoir* is literally a 'place for sulking' but is also commonly used in both languages to refer to the opulent bedroom of an experienced and sexually available woman.

    Further to this strand of prurient influence, we might speculate that the word *pudendum* has a role to play. Literally this means 'thing of shame' but if the 'lips' (*labia*) of the *pudendum* were to 'pout' (as the oral pout always implies—hence the fact that men are rarely said to do it) then this would be a very serious act of *im*pudence. Hence the ribald undertones of the

Unscrewed £e top, drew out £e plastic wand,
    And dabbed €ree globules on her lower lip.
$e spread it round wi£ care—$e wasn't fond
    Of how £e stuff had tasted when a drip
Fell on her tongue one time. Its tint of blonde
    Was not unlike a Silk-Cut filtertip.
Against her skin (£e $ade of a cigar) £ough,
    It made her look £e negative of Garbo.

Friar's *admonishment* of the young heroine in the 1597 Quarto version of *Romeo and Juliet* (III.iii.143-4): 'But like a misbehav'd and sullen [swollen?] wench, Thou pout'st upon thy fortune and thy love'. The version ('But like a *mishaped* and sullen wench, / Thou *puttest vp…*' [my emphasis]) in the Folios simply switches the gender of the genital double-entendre in order, perhaps, to reveal the pubescent boy-actor underneath the frock.

129.3 *fond*: This adjective denoting liking actually (and somewhat paradoxically) derives from the past-participle of the verb *to fon,* 'to lose flavour' or 'to develop an unpleasant taste'. *Fonned* therefore meant 'insipid or sickly' and only came to mean 'having a strong affection for' after a long period spent denoting a state of foolishness or genuine insanity. This is something of which this poet is clearly aware. He is intent, for revolutionary reasons, on upsetting the stability of our linguistic appropriation of the world by forcing us to inhabit this world of shifting semantic sands.

129.6 *Silk-Cut filtertip*: So named, one assumes, for a superior form of filter mechanism using silk that the poet thinks could plausibly replace the filter mouthpieces on cigarettes: currently made either from cotton wool wadding (as in the Benson and Hedges *Parliaments* so often alluded to in this poem) or else (in the case of Lorillard's *Kent* brand) from a potentially far superior material called 'micronite'. (see 35.7 *filtertips*)

129.8 *Garbo*: One of the so-called 'stars' of Hollywood whose zenith was reached during that heady period of transition from silent cinema to 'talking' film. Always a remnant of the former laconically inhabiting the latter, Garbo still belonged to that moment in cinema when capturing the human face plunged audiences into the deepest ecstasy, when one literally lost oneself in a human image as one would in a philtre, when the face represented a kind of absolute state of the flesh which could be neither reached nor renounced. It was not a painted face, but one set in plaster, protected by the surface of the colour, not by its lineaments. Amid all this snow, at once fragile and compact, the eyes alone, black like strange soft flesh, were two faintly tremulous wounds. This face, not drawn but sculpted in something smooth and friable, that is… at once perfect and ephemeral, came to resemble the flour-white complexion of Charlie Chaplin, the dark vegetation of his eyes, his totem-like countenance.

The temptation of the absolute mask (the mask of antiquity, for instance, before it ever got its disturbing modern name) perhaps implies less the theme of the secret, the clandestine, or the occult (as is the case with Italian half mask) than that of an archetype of the human face. Garbo and Chaplin offered to one's gaze a sort of Platonic Idea of the human creature, which explains why (aside from Chaplin's deliberately *false* moustache) their faces are almost sexually undefined, without however leaving one in any doubt.

One must assume it was this correspondence that Garbo's uncle Al was attempting to make implicit when he fashioned his nephew's silent character on Vaudeville. By the time they were coming to prominence on Broadway in the early 1920s, the reversion to the use of the family name of 'Marx' by Adolph (Garbo) and his brothers, Leonard (Chico) and Julius Henry (Groucho), seemed a serendipitous piece of topical satire that made light of grave events in Russia. Here, however, this serendipity of nomenclature has been adopted for much more worrying purposes. *Garbo* was so named presumably by way of ironic reference to the character's outmoded dress: his top-hat and cane, his *garb*. In Italian, however the word *garbo* literally means 'grace'. 'The negative of *Garbo*' is therefore being introduced to combine the ideas of 'anarchic' comedy with a genuine revolutionary intent: the opposite of *grace*. It is, in fact, the image of the poet: a shady revolutionary, like a reversion of Al Jolson in the *Jazz Singer*, blacked-up, not just for entertainment's sake, but as a rebellious negroid *maskhara*, a bolshie collier, a sooty metalworker from the Midlands whose weapon of revolution (and whose *voice*) is as much the honking phallic cane of a Vaudeville clown as it is the hammer with which his ancestors coined their counterfeits, and the brushes with which his transvestite antecedent is to *counterfeit* her 'reginal' *countenance*.

*　　　　　*　　　　　*

It finally became too sickening to bear. I slammed the door and slid the bolt across, fumbling with the latch at the top and failing to relock it. I ran back up the stairs, two at a time, my thighs and calves burning with the pain of underuse. Considering the cautious difficulty of my descent, I was surprised how easily and how instinctively my feet seemed to find the steps: as if—now that I was travelling back towards the safety of my room—they knew the staircase intimately in the dark. I did not slip once, or miss a single step. I arrived back at this room—this illusory haven of mine—and collapsed exhausted and quivering on the sheepskin rug.

That was the first night of the dream.

Perhaps it cannot be called a 'dream'. Now that the covetous flames have begun to caress my skeleton, I realize this dream *long ago ceased to be extricable from any other function of the mind. I assume there must have been a time in which it only happened when I was asleep. It underwent a minor adaptation every day, of course, as the fiery ending approached ever closer, and as my struggle with this poem drew towards a close. I no longer sleep, of course, not for many days; or rather it is many days since I remembered the last time I woke up. Precisely what my state of consciousness might be according to a psychologist I would not like to guess. I assume people do not normally reflect upon recent events when at such an advanced stage of immolation, let alone retain the motor functions necessary to write them down. Suffice to say, I long ago surrendered to the undeniable fact that the simultaneous equivalence of both my waking life and the infernal conclusion of this dream would be the culmination of both…*

*　　　　　*　　　　　*

130

> £e stuff went back inside £e bag $e kept
> >Her bits and bobs in: didn't have £e time
> To find a home for €ings—$e'd overslept.
> >$e brea£ed, looked back, and whispered 'hi'. First sign
> Of madness, talking to yourself. Except
> >$e did it every day and $e was fine.
> In fact, if you can live in eerie silence,
> You must be capable of quiet violence.

130.7-8 *eerie silence… quiet violence*: Another indication of the threat lurking in the previous allusion to Garbo Marx.

* * *

I am in this same building, or something very similar. I explore its hidden rooms and corridors. I am an expert explorer. There is nobody who knows the building in my dream the way I do. I can tell you, for example, that a hole behind a map of the Peloponnesian Wars in a teaching room on the fifth floor leads indirectly to a cavity beneath the stairs. Each staircase has, in fact, another hidden staircase underneath it, or beside it, which can be accessed from this first. I can move through these seemingly impassable spaces with vigorous skill, and in secret, bounding over the torrents of pipes and wiring like a salmon leaping weirs.

To begin with—despite the odd means of accessing them and their continually fluctuating topography—the rooms in the building are no more numerous or unusual than the real rooms of the college. As the dream progresses however, the building telescopes in all directions, the spaces it contains becoming increasingly diverse.

The first new areas are invariably bleak and homogenous dormitories. In the middle of each corridor of these are situated (without exterior doors to protect one's modesty) large interconnected public bathrooms. If inured to the remnants of raw human bestiality they contain, one is capable of passing between these bathrooms to access every floor and corridor of the dormitories which are—according to the signs—officially closed off from one another to prevent the intermingling of male and female residents. It is possible, in fact, to move quite quickly through the plumbing. The most convenient accesses to which I hardly need to name.

From there, the types of rooms one can discover multiply exponentially. There is often, and by turns: a massive multi-departmental library entirely transparent in structure, a drill hall, a gymnasium, a drained swimming pool with a bicycle and beer bottles in it, a garage that used to be a stable, a nursery full of clockwork toys, a walled garden with a peach tree, a noxious laundry room, a kitchen, a bubbling laboratory, a chapel, a hospital ward for geriatrics, a schoolroom, a greenhouse containing nothing but refrigerators and electric cookers, a basement where boilers, furnaces and generators hum and hiss and ooze orange grease from their seams… all of which are found by hurrying through a warren of secret passages and ventilation shafts that seem to develop an infinite number of illogical internodes as the building grows.

* * *

"Well, actually I wanted *Meta*: the artist from last night."

She laughed, "I'm afraid she isn't here now, bab. She isn't even *Meta* on a Sunday. She's called Charlie. What d'you want her for anyway?"

"It's a long story."

She crossed her legs & folded her arms. Then she just waited. I didn't want to go through the whole thing again. I'd had my fingers burned by Eels. So I sat there dabbing at my thick, tingling bottom lip.

She cracked first: "You don't want to trust anything *Meta* says, darlin: she's a drag-queen. You should never trust what a drag-queen says... I know it sounds terribly un-PC, but it's a bloody good piece of advice. It's not that you shouldn't trust a drag-queen. I'd let Charlie take my kids on holiday or organise a mortgage for me. It's just you don't want to trust a single thing they say when they're in character. The fact is, *Meta* doesn't say anything she hasn't picked up from a film or copied off a record."

I frowned, which also hurt. "That explains a lot."

"Why, what did she say to you?"

"I was looking for someone. She told me to meet her today & she'd help me out. She seemed to know who I was talking about. I thought she did. Which made a nice change. But the address she gave me didn't exist. Not really."

"What's your name, love?"

"Sam."

"Listen, Sam. Forget about *Meta*, she was probably practising a routine on you. I'm quite surprised she didn't take you home with her, to be honest... nice boy like you."

I didn't say anything. I didn't want to tell this woman I'd keeled over with exhaustion & slept on one of her sofas last night. I didn't want to explain to her about the poem. I didn't know how to tell her that I wouldn't have been interested in going home with a drag-queen. But one other thing was certain. It'd take a lot more than a bit of worldly advice from an older woman to make me forget what had happened to me during Meta's show.

"Who were you looking for anyway?"

"A bloke called Zomby: a poet. People said he'd done readings here in the past."

"You're looking for Zomby?"

"Yeh."

"I remember Zomby. You should've come straight to me. I was on the door last night."

I fidgeted a little in my seat at the thought she might've seen me come in on my own. She might even have seen me leave this morning.

> Retightening £e silk belt round her waist,
> $e wi$ed $e could be just an inch more €in.
> But £en, £e gloss had left an aftertaste
>   A bit like diet tonic saccharine,
> So off $e went to fill her made-up face
>   Wi£ food, one foot luxuriating in
> A €ousand tufts of woollen carpet-pile;
> £e o£er peeling off £e ba€room tile…"

131.4 *diet tonic saccharine*: There is a common misspelling here. *Saccharin* (without the final *-e*) is, according to the OED, the common name of the 'anhydride of saccharic acid' ($C_7H_5NO_3S$), 'an intensely sweet substance obtained from coal tar' used most commonly to sweeten the food of diabetics. It naturally gets in name from the adjective 'saccharine' meaning *very sweet*, but must be definitively differentiated from the noun 'saccharine' which means *sugar* and therefore the very substance for which it is a substitute. The poet is suggesting here that people in the future take this chemical as a 'diet-tonic', that is: a medicinal compound which reduces one's weight. The reasons are obvious. As are the reasons for the typical confusion of the genuine and the counterfeit.

*   *   *

These rooms each contain an unusual variety of surfaces—some moving and some stationary—between which one can jump, with very little effort, to get from one secreted entrance or exit to another, or in order to avoid a vast array of almost comically unrealistic hazards. There are also various ladders and ropes for one to climb, chutes to slide down, rotating doorways to negotiate and so on. There is a halcyon period in which the whole place seems to be a wonderful surrealistic kindergarten playground.

This sense of joyful exploration and pleasure in the superhuman ability to move and navigate instinctively about the rapidly expanding environment inevitably becomes, however, suddenly and terrifyingly soured. There is some kind of an event—impossible to remember—which makes you realize you are not alone: there is something chasing you…

This revelation is terrible. The terror resides not so much in the dread of being caught by the pursuant identity as in realising that, previous to its materialisation, you had been quite alone: until this thing that hunts you arrived to give some meaning to your actions, you came from nowhere and were going nowhere. As you fly faster and faster and with greater skill and knowledge through the building, trying desperately to find an exit—speaking like a teacher to yourself: lecturing, as it were, a younger version of yourself, with a quite self-deluding air of alacrity, in the ancient knowledge of survival—there are three things which become progressively apparent.

*   *   *

"Zomby was a character alright. He called himself a *guerrilla artist*. He did all sorts of stuff: slam poetry, flyposting, graffiti, pamphlets... he used to pretend to be this militant queer terrorist who believed in outing all public figures, putting heteros in concentration camps & making all forms of potentially conceptual intercourse illegal. He did bizarre rants about the beauties of invitro fertilisation & human cloning; that & some pretty bizarre pornographic imaginings about futuristic cyber-orgies. Imagine a cyber-punk nightmare clone of Peter Tatchell. He was also running a weblog that claimed to be written by a rent-boy. It was supposed to be anonymous but everybody knew it was him. He obviously had no idea what it was really like being a rent-boy. It was just an excuse for a bit of stress-relieving indiscretion at the weekends. Everybody seemed to tolerate him because they thought he was a joke. The Ali-G of the bizarre gay scene. I wasn't so sure. I thought he was bit cracked. I put him on once or twice though: as support."

"When was this? The person I'm looking for disappeared a couple of years ago."

"Yeh, that fits. He was only around on the circuit for six months or so. & that was at least two years ago. I haven't heard anything from him since. He used to talk about going to Iraq, but nobody believed him. He said he was planning something big. He warned people he was going to disappear. He tried to make out it was dangerous & controversial, but most people assumed he was just a screwed up closet who was planning to come out. Once he had, I suppose he realised he wouldn't need to go round violently hating straight people at the weekends. He could jack it in."

"Actually I was kind of hoping he'd only appeared a couple of years ago — when my guy hopped the nest — & was still around for me to find."

"Sorry."

"Could he have been planning to write something?" I didn't want to say what. Not yet.

"It's more likely than the idea he ran off to Iraq to fight the Yanks. He thought he was a writer... but then he thought he was a lot of things."

"How about counterfeiting? Did he ever get involved in that? Or maybe making his own coins?

"Why do you ask?"

"You see, I think my guy was interested in using coins & tokens as a form of publishing. There's a book... well, that's not really important. The point is that Singh, the guy I'm looking for, was obsessed with two things: drag-artists & counterfeit coins. I think he might have been planning to have his own one-pound coins made."

"It's certainly possible. It's the sort of thing he might have done. As long as he could afford it. He once went round a supermarket putting the price-sticker for their own-brand budget baked beans on top of every barcode he could find. He got in trouble for it. Who is this person you're looking for anyway? You say he's called 'Singh'. Is he a Sikh?"

> (In case some readers didn't realise,
>   My storyline's a sacrilege of Pope.
> I must confess, I've wholly plagiarised
>   'The Rape of the Lock.'—I'm too much of a dope
> To hatch £ese plots myself.—Was £at unwise?
>   I know I haven't got a snowball's hope
> In hell of matching its anointed couplet;
> £ese tupny-ha'pny rhymes won't even trouble it.

132.8 *tupny-ha'pny rhymes*: If sincere, this might have been a moment of rare insight. It is not, however. There is nothing more *faux* in this poem than its modesty and its naïvety. 'Sacrilege' and 'anointed couplet' are heavily sarcastic and congregate around an infantile play on 'Pope'. The whole point is to dissolve the difference of value between the sovereign and the *tupny-ha'pny* and therefore to inveigle the anarchist logic that opens sovereignty to every *private mint*. Such a conception also refuses to differentiate between true poetry and the bawdy doggerel of the backstreet balladmonger. Every man can be, not only his own King and Queen, but his own poet laureate. The allusion, once again, is to *The Threepenny Opera* of Bertolt Brecht. This poet sees the German Socialist as improving on the work of Gay and himself as doing something similar with his egregious vandalism of the work of Alexander Pope. It would be laughable if it were not so worrying.

133.1 *flush*: Professor Weekley calls this 'a very puzzling word' (*An Etymological Dictionary of Modern English*, London: J. Murray, 1921). It certainly is. As usual it is being employed here for precisely the reason of its dialectical ambiguity. The oldest form of the word in English is the verb *to flush* which, before any other etymological vagaries are introduced, already has two entangled roots: a variant form of *to flash* 'to emit or reflect a sudden burst of light' and what is presumably an onomatopoeic verb derived from hunting jargon *to flush* 'to fly up suddenly (like a flock of disturbed birds)'. It is from an extension of this latter form into the transitive that we get the phrasal construction *to flush out* and the old collective noun *a flush of ducks (in flight)*; although it is already possible to see how a sudden flight of ducks (or musical swans: see 12.1 *The Swan*) might just as easily be understood to 'flash' in the sun as to make a *flushing* sound with their wings. Another idiomatic nominal usage is to be found in 'the first flush of spring', where the sense of 'shooting up' is presumably applied as a cliché of poetic hyperbole to the 'shoots' of plants. Again, however, I think it likely that this has happened not as a means of pure metaphorical germination but under the fecund influence of a degraded version of *to flourish*.

The most common nominal usage today, of course, is the *flush* on a toilet. This comes from the analogical employment of the original verb in reference to a *spurt*, a sudden rush of water, or a *flash flood*. It is also from this development that we are supposed to get the adjectival usage meaning 'rich', 'full' or 'perfectly level': the theory being that it conjures up the image of a river basin through which water is rapidly *flushing* and which is, therefore, 'full right up to the brim of the bank'. At this point, however, it is impossible to ignore the influence of the French term *un flux* meaning literally 'a flow' but imported into English in order to denote a hand in a card game involving a set of cards all of the same suit. This third etymological tributary (*flux*: 'flow') must feed into all uses that suggest a surge of fluids: whether of water, the blood of the human body, the saps of the natural world, the circulating currency of a financial system or any abstract notions that metaphorically assume fluidity of motion. Hence the adjective *flush* stands at the meeting of at least three tributary senses, where etymological waters mingle to create dizzying eddies and perilous undercurrents of semantics.

Here the word seems, on the surface, to mean simply 'replete' or 'rich' with genius. It manages, however, to suggest that the waters of the Thames, *up* which Pope's second Canto *meanders*, are flooded and rushing fast with dangerous implications of an awful future: not just the trivial game at cards that will bring about the equally trivial downfall of Pope's heroine, but with the blood of the *Meander* as envisioned by Cassandra. We should not forget the original meaning of *genius* (before the French confusion with *ingenium* and the influence of *Sturm und Drang* philosophy), which was: 'an attendant spirit or demon' 'the *begetter* of fate'. *Thygrim multo spumantem sanguine cerno* says the Sybil at Cumæ, and it is precisely this kind of thing that the phrase *flush with genius* implies. If Britannia is *flush with genius*, it is because she has a demonic counterfeit in her purse: one that foretells the moral carnage flowing from the downfall of the British Empire.

To turn to a rather more delicate (but not unrelated) matter concerning Professor Weekley, it is worth pointing out, I think, that *flush* is one of the favourite words of his ex-wife's second husband, D. H. Lawrence. Weekley's puzzlement at, and Lawrence's relish in, the chaotic depths of meaning this word combines and signifies are two sides of the same coin. Much of Lawrence's delight in everything bestial and instinctive, and his rejection of rationality and British pragmatism, is, one suspects, a continuation into the writing of a diabolical erotic pleasure taken by the libertine daughter of German Romanticism and her spiteful young lover in bating the dignified, cautious empiricism for which Professor Weekley so gallantly still stands. I could quote a hundred instances in Lawrence, but this one will suffice:

> The human will is free, ultimately, to choose one of two things:
> either to stay connected with the tree of life, and submit
> the human will to the *flush* of the vaster impulses of the tree;
> or else to sever the connection, to become self-centred, self-willed, self-motived—
> and subject, really, to the draught of every motor-car or the kicking tread of every passer-by.
>
> ('Free Will' from *Pansies* 1929, *my italics*)

It is perhaps unfair to lump Lawrence in with the poet of this piece. There is a sense of inevitable, pre-determined chaos inherent to this poem in comparison with which even Lawrence's Bergsonian restriction of free-will is made to look like harmless humanism. *The Birmingham Quean* appears to suggest that where a total collapse of sexual morality and psychological discipline applies, no real difference exists between the *sub*human anarchy of 'submitting the human will to the flush of the vaster impulses of the tree of life' (Bergson's *élan vital*) and the *super*human anarchy of becoming entirely 'self-centred, self-motived and self-willed' (like Nietzsche's *übermensch*). Rather than subject to the kicking tread of every passer-by, the Quean becomes both the *subjective* and the *objective* embodiment of a fated, universal prurience inherent in the animalistic concept of total psychological and corporeal liberty.

133

> Pope's Second Canto, flush wi£ genius,
>   Meanders up £e Thames to Hampton Court.
> My budget only stretches to a bus
>   From Calthorpe Park to Sherlock Street—a $ort
> Hop on £e Thirty-Five—to ferry us
>   Towards a ra£er less salubrious port
> Of call: A TV karaoke bar.
> Our pound-coin, £ough, was swerving round a car

One cannot help, however, but be reminded by this passage of one more example from Lawrence in which the orgasmic *flush* comes as the ultimate pathetic fallacy of death and rebirth that is supposedly the reward of surrendering entirely to the instinct.

> Wait, wait, the little ship
> drifting, beneath the deathly ashey grey
> of a flood dawn.
>
> Wait, wait! even so, a flush of yellow
> and strangely, O chilled wan soul, a flush of rose.
>
> A flush of rose and the whole thing starts again.
>
> ('The Ship of Death' IX 10-15)

133.2 *Meanders up the Thames*: Hans across the ocean / Shand's across the sea [Poet's note]

The Meander, as previously noted (above and 12.1 *The Swan*, 13.2 *forward*), is used by this poet to combine the idea of the treacherous 'flux of time' with the symbol of the river across the battlefield of Troy, foaming (like the Tiber) with much blood. Here there seems to be a paradoxical implication that the narrative is moving *upstream* in time, and therefore towards the past, but that the events depicted have yet to come about. The ensuing two stanzas concern themselves with a torrid explanation that the expected bus-ride to the pub (*The Swan*) in which the climax of events is to take place, is not in fact the one narrated. This is because the Quean/Coin narrator could not possibly have witnessed it. Instead we are given the bus-ride home again—the return journey—and informed that, consequently, the dawn scene we have just read is not the morning of the darts match at all, but the morning after.

All this is rather confusing and unnecessary, one might think, but the poet is much more intent on provoking confusion than he is in aspiring to clarity. His own note provides a clue. 'Hans across the ocean' is an allusion, I think, to Hans Reichenbach, the German logical positivist who died earlier this year. Reichenbach left Europe when the Nazis came to power and emigrated ('across the ocean') to America. His contribution has been to give Einsteinian physics a thorough philosophical grounding so that it can be extended beyond its scientific basis into questions of epistemology and morality. Essentially his life's work seems to have begun as an attempt to consolidate Einstein's position in the debate with Bergson on *time* by providing the philosophical elements it needed to nullify Bergson's objections. By the end of his life, however, Reichenbach's opinion seems to have diverged from the implications of static or symmetrical space-time in Einstein's relativity theories, which had been the major sticking-point for Bergson. As he aged, Reichenbach asserted that time has only one real direction (however it might be perceived) as provable by the universal proliferation of entropic decay. Everything, says Reichenbach (approaching his own death) is decaying and dissipating, and time is the progress of this decay; instances of 'negative entropy', as in fertile *polyphiloprogenesis* (the kind of thing Bergson would put down to the *élan vital*), are simply statistical anomalies based upon relativized processes of data gathering. In short, much more than Einstein ever did, Reichenbach saw himself as the implacable (realist) opponent of Bergson's (idealist) *durée*.

'Shand's across the sea', presumably refers to Alexander Shand: a minor English philosopher and an early exponent of the new fields of psychology and sociology at the turn of the century; he was a founder-member of both The Psychological Society and The Institute of Sociology. He developed an early 'neurological epistemology' and was particularly interested in the interplay of emotions and reasoning in the cognitive, causal processes of intention (and therefore the philosophical debate on free-will.)

These figures are probably being combined to bury their philosophies (at sea) rather than to praise them. Instead, the logic of the Tarot (the *flush* of past and future) is to be asserted in order to cast Reichenbach and Shand in the decaying role of Phlebas the Phoenician (the 'drowned man' of Eliot's *Madame Sosostris*):

> O you who turn the wheel and look to windward,
> Consider Phlebas, who was once as handsome and tall as you.

This rejection is natural (for an anarchist occultist) when you consider both Reichenbach and Shand's philosophies insist upon the asymmetrical continuum of spatial time (in Shand's case because his *free-will* relies on intention—whether conscious or not—being a causal neurological event which instantaneously *precedes* an action in the human mind). This poet relies upon the contrary belief that time can be made subject to the will as much as the will to time. Inculcated in this *magical* belief—a bizarre extension into the occult of Bergson's *durée*, combined with something taken, one supposes, out of Wittgenstein—is the desire to change the intentions and perceptions of others simply via the effect on the reader's consciousness of the strange use of words. His anachronisms of narrative time and reversals of direction are meant, quite literally, to make the reader change his perception of the passage of time and therefore how he understands (at the fundamental, instinctive level) cherished notions of free will, cause and effect, logical consequence and, ultimately, of morality. It is an attempt to manipulate, to revolutionary ends, the Bergsonian *instinct*.

133.7 *TV karaoke bar*. See 32.6 *karaoke div*

> In Sloggy's clingy nylon tracksuit pants
>> As Tanya caught £e bus: £erefore £is scene
> Can not be told by her. But, to enhance
>> £e overall impression of our Quean,
> I €ink I'll let her come at it askance:
>> £at is, to tell Mercator what $e's seen
> Aboard £e last bus home—£e o£er way:)
>> "I still remember it like yesterday…"

134.1 *clingy nylon…*: Another indication of the femininity of Jeff Sloggy. Nylon is, of course, the best known of the new synthetic fabrics and is archetypally used as a more durable and elastic alternative to silk in the manufacture of women's tights and stockings. It might be described (colloquially) as *clingy* for two reasons: firstly because its elasticity allows it to be stretched a great deal to create a very *tight* fit, and secondly because it is an excellent medium for static electricity and therefore capable of being lent (by friction) a literal electromagnetic *clinginess*. The sexually suggestive nature of these things is obvious. It is entirely in keeping with the ubiquitous prurience of the society depicted that the part of the *tracksuit* (the garment that allows constant *access* to the wearer; see 42.3 *tracksuit* and 50.7 *tracksuit top*) in which the Quean/coin is held should be a ludicrously feminine pair of nylon *tights* (or as the Americans would call them, *pantyhose*).

134.4 *overal*: era 12

134.4 *impression*: An infantile pun on the mis-striking of the Quean's effigy. When one considers its various polysemes, however, the word turns out to be an important one. The poet intends his work to take effect by stamping a new *impression* into the medium of the reader's consciousness by forcing him to 'do an *impression*' of the *Birmingham Quean*. The fact that the piece might also be described as *impressionistic*—especially the marginal stanzas that occur during the bus-ride, which recall the light-effects employed by painters like Turner and Monet—in no way detracts from this forcefulness of intent. The elements of vagueness or blurring are not accidental or lazy but designed to employ the reader's own imagination to give shape and structure to the piece and thereby impose a reflexive *impression* of the poet's revolutionary æsthetic on his mind by (as it were) gambling more of his own psyche on the venture.

*   *   *

Firstly, you cannot do anything to stop it gaining on you. Secondly, you have no choice but to keep running. Thirdly—and most devastatingly—there is no way out without its help.

You stop to catch your breath. It does the same. You turn to look at it. It glares back. Your eyelids widen and you run again, leaping from foothold to foothold with simian agility. It follows in your footsteps. 'It is the fire;' says the voice-over: *'It is you…'*

*   *   *

"Er, no, not really. Well, his dad was Sikh, but he..."

"So who is he? What's his first name?"

"Amrit. He's the ex-partner of a woman... a friend. He ran away just after they had a kid. She wants him back. I thought he might be this Zomby. There are a lot of similarities."

"Well, well, Zomby had a family did he? No wonder he was so screwed up. If Zomby really was this Amrit Singh, that is. I never would've taken him for an Indian. Not even half Indian. I suppose he did have quite dark colouring. Have you got a picture?"

My fingers dropped slowly from my lip, where they'd been hovering gingerly for the past few minutes. They began to tingle slightly as the blood ran back into them. When you're leaking blood, you can forget that the stuff is not just supposed to be kept inside your body, it's also supposed to flow around & get things done.

I was desperately searching my memory. I shook my head: "You know... I'm not sure I've ever seen one myself."

"You can't even describe him?"

"It never seemed important."

"It never seemed important? You mean to tell me you've never even seen this man you're looking for? Not so much as a photo? You have absolutely no idea what he looks like? You're not much of a Sam Spade, now are you bab."

I laughed, feeling I deserved the twinges it created in my diaphragm. It was daft. She was right. How could I have come this far without so much as an internal visual image of the man?

Maybe I didn't want to know what he looked like. I was obviously jealous of him: of the power he still exerted over Hannah. Maybe I was terrified of how alluring he might turn out to be. Secretly, I must have feared I'd have considered myself no competition. It was just easier not knowing what he looked like. But it was absolutely mad that I'd attempted to find him in those circumstances: just a name, a signature, a style of writing, entirely without any physical extension into the material world off which the sunlight might reflect or which might stir the air or excite the skin of the woman I loved.

I realised, when I'd reached out & touched Hannah's body for the first time, as she gazed out of her kitchen window at the darkened garden, imagining him out there, that I'd seen nothing but her reflection. She'd been staring through the shadow that my outline made towards the bushes, seeing him there, knowing what he looked like. But the focus of my eyes had been anxiously fixed on her. It wasn't lust. It wasn't a desire to watch my own hand drag aside the green material to reveal her naked breast. In fact the situation had quickly become entirely without desire for me. It was too screwed up. & I was far too drunk. Instead it was a desperate fear of actually seeing Amrit Singh out there like some kind of handsome, brooding Heathcliffe glowering a challenge at me through the gloom.

She starts… (oh, by £e way, please don't forget
  £at every€ing you've heard since Tanya woke
Can't possibly have happened to her yet:
  £e Quean was £ere to watch as morning broke
But Tanya and £e coin still haven't met;
  And £is is long before £e Quean first spoke—
Or even learned she could… so here's £e score:
£at was £e morning after; now's £e night before:)

---

       *   *   *

I awoke in the pink gleam of dawn. It was an unpleasant feeling. I had become almost entirely nocturnal during the previous winter and was much more used to coming back to consciousness at dusk. My eyes were bleary, the lashes gummed with mucus from the tear ducts. The colours in the room seemed false, like poor Technicolor. Amongst what had previously been a rather dun environment of browns, my undiscriminating gaze found nauseating patches of blurred but vivid reds and blues. I was helpless and weak. There was a sensation in my right hand, on which I had been lying, that suggested it was clinging to a single microscopic strand of hair which was nonetheless as rough and massive in its tender grip as a naval rope in the hand of a child.

The adult clinging to the little finger of the baby is the baby clinging to the little finger of the adult man.

Beneath my cheek I felt something rough and cool which crackled loudly in my ear against the stubble as I moved my head a little to examine the small patch of moisture—about the size and shape of a poppy—which had darkened the chestnut surface of the stuff beside my mouth.

I lay paralysed. Blink by blink, my surroundings struggled back into focus. The definition sharpened gradually and I discovered that the reds and blues I had cringed to see well before I could give them shapes existed solely on the crackling surface underneath my face. They turned out to be words scrawled in coloured inks on what I slowly realized was a sheet of white paper pasted to the interior of the brown parcel roll I had dislodged from its resting place in the previous night's haste. The words were half-embossed in the surface by the pressure required to force the sticky ink to roll around the ball of the nib; consequently the dawn light seemed to define the perimeter of each lexical indentation. The words glowed like legends in a stained-glass window.

In red against a page of bluish white, I read:

    £en you could really lick arse with your doggerel.

I frowned and narrowed my eyes to focus. Then:

    Recycling bin for use as Royal bogroll:

       *   *   *

The rest of our conversation became a kind of therapeutic exercise in the construction of an air of amused sympathy for my absurd plight. We agreed I was no kind of Private I. She called me a taxi & I recounted some of my daft escapades throughout the past two days for our mutual entertainment while we waited for it to arrive. I was actually crying with laughter when I told her about the ABRA conspiracy. I was feeling very stiff by now, but I made a valiant attempt to do an impression of the teenager in Eels's flat. I was never going to manage though. I just kept cracking up. Every time I did, I remembered a kick or a punch as the pain of it jabbed me once again. & this made me laugh all the harder. I think I was a bit hysterical.

"You know those two blokes who attacked you..." she asked, as I began to wind down like the all-clear after an air-raid, "are you sure that wasn't the same two jokers from the flat? Eels & his mate?"

I caught my breath. She had a point there. It might very well have been. It made more sense than some random homophobic attack. Maybe they'd just meant to mug me or something. & then I'd started laughing & it'd pissed them off. I wasn't laughing now.

The telephone rang. It was the taxi.

"Sam," the manager said (I never found out her name, unfortunately), "take my advice..."

I struggled to my feet. She helped me. I wanted her to say: *put the poem back where you found it*; I wanted her to say: *give up playing the detective*; &: *go back & tell Hannah you're in love with her*.

"... think about prosecuting. I don't like people getting jumped outside my club. I want to stop this kind of thing from happening. I wish more people... well, just think about it."

I promised her I would & left. I asked the taxi driver to take me to the University. I had to try & take the poem back. It was going to be hard to give it up without even taking a copy, but I knew it had to be done. He dropped me just outside the janitor's hut at the entrance to the main campus. That was probably a mistake. I was bound to draw attention to myself hoisting my tattered, blood-stained lower body out of a private hire cab with a face like a method actor gearing up for the lead role in a Sylvester Stallone biopic.

I only got as far as inserting the main door key in its lock. Then I felt a light hand on the side of my arm.

"Excuse me sir. Sorry to bother you. But can I just take a quick look at your staff card."

I turned. Or, rather, I was turned... to see a short man in thick, square glasses & a generic blue Security uniform.

"Actually I don't have one. I'm... I'm doing a favour for a friend."

"I'm going to have to ask you where did you get the key from."

"It's my friend's. He works here... well, he used to work here."

"£e stiff pub-door propels Britannia back
　　Up Hurst Street like a heavy pinball flipper.
£e bus pulls in. $e squawks like a macaque
　　For it to wait and leaves behind her slipper
(€ink Cinderella), managing to tack
　　Against £e wind, £e kerb about to trip her
As some Prince Charming grabs her quadriceps
To gently pu$ her up £e €robbing steps.

136.2 *pinball flipper*. The double doors of *The Black Swan* are a portal in time. Most of the character-movement in the narrative concerns motion to and from this pair of doors and the occasion of passing through them always coincides with a switch in (what I suppose we must call) narrative *space-time*. The idea of a *wormhole* is rather typical of the kind of thing introduced to *Science Fiction* by Einstein's theories of relativity. There is a good deal of evidence here that the doors are not seen merely as the threshold of a *passageway* however—a passive *tear* or *loop* through which the characters' energies are to take them—but as a kind of catapult which also aggressively provides the impetus required to cross its own temporal *liminus*. Later the doors are to be described as 'flapping' like a pair of wings: an obvious enough metaphor in the circumstances. Here, though, they are not *flappers* but the *flippers* of a *pinball* machine.

Pinball is the name Americans have given to a new commercial, *slot-machine* version of the game Bagatelle. One inserts a coin into the *slot* of the machine (see below: 137.8 *the slot agape*) and receives in return a number of steel ballbarings which can be propelled by means of a sprung piston, one by one, into the tilted body of the contraption to watch them progress down the board, chaotically buffeted by patterns of *pins* and sprung obstacles as they approach the hole at the bottom. Unlike Bagatelle, the idea of the game is not to get the balls into holes of higher rather than lower value but to postpone for as long as possible the ball from falling into the one and only hole in the board. To do so is to *lose*. As a marginal aid, the large hole is partially covered by a pair of *flippers*—thin triangular blocks on hinges—that can be made to go up or down independently by means (respectively) of pressing or releasing a button on either side of the box.

Psychologically speaking, the idea of this game is to make the player feel as if the ball is somehow alive—that its motion is the index of life—and that to let it fall down the hole (and therefore to stop) is to allow it to die. More than this, one is asked to sympathize with each ball as if it were a polished symbol of one's own life, like a tragic hero; the struggle to *keep it up* being a distillation of the struggle to stay alive. Consequently one is led into feeling that the progress of the ball around the board—patently chaotic, or at the very least subject to far too complex a mathematics of motion and probability to be in the least predictable or controllable—is somehow one's own responsibility: the result of one's own choices; the trace of an ongoing struggle with the vagaries of fate to gain the upper hand.

The commercial genius of this diabolical confidence trick is clear. There is a desire in every sentient being for the skill to confound death. The gullible are led into feeding the machine more and more money as a Faustian act of faith in some freakish effect of quantum mechanics or gravitational relativity that will one day allow them to belay the inevitable indefinitely: to become immortal by stopping the ball from ever going down the hole. As they do so they become more and more convinced of a lie: namely that they are becoming increasingly skilful at exercising their free-will, and that their will therefore has come to extend beyond the realms of what is scientifically possible. Quite the contrary is true. The will is made subject to a profit-making enterprise which reduces it to an intrinsic function in a spectacle of sheer futility.

The poem is quite similar. The chaotic switches in time, place and point of view have a veneer of logic that might convince the reader he is in control. He is not. Instead his consciousness is buffeted from one place to another as it slips, inexorably, towards a semantic and moral *black hole* from which the flapping doors of the pub make only a mocking gesture of protecting him. The desire of this poem is to addict the reader's imagination to repetitive spectacles of futility, analogous to an addiction to the pinball machine, so that he ends up in thrall to a nihilism that is the necessary prerequisite of its anarchist ideology.

As a symbolic act of defiance, I would urge the reader to reject the American term *pinball* (yet another amphibious pairing) in preference for the British *bagatelle*. This word, from French, means 'a trifle' 'something of no intrinsic value'. Until recently, it was idiomatically and pleonastically paired with 'toys'. As Francis Bacon might just as well have said at the end of his typically bombastic little essay 'Of Masques and Triumphs': 'But enough of these *bagatelles.*'

136.6 *tack against the wind*: This is another reminder *The Royal Yacht Britannia* (See 51.4 *as up she rises.*) Despite its name, it is not a sailing vessel at all, of course, but the idea of this *Britannia* tacking against the wind is designed to make the typical association (still to be seen on the copper coinage) between the national icon and the traditional sailing vessel of the Royal Navy at the height of the Empire. Phlebas the Phoenician is also recalled once more. To *tack* is not just to 'look to windward' but to 'head to windward' and also, therefore: upstream, towards the stars, towards the past.

136.8 *to gently push her*: As in 47.7 *to somehow perfectly repair*, one must assume this split infinitive to be quite deliberately employed. It is not one of those occasions when avoiding the construction would be awkward or unwieldy; 'to push her gently up the throbbing steps' seems a perfectly acceptable alternative. The slight imbalance of prosodic emphasis this would cause is hardly distracting enough to be considered unæsthetic. It is, of course, only by conformity to an arbitrary convention of good taste that one is urged consistently to avoid the split infinitive. Wilful non-conformity is worse than ignorant oversight however. It would be something relatively tolerable in a member of the *nouveau riche*, but symptomatic of an irritating lack of manners in an educated man, for him to use a knife and fork at High Table to *pointedly* dissect his asparagus.

                                137

                At £is point, I experience a bru$
                    Wi£ destiny: £e manicured forefinger
                Of Tanya's right hand trails around £e plu$
                    Interior of her suede purse to linger
                Above my head; and, in a sudden ru$,
                    $e plucks me out, presenting me towards £at €ing a
                Bus driver has beside his cubicle
                For coins. £e slot agape, a cuticle

137.6 *she plucks me out*: From St Augustine's *Confessions*: 'I entangle my steps with these outward beauties, but Thou pluckest me out'; Augustine is echoing God's own challenge to Satan in Zechariah III.2: 'is not this a branch plucked out of the fire?' (see *The Waste Land* li. 309, and the poet's note). As usual, this poem's (anti-) ethos of blasphemous sarcasm reverses the logic, the scale and the morality of Augustine's panto-redemptive vision.

137.8 *the slot agape*: *Slot* is quite possibly related to both *sleuth* and *slut*. I would rather not, however, subject my fingers to the task of traipsing through the philological tomes in search of evidence like the rumpled slacks of a *gumshoe* in a nasty little American *crime movie* embarking upon a wild goose chase at the behest of a sultry *femme fatale*. Why should I care if these correspondences are genuine when the poet patently does not?

The picturesque adjective *agape* is supposed to suggest a jocular expression of surprise or shock on the face (as it were) of the receptacle for coins, provoked by the large sum of money it is about to receive. As well as cartoonish comedy, however, this image manages to carry all the usual connotations of sex and death. The *slot* is *agape* like 'the maws of doom' (or, indeed, the hole at the bottom of a *pinball* board: it is described in the next stanza as *the gawping tomb*) and also like a crude icon of aroused vaginal dilation.

Slot machines have always contained such tainted implications in their mysterious innards. Whether they be 'fruit' machines, 'one armed bandits', 'jukeboxes', 'sweepers', 'fortune tellers' or (more obviously) 'what the butler saw' *peep shows*, all coin-operated entertainment machines on the pier and in modern 'amusement arcades' are driven by a principle of prurience. There is very little difference between these mechanisms and prostitutes. It is literally the insertion of the coin in the orifice—the perfect combination of the erotic and the monetary—which *arouses* the activity of these things. Thus men's fanstasies are fleetingly fulfilled. They understand the association instinctively. The desire of the gambler is for the machine to be *fertile*: for his monetary *insemination* to fall on fertile earth in the internal mechanisms and give birth to a valuable litter. The desire of the onanistic user is for futile pleasure and futile waste. If one watches how men feed their money into the slot, this connection soon becomes apparent. There are as many ways of treating a *slot* as a *slut*. An ingenu will drop the coin in tentatively, nervously; sophisticated players will employ a lingering, teasing grip: tricking themselves they are in control; overwrought men will feed the thing obsessively… too fast, too much; others absent-mindedly, with a casual wrist, to give the impression they could hardly be bothered; and a drunken Irish navy will brutally force into the hole whatever change does not evade the deep plunge into his pockets and his fumbling grasp, then beat the side of the machine with a thick port-and-stilton palm as if it were a recalcitrant dockside whore.

EDGBASTON

"I think you'd better come over to the lodge."

"Er... I just wanted to drop something off. It wouldn't take a second. Maybe I could..." I was about to offer it to him to do. Then I could go. But something stopped me. There was no way I'd be able explain why I wanted him to put the poem back in the cupboard without telling anyone. Where had it come from? Who was it for? Could I even trust him with a task like that? I didn't have any option. As far as he was concerned I was a beat-up looking young bloke with a local accent, a swagbag & a flimsy excuse for having a key to a building which probably contained thousands of pounds-worth of computer equipment. I went with him. What else could I do?

He walked behind me, trying to disguise his irritation at my slow progress, & also probably a bit of apprehension, with a cheery whistle.

"A friend of yours gave you the key, you say?" he asked when we turned the corner to within sight of the main janitor's lodge. Various uniformed men with walkie-talkies were sitting or leaning against a counter in there.

"Yes. His name's Amrit Singh. He used to work in the English Department."

"Don't know as I recognise the name." He opened the door & showed me in. The guys in there halted their conversation when they saw me. He asked one of those on seats for a list of Arts Faculty staff, then guided me through to a small, private room at the back.

"Well, he was just a Teaching Assistant, not a permanent member of staff." I said as we went down a narrow pink corridor. There is something very unsettling about pink in an environment of security enforcement. Even in a place as relatively laid-back as a University Janitor's office. You wonder what it's there to cover up.

"I'm sure we'll get this sorted out. You'll understand you look a bit suspicious though... "

"Er, yes, I've been... I was beaten up. I was on my way to the train... I live in Glasgow."

"... I'm afraid we're going to have to ask this friend of yours to come down here & vouch for you. What did you say his name was?" He pulled a plastic chair towards me.

I took my rucksack off & gingerly sat down. "Amrit Singh. But I don't think you're going to find him on any staff lists. He left two years ago &, as I said, he was only part-time."

"We'll see," he said. He kept repeating it: "we'll see, we'll see." & then, extremely worryingly, he added, "I shouldn't worry."

He found the right page & ran his finger down it. Nothing. He ran his finger down it again: more slowly this time. Still nothing.

"I'm afraid I haven't got any Singh on my list." He sounded genuinely apologetic.

"No, like I said..."

"& we have all the Teaching Assistants as well, not just the permanent members of staff."

Between my edge and £e approaching doom,
   I try to wriggle free somehow, to break
Her grip, to steer clear of £e gawping tomb.
   I slip… and £en… $e notices I'm fake:
Her favourite back-to-front Regina, whom
   $e wouldn't want £e bus driver to take;
$e hesitates, makes out $e's in a muddle
£en pays 2p and joins £e night-bus huddle.

The fact that this phrase is being used in full knowledge of the Greek term $\alpha\lambda\acute{\alpha}\pi\eta$—in Christian theology, universal Christian love, as differentiated from erotic lust—which is a homonym of *agape* in English, is quite in keeping with the poet's virulent pagan iconoclasm. It is the equivalent of a vandal daubing grotesque genitalia onto a religious icon.

138.8 *2p*: This is probably just a simple spelling error. It should, of course, read '2d': a much more likely tariff for a bus journey than a pound; no doubt the intention is to demonstrate just how drunk this lush has become by having her consider paying a sovereign to get on a bus. The mistaken use of the lower case <p> for the lower case <d> (as it were, by rotation) is almost as common amongst young children and the semi-literate as is the mistaken use of lower case <b> (as it were, in this case, by reflection). There are, however, other examples in the poem of 'deliberate mistakes' of this kind employed as a mimetic evocation of the minimal education (and in this case also the alcoholic intoxication) of a character.

          *   *   *

These lines, especially in isolation, were semantically obscure. The critical annexe of my mind came suddenly to life however, reminding me that they were probably intended as a couplet: a particularly unpleasant and unsuccessful feminine rhyme which the punctuation and grammar suggested I had read in the reverse order. I heaved myself onto my elbows and cocked my head to read the right way up. The portion of the brown paper which had unrolled when I knocked it over, and which I seemed to have used as a pillow, revealed a sheet of letter paper pasted to its surface. Onto this was printed the heading 'Canto One'. Underneath it a dedicatory stanza had been scrawled (if an undignified volley of petty, semi-articulate spite like this deserves such a title). I am no longer capable even of turning this roll of strangely fire-resistant paper over. (My smouldering frailty is quite repugnant to me.) The following quotation is therefore included only to remind myself of what it said. (I will ignore the compositional corrections):

    £is poem's going out to Andrew Motion
       Who couldn't tackle 'Johnny Wilkinson'.
    Perhaps I haven't any right to question
       What England's rhyming Rumplestiltskin's done,
    But, Andy, couldn't you best serve £e nation
       By stuffing poems of £at ilk in some
    Recycling bin for use as Royal bogroll:
    £en you could really lick arse wi£ your doggerel.

          *   *   *

"Yes, I'm sorry, listen... the thing is that my friend Amrit Singh hasn't worked here for over two years. He's in Uganda looking for his father. His father was a Ugandan Asian, you see, who Amrit's never met. He can't even be sure he's alive after all the trouble with Idi Amin in the seventies. Anyway, a couple of years ago Amrit's wife... his partner... had a son & Amrit took it upon himself to go to Uganda & try to find his own father & tell him he'd become a grandad..."

"So he's not going to find it very easy to come down here & vouch for you then?"

"Er no, but anyway he asked me to pick something up for him from the TA staff-room..." My mind raced to remember something that was actually still in room 426, just in case he wanted to accompany me up there: "a year's worth of editions of the London Review of Books that he wants to keep. He left them on the bookcase before he went."

"So along you come... all beaten out of shape... with a rucksack on your back..."

"I know it sounds ridiculous."

"Are there any other members of the department I could call?"

He really seemed to want to help me out. I couldn't think of anybody though. I could remember plenty of first names. That hour of gossip I'd been party to, when Lynne was round at Hannah's flat, had furnished me with enough material for a short David Lodge novel. That was only the night before last. Christ, I could tell you which ones were sleeping together behind each other's backs, which ones kept bottles of vodka in their filing cabinets, which ones were destined for promotion, & which ones had spent ten years writing a single article. I could tell you inside leg measurements, bathing habits & the due dates of unexpected offspring. When it came to surnames & official titles though, I was buggered.

"I'm sorry, son, but I'm going to have to call the Police." He took a mobile phone out of a plastic holster clipped onto his belt.

"You just need a member of staff to vouch for me, that's all?"

He paused, about to dial. "That's it, yeh."

"What about somebody from the Sociology Department? Would that be ok?"

"I suppose so."

"Ok," my heart sank, as they say, but I tried not to let it come through in my voice, "Hannah Arden. She teaches in Sociology, I think. Whatever department it is that the old Centre For Cultural Studies was in."

He was on the Sociology page. He found her pretty quickly. "Here we go," he announced, "Miss Hannah Arden. I've got her home number here. We'll have this sorted in no time...

"... it's ringing..."

My pulse began to thud faster in my skull: a big black slave with pectorals like outsize conkers thumping the dual drums of my temples on the Egyptian galley of my cranium.

> £e heaving, humming single deck is rammed
>> Wi£ passengers who sway along £e aisle,
> £eir damp fists grasping neighbours' $oulders, crammed
>> Against £e plastic seatbacks, double file;
> A heavy knee-joint buckles; £en it's jammed
>> Back in: to hold a tipping head a while.
> Britannia, in £e middle of £e scrummage,
> Can feel a stray hand have a crafty rummage.

---

139 This stanza seems heavily influenced by the earthy visions of peasant celebrations in the paintings of Pietr Brueghel The Elder. One in particular springs to mind. The *Kermess* depicts a feast day (a *kerke-mess*: 'church-mas') held on the date of the consecration of an important church. (St Giles's Fair in Oxford follows precisely the same idea.) Revellers with heavy limbs and rosy jowls kiss and dance and vituperate. Leaning into the face of a bagpiper with bulging bag and cheeks, perhaps to repeat an expectorant request, a leaden-eyed drunkard grasps a rotund jug of booze by one of its four handles as if to steady himself with the same weighty substance that has produced the need for such a counterbalance. Largest in the frame, towards the right, a hearty young buck with a sheathed sword at his side and a feather in his cap leads a woman with a plump purse beneath her yellow pinafore at a jaunty gallop into both the party and the painter's composition. It is an obvious invitation to join in with all this heady, fecund ribaldry. We too are being led into the dance.

The insistent repetition of 'rammed / crammed / jammed' here suggests acute containment, but does so in a bawdily ironic way which precisely mirrors the rebellious vision of anonymous peasant abandon in Brueghel's work. In fact the suppression (of the tight belts, thick-sided pitchers, social decorum) serves to heighten the burgeoning sense of revolutionary desire swelling in their bellies, their windbags, their frothing drinks and their warmed underwear. This is even true of the picture-frame itself. Unlike a comparatively tame painting on the same theme by Brueghel the Younger—*Peasant Wedding Dance* 1607—Pietr Brueghel's work rarely *contains* the figures it depicts. The peasants seem to burst out of the sides of the frame like their beer-filled paunches out of their breeches.

The true extent of the counterfeit pound's ability to share the perspective of (*join in the dance* with) the person she is touching (Britannia, and in turn those who touch Britannia) is revealed for the first time here. We are allowed, at least, a tiny glimpse of its terrifying potential. The *pounding* rhythms of those im*pounded* in the bus leak into the rollicking metre as the pound-coin's consciousness mingles with those of the other passengers. She wants them to touch her mistress so that she can enter them. She passes through their nerves like a principle of abandonment to desire. The coin is almost the drunkenness itself: a bacchanalian libido capable of transforming a collection of disparate and addled minds into a telepathic orgy of undifferentiated depravity. We should beware of an arrogant belief that we can stay apart from this. Our imaginations are capable of being imprisoned in the same nightmarish fantasy of carnivalesque anarchy to which it wants us to submit.

Brueghel's paintings are no doubt a powerful influence on the poem. The relish taken in depicting chaos, corporeality, mass insanity and the rejection of authority is shared by both. In Brueghel, however, there is always an over-arching moral implication: a universal satire which sits uncomfortably alongside the *gusto* (as Hazlitt would have it) of such bucolic celebration.

An important poetic influence (one which I take to be indirectly inspired by precisely the same painting) is probably the poem 'Bagpipe Music' by Louis Macneice (1938):

> It's no go the merrygoround, it's no go the rickshaw,
> All we want is a limousine and a ticket for the peepshow.
>
> Their knickers are made of crêpe-de-chine, their boots are made of python,
> Their halls are lined with tiger-rugs and their walls with heads of bison. [etc.]

It would be natural for a young poet with revolutionary pretensions to be inspired by the *New Signatures* group. Macneice's work never loses that Swiftian satire that Brueghel shares, however, and there is no suggestion as far as I can see that he supports what he actually understands to be social degeneration into *brummagem* anarchy: 'The glass is falling hour by hour, the glass will fall for ever / But if you break the bloody glass you won't hold up the weather.' The worst one can say about Macneice's piece of glowering local colour is that it appears to resign itself, rather melancholically, to the canting philistinism and prurient amorality he saw growing up around him (he was a lecturer in Classics at Birmingham from 1930 to 1936, we should remember) and in which this poem so gratuitously revels.

A final thought: *a tipping head* might be glossed as the Queen's effigy on a coin given as a gratuity. In this case, such a gesture would certainly represent what the French call *un cadeau empoisonné*.

And so can I: I see what Tanya sees;
 It's like her senses have become my own:
I feel £e fingers in her buttocks squeeze
 £e fle$. I know, as if I've always known,
£e stance to take, £e moves to make, to tease
 A piss-head like a bulldog wi£ a bone.
$e twists beyond £e remit of his te£er
And grabs a handful of black jacket-lea£er

---

   *   *   *

It was not immediately apparent—despite the use of the Ottava Rima form, the flippant polysyllabic rhymes, the anti-royalist attack on a putative Poet Laureate (the absurd Dickensian name of whom I took at the time to be an intimation of fictionality)—that this was just a feeble attempt to mimic Byron. Feeble as pastiche, perhaps, but I soon discovered its disturbing potency in other areas.

It seems unmistakably derivative today, but at the time I was intrigued. Even then I had little hope of finding anything of real quality if I read on. The prospect of unravelling more of this bizarre and tasteless verse was nevertheless almost sinfully intoxicating. I felt compelled.

I struggled to my feet, taking the roll of parcel paper with me in my right hand, and swept the books and papers off the desk with my left. My vision darkened for a second but I countered the effect by quickly dropping my chin towards my chest. The blood rushed back into my brain. Having propped the rest of my books against the sturdy volume of the OED, I used the two ceramic book-ends to confine the parcel paper as I unrolled it like a scroll and began, quite rapaciously, to read.

This is precisely the way I have it set up now, as the inferno spreads around me—the two rolled cylinders sitting in the white glazed angle of the two opposing book-ends—except that this time the rolls are underneath the paper. I am now writing back to front however—the beginning of this foreword being, as you can see, written on the backside of the last page of the poem—I therefore still perform precisely the same action to move the paper on as I did when reading through the obverse face: that is, I have to turn both cylinders clockwise, my fingers tucking underneath the right hand roll with each rotation.

I am still capable of the rational deduction necessary to realize that if you can read these words you can probably just as easily turn over the thick brown scroll to find for yourself what it was that I discovered. I would be very surprised in fact—in the hypothetical and paradoxical future in which this document somehow survives the fire it exists solely to ignite—if you had not done so already. I am also acutely aware however that I can no longer remember (or indeed exist) without writing, that the only way the past (whose simultaneous creation and annihilation both myself and this document have come to embody like a gruesome pair of still-born Siamese twins) can cling to the last few gasps of life is if I manage to inscribe it here. My scribblings hold back the ultimate end of a blaze of which they are in fact the heralds and the first voracious flames.

   *   *   *

"... hello, Miss Arden, sorry... Oh it's an answer machine," he said. He took the phone from his ear, without hanging up, & rather helplessly repeated, "It's an answer machine."

He was about to hit the red button.

"No, wait... sorry... may I?"

He shrugged & handed me the phone.

"Hannah?... Hannah, are you there?... it's Sam... please pick up the phone..."

The janitor was embarrassed. He looked at the space where, if there'd been a God, there would also have been a window that accorded a man sat just where he himself was sat the perfect view of something really deserving of a security professional's attention.

Sam?

"Oh thank God." it could have been either of us men who said those words.

Where are you?

"I'm at the University. I need your help."

In Glasgow?

"No, I'm still in Birmingham. I need you to come down. I'm at the Janitor's Lodge."

I thought you'd gone home?

"I know. I was... I was looking for Amrit. Can you come? They need someone to explain why I've got a set of keys. They think I'm a burglar. They want to call the Police."

The janitor began miming with his face that this wasn't necessarily so, then went back to wishing there was a window in the office.

You've got a set of keys? ... Okay, I'll be right over. You really pick your moments, you know.

She rang off before I had a chance to thank her. She turned up less than fifteen minutes later with the kid in a buggy. I was waiting sullenly in the foyer of the janitor's lodge when she reversed in, chattering away to her laconic son. She dealt consummately with the janitors. A big fellar peepoed the boy a few times, then let him play with his peaked cap. She had them eating out her hand. She just tutted & shook her head when she saw me. "We'll have to get you cleaned up," was all she said. It was hard to tell which of us she meant.

They gave her a mild ticking-off about security regulations & that was that. I held the door open for them, wincing as she repeated her gratitude to the 'lads' & steered the buggy underneath the shaky arch formed apologetically by my arms & torso.

Hannah continued chattering away to Sammy as we walked. She was encouraging him to pronounce the names of things we passed. I felt it was at least as hard for me to speak as him. Both of our lips kept struggling to form the shapes that would result in the first sound of a word for something real, but nothing came out. It occurred to me that he was quite old not to be speaking. Maybe he was autistic? Then again, I was over thirty & I couldn't speak myself.

Belonging to a bloke who's pretty fit,
  Reclining just in front of her beside
His wife. He asks her if $e'd like to sit...
  Before he can get up, $e steps astride
His lap and hitches up her skirt a bit
  And perches on his knee: '€anks for £e ride,'
$e whispers in his ear, 'I'm sorry if
My little bottom makes you slightly stiff.'

---

141 Poet's additions:

　　　　　　She perches like she's on a carousel,
　　　　　　　　Acanter. Something vaguely roseate
　　　　　　Beyond the steamed-up windows, like the bell
　　　　　　　　Of an advancing jellyfish, pulsates,
　　　　　　Diffusing light that makes the carriage swell
　　　　　　　　And ebb in unison as it vibrates:
　　　　　　A UFO? the moon? the central mosque?
　　　　　　Or just a streetlamp or a phone kiosk?

　　　　　　The driver turns the wheel and looks to rightwards
　　　　　　　　Considering the headlights—shiny pennies
　　　　　　(A Comet van transporting white-goods
　　　　　　　　From store to showroom, on the late run) when his
　　　　　　Foot slips. Rudeboys, huddled in their night-hoods,
　　　　　　　　Bob in the wake, like gondolas in Venice,
　　　　　　The slipstream frisking them as the bus swerves.
　　　　　　The driver shivers to rejig his nerves.

- *Acanter*. A neologism as an adjective; derived presumably from the noun *canter* 'a slow gallop'. The word is an abbreviation of *Canterbury trot*, so-called because it is traditionally the pace at which the pilgrims rode on the way to Canterbury. It is also, therefore, the probable prosodic *pace* of Chaucer's *Canterbury Tales*. Two things occur from this association. Firstly, it is obvious that Britannia can be seen as a descendent of the characters (and, indeed, the tellers) of the bawdier of Chaucer's tales. Secondly, and most importantly, *acanter* could also theoretically mean 'in the process of talking slang' or (more basically) 'singing'. It is crucial that the drag-queen is not just *acanter* in the sense of bouncing provocatively on the knee of the stranger in the leather jacket like a child on a merrygoround, but also in the sense that she is (as it were) *achatter*. As usual, this can also be said of the reader of the piece: he is *singing the cant* of the poem and, as such, is perched in the saddle of *cantering* carousel that is taking him on a diabolical pilgrimage to… the devil knows where… at this point we seem to be going both to 'the ends of time' and 'twenty thousand leagues under the sea'.

- *the central mosque*: The notion of Birmingham's traditional role as an anti-Episcopal city is being emphasized in the most acute manner possible here. (This is something that made it, for example, the most important target of the Oxford Movement in the 1830s who—during the period of The Birmingham Political Union, Chartism and moves towards disestablishment—built and consecrated a number of High Anglican churches in the area surrounding the rapidly expanding hub of opposition to Tractarianism.) The suggestion is, one assumes, that the most prominent building in the town centre of the future is just as likely to be a place of Muslim worship as an Anglican cathedral; its clerics turbaned, caterwauling imams as the servants of the Apostolic church in surplice and baretta.

- *The driver.* "Sharon" [Poet's note] The poet is revealing his ignorance with this note. The intention—as demonstrated by the allusion to Eliot's 'Death by Water', the mention of gondolas and the likening of the headlights of the 'Comet van' to *shiny pennies*—is clearly to liken the bus driver to Charon, the ferryman of the Styx. This is another near oxymoronic grafting of symbolic characters: in this case of Charon onto Ariel, the *conductor* of ceremonies in Pope's version of the journey. This Ariel/Charon has, as his followers, not the sylphs of the air but the shades of the underworld, sarcastically associated with the peers of the realm: the 'rudeboys, huddled in their night-hoods'. The driver's 'shiver' to 'regain his nerves' is supposed to mimic our own *frisson* in response to this uncanny scene that *swerves* into the marginal annotations. One is left in little doubt that it is the reader himself who, momentarily at least, is meant to take on the role of the driver. As the re-enactor of the written word, the *conductor* of the canto, the reader is to become Ariel/Charon. The fact that these aquatic stanzas were added as an afterthought (they were not 'cut' like many other stanzas: they have no numbers and were handwritten onto the brown paper) only adds to the treacherous nature of the poem's semantic undercurrents.

*   *   *

I confess however—and this is probably the right time for confessions—to a twinge of patriotic pride in my ability to maintain a certain syntactic poise in the egregious circumstances. This leads me to conjecture that the English Language itself has been the real source through the ages of this nation's courage under fire. For that reason alone it might be worth my perseverance in the face of an unconquerable enemy. The maintenance of grammatical precision is a patriotic duty: even in defeat.

Wait until you see the whites of their eyes.

Inside the parcel roll, then, were 60 sheets of letter paper, each of which had printed on it 4 stanzas of Ottava Rima. The method of printing was unusual. On first perusal it appeared slightly speckled. To get a closer look, I screwed one of the objective lenses off my binoculars for use as a magnifying glass. Neither the characteristic 'embossed' appearance one expects of typeset printing nor the anaglyptic sheen of lithography was apparent. Instead, from the evidence of the slightly inconsistent texture, the ink seemed to have been applied as if through an extremely sophisticated and accurate template using some kind of vaporising spray. The mind boggled at the extent of painstaking labour involved in producing what was in fact a rather disappointingly imprecise effect.

*   *   *

> So £ere $e sits and banters wi£ her friend
> About £e slappers on £e different buses:
> 'Which is £e one £at goes to Lickey End?'
> $e quips, '£e 69? £at's full of hussies
> Saturday night.' $e wriggles to unbend
> Her aching back (supposedly); $e fusses
> Intently at her waistband wi£ a €umb
> And $ifts from side to side so £at her bum

---

*   *   *

Each of these sheets was pasted carelessly onto the brown paper, leaving most with a heavily wrinkled surface like the skin of an albino pachyderm wallowing in mud. Onto these sheets, around the stanzas, there were corrections and suggestions scrawled in red ballpoint pen and, in blue, oblique working notes, the occasional eccentric cross reference and various bizarre citations (most of which I confess I neither recognized nor managed to root out). Considering the document's sequestration in the attic-space of a room which had not, as far as I could discern, been opened since the war, this use of what I have long considered a particularly dubious technological innovation was something of a mystery. I was sure the biro had been invented only very recently. It was only three years, for example, since I had used a red one for a trial period of marking: long enough to leave an unsightly tumulus of flesh on the left slope of my middle finger.

My immediate supposition was, therefore, that it was a very contemporary piece of work which had been meticulously concealed in a forgotten backwater of the College in order to have precisely the uncanny effect of anachronism on its discoverer that I was dutifully suffering myself. I soon ascertained that the content of the poem was entirely consistent both with a thematic environment of disturbed temporality and with such an over-elaborate gimmick. It seemed, at first at least, perfectly obvious this was a piece of satirical 'Science Fiction', derivative of Wells, Huxley and Orwell.

It was much more abstruse however: all three of these eminent C20[th] novelists had learned from Swift and Butler the necessity for stylistic clarity and precision when presenting the fantastic society as satirical metaphor. Instead, it was linguistically bizarre, politically tendentious, narratively and tonally inconsistent, morally equivocal and descriptively overblown. I had to concede, however, that it was presenting a vision of a future with which this degraded verse was entirely concomitant. The trashy unpleasantness of the sneering parodic style—with all its creaking puns, its putrid slang and its terrible Byronic rhymes—suited perfectly the debased environment depicted.

For all its abhorrence, and quite despite my better judgement, the poem exercised an irresistible fascination for me. Little by little I found myself in its thrall. I worked on nothing else. I had soon prised all the lenses out of my binoculars for use in examining the poet's less easily decipherable scribbles and doodles, and consequently no longer even took consolation in the uncomplicated transactions of the quadrant's birdlife.

*   *   *

It wasn't until she'd paid for the bus & we'd taken our seats that I attempted an apology.

"Look, Hannah, I'm sorry... I'm a twat. I know... I should've told you. I should've asked you... It's just that I've uncovered a lot of information. There's something you should see." I began to open my bag. She turned to me with a pitiful look, & glanced over her shoulder.

I stopped & scanned the bus. Everyone was staring at me. They pretended not to be, but they all were. They were probably just feeling sorry for me, but for a moment I couldn't shake off the thought of them as ABRA agents, willing me to pull the poem out of the rucksack, chanting some diabolical mantra to themselves like Tolkien's ringwraiths: *Heeza nimbecile... Heeza fuckinimbecile... Un-Roll The Scroll!... Un-Roll The Scroll!*

I closed the bag again. We kept a silent vigil all the way to Moseley. In fact, no-one said a single word that I could hear except to pay the driver or to thank him for the ride. Such a protracted silence is almost unprecedented on a Birmingham bus. I couldn't help but think it was all to do with my debilitating presence. I was the elephant (man) on the bottom deck.

Back at her flat, Hannah handed me a towel & pointed me towards the shower.

"I hope you've got clean clothes," she said, "you're not getting any of Amrit's."

I nodded. Was that a good thing?... in that it suggested she'd stopped thinking of me as his replacement? Or did that mean she wasn't interested in me any more?

The hissing torture of the water-jets against my cuts & bruises soon put an end to such nuanced questions. I travolted for a couple of minutes in that cubicle of steam, gasping at each new spasmodic indignity the unrelenting fingers of hot water could inflict, until I felt myself sufficiently chastened to tackle a discussion of the events of my last visit.

I dressed slowly & precisely, careful to avoid applying anything that might result in my smelling like Hannah's ex. Then I padded into the kitchen on bare pink feet. The child had been wheeled into the study for a nap. I hung my damp towel over a chair & leant my rucksack on the table-leg closest to Hannah, then sat down to put my socks & shoes on.

"What on Earth happened to you, Sam?"

"I'm sorry. I was...embarrassed. I don't suppose we should've done what we did."

"We were drunk. Forget it. I didn't mean that: I mean what *happened* to you?"

"Oh..." she seemed to have shrugged off the events of the other night a little too easily for my liking. I couldn't just forget it. I wasn't going to talk about it now though either: "... it's a long story. It doesn't matter, I'm fine. But you should take a look in my rucksack. There's something in there you should see."

I was intent on my shoelaces, but I could hear with unusual clarity as she unclicked the plastic buckles of the rucksack & loosened the cord around its waterproof flap. I almost shuddered — the way you sometimes do when knocking spirits back — as she drew the roll of parcel paper out of the bag. She placed it on the table. "You mean this?"

"Yep..." I sprang up & moved towards it, "I think we'll find our man in there."

> Can rub against £e poor guy's denim €read
>   And, as his interest seems to reach its firmest…
> Hold on a bit (as Pushmepullyou said
>   To Ouroboros at £e Taxidermist)
> I €ink, perhaps, we $ouldn't get ahead
>   Of ourselves. If I'm to carry on in earnest,
> I really $ould get off £at bus mid-sentence
> And cut back to £e scene of Tanya's entrance…"

143.3-6 *as Pushmepullyou said… we shouldn't get ahead of ourselves*: At first sight this is just a tastelessly contrived attempt at wit. It is, however, gruesomely redolent of the musty atmosphere of the Curiosities Tent at the Carnival. I remember, with a taste of rising nausea, a stuffed two-headed weasel at a travelling fair which an irresponsible 'uncle' had allowed me to glimpse as a boy. Of course, I realize now that the clichés of these phantasmagoric expositions—the conjoined mammal (*Pushmepullyou*) and the auto-consumptive snake (*Ouroboros*) being prime examples—are routinely staged and counterfeited, but as a child I was terrified: not by the customary fear of the reanimation of this beast, or of a malign desire on its part to nest beneath my bedsprings—such possibilities seemed entirely unlikely (even to the mind of an impressionable youngster) considering how mangy its fur had appeared and how crudely it had been secured to its thick oak base—but of a second head of my own growing from the portwine birthmark covering my clavicle as I slept. I refused to close my eyes for three days in a row.

I am beginning to experience precisely that same sense of dread. If it is at all possible—I realize it is not—this poem seems to be transforming my imagination into both an Ouroborus *and* a Pushmepullyou. In what direction time is moving at this point, I can no longer be certain: it appears both to be eating itself and to be attempting to move in opposite directions.

Of course, the traditional epic narrative is always somewhat Janus-headed. That said, the structure even of the *Odyssey* is eminently logical. Odysseus's tale catches up with itself and in doing so overcomes the chaos brought about by the capricious buffetings of Poseidon, and then his journey is released to carry on back to the point at which it started. The only way the narrative of *BQ* could ever be described as 'logical' however, would be if there truly were no difference between the future and the past: as if both were destinations on the same bus route in opposite directions—a circular bus-route, with no termini, such that travel in either direction (clockwise or anticlockwise) becomes a journey via which one might approach the request-stop of the present. Spend too much time on such a bus, in either direction, and you forget which *present* is the stop where you climbed aboard and at which stop you intended to get off. The *present*, in this anarchic nightmare, is wherever the Poseidonish driver decides to pull up next and Britannia—as Athena—turns out to be his conductor, and no friend of ours.

*   *   *

I soon graduated from simply reading the thing to inscribing my own annotations directly onto the brown paper beside the pasted sheets of poetry, continuing over to the back of the paper where I thought it necessary to reveal the extent of the poem's strange effects on my imagination. Why I started this I can only conjecture, but once I had begun I knew only that I must complete the task.

*   *   *

She didn't unroll it. She peered at it like it was a dinosaur bone. I was relieved. "What is it?"

"It's a poem. It was in his office. Notes as well. Do you want to see?... Hannah?"

She didn't reply. She just nodded & proceeded to unravel it. She read a portion at the back (which was still the first bit you came too; I hadn't rolled it all the way over yet) then shifted a random amount of it along, to about halfway, making two cylinders on either side of the exposed sheets. She seemed quite adept at this. I was all fingers & thumbs when I'd done it in the University library.

She just glanced, not really taking in the content. If she was nervous, she wasn't showing it. Considering the fact she refused even to look at the stuff from the study, she was treating this with a suprisingly composed air of meagre curiosity.

"What's it about?" she asked.

"Well it's a parody of Byron's Don Juan. It's narrated by a counterfeit coin & it's about a dart-playing drag-queen called Britannia Spears. The bit you've got there is on a bus-ride home from the pub. There's more to it than that. But that's the basic gist..." She frowned incredulously at me. "The point is... I think it shows that Amrit, might, possibly... be gay."

She laughed & waved aside the suggestion with a regal waft.

"No, really. It's about counterfeit & drag: covering the truth & revealing it."

"Sam, that doesn't prove anything. This isn't even Amrit's handwriting."

"Well it's changed, but you can see the similarity. He's just using a different pen."

"I can tell you for a fact this isn't his handwriting, Sam. What's more, it's absolute nonsense. Look at this: firmest... taxidermist... carry on in earnest. That's it, isn't it. It's like Carry On Being Earnest. Kenneth Williams as Oscar Wilde. Amrit wouldn't write a thing like this."

"No, really, I found it in his cupboard at work. I was trying to put it back when I got caught. & you know what else I discovered today? There was a poet who hung around the gay scene until a couple of years ago & called himself Zomby... ring any bells?... It's obviously Amrit. Amrit's project was the Zomby project. Amrit is this Zomby. Before he disappeared, he told everyone he was going off to work on something big. I'm certain this is it."

Hannah let the rolls go. They thudded back together. "Sam, forget it. It's a goose chase. This thing is a load of trash. & it's nothing to do with my ex-partner."

"Honestly, if you just let me have a picture of Amrit I could prove all this. You realise I've never even seen one myself. I've been looking for a man I wouldn't know from Adam."

"You know I can't. I told you when you first came that I'd destroyed all the photos of him."

"You didn't. You never said anything of the sort. I never even asked you... More fool me."

"Yes I did, I told you there'd been a time when I couldn't bear to see his face."

"Why are you lying to me? Why does everybody seem to lie to me these days?"

"Maybe they're not lying to you, Sam. It's you who refuses to see the truth."

(Okay, here comes ano£er switch in time.
    Perhaps you €ink I $ouldn't interject
To point £ese segues out. But, frankly, I'm
    Aware £at certain readers do expect
A narrative to toe £e temporal line.
    So please take just a moment to reflect
£at every€ing ensuing happened prior
To when Britannia's bus came whiffling by her…)

---

    *   *   *

As I waded through the work, my recurrent dream began to undergo a transformation. No longer was the building through which I moved just a building; now it was a city. It was the Birmingham of the poem: a Birmingham changed beyond all contemporary recognition. It was a metropolis of towering concrete highways on colossal legs that bestrode the canals like brontosaurs. It was a warren of subways and alleys and underpasses whose tidemarked walls were infested with multilingual, multicoloured palimpsests of occultish graffiti. The skyline—glimpsable occasionally through the gaps between the roads and rivers, the bridges and tunnels and canals tangling incomprehensibly like the complex pipes and wires of its acrid factories—was replete with cylinders and ziggurats and Arabian domes that glowed in the city's blinking neon light.

There was hardly a stationary surface in the whole environment. Even the canals were coated with the restless cyclones of spilled engine oil. The city was enmeshed in a warp and weft of paternosters, escalators and conveyor belts; trains rushed through tunnels which became tubular viaducts; trams turned into buses and buses into trams. There were intermittent stations and places of interchange but invariably the destination you were trying to reach would be bypassed or flown-over or tunnelled under and you would need to throw yourself physically from one means of transport—heading for some atrocious sounding terminus like 'Bangham Pit'—to another—bound for 'Warstock', or somewhere equally unpleasant—as the carriages came close enough to one another on either side of an opening of sufficient proportions to allow the features of the other passengers to become almost distinct.

The interior voice of instruction became the facetious narration of the poem's Birmingham coin. Its whining vowels and tapping, buzzing, hissing consonants tormenting the ears and setting the teeth on edge like the cacophonies of industry that forged it.

Again, the sudden sense of the pursuit would bring a wave of loneliness: not now because of a tangible emptiness; instead because you realize there is nothing but movement, there are so many passing through the various interweaving channels that each one is nothing but another particle in a circulating current.

It catches up with you again. You stop to look. It glares. You dive away into the flow. It follows.

'It is the fire.'

'You're it.*'*

    *   *   *

I lost my temper at that: "*I* refuse to see the truth? You're the one who can't admit the fact your boyfriend was a shirt-lifter. You don't actually want to find Amrit at all, do you. You're quite happy with things the way they are. You can live in your romantic fantasy that he was a genius hovering on the verges of insanity, that his work became too brilliant & deep: too close to some dangerous secret, & then his sensitive mind collapsed under the strain." I was speaking quietly with a nasty, sarcastic edge. She just stared at me... hard.

"But all that would be destroyed if you were to find out where he really was. You'd be forced to admit he was a closet homosexual all along: one who couldn't show you his work because it would reveal the truth. In fact, I think you probably knew. The two of you had it all worked out: it would remain unspoken between you, understood but unspoken... unwritten even. That's why you couldn't look at his writing. You were afraid of finding *this*."

"What do you want me to say, Sam? Why are you so upset? Amrit didn't write this. Amrit wasn't gay. You've imagined it. This is all about the other night, isn't it?"

"No. For fucksake Hannah, look, *The Birmingham Quean* is the only half decent thing I've read of Amrit's. If you really think he didn't write it, then I can only tell you this: the Amrit Singh you want to remember was a loser. If you think *this* is rubbish, you should look at the stuff in the study. It's pretentious. It's vague. It's repetitive..." I was moving towards the study, "& it hasn't a hope in hell of amounting to a hill of beans." I shoved the door aside for emphasis. The kid was in there. The door hit the handle of his buggy & he began to cry. I grabbed a random sheet or two & threw them on top of the brown roll. "Read that!"

She didn't look at them. She was already on her way to rescue the cawing infant. Seconds later, she strode back into the room with her son clasped against her shoulder, facing forwards so that both of them were looking at me. He was still bawling. She said nothing. She didn't need to. I started to gather up my things & shuffled over to the brown roll. I looked back at her. There was something primeval about that tableau: a woman with a child wailing at her side like a charging grenade launcher. I left the poem where it was, & walked straight out.

When I had chicken pox as a boy, my mom put calamine lotion all over my upper back & chest. She thought it would help. What she hadn't noticed was that it was years out of date. It was thick & stringy & dark pink. It made me feel like I was wearing elasticated braces bolted from my shoulders to my solar plexus. I found it very hard to breathe for the next two days. In fact, it was considerably worse than the itchiness of the disease. On my way out of Hannah's flat that afternoon, I felt as if that old calamine lotion had been reapplied.

As I turned away, I couldn't decide if it was Hannah dragging me back like that, making my progress away from her door so difficult, or if it was the poem.

I didn't have to wait long for an answer. I was only halfway up the drive when the door reopened. There were two dull thuds in short succession & the door slammed shut again. I turned to see two brown cylinders: one balanced on the doorstep, the other just over its lip, suspended by the tension of the paper. I strolled back to it. I felt no pain or difficulty, no resistance of any sort, as I bent down into the soft shade of the porch & picked it up.

Section 2(a)

Fly, Fancie, *Beauties arched* Brow,
Darts, wing'd with Fire, thence sparkling flow.
From Flash of Lightning Eye-balls *turn;*
Contracted Beams of Chrystal burn.
Wave Curls, *which Wit* Gold-tresses *calls,*
That golden Fleece to Tinsel falls.

(Edward Benlowes, 'To my *Fancie* upon *Theophila*, in *Theophilia, or, Loves sacrifice, a divine poem*. London: Printed by R.N., sold by Henry Seile and Humphrey Moseley, 1652: ll. 1-6.)

fig. 5: Queen's effigy as head of John Dee's alchemical glyph

₤e tilting locals almost dropped ₤eir beers
    (And made an effort not to drop ₤eir jaws)
As six-foot, kitten-heeled Britannia Spears
    Came tottering €rough ₤e Black Swan's flapping doors,
Metallic ringlets pinned behind her ears,
    Her dress a Union Jack of sequinned gauze
Which floated over loosely knit chenille
And plunged towards her bottom to reveal

145.3 *kitten-heeled*: It is no surprise that female sexuality is habitually compared to certain predatory mammals: the fox (as exemplified above), the mink, the cat. These are creatures whose soft fur and instinctive corporeal self-indulgence disguises an unpredictable, sly and deadly nature. Beneath the soft pads of those stealthy paws there are retractable claws. Women of a particularly vampiric sexual nature make no apology for recalling this association. The wearing of fur, the filing and painting of long fingernails, the application of scarlet lipstick all reveal a woman to be red, if not in *tooth*, at least in *lip* and *claw*.

    In this case, however, I think it unlikely that Britannia would actually be wearing a cat's pelt. *Heeled* is used here not to refer directly to a part of a shoe (one that would not be in the least suited to such a soft material as kitten-fur), via a typical American metaphoric extension, to mean 'armed'. If a man is *heeled* in popular US crime-fiction, he is carrying a weapon. It can also refer to money. If a man is said to be *well-heeled* it is because he is *armed* with a good deal of cash. *Kitten-heeled* is therefore probably intended to mean Britannia is brandishing a striking cat-fur... perhaps in the form of a purse. We can imagine what kind of cat it comes from: one of those fat, pampered balls of fluff that cosies in the laps of such predatory females—animals whose snow-white pelts act as an ironic contrast to the blood-red claws that play amongst their tufts. A colourful gloss might be *armed with a pussy*.

145.4 *Came tottering through*: The insertion of this anapæst (as opposed to the elision *tott'ring*) into a line of iambs manages to trip the tongue on the alveolar ridge in a fashion mimetic of the denoted action. The poet uses these indexical correspondences of articulation and movement to force the reluctant reader to enact—via a kind of gestural mimesis—the role of the character depicted. We are therefore coerced into plumbing the depths of physical depravity encoded in the ghastly future he predicts. (See particularly 247:4—'Slow thighs jigging to an offbeat rhythm').

145.5 *Metallic ringlets*. Obviously this connotes all the myths encapsulated in Tolkien's work in progress, the *Nibelungenlied* and Plato's 'Ring of Gyges' previously explored in 17.3 *inkling*, 37.3 *signature*, 47.8 *ring* and especially 38.2 *nickel-brass*. When applied to feminine *locks* (a word fascinating in itself), *ringlets* suggests the treacherous temptation of gold coin. Milton, in Satan's vision of Adam and Eve from Book IV (li. 301-11), has:

    Hyacinthin Locks
Round from his parted forelock manly hung
Clustring, but not beneath his shoulders broad:
Shee as a vail down to the slender waste
Her unadorned golden tresses wore
Dissheveld, but in wanton ringlets wav'd
As the Vine curles her tendrils, which impli'd
Subjection, but requir'd with gentle sway,

> And by her yeilded, by him best receivd,
> Yeilded with coy submission, modest pride,
> And sweet reluctant amorous delay.

The attentive reader will recognize this as one of those moments upon which the veneer of Milton's supposed militant refusal of rhyme in his epic is revealed to be a little flimsy: *waved, implied, sway* and *received, pride, delay* is self-evidently a rhyming pattern. Perhaps this is the wily (so-called) 'puritan' submitting to the elegant Restoration æsthetic as a way of echoically capturing the beguiling nature of the *wanton ringlets*, (with their complex and ironic play on subjection.) This is not just a difference of sex, this is quite evidently the differentiation of 'roundhead' and 'cavalier': the former with hair *not beneath his shoulders broad*; the latter sporting a flamboyant wig that *wav'd / As the vine curls her tendrils*. (See I Corinthians 11:14-15, where St. Paul opines that in man long hair is 'a shame' but in a woman 'a glory.') In effect, Milton is ironically donning a wig of curly Caroline *rhymelets* in order to capture the satanic desire for primitive woman. The poet of *BQ* takes this to an extreme with his *metallic ringlets*... I have begun to wonder who exactly this poet might be...

145.6 *sequinned*: Originally the 'sequin' was the *zecchino*, a Venetian gold coin whose name derived from *zecca* (the mint). The fact that this word finds its etymological root in Arabic *sukkah* (die for coining) is demonstrative of the vital connection between Arabic words and monetary economics in the history of European civilisation. The path towards this borrowing is revealed by its synonyms; coins and words are both altered as they pass from hand to hand and mouth to mouth:

The *zecchino* was the Venetian equivalent of the Turkish *sultanin*, also known in the Arab world as the *scherifi* (from *sharif*, meaning 'noble' or 'glorious'). Another Italian corruption of this latter name—*saraffo*—led the French copiers of the coin (the equivalent of the Spanish *real*) to assume it had been named after a *seraph*. They had obviously misinterpreted the Arabic for 'noble' as the Hebrew for 'angel' (and not without some justification). Louis XI therefore struck a new coin of the same value called the *angelot* depicting the archangel Michael—something which would have been anathema in a Muslim society that took the commandment forbidding graven images very seriously—and it is from this French error that Edward III's introduction of the *angel-noble* into English currency obviously derived.

Crucially, from its first utterance, this English coin was thought to have healing powers. It is the original *touch-piece*. So, after the creation of the Anglican Church, the divine right of Kings came to be exemplified by the healing touch of the King's effigy on the obverse of this denomination of the common currency. It was consequently minted in great numbers in the reign of Charles I, but was pointedly discontinued during The Protectorate. This was, I think, the most important single act of Puritan iconocalsticism: something which exemplifies just how alike the Puritans were in ideology to the original minters of the *sherifi*. It would take a more knowledgeable historian of Medieval Europe than myself to delineate its processes, but there can be little doubt (considering their similarities of religious practice, belief and commerce) that the influence of Mohammedanism on the origins of fanatical Protestantism is virtually instigatory. The English Puritanism that forged the United States finds many direct analogues in the zeal of Islam.

Another disturbing consequence of the influence of this Arabic word *sharif* on English is to be found in the word *sheriff*. The standard etymology suggests the word predates the Norman conquest and derives from *shire-reve*: a local legal representative of the King whose title in French would have been *viscounte*.

> Her back, mahogany and muscular—
>   As broad and brown as Ainsley Harriot's,
> $e'd hardly have been more spectacular
>   Aboard a Boadicean chariot
> (£at's 'Boudiccan' in £e vernacular,
>   According to some Classics Laureate).
> £e gold wig might have seemed like overkill,
> But £en it worked for Cecil B. De Mille…

It is inconceivable, however, that those involved in trade and dispute with the Moors in Spain and the Arabs in the Holy Land could not have noticed that the Arabic *sharif* was used in both societies as an honorific title for a local potentate with very similar duties to the (so-called) *shire-reve*. Quite apart from the obvious influence this Arabic term could have had on the phonetic development of an extant Saxon title, I would suggest the evidence (provided by the Mercian coinage of Offa, for example) of Arabic influence on Saxon development demands that we do not discount the possibility of *shire-reve* being an Old English folk-etymology for an Arabic loan-word. The Sheriff of Nottingham was the *Sharif* of Nottingham.

But the reason for its appearance here is even more disturbing. In the glint of these flashy adornments, the poet is revealing his true identity. Britannia's procession into this section of the poem is as a trashy botch-up of the Queen of Sheba: a Gypsy Queen with an outfit covered in metaphorical gold-coin. And the poet is the King to Britannia's Queen. Here I think we finally discover his true identity. He is neither a contemporary satirist nor a contemporary anarchist. This poem was written at the same time as the greater part of the other uncatalogued archive material here in my room: the nineteen twenties. It is the work of a man who believed he could genuinely see into the dismal future it depicts. I do not have the stomach to explain in detail yet, but there was a student of this college I knew as an undergraduate who was supposed to have 'unlocked the secret of the future.' This esoteric knowledge he had gleaned, it was said, by befriending the leader (the King, or perhaps the *sharif*) of the local gypsy community. At the time, nobody (myself included) took this at all seriously. I am no longer sure about this, however: nor any of my past judgements. The student's name was not important, but the Gypsy apparently called himself *Ryley Bosvil*.

George Borrow has this to say (*Romano Lavo-Lil: Word-Book of the Romany…*):

> Ryley, like most of the Bosvils, was a tinker by profession; but… he was amazingly proud and haughty of heart. His grand ambition was to be a great man among his people, a Gypsy King. To this end he furnished himself with clothes made after the costliest Gypsy fashion: the two hinder buttons of the coat, which was of thick blue cloth, were broad gold pieces of Spain, generally called ounces; the fore-buttons were English "spaded guineas"; the buttons of the waistcoat were half-guineas, and those of the collar and the wrists of his shirt were seven-shilling gold pieces. In this coat he would frequently make his appearance on a magnificent horse, whose hoofs, like those of the steed of a Turkish sultan, were cased in shoes of silver. How did he support such expense?… by driving a trade in *wafodu luvvu*, counterfeit coin, with which he was supplied by certain honest tradespeople of Brummagem

Here, without a shadow of a doubt, is our poet.

GLASGOW

There's something energising about the gloom that shrouds the West of Scotland. It's as if the furtive business of humanity, hidden almost permanently from God's little sunbeams, is given an unusual fillip. If it's a paradox then it's a natural one. There's nothing more productive than a colony of rats or mushrooms. A fact which seems to echo in the higher organisms what evolutionary biologists (some of them at least) are now suggesting about the earliest forms of life: namely, that DNA may not have first developed in the proverbial primeval soup — a rockpool of amino acids heated by the sun — but somewhere much more dank, somewhere with a strange acidic accent the sun can hardly understand: a cave. Despite what all those upright photosynthesisers will insist, most forms of life prefer it dank. Human life is seemingly no exception. & Glasgow is defin*ately* dank.

There's a smell in this city. When I first arrived, my Brummie nostrils guessed it might be Bovril or Marmite, or some kind of cheap industrialised meaty pie. In fact it's the malt fermenting for the whisky: the smell of furious clandestine reproduction. There are breweries elsewhere — it's not as if we don't have them in Birmingham — & distilleries all over Scotland, but it's only Glasgow that ever smells like this. There must be some kind of reaction that takes place when the gas expelled by fermenting semi-germinated barley escapes into its thickened air. The residues of life & death, of work & waste, that coat the city's sandstone & concrete, & the glistening surface of the Clyde, must have transformed themselves over the generations into various kinds of active yeast. Every time a cloud of nascent alcoholic steam is released into the drizzly microclimate, these organisms struggle back to life to create a sickly sweet chain-reaction of negative entropy. Just like human beings, yeasts like it dank.

This is precisely how Glaswegians interact. They allow their humanity to fester; they nurture it in the gloom. Then they get together to release it into public where it creates an intoxicating crescendo of solidarity as they bulge & froth with an unlikely but irresistible optimism that cannot be contained.

All of which makes Glasgow sound like the spiritual home of drunken ribaldry. If it is, it's also the home of buttoned-up Presbyterianism. It has much stricter bye-laws concerning drink & sex than Edinburgh, for example. & John Knox may be associated in most people's minds with Auld Reekie to the East, but if you want to find his most imposing monument you have to climb the gloomy hill that marks the edge of the East End of Glasgow, overlooking the old High Street. This hill has the best blood-&-thunder name of any place in Scotland. It's called *The Necropolis*. Cue the organ. Or, rather, cue an acapella psalm from the Free Church. Glasgow is the cumulus frown as much as it's the thunderclap laughter or the persistent (pitter) patter.

But these things can not be separated. The dour shadow cast by the Kirk & the Necropolis is just another reason for a bit of levity & camaraderie. If things get done in Glasgow, it's as much despite the Protestant work ethic as a result of its supposedly bracing influence. As I said before, life likes it dank.

>   Britannia's stride was magisterial.
>   A fla$bulb aura seemed to wink at you,
>   Reflected in £e bright material
>   Cascading from her $oulder to her $oe.
> $e looked untouchable, e£ereal,
>   A Gloriana in red, white and blue.
> $e glittered €rough £e smoky room in slo-mo:
>   A magic moment fit for Perry Como.

146.8 *Cecil B. De Mille*: Epic American film-maker; casts Bible stories in monumentally crass Technicolor. His most recent film is *Samson and Delilah*, in which Victor Mature sports an absurd long, curly wig.

147.2 *flashbulb aura seemed to wink at you*: It is typical of the reversals in direction of light and the transitivity of the gaze in this poem that the dress appears to be a host of 'flash photographers' such as swarm around glamorous Hollywood *film-stars* like mosquitos around a flame. This is all part and parcel of the reversal of time in the Gypsy King's occultist vision. Rather than the object of photographic attention, this uncanny Britannia is wearing on her body a threatening mass of flashing eyes: *evil-eyes* perhaps, or an insectoid compound eye. The verb 'wink' is used quite pointedly to reverse the etymological progress of the word 'twinkle' from the viewer to the object: eye to star. The 'twinkling of an eye' is, of course, an idiom synonymous with instantaneity. And the flash-photograph is the obvious analogue for the captured moment. If it is Britannia's dress which takes these *snapshots* then, it is we who have become the objects of the temporal capture: we are being pinned to a single instant of dreadful revelation by her passing like butterflies in a display-case. The *flashbulb aura* is an orgy of lascivious *clin d'œils* whose insinuations of prescience and material intimacy are the matrix of a demonic Americanisation of the Union Flag.

147.8 *Perry Como*: A popular American singer. This is self-evidently a reference to his most recent song: 'Don't let the Stars get in your Eyes', which was the best selling record for February and March of this year. The clear contemporaneity of this allusion should not fool the reader into a belief that the poem is the work of a contemporary writer. The prediction of those things upon which bets might be placed are the staple of the fairground fortune-teller. In America, I am led to believe, money often changes hands in wagers upon who is going to 'top the *hit-parade*.' It is therefore the business of a figure like Ryley Bosvil to know such things. What is truly terrifying, however, is the implication that Bosvil had fore-knowledge of the poem's discovery in 1953. Not only can Ryley Bosvil see a twenty first century overrun by moral degradation and perversion, but he knows exactly when and where a man like me will stumble across his dire predictions. There could be no better supporting evidence for the veracity of his vision of the future.

   I can hardly bring myself to go on.

It's a strangely enlivening atmosphere. When I got back to Glasgow, I also got back to work. It wasn't paying work. It rarely is. It was work on *The Birmingham Quean*. I beavered away in my basement flat (*moled away* might be a better phrase), my productivity increasing in inverse proportion to the dwindling October sunlight. Occasionally I'd glance up at the weather through the overpainted railings that protected the top third of my window from West End Park Street. Otherwise my gaze was squarely fixed on the brown roll.

At first I tried to reconcile the poem with the theory. I read it in tandem with Bakhtin & Bloch, Benjamin & Adorno, Derrida & Deleuze, Bhaskar & Habermas, Butler & Cixous. This was successful enough, but it was a bore & taught me nothing really new.

Then something truly significant happened: I discovered RH Twigg. I know it seems unlikely, but it had taken me all this time to get round to tackling the notes. The handwriting was pretty hard to read &, if I'm honest, I'd been avoiding it. I assumed the 'scroll' was a working document: a late draft of the poem that had been made to aid preparation of the final manuscript. (After all, Singh had prepared a similar thing for *The Fiction Party Manifesto*, with four different translations of the Marx-Engels original pasted a page at a time into an A1 flipchart.) The idea was presumably to create *synoptic* effect: 'everything seen at once' (a bit like a filmmaker's *storyboard*). I assumed the notes were just self-reminders of a complex intertextual hinterland: never intended for publication.

For some reason, about a fortnight into the work, my gaze strayed into the annotations at a point in stanza 103 where there was a passing reference to the dangers of laser-treatment of facial hair. I don't know what I was expecting to find: maybe something like a cross-reference to Elizabeth Grosz's *Volatile Bodies*. Instead, there was a bizarrely anachronistic explanation of the word 'laser' which relied on the idea that the note was written before the invention of the high-intensity beam of light. I hunted around for more like this & found the notes were teeming with them. It was like an anachronistic game of *Call My Bluff*. Some were bizarre & contrived, like *karaoke*; others, *blow-job* for example, made me laugh out loud, despite being cheap cracks.

Obviously there was satire involved. Singh was taking a swipe at the traditional lexicography business: particularly the OED, with its constant claims of contemporary relevance based on the unprecedented numbers of modish neologisms included in each 'update', whilst its philological culture remains fettered by an obsolete historicism. Twigg's efforts were rarely more embarrassing than the real thing. If you look up 'moonwalk' in the 2002 revision of the full OED, for example, it reads: 'A kind of exaggeratedly slow dance intended to evoke the characteristic weightless movement of astronauts walking on the moon. The dance is associated principally with Michael Jackson (b. 1958), U.S. singer.' Now that's what I call going backwards whilst making out you're moving forwards.

£e wig was not unlike a golden fleece.
    It was a copper-colour corkscrew perm,
A kind of gilded DNA hairpiece,
    Each curl half like a spring, half like a worm:
Too rigid to be tousled by a breeze
    But loose and li£e enough to bounce and squirm
Benea€ two sticks £at held it up like noodles—
Not quite a $eep's skin… more a golden poodle's.

148.1 *golden fleece*: To return to the theory discussed above (35.3 *Tarantino*) that this legend derived from a Kolchisean practice of using sheepskins to filter gold from local rivers, it might be seen to make internal sense if we compare the 'catching' of the precious metal in the wool's thick knots with the 'trap' set by Ætes for the hero, Jason. In a poignant irony, Jason can overcome these trials only with the help of Medea, the King's sorceress daughter: an even more treacherous 'trap' for the hero, it turns out, than the 'impossible' tasks set by her father. Medea's first act of jealous rage, before slaughtering her own children and returning to Kolchis on a chariot drawn by dragons, is to poison an expensive dress and a golden wreath given to her rival, Glauce, as a wedding present. Britannia's Union Jack frock and gilded wig are a clear allusion to these deadly accoutrements. Instead of the beautiful young victim mortally adorning herself with them though, it is the dark Medean sorceress herself who wears the poisoned items and those who see her pass who are to be entrapped by its venomous snare. Such inversions of effect are a staple of Bosvil's *argot* (a word which itself seems to derive from an ironic association with the *Argo* and the *Argonauts*; as indeed does the word *jargon*, which also has a mysterious connection with the esoteric 'language of the birds.')

148.3 *DNA*: The Romany necromancer displays his virtuoso prescience once more. Deoxyribonucleic Acid was only discovered and named in the 1930s and was described as a 'double helix' by Crick and Watson in a much vaunted article published this year "A Structure of Deoxyribose Nucleic Acid." (*Nature*. Volume 171. Pages 737-738.) The news of this extraordinarily unsettling discovery of the spiral structure that contains the code of life itself was being continuously discussed on the Home Service at precisely the same time that the above-mentioned *hit* by Perry Como was playing almost as regularly on the Light Programme.

    I know this because I managed, during the colder and lonelier months at the beginning of the year, to install a wireless set in my office. It was my only solace when the songbirds became scarce. I have recently put it beyond use, however. I cannot ignore the dreadful portent of the future it seems to carry. It is almost as if the broadcasters and the ghost of Ryley Bosvil were *in cahoots* (such dire American terminology is the only way to represent a diabolical allegiance of this kind). I have begun to believe I can see his outline described in the subtly excited molecules of air surrounding its brown, porticoed speaker-cabinet whenever the radio crackles into life.

    And what tremulous, writhing portents they are. In the next lines, these genetic *anglaises* become, at once, the springs—the clockwork mechanisms—of a satanic time-machine and the serpents crowning a Medusan head. We know we must look away. Instead we stand transfixed.

148.4 *half like a spring, half like a worm*: Crick and Watson's model of DNA has two spirals revolving around the same axis. These two spirals combine, in Bosvil's vision, as a marriage of technological industry and demonic nature: the spring and the worm. We should not forget that the *ægis* of Athena and the head of the gorgon (the manufactured bronze shield and the visceral snaked head) are similarly conflated in Classical mythology into a single object: its definitive protection of Perseus being as a mirror, rather than simply as a shield. Minerva is traditionally depicted by the Romans as having the head of the Gorgon on her breast-plate. It is as if the power of the *ægis* is literally the *reflection* of the Medusa. In this case, however, we are to understand the Gorgon to have defeated the emissary of Minerva and to be wearing his exploded *ægis* on her head. As such, this *Britannia*, is not just a Negro male dressed as the noble female spirit of Great Britain, but the Medusa posing as an *avatar* of Athena… just as the counterfeit narrator poses as (one of the elements, at least) of her *ægis*.

The whole idea of DNA seems to suggest that a man's future is encoded in the basic structure of his molecules. That has terrifying enough consequences in itself for the notion of free-will and the immortal soul. In Bosvil's vision, however, the future DNA encodes is revealed to be an even more dreadful fate of demonic victory over the divine. I have no doubt he not only predicted the discoveries of this poem and the molecular structure of the primary chemical of life would coincide, but that he arranged it to be so. How he went about this I can only speculate. It is certainly not beyond the bounds of possibility that there could have been some ghostly influence on my discovery of this room and its contents over the past few months. Events certainly conspired to an unusual degree.

It is this poem itself, I suppose, which is the real Gorgon. Its stanzaic structure of entangled lines is its writhing head of DNA. I have tried to look away. I am already petrified. It is too late for me. For you?

> A man, £ough, $ouldn't underestimate
> > £e power coiled in each follicle
> To twist £e unsuspecting victim's fate
> > Into a see£ing me$ of helicle
> Entanglement. It's always far too late
> > Before he realises it's... umbilical.
> You just can't tell how treacherous a girl is
> Until $e's got you by £e $ort and curlies.

149.4 *helicle*: Not just a random misspelling of 'helical', I think, but one intended to conflate all of the following: *heliacal*, the state of a morning or evening star on the point of emerging or disappearing into the sunrise or the sunset; *heli(con)ical*, the shape of Mount Parnassus (a spiralling cone like Yeats's *gyre*); *hell-ical*, a putative synonym for 'diabolical' or 'infernal'; *hell-(ic)icle*, a portmanteau of 'helical', 'hell' and 'icicle' which casts the Underworld as a descending spiral of ice. The ringlets of this diabolic *anti-muse* therefore manage to invert the spiral Helicon of the Muses to suggest the downward spiral of Dante's *Inferno*, which infamously culminates in the ice into which has been embedded Lucifer, the aspiring *Morning Star*.

The Bolshevik English newspaper of that same name would doubtless insist that we make reference here to Marx and Engels' dialectic: 'spirals of change', 'negation of negation', and other such dour communist Germanicisms.

149.8 *short and curlies*: According to Partridge, this is forces slang from the recent war referring to the pubic hair as a point of such intimacy on which to be gripped that it suggests the impossibility of escape. It is more often used to mean metaphorical capture—in senses of unavoidable obligation or unassailable argument—than any physical sequestration. Here the intimacy is infinitely more disquieting. The *short and curlies* are not just the pubic hairs but the molecules of DNA. One thinks of Hardy's Jude tricked into marriage and a doomed existence by the unwanted pregnancy of a ruthless, venal and insensitive woman of greater experience.

Deciphering more of the handwriting soon revealed that there was much more to Twigg than ironic lexicography. In fact, there were three different bodies of text this character had putatively written. These corresponded to three phases in his relationship with the 'primary text'.

The first section (although the last in physical position) was the 'Foreword', from which we could discover his name & the time & place in which he was supposedly writing: Oxford 1953, at a fictional College called 'Temple'. This claimed to have been written before the editorial annotations themselves. It set out in bombastic terms his initial attitude to the poem: one of support for what he believed to be a controversial but much-needed work of dystopian science-fiction, in the tradition of Wells, Huxley, Orwell & so on. The fact that he attempted to propound the literary merit of this addition to the genre by tracing its influence to Jonathan Swift is a characteristic witticism on Singh's part when you consider Twigg's own position as an updated Martinus Scriblerus.

Secondly, there were the notes themselves, which charted the collapse of his belief in the poem as a conservative satire of a derelict future. Having passed through several stages of increasingly histrionic interpretation, like the circles of Dante's hell, it was the notes themselves that collapsed into paranoid hallucination as his mind broke down under the strain of a protracted realisation of the 'truth'. The *Call my Bluff* stuff gave way to feverish speculations about time travel, magic & esoteric knowledge. Aside from the Scriblerian examples, the most obvious influence on all of this was Vladimir Nabokov, who even made an appearance (in a letter) towards the end of the notes.

Lastly came the *Fire* narrative: a weird account of his life & the events leading up to its end that were supposedly being written as he burned to death. At times it seemed the fire was just a psychic foreshadowing of mortality, at others that it was genuine ongoing *spontaneous combustion*, & even that Twigg was writing whilst already dead. This last narrative existed at the temporally & psychologically opposite pole to the 'Foreword'. It was the end-point of the collapse. Stylistically it seemed to have come full circle, though. There was a sense of relief & resignation that returned control to his prose. (Quite unlike the way you'd actually imagine a man on fire to express himself. At times it read like CP Snow or Anthony Powell, at others like Evelyn Waugh or Nancy Mitford. Only when he recounted the various stages of the *dream* did strange echoes of Henry Green, William Burroughs & Iain Sinclair pop up.) Neither was this section confined to the bit at the end of the roll where the sheets of poetry ran out (in fact, this was where the Foreword appeared). Instead, it was interspersed throughout the text as if Twigg were supposed to have filled in all the remaining gaps whilst reading back the poem in the light of what his imminent death had persuaded him was a conclusive understanding of the text.

What this was all about was not immediately obvious. The idea of producing a time-paradox version of *Pale Fire* might glibly be explained as postmodern anti-historicism. But that wasn't it. This was a text in which an internal critical commentator suffered a nervous breakdown as a result of an attempt to explain a poem that he came to believe was a genuine representation of a future (50 years away) in which nothing is actually 'genuine' at all.

>   It was £e wig £at Sloggy noticed first.
>   He hated all £e benders in £is boozer.
>   £ese freaks could take away a punter's €irst,
>   Or worse… £is tart's panache did not excuse her.
>   Why couldn't it just get itself reversed?
>   But Sloggy wasn't just some ugly bruiser;
>   He made a decent living out of queers—
>   Wi£out £em he'd be buried in arrears.

150.1 *Sloggy noticed first*: The previous four stanzas, and the entire ensuing passage, are revealed to be covertly filtered through Jeff Sloggy's point of view.

In narrative fiction this is a relatively common convention. Even where characterized narrators are concerned, it is usually assumed that the ability to view a scene through the epistemic position of another character is an act of speculation (or simply a narrative convention to be put down to 'poetic license') rather than evidence of genuine extra sensory perception. This poem, however, makes a point of foregrounding and discussing these shifts and blends of psychological and ideological perspective. It claims that the coin's ability to perceive events is achieved as a kind of parasitic symbiosis with the character in whose *possession* it finds itself at any given moment. In fact, this manages to reverse the concept of *possession* entirely to suggest that the 'owner' of the coin does not 'possess' the coin so much as it is capable of *possessing* its owner.

The coin is only beginning to discover the nature of its own strange existence in this work (which purports to be only the first canto of a much larger piece) and we see just the first glimmers of its unsettling development from a passive viewer of the scenes, through the eyes of the character whose mind it inhabits, to the influencer (and perhaps even the controller) of the actions of that character. The occasional narrative confusion is, one supposes, designed to mimic these first bewildering hours of the coin's psychological development and its struggles for more and more influence. There is a habit made of these sudden reminders of the character's point of view which drastically alter the way one understands the previous scenes to have been received. The reason is that the poet wants us to feel like the coin, or at least to contrast our experience with its own. Our roles as readers, moving through the various intermingling points of view, is directly analogous to that of the coin; the difference being that, however hard we struggle, we exercise no control.

Instead it is the spirit of Ryley Bosvil, as encoded in his incantations, which is slowly coming to influence our minds. Like Sloggy, we have the Birmingham Quean in our possession and, as a result, *we* are gradually being possessed by *it*. At the moment, like Sloggy, it is only colouring and distorting our views of the world as it mingles with our consciousness. What it really wants, however, is to take control. This is how, one must suppose, Bosvil actually sees into the future. He possesses the minds of those who inhabit it and uses their perceptions to encounter it. It is a kind of inverse necromancy: he is a dead spirit who sees the future through the eyes of those who accidentally summon him to tell the futures he predicts. His greatest trick is to make those futures come about by forcing his victims to influence their progress. Make no mistake. We are all becoming his victims.

150.8 *buried in arrears*: It should not go unnoticed that this phrase perfectly represents the situation in which the narratee, Tiberius Mercator, finds himself. This character is little more than a personification of the inevitable bankruptcy suffered in this degenerate society by those who refuse to indulge in immoral business practices. It is worth reminding ourselves of this narrative situation. Much of the history of Sloggy's business career to follow is presumably intended by the coin/quean as an example of good practice and an implicit admonishment of Mercator's futile ethics.

There are other, more important, implications though. Firstly, it should not go unnoticed that this phrase carries a (typically paradoxical) connotation of anal penetration: (paradoxical because without any *queers*: 'sodomites', it would actually be impossible to commit sodomy.) A more obvious and a more disturbing pun, however, suggests the sense 'buried inner ears.' The fact that the *phonetic anagram* 'inner ears' is buried within the term *in arrears*, and also the fact that it is only in our *inner ears* that this phonetic burial can be uncovered, makes the phrase reverberate with particularly uncanny resonances. The most important part of the inner ear, as far as the human sense of balance is concerned (and even, it has been suggested, our sense of temporal equilibrium), is called the *labyrinth*. The amphibolous language and ideology of this poem is a monstrous vision of the future, channelled by Bosvil to implant itself in our labyrinths like the Minotaur of Crete. If we venture into such dismal realms to confront the creature, we will find ourselves, like Theseus, not only lost in Crete, but lost in time.

Which brings me to the literal meaning of *buried in arrears*: 'interred in that which is behind.' There is a belief amongst one of the American Indians tribes (I forget which) that a man moves backwards rather than forwards in his life. That is to say—and the logic is particularly cogent—that the inability of man to see into the future suggests that the future is behind him, not in front of him. The past is before him and receding towards the horizon as he himself retreats in the direction of the future. For a man to be obsessed with what is to come he must therefore attempt to turn his back on the past and, in the process, lose his memory. Each act of attempted prescience is consequently a futile act of forgetting. For these people to be *buried in arrears* is to be buried in the future, not the past. It is to turn one's back on one's ancestors and the guidance into the future they provide. This is what they believe had happened to the European settlers who took their land, and were looking always towards the West and away from the sunrise of their origins.

It is the implicit aim of this poem, and its Gypsy composer, to bury the reader in such *arrears of the future*.

> It started wiþ þe phone-sex story lines:
> Like *12 inch Pizza Boy*, *Piss on þe Piste*,
> *All Hands on Declan*, *Minors down þe Mines*,
> *Defrocked: Confessions of a Collared Priest*,
> *A Bareback Rodeo*, *Þe Thai Þat Binds*,
> *Þe Way of Þe Exploding Fist*, and *Grease Artiste*.
> He advertised þem in þe pinko press
> But upped his turnover wiþ more finesse

151.8 *upped his turnover with more finesse*: This has something to do with cards, I think: Tarot cards perhaps. These are, after all, the staple props of a Gypsy fortune-teller. A *finesse* is a specific act of sophisticated bluff in Bridge, a game in which one decides the level (higher or lower) of the card one 'turns over' in a 'trick' depending upon complex predictive speculations. Obviously, the surface meaning derives from American business speech: a simple gloss is something like 'increased his profits in a more sophisticated manner', but the esoteric card-gaming connotations suggest a more fundamental underlying metaphor of logical/moral reversal (*turnover*) and showy duplicity (*finesse*) which are the mainstays of Gypsy obfuscation.

*   *   *

400 years ago, almost to the day, the anti-Nicean firebrand, Miguel Servetus, was burnt at the stake by order of the burghers of Geneva. His prosecution for heresy had been carried out by Jean Calvin, the radical protestant reformer under whose auspices Servetus was seeking sanctuary from a previous death sentence passed by the Inquisition at Vienne. The fire that ended the life of this Unitarian pioneer was kindled with copies of his own book: Christianismi Restitutio. *The obstinate Servetus is reputed to have met calls for his last-minute repentance with a recitation entirely from memory, amidst the flames and smoke, of a long passage from this histrionic and eclectic tract. Amongst the theological ranting, the book actually contained one genuine scientific breakthrough: the first description by a European writer of pulmonary circulation. Unfortunately (for posterity), it was not this extract that he chose as his last words. As his flesh burned and his throat choked, he revisited verbatim a bombastic critique of Augustine's anti-apocatastasisism. Despite the respiratory exertions involved, it took him a considerable amount of time to asphyxiate (the usual cause of death in these circumstances). Legendarily he did not lose consciousness at all before the moment of his death. Witnesses claimed to have seen his newly shaved head grow back a beard of flame as he continued to billow fuming, unintelligible Latin. Just before the blood ceased pumping to and from his lungs, refusing (as only he could have understood amongst those present) to seep through any theoretical perforations in the septum, charred pages of the book from which he was quoting began to detach themselves from their binding and spiral up towards his shoulders like black vultures. At the critical moment, one of these errant leaves of ash covered his face, smothering the climax of his loquacious career. The more informed amongst those present recognized this as divine retribution for his heretical account of the annunciation.*

*   *   *

Twigg was obviously supposed to be a figure of fun, even of strong satire: he was caricaturally racist, sexist, elitist & conservative. However, he had one saving grace: an acute sensitivity to the poem. His slow breakdown under its spell suggested the opposite of the usual poststructuralist rejection of origins. Instead the acute violence carried out by postmodern twenty first century culture (in versified guise) was being seen to have a disastrous effect on the period of history from which it sprang.

Curiously, Twigg's explanation for the cause of what he considered to be the chaotic & degenerate society depicted in the poem could just as easily have come from the kind of radical left-winger we assume produced the poem itself: it was the result of postwar Imperial American ultra-freemarket capitalism. At times Twigg's anti-Americanism sounds almost Bevanite. *The Birmingham Quean* might just as easily have been intended as a eulogy for a lost society, for lost morals & lost intellects, as a satire of them. If so, it would seem to have been both radical & acutely conservative. (Something not without precedent in English 'radicalism'. Think of William Cobbett, William Morris, Orwell, & so on.)

Whatever its political intentions, one thing seemed clear: this was the work of Amrit Singh. Maybe these multiple contradictions were evidence enough in themselves, but Twigg's similarity to the tramp of the *Zomby* project was also striking. Just like the tramp, he was a prematurely ageing man: apparently a relic of an earlier time inhabiting a world with which he shared only the occasional glimmer of mutual understanding (despite its frustrating proximity). Twigg went round & round in circles, tracing the byways of *The Birmingham Quean*, just as the tramp trudged the gullies & towpaths of the city in *Zomby*. (Could Twigg be another version of Singh's missing father? More a grandparent perhaps...)

Obviously he was quite different to the tramp: his opposite in many ways. He was nothing but words, whereas the tramp was wordless. He was deeply affected by his encounter with another time, whereas the tramp remained almost insensible. Most of all, Twigg was an anachronism in the opposite direction: not a misunderstood icon of a utopian future but a man stuck in the past (but inserted in the future). There seemed to be at least three levels to this. Firstly, he was trapped in his contemporary frame of the early 1950s; secondly, he was (within the 1950s) physically sequestered in a room crammed to the rafters with miscellaneous college papers from the interwar period & wallowing in nostalgia for his own youth; thirdly, his primary research interest in mid seventeenth century poetry meant that he was intellectually mired in a period 300 years previous (a period which was itself riven with reactionary traditionalism in response to revolution.) As such, Twigg was the victim of a violent historicism that made him a self-aware caricature of History itself.

This is probably an overstatement, but it was Singh's own overstatement. Twigg was just an act: 'period camp'; overstatement was part of the drama. At no point did Singh allow the reader to forget how fake he was. The silly explanations of new words, especially the sexual terms, came across with much of the faux naivety of the drag-act. But we'll return to this idea. More pressing is the question of Twigg's numismatic obsession.

By getting teenage kids, whose goods he fenced,
    To ring £e numbers when £ey robbed a place
And leave £e stories running: ninety pence
    A minute, keeping up a steady pace,
Would soon become a staggering expense
    If no-one on £e crime-scene could replace
£e phone receiver for a day or €ree—
Whoever did, would find a gay orgy

152.1 *teenage*: 'Teenager' is slack American slang for a person whose *age* ends in the affix *–teen*. That is, youths between 13 and 19 years of age. 'Teenaged' would be the obvious adjectival form. Here the *–d* has been dropped, presumably, to resist the poetic convention of producing the word 'agèd' as a trochee. However, it also manages to emphasize precisely that ambiguity which the bisyllabic 'agèd' helps to avoid. Namely, the possibility of its being mistaken for a word with the *–age* suffix (imported from the French, and therefore pronounced <a:j>). This ending nominalizes certain French verbs: the result of the verb *masser* is a *massage*; the result of *camoufler* is *camouflage*. Many of these words were loaned into English only in their nominal forms and therefore became doubled as verbs. One can therefore be said *to massage* and *to camouflage*; the upshot being the rather ugly adjectival forms: 'massaged' and 'camouflaged', which in French are *massé* and *camouflé*. Obviously, the implication is that there might be some similar transitive verb *to teenage*. What precisely this might involve, and what might be its effects upon the sufferer, one shudders to think: perhaps some form of accelerated (or else arrested) physical, psychological and moral development. (Perhaps both.)

152.1 *fenced*: This is criminal cant for dealing in stolen goods. The most infamous *fence* in history, and the man for whom the term could very well have been coined, was Jonathan Wild 'The Thief-Taker General of Great Britain and Ireland' in the early eighteenth century. This character was a famous enough rogue to be the direct object of two of the most important satirical works in the period directly following his death: Fielding's *Jonathan Wild, The Great* and Gay's *The Beggar's Opera*.

    All the polysemes of the verb *to fence*—'to engage in skilful swordplay or other cunning forms of combat', 'to erect a barrier around or to *countermure*', 'to receive stolen property', etc.—are ultimately derived from an abbreviation of the noun *defence*. It seems a little odd that these did not all come under the heading of the more logical abbreviation *fend* (of the verb *to defend*). But then such confusions of parts of speech are common in lexical development (see prev.). No two words are ever very happy meaning the same thing, however. The result is that the verb *to fence* seems to have become a term with much more aggressive and ingenuitive connotations than *to fend*, which feels a little pusillanimous by comparison. Crucially, the criminal *fence* seems to be so named for an ability to combine all of these qualities. Sloggy's sly practice of storing stolen goods on dangerous building sites is at once a way of *fencing them off* (by erecting scaffolding and signage) and of *fencing* with the (much less skilful) authorities. His cunning directly recalls that of Jonathan Wild. It should come as no surprise to the reader that Wild also came from Wolverhampton.

152.6 *crime-scene*: The term *the scene of the crime*, of which this is obviously a conflation, is one transferred from fictional use to genuine Police use, rather than vice versa. That is to say the clichéd phrase of the *whodunit* predates the application of any such term in real life to the area in which a crime under investigation has supposedly taken place. Agatha Christie was the first to use it, making a rather convenient allusion to theatre to pre-empt the gauche theatrics of her detective hero, Hercule Poirot (a character who, incidentally, I am convinced owes a great deal to M. Paul Emmanuel in Charlotte Brontë's *Villette*.) It is, of course, the whole point of this particular sub-genre of *crime fiction* that the reader should be encouraged to predict the detective's eventual *redramatisation* of a murder (or a series of murders) that has already taken place. So it may seem surprising that it has taken until now for any such drama to appear in the theatre. The reason is obvious though. It is quite impossible to suppress the knowledge of *who dunit* in such a public forum. The entire interest of anything in this flimsy genre dissolves the moment that single piece of information is revealed, and it is only via the intimacy of silent reading that it can be kept secret. We can safely predict that Christie's *The Mousetrap*, which has just opened on the London stage, will not have long to run.

A scene of a play, not unlike the context of a murder, is a treacherous environment. Things are not what they seem; it is the site of duplicitous performances and counterfeit objects. If this is what is implied by the phrase *the scene of the crime*, it seems a perfect name to give the setting of this poem's climax. We should also recall the room in which this story is being told. It is a kitchen strewn with its owner's few belongings and in which he was intent on murdering himself. It is clear how he is therefore likened to myself, and any other reader, at this point. We too are the victims in the midst of this poetic *crime-scene*, strewn with desperate marginalia. The difference is we know *who dunit*: it was Ryley Bosvil.

*   *   *

I mention the morbid anecdote of Miguel Servetus because my room is full of the same whirling flocks of incinerating literature. I can hear their manic warbling as they search for a roost in the overexploited eaves. It is hot enough by now for entire slim volumes to take flight amidst the college papers—collections of poetry, for the most part, though some are plays and essays. The room has become the disintegrating memory of a madman. I used to have a system whereby my recollection of an apt quotation could be quickly prompted by reference to shelf number, chapter, page and paragraph. If I needed a point of reference, I would know precisely where it could be found simply by looking at my bookcases: they were arranged as a logical diagram; I would turn to it in seconds. It was a trick I used to impress the keener sort of student. Such prowess has long-since left me though. The remnants of my memory and my library, left to me after the summary eviction from my rooms, are scrambling around my ears like fighter-planes. Fire mixes, confuses and disintegrates before it finally annihilates the dizzying morass it has produced.

*   *   *

Narrated, blow by blow, amidst £e mess:
"£at's right, boy, lick it up and down £e seam
£en put £e WHOLE €ing in your mou£—Oh YES!"
£e tru€ was Sloggy €ought it was a scream.
Financially, it was a big success,
But Sloggy's personal interest in £e scheme
Was €inking he could charge some Christadelphian
For *'Kiss my Hard-on' by Fellatio Nelson.*

153.1 *blow by blow*: This is a metaphor derived from the terminology of American radio commentary on boxing matches. The putative narration over the telephone line of a pornographic scene has obvious similarities. Despite the possible sadistic depravity suggested by the titles listed in stanza 151, and the conventional homoeroticism of the pugilistic spectacle (Byron himself, we should remember, is supposed to have carried with him wherever he went the muscular miniature portrait of a famous contemporary prize-fighter), I do not think we are to suppose the events depicted to be genuinely violent. The implication is, rather, that the mode of speech is likened to the excitable machismo of American sports commentary. Bosvil knows as well as anyone how the pace and tonal qualities of language can have emotional and even physical effects upon the hearer. These are the mechanisms an *enchanter* uses to infect our minds (the word means 'he who sings'.)

153.1 *Narrated... amidst the mess*: An allusion to the frame narrative of Tiberius Mercator.

153.4 *scream*: A cause of explosive or shrill laughter. But the threat inherent in such words is never far below the surface of this poem. I think I am right in identifying its first recorded nominal use as this from *Macbeth* (II.iii.57-61):

> LENOX. The Night ha's been vnruly:
> Where we lay, our Chimneys were blowne downe,
> And (as they say) lamentings heard i'th' Ayre;
> Strange Schreemes of Death,
> And Prophecying, with Accents terrible,
> Of dyre Combustion, and confus'd Euents

My nights have been like this for weeks.

153.7 *Christedelphian*: Literally *brother of Christ*: a member of the Thomasite anti-Trinitarian sect which promotes literal belief in the Bible as the unmediated word of God and denies both the divinity of Christ and the existence of Satan and Hell. It is a characteristically Trans-Atlantic religious movement, conceived as it was by John Thomas who emigrated to America in 1832, where he developed his radical Protestant theology, only to return and transplant the sect into the fertile radical Non-Conformist soil of the England's industrial heartland: most notably, and most successfully, in Birmingham.

153.8 *Fellatio Nelson*: I need hardly point out that Admiral Nelson's final words were '*Qismat*, (and not *Kiss me*,) Hardy'. The tawdry implication that all officers in the British Navy are homosexual is being acutely magnified by this vilely punning extension of the conventional mishearing. Bosvil is intending us to mine the truth, however. He knows the discoverer of his prediction will be a critical reader. He knows I will understand that Nelson's real final message to the world was the Arabic for 'fate'. Bosvil wants us to realize that our own *fate* is one in which the martyrdom of our nation's greatest naval hero is to become defiled as a grotesque tableau of homosexual oral intercourse.

Aside from a likely desire on Singh's part to combine the theses of two influential scholarly books — Marc Shell's *The Economy of Literature* & Anthony Grafton's *Forgers & Critics* — there was a sense in which Twigg's numismatic obsession had a truly reflexive quality. It was telling that Twigg should share with the Renaissance Humanist Joseph Scaliger an interest in rational historicism backed up by the notion of the coin as the pre-eminent 'authentic' object. The historical importance of the coin (made of unreactive metal) derives from the fact that it lasts. For traditional historians, fascinated mainly by the wielders of power, coins are the archaeological objects par-excellence. They are the tools & texts of potentates, & they remain pristine a good deal longer than most other bits & bobs. Dig up a coin & you're literally digging up a bit of history. Perhaps Twigg was not intended to be just a historian of coins, but himself a kind of coinage. He represented the notion that discrete historical objects — like himself — embody a permanent & unchangeable history insofar as they resist decay: either the literal decay of erosion (ageing) or the metaphorical decay of diminishing knowledge.

This was a poignant irony. If Twigg was a coin, he was a shoddy fake. There were hundreds of self-conscious jokes that made this clear. His denunciations of the counterfeit narrator, for example, were always made to coincide with ironic misunderstandings of decimal money. But the most consistent revelations of Twigg's false nature occurred at the stylistic level. He wasn't just a counterfeit. Unconsciously, Twigg was also a plagiarist.

For me, this was the least dismissible piece of evidence that Singh was responsible for R.H. Twigg. It was precisely the same method of 'rewriting' at work that had characterised the *Zomby* project & *The Fiction Party Manifesto*. There were hundreds of examples: too many to trace here. But one in particular stood out. The very first thing attributable to him was a Virgilian epigraph: 'Wars. I see terrible wars / & the River Tiber foaming with much blood.' This was a quotation, rather than plagiarism, of course, but the 'Foreword' that followed it was far from original; it was a *détournement* of Enoch Powell's so-called *Rivers of Blood* speech (so-called because of a poor translation by a scaremongering press of the Virgilian epigraph spoken in the original Latin during Powell's pretentious/portentous speech).

This was typical Singhian black comedy. (I use the term pointedly.) Twigg was being likened to the pariah of English Toryism. The fact that Powell had disgraced himself by playing the Sibyl of Birmingham, whilst Twigg was commenting on a 'dire vision' of a *Brummagem* future, was part & parcel of the joke. But it wasn't just a matter of condemning Twigg by association with another nostalgic, intellectual, ultra-conservative racist. There was a sense of nostalgia in Singh's own satirical method that seemed to bring him closer to both Twigg & Powell, for all their ideological anathema. There were overtones of admiration — the kind you might have for a worthy advisory — in what was nevertheless a withering attack. Where the *Zomby* project had re-written for theoretical reasons, here the method was used as a means of characterisation. Twigg's *arc* was that of a self-conscious bulwark of 'authenticity' against the relativist forces of postmodern culture who suffers a collapse as he realises his own fakeness. You couldn't help thinking Singh felt sorry for him. After all, Twigg was Singh's own drag-act.

It wasn't always queer porn he'd sold.
    He'd started wi£ a simple lightbulb trick.
(He borrowed it off Pete £e Feet, £is old
    Inebriate he knew—a lunatic
Who went round barefoot even in £e cold
    Because an acid trip once made him sick:
He €ought his bro€el-creepers had caught fire—
    A premonition of his funeral pyre).

154.6 *acid*: No doubt this is a slang term for some form of cheap, vinegary alcoholic drink which has acted as an emetic on this mendicant alcoholic character (what the Americans would call a *wino*). It is a philological curiosity that the word 'alcohol' derives from the Arabic *al-koh'l* meaning 'Stibium' (more accurately, Antimony Trisulphide, the naturally occurring dark grey ore of that strange metal). It was used by the Arabs, in a calcined and powdered form, for two things: firstly as a cosmetic black stain for the eyelids, and secondly in a ethanoic suspension (by doctors) as an emetic medicine. It is obviously from this latter preparation that the word was eventually used to mean distilled liquor. It is the former use that reveals its etymology though, and thereby its importance as a driving principle behind this poem:

In Ezekiel XXIII, a complex analogy is drawn between two harlot-sisters, called Ahola and Aholiba, and the cities of Jerusalem and Samaria (the capitals of the two schismatic Jewish nations: Judah and Israel). The idea is that trade relations with neighbouring states (Babylon and Assyria), leading to dalliances with their religious and cultural practices, are equivalent to 'whoring' with their 'paramours' and their 'desirable young horsemen… whose flesh is as the flesh of asses and whose issue is like the issue of horses'. The inevitable result is defilement and destruction at the hands of these bestial heathens, sanctioned by God (addressing Jerusalem/Aholiba through Ezekiel) as punishment for such impure adulteries.

> 33 Thou shalt be filled with drunkenness and sorrow, with the cup of astonishment and desolation, with the cup of thy sister Samaria [Ahola]…
>
> 40 And furthermore, that ye have sent for men to come from far, unto whom a messenger *was* sent; and, lo, they came: for whom thou didst wash thyself, paintedst thy eyes, and deckedst thyself with ornaments…
>
> 44 Yet they went in unto her, as they go in unto a woman that playeth the harlot: so went they in unto Aholah and unto Aholibah, the lewd women [Samaria and Jerusalem].

The Hebrew verb translated by the King James Bible as 'paintedst the eyes' is *kākhal*, uncontroversially identifiable as the etymon of the Arabic *al-koh'l*: 'that with which one paints the eyes'. The connection between this idea and that of strong drink—and indeed between the drunken 'cup' and the lascivious overflowing female genitalia—is also made quite explicit in this Chapter. One cannot help but think of the Britannia of this piece as a shameless and unpunishable creolization of the painted Aholiba.

Antimony itself has been subject to a curious French folk-etymology, supported even by Johnson, which breaks it down as *anti-moine* 'against the monk' and leads it to be called *monks-bane*. It was, in fact, first used as *antimonium* (a synonym for Stibium) by the Alchemist Constantinus Africanus of Salerno (who appears in Chaucer's *Merchant's Tale* as 'cursed monk daun Constantyn'). It was probably a medieval Latin corruption of some other Arabic word. Very many alchemical terms are, including the word *alchemy* itself. An even more absurd analysis, but one that finds resonances in the present work, might cast the word as *anti-money*.

154.8 *funeral*: era 13

154.8 *pyre*:

> Content
> To find there was ephemeral work to do,
>
> Ephemeral work I did. The skies were rent
> And I took notes; delicate whippets of fire
> Hurdled the streets, the cockney firmament
>
> Ran with flamingos' blood and Dido's pyre
> Burnt high and wide and randy over the Thames
>
> (Louis MacNeice 'Canto IV': ll. 77-83)

The flamingo—the leader of the Aristophanic chorus—crouches over the 'brummie firmament' of this poem like a gruesome inversion of a bird: self-sacrificing, bizarrely fledged in flame like an embodiment of the destructive power of racial, sexual and philosophical ambiguity. The pyre of Dido is the *Phoenician* fire, the birthplace of the *Phoenix*, the lifeblood of the *Phoenicoptera*...

*   *   *

The effect of this imminent metaphor is so acute that I can imagine my entire memory—not just of literature, but of life itself—swirling in the raging vortices of convection that surround me. That is to say, all these fluttering leaves of winged ash harrying the fringes of the blitzkrieg seem so similar to the recollections of my life that I have no trouble imagining them all to be the pages of my still unwritten memoir. It is not merely my present self that is burning. It is 'the life' as well.

They say your life passes before your eyes as you die. This is nothing of the sort. Rather than becoming more present, the events of my existence seem to retreat from vision, ascending like the burning pages in a tangled lattice of helixes towards a blurred apex of intangibility. Imagine cinematic images of ordnance falling from the bombers onto Dresden, London, Birmingham... but played back in reverse. And yet, the story seems more coherent as my ability to inhabit it (or even to relate to it) recedes. It is no longer my life. At least, it is not a real life. It still, however, feels like mine to tell. It is one that must be told before the end.

*   *   *

You need some bulbs wi£ decent packaging
   —A dozen of £em in a cardboard tray—
An anti-static duster and some cling-
   Film; and it's quite important you portray
Yourself as Johnny corporate marketing,
   So $irtsleeves, nametag and a dossier
Of branded products doesn't go amiss.
You choose a leafy street, and what you do is £is:

155.3-4 *cling-/Film*: Transparently, there is a flimsy self-referential pun contained in this awkward enjambment. To necessitate such an odd attraction across two lines of verse with the bisection of a hyphenated term is tasteless enough. But when that term apparently refers to some thin sheet of rubber (or one of the new plastics perhaps) used to test the efficacy of an 'anti-static duster' by measuring the residual adhesive effects of static electricity upon that material, it is obviously supposed to be a joke. The hyphen, that is, becomes like a *film* that *clings* to the proceeding line, thereby suggesting that a semi-magical electromagnetic attraction is at work.

It is not funny. Instead something very worrying springs to mind. Bosvil must be hinting, by analogy, at some diabolical force of attraction that exists between the poem and the (charged) 'film' of the reader's imagination. In the culture of his intended readership, that is, the imagination is a 'film' in the sense that it is likened to a diaphanous *liminus* between the senses and the soul (actually something of an epistemological commonplace) and also (and much more importantly) in that it is envisaged as the result of the overpowering effect of the ubiquitous 'moving image' upon the human mind in the culture he is addressing. Film (as in *cinema*), Bosvil is suggesting, has primed the imagination to be ineluctably attracted to his dire predictions. It is almost as if the imagination is itself literally made of celluloid (or some other more sophisticated material based upon modern plastic) and that this material—this *film*—has been charged with an awful attractive force that makes it *cling* to a future which it has itself created.

> I am moved by fancies that are curled
> Around these images, and cling:
> The notion of some infinitely gentle
> Infinitely suffering thing.
>   (T. S. Eliot *Preludes*)

*   *   *

This is how it was to have begun…

When Hermione Gordon agreed to marry me, somewhere between Bletchley and Willesden Junction in the dining car of a London and Northwestern train, it was because she considered me 'deep'. In 1923, this was a very modern thing to be. Twenty years later, when she finally left me for a South African archæologist with a parenthesis in Burke's Peerage, *she revealed that my apparent 'depth' had long-since lost its charm: what she had ever seen in me, she mused, was 'quite unfathomable.'*

*   *   *

A core feature was the Oxford/Birmingham dichotomy. This idea grew from Twigg's understanding of seventeenth century history. Simply put, Twigg saw Oxford (the capital of Charles I in the Civil War & his son during the Exclusion Crisis) as the bastion of a conservative tradition which was the source of its pre-eminence in original research. Intellectual advance was exclusively the result of furthering existing knowledge (rather than undermining it): hence Oxford's success. On the other hand, Birmingham (the armoury of Parliament, the revolutionary source of counterfeits, the heartland of Industrial Revolution & modern economics... Chartism... mass immigration) was Oxford's neighbourhood nemesis.

Again, this might just be understood as Singh the brummie taking a swipe at Britain's stuffier academic institutions. Yet he knew it was unfair on both cities to characterise one as all dreaming spires & royal cloisters & the other as just foundries & towerblocks. It was Twigg's mistake, not Singh's. Twigg's inability to understand how people, places & cultures can contain contradictory qualities was the crux of his wrongness in Singh's eyes. His desire to divide ideas into binary oppositions of this sort — & to resist the insidious tendency for paradoxical *cleavages* of these oppositions — was literally his *raison d'être*.

This fundamental fault of Twigg's stemmed from a need to *gender* everything. For Singh, binary oppositions were always *genders*: Oxford & Birmingham were no exception. Essentially, he wanted to insist on the reduction of dialectic to a sexual metaphor — thesis & antithesis were just another way of saying male & female. White & black, rich & poor, *self* & *other*, even history & fiction: all these things were *genders*. The idea of *drag* was therefore the most fundamental (& philosophical) of transgressions.

Crucially, such 'cleavages' upset the notion of the 'family tree'. Here was Twigg's ruling principle. It was no doubt also the source of his ironic name: he was a *twig* (the offshoot of an offshoot), & one who claimed to understand (to *twig*) things by placing them within a strict taxonomy of knowledge. If we were to trace his philosophical descent in this regard the line would run something like the following: Aristotle's *categories*, Porphyry's *tree diagrams*, John Wilkins's *tables*, Linnaeus's *taxonomy*, Burke's image of the *tree of society* & August Schleicher's *Stammbaum* theory of linguistics. Common to these intellectual models is the notion of genetic hierarchy: i.e. the impossibility of *reverse* connections between subordinate (child) & superordinate (parent) categories. Hence the idea of 'branching'. In the core example — the 'family trees' of royal pedigree — any such *abominations* are politely obscured... even when, as Oedipus reveals, they are almost their guiding principle. (Freud tended to ignore this specifically political attribute of Sophocles' examination of tyranny & incest.)

It was Darwin, & then August Schleicher, who brought together the taxonomic tree & the tree of descent. Both men thought it ultimately possible for present taxonomies to be revealed as literally (& not just metaphorically) 'family trees'. The theory of evolution would show that present tree diagrams of 'category' were the result of (perhaps even directly equivalent to) historical trees of 'descent'. In (anti)structuralist terms, synchronic structures were merely the traces of diachronic ones: the pattern of history *was* the pattern of the present day.

You take £e first door down and ring £e bell.
 If someone answers (usually a '$e'),
You smile and say you haven't come to sell
 Her any€ing; instead, your company
Will give her trial bulbs for free; you tell
 Her £ey last longer and, importantly,
£ey never leak £is awful tungsten plasma
Which lab-tests prove can cause your children asthma.

156.7 *tungsten plasma*: Aside from the basic substance of blood, 'plasma' is a word used to describe a gas in which there are an equal number of positively and negatively charged ions. The glow caused by the interactions of these ions when a current is passed through the gas has led to the recent innovation of 'neon' lights—those tubes of orange-pink luminescence so redolent of rampant American advertising—which many commentators in the scientific community insist will one day replace the 'tungsten-filament' lightbulb, being safer, longer lasting and more economical. It is also the effect that creates what we call 'lightning'.

'Tungsten' derives from the Swedish *tung* 'heavy' and *sten* 'stone', and is an alternative name for both the element *wolframium* (W), and the ore in which it naturally occurs: *wolfram*. It is this ore (manganese tungstate) which is used to make the filaments for lightbulbs. Essentially what has happened is that the Swedish term has been used to replace the German *wolf-rahm* ('wolf-cream', presumably a polite reference to semen). Both are old miners' terminology (see 38.2 *nickel-brass*). Typically, the romantic German version carries the idea of an insidious threat lurking in the material: it is 'that which engenders wolves.'

Sloggy's oxymoronic graft of these two opposed ideas—wolfram and neon plasma—is, on the surface of things, a bit of cheekily impossible pseudo-science: the mark of a virtuoso confidence trickster scoffing at the ignorance of his victim. The whole point of Coolidge's use of tungsten to improve the carbon lightbulb filament (Eddison had even experimented with human hair) was precisely that it was a metal with a very high melting point. The temperature at which it would have to be kept in order to become a 'plasma' is astronomical. There is obviously more to it for Bosvil, however. The idea of charged ions creating a magical effect of irresistible attraction has been used in the previous stanza to liken the human mind to the celluloid of cinema film attracted to the visions it projects (into the future). Now we find an analogical reference to the light source which makes that projection possible.

(It is not at all irrelevant that Joseph Wilson Swan, the man whose carbon filament bulb Eddison only adapted, also revolutionized photography with the invention of bromide paper; nor that the true inventor of the electric lightbulb was Humphry Davy—the maker of the miners' lamp; nor, indeed, that the first building in the world to have electric lighting, in 1882, was the new Birmingham Town Hall.)

There is an almost intolerable notion of feedback inherent in this idea. (One can hardly refer to it as an 'image'.) The human mind is at once a 'film' (which carries a series of daguerreotype images of the world that combine into a false consciousness) and the 'projector' of that film. The imagination is both the *lamp* and the *pictures* of the lightbox that produces images to which it is itself attracted by some mystical interaction of charges and (bizarrely) *from* which it receives the electrical current to light the *plasma* contained in the bulb of the skull to continue the projection. And behind all of this lurks a gypsy wolf, singing of the future destruction of civilisation in the hum of an impossible tube of luminescent *wolfram gas*… baying for blood.

Twigg felt the literary canon was this kind of tree. The critical analysis & evaluation of a text was designed to reveal the extent to which its form & content represented proper self-positioning within the relevant part of its family tree. That's to say a writer should be aware of his own literary 'line' &, his potential place within it, in order to take up that hallowed position in the canon. (T.S. Eliot would be Twigg's example of a poet who had succeeded. In this respect, at least, he was a Leavisite.) Such self-awareness need only be implicit, of course. The role of the critic was to dig for this kind of treasure.

Twigg was no determinist, however. It was never just a question of whether a text failed or succeeded to represent inevitable truth. There was a third option. Singh's characterisation relied heavily on the fact that Twigg found in history, literature & society a 'degenerative' force that wanted to destroy this process of 'growth'. Just as human beings could intervene in evolution (with artificial breeding... not to mention genetic engineering), they could use words to intervene in History. There were revolutionary uses to which language could be put which undermined both the progress of this evolutionary model, & the model itself.

Most obviously, he would see this occurring in the 'false historicism' of revolutionary propaganda, for example, but fiction & poetry were equally dangerous: perhaps more so. In the literary arts, these nasty things were not merely characterised by 'degenerative content' in their ideas & portrayals, but by 'degenerative stylistics'. The effects of metaphor, word-play, semantic cross-pollination, syntactic jiggery pokery, allusion, parody, dialect, & so on, were all seen as potentially disastrous. All tools available to the writer could be used to defy the proper hierarchies of language, history, society & art just as easily as they could be used to assert them. Twigg suspected that his *culture* (a shorthand for this cluster of ideas) was infected with a derangement that was a threat to the *tree*: not just something that wanted the tree to stop growing, or to fell it, but which wanted it to grow in an abominable way. It was the responsibility of people like Twigg to weed this out.

Borrowing terms from the darling of post-structuralist philosophy, Gilles Deleuze, we could call this hidden disease the *rhizome*: the root structure which, unlike that of most trees, forms a web of random internodes with no hierarchical arrangement of any sort. The rhizome makes connections which apparently should not be made. This kind of thing, says Deleuze, is what really underlies language & culture, not the 'logical' roots of a tree. If Twigg had been a real person, he couldn't possibly have been influenced by a metaphor of 1980s high postmodernism. But he was not real, & the fact that he came to realise this was the core of his tragedy. When he encountered *The Birmingham Quean* — believing his job to involve the denunciation of precisely the kind of malign influence he never had the opportunity to find in Deleuze & Guattari — he thought he'd uncovered a kindred spirit. Here was a scorching satire on the kind of future that might be brought about by the dreadful literature & culture it was parodying. Here was a text that gave the disease a name: Birmingham.

£ere *is* a small deposit of five pounds,
    But $e can have a refund in a week
Because you're coming back to do your rounds
    And if $e'd ra£er have £e bulbs £at leak,
To save some ca$, or on whatever grounds,
    You'll happily replace £em wi£ 'antiques'
And pay her £e deposit of five quid,
    Al£ough you'd hate to do £at to her kid.

---

        *   *   *

At the time, however, the rather sullen and unflattering nature of my proposal had been a perfect indication of its peculiar suitability. I was gazing out of the window, comparing the relative velocities of parallaxing hedgerows and considering the idea of National Time. Meanwhile, she was detailing the shortcomings of her male peers, to the polite accompaniment of cutlery on porcelain. I interjected suddenly (I surprised myself as much as her): 'I don't see why one should consult your father.'

'Daddy?' she said, 'What about?'

'Marriage. I've been thinking...'

'Oh, darling, what a fabulously wicked idea. Let's do it. Let's not tell Mummy and Daddy a thing.'

And that was it. Daddy was consulted in the end, of course—and asked for money—but this minor retreat into convention did not undermine the 'depth' that was apparently my winning attribute in any way. The fact that most of her friends were flabbergasted by the match was part and parcel of the strange attraction. I know full well that they considered me laconic, bookish and (if I'm frank) quite ugly.

To be fair, I was all three. I thought prose far more enlivening than chit-chat, and tended to involve myself with the former far more often than the latter. As for my physical appearance, it had to be admitted I did not measure up. I was short and thin, but with a rather childish paunch just visible above the belt. The mirrors people invariably kept in their entrance halls in those days (perhaps expressly for this purpose) would cruelly remind the more unprepossessing sort of new arrival that his face was nothing to behold: the complexion sallow and clammy like beeswax, the hair prematurely thinning, the eyes a murky grey, the eyelids heavy, the lips thin and dry, the nose more gnomic than gnomonic, and the chin defined only by the lateral motion created by the occasional grinding of the Neolithic teeth.

I was acutely aware of my inelegance beside her gleaming, tennis-playing friends, but pretended to care nothing about appearances and even less about apparel. As a consequence they called me 'the manikin'. This was to be expected, however. Her friends were 'shallow'. If for no other reason, she married me to prove that she was not. But there was more to it than that...

        *   *   *

All of which makes Twigg sound like the straight man to a *queer* poem: a stick-in-the-mud antithesis. But that wasn't it at all. Singh's secret affection for Twigg came through in his performance. He could never leave such a poker-faced dichotomy un*dragged*. Twigg's part was pathetically human. His role was to discover just how wrong he'd been. In doing so, he came to realise he was an integral part of the whole tangled *rhizomic* performance. After all, it was Twigg who formed the most paradoxical of 'internodes'. He stood at one end of an impossible bridge between periods of history. Amongst the miscellaneous college archives, he'd found a poem from fifty years in the future. Things like that don't happen to just anyone. Towards the end of analysing it — tracing its webs of allusion & metaphor — he came to the conclusion that this critical activity itself was somehow responsible for bringing about the future that had spawned it. Twigg, more acutely even than Britannia Spears & her poem, was a travesty of history. To put it bluntly, Twigg was a drag-act who found out he was a drag-act. The knowledge broke him. Only as he burned did he achieve a rather weird solace in the thought that he, & everything he knew, was just as fake as all the contents of the poem. Consequently, nothing mattered.

It's pure melodrama to say so, I realise, but something similar was happening to me. *The Birmingham Quean* was driving me insane. Soon after the discovery of Twigg, work that had been nothing more than a convenient distraction from my own stalled thesis quickly turned into a serious addiction. Why this should be I can't be sure. The thing was flashy pseudo-intellectual rubbish. It really didn't deserve the time I'd spent on it. What's more, I'd only stumbled across it as part of an elaborate attempt to get off with the author's ex-girlfriend. What the hell was it that kept drawing me back? Just like Twigg, I could cite mitigating factors: the lack of a partner, the lack of intellectual direction, the lack of a job... Still, I knew perfectly well I should be writing my own stuff instead, but there was always some excuse to get the brown roll out each morning & wrap myself once more in its sticky tissue of illogic. 'Just to look at for a bit,' I'd say, 'just for an hour;' then, 'just till lunchtime'. It was always dark before I ate. I'd usually wolf down something malleable pummelled into a hunk of stale bread, hunched over the manuscript. A few hours later I'd lose consciousness, my cheek slapping itself onto the crumby paper like a cold, grey fishcake.

Over time, the obsession became almost military in its scope & devastation. Every night I'd slip into a dream in which the gleaming traces of Singh's biro were advancing slowly across my field of vision like lines of redcoats snaking through mountainous terrain. I'd find myself planning strategies: teasing out the balances of power within the vast web of cultural cross-references; devising long & careful sequences of reading... priorities of analysis, angles of attack. I was field-martial in an attritional campaign of literary criticism. I'd forgotten why the war had started, but an unshakeable desire to join battle afresh each morning — to make a few more yards with some new initiative — always stopped me from getting on with my own work. Each time I managed to open the computer file that contained my embryonic thesis, I'd find myself firing off speculative volleys of bullet-points about *The Birmingham Quean*. It wouldn't be long before the brown roll trundled out & I'd find myself back in the thick of the melée.

So, if þe bites, þen round þe house you go,
    Exchanging bulbs and friendly chat; and þrough
Her life you pass to leave a healþy glow
    In all her rooms (and boþ her cheeks) as you
Take special care to dust þe old bulbs so
    You can replace þem looking good as new.
You settle up; þe sees you out; and þen…
You take her bulbs nextdoor… and start again.

---

*   *   *

When we first met, she admitted, she had considered me at best obnoxious. We were both invited to a shooting party in Scotland in the autumn of 1922. No-one understood why I was there. Hermione was the only one confident enough to ask. I had spent the best part of the day trudging around a hummocky bogland with the female entourage, deflecting girlish small-talk with curt self-deprecation and surreptitiously dipping into Dante (just as the hunters would take nips from hip-flasks) whenever the occasion presented itself.

The sun was sinking fast and the temperature dropping. After missing yet another grouse by several feet (she was the only woman shooting) and without turning from her inspection of the terrain, she asked: 'what are you even doing here, Mr Twigg? Do you realize I don't know your Christian name, for heaven's sake? You don't even have a gun, man.'

What was I doing there? It was a good question. The truth was that Alexander Fitzmorris, the student for whom the sporting weekend was to be a 21st birthday celebration, was the only person who genuinely thought of me as a 'friend from University'. The feeling was not exactly mutual.

We first encountered one another in Wadham College Chapel on the 18th November 1921 at a memorial service to mark the fifth anniversary of the end of the Battle of the Somme. We were neighbours in the stalls. During the first verse of 'Jerusalem' (quite how this tasteless snippet of millenarian doggerel became the nation's favourite hymn I will never understand) I noticed tears streaming down the cheeks of the slightly chubby, dark haired fellow standing next to me. I felt suddenly ashamed of both myself and of him. His histrionics and my stony numbness seemed equally inappropriate responses to the proceedings. We were somehow implicated in one another's shame.

At 'dark satanic mills', I decided to act. I patted myself down, looking for my handkerchief. (I have never been one of those dubious types who always knows precisely where his hanky is.) It was in my trouser pocket: rumpled in amongst my change, but mercifully unused. I thanked God—in an apologetic way—and slipped it into his trembling left hand as organ descants flitted between the Jacobean eaves.

*   *   *

There was only one way I found to get out of the war. (Though it was obviously a Catch-22.) I could distract myself by collecting things from the 1950s: films, books, newspapers, clothes, pictures, ornaments, food-tins, money, anything. This was what I guessed Singh must've done in writing the Twigg stuff in the first place. For some reason, I felt I might understand the piece & its writer better if only I could reproduce the activities that had created it. That was what I told myself. The discovery of R. H. Twigg had given me a new insight into the 'retro' nature of the *Birmingham Quean*. Slowly my obsession with the poem mutated into an obsession with these accoutrements of *period-drag*. More than that: I actually began to inhabit a semi-delusional world of early fifties' style, morality & preoccupation.

Let's be clear, we're not talking about American 1950s nostalgia here: greased quiffs, pink finned Cadillacs, jukeboxes, poodle skirts, college bomber jackets... This was strictly ration-book retro: coronation chicken, button-down braces, BSA bikes, leather casers & Larry Adler. It was *The Lavender Hill Mob* rather than *The Wild One*.

The distinction was important. It was probably the whole point. In Singh's view (& in Twigg's), the year 1953 was a pivotal moment in the transformation of Britain from autonomous Empire to American dependency. This had already happened, of course. The ruthlessness of American negotiators towards their crippled creditors at the summits of Yalta & Bretton Woods in 1944 had seen to that. It might also be argued that the situation is not fully consolidated — not fully acknowledged, at least — until Suez; thus making 1956 the true year of the national nervous breakdown. But it was the irony of the coronation — an event that swept the mortally wounded Empire with a histrionic royalist relief like a desperate burlesque of the Restoration — that provided the pivotal tableau. Simultaneously, Britain was testing its first 'independent' atomic bomb. Both performances were the roars of a paper tiger whose puppet-master was America. (They were as unconvincing as James Bond, who stirred but didn't shake the world that year with his appearance in *Casino Royale*.) Deep down everybody knew it. Hence the paranoia.

It's a critical commonplace for the explosion of neurotic science-fiction in the 40s & 50s to be put down to the Cold War. The Faustian scientists were the Manhattan project; the flying saucers were Soviet A-bombers; bodysnatchers were just Reds under the bed; & so on. What is less often acknowledged is the palpable fear of America expressed in British Sci-Fi of the period. It was not the Soviet Communism, but American culture that was really mounting an insidious invasion. I'm certain — so was Singh — that it was this fear which informed work like the novels of John Wyndham & Nigel Kneale's *Quatermass* television serials. Key to Wyndham's novels is the theme of a hidden threat that rides in shotgun on the back of some marvellous event (something apparently beautiful or beneficial). The invasion of England by the Triffids (after everyone has been blinded by a meteor shower) seems to owe much more to the real 'invasion' that had occurred a few years previously (of American troops), than to the imagined invasion by Nazis or the USSR. Britain had never been 'blinded' by the propaganda of Fascism or Stalinism, but it had fallen hook line & sinker for America's big lightshow.

> As good as Sloggy was at £is, £e ca$
>   He got was crap. He'd never seen £e point
> In wasting all £at effort and panache
>   Until he took £e chance to case a joint
> One time, and tipped some burglars off and sta$ed
>   £e stuff £ey robbed. And after £at, he coined
> It in. £e storage was £e real earner,
> And Sloggy proved himself a speedy learner.

159.1-2 *the cash / He got was crap*: 'Crap' was originally a synonym for 'chaff'. Its usage in the sense (5. in the OED) of *money* predates the common vulgar usage as *excrement* which has, no doubt, appeared under pressure from the name of the famous water closet design and production company of Thomas Crapper. Typically, there is a reversion to the older form here alongside a deliberate confusion of the etymology of 'cash': a Portuguese confusion (it turns out) of the Latinate *capsa* 'coffer'—which gives us modern French *caisse* and Portuguese *caixa*—with the Sanskrit *karsha* 'a weight of silver or gold equal to 1/400 of a tulā' (Williams)—which gives us Tamil *kāsu* and Singhalese *kāsi*, both small denomination coins. The early Portuguese traders in the Far East obviously associated the later word, by folk-etymology, with the former and used *caixa* to mean small change in any Far Eastern currency. Hence the confusion. It is from India that the importation into English derives. Portuguese influenced areas in the South of India, up until British rule unified the subcontinent in 1818, had a monetary system in which the *cash* was the smallest denomination (being 1/80 of a *fanam* and 1/3360 of a *star pagoda*).

A gloss in contemporary colloquial English which captures the two ideas of *small coins* and *cereal husks* might be: 'the change he got was peanuts.'

This example reveals just how important it is we should retain a constant awareness of the destabilising influence Eastern languages and culture are having on our own. The dereliction Bosvil invites and relishes comes—just like the Caribbean Indians behind Guyanese Communism—from both East and West at once. The gypsies, we should not forget, were originally from India.

*   *   *

This small act of kindness had nothing like the desired effect. I assumed the fellow would pretend the hanky was his own and undemonstratively wipe his eyes, blow his nose and pull himself together before enduring the second verse. Instead, his whole hysterical performance seemed to take encouragement from my intervention. He turned to me mid-cadence, his slightly piggish nose still drooling, and with a look of astonished gratefulness, mouthed a 'thank you'. He then proceeded to sing and weep with even greater gusto than before whilst holding the thing out in front of him on his upturned palm like some kind of tragic stage prop. It perched there, fragile as a butterfly, permanently on the verge of fluttering away under the influence of his shuddering intonations. Between each bellicose line of the second verse, the handkerchief approached his snivelling features, only to be withdrawn again so he could swell into the next with extra vigour.

*   *   *

Even more convincing is the trope of 'the thing that came back bad.' it's obviously true that Quatermass tampering too far in science — resulting in the discovery of a malign shape-shifting alien — is an analogue of WMDs. It was written at the height of Aldermaston's so-called ABC (Atomic, Biological & Chemical) experiments. There's something more, though. Quatermass's rocket is definitively a 'space-ship'. It's like an exploratory vessel of the sixteenth century heading for the West Indies. It comes back with the twentieth century version of syphilis: a protean contagion. Here is the primal fear of America. It's a short step from this to the nightmare of the US as the demonic offspring of the British Empire: the prodigal son returned... the thing that came back bad. The self-conscious focus on the medium of television itself is crucial. Kneale's climax was the live broadcast of a fictional live broadcast from Westminster Cathedral: the place where only weeks before the nation had watched the Queen crowned on their new television sets. BBC Television was obviously still very British at the time, but the looming prospect of commercial TV (Lew Grade's ATV was the wonderful meteor-shower everybody was expecting) revealed this to be the American medium par excellence. Consequently, the supposed power of the coronation spectacle (as a much-needed patriotic fillip) relied very heavily for its dissemination on a very American means of mass communication. *The Quatermass Experiment* was even more popular than the coronation itself. It made maximum play of this America/TV complex. If any clearer expression could be made than this of a fear (an almost self-censored neurosis) that the heart of the British Empire had been taken over by an insidious alien force brought into its inner sanctum (& its living-rooms) by its own people, I find it hard to imagine how.

Perhaps Wyndham's *Midwich Cuckoos* is the only real contender. Here the quiet Middle-English village — the pastoral breeding-ground of the Empire, rather than its spiritual heart — is threatened by its own strange offspring. The children are easily identified as Nazi or Communist allegories, but I think Singh read them with American accents (the sound of commercial television & nuclear threat). They are the golden-eyed harvest of an infertile realm, like Britain's adopted post-war 'wealth'. We might be thrown by their rather un-American lack of individualism but we should remember that a colonial American culture would have seemed peculiarly (even acutely) homogeneous to postwar Britain. Colonising cultures always do. & it wasn't American people that were feared, so much as America's culture & economy. These are not conquerors, remember, they're cuckoos.

Singh positioned Twigg's narrative on the crest of this wave of early 50s sci-fi paranoia. The year 1953 marked the high watermark of the flood. As well as *The Quatermass Experiment*, it saw the release of Ray Bradbury's *Farenheit 451*; Kurt Vonnegut's first, *Player Piano*; Evelyn Waugh's ill-advised foray into the genre, *Love Among the Ruins*; John Wyndham's *The Kraken Wakes*, Arthur C. Clarke's *Childhood's End*, Isaac Asimov's *Second Foundation*, Pohl & Kornbluth's *The Space Merchants*, Alfred Bester's *The Demolished Man* (the winner of the inaugural Hugo Award), & (most explicit in its examination of American imperialism) Marghanita Laski's play *The Offshore Island*. Twigg's initial reading of the poem & his own time-paradox experience are therefore perfectly in keeping with contemporary popular literature.

Þe game was all about avoiding heat,
    And Sloggy worked out Þat a building site,
Especially in Þe middle of Þe street,
    Bizarrely, seemed to go unnoticed right
Beneaþ Þe feet of Bobbies on Þe Beat,
    Who never seemed particularly bright:
Þey rarely made him fill a manhole in,
'N' were buggered if Þey'd climb up scaffoldin.

---

*   *   *

Relief came with the final organ solo. It is a gratifyingly short hymn. That day, however, it had seemed almost interminable. My neighbour smeared the square of linen beneath his visibly leaking nostrils without exhaling and attempted to return it to me. I declined, trying to appear more generous than disgusted. After the ceremony, he introduced himself as Alexander Fitzmorris and I agreed to let him buy me lunch.

We discovered that we both had elder brothers who had served as lieutenants in Rawlinson's Fourth Army. They had both died on the Somme. They probably never knew one another, though: Alexander's had joined with reinforcements in October; mine had died in the first week (though probably not, as my mother insisted on assuming, the first day—she considered the matchless carnage of July 1st to be divine acknowledgement of the gravity of her own personal loss).

From that point on, we met occasionally for meals or tea in term-time, always at Alexander's instigation and never more than once a week. We would discuss our work and plans: predominantly his. He enjoyed the thoughtful debate, he said. He was a biology undergraduate and attempting to reconcile evolution with his Christianity.

This was something I also had an interest in. My recent dabblings with amateur ornithology had suggested to me that 'natural selection', while it was self-evidently true (no creature can mate without surviving to do so; survival characteristics are therefore obviously strengthened), was neither the sole nor the most important driver behind 'evolution'. A huge variety of strange and beautiful creatures had become yet more strange and yet more beautiful without any necessarily positive impact on their survival rates. In my more optimistic and spiritual moments I would put this down to an æsthete God. More often though, I considered it the result of something much less edifying. It was, as Darwin's theory of 'sexual selection' suggests, all to do with male display and female choice. The sexually attractive features of a species—long tails, bright plumage, extravagent songs, aerobatic prowess—were arbitrarily promoted by female choice of partners. This need not have anything whatever to do with practical survival. Often adaptations came as positive drawbacks: long-tails a hindrance to flight, bright plumage to camouflage, and so on. It was survival of the 'most ostentatious' rather than the 'fittest'.

*   *   *

But it wasn't just the Sci-Fi of the period that carried this nagging fear of the States. A genre as quintessentially British & apparently heartwarming as Ealing Comedy was just as riddled with the complex. The two films made by Ealing that year — *The Maggie* & *The Titfield Thunderbolt* — gained all their power of sentimental escapism by championing remnants of a pre-war British society (of two different sorts) in defiance of both their supposed obsolescence & the overweening influence of modern (modernising) America.

In *The Maggie*, the captain & crew of a clapped-out 'Clyde puffer' give the run-around to an American financier (with the topical name, Calvin B. Marshall) who acts as if money can achieve anything. The decent but deluded American is eventually forced to write off the debt they owe him for both cargo & (by now) the vessel itself. It's a clear allegory of British war-debts. The puffer is postwar Britain: small, grimy, unprepossessing & run into the ground. Even if Marshall (& America itself) comes to own the boat & everything it holds, the puffer still spiritually belongs to the smart but disempowered sentimentalists who are its crew. It's pure escapism that the American comes to understand this 'truth' in the final scene & gives the money back. The USA obviously did no such thing. The real Marshall (in)famously handed British loan repayments over to West Germany.

In *The Titfield Thunderbolt*, this idea also exists at one remove from the narrative. The story is of a small private railway in the countryside competing with a grasping city bus company for control of a minor commuter route. When their locomotive is sabotaged, the railway enthusiasts are forced to fetch the original Edwardian engine that worked the route. The whole village turns out to wheel it down the steps of the museum. The parish vicar is the driver. At one point during the inspection day, all the passengers are forced to push the train along the tracks because the engine has broken its temporary coupling. You get the idea. Crucially, though, the film is a very English parody of an American 'Railroad Western': a fact which is made quite explicit when the Television in the village pub shows a clichéed saloon scene — with three cowboys round a table discussing how to stop the railroad being built whilst a bawdy waitress in lots of skirts flamboyantly doles out the rye. (In the midst of a cosy village local, all that Western whooping sounds like an air-raid siren.) This scene is then immediately burlesqued with a parallel (antithetical) tableau in the pub. At that point the television blinks out to leave a card saying 'Normal service will be resumed'. This is an obvious cinematic dig at the small screen, but it's one which explicitly identifies the television as the source of an insidious American culture which is being openly defied.

The Thunderbolters win through, of course, as does the nostalgic pre-war Ealing ethos. Everything about these films is designed to emphasise Britishness in terms of its fundamental difference from an American aesthetic. This is probably why they're so appealing now. It's not just that we can get lost in the idyllic naïvety of a 1950s full of bicycling bobbies, red telephone boxes & improbable class-cooperation. It's also that these films were designed to have precisely this kind of nostalgic effect at the time they were released. Fundamental to the atmosphere of modestly eccentric rebellion was a rejection of the American accents, stars & narratives that dominated British cinemas at the time. It was nostalgia then. It's nostalgia now.

> And £en £ere was £e old asbestos scam:
>> You run a team disposing of £e stuff—
> You need certificates, but you can $am
>> £e paperwork convincingly enough
> To fool £e owners: £ey don't give a damn
>> Once £ey've been softened up wi£ legal guff
> (It's not asbestos you remove, it's fear;
> You spread it, £en you make it disappear)—

161.1 *asbestos*: Another name for the mineral *amiantus*. See 35.7 *filtertip*. In fact, my passing reference in that note to the fact that the use of *asbestos* is a paradoxical folk-etymology, seems heavily portentous now. I am serious considering an attempt to destroy this document by means of fire. Whether this would be possible, and what might be the consequences, I do not know. The thing seems quite capable of being both *amiantine* and *asbestous*: unignitable and unquenchable.

161.1-3 *scam... sham*. See 26.5 *shame* and 32.4 *sham*. The word *scam* is another of the cognate forms, closer to the Scandinavian root. The set is only complete, however, when we add *scamble* or *shambles*. This term originated as a word for a 'counter': a table for counting money and for exchanging retail goods for cash. This followed precisely the same process of phonetic change from *sk-* to *sh-* under Anglo Saxon influence as *sham* and *shame* and became refined in Middle English (under pressure from the French *compter* forms) to mean a table in a meat-market and finally an area for butchery or an abattoir. The metaphoric usage (as in 'this thesis is a total shambles') is a full-blooded reference to the pungent gore and offal one imagines strewn about such a place. The words are intimately related. *Scams* and *shams* are naturally related to the marketplace, especially that most visceral of trading environments, the flesh-market. *Shame*, as Macbeth literally demonstrates, is traditionally conceived as the ineradicable stain of blood. This poem is all of these things: a *scam*, a *sham*, a *shame* and a *shambles*.

*   *   *

Alexander rejected this line of argument. He was stuck between two absolutisms. Somewhat as a result of our discussions, I admit, he abandoned his eminently sensible (and theologically orthodox) 'omniscient instigation' model for a vain attempt to describe natural selection as the sole mechanism of (ongoing) divine creationism. Most importantly, his ideas relied on denying anything non-purposeful about evolution. The Earth was God's creation: a cauldron of evolution whose environment was designed (by means of his laws of physics and chemistry and so on) specifically as the place in which man (and whatever was to follow man) could be produced... by means of natural selection. The goal was divine consciousness. In order to hold an (ultimately Hegelian) argument like that you have to assume there to be no blind alleys or false starts. All life must serve some purpose to this end. Females were in no position to make pointless, arbitrary choices, whether or not they thought they were.

*   *   *

There's a tricky subject to be broached. Ealing Comedies (& similar films made at Shepperton & Pinewood) were the constant backdrop to my retro fantasy. I watched them over & over. I got the greatest pleasure from the sights & sounds of the streets & houses, the pubs & workplaces & railway stations. Scenery & sound-effects were much more important than the action. I got an almost opiate effect from the feeling that I could inhabit the world portrayed: I was walking those pavements, catching those trains, chatting with those affable peelers. I was an Ealing extra. As all great escapism should, it washed away the sense of imminent threat that seemed to characterise contemporary life.

But there was something worrying that couldn't be ignored. There was a dubious feature of those streets & boats & railway carriages that was fundamental to their appeal. Not only did they contain few traces of America, they also portrayed none of the effects of Windrush immigration. I had to ask myself if this was what I really wanted. Was I secretly hankering after a Britain quite unlike the one I'd grown up in: with its Mosques & Gurudwaras & blues parties? Had Ealing become a xenophobic vision?

I seriously hoped not, but I couldn't deny that nostalgia of this kind went hand in hand with quiet English racism. Singh understood this perfectly: much better than I could myself. Central to his thinking was the argument that fear of immigration in the 50s & 60s (the same fear that now breeds a yen for that period just before immigration took hold) was principally a result of what Freudians might call 'transference' or 'projection'. What the British were really afraid of was the new colonial power: America. The key feature of immigration was its role as both a symptom & a catalyst of the Americanisation of Great Britain. What theorists nowadays might call 'the post-colonial diaspora' was not seen as a barbarian horde, but as a new colonial avant garde. We shouldn't forget, as the theorists have sometimes done, that for Britain the single most significant post-colonial nation has always been the United States. One sentence in particular from Powell's infamous speech — repeated in slight modification by Singh himself in Twigg's 'Foreword' — brings this fear to the surface: 'That tragic & intractable phenomenon which we watch with apprehension on the other side of the Atlantic but which there is interwoven with the history & existence of the States itself, is coming upon us here by our own volition & our own neglect.'

If British racism was just a sublimation of the fear of Imperial America then the Twigg-act was an attempt to *out* it. It wasn't just a matter of permitting Twigg to say those things that British culture of the 1950s had self-censored, but that the whole retro-drag performance was itself a way of uncovering the tendency for contemporary British society to seek sanctuary from the new colonialism in a milieu of vague nostalgic racism.

It certainly had this effect on me. I found myself taking furtive hits of the past, the guilty pleasure of which involved a kind of mental self-flagellation at the politically incorrect desire it revealed. It was masochism. Unlike Singh, I couldn't think of this as drag. Drag's nothing if not ironic. But the nostalgic desire was as real for me as the revulsion at a 'degenerate future' was for Twigg. There wasn't anything in the least ironic to it.

> £ey need to self-declare contamination,
>> (£ey'll do it willingly if you're at pains
> To outline £e potential compensation),
>> And once £ey have, your boys take up £e reins
> And cordon off £e site. A big alsatian
>> Behind £e gate and signage £at explains
> All access is denied by High Court Order,
> And local cops are fucked. He'd even stored a

---

* * *

Another consequence of Alexander's naïve thinking was that he considered man's impact upon the process to be one of positive cultivation. Human interventions—animal husbandry, hunting, botanical hybridisation and... so on—were accelerations of spiritual evolution. When he invited me to his birthday shoot, therefore, it was as a kind of demonstrative experiment in which I was to take part. I would, he assured me (assuming it would be my first shoot, I suppose) see the teleology of evolution at first hand. I could think of no polite excuse, so I agreed to go.

Needless to say, when Hermione asked me what I was doing there, I did not tell her any of this. I considered some kind of witty rejoinder—'didn't you know? it's traditional for Scottish hunting parties to contain at least one Dante reader', or something of the sort—instead, I simply tucked my slim volume back into my jacket pocket and apologized: 'I'm sorry, very impolite of me.'

'I suppose you think it unseemly for a woman to be doing this,' she said.

'Not at all, my mother shoots.'

She turned and regarded me over her shoulder with an air of genuine surprise: perhaps just as astonished that anybody from a family capable of producing offspring as unbucolic as myself might shoot as to discover the person in question was actually a woman.

'Really?' she replied, 'is she any good? I can't seem to hit a thing. They don't teach us how it's done, you know.'

'That depends on what you mean by 'good': good for the birds or good for the bag?'

'I would have thought that was obvious.'

Alexander piped up: 'Twiggs prefers to sketch birds than to shoot them, Hermie, he's a bit of a birdwatcher in his spare time.'

'Is he?' she looked me up and down, 'which bit, I wonder?'

There were chortles amidst the tubular resonances of empty cartridges ejecting from their chambers... the frothy panting of the dogs.

* * *

It's not that I became convinced by Twigg. How could I? It was more that his unconvincing nature somehow increased my empathy for him: the pathos of his existential dilemma boosted my ability to feel that same desire to reclaim a past that was already slipping out of memory. But at least Twigg could get out of his personal bind with the realisation that he was just a fake. Singh's double-bluff left no such opt-out clause for me.

I became obsessed. I collected things from 1953. I wore the clothes & learned the history. I discovered it was the year in which Stalin died & the Korean War ended. To complement the coronation of our own Regina (not as 'empress' but simply 'head of the commonwealth'), Harrow old-boy Hussein bin Talal was crowned King of Jordan, Eisenhower was sworn in as the first Republican President of the USA for a generation, Kruschev began to pull the strings in the USSR, Nasser did the same in Egypt, Castro made his first attempt for Cuba & the CIA were up to their arms-dumps in Iranian regime-change. Cambodia got independence from France, but Indochina & Morocco weren't so successful (yet). The Mau Mau killed Kikuyu families in the Kenyan village of Lari. Before collecting his Nobel Prize for Literature, Churchill emerged from a 'black dog' depression only to emulate the brutal Soviet suppression of a workers' revolt in East Berlin by sending troops into Guyana — at the behest of the United States & the Booker sugar company (now known as the creators of another prestigious literary prize) — to overturn the result of the country's first democratic election, which had inconveniently returned a socialist alliance of the local Black & Indian 'English-speaking peoples' to power. As a sweetener to a public kept mostly in the dark, he did away with sugar rationing. Whilst Britain's first nuclear triumphs rumbled across the Australian desert, the Politburo announced they had the H-bomb & the Rosenbergs went to the chair for it. It was also the year in which Everest was 'conquered' & DNA was 'described'; the world's first sex-change operation & 3D movie were both completed; Derek Bentley was hanged for saying 'let him have it' &, on the last day of the year, colo(u)r television sets went on sale in the States.

It doesn't take a genius to recognise this as a pivotal year in the Cold War, not to mention the end of European empire. It also saw the publication of two of the most influential scholarly books of the post-war period: Wittgenstein's *Philosophical Investigations* & Milton Friedman's *Essays on Positive Economics*. It was also a pivotal year in the history of literature & criticism. In France, Alain Robbe-Grillet pioneered *le nouveau roman* with *Les Gommes* & Roland Barthes released his first: *Le Degré Zéro de l'Ecriture*. Meanwhile, Beckett's *En Attendant Godot* opened at the Théâtre de Babylone & Jacques Derrida was admitted to study under Foucault & Althusser at the Ecole Nationale Superieure. In America, M. H. Abrams unveiled his seminal study of Romanticism, *The Mirror and the Lamp*, Charles Olson published his first collection of poetry *In Cold Hell, In Thicket*, Arthur Miller brought *The Crucible* to the stage, Saul Bellow released *The Adventures of Augie March*, Hemingway won the Pulitzer Prize for *The Old Man and the Sea* & William Burroughs (under the nom-de-plume 'William Lee') published both his first novel *Junkie* (though, just like Singh, he preferred the spelling *Junky*) & its blacklisted sequel, *Queer*. A new generation of Bolshie Black writers also emerged: James Baldwin brought out *Go Tell it on the Mountain* & Ralph Ellison *Invisible Man*... & all this as McCarthyism hit the TV screens.

>   Sikorsky helicopter for a bit,
>   And £ere was bollock all £e pigs could do
>   Wi£out equipment and a High Court writ.
>   He got a visit from £e boys in blue
>   But pretty easily got rid of it
>   Before £e legal paperwork went €rough.
>   £e fencing and £e porn were bo€ safe bets
>   But Sloggy saw £e future on £e net.

163.1 *Sikorsky helicopter*. The common brand of helicopter made by the company of its Russian-born inventor.

163.2 *pigs*: A slang term meaning *plain-clothes policeman*, derived from a usage of 'pig' to mean *sixpence*, a colloquial synonym of 'tanner.' Presumably this refers to the traditional remuneration received for serving in this capacity and differentiates the officers in question from the uniformed 'coppers' by this means.

163.8 *Sloggy saw the future on the net*: I cannot imagine Bosvil being any more explicit. This is obviously intended to mean the character has gained some sort of supernatural prescience with the aid of what is seemingly a sado-masochistic technological contraption called 'the net' (or elsewhere 'the web'). One imagines an elaborate tangle of electrodes with 'pegs' and 'clips' that attach it to the user's tortured flesh. (The latter word is used repeatedly… we should not ignore the fact it is another *antagonym*—another Freudian 'primal word'; another *counter*—to *clip* is at once to 'sever' and to 'connect'.) The device must create spasms in a multitude of specific neuroligically active points on the body (in a way analogous to Chinese acupuncture), inducing a psychoactive effect which can alter human consciousness sufficiently to allow the user to 'see into the future'… or at the very least to believe he can. This is presumably a sophisticated extension of the electric shock therapy given to sufferers of chronic neuroses and psychoses by psychiatrists: one which reverses the usual effect to create an acute psychosis equivalent to (or mistakable for) visions of the future.

It seems from the following stanzas—the most vulgar Bosvil has to offer—that the specific excitement of sexual areas of the brain and body is intrinsic to the effect. The Marquis de Sade himself often drifts into the kinds of megalomania and (near paradoxical) reveries of extra-sensory perception that might provide a clue to the origins of this deplorable practice. Furthermore, it is impossible to avoid the implication of an analogy between the effects of this machine of transcendental self-torture and of the poem itself. We are not merely gaining the results of a vision here; this is also an elaborate, tangled, pulsing machine of doggerel verse designed to have a neurological effect upon the reader. We are not supposed only to receive a report of the diabolical future, but to experience it for ourselves, in all its agonising, fleshly detail. The terrifying accoutrements of torture—the *net*, the *web*, the *m.pegs*, the *links*, and the *clips*, designed to give us *web-sight*—are like the lines and stanzas, the hideous interweaving of *brummagem* phonetics and semantics from which—like the future itself—one cannot escape. If this poem is a *net*, we are the fish; if it is a *web*, I am the fly and Bosvil is the spider. The more I struggle, the closer he approaches.

Compared to such radical stuff, the relatively temperate sea-change that occurred in British literary criticism may not seem all that noteworthy; but when Raymond Williams published his seminal article 'The Idea of Culture' in *Essays in Criticism*, a genuine revolution was being heralded. This wasn't just the beginning of English Marxist Criticism & the driving force behind British Cultural Studies, it was also a virtuoso parody. Well before the French & American postmodernists were playing up this kind of thing, Williams irreverently deconstructed the work of one of English letters' biggest hitters: William Empson. The previous year, in the pages of the journal *English*, Williams had reviewed *The Structure of Complex Words*, & it was precisely the method he found in that book — of painstakingly listing the polysemes of a resonant word & picking out their various multiple effects in literature — that he was aping in this essay. He did to 'culture' what Empson had done to 'clown'. It made for a subtle but acute *piss-take*. Everything Williams was saying defied Empson's non-sociological, non-political approach. He moved radically away from Empson whilst simultaneously burlesquing him. It was as if he'd stolen Empson's entire structure (like Elgar writing his first symphony with exactly the same form as Mozart's 41st) simply to denounce him & his whole approach. To take another example from the same year (mentioned in the poem) it was like Bacon's deconstructive *Study after Velázquez's Portrait of Pope Innocent X*. &, of course, this was precisely how Amrit Singh went about things too.

In short, I think Singh saw 1953 as the beginning of the Postmodernist era. To be clear about this, Singh's idea of Postmodernism necessarily contained both the *hyper-modernist* radicalism found in art & politics (including *neo-Marxism*) & the antithetical *hyper-conservatism* (self-consciously exemplified by books like Leo Strauss's *Natural Right & History* & Henry Hazlitt's *Time Will Run Back: The Great Idea*). Nostalgia & radicalism were the paradoxical counterparts in what he called the 'oxymoron of Postmodernism'. It was as much about *The Lord of the Rings* as it was about *Lolita* (both in the final stages of preparation at the time). Postmodernism was *moonwalking* through history (as Heidegger would never have put it). It was going backwards & forwards at once.

If this was what I was doing with my own retro obsession, then it was through no great skill. You'd think, at the very least, a 'hobby' like this might get me out of the house from time to time. But no such hale & hearty act of courage is necessary these days. All the objects I obtained were bought or borrowed via the internet. Books & films were easy to come by, but I also found enough collectors' sites & online auctions to satiate my desire for period nicknacks.

One site in particular had a profound impact on my fragile mental state. It was the gateway of a strange lesbian 'micronation' called *Aristasia*. This is a bizarre counterculture — perhaps not a counterculture at all; perhaps just the product of one or two people's imaginations — in which women adhere (ironically or not) to the idealistic notion of a world in which there are no men. There's more to it than this, however. It's not a genderless world at all, but one in which the two sexes are *blonde* & *brunette*. The former being 'about six times as feminine as the average modern woman' & the latter 'about twice as feminine...'.

164

> Already, he'd set up a listings page
>   Wi£ links as appetising and diverse
> As, 'Sweet Latino Tranny comes of age
>   By taking on €ree bikers, unrehearsed,
> From Jeff'; 'Jane sent £is slave-girl in a cage';
>   '2 doctors give injections to a nurse';
> 'A massive age gap in £is interracial,
>   Tri-sex, pierced, midget double facial'…

164.3 *Latino Tranny*: One assumes this is the *nom de guerre* of an infamous prostitute of the future. Curiously, it seems to be an abbreviation of *Latin Translator*. Perhaps this is a variation of the euphemism discovered recently to appear on clandestine advertisements for prostitutes in London: 'French Lessons'.

164.5 *slave-girl in a cage*: An obvious Sado-Masochistic image. The appalling pun on 'injections' in the following line also suggests the deliberate inducement of pain.

164.8 *tri-sex, pierced…*: One shivers to imagine what this might mean. The idea of the trident of Britannia penetrating one's flesh as one reads can not be far from Bosvil's dire intentions. 'Midget double facial' suggests a grotesque circus freak: a stunted adult with a Janus head… the kind of gruesome pickled body of a still-born Siamese twin which is the epitome of the amphibolous nature of this work.

*   *   *

That evening I quietly plotted my revenge. Hermione introduced the odd sarcastic comment about 'the conscientious objector' over dinner. She had a number of admirers willing to indulge her penchant for 'manly' conversation. Evidently, her lack of skill with a firearm did not tarnish the boyish modernity of her keenness to brandish one: whether in the glen or in the conversation. We had rabbit pie. She asked if I mightn't be more inclined to hunt a rabbit than a bird: recognising a fellow creature of the underworld. Maybe I would find one easier to hit, seeing as they only moved in 2 dimensions, like the words across a page. And there might be certain advantages to a pair of eyes that was slightly closer to the ground, *she supposed.*

I made some dry reference to Lewis Carroll. This won me general tolerance and (far more importantly) the right to remain almost entirely silent until I could politely offer my excuses and retire. I was barely half way up the stairs when Alexander launched a dutiful rear-guard defence of my invitation.

Next morning, out on the chilly moor by seven, I asked Hermione if I might carry her bag. She frowned a little, nostrils flaring in the ozone-rich atmosphere, but accepted the offer. I stood a little back from her and watched as she dropped her first two cartridges into the twin chambers of the gun with a childlike gesture… like a wizard casting spells. She was half-silhouetted against the pink sunrise.

*   *   *

The other core feature of *Aristasia* is its apparent total rejection of all the supposed social advances that have occurred since the 'Eclipse' of the 1960s. Its ideology (which is sophisticated enough to include a religion & a fictional global politics) is consequently extremely conservative. Not only that, the whole thing is acutely paradoxical when you bear in mind that Aristasia exists almost exclusively as a modern internet phenomenon & is precisely the kind of homosexual fantasy that would probably have been outlawed, or at the very least censored, before the liberalising legislation & case-law of the 1960s. Oddest of all, Aristasia appears to denounce the same post-war countercultures that are obviously its own heritage.

Aristasia Pura (the fictional utopia as distinct from *Aristasia-in-Telluria*, which is what they call the countercultural reality) is actually a whole empire containing various 'provinces' which 'correspond to various periods in History'. The most 'populous' of these (the so-called *Western Nations*) are decades from the first half of the twentieth century, but there are also *Arcadia* (which is basically Victorian), *Amazonia* (which is vaguely 'ancient') & *Novaria* (which is futuristic). This is a kind of paleoconservative pan-retro counterculture (with a bit of futurism thrown in for paradoxical good measure). Perhaps it should come as no surprise that it first appeared in Oxford in the 1970s.

The modern media, & the culture it has produced, Aristasians call 'The Pit' (something without which they could obviously not exist) & anything emerging from the politically correct world of the chattering classes — or contemporary theory, sociology, journalistic comment & the like — they dismiss as 'bongo'. It's not hard to find racist (even fascist) undertones in all of this. 'Bongo' is a term with undeniable Afro-Caribbean implications, whilst *blonde* & *brunette* are self-evidently racially specific categories (even — perhaps especially — if they're used metaphorically).

Despite this, I think Singh would have warmed to Aristasia. He would have seen it as a quintessentially postmodern phenomenon: its paradoxicality as the core of its nature & appeal. Despite the pluralism of the retro 'provinces', the foundation period for the Aristasian ethos was clearly the 1950s of *Quirinelle*. It was from here that most of the terminology, the aesthetics & the fetishised icons were originally gleaned. Singh wouldn't have found this difficult to explain. The fifties was the decade just before the 'Eclipse'; it was the halcyon moment that preceded the fall; & it was — in the coffeebars of the *bongo* beatniks — the breeding ground of the first postmodern countercultures that would lead to Aristasia itself. It was this fifties connection that attracted me, of course, & the risky politics just added to the guiltily erotic glamour of the girls' school fantasy. I suppose this is the kick for gay skinheads & the like. But it was no less troubling for having analogues. The ironies were quite impossible to pick. Whether it was just *drag* (St Trinianites into a bit of spanking) or a sincere ultra-Tory post-feminist movement arising from public school lesbianism was very hard to tell.

Still, I found myself going back to Aristasia's *Elektraspace* more & more regularly as the days went by.

But £en Pete Townshend got £e kitchen sink
　　€rown at him, which could be calamitous.
For Sloggy: now you'd wind up in £e clink
　　For simply testing your parameters
Of tolerance by clicking on some link
　　To watch (say) *se-male teenage amateurs*.
£e man had single-handedly besmirched
£e name of single-handed web research.

165.3 *wind up in the clink*: 'End up in prison,' but the sadistic overtones of these stanzas force one to imagine 'the clink' to have become, by extension, another instrument of torture like the medieval *rack* that is 'wound up' to inflict agony on the victim. (Though perhaps it is the electric current that is 'wound up' and 'the clink' is simply another name for *the web* or *the net*.) And there are further multiple senses bound up in this phrase: 'clink', as an onomatopoeic noun, is a pejorative term for both jingling rhyme and jangling coinage. It can also be used in reference to a small crack or fissure, especially in newly cast metal (hence the need for the *annealing* process: see 36.5 *Our skin anneals*), and is therefore semantically similar to 'chink'. Spenser captures this clinking assonance of sound and sense in *The Shepheardes Calender*; Piers, in May, tells of how the 'false Foxe' in the guise of a mendicant friar comes to the door of the Kid and begs for alms:

> Well heard Kiddie al this sore constraint,
> And lenged to know the cause of his complaint:
> Tho creeping close behind the Wickets clinck
> Preuelie he peeped out through a chinck:
> Yet not so preuelie, but the Foxe him spyed:
> For deceitfull meaning is double eyed.

Spenser's own annotations, if they really are his own, explain 'clinck' as a keyhole, the diminutive form 'clicket' having purportedly been used by Chaucer to mean *key*. This usage perhaps explains the movement of the onomatopoeic 'clink', via the sound of the key turning in the lock, to *gaol*. Wedgwood suggests a similarly logical progress for 'chink' from *short, sharp metallic sound* to *fissure* or *crack* on the grounds that the former is the sound of the occurrence in metalworking of the latter.

　　The key to the Spenser passage lies in the revelation of concealment and the reversal of the spying gaze. Like the vulnerable Kid in this anecdote, I feel myself peering through the chinking, clinking rhymes of this poem at the duplicitous Bosvil whose double-eyed meanings fox me, expose me and finally imprison me in the dreadful fate which they predict.

165.5 *tolerance*: era 14

165.5 *clicking on some link*: These onomatopoeic assonances rattle like Marley's chains… Jacob's… Christopher's. Was Dickens thinking Scrooge was *Shakespeare*?… This is truly Hell on Earth.

165.8 *single-handed*: Maybe a further grievous wounding of the flesh is carried out for the sake of a glimpse into the future. Like the devotees of Mithras who self-castrated in their rite of passage, users of *the web* may have one of their hands cut off like Arab thieves. Perhaps a surgical grafting of the machine into the neurological system of the user is necessary, requiring the amputation of a hand.

There's something I should explain... confess, in fact. In the sporadic periods of loneliness during my life, I've occasionally been known to *cyber*. The term is usually a prefix, but as a verb it means *to fuck*. As in most environments, the cyber world has its simplest paradigm in sex. Cybersex is a grand term, but it *is* more than wanking. Another person uses words to make you come — directly, personally & only to you are those words addressed. Words, always the same ones, moving from the early tentative euphemisms, through a clarification of boundaries, delight in recognition of similar tastes, then an inevitable flurry of fingerings through the sexual dictionary we usually keep for a punched pillow or a favourite friend. At points the phrases are conditional: 'I would if I were with you'; others are questioning & present: 'What are you touching now?'; but the most incendiary are the fantastical sentences which are not true: 'You're inside me.' I'm sanitising these statements so as not to titillate myself. But, unsanitised, I'm ready to admit, a clever typist has been able to arouse me beyond anything 'real life' has ever offered.

But I came to the decision, a year or so before my return to Glasgow, that it would have to stop. It was a self-deluding compulsion. There were so many lies, & possibilities of lies, bound up in cyber that I was left feeling the whole experience was characterised by wilful denial. The point of the exercise was the thrill gleaned from honesty through secrecy — & the sense of liberation the masquerade could give me was addictive — but this was more than sex in a blindfold. If I was honest with myself, I had to admit that for many of the people involved the appeal came directly from the ability to conceal their real age, their physical attributes, & (crucially) even their gender from the sexual partner. & it was precisely this dark zone of ambiguity that generated the illicit thrill. I knew full well I was playing into their hands. I'd deliberately keep my responses sufficiently oblique or universal to allow whoever it was to think I was... whoever they thought I was. This obviously begged the question: who do they really imagine is 'wording' them like this. More to the point: who do *I* imagine 'wording' me?

It was only when I found Aristasia that I rediscovered the desire. Suddenly, & for the first time, I was capable of indulging the deepest of my fantasies. I suppose — it feels sordid to admit it, but I suppose I must — I've always been attracted to lesbianism. Let's be clear, though, I absolutely do *not* mean the fake girl-on-girl action churned out on a daily basis by the porn industry. It was real lesbian erotica I secretly adored, despite the difficulties involved in finding it, especially those images from a time when the relationship with the camera & the viewer of the illicit prints was much more reverent & intimate.

I've never thought of sex as an expression of my masculinity, or even my *maleness*. It's quite the opposite, in fact. The experience of mutual pleasure has always come with a sense that it can somehow transform my gender: pluralise it; switch it. I don't think this has ever been an extended penetration fantasy: the notion that I've literally 'got inside the skin' of my partner... *possessed* her. Not only is penetration unnecessary, it's sometimes a turn-off. Instead I imagine myself to have become another woman: not even myself feminised but an original collaborative creation of every other partner with whom I've shared this same sensation. I suppose I imagine I'm a lesbian.

Which was a $ame, because it ran itself.
£e websites simply paid him to include
£eir links to m.peg clips. £e URL
Was all he asked of £em, and some€ing lewd
Describing it, so customers could tell
Which films might suit £em. Veena Wellspring, who'd
Allowed our man exclusively to glimpse
Her latest project—*dominatrix pimps*—

166.1 *shame*. See 26.5 *shame*, 32.4 *sham* and 161.1-3 *scam… sham*.

166.3 *links to m.peg clips*. Besides the obvious idea of crocodile clip electrodes—which certainly resemble the modern sprung clothes pegs—it is possible *m.peg* connotes the American game of juvenile machismo called 'Mumble the Peg', which I believe involves throwing knives at a treestump. How this might be translated into a psycho-sexual practice designed to alter consciousness I would rather not imagine.

166.3 *URL*. Again, one hardly likes to guess what dreadful sort of mechanism this might be. I refuse to speculate on the lurid acronymic possibilities. The chance that it could be a 'rebus' has not eluded me. The implications are too unsettling to contemplate.

*   *   *

There was certainly something appealing about the way she conducted herself. Perhaps I was beginning to realize what the others saw in her. She was by no means the prettiest girl at the shoot, but there was another kind of beauty to her: a fascinating quality best seen in this half light. She had a physical self-confidence to which the average young man, let alone the average young woman, could only aspire. The way she brushed her hair back, shifted weight from one foot to the other, or simply scratched her knee seemed to involve no effort or deliberation. It was this that made one want to be with her. Perhaps I imagined I could partake of this simple power: if I could be next to her, I might also become a little more like *her. There was certainly a magic there that people wanted to be around. It was as if there were no dilemma of free-will or determinism in her mind or body: no split of mind and body at all. That sounds preposterous, but I mean simply that everything she did seemed pre-ordained, but also entirely her own, instantaneous decision. Maybe this was as true of her breathing and her heartbeat as it was of her gestures and her words: a perfect hybrid of intellect and instinct.*

It was even true of her shooting. She was useless at it, of course, but the way that she was useless was entirely natural. It would not be hard to teach her. And here I saw the opportunity for my revenge. After her first two shots (and misses) of the day, I whispered (without seeking her permission to offer my advice):

'Just relax. Don't try too hard.'

'What?'

'Don't try too hard.'

*   *   *

It was the access it gave me to this age-old fantasy that first brought me to Aristasia. I learned through tentative trial & error to identify the girls to whom the woman I was imitating might be attracted... & attractive These were brunettes who liked brunettes. This form of *meta*homo-sexuality was unusual but tolerated. Most importantly, before I could be initiated into genuine Aristasian cybersex, I had to learn the vocabulary & the archaic syntax. With cyber you always need to pick up the idioms to be successful, but the Aristasian (in)version involved unlearning all the jargon & the abbreviations that the medium itself seemed to demand. That's not to say it was extremely formal; more that its colloquial qualities were based strictly on a type of mongrel period-slang from which everything originating in the 1960s onwards had been eradicated. (Though Aristasian slang itself was obviously exempt from censure.) I learned to refer to all such manifestations of *the pit* as *bongo*, or at least: *a bit infra*.

It was noticeable just how much this process had in common with reading (& presumably also with writing) R. H. Twigg: the inverse logic, the time-paradox, the rejection of Americanisms, the denunciation of an unpalatable 'future', the caricatural conservatism, & so on. The following is a good example of how Twiggishly Aristasians express themselves (taken from the *Aristasian Embassy*'s official glossary of terms):

'*Racinate*... Just as the deracinated objects of bongo design, from cars to music, help to create a deracinated consciousness, so the artefacts of the real world are both *racinated* & *racinating*. Thus, when we surround ourselves with real things, watch real films, listen to real music, regularly read up-to-date magazines, dress in real clothes, make our homes as real as possible, we work a subtle magic on our souls.'

For 'up-to-date' & 'real' read *old* or *retro*. This was queer historicism: not in the Jonathan Dollimore sense (of the history of the queer) but in the Twigg sense (of queer historical praxis: *recherché* period drag). To get involved in it was to take part in a *travesty of history* in a far more literal & assertive way than the phrase would normally allow. The experience was intoxicating. I'd find myself going back to the same site every time I turned on my pc. My right hand seemed to control the mouse entirely independently of any intention the rest of me might have to get on with some proper work. By the time it came to typing words, my fingertips would have long since surrendered to the desire. They would feverishly tap out my lies & provocations in temporally bowdlerised English, decorated with a smattering of Aristasian Oldspeak.

If I had to explain why this bizarre counterculutre had come to hold such an overwhelming fascination for me, I suppose I'd have to insist on the imaginative effect of being sexually & historically pluralised. Aristasia & *The Birmingham Quean* were doing the same thing to me. Unfortunately, I don't think the effect they were having was the one that Singh would have intended for his work. My cyber-experience was not 'fiction' but 'lies'. Rather than the pluralising fiction Singh was after — one that always revealed itself to be a fiction; one that might also be called *drag* or *brummagem* — I was simply being disingenuous. I was trying to *pass*. Not to beat around the bush: in Aristasia, I just lied & wanked.

> During a furtive conference tête à tête,
>> Had personally endorsed £e site because
> Vaginal ejaculation on £e net
>> Would be democratised and free, and £us
> Her profile as a sexual suffragette
>> Could profit by association… plus,
> £ese kinds of hastily forged loyalties
> Did untold wonders for her royalties.

167.3 *vaginal ejaculation*: A deliberate oxymoron, calculated to disgust with its aggressive portrayal of the feminine sex. One can hardly force the vocal organs to expectorate the phrase. This terrifying future seems to have in store a hybridisation of the human genitals—either by evolutionary change or more likely by surgical intervention—so that a constituency of hermaphrodites comes into existence, capable of such a mind-boggling impossibility. The effect is reminiscent of the grotesque physical mutations in Brueghel's 'Dulle Griet'. One cannot help looking, and, in looking, being captured and enslaved as one of the tortured souls figured in the scene of succubine excess.

167.4 *democratised and free*: The fact that the concepts of democracy and liberty have become debased so far in this future as to be retained only for sardonic use in reference to grotesque forms of anonymous casual sex should come as no surprise. Communism, Anarchism and so-called political innovations of all sorts have long since existed purely as pretexts for sexual libertinism. This is the result: a world in which sexual intercourse is universally hedonistic, non-reproductive, anonymous, masturbatory, vicarious, sado-masochistic and mechanized.

167.5 *sexual suffragette*: This twists the knife inserted in the previous line. The suggestion is that 'suffrage' (a supposedly noble desire for equality of power) has been *countered* by an aggressive folk-etymology to become '*suffer*-age': i.e. a synonym for 'suffering'. A *suffragette* therefore becomes a terrifying caricature of a woman prepared to 'suffer' physical pain (as did many of the militant suffragettes involved in hunger strikes and so on) for the sake of her own and others' pleasure. It becomes the antonym of the previous coinage *dominatrix*. That is to say it epitomizes the surrender to, rather than the exercise of, power. The fact that the two terms might very easily be swapped—each capable of being used as the subject or the object of the infliction of pain—is yet another of the amphibologies at work.

167.8 *royalties*: Veena Wellspring is implicitly cast as yet another image of the Quean. The real Dominatrix-Suff(e)ragette of the piece is obviously Britannia Spears.

    *   *   *

Of course, she tried all the harder next time round. She wanted nothing more than to prove me wrong. Two partridges scrambled out of a thicket of bracken to our left in opposite directions, their wings emitting intermittent bursts of action like sputtering propeller engines. She hunched her shoulders, screwed her eyes and thrust her gunbarrels towards one of them, as if attempting to harpoon it.

BANG!

She missed by yards.

    *   *   *

I realise now, that I've also been concealing something absolutely crucial from the reader. Perhaps my experiences have left me treating the projected audience of this tortuous account the way I would treat a chat-room partner. I've been deliberately vague in order to create a coherent image you might want to engage with on a deeper level. But I doubt that anybody's ever going to read this thing except for me... & if I can't be honest with myself...

It wasn't just any brunette that I was looking for in Aristasia. It was Hannah Arden. I'd occasionally get scanned images of the girls, but pictures never had any real impact on me. I would still imagine Hannah. Not that I really thought that she'd be there, but the words could fool me for a moment. They had an electrifying effect. The closer the exchanges came to the way I remembered Hannah speaking — those sassy comments shimmering through her lips in the autumn sunlight that lent the Shakespeare Institute's conservatory a thin gilt film — the closer I came not just to physical pleasure, but to something genuinely joyful.

The shame that followed disengagement was a recurrent memory: an analogue of how our first conversation in the pub had descended into impossibility, how she'd moved further & further away in those last moments precisely because of my inarticulacy, my insensitivity, my basic meanness of spirit... how every one of our encounters had suffered in the same way since that day. The technologically enhanced daydream of using words (& words alone) to make a woman like her want me, love me even (if only for a few hours), was the apotheosis of that age-old fantasy where you replay some encounter in your mind the way you would have acted if you had a second chance. Never once did I write: "I feel dizzy. I'm too drunk tonight. I think I might vomit." That would have been far too much like real life. As the effect of the endorphins dissipated, this unpalatable realisation would always hit me a little harder than it had the time before.

One thing was clear, though, I may not have got any closer to finding Amrit Singh, but I'd certainly got closer to his way of thinking. Both of us seemed to be addicted to the fleeting liberation we could find by venturing into a pluralising counterculture. More importantly though, for both of us, the experience was a meagre substitute for something else: not some idealistic abstract notion of *contrapuntal reality* or *multiple truth*, but an actual woman. What Amrit Singh & I had both really wanted was Hannah Arden.

There were two unavoidable differences though. Firstly, in every sense except for the most obvious, Amrit Singh could still claim to *have* Hannah Arden. It was torture to recall how she'd been aroused when I touched her... only because it made her think of him. Secondly, it was increasingly clear that *The Birmingham Quean*, the thing that had control of my imagination (just as he still had control of Hannah's), was Amrit's work. The idealistic theory that underpinned it — the only thing that might have offered a way out of my conundrum — was something I seemed to have been cursed to understand (in part, at least) whilst remaining entirely incapable of buying in to it in any therapeutic (or even palliative) way. The trouble was I understood the theory & its creator far too well; I understood precisely where Singh's ideas had come from & precisely what was wrong with them.

> Like Veena, Sloggy wanted to control
> £e intellectual property in porn.
> For £at, he knew he needed to get sole
> Production status—maybe he could spawn
> An empire £at way. He could enrol
> Support from bit-part boys whose gifts he'd drawn
> On heavily to help him come £is far,
> But really £ey would need a bonafide star

168.2 *porn*: The –awn rhymes in this stanza suggest an implosion of the homophone pair 'pawn' and 'porn'. This is probably commonplace in the imaginations of these kinds of people. Both terms are self-evidently about exchanging what one might call 'intimate family belongings' for money. Sloggy's desire, described here, might quite accurately be characterized as wanting to be a 'pornbroker'. The social connections between pawning and prostitution implicit in this neologism are obvious. Neither seem to carry any shame in Sloggy's circles.

168.4 *spawn*: A seedy choice of verb in the circumstances. Empires are usually *built* rather than *engendered*… though *spawning* might be considered a particularly gypsy way of (literally) conceiving of empire: for people of a primitive mentality the idea of *empire* might be no different to that of an enormous *tribe*.

168.8 *bonafide*: Strange that the English language seems to borrow so many foreign words denoting authenticity: *echt, pukka, kosher*. With the exception of this example from the *lingua franca* of Latin, one might suggest that the use of foreign words in this context carries a metonymic implication of doubt towards the authenticity of products derived from the cultures in which the source languages are spoken. Perhaps, that is, we need these words in order (so the analogy might run) to haggle with the dubious stall-holders in bazaars and continental markets where counterfeits and shoddy goods are known to be rife.

Bonā fidē literally means 'in good faith' and is therefore equivalent to the commonplace defence against the charge of receiving stolen or counterfeit goods. Clearly, the 'star' in question is in no way *bona fide*. One is reminded of Venus, the false, dissembling star which vainly rivals the sun; the *light of the morning*. Lucifer.

*   *   *

'Really: don't look at the bird, look at where it's going. And relax. Just squeeze the trigger.'

This was really irritating her already. She snatched two more cartridges from my proffered box and inserted them vehemently. She missed another pair of birds: one of them a large black grouse who flashed his pom-pom at us less than thirty feet away before tearing into flight.

'Have you just come along to gloat, perhaps?' she asked. 'Why don't you show me how it's done. You seem to know so much about it.' She held the gun out to me, hinged over her grimy brown suede glove.

'I don't.' I said. 'Besides, I think we're on the move again.'

'Well, I'll thank you to keep your comments to yourself, in that case.'

*   *   *

Countertheory owed far too much to Queer Studies to be really convincing. Singh's desire to problematise all forms of arbitrary category & his identification of gender & sexuality as the core features of ideological identity-creation are Queer Theory's central principles: some of his observations might have come straight out from between the recto-verso sheets of Judith Butler or Eve Kosofsky Sedgwick. He saw himself as moving beyond the merely 'plural' or 'mutable' ideas of sex that seem to form the two main fundamental versions of 'queer', but his model of *contrapuntal* performativity was not so dissimilar to the kind of thing that critics like Michael Warner harp on about.

He'd have liked to think that what he was engaged in — fiction — was even more liberated & liberating than the activities of Queer reading. Basically, he understood Queer crit. as something that had mutated from a type of Deconstruction — one that exposed latent qualities of non-normative sexual desire associated with a text: basically post-structuralist 'outing' — into a type of New Historicism: one that revealed a text's resistance to the various ideological categories of sex & genre imposed upon it both by its contemporary *epistème* & by more recent 'publics'. For Singh, both of these types of reading suffered from an inability to *join in*.

It was crucial to his understanding of literature that the permanent truth behind fiction was not universal difference — that characteristically queer combination of Freud (or Lacan) & Derrida — but universal similarity (& simultaneity). Basically, Singh thought everybody throughout history had always wanted to *multiply* themselves: i.e. to become *dividual*. The contrapuntal nature of *comedy* (in the oldest & the broadest sense... 'the communal song'... anything approaching Bakhtinian *heteroglossia*) was a way for this intrinsic human socio-sexual quality to assert itself. Whatever the politics of writers, the dramatic qualities of their writing had served to defy ideological forces that for one reason or another wanted to subdue their revolutionary potential. The orgiastic carnival of *dividualism* was not only trans-historical but it literally transcended history.

Queer historicism, he would argue, relied on a fairly stable idea of time & historical distance in order to show that social categories & identities we take for granted now had not existed in the past... or, at least, they'd not been quite the same. Queer history denied any *teleology* or *progress* but still had a 'sequence' & 'periods'. Singh's fiction, on the other hand, *queered* historicism itself. Periods in history (even dates, like 1953) were seen as arbitrary categories: the result of an ideological 'fencing off' of the timeless utopian possibilities to which fiction could give us access. Singh, you might say, wanted to denounce *time* itself: that existential chimera that Stephen Hawking glibly defined as "what stops everything from happening at once." Derrida's *La Fausse Monnaie*, in which the notion of time is explored alongside Baudelaire's meditation on counterfeit, was obviously an influence. R. H. Twigg was an attempt to do to time what Britannia Spears did to sex & race: to reveal it as a tool of ideological oppression & defy it by making 'everything happen at once.' For Singh, *now* & *then* were just another pair of genders to be dragged. For all his desire to transcend Queer Theory, it's pretty clear that his counter-theory was still subject to its central flaw. The reason for this was that Singh's best critical observation was never used to analyse his own work...

To rake it in; and here, framed by £e doorway,
    £ere stood a tart wi£ an outrageous glamour
£at astoni$ £em as much on Broadway
    As any one-horse town in Alabama.
Just looking at her was a kind of foreplay.
    He chuckled audibly above £e clamour.
$e looked him up and down like an amœba.
So who'd $e €ink $e was, £e Queen o Sheba?

169.2 *outrageous*: It is perhaps understandable that one of the most common folk-etymologies in English suggests this word to be the result of an inverted phrasal verb *to outrage* 'to rage (out)'. It is from this false idea that we get the inelegant adjective *outraged*. In fact the word *outrage*—which therefore gives us the only really justifiable adjectival form *outrageous*—derives from *ultra-age* 'the state of being *ultra*': 'too much' or 'over the top'. It might therefore be a perfect word in the circumstances, no less apt for being so pertinent to the poem itself. Typically, however, Bosvil intends her *glamour* to be *outrageous* also in the sense that it 'causes an outrage': a phrase which perfectly exemplifies the *outrageous* folk-etymological usage. Do not imagine for a second that Bosvil does not realize the effect this has on a reader like myself. It is precisely by chipping away at the integrity of the language—the only tool I have with which to reason—that he means to bring me to his level. I cannot claim to be optimistic that I might defy him. I see the flamingo looming on the horizon like a sunrise dripping semantic blood through the Faustian firmament.

169.2 *glamour*: A Scots corruption of *grammar*, in the sense of occult learning or necromancy, introduced into the canon (alongside the alternative *gramarye* and the related *færie*) by Sir Walter Scott. The following example from Burns's 'Captain Grose's Perigrination' (iv.) is both a perfect delineation of the usage and a very apt epithet for Ryley Bosvil and his ilk:

    Ye gypsy-gang that deal in glamor,
    And you deep read in hell's black grammar,

169.3 *astonish*: These kinds of etymologically entangled words seem to thrive in a future of ambiguities and contradictions. 'Astonish' and 'astound' and 'stun' are weeds which are impossible to tease apart, and their lascivious roots (Latin *attonāre* = 'to strike with a thunderbolt', Old English *stunian* = 'to resound', Early Middle English *stānen* = 'to pelt with rocks' or 'to petrify') spread and intertwine over large distances in order to take hold in the stoniest of ground.

    A common sight in British cities since the war has been the daffodils and thistles and rose-bay willow herbs spreading across the uncleared bombsites and poking through the rubble. These plants, especially the latter—whose slender height and plump tongues of clustered purple blooms seem to mock the destruction, have an uncanny ability to take root in an entirely soilless environment. Some even flourish at the very tops of bombed-out buildings, forty or fifty feet from earth, clinging to the crumbling, blackened windowsills and rusty gutters. In this respect they are almost lichen-like.

    But lichens do not have roots. A lichen is a symbiosis of fungus and algus. Or perhaps it is more accurate to say that a lichen is an algus with a parasitic fungus which allows it to grow as it does. This stuff has long been a source of fascination for me, not to mention fear and disgust. It seems capable of infecting any surface it desires. One would not be surprised to discover it thriving on the moon, or spreading onto human skin. It is for this reason that the Greeks named a variety of eczema after it: a variety I have found recently thriving in one of the more intimate areas of my body. I cannot discount a connection between the influence of the poem and this latest dermatological eruption.

Nor, I think, can we discount the possibility that the Nazis deliberately sent some variety of malign spores over on their V2 rockets, the explosions being designed merely to disseminate an insidious organic attack which is only now beginning to flourish. They had, we are led to believe, every intention of adapting the rockets to carry nuclear bombs. So why stop there? 'Atomic' weaponry is only the A of the ABC of modern warfare: the other two being 'Biological' and 'Chemical'. Both the Americans and the Soviets have developed all three. It is well known that both sides have German scientists in senior positions within their military development programs. Who knows what they might have tested in the blitz?

169.4 *Alabama*: This Southern State contains another dusky city named after its Central English prototype. The tastelessly explicit intention of its founders was to emulate the workshop of the British Empire. It is only about half the size, but its sheer existence serves as a reminder of Birmingham's importance as a pioneer of the American commercial, industrial non-conformist city. It should not be ignored that a revolutionary movement called the Southern Negro Youth Congress, operating from a headquarters in this town under the Liberal disguise of opposition to racial segregation, has recently been closed down by the FBI. That similar threats will soon arise in our own second city is beyond all doubt if Bosvil is to be believed.

169.7 *amœba*: According to the OED, 'A microscopic animalcule (class *Protozoa*) consisting of a single cell of gelatinous sarcode, the outer layer of which is highly extensile and contractile, and the inner fluid and mobile, so that the shape of the animal is perpetually changing.' The word derives from Greek ἀμοιβή meaning 'alternation'. An *Amœbæan Eclogue* is therefore the name for the Virgilian form of pastoral dialogue used in Spenser's *Shepheardes Calendar* (cf. 165.3 *wind up*...) We have moved from lichen to amœba and back. William Empson's extension of the 'pastoral' to include *The Beggar's Opera* is worth bearing in mind here.

*   *   *

We tramped in the direction of the coppery hills to our right. The wind stung our eyes. She broke the silence first:

'I don't know how you think...'

'I apologize. It's just that you complained that nobody taught girls how to shoot.'

'I don't know how you thought you could be of any help.'

'I was just offering some advice.'

'And what makes you *the expert? Or are you just a natural busybody? You don't even shoot yourself.'*

*   *   *

> He wasn't sure $e was cut out for it.
>   Perhaps a businessman like him could mould
> £e raw material a weenie bit,
>   For maybe ten or twenty grand all told—
> A touch of nip and tuck, yknow, £e tit
>   -Job, electrolysis, fle$ out a fold
> Or two, and Fanny's (surgically) your aunt;
> Well, Bob's your uncle still… but wi£ a girlie slant.

169.8 *Queen o Sheba*: For Bosvil, the ostentatious irony of casting Britannia Spears as The Queen of Sheba has much more to it than Sloggy's own dismissive sarcasm reveals. Unlike his anti-hero, who is merely adopting a colloquial cliché, Bosvil is aware of his own sardonic recruitment to the role of Solomon. The relationship between these two monarchs is crucial in two regards. Firstly it is the fundamental to the supposed theological legitimacy of the kingdom of Israel. And secondly, it is the source of the claim of Creole Rastafarianism that Emperor Haile Selassie of Ethiopia (and previously of Bath) is God on Earth.

To deal with the first of these tenuous points, contemporary Zionism relies on Sheba's acceptance of the Kingdom of Solomon as a precedent to counteract Arab resistance to the State of Israel. Sheba, in I Kings 10 and II Chronicles 9, is clearly identified as the great Arab neighbour (though obviously pre-Muslim): a nation of comparable (probably superior) wealth and power to that of the Jews. The arrival of the Queen in Jerusalem, amidst the proverbial quintessence of opulence, is as an explicit challenge. Imagine the motorcade of President Naquib processing through the streets of Tel Aviv. The gulf between the ideologies of Jerusalem and of Sheba is in fact even greater. Sheba is a strict matriarchy, one whose name is derived from that of a dark goddess of the moon, *Shayba*: (waxing a young maid; full a pregnant mother; waning an old crone). The Queen seeks not merely to assay the quality of this particular king and his society, but the whole idea of a king and a society capable of being ruled by one (on Earth as it is in Heaven). In such circumstances, the fact that Solomon's wisdom alone convinces her not only to accept the existence of a patriarchal monotheist nation, but also to shower its king with enough gifts (of gold incense and myrrh) to usher in a period of unparalleled prosperity, suggests an inherent power of divine reason well beyond any worldly capability to resist it. Reading in the Torah, modern Jews (obsessed with ancient precedent) can therefore find something like an Arabic Balfour Declaration has already been made.

Bosvil is allowing us to glimpse this idea as a vision of his own cacotopian Zion in Birmingham. (From hereon in, I adopt Jeremy Bentham's *cacotopia* to mean 'a diabolical or evil utopia', as envis-aged by someone with malign intent; as distinct from *dystopia*, which is an ironically immoral or dysfunctional utopia, envisaged with satirical intent.) The dialectic of Sheba and Jerusalem is not merely parodied in the interactions of Britannia and Sloggy; it is pointedly analogized.

Obviously, the relationship is inverted in almost every aspect, however. I do not think I need explain precisely how. Exegeses of similar effects are well enough rehearsed by now for the reader to have become accustomed to them. Suffice to say Britannia Spears is as much a faux Solomon as a faux Queen of Sheba.

This brings me to the second point. There is a clear implication here that the Guyanese Britannia is to be associated with the lineage of Menyelek and the worship of Haile Selassie. She is a kind of God(dess) on Earth. This is not a literal thing of course. We should remember that the entire logic of this poem seeks to detach any such real or noble claim to legitimacy (however false) in favour of the move towards an entirely symbolic, self-determined and mystical value as represented by the counterfeit coin. Instead of being the genetic result of the union of the Queen and Solomon, therefore, Britannia is both King and Queen, black and white, Rastafarian and Christian in that she/he is a Creole drag-queen.

This idea might benefit from some careful illumination. Solomon is traditionally associated by Christian theologians with Jesus. For this reason he also became the ideal monarch for the British constitution. That is to say that Psalm LXXII (in which David seemingly prophesies the idyllic reign of his son) is taken by Christian scholars to be prescient of Christ and his ultimate kingdom, and the life and reign of Solomon as an analogical prefiguring (on the part of God) of the result of the second coming of Christ. Crucially, the tribute of the Queen of Sheba is often cited in scripture as the proof of Solomon's legitimacy in this regard:

> And he shall live, and to him shall be given of the gold of Sheba: prayer also shall be made for him continually; *and* daily shall he be praised. [Psalm LXXII:15]

> The queen of the south shall rise up in the judgement with this generation, and shall condemn it: for she came from the uttermost parts of the earth to hear the wisdom of Solomon; and, behold, a greater than Solomon is here. [Matthew 12:42]

Inherent in the idea of Solomon is that of 'a greater than Solomon.' Naturally enough therefore, from the moment of its inception, the Anglican Church saw its ideal monarch as one like Solomon: the embodiment of the prophesy of Christ's second coming and the epitome of the link between wealth and wisdom. The moment of justification in Sheba's tribute is obviously the precedent for the gifts of Epiphany. But it is the use to which Solomon puts the Queen's gold which provides the crux. In the passage that directly follows I Kings 10:1-13, we find this: '16 And king Solomon made two hundred targets of beaten gold: six hundred shekels of gold went to one target.' Solomon, that is, creates a fixed-rate gold-standard currency. The stability and fairness of Solomon's reign is consequent upon the use to which he puts his gold reserves (the result of tribute paid to him by those in gold-rich countries who, like the Queen of Sheba, recognize his divinely granted legitimacy): i.e. both to adorn God's temple and to create a stable currency from the combination of Sheba's gold and Solomon's holy 'stamp'. Solomon's currency is just like his Abassynian bloodline: Sheba's substance with Solomon's stamp.

And this is precisely the ideal carried by the stamp of the British monarch on her coin. It is inherently to travesty such an aspiration to the embodiment of noble legitimacy that Bosvil has a mis-struck effigy of the English Queen on a cheap alloy introduce a bastardized tableau of Solomon and his Queen. The epiphanic nature of 'the first glance' becomes a caricatural performance of mutual mock-disdain. At the moment their eyes meet Sloggy and Britannia react in precisely the same way: as if they were mirroring each other. They are mutually revealed (it is perhaps too obvious to require utterance) as two sides of the same coin: a diabolical counterfeit of Solomon/Sheba; not the incarnation of the Bible's Messianic prophesy, but the incarnation of Bosvil's anti-Messianic one.

It is not at all irrelevant to the ensuing frenzy of Aristophanic pastiche that the Queen and Solomon are legendarily believed to have communicated by means of a talking Hoopoe.

Now Sloggy came to €ink of it, in fact,
    £ere might be money in £e actual op.
£ere must be some asylum-seeker quack
    Who'd do £e business for a grand a pop,
Or passports for his offspring in Iraq.
    And he could pioneer £e cut-price chop:
Just scribble out a five grand cheque to me—
I'll do a quick, discreet penectomy.

---

170 This stanza abounds in gambling slang with bawdy overtones of cosmetic surgery. A *grand* is a thousand pounds to a turf accountant; *all told* is a croupier's term referring to the counting of betting chips; *nip and tuck* means something similar to 'neck and neck'; and so it goes on. For a possible source of this kind of tasteless nonsense one might look to a scene in Howard Hawks's *The Big Sleep* in which Humphry Bogart and Lauren Bacall indulge in a crudely encoded flirtation using the vocabulary of horse-racing.

170.1 *cut out for it*: A tailoring analogy which draws attention back to the dress and the concept of trans*vest*ism. The surgical double-entendre is crude in the extreme.

171.2 *op*: I recently had the misfortune to peruse a copy of *Italian Visit* by Cecil Day Lewis. I stopped reading at the point at which this sharp medical abbreviation was used as scalpel in the emergency syllable-ectomy required to keep alive a flippant tetrametric couplet that would have been better left to die: 'I'd not advise you to believe / There's a slick op. to end your grief.' The similarities of this to the style and content of the present stanza are quite obvious. It is no longer easy to tell in which direction the influence might have flowed. Perhaps Bosvil, in another of his characteristic switches of direction, is demonstrating his ability to pre-empt both the very existence of the *pylon poets* and their debilitating pink influence on the future of English poetry by hinting at his own (impossibly anachronistic) influence on *them*.

171.3 *asylum seeker*: This is perhaps one in search of immunity from prosecution—a criminal on the run from the authorities—in *seek* of *asylum* under the auspices of local gangster who wants to style himself as a benevolent potentate. The choice of countries is telling. Iraq is a nation whose growing stability over the past few years is a direct result of the steady influence of a British style of constitutional monarchy over both the Imperial designs of the Ottoman Turks (in league with Germany), and the petty wrangles of various local *shayks*. The recent democratic elections and crowning of young King Faisal II are a matter of great hope in a region dogged by troubles of a revolutionary and inter-tribal nature. And it is the despotic petty warlords and the ideological revolutionaries (like Sloggy and Bosvil) who have most to lose from British success in nurturing this admirable polity. The fact that Bosvil is trying to invert the notion of a refugee from a dictatorial or war-torn state in this supposed figure of a criminally unqualified medical practitioner on the run from a stable, wealthy and peaceful nation is just another example of his mindlessly destructive vision of the future.

Offspring is perhaps a veiled reference to Iraqi oil. It is, in fact, precisely as a result of the wealth gained by Iraq from the British-controlled Iraq Petroleum Company that has made its social transformation possible.

171.4 *a grand a pop*: Again this is American gambling cant—*one thousand dollars per bet* (ie. $1000 is the minimum stake.) This future world seems full of hazardous games of chance and, as his narrative progresses, the poet seems continually to *up the ante*. This is becoming, as they say, a little too rich for my blood.

In one of the Zomby documents, Singh pointed out that Mikhail Bakhtin (always his most enduring influence) had never really understood epic poetry. Singh's pan-historical belief in the counterpoint of comedy relied on rejecting Bakhtin's view that *heteroglossia* was a recent literary feature of a 'new, democratic' form: the novel. Bakhtin's *dialogic imagination* hinges on comparing (monologic) epic poetry unfavourably with (dialogic) modern prose-fiction. Singh pointed out that Bakhtin's mistake was to assume that the dramatic elements of narrative verse need to be contained in the verbal content of a text in the same way they exist within a novel. Bakhtin judges epic poetry on how good it is as novel-writing. Singh cogently argued that the novel — as a result of its material form (mass-published, small-format printed volumes) & its means of reception (mostly private, silent reading) — acts as a 'gravity sink' into which the previously public dramatic contexts of oral narrative are subsumed. As the novel progressed, this effect became more & more acute, & more & more of the 'contexts' of a work (social, critical, performative etc.) had to be included in the text itself. The novel necessarily became more sophisticated, multilayered & 'dialogic' precisely because the post-enlightenment society that produced it was in the process of losing these interactive features of social complexity where narrative performance was concerned. The novel was forced to 'people its own solitude'. (This process is particularly evident in the verse-novel *Don Juan*.)

Singh's triumph here was to reveal the novel as less rather than more 'democratic' than narrative verse. The apparently socialising aspects of multivocality were described as an internal reaction to an intensely *anti*social artform. Comedy was asserting itself despite (rather than as a result of) the 'inward turn'. To expand the sexual metaphor, the novel was a masturbation-aid more than a forum for intercourse. Its socialising qualities were totally fantastic. & yet they were somehow capable of acting as imaginative resistance to their own form & asserting *dividualism* in the midst of the archetypal individualist artform. They were a contrapuntal Fifth Column in the principal superstructural edifice of 'solo psychology'.

Singh tried to use this argument to justify his own transcendentalist theory: contrapuntal stylistics was a revolutionary impulse intrinsic to humanity 'despite' history... the permanent *counter* of individualism. The reflexive & relativistic elements of the so-called postmodern novel were a challenge to the same acutely introverted culture which had created them. The trouble was, Singh was incapable of seeing just how much this theory itself was an extension of the same old individualist fantasy of internal democracy.

Queer theory takes as a core principle the Freudian dislocation of pleasure from 'the object of choice' & therefore fools itself that it transcends bourgeois norms whilst succumbing to the apotheosis of romantic introversion. Singh's *dividualism* — the single mind multiplied into a social counterpoint — was also just an extension of the antisocial effect he quite rightly recognised in the novel. If the novel was all about fantasising social (& sexual) interactions as a way of actually avoiding them in life, then Singh's *synacoustis* was a way of deafening himself to his social context. Ok, he hypothesised a Habermasian 'ideal speech situation' in which internal counterpoint had extended into the public sphere, but this was just an armchair utopia: as Hannah could testify, Singh rarely spoke to anyone... not even her.

> A snip at half £e price. £ough Sloggy knew
> 　Britannia wasn't into surgery.
> He reckoned $e'd be likely to poo-poo
> 　£e whole €ing if you tried to urge her. He
> Was sure £at getting Tanya to go €rough
> 　Wi£ £at would take some kind of burgalry.
> It's hard to get a geezer to down tools
> And let you walk away wi£ his crown jewels.

172.1 *a snip at half the price*: Bosvil's squalid wit is nowhere near as incisive as he seems to think. His attempt to bolt together such cheap double entendres of cash and surgery like the blades of scissors is irreparably blunted when applied to this illogical epithet. I wish it could be cut.

172.3 *poo-poo*: This is usually spelt *pooh-pooh*. Its use like this as a transitive verb stems from its position in the language as the quintessential dismissive interjection, something which led Max Müller to coin the term *Pooh-pooh Theory* to refer to his suggestion that human speech derives ultimately from the competitive interplay of non-denotative interjections of this sort. The linguistic environment of this poem depicts a world in which speech, detached from any stable symbolic function, is reverting to this cacophony of squawks. Unfortunately, at this stage I find it quite impossible simply to pooh-pooh it.

172.2-6 *surgery… urge her. He… burgalry*: This dreadful rhyme is not, I think, concluded with a spelling error. *Burglary* is quite often metathesized like this amongst those classes most prone to commit the crime. In this form, however, the word achieves the rhyme (already desperate) even more weakly than it otherwise might. I can think of two explanations: firstly, it is possible the erroneous pronunciation has spread like a canker into the English of the future and infected the orthography; secondly, it would be entirely consistent if Bosvil were mischievously disinterring the obsolete word 'burghalry'—an old synonym for the French term *bourgoisie*, which owes its ubiquity to the translators of Karl Marx—in order to lace the work with echoes of a bloody-minded ideology.

172.7 *geezer*: Originally *guiser* = 'one who guises', 'a masquerader'; in this case, *a travesty*.

172.7 *down tools*: From the argot of trades unions, *to withdraw labour*, but used entirely ironically about a transvestite whose only gainful employment seems to be gambling and trading (perhaps even in his own body) on the black market (if such a concept still exists). The only 'tools' a 'drag-queen' has are the items of his costume: his *drag*. Perhaps one might therefore gloss this line as 'It is difficult to persuade a *travesty* to undress.' This would certainly tie in logically with Sloggy's violent intentions.

172.8 *crown jewels*: A vulgar epithet for the male genitals which carries sordid anti-royalist possibilities. Bosvil makes us see, through Sloggy's quasi puritanical eyes, this repulsive succubus of a Queen as abominably 'crowned' with male genitalia. The justification of Sloggy's desire to castrate is therefore likened to Milton's justification of the decapitation of Charles I, but the pomposity is immediately deflated by the image of Colonel Thomas Blood, the infamous double-agent of the Commonwealth and the Restoration who, disguised as a parson, stole the Crown Jewels from the Tower of London in 1671, only to be captured and then mysteriously pardoned and stipended by the King.

Again we see the layers upon layers of this squalid masquerade.

If anybody understood Singh's solipsism it was me. My sordid Aristasian experiences were grist to its mill. I'd become increasingly withdrawn & unresponsive to the outside world as the weeks had drawn on. I might want to blame the novel itself for my recession into this hermitic environment, but it wouldn't be entirely fair. The truth is that Singh's work had only revealed to me just how much I'd been suffering from this pathology all along.

I began to imagine my consciousness as the surface of a wishing-well, just beneath which the (first person) 'I' was floating in the dinge like the sole surviving carp: slow & fat. Events, words, relationships were just like coins & raindrops falling from above, only coming into existence as they impacted on the surface & caused waves to pass through the meniscus. If the influence of Singh & his reclusive don had made me sink even deeper into my few cubic feet of eutrophying bilge (so that I could watch the ripples & imagine them to be a show put on for my own personal entertainment) then at least *The Birmingham Quean* had revealed to me just how much this stagnant psyche was my inevitable cultural inheritance.

This, I thought, was what everyone was like these days. Sex was absolutely at the heart of it. Human consciousness had retreated so far into the 'self' that even our skins (even our *privates*) could touch each other when our thoughts & words did not. Pretending they did — imagining there to be some telepathic communion that never happened — was simply fantasising. When Singh said 'the human being is a group; to be human you must be *dividual*' it sounded nobly communitarian, but it was really just the philosophical equivalent of an orgiastic masturbatory fantasy: typical of an isolated twenty first century male psyche bent on sexual self-destruction. (No pun intended.)

Like all queer theorists & post-structuralists, Singh was suffering from the same acutely individualistic malady he purported to oppose: the desire to encompass humanity in a single mind. According to these same theorists, such grasping universalism was the central flaw of the Enlightenment. & yet, they fall in the same trap. (You might even say it was a 'colonial' attitude.) The queer version, or the (*post*-colonial version) may not want to organise the world's societies hierarchically, but they still want to take our voices home & keep them on their personal bookshelves. These kinds of contradictions abound. The desire for individual privacy has increased throughout the period in which technologies of surveillance & communication have become increasingly available. Singh revealed, by exemplifying it, just how much contemporary theory & modern literature had supported the same *priv(atis)ations* of identity they were meant to counter. *The dialogic imagination* had become something an individual could experience (unnaturally & antisocially) in isolation.

Singh was right about one thing though: drag & fiction are intimately related. But only queer theory could be self-deluding enough as to suggest that drag (an attention-seeking, individualistic performance) is a sophisticated act of philosophical/political 'transgression'. Drag is sexual display. It's an act typical of a culture in which people want sex without intimacy. It's all about privacy dressed up as extroversion: an armour of caricature & cliché that admits *sexual* but not *social* intercourse. Drag says: 'we fuck, but we don't really talk.'

> And Tanya didn't want to dock her dick—
> > Not like some girl who says $e'll slit her wrists
> Unless $e can become a plastic chick
> > By crawling in some magic chrysalis
> In Thailand where you get a little snick,
> > A new vagina, and a clitoris.
> Genito-reassignment surgery
> Is not as cool as it's cracked up to be.

173.1 *dock her dick*: Here the *tick-tock* of the normal passage of time is echoically reversed. The fact that this occurs simultaneously with an explicit reference to penile castration intimates a direct connection between sexual and temporal reversal. This is a belief long-held, of course: think back (and forward) to Tiresias. This is clearly the major portent of the poem. It is a joke of staggeringly black proportions that the desire to know and to control what is to come—to surrender (as Marx has done) history to prescription; to hurtle ravenously towards the future without a proper respect for the present or the past—should result in a future which is sexually, morally and existentially degraded directly as a result of this desire to achieve itself.

173.6 *clitoris*: According to the OED, 'a homologue of the male penis, present, as a rudimentary organ, in the females of many of the higher vertebrata.' An etymon is virtually impossible to find.

*   *   *

The truth was—my reluctance notwithstanding—I was something of an expert shot. My mother's family had a small estate in Somerset on which they kept pheasant. My grandfather, a minor industrialist from Shropshire, had spent his whole retirement shooting, reading about shooting, collecting antique shotguns and the like. When my father went to the Falkland Islands for a year, I got my opportunity to learn. My brother was at boarding school, but my father considered me too young to go away, at the ripe old age of 11, and insisted that I stay with my mother and attend our local day school. She kept to his odd desire, insofar as she did not send me away, but we moved in with my grandparents in Berkshire instead. I did not go to school at all until the following spring.

Needless to say, I loved it. My grandfather taught me to shoot with a short-stock sixteen gauge and we spent almost every day that autumn bagging pheasant. Besides chess with Arthur in the evenings, the shooting was my only occupation and my only education. My mother seemed not to mind. She would come along herself from time to time. She had a natural talent for it; as did I. My grandfather on the other hand, despite his zeal, was never very capable before a moving target. Once I had gleaned the basics from him, and got to grips with my gun, I began to outperform him to an embarrassing degree. I put this down to the fact that it did not excite me at all.

Grandfather would insist, before it became quite plain there was nothing he could teach me, that the idea was to imagine yourself as the bird, feel the way it moved, learn to predict its movements. He had read this somewhere. I pretended to listen intently, then simply did the opposite. The bird was panicking, flapping off furiously to escape the beaters. I knew instinctively this was the wrong way to feel. Instead, I would treat a startled pheasant as an abstract target, its motion as a geometric arc. This was not achieved by focusing on the bird—as might an ornithologist, attempting to identify its sex and age by reference to minor variations of the plumage—but by relaxing the eyes so that concentration was on the field of the sky and the bird became a characterless blur, unidentifiable even as a species. The rest was a casual sweep of the gun along the bird's trajectory and a gentle increase in the pressure on the trigger. My skill at this was the polar counterpart of my grievous inability at chess. I would hit a bird almost every other time. My grandfather was forced to ration my ammunition very strictly. His excuse was that excessive repetitions of the recoil effect might damage a young shoulder.

'I have shot in the past,' I told Hermione, 'It's just that I choose not to now.'

'Are you some kind of a vegetarian?'

'It's simply not a fair contest. The birds can't shoot. Fortunately, neither can most humans... I'm not so fortunate.'

She was looking straight at me now. Her eyes gleamed with a ruthless, hungry kind of beauty. 'So what, in your opinion, am I doing wrong? And don't tell me to squeeze the trigger rather than pulling it.'

Hermione's problem was the opposite of my grandfather's. Instead of trying to 'be' the bird, she was trying to 'be' the gun. She imagined herself to be loaded—perhaps 'charged' might be the better word—and she attempted to shoot the quarry with her eyes. The tension in her body was released with every discharge and reinserted with every new red shell. She was an extension of the gun, rather than the other way around. Doubtless this was a defiant compensation for the lack of 'manliness' she assumed was required to wield the weapon. She was aping those supposed masculine virtues of expansive vigour, steadfast muscularity and focused concentration, as if the power to kill had to come from inside herself rather than inside the gun... as if she were wielding some kind of hefty pikestaff. In fact, a shotgun requires more of what one might call 'femininity' in order to be used successfully. Shooting is all about casual grace, gentleness, looseness of grip, fluidity of movement: in essence, a *light touch*.

'You should relax.' I told her, 'You're letting the gun turn you into something that you're not. You're all puffed up by it. Just be yourself. And don't try too hard. Smile when you shoot.'

I understood this all too well. At first, an eleven year old boy with a gun feels like a god. Eventually the novelty wears off; the sense of transferred power is revealed to be a humdrum fantasy. Only then does he become any good at using it. The true reason for my refusal to continue with this aristocratic pastime was an awareness that the discovery of an unlikely prowess also unearthed something much more worrying in me. It was an ability to extinguish my natural empathy for other living creatures that made me good at killing them. It was practised callousness. The implications were terrible. A functional detachment from other lives is very similar to a functional detachment from one's own. Perhaps the former is dependent upon the latter. Mastery of the gun is actually a surrender to its thoughtlessness, its absence of humanity. It is not the gun that kills, they say, it is the man. But in order to be any good at it, the man must be as cold and mechanistic as his weapon. The two become quite indistinguishable.

*   *   *

174

> As Tanya strode across £e sticky floor,
>> Her girlfriends flocked around her, twittering,
> £eir bodies draped in acetate, velour,
>> And viscose; rayon chiffons fluttering
> In breezes from £e ceiling fan. One wore
>> A poodle-clo€ crop-top, a navel ring,
> Pink vinyl hotpants and a fea£er boa
> (Which somehow edged her neckline even lower),

174.3-4 *acetate... rayon chiffons*: These are synthetic fabrics. *Acetate* and *viscose* are both plastic preparations which can be spun into *rayon*—a generic substitute for silk—*velour* is synthetic velvet. These 'twittering', 'flocking', 'fluttering' birds have plastic plumage.

174.6 *navel ring*: Perhaps this is a precious metal ring attached somehow to the skin so as to surround and emphasize the exposed navel, banding the absent umbilicus the way it might a finger. Turkish 'belly dancers' often adorn the navel with a gem lodged amongst the fleshy skin, but this practice manages as much to disguise the umbilical scar as to draw attention to its existence. A ring around the *omphalos*, however serves precisely the opposite purpose. It provides it with a *frame*: makes a spectacle of it.

All three words for this uncanny part of the body—this twisted evidence of gestation—have a similar derivation: *navel*, *umbilicus* and *omphalos* all refer to the 'boss' of a shield and the 'hub' of a wheel. Obviously, the Latin and English/French words are used by analogy with the Greek. Crucially ὀμφαλός was also used by the Ancient Greeks in reference to the stone at the temple of Apollo at Delphi which they supposed to be the centre of the flat Earth—conceived as a shield or wheel—and therefore the centre of the cosmos around which everything rotated.

It is obvious how this idea might appeal to Bosvil. His Birmingham is also conceived as the centre of the universe (the universe being defined as that which is capable of having a place like this as its centre). We are also back in the auspicious metaphorical territory of the shield of Æneas, the armour of Achilles, the ægis of Athena/Minerva—the *omphalos* of which is traditionally represented on the coinage as the mouth of the Gorgon. So here we have the boss of the goddess's shield, ringed with gold as the sweaty navel of a grotesque Medusan transvestite and as the hub of a revolutionary *brummagem* universe.

What really disturbs me is the impression I am given that in providing a painstaking exegesis of such dreadful stuff (in my current state of self-inflicted sequestration) I might myself have begun to worship at this derelict corporeal temple like some delusional *omphalopsychite*. The god I have come to worship is one that seeks to undermine such eminently sensible English Christian Philosophy as the *Omphalos* of Philip Henry Gosse (the subject of Edmund Gosse's *Father and Son*) (see 175.2 *flamingos*). Perhaps the god of Ryley Bosvil is no god at all: merely an idol... the phoenikopteros.

174.7 *pink vinyl hotpants*: One assumes there to be some ingenious material based upon polyvinyl chloride which gives these trousers an internal energy source, thus making their temperature regulable. Perhaps this has a direct correlation to an ability to change their colour across the traditional analogical spectrum, from blue-cold to red-hot. The use of the Americanism, *pants*, serves to emphasize this sense of heat (in what is presumably a proprietary brand name) in that it catches a whiff of the homophone *to pant* = 'to breath rapidly as if hot or physically excited.' cf. 'hot thick pants' in Coleridge's *Kubla Khan*. If any such respiratory excitement were to occur in me it would be as a result of growing panic rather than arousal.

Singh's extension of drag from sex into history served only to accentuate the flaw in the fantastic theory he wanted so desperately to believe. It's a staggering paradox of an argument to suggest that fake history (a retro drag act) is better than the institutionalised *non-fiction* version on the grounds that it counteracts a 'travesty of history' which insists on imposing an external relationship (in terms of sequence & causality) on past & present: a relationship ideologically maintained in order to restrict faith in our ability to 'make history' (& therefore effect social & political change). It simply isn't the case that we can inhabit two or more time periods at once. That (for Stephen Hawking) is the whole point of time & (for Heidegger) the key to the philosophical pre-eminence of History. More importantly, it's obviously a moral error of revisionist propaganda to seek to change the present by changing the past. Historical fiction is only a short route-march away from fictional history.

All of which would obviously not need to be said if Singh had simply accepted that his writing wasn't 'true'. But he would never have done any such thing. *The Birmingham Quean*, if it had any single theme, was about the 'truth of fiction'... the 'authenticity of counterfeit': that much was clear. Something else was clear, though: it was quite impossible to denounce the drag-act of R. H. Twigg (to denounce the theory that underlay it) without starting to sound rather like the old duffer himself. I've already fallen in the trap. The trouble is, that to reject Singh's *queering* of history — his *countering* of it; his desire to make narratives & voices from different periods artificially polyphonic — seems to require the same kind of reassertion of a strict sequential, causal relationship between past & present that is the mainstay of Twigg's own rigid version of historicism. For all the undeniable weaknesses of Singh's utopian theories, his rhetorical prowess could not be doubted. He'd planned the thing so that you had to go along with the travesty of a stuffy fifties Oxford don if you didn't want to end up turning into something similar.

Actually though, my rejection of Singh's fantastic idealism in these terms had probably come straight from Hannah. The pragmatic criticisms were hers — precisely the ones she'd used to wave away my foolish attempts to get into her good books that awful night with my own travesty of her ex's other-worldly philosophy. There was obviously some of Hannah in R. H. Twigg, & the fact that her rebuttals had occurred to me during this lonely period was very telling. Just how thorough her influence on my mind had become only dawned on me gradually as I discovered the same thing in Singh's creation. It was even more telling that my admiration for his unlikely ability to enthral me with this piece of work, despite my critical objections, was enough to dismiss the opinion of the woman I'd fallen in love with. Hannah hadn't even gone so far as to agree with me that Singh had written *The Birmingham Quean*. She'd implied she thought it was beneath even him to create such a self-indulgent gallimaufry of pretentious twaddle. (Though perhaps she'd glimpsed herself in it.) So, while I crawled the net for the merest erotically-charged hint of her, I was simultaneously cheating on her with her ex-boyfriend's queer novel: revelling in the sheer opulent unacceptability of it all to her ideas... as if to do so was to break down her resistance; to make her submit to an absurd transcendental fantasy that Singh & I were oddly capable of sharing.

And patent-fini$ed plastic snakeprint boots.
$e spread her arms out like flamingos do
And flagged her head in disbelief, as hoots
And coos of admiration from £e two
Behind her in £eir spandex siren suits,
Descended to a light *to-wit to-woo*,
Allowing everyone to hear her screech,
Click on a mike, and launch into a speech:

175.2 *flamingos*: In Aristophanes' *The Birds*, Epops (the Hoopoe, incarnation of the incestuous rapist King Tereus) introduces the first bird of the avian chorus by tossing Peisetairos ('persuader of men', associated with the crow) a titbit of ornitho-etymology. 'Crikey!' screeches Peisetairos, spotting the strange purple bird that arises from a bush at Epops's beckon call, 'He's so fine and φοινικιοῦς!' 'Of course,' crows Epops, 'that's why he's called φοινικόπτερος.' (272-3)

The OED retains the word 'phoenicean' (cf. 'Phoenician') meaning 'purple-red' or 'crimson' to accommodate a single C19th occurrence where it is pompously applied in reference to the colour of a bird. '**Gr.** φοινίκεος' explains the etymological parenthesis. Either author or lexicographer must have had Aristophanes in mind, but which (or whether both) is hard to say. Similarly, the OED finds it difficult to decide whether uses of 'Phoenician' meaning 'crimson' arise from the murex-dyed wool the Phoenicians were famous for exporting or whether the name *Phoenicia* itself derives from Greek for 'the red land' 'the φοινίκεος land'. Was the dye (the *tincture*) named after the land or the land after the dye? [Another theory has Phoenicia as *the red land* to the Greeks because it is 'the land of the rising sun'—a signification which mimics our application of this epithet to modern Japan in combining a reference to the internal pre-eminence of the sun-god Baal in Phoenician culture with a western (in this case Greek) view of Phoenicia's oriental strangeness. Phoenicia is South East of 'here'. We steer towards the rising sun. This theory has obviously undergone infection from the *phoenix*...] Despite the even-handedness of the note under 'Phoenician', the fact that the compilers of the OED divide 'phoenicean' (with no intial capital) from it as a separate headword implies a strong attachment to the latter theory. 'Crikey!' Peisetairos says 'he's so fine and so *phoenicean*! EPOPS. Of course, that's why he's called *phoeniceanwing*' (OED—'**1857** *Fraser's Mag.* LVI. 579 The wings are of a phoenicean colour, that is to say, reddish verging upon fulvous.')

But what exactly is the *phoenikopteros*? There is as far as I can tell only one other occurrence of the word in Ancient Greek texts: a similarly ambiguous reference in Cratinus's *Nemesis*. It is certainly not included amongst the exotic birds listed by Herodotus. Famously, though, the other bird derives its name from its *phoenicean* (or perhaps *Phoenician*) characteristics does make an entrance in the *Histories*... but more on the *Phoenix* below.

By the time *phoenicopterus* finds its way into Latin, there appears to be a unanimity of reference. One of Martial's epigrams, entitled *Phoenicopterus*, reads:

Dat mihi penna rubens nomen; sed lingua gulosis
Nostra sapit: quid, si garrula lingua foret?

> I get my name from my red wing;
> The gourmets prize my tasty tongue:
> But then, what if this tongue could sing?
>
> (my translation)

This is certainly supposed to be the *flamingo*: the bird with by far the largest of all avian tongues, which it uses to pump the brackish marshwater through the complex horny plates that line its bill in order to extract the tiny red crustacea which lend its plumage that characteristic (and definitive) pink tint. Roman aristocrats used to eat these lumps of grey gristle: as much, one suspects, as a display of Epicurean excess (requiring the slaughter of multitudes of the exotic birds for one course of 'delicacies'), as for the attainment of any true intrinsic gastronomic experience. (Though, to this day, both the Italians and French have retained a strange taste for the gizzards of ducks and geese.)

It is curious to imagine what Martial thinks the flamingo would sing, were it sufficiently *garrulous*. He is quite pointedly recalling Philomel and Tereus, of course. The insinuation is that the flamingo carries a dark secret. There is further evidence that the bird was considered mystical and portentous by the Romans. Suetonius says of the death of Caligula:

> prodigiorum loco habita sunt etiam, quae forte illo ipso die paulo prius acciderant. sacrificans respersus est phoenicopteri sanguine

That the Emperor should be sacrificing a flamingo at all is telling—a self-evidently (and typically) excessive gesture—the fact that the splashing of the flamingo's blood on his robes should be taken as a portent of his impending death reveals even more. Roman society had perhaps been swayed by the seeming etymological link between the *phoenicopterus* and the *phoenix* (the bird which so preoccupied Ovid and Pliny).

Like the *phoenikopteros*, the *phoenix* might just as easily be the *phoenikious* bird—the scarlet-purple bird—as the bird (originally) from Phoenicia. Or perhaps it is the other way around. Perhaps the *phoenix* is the essence (the fiery *tincture*) of the colour which gives the other things their names. In Greek, φοίνιξ meant two things: the mythical bird that regenerated every 500 years in its pyre/nest, and the tree, the Date Palm (*Phoenix dactylifera*) (see 'date' 227:7). It is possible the bird was supposed to live in a tree of this species, or else merely that the tree was metaphorically identified with the legendary bird as a result of its geriatric reproduction and its legendary ability to regenerate when burnt down to the root.

The most cogent linguistic argument, however, (I do not think we can except *date* as 'the red fruit') runs that the Egyptians (from whom all of this mythology was procured) had their own etymological connection between the bird and the fruit tree. Their name for the Phoenix was *bennu* and for the Date Palm *benra*, which gives us the Coptic *benne*.

The hieroglyphs that represent the *bennu* look nothing like the Greek eagle-like conceptions of the Phoenix. The bird in question was almost certainly the Purple Heron. This solitary species is smaller and shier than its more common grey cousin, but individuals can be found hidden amongst the reeds in the marshlands bordering the Nile. Like the Flamingo, the bird has a characteristic scarlet patch on its wings, from which it gets its name.

It is worth remembering that the word 'purple', which has come to refer in loose English to everything from 'claret' to 'violet', derives from the French *pourpre*, which retains its specificity of reference to 'dark red' ('*phoenician* murex-red'... *phoenicean*), whereas *violet* is used for the majority of shades we now call 'purple' in English.

'Okay you glamour-pussies, listen up.
    £is isn't some€ing £at you'll want to miss.
Turn down £e jukebox, Clive—£at's it—turn up
    £e decks as well please, Honey, sticky kiss.
You butch girls at £e bar; and you—done up
    Like someone in Phil Collins' Genesis;
And you: £e sun-tan wi£ £e signet ring
Your jewellery's some€ing, but your skin's bling-bling

The French names for the two main types of Heron are therefore particularly revealing in their recollection of the Phoenix association; they are *l'heron cindré* and *l'heron pourpre*: 'the Ashen Heron' and 'the Phoenician Heron'. To the Egyptians the *bennu* must have seemed like the fiery infant born of the ashes of its parent. Thus a mythology is engendered; the Heron becomes the Phoenix in the flames of the imagination.

It might well be this bird that Aristophanes means. The definitive wing-patch of the Purple Heron is distinctly φοινικιοῦς. It also 'lives in the marshes', something the playwright explicates.

Wherever the confusion starts—in Athens or in Rome—confusion there is in abundance. This is something that often happens in the translation of birds' names. One need only trace the various offerings for the Hebrew *qa'ath* in different versions of the Bible to discover how haphazard it can be: there is everything from 'pelican' to 'little owl'. The 'birds of the air' defy the languages of man.

No bird is more dubious in this respect than the Flamingo. Its confusion amongst the Romans, the Greeks and the Egyptians with the Phoenix and the Bennu is mirrored in the confusion of its own linguistic pedigree. *Flamingo* is supposedly derived from the Spanish *flamenco*, which is, of course, also the name of a the traditional dance music of Andalusia. How this comes to be the case is somewhat puzzling. Skeat implies that the (Hatzfeld-Darmesteter) etymology in the OED, which suggestst the word derives in Romance languages from Latin *flama* 'flame', is false. Instead he insists *flamenco* is a modification of the Middle Dutch *Vlaming* 'Fleming', a native of Flanders. This finds its way into Spanish during the reign of Charles Quint (originally from Ghent) whose courtiers were known for their sartorial *flamboyance* (an entangled word itself) and the sunburnt pinkness of their complexions. The transference of this word onto both the Andalusian Gypsies whose music it names, and onto that most flamboyant of birds, the *phoenicopter*, apparently occurs via some kind of mildly pejorative metaphor: akin to the French naming the English *rosbifs* after their sunburnt skin.

This is no simple matter. The Provençal form *flammant*, used by Rabelais, appears to pre-exist this association of the Flemings with the gangling bird and the extravagant Gypsy dance. Furthermore, there is a Provençal poetic Romance called *Flamenca* whose heroine is evidently named for her glowing complexion (my translation):

L'autrui beutat tein es effaza	All other beauties would seem pale and weak
Li viva colors de sa fassa	Beside the living colour of her cheek.

This kind of thing is constantly repeated in the poem. Crucially, it is not at all clear whether Flamenca's beauty is supposed to be derived from a relative paleness of her complexion (making her bright *blush* the focus of her *flaming* beauty) or (in complete contrast) from its relatively swarthy nature (which would make her seem more like a smouldering Gypsy-woman). Experience suggests the former, but this same ambiguity turns up in a number of the Shakespearean Sonnets to the infamous 'Dark Lady', and it could easily be cleared up by a poet intent on racial disambiguation. The point being that the latter interpretation would suggest a link between the 'flamboyance' of the *flammant* and the dark Gypsy temptress of the dance. If we suppose there to have been a word for the bird in Spanish, predating the arrival of the Flemish court and related to the Provençal—**flamenc*, let us postulate—and a similar traditional idea of the Gypsy *Flamenca*, then we can speculate the reverse process to have occurred in the creation of the word *flamenco*. Namely that it was a humorous folk-etymological response to the immigrant Flemings to call them Flamingo-Gypsies. It is obvious why Bosvil would want to champion such a thing.

In fact it is impossible to decide between these possibilities. It is at once the flame-bird, the Flemish bird and the dancing Gypsy bird. Most etymologists would choose to pass this off with a question-mark. That is to say they would simply express doubt about the derivation by placing a question-mark at the beginning of the etymology, and move on. (See 13.5 *rift*). I can not be so sanguine in failure. The impossibility of deracinating the weeds that entangle this word—even of telling the weeds from the true plant—is a fundamental failure of philology. Ours is a discipline designed specifically to avert such folksy instances of *paranomasia*, to demonstrate empirically the evolution of language and thereby stem the deleterious affects of ignorant folk-etymologies. The flamingo mocks our failure. This bird defies the stability of human language to such an extent that etymology itself is felled by her inverted leer. The Flamingo is not satisfied with the failure of language to capture her in its semantic nets; she wants all etymologies to begin with that mark of doubt.

In Spanish they have two question-marks: one to conclude an interrogative (as in English) and the other to introduce one. This second question-mark is upturned. It looks like this: ¿ I do not know the name of this *inverse eroteme* in English or in Spanish. Perhaps it has no name. If not, I propose we call it the Flamingo. It has its long, curved neck bent downwards; its inverted head half-submerged in the brackish marshes of semantic uncertainty. It stalks the fringes of every etymological swamp, confusing the coastline between the solid ground of history and the reflective surface of a liquid myth. It is Bosvil's bird.

It is as if this linguistic abomination (like the counterfeit narrator herself) had been created by an illicit encounter between plural 'dads'. As such, the flamingo is not just the metaphorical result of some obscene bohemian fantasy of unnatural generation, but a word that acts to undermine the very substance of the 'Stammbaum' theory of August Schleicher upon which the entire study of historical linguistics hangs. In fact, the flamingo's flouting of the bifurcating structure of the taxonomic tree, which Linnæus had inherited (perhaps via John Wilkins) from Porphyry's diagrams of Aristotelean 'Categories', impacts on something even more important than Schleicher's Tower of Babel. When P. H. Gosse reconciled evolution to the *Jesse's Rod* of divine creation, in *Omphalos*, it was in terms of justifying in theological terms precisely the same extension of taxonomy into the (divine) dimension of 'time' that Schleicher had uncovered in Darwin. According to the mystery of Rouen, remember, the Sibyl of Cumæ, the keeper of the Golden Bough, is included with Isaiah on the Rod of Jesse as foreseer of the birth of Christ: the fruit of the tree. Simply put, the biological taxonomy combined with evolution is the tree of knowledge itself: the pattern of God's creative thought growing out through time to form the infinite variety of his creation. The flamingo's thorny alternative—with all its historical travesties and its tangled, abominable generations—is Satan's most absurd burlesque.

You're almost $iny as Ron Atkinson;
    And you—£e Sou£side Rudies—irea bwoys?
Why suck your tee€ when you could practise on
    £e real deal, sugar? $ut your noise,
And put away your toys; you too Wins*ton*.
    If you could all let go your saveloys
A sec... okay, my little troop of fairies,
I'll tell you who £is Queen of ladieswear is.

I cannot end my note on the flamingo here. There is something more... something even more tawdry and terrible. We must return to Aristophanes' *The Birds* to find it. This is a play—perhaps the apotheosis of Greek Comedy—in which an old tramp, the personification of rhetoric, defeats the gods and upturns their judgements on Œdipus and Tereus. Not only is this conceived as the ultimate political transgression—the siege of heaven carried out with the help of the birds—but simultaneously as the ultimate sexual transgression. *Cloudcuckooopolis* is evidently a realm of total phallic liberty; the birds are ruled by an incestuous rapist and are grotesquely ithyphallic in nature. Whatever species the Phoenicopter is, its appearance is quite obviously a penile joke. Just like the translator, the two old men are not sure they recognize the first bird to stretch its long, red length up from behind the bush. They ask Epops. 'He is not one of the birds you would know,' the King replies, 'he lives in the marshes' (very possibly a bawdy vulvic reference). 'Crikey,' blurts Peisetairos (rather awe-struck it would seem), 'he's magnificent and purple'. 'That's why he's called the Great Purple Cock', jokes Epops/Tereus. (His joke is a folk-etymology.)

The play teems with incessant flocks of these dire sub-witticisms. Eventually, of course, Peisetairos convinces the birds to build an enormous edifice to countermure the Earth against the gods. In the process he symbolically rediscovers the sexual potency so obviously missing in the early exchanges. So successfully does he manage this that Zeus is forced to surrender his mistress to his reinvigorated lust. The implication is clear. Peisetairos has enlisted the birds—whose liberty (and libertinism was proverbial)—to unthrone the father of the gods and take the stepmother of the gods as wife. Thus Aristophanes travesties a return to the Golden Age at the hands of the unchecked sexual and political hubris of the human individual. This is no satire however. It is no more a satire than this poem is. Aristophanes' play is the ultimate expression of fabulous, revolutionary wish-fulfilment. In that play, as here, the first bird of the chorus is the *phoenicopter*.

Today the bird seems just as redolent of sexual deviance as it may have done to Aristophanes. Perhaps this is a result of its adaptational inversion: the flamingo is a bird whose head is upside down; why not its sexuality? On the other hand, we might speculate that it is the bird's extravagent phallic appearance—its elongated neck and legs, its garish pink—which makes it so attractive to the perverse of inclination.

All of this, however, is to forget the real deviance of the flamingo. The flamingo's true (untrue) nature is to be found in its names. It is the *fake firebird* and the *phoney phoenix*. The phonic disruptions inherent in its effects upon the language reveal it to be a cheaply alloyed counterfeit of the Queen of birds. Not only does it travesty the phoenix, it occludes the entire concept of *phoenicity* by refusing any singular etymon. In other words, by faking *phoenicity* (not in order to *pass* as a Phoenix, but in order to disrupt the whole idea of the Phoenix with a multiplicity of counterfeits), the Flamingo kills both beauty and truth.

This sounds a histrionic claim, but there is more to this than mere philological curiosity. There is an ancient symbolism of birds, adopted by the Neoplatonic practitioners of

Alchemy, within which the Flamingo (the *phoney phoenix*) encodes something truly diabolical. Shakespeare's 'The Phoenix and the Turtle', for example, is misunderstood by those who read it merely as an allegorical denunciation of Elizabeth's execution of Robert Devereux, ignoring its allegory of failed alchemical transmog-rification: in terms which, at the time, would have been quite readily decodable by the initiate.

It is a critical commonplace to deny that the 'bird of loudest lay', which begins the poem with a call for all birds of 'chaste wing' to assemble, can be the real (new) Phoenix. The poem is quite unequivocal (on this point if on no other) about the failure of the Phoenix to regenerate. What is never mentioned, however, is the fact that the other birds are all conventional symbols of various stages of transmogri-fication, the last of which is always the Phoenix: (representative of Gold, Christ and the introspective perfection of the Alchemist himself). The Crow or Raven is always the first. The myth alluded to of its ability to self-engender from its own breath was rarely taken seriously (as commentators seem to assume) but commonly understood as a standard alchemical code for the sublimation processes in the creation of compounds of antimony. There is a predictable mention in Jonson's *The Alchemist*: Face re-enters (II.iii.67-70) after supposedly carrying out a stage of the experiment—

> SUBTLE   How now? what colour says it?
> FACE   The ground black, sir.
> MAMMON   That's your crow's head?
> SURLY   Your cockscomb's, is't not?
> SUBTLE   No, 'tis not perfect. Would it were the crow.
>   That work wants something.

The next stage is the Swan (as is Shakespeare's) then the Peacock, the Pelican (both of which are conspicuously absent) and the Phoenix. The stages of the *Peacock's Tail* and the *Pelican in her Piety*, which are the necessary precursors of the creation of the Golden Phoenix, can only follow after the coupling of the *King* and *Queen*. Again, this event is explicitly absent (li. 59-61):

> Leaving no posterity:
> 'Twas not their infirmity,
> It was married chastity.

This could quite uncontroversially be glossed by a contemporary reader of the *Rosarium Philosophorum* as a failure of reaction at a crucial stage of the aureofaction process. This reaction is, for the Neoplatonic philosophy of the alchemists, the core event in the creation of the *One* from the 'two distincts' discussed in precisely the relevant terms in the stanzas preceding the Threnody. The poem is therefore (at one level of reading) a satire on a typical alchemical failure to 'recreate the Phoenix' caused by the non-reaction of the 'King' and 'Queen'. The political allegories are obvious. It is crucial to remember, however, that the process of transmutation is as much a question of approaching divinity (in the Neoplatonic sense), nobility, enlightenment and so on, as it is of creating gold. But what is created in the new Phoenix's place? 'the bird of loudest lay'. It is irrelevant to attempt a final decision on the particular species referred to. The point is that there probably is no particular species 'of loudest lay'. On the surface, the line simply reads: 'Let whatever bird has the loudest voice / Sing both a eulogy for the dead birds and a fanfare for itself.'

>It's Birmingham's doyenne of TV darts;
> $e's won a €ousand matches €rough £e years,
>And who can say how many Brummie hearts
>   Her cupid arrows still intend to pierce?
>$e's long been £e big €ing around £ese parts:
>   Please pay your tributes to... BRITANNIA SPEARS.
>(And since I've done £e job of namin her,
>I'll wi$ success to all who sail in her.)

To understand more specifically what might meant by 'loudest lay', however, we need to note the complex play on words. First of all, 'lay' could mean the production of an egg. *The Philosopher's Stone* was often referred to by Alchemists as *the cock's egg*. The cock being certainly the loudest of domesticated birds, and the result of its 'lay' being semantically simultaneous with this loud 'crow', the satirical alchemical association with the phoenix could be all the more acute. More pertinently, 'Lay' was a contemporary aphetic form of *allay* 'alloy', and 'loudest' could as easily have meant 'shiniest' as 'of the greatest acoustic volume'. Hence, this particular *phoney Phoenix* is a flashy alloy passing itself off as gold: the result of charlatan aureofaction. The bird is also quite obviously a fake Queen. Shakespeare (or whoever wrote the work ascribed to him amongst his shady Marlovian circle) is applying cheap gilts of satirical irony, layer upon layer.

It is implicitly to identify the sexually dubious flamingo with the *phoney Phoenix* of this anti-purifying incantation that Bosvil imports the same sophisticated, multi-layered argot. The flamingo is the counterfeit sovereign, the drag-queen amongst birds. To let its name slip is to let slip a pointed hint at the intention of his work. His is the poetry of inner-transformation. The effect is more than analogous to that mystic link between the alchemical transmogrification of matter and the metamorphosis it is designed to carry out within the alchemist's own mind. Instead of purifying and integrating our psyches, Bosvil gives us this poem as a deliberately unconvincing theatrical performance meant to transform us psychologically into the same cheap alloy of fake *phoenicity* the Shakespeare poem calls 'the bird of loudest lay'.

As a result, we ourselves become the flamingo: the epitome of the tasteless and garish in nature; the species whose pungent prurience of form makes us doubt once and for all the hand of God in our creation on æsthetic grounds; the bird whose name upsets all etymologies, all family trees and all taxonomies; whose stinking, orgiastic 'cities' are the most vehement parody imaginable of the perfumed, noble, virgin solitude of the Phoenix; the bird who patrols the liminal zone between histories the way Cloudcuckooland sets up a toll on the frontier of Heaven and Earth; to pile Pelion upon Ossa, the bird whose trashy alloy symbolism is the very token currency of lawless transaction in a *black economy of time* that Bosvil operates to make it possible for me, in 1953, to buy into a future that will hatch from the foolsgold *cock's egg* of its 'loudest lay.'

175.5 *spandex siren suits*: One assumes the constant threat of nuclear war hangs over this society and a bloody-minded encroachment of the vagaries of fashion into the design of even the most grimly practical of garments (to be worn during aerial bombardment) means that they are now constructed in some deliberately impractical material with the lurid name of *spandex*: presumably a colourful, reflective or luminescent fabric.

175.6 *to-wit to-woo*: '*Scilicet* to seduce', but also the standard English onomatopoeic imitation of the owl. The two ideas are intimately related. In Classical mythology the owl suffers from the contradictory attitudes of the Greeks and Romans. For the Ancient Greeks, the owl—

principally the Little Owl (*Athene noctua*)—is associated with the goddess Pallas-Athene, and therefore with poetry, wisdom, virginity and war. (See 41.4 *shield*, 148.4 *half like a spring...* and 174.6 *navel ring*). It is for this reason that Attic coins commonly carried its image on the reverse. In Roman mythology, however, the most important species was the Barn Owl (*Aluco flammeus*), otherwise known as the *screech owl*, on account of its discordant cry which was purported to prophesy doom. It is this bird that is obviously Shakespeare's 'shrieking harbinger of doom': a reference that recalls a sound-effect cliché of the Jacobean Tragedies whose phantasmagorical triumphs he would soon be wallowing in. The motif is rife, but its stereotype is the moment in the second act of *Macbeth* where the regicidal first scene is immediately followed by one we are to interpret as simultaneous with Macbeth's murderous soliloquy. The bell that tolls after the Thane of Cawdor has sunk his dagger in the King's heart is replayed in his wife's imagination as a clichéd pathetic fallacy: the screech of an owl at the moment of death:

> Hearke, peace: it was the Owle that shriek'd,
> The fatall Bell-man, which giues the stern'st good-night.
> (II.ii.3-4)

Despite Middleton's *The Witch* and Webster's various morbid offerings, it was probably John Marston who best exemplified the Jacobean penchant for spectral horror whose cobwebbed eaves provided a permanent roost for the Senecan symbolism of *Aluco flammeus*. For this reason, Samuel Johnson called him 'a screech-owl amongst the singing birds.' In *Antonio's Revenge* (a tragedy which ran in direct competition to *Hamlet* on the opposite bank of the river at St Paul's and whose burlesque features were as gruesomely absurd as anything the present poem has to offer), the eponymous revenger sets the scene for the ensuing bloodbath with the following formulaic evocation of the witching hour (III.iii):

> Now barkes the Wolfe against the full cheekt Moone.
> Now Lyons halfe-clamd entrals roare for food.
> Now croakes the toad, & night owles screech aloud,
> Fluttering 'bout casements of departing soules.
> Now gapes the graues, and through their yawnes let loose
> Imprison'd spirits to reuisit earth:
> And now swarte night, to swell thy hower out,
> Behold I spurt warme bloode in thy blacke eyes.
> *From vnder the stage a groane.*

Before such phantasmagoria had really come into fashion though—coincidentally with the publication of *The Phoenix and the Turtle*, in which Shakespeare appears to cast himself in the role of 'shrieking harbinger of doom' and implicitly blames this transformation on the political environment—a speech to accompany and introduce the atmospheric stage-effects required to portray an act of necromancy (the art of predicting the future by speaking to the dead) had already become a standard formula on the Elizabethan stage. (John Dee was doubtless the inspiration.) It is from here that Marston's version obviously derives.

Now here's £e winners from our disco-tent,
 It's Gloria Summers and Susannah York…'
Oh, we are fam-i-ly, £e sisters went,
 £e pub's applause died down and punters' talk
Flowed back. As Tanya made her brisk descent,
 A Chinese girl in some€ing like Bjork
On *Homogenic* (people call her *Gay$a*
 —$e's always first to come up and embrace ya)—

The earliest example is in Shakespeare's *Henry VI, Part 2*. It is the perfect reflection of Bosvil's own desire to be brought back to life by this necromantic incantation in order to effect the doom it farcically predicts (Craig 1904):

Act 1, Scene 4 GLOUCESTER's garden.
Enter MARGARET JOURDAIN, HUME, SOUTHWELL,
    and BOLINGBROKE

HUME
Come, my masters; the duchess, I tell you, expects
performance of your promises.

BOLINGBROKE
Master Hume, we are therefore provided: will her
ladyship behold and hear our exorcisms?

HUME
Ay, what else? fear you not her courage.

BOLINGBROKE
I have heard her reported to be a woman of an
invincible spirit: but it shall be convenient,
Master Hume, that you be by her aloft, while we be
busy below; and so, I pray you, go, in God's
name,
and leave us.
       Exit HUME

Mother Jourdain, be you
prostrate and grovel on the earth; John Southwell,
read you; and let us to our work.

   Enter the DUCHESS aloft, HUME following

DUCHESS
Well said, my masters; and welcome all. To this
gear the sooner the better.

BOLINGBROKE
Patience, good lady; wizards know their times:
Deep night, dark night, the silent of the night,
The time of night when Troy was set on fire;
The time when screech-owls cry and ban-dogs howl,
And spirits walk and ghosts break ope their graves,
That time best fits the work we have in hand.
Madam, sit you and fear not: whom we raise,
We will make fast within a hallow'd verge.

Here they do the ceremonies belonging, and make the circle;
BOLINGBROKE or SOUTHWELL reads, Conjuro te, &c.
It thunders and lightens terribly; then the Spirit riseth

SPIRIT
Adsum.

MARGARET JOURDAIN
Asmath,
By the eternal God, whose name and power
Thou tremblest at, answer that I shall ask;
For, till thou speak, thou shalt not pass from hence.

SPIRIT
Ask what thou wilt. That I had said and done!

BOLINGBROKE
'First of the king: what shall of him become?'
    Reading out of a paper

SPIRIT
The duke yet lives that Henry shall depose;
But him outlive, and die a violent death.

  As the Spirit speaks, SOUTHWELL writes the answer

BOLINGBROKE
'What fates await the Duke of Suffolk?'

SPIRIT
By water shall he die, and take his end.

BOLINGBROKE
'What shall befall the Duke of Somerset?'

SPIRIT
Let him shun castles;
Safer shall he be upon the sandy plains
Than where castles mounted stand.
Have done, for more I hardly can endure.

BOLINGBROKE
Descend to darkness and the burning lake!
False fiend, avoid!
    Thunder and lightning. Exit Spirit

175.8 *mike*: A phonetic abbreviation of *microphone* (cf. 20.4 *earwig*). Perhaps there exists in this future a piece of technology which allows the 'mike' to act as an instrument which somehow materializes the spoken words: as lightning-conductor to sorcerous semantics. Maybe it is only by speaking the poem into a machine like this that anyone could be responsible for summoning Ryley Bosvil.

    This is obviously absurd. But the absurdity of it is nowhere near as comforting as one might like.

176.1 *glamour pussies*: Black-magical cats (see 169.2 *glamour*), the traditional 'familiars' of witchcraft, particularly in the performance of necromancy.

176.3 *jukebox*: Another of the 'slot machines' with which America is infiltrating a profiteering prurience into our places of leisure (see *slot agape* 137.8). In this case, the result of the *coin-operation* is to play the kind of musical recording to which youngsters want to dance (if one can call all that ritual waddling and flapping to accompany the anatidine cacophony of *big band jazz* 'to dance'). This seems innocent enough at first but when we consider that the word *juke* derives from a sub-literate Negro term for 'brothel', and ultimately a West African verb *dzug* 'to live in wickedness', we can see just how easy it might be for the Bosvilesque influence of brutal interracial intercourse implicit in the dollar and its automated vehicles of depravity to turn the chapel of English popular culture, the local pub, into such a wretched hive of scum and villainy.

176.3-4 *turn up / The decks*: 'Turn the playing cards face up'. Cribbage-players, or their ilk, are being asked for some reason to reveal their hands at this point. Perhaps the idea is that they stop playing in order to gamble on the outcome of the darts match instead. By now, however, we should recognize the queerness of such a request as indicative of some occluded meaning. I have previously made reference to the possibility of the whole poem being an encoded card game or trick: (21.3 *psyche*, 22.5 *cards*, 39.6 *palm em off*, 50.7 *tracksuit top*, 133.1 *flush*, 151.8 *upped his turnover with more finesse*). To take the idea a little further, maybe all these thinly veiled references are instructions to an esoteric reader, schooled in such things, to perform some ritual of the Tarot during the incantation in order to hasten the summoning of Ryley Bosvil. The reflexive nature of the present example makes this seem all the more likely. For an obscure code to work it must contain a *keyhole*: some indication of the kind of code it is. (See 79.3 *radio-alarm*.) If we suspected this to be such a *keyhole*, we might gloss it (via an understanding of the history of the word *deck*, from Old Teutonic *decke* 'operimentum') as 'lift the veils', 'uncover what is hidden'. The bawdy connotations are part of the effect.

Swooped down as quickly as a peregrine,
   (Her nose was not unlike a falcon's beak)
And clawed £e $oulders of our heroine.
   $e kissed £e air £at hung by ei£er cheek.
Her eyelids fluttered where £e air blew in
   Around Britannia's bowsprit, so to speak;
$e stepped away to do a little bow,
   But Tanya $rugged: £ere's no need to kowtow.

176.4 *Honey*: Oozing American term of endearment. But also what Hercules must feed to Cerberus to gain entrance to the underworld. Intimately related to both is the crude euphemism for female genital excretion.

176.6 *Phil Collins' Genesis*: I assume Phil(ip) Collins to be the inheritor of the William Collins Publishing company in Scotland, who are renowned for their scriptural publications. Notably, these include certain unashamedly populist books, such as the recent *Children's Illustrated Bible*. In the guise of a drag impresario, Bosvil is mischievously likening the addressee to one of the stylized depictions of man's original ancestors from the first book of the Old Testament (begging a comparison of himself to 'counterfeiting Satan').

176.7 *sun-tan*: see 36.2 *bronze our features* and 36.5 *Our skin anneals*

176.7 *signet ring*. The historical origin of both the coin and the legal autograph. (See 29.3 *blanks*, 37.3 *signature* and 38.2 *nickel-brass*). There is also a play on *cygnet* to remind us where we are (see 12.1 *The Swan*).

176.8 *bling bling*. Perhaps an emphatic adjectival iteration of a local form of *blink*. If so, the image is probably designed to recall the 'flashbulb aura' of Britannia's dress (147.2) which 'seemed to wink at you'. Again, the figure of transferred epithet hinges on a switch of transitivity. It is the dazzled viewer who is made to 'blink' repetitively, but it is the flashy object causing this response which is described as *bling bling*. It would obviously be applied quite naturally to a 'signet ring' incorporating *bright-cut* gems. The comedy of the line therefore derives from the somewhat illogical idea of skin so tanned by the sun that it outshines the bearer's ostentatious jewellery. But this is not merely a lurid joke. *Blink* thinly veils its original meaning: 'blind', 'deception', 'trick'. As a verb, it is still used in certain rural Scottish and Irish dialects to mean 'to cast the evil eye'. The iteration is remarkably spell-like.

177.1 *Ron Atkinson*: Much of the ensuing stanza is written in a way that suggests it should be performed in a kind of Creolian *patois*; this might therefore be an illiterate reference to the West Indian cricketer Denis St Eval Atkinson. The speaker is comparing the sunburnt skin of the addressee (perhaps previously likened to the tanned slaves of the Pharaoh in Genesis) to that of the mulatto Atkinson. Use of the adjective 'shiny' is yet another reversal of the direction of light-radiation in the poem. The skin in question is, in fact, darkened rather than rendered more luminous by the effects of Ultra Violet radiation from the sun.

177.2 *Southside Rudies*: I presume, from the ensuing Caribbean argot, that this is the name of a criminal gang comprising of West Indians. 'Rudies' perhaps combines the senses *rude* and *ruddy* to signify their manners and their burnt complexions. Though it may be a misspelling of 'Rubies'; this latter reading would certainly appear appropriate to the ostentatious jewel-imagery of the scene, and the mistaken mirror-reversal of a lower case <b> as a lower case <d> is the commonest of orthographic errors amongst the uneducated.

177.2 *irea bwoys*: Some form of canting shibboleth no doubt. Bosvil's people utter little else.

177.4 *real deal*: As well as the whining Birmingham effeminacy of the double diæreses (cf. 47.3 *nail-file*) it is also the case that such drawling effects of variable vowel-pitch stretch the ductile substance of the Creole dialects of the West Indies. The Birmingham accent, the caricatural effeminacy and the immigrant *patois* form a viscous melange in the diabolical melting-pot of Bosvil's future: one whose relationship between sound and sense completely undermines the kind of authenticity that is the butt of this phrase's sarcasm and makes the reader's mouth into a zone as degenerative in inauthentic as *The Black Swan* itself.

177.5 *Win<u>ston</u>*: (As prec.) the reversal in prosodic emphasis achieves the same sort of effect. The given name of the Prime Minister is, for obvious reasons, a particularly common one to be given to the male babies of a new wave of immigrants bent on 'integration'. The fact that they invariably pronounce it wrongly in this way, reveals just what a travesty of the nation (just what a reversal of its emphasis) might be made by the kind of 'integration' that has encouraged increasing numbers of these little brown Win*ston*s to be conceived in the heaving boarding houses of Birmingham's shady suburbs.

177.6 *saveloys*: 'Cervelat' sausages—dried and highly spiced like the Spanish *chorizo*, the French (who introduced them to this Caribbean culture) slice them thinly and serve them as an apéritif. Instead, one assumes, these dusky gangsters clench them in their bejewelled fists and gnaw them slatheringly with their canines like American cowboys do strips of *jerky*.

* * *

That morning, with a little more encouragement from me, Hermione bagged eight birds—seven partridges and a willow grouse—twice as many as any of the men. I asked her not to tell them it was anything to do with me. This was, I thought, the key to our relationship. There was instantly a bond between us. It was a dark shared secret. I had not admitted anything to her about my true feelings where shooting was concerned, and yet she seemed to understand. It gave her something like a feeling of empowerment. On the other hand, my coaxing her 'to be herself' suggested I might possess a similar understanding of her own hidden hopes and fears. This was, I suppose, the moment she ascribed to me that all important quality of 'depth'.

She found it easy to comply with my wishes. She had quite a talent for the traditional false modesty. It was luck, she explained, the beaters had been sending all the birds straight at her because she was a woman, it was an unfair contest. This was all designed to rub salt in the wounds of male pride, of course, but I recognized that last part was for me. I grinned into my soup.

* * *

            £en all £e o£ers pecked her cheeks and squawked.
                £ey jabbered feveri$ly all at once
            But $e could follow it; somehow $e talked
                To each of £em, bo€ like an audience
            And one by one. And Sloggy, £ough he balked
                At all £e twittering of £ese deviants
            And wanted desperately to make £em zip it,
            Just couldn't help but pick up £e odd snippet

177.7 *fairies*: Etymologically, fairies (from *fays*) are descendants of the Fates, who appear in English mythology as the *weird sisters* for the same reason (*wyrd* being Old English 'fate'). The legend of Macbeth in Holinshed refers to 'The prophesie of three women supposing to be the weird sisters or feiries' (*Chronicles* 1577 p.243, margin) and it is from Shakespeare's version of this in *Macbeth* I.iii, the *weyrd*, *weyard* or *weyward* sisters (Folios, under pressure from *wayward*, to contrast ironically with *homeward* two lines before its first appearance) that the modern *weird* gains currency. It is emended variously to *wizard* (under pressure from *wise-ard*) in certain early dramatic editions, but Theobald's version *weïrd* is the authoritative one.

Theobald's explication of the diæresis is perhaps unnecessary but indicates precisely the reason for the Folios' ambiguity. It also reveals something of deeper relevance here. The fact that the Old English for *fātum* is being given this emphatic and exotic prosody uncovers the intimate relationship between the *queer* diæreses of *The Birmingham Quean* (see passim) and the doom that Bosvil seeks both to predict and to prescribe. These *weïrd* articulations (notice how *word* itself seems to be stretchable across two syllables to hyper-demonic linguistic effect) are the vocal gestures of the spell. One must suspect a similar phonetic *weÿwardness* to be at work in this couplet of potentially dodecasyllabic lines. Like so much Scotch mysticism (see 43.6 *jape* and 169.2 *glamour*) this diæretic version of *faërie* was reintroduced by Walter Scott. The word is a near homophone of *fiery*, and as such (to complement the obvious allusion to Spenser) it connotes the 'fiery' Queen of Wands in the Tarot: the archetype of the clairvoyante. Perhaps for this reason, this trisyllabic polyseme only really maintains much currency amongst occultists. Its transference into the mainstream in Bosvil's vision is implicated in its encroaching usage to mean 'male homosexuals': whose affected metropolitan speech sardonically reproduces this pejorative term in an exaggerated and elongated fashion. It is in this way that such *haggard* deviants as these drag-queens can become the *fates*: the speakers and enactors of *fātum*: 'that which has been spoken'. The literalising connection between the act of speaking and the manifestation of doom (the proverbial *self-fulfilling prophesy*) implicit in the word, is captured in the English saying *after word comes weird (fair fall them that call me Madam)*: the definitive threat of the *faërie*.

178.1 *TV darts*: How, precisely, the television interacts with the bar-game is hard to imagine. Surely we are not to understand that the broadcasters bring their cameras into public houses to 'televize' the games the drinkers play. Perhaps a television set is a traditional prize for winning a tournament.

178.5 *she's long be the big thing around these parts*: One imagines a licentious gesture.

179.1-2 *Now here's the winners… Susannah York*: This derelict misquotation of the opening lines of Shakespeare's *Richard III* fills me with apprehension. The only way I can make head or tail of it is to assume 'winner' to be used in the Northern dialectal sense of *dweller* and that 'disco-tent' is intended to refer to a circular marquee such as the *big top* which definitively *encircles* the circus. The speaker is therefore playing the role of *ringmaster* (*ringmistress*, if such a thing exists); the line might therefore be glossed as: *next to arrive are the inhabitants of our big-top*. Their names are merely convenient echoes of 'Made glorious summer by this son of York' in the style of a (particularly) 'bad quarto'.

179.3 *sisters*: Having spoken the future, *Macbeth*'s weird sisters (who Holinshed tells us are in 'strange and ferly ('frightful') apparel' vanish from the first act of the play just as these bizarrely bedecked sisters do from this poem 'as breath into the wind'. 'The Earth hath bubbles, as the Water ha's,' says Banquo, 'And these are of them.' (I.iii.79-80). Macbeth's tragic flaw is to treat their words not as froth but as *fātum*: just as Faustus need only disbelieve the determinism of Mephistopholes's contract and repent to avoid damnation, Macbeth becomes the tragic agent of his own doom only because his wife convinces him it is his destiny.

Banquo continues to offer sceptical explanations: 'Were such things here, as we doe speake about? / Or haue we eaten on the insane Root, / That takes the Reason Prisoner?' (81-3) He means the mandrake root, of course: the juice of which the enchantress Circe used to turn Odysseus's men to swine. Then: 'What, can the deuill speake true?' (105) and 'oftentimes, to winne vs to our harme, / The Instruments of Darkness tell vs Truths, / Winne vs with honest Trifles, to bestray's / In deepest consequence.' (121-4)

I am beginning to feel myself to be engaged in a similar cosmic struggle with a necromantically revealed doom. This ghoulish Britannia is Hecate; these 'fairies' are her 'weird sisters'; this grotesque rhyme is their demonic incantation; the reader is Macbeth and must enact their gruesome vision of the future for it to become reality. I have no Banquo (progenitor of the Stuart monarchy) and I cannot be sure my *moly* of philology has not been transformed by Bosvil's *flamingo* into my own 'insane root'... my *mandagora*.

179.4 *punters*: Again, this is the language of the bookmaker. The audience in the pub are like the 'audience' of the poem—we are gambling simply by listening. One wonders what precisely is at stake.

179.6-7 *Bjork... Homogenic... Gaysha*: It is hard to tell whether this is some kind of invented language. It would not be unprecedented. Professor Tolkien has created just such a thing in its entirety (including a literary canon) for his new book. *Bjork* looks distinctly Scandinavian. What it might mean, I cannot be sure. *Gaysha* might just be a misspelling of *gayshe*, a diminutive form of *gash* 'goose', so 'gosling'. One can only guess that the material (*Bjork*) worn by this character is some form of Scandinavian eiderdown from a synonym of which (*Gaysha*) the wearer gets his/her nickname: *ferly apparel* indeed.

180.1 *peregrine*: The most valued bird in falconry for its unrivalled swoop. The name is cognate with 'pilgrim' and derives from Latin *peregrinus* 'foreign' or 'exotic'. See next.

180.2 *falcon*: The name for this family of birds of prey derives from Latin *falx* = 'sickle', owing to the resemblance of their talons to reaping-hooks. No doubt the red painted nails of this *quean* are being likened firstly to the bloody talons of a falconer's raptor ('falcon' is only applied to the female of the species; the male, being one-third smaller, is a *tiercel*), and secondly (by etymological recovery) to the red weapons of Mao's bloody Communist revolution in the character's native China.

This is a portentous tableau: the Maoist harpy diving to sink her sickle-claws in the shoulders of Britannia, pecking her on the cheeks like Judas in Gethsemene: Jenny Diver in the Newgate Tavern.

> About Þeir conquests in Þe local gay-bars:
>> Þese sluts had talking smut down to an art;
> Þeir one-night-stands were Herculean Labours.
>> He turned away and was about to start
> AnoÞer conversation wiÞ his neighbours
>> About a motor in Exchange & Mart,
> Or racing—how his horse in Þe Gold Cup did,
>> Or Princess Anne [in court], when he was interrupted.

180.6 *bowsprit*: The jocular use of a term from naval architecture to refer to the African retroussé nose of this 'Britannia' is presumably calculated to remind the reader of the recently launched eponymous Royal Yacht. The fact that *Britannia* has no bowsprit (being a modern engine-powered ship rather than a sailing vessel) is entirely consistent with the demonically anachronistic nature of this poem's attempt literally to divert the proper course of history.

181.1 *others pecked her cheeks and squawked*: like Jenny Diver, Mrs Coaxer, Dolly Trull, Mrs Vixen, Betty Doxy, Suky Tawdry, Molly Brazen…

> Even all the nation of vnfortunate
> And fatall birds about them flocked were,
> Such as by nature men abhorre and hate,
> The ill-faste Owle, deaths dreadfull messengere,
> The hoars Night-rauen, trump of dolefull drere,
> The lether-winged Bat, dayes enimy,
> The ruefull Strich, still waiting on the bere,
> The Whistler shrill, that who so heares, doth dy,
> The hellish Harpies, prophets of sad destiny.
>
> (Spenser *The Faerie Queene* II.xii.37)

Acrasia, the setting of this dire *Parliament of Fowls* (the clear precursor of the Jacobean aviaries of hell), is as much a queer mixture of excess and impotence as Bosvil's Birmingham. Spenser's 'Bower of Bliss', like *The Black Swan*, is a paradoxical *travesty* of an exotic *motherland*: sterile, artificial, and yet of a seductively grotesque fecundity. It is associated with the 'plantations' in the New World: the eventual source of another 'flight of harmefull fowles' that Bosvil's vision has brought home to roost.

181.7 *desperately*: era 15

181.7-8 *zip it… snippet*: Sloggy fantasizes the ability to *stop up the access and passage* to 'the twittering of these deviants' by closing a zip-fastener on their mouths. 'Come, you Spirits, / That tend on mortall thoughts,' says Lady Macbeth (I.v.43-4), perhaps addressing the audiences of her soliloquy as the real *murthering ministers*, 'vnsex me here,' and by *here* she means *on this stage, 'under my battlements'*, and *this part of my body*: hence 'Stop vp th'accesse, and passage to Remorse / That no compunctious visitings of Nature / Shake my fell purpose' (46-8). Sloggy's zip-fastener might therefore be used to close another orifice. And the teeth of 'zip it' mesh together, in an artificial rhyme, with 'snippet' to remind us of Sloggy's fantasy of literally enervating the threat of this coven with surgery.

For all its distasteful barbarity, one cannot help but sympathize with Sloggy's attempt to imagine a red-blooded way out of this tight corner. His predicament, after all, is not so dissimilar to ours.

182 CUT

'... Don't get your knickers in a twist. It says you're
   Coming on too strong is all. The bloke's
Just worried that he's never gunna measure
   Up to *you know who*. You'll have to coax
Him out his shell by showing him the pressure
   Isn't on him to perform. Just crack some jokes
And keep him off the booze. When mine gets drunk he
Loses courage: softly, softly, catchy monkey.' ...

183 CUT

'...The other day, I'm in a greengrocer's:
   "A cucumber and some Pink Fir potatoes,
Please" I say. The owner swallows his
   Last swig of tea and says, "this isn't Waitrose,
Bab; we don't do fancy spuds; just this
   Then is it?", handing me the cucumber. His wife goes
"Want that sliced and wrapped in polythene?"
"No thanks, my love" I say, "I'm not a slot machine!"'

184 CUT

'... He told me it was never gunna work;
   It wasn't something that was meant to last;
A bit of fun was all (he had the smirk
   To prove it), "honestly, it was a real blast,"
He said, "thank you for managing to perk
   Me up..." "He *said* that?", "now let's put this in the past;
It never felt like part of something bigger."
Which made me think of his wee part and snigger.' ...

185 CUT

For the most part it was stuff like that: on sex
   And men and dicks. Is that what normal birds
Are like when they're alone? In most respects,
   He thought it was. He'd often overheard
The gossip when he used to work the decks
   On ladies' nights; it wasn't any more reserved
Than this; these tarts weren't any wilder;
In fact, Britannia's story was much milder...

186 CUT

'... And then this old flame, kneeling at her door
   Sings showtunes to her at the letterbox
And tells her she was beautiful before,
   But now he thinks that she's a total fox;
She's grown into her body; she's much more
   Than just a pretty girl in pretty frocks:
Her legs, her breasts, her hands, her neck, her face
Are thought and kindness, power, skill and grace.

187 CUT

'It's all just cobblers—clichés—but could you
   Resist him if you thought he really meant
The things he said? Does stuff like that come true?
   Say if a man said you were heaven-sent
For men to love, then maybe, for a few
   Hot minutes, could you be? At least until he went.
Trust me, an Irishman who's kissed the blarney
Can make a woman feel like Isabelle Adjani.

188 CUT

'So Fingal strokes her door and tries to touch
   Her through the wood, as if he's measuring
Its flimsiness. He massages so much
   That she can almost feel him pleasuring
Her on the other side. And he is such
   A lovely man, with you or me: a sure thing.
But she can't let him in. Push comes to shove,
She's somebody who always needs to be in love.

189 CUT

'And now she is... with someone else. The men
   Who were the secret objects of her lust
When she was in the shower—even when
   She moved her boyfriends in—have gone. They sussed
Her in the end of course; time and again
   She'd wind up on her own. But things have changed; now just
Her boyfriend's soap can make her eyeballs swim
And she'll just rub it on herself and think of him.' ...

190.6 *motor*. This is a rather old-fashioned way of referring to a car which, since the last war, has become increasingly rare owing to the obsolescence of the previous necessity to mention any other (that is *unmotorized*) form of car. The fact that this 'motor' appears in *Exchange & Mart*, a magazine dedicated to the classified advertisement of second-hand goods, suggests that the car in question might itself be rather old-fashioned. The anachronism comes full circle: where 'motor' was used at the beginning of the century because it was a new idea, it is used in the next millennium to differentiate its antique technology—the internal combustion engine—from whatever new-fangled nuclear propulsion system the latest vehicles employ. This linguistic *knotting* of the lines of temporal progression seems to be part of the poem's diabolic code. I am beginning to suspect the untangling of its Gordian complexities to be beyond this humble hermeneut.

> Some geezer wearing Reebok and Joe Bloggs
>   Stood up and muzzled Sloggy's repartee
> About £e country going to £e dogs
>   By mumbling it was time he went to see
> His mom, who was about to pop her clogs."
>   (I'm sorry £at was put so callously;
> A Briti$ poet ought to have more tact.
>   Except, of course, £ere's no such €ing. In fact,

190.7 *the Gold Cup*: It seems rather late for Sloggy to be discussing the Cheltenham Gold Cup, which takes place in March, and if this is June 2nd, the Gold Cup at Royal Ascot—which would be the most likely horse-race to suffer an attack at the hands of such an obstinately anti-monarchist tract—is not going to happen for another two weeks. The most probable major race to occur around this date would be the Epsom Derby, in which, for the first time, the newly knighted Sir Gordon Richards finally triumphed this year aboard Pinza. Such iridescent moments of contemporaneity seem impossibly distant to me… unattainable.

The point, of course, is that the racing calendar—one of the most fundamental of organising principles in British national life—has been wilfully disturbed by this skewed vision of the future.

190.8 *Princess Anne [in court]*: I find it hard to stomach that our Royal Family should receive such a savaging in the maws of this rabid Romany that its youngest member, Her Royal Highness the Princess Anne Elizabeth Alice Louise, should be dragged before the court in his vision; an ignominy not suffered by any of her predecessors since Charles I was charged with treason and decapitated to slake the bloodlust of misguided puritans and the maniacs of nascent Socialism. The poet's dogged determination to bring into being both himself and the anarchic future in which he prowls has left its stain on the reputation of a mere toddler like a gaping bite-mark in her innocent young flesh. These terrible hallucinations are passing before my eyes like the tortures in Orwell's Room 101. I cannot tear my gaze away. Its teeth have sunk deep in my imagination and its jaws have locked.

191.1 *Reebok and Joe Bloggs*: 'Reebok' is Afrikaans for *roebuck*, a small African antelope, *Palea capreola*—I assume it is used here in reference to some item of clothing made from the hide of this animal. 'Joe Bloggs' is probably some kind of rhyming slang for *clogs*, the rudimentary wooden soled shoes worn, until recently, by the lower classes in the North of England. Their use today is restricted largely to a small minority of Marxist *saboteurs*. The combination of these two items of clothing doubtless signifies the political antagonism of their owner, and this society in general, towards political traditions of the British Empire.

191.5 *to pop her clogs*: Presumably a crude euphemism for *to die*—a dialectal version of *hang up one's boots* which carries a sentimental glorification of a proletarian symbol.

The situation was insane. I knew it was. & yet I carried on, caught between the devil of Singh's exotic *synacoustis* & the deep blue sea of Hannah's humane realism. Singh would say they coexisted in me like two contrapuntal voices. I was more in thrall to this kind of thinking than was healthy, I suppose: not least because it was something I could access without needing to involve myself in the messy business of real human interaction. I was becoming just like Singh... except I knew exactly what was wrong with me. The suspicion that I'd gained this knowledge only from reading *The Birmingham Quean* was probably what kept me coming back. It was a kind of masochism. I took the novel as a drug — just like the Aristasian encounters — & the profound sense of guilt that remained after my pseudo-transcendental hit was almost the whole point (like drinking for the hangover). Only in these moments of critical disengagement could I bring myself a little closer to the woman I loved... her thoughts if not her body & her life.

It's typical of Singh's skewed idealism that he should recognise this kind of internal conflict & actually attempt to promote it in the reader's mind. It's also typical of his comedy that he should choose to do so in such a surreal way. The object that Twigg's imagination seized upon in order for Singh to reveal his theory a little more explicitly was not a central feature of the poem — an obvious choice would have been the counterfeit narrator, or the drag-queen herself — but something tangential & almost definitively absurd... the flamingo.

In fact, Twigg's obsession with the flamingo — both the bird & the word — might almost be identified with Singh's core thesis. Clearly its queerness as an icon was the important thing. Twigg's period-drag act ironically involved the histrionic rejection of an entire avian family which represented the same gaudy performativity as he did himself. He viewed the bird's name as the result of an abominable form of polyandrous generation & the garish animal itself as emblematic of an anti-essentialism which defied all that he must consider sacrosanct: objective truth, *Linnæan* hierarchy, linguistic origination, *Stammbaum* philosophy, & (by extension) noble heredity, heteronormativity, racial purity & intrinsic value.

If Twigg were a contemporary of Singh's, we might put this down to a popular culture that has cast the flamingo as the queer bird *par excellence*. Think of John Waters' *Pink Flamingos* or the gay tango club in *Police Academy*. The flamingo *accent*, as they call it over there, stalks the homes & gardens of small-town puritan America like the blushes of its repressed sexualities. It's obviously a kitsch gesture of transgression — a flirtation with that which is beyond the pale. & it's rampant: over 20 million plastic lawn flamingos, designed by sculptor Donald Featherstone in 1957 have been sold since their release.

There is also a practice known as 'flocking'. This involves ordering a large number of these things to be placed on someone's front lawn overnight. When they part their curtains in the morning, it's to greet an almighty pink shock. Imagine rugby players putting make-up on the face of a catatonic team-mate. (Now think of Lacan's *mirror-stage*.) The reason for all this is doubtless that the bird is big & pink & *fabulous*. Whichever way you look at it, the flamingo is camp. Those who believe in *intelligent design*, must suspect the *phoenicopter* to be God's big coming out party. At the very least, he's giving us a good flocking.

'A Briti$ poet' is an oxymoron.
   £e Briti$ skill wi£ words is *not* to say
But *still* to speak, as if £e nation swore on
   £e King James Bible £at £e tru€ would stay
Disguised and we would base our rule of law on
   A pledge to keep enlightenment at bay.
All honesty is bani$ed wi£ £e brickbat
Of *de rigueur* inconsequential chit-chat.

---

      *   *   *

After Alexander's party she came to visit me in Oxford. She came alone and uninvited, briskly bearing gifts. This was a pattern that continued every other weekend of the Michaelmas term. She even brought me flowers from time to time—to brighten up my room: not that she was allowed that far into the college. I suppose you would have to say she courted *me. She took great pleasure in the audacity of this. Of course, we would always have a meal with Alexander on the Saturday, and it was to see him that everyone assumed she came to Oxford, but every Sunday we would spend alone. We would go to church together (both of us still went in those days) and then walk along the canal, or take tea at Lyons', or attend an afternoon concert.*

It was not until her final visit of the year—in the first weekend of December—that we broached the subject of our family backgrounds. We had been wandering along the High Street towards the Magdalene Bridge when the wind had picked up and a stinging sleet had driven us to seek out the shelter of the hothouse at the Botanic Gardens. We hurried through the walled garden and made a beeline for that curtain of heat that sustains the desert plants. It made us gasp as we swung open the wrought iron door. We found a bench beneath a huge taupe cactus bristling with thorny chevaux-de-frise *and sat beside one another, trying not to pant too audibly. Despite the relative comfort of the place in such inclement weather, we were the only people there besides a hunched curator who was pacing the perimeter. The succulents cast twitchy shadows beneath the swirling grey weather, as if not entirely convinced of the protective qualities of their thin glass roof. We sat in silence for a while, allowing the fierce heating to dissolve the pricks of cold mottled in our cheeks.*

'You should come to visit over Christmas,' Hermione began, at last, 'there are always hordes of visitors.'

'Where?'

'My parents'. My father's a keen botanist himself. You might actually get on.'

I chuckled.

'He's actually always been very supportive of me. Mummy mostly disapproves. She thinks I'm a tomboy. She blames my father. She's forever quizzing me about my views on 'floppers' (she thinks the name comes from the floppy hair, poor thing) and universal suffrage. She's just testing the water. I can't resist teasing her a little though.'

      *   *   *

& it's not just a matter of camp aesthetics. At the risk of extending the abject blasphemy even further, we should note that if God made the flamingo, he made it genuinely queer. The sexual life of the flamingo is one of the most flexible & varied of all bird's. During the mating season, flamingos form the largest flocks on Earth: over 1 million Phoeniconaias minor return each year to form a huge nesting 'city' (with roughly the same population as Birmingham) at Lake Natron on the Kenya-Tanzania border. Within this metropolis every possible permutation of sexual/parental partnerships can be found: same & mixed sex relationships of pairs & groups of birds. It is true that the mixed-sex couple is by far the most common. But it's also true that the percentage of same-sex couples is roughly the same as that found in liberal human societies (about 8%), & that there are certain practical advantages to same-sex & multiple partner relationships (in terms of territorial control & nest protection) which would tend to support the theory that these sexual practices result from natural selection. They would certainly be very queer if they were the product of an intelligent design at the hands of a God who only saw fit to condone traditional marriage.

It's interesting to speculate what might have been the outcome in America if the film La Marche de l'Empereur had been, instead, La Marche du Flammant Rose. The hatchlings of the Lesser Flamingo do in fact walk large distances across the forbidding salt flats of the Rift Valley before they learn to fly. It's an epic mince across the wilderness; it would make equally compelling cinema. Perhaps, instead of Southern Baptist churches & Bible classes on group bookings, we might have seen Gay Pride out with the Darwinists.

So much for the 'signified'. The queerness of the signifier was equally important to Twigg's discomfort. Here was where the obvious debt to post-structuralism owed by queer theory & by Singh himself became most clear. The etymological polyvalence of flamingo suggested to Twigg that the word came from an insupportably queer (tetraparental) linguistic family. His inability to disambiguate the word's 'roots' expanded in his mind into a fundamental crisis of his philosophical approach. This extrapolation of an entire epistemological breakdown from a miniature linguistic problematic (Deleuze & Guattari's heterogenesis) is post-structuralism's characteristic manoeuvre. Implicated heavily was one of the most important post-structuralist essays in English literary criticism: Derek Attridge's 'The Romance of Etymology'. Twigg's idea of preceding all etymologies with a question-mark came directly from this source. It was a typically Singhian comic touch that this idea should be modified so that the question-mark to be used was the upside-down one that introduces interrogatives in Spanish & that this arbitrary symbol should be called the flamingo: a word which had itself become an icon of the collapse of etymology into fiction that the symbol would be employed to demonstrate.

Obviously, Twigg could not have been consciously aware of either the theory or the cultural iconography involved. The Course in General Linguistics had no kind of currency in British Universities at the time; Roman Jakobson was at Harvard but largely unknown at Oxbridge; & Barthes' 1953 Le Degré Zero de L'Ecriture was much more to do with Sartre than Saussure. So much for structuralism. Even the association of the colour pink with homosexuality — though innovated by the Nazis in history's most acute example of evil done in the name of maintaining an ideology of rigid categories — did not reach popular currency until the 1960s.

We can't address £e terminally ill
    Because we know our words can't make £em well.
It's like £e mention of £e future will
    Upset some infinitely fragile spell—
£e lies £at keep a man alive; we'd kill
    Our family wi£ £e tru€ and go to hell
To spend eternity dunked in a tar-pit.
Instead, we sweep it all under £e carpet.

193.7-8 *tar-pit... carpet*: A terrible couplet, possibly the weakest in the piece. It could never give me succour to denounce it though; the more debased and tasteless this poem gets, the more debased and tasteless the world it comes from seems to be, and the more afraid it makes me that I might in some way contribute to the inception of this *fātum*.

*   *   *

'Daddy wants me to take up the family business. He's an art-dealer: exotic antiques mostly... import, export kind of thing. Been teaching me for years. I know simply everything there is to know about Chinese Dynastic pottery. You wouldn't think it to look at me, I know. But then you can shoot. I'd sooner have expected you to tango.'

It was very hot and dry. I fidgeted and smiled weakly at her apt comparison.

'Mummy doesn't like the idea at all. A young lady trading on the foreign market: it's decidedly outré. Poppycock of course, but you've got to feel for her. She doesn't really have a say. She thinks it's all the fault of Valentino.'

'*My* mother wanted me to take up economics.'

'Good grief!'

'I know...' I didn't though. How I'd been tricked into revealing the details of the quintessential embarrassment that was my family background, I couldn't work out... 'I even began to study Political Economy.'

'You wouldn't like to tango, would you? Perhaps the keeper has a gramophone'

'Seriously. I detested it. It wasn't so much the subject itself as the reason I was doing it. You see, it was my brother's subject. He'd been there a bit less than year when he enlisted. Mother desperately wanted me to finish what he'd started: to make it seem as if he'd not been totally extinguished. It seemed like the whole point of my existence.'

'You poor thing...' She took my hand between her suede gloves and squeezed. How she could keep them on in this stifling aridity I didn't know. The nap of them was irritating, but it was mitigated by the rare thrill of physical contact. She wanted to encourage me to carry on. I had to oblige.

'Eugene was always more robust than me. He was a bully to be honest. He must have been disgusted to be cursed with such a bookish little brother. I confess, I was really quite gratified at first when we got the news that he'd been killed in action. I could just imagine some German big brother in a rage doing to him what he'd routinely done to me when we were younger. I didn't really understand war. I felt guilty about that. It was probably the reason I tried so hard to please my mother afterwards.'

*   *   *

Twigg could certainly never have known about the combination of these two areas (post-structuralist theory & non-normative sexuality) into a discipline called *queer theory*. His classical education nevertheless allowed him to explore the *queerness* of the flamingo in terms of its role in Aristophanes' *The Birds*. This play — the piece that Erich Segal argued (in anti-Oedipal terms very similar to those parroted by Twigg) was the last true 'comedy' — is as camp as anything the twentieth century turned out. Twigg identified it as the source of the scholarly folk-etymology of the word *flamingo* (from Latin *flamma*... hence the 'flamebird') & put the error down to a Latin mistake of identifying the *phoenikopteros* (the ithyphallic leader of the Aristophanic chorus) with both the pink long-legged bird & the mythical *phoenix*. The fact that Linneaus had given the flamingo 'family' status & perpetuated the Roman error by placing it under the heading 'Phoenicopter', put Twigg's whole taxonomy of knowledge at risk from the debilitating effects of this problematic bird.

But for Twigg the flamingo wasn't just a bit *queer*, it was more than that: it was the *phoney phoenix*. The *phoney phonics* that had led to this mistake were as much the dissembling substance of the flamingo as were its garish feathers. The reason he could argue such a fleeting reference to have been a thematic crux of *The Birmingham Quean* was that the 'phoenix' — within the covert alchemical symbolism he believed to have been imported from Shakespeare's 'The Phoenix & the Turtle' — referred to the final product of successful transmogrification: not just gold, but also the fusion of the *king* & *queen*, the embodiment of the resurrected Christ, & the state of internal perfection concomitant with the last stage of the esoteric process. A malign & absurd travesty of such a thing was designed to achieve the opposite. Its *phoney phoenicity* was even worse to his way of thinking than a counterfeit sovereign or a multiracial transgendered homosexual.

Most importantly, we were probably intended to spot in Twigg's obsession with the false, pink *flamebird* the first flickers of the 'fire' that killed him. This link became increasingly apparent to me as the nights drew in & my reading neared the end of Twigg's weird annotations. I'd usually rest my eyes for a while in the late afternoon by peering through the filthy basement window at a sunset smouldering above the West End & ponder the question of Twigg's fire. It was always possible that Singh had intended the reader simply to accept the premise that somebody could write a memoir whilst spontaneously combusting. More likely, though, was the interpretation suggested by this link between the flames & the flamingo. The fire was probably easier to accept as a metaphor for some kind of fever (& accompanying delirium). It was *pyretic* rather than literally *pyrotechnic*. I often felt the same way. It was probably the cold & damp that made me shiver despite a warm cup of tea, but I couldn't be so sure. Presumably Singh would have wanted us to put this down to a psychosomatic effect. The result of his *queering* of the central tenets of *Stammbaum* philosophy (with the 'germ' of the flamingo) is that Twigg 'comes over queer'. The effect is all the more profound for impacting on the truth-conditionality of his writing, transforming his style into a deliriously metaphorical fiction. In this way, he comes to feel the whole thing is his responsibility; that it (the *fire*) is inside him... that it's billowing out of him like the breath of a dragon... that it's *catching*.

  £is 'nation' is our geriatric mo£er.
   $e keeps reminding us $e's going to die.
  And no-one has £e streng€ of will to smo£er
   Her life £e way $e wants, or even try
  To talk about £e €ing. We choose ano£er
   (Less awkward) subject and protract £e lie.
  We blow £e surface of our tea and smile
  And pass £e time, and suffer in denial.

---

   *   *   *

'Mummy's little soldier.'

'I suppose so. My father was a soldier too. He certainly didn't want that for me though: his first son had lost his life in France and he'd lost all his joy for it at the Battle of Spion Kop. He was particularly keen I should go to Oxford. It was his Alma Mater. He used to conspire with me, filling my head with dreams of intellectual refinement as an escape from the cut and thrust of gentlemanly business that Mother wanted for me. She needed me to regain the life my brother lost. Father needed me to do the same for him. Maybe I really did expect the dreaming spires he'd told me about. But when I got to Oxford I found more of the same. It was a place still living in the shadow of the war. It was all about living up to the manly virtues of the martyrs: quite impossible, and everybody knew it.'

'They might do as well to live up to the womanly virtues of those left behind.'

'Yes, I suppose they might... I wasn't at all bad at economics, but I soon stopped studying it. I would read anything I could get my hands on, as long as it had nothing to do with public finances. That was when I discovered Prufrock... T. S. Eliot?'

'Ah, yes... you plunged into the heady world of poetry and haven't surfaced since.'

'I have heard the mermaids singing, each to each.'

'Have you indeed. I heard Ivor Novello do "My Dearest Dear" at the Dorchester... I requested it.'

I laughed. She squeezed my knuckles with her bottom hand. I felt a surge of desire for kinship with this confident young woman. Her comment was the perfect example of an easy intelligence that I, for all my intellectual rigour, could not aspire to. It concealed real ignorance, but it did so in an ironic, sympathetic way. The feigned stupidity of her response had pricked both of our (quite different) pomposities whilst expressing a deep feeling for my awkward revelations and my apprehension in this tricky situation.

'Romantic' one would have to call it. It was undeniable that I wanted more of this same feeling: this unprecedented self-assurance I seemed capable of borrowing from Hermione whenever we were in each other's company. And there was more, of course. I wanted to slip my hand out from between her gloves and push it round over her hip to rest in the soft curve of her waistline. Her body seemed almost to have been designed to cradle mine.

   *   *   *

This is always the effect of fiction. The pleasure of it comes from feeling the events, the characters, the settings, even the words themselves spontaneously occurring inside you. It's not like someone's speaking to you: more that your internal voices are dramatising it themselves. The effect catches; it spreads. The same thing's true for writer & for reader. The cliché of 'firing the imagination' is a cliché because it's so apt. I'd learned from the *Zomby Project* that for Singh, this thing he wanted to spread like wildfire wasn't simply 'pleasure' (in its vaguest sense) but something more devastating: something that would irresistibly & irreversibly bring down the kind of individual, positivist ideology that Twigg ironically expounded.

It was ludicrously ambitious. The terminology he'd created to describe these ideas was particularly pompous. His style he liked to call *synacoustis* (like *synopsis* 'seeing together' but transformed into the auditory/musical sense so that it meant something almost diametrically opposed to the common usage: 'concise summary'). But his favourite name for the desired psycho-political transformation was *dividualist ethonomics*. This was pointedly the antithesis of *individualist economics*: a way of thinking that replaced economy with ethics, competition with counterpoint, 'the antagonistic transaction' with 'cooperative interaction', Game Theory with Music Theory.

I was all too well aware it was a utopian fantasy, but if my own growing yearning for the same idealistic victory of plural process over singular product was anything to go by, there was definitely something worth salvaging in Singh's refusal to abandon both socialist idealism & a desperately unfashionable postmodernist approach. There was something undeniably attractive about the tall tale that these twentieth century theories had simply been the final stepping stones towards the fictional revolution that would be the next stage in the Enlightenment: something they seemed (romantically) to have abjured. If the effects of Singh's fiction didn't have a hope in hell of bringing a grand vision like *dividual ethonomics* to the wider world, at least *within* his fiction we could fantasise a situation in which such disparate philosophers as Deleuze, Habermas & Roy Baskhar were reconciled. More than that: we could fantasise a change in our political consciousness at a less pretentious level that might communalise our imaginations, histories & beliefs & make capitalism seem as much of an embarrassing anachronism as communism had become since the toppling of the Berlin Wall.

I wallowed in the escapist self-indulgence of it all. Congratulating myself at my ability to recognise the parodies & pick the ironies: not all of them, of course, but just enough to give that smug sense of superiority & justify my withdrawal from a society whose most crucial flaw was an inability to appreciate what Singh had revealed... not just its flaws, but its possibilities. If anybody could've seen me in those last moments — in a striped grandad shirt; a short, flecked sleeveless sweater; turned-up flannel trousers with button braces & an old pair of pin-hole brogues — pouring over a roll of manila parcel-paper, they could've been forgiven for thinking I'd turned into R. H. Twigg myself.

I was ripe for a fall. When it came, it came as a relief. Just like my bruising brush with homophobic violence outside the Pussy Club, it hurt... & badly... but it woke me up.

A poet can become an 'anti-Brit',
> However. Anyone can speak £eir mind
About £is 'nation' and resign from it.
> I've spoken mine, and I've become resigned:
I can't keep up £e lie £at I'm £e grit
> £e oyster turns to pearl. I'll have to find
Asylum in some place across £e sea
And pray £ey pardon my apostasy.)

195.7-8 *Asylum... apostasy*: To speak in such religious terms about exiling oneself from one's nation is ungratefully to thumb one's nose at the antidisetablishmentarianism which has cemented the British Constitution since the Restoration.

*   *   *

I gently pried my hand loose and retracted it to grip the hem of my own pullover. I was very hot by now. I considered taking the thing off, but the usual inner voices of decorum intervened. It is impossible to pull a woollen garment over one's head in such circumstances without appearing to have been dragged backwards through the local flora. I let it go again and folded my arms. As I did, Hermione leaned quickly forward and touched her nose (pink and warm from the rapid change in climate) against mine. She held that position for a second. I felt her breath mingle with my own. The rhythm of both accelerated a little as her smile faded. Gradually, she tilted her head and slid the very tip of the nose around the curve of my nostril until our lips touched almost imperceptibly. I tried to untangle my arms (suddenly leaden with desire) in order to emulate the famous Rodin sculpture. She pushed her breast against my left elbow and held the other in place with her right hand, pressing me back into the recess of the cactus-bed that accommodated the wrought-iron bench. And in that awkward pose, sprawling on the polished slats, we kissed.

Is it merely hindsight?... perhaps I had absorbed the fanciful clichés that abound in the kind of romance-fiction for which I had unconcealed contempt despite my secret reliance on it for any information about how this kind of thing was done... but I am sure that at that moment—during that first kiss—I understood almost by osmosis the entire pattern of our ensuing relationship. By some obscure means—in the delicious, melting action of our lips—I knew we would be married and I knew that it would never last. Within the very vibrant promise of love was the understanding of its illusory nature. Ours was a marriage doomed to fail because of the artificial premises upon which (from this moment onwards) it would necessarily be based.

In her lips I tasted all her future disappointments and adulteries. I knew that my acquiescence to her way of life would come ultimately to disgust her as much as it now filled her with the kind of pleasure one can only get from discovering a fillip to one's own supposed trajectory of development. As she kissed me, I became physically aware (as if this kind of prescience can be carried by the blood) of an inevitable future in which she would do the same with other men: at first merely as a means of inciting that primal (Lawrencian) manliness which she continued to believe existed in me; later merely out of exasperation at its apparent absence; eventually in order to replace it.

*   *   *

I'd been out to the shops. I still did this occasionally. I'd considered ordering my shopping on the net, but it would've been even more disturbing, I'd decided, to have to deal with a delivery man knocking on my door with a crate full of the sorry objects that tended to provide my sustenance these days — pork luncheon-meat, Bird's custard, tinned peas, crab paste, suet pudding — than to line them up on the supermarket conveyor-belt.

I got back home just as the plastic bag-handle had mutated my fingers into the thick, blue-black digits of a gorilla. Before I'd even heard the closedoor shut behind me, I noticed my own front door was dented & wide-open. The frame was split. A chunk was still attached to the mortise bolt, the pale flesh of the timber exposed beneath its skin of black gloss. A surge of adrenaline hit me like a shot of the cheap whisky I'd just bought. I dropped the bag in my left hand, & let the keys slip out of my right as I stumbled into the flat. The thought never occurred to me there might be someone inside: someone dangerous. I was only interested in one thing.

The place was no more untidy than usual. It smelled of stale cigarettes... not like they'd been smoking in the flat, but like they'd just put their fags out before they did the job. They couldn't have been gone long. There were various books & bits of clothing on the floor, but that was nothing new. My pulse tapped at my temples as I made for the table by the window, half tripping over a brown sofa cushion as I went. Serene as ever on the laminate surface, like some kind of *Lotus Sutra* — two tea-stained mugs holding its rolled ends apart — sat *The Birmingham Quean*. I slumped into my chair & breathed a shaky sigh.

After propping up my aching eyebrows for a minute or two, I took stock of what was missing. The only thing that appeared to have been taken was the only thing of real value in the flat. They'd even left the stereo — I suppose it did look like a control-panel from *Blake's Seven* — & my equally archaic record collection. All they'd had the time or the inclination to make off with was the computer & my rucksack to carry it in. The fact that my first thought had not been to check on this crucial tool — the thing, after all, that contained the vast majority of my own research — was very telling indeed. Instead, I'd made a bee-line for Singh's obsessional manuscript like a junky scrabbling for his stash... a miser for his gold.

I leaned against my filing cabinet & gulped whisky from the bottle. I had to face it: they'd taken my entire PhD. The files were backed up, of course. But I'd left the CD inside the burner next to the laptop & that'd gone as well. I began to rifle the drawers, like a burglar myself. Besides the original proposal, & a sketchy draft of the first chapter, the only hard-copy I had to show for two years of research was that paper on *King Lear* I'd given at the Shakespeare Institute. That was it. I knelt amongst the debris & read it through. Rather than in my burgled flat, I imagined myself back at that beeswaxed lecture theatre, searching the faces of the conference for positive reactions. Then I tried to picture Hannah there. If anything could remind me of her image, it was this. But nothing happened. It was disturbing. How could I be in love with a woman whose face I couldn't picture amongst thirty or so others that seemed very clear?... Then it dawned on me. This was no Proustian dilemma. The reason I couldn't place Hannah at that lecture theatre was that she was never there.

"€ings went all quiet at £e bar until
  £e bloke had left—£ere's no€ing £ey could say
£at wasn't sympa£etic overkill,
  But also wouldn't tend to underplay
£e gravity of it; £ey knew £e drill—
  You swill your beer, wait till he's away,
And £en you swallow down profundities
Wi£ lager dregs and ask whose round it is.

196.3-4 *overkill... underplay*: The first half of this pair is American military jargon of the nuclear age. It refers in statistical terms to the excessive use of 'firepower' to kill the enemy when methods of mass-incapacitation might be more effective (though no more humane). Its modification by the word 'sympathetic', in the gratuitously morbid context, is crass irony of the lowest order. *Underplay* is being used in metaphoric extension to mean 'provide scant acknowledgement of'. Literally, it means to bid deliberately low in Bridge or Whist in order to achieve the 'contract' by losing tricks. By now I feel it an unnecessary risk of critical explication to delineate the dire consequences possibly emergent from the combination of these things.

196.8 *lager*: A pale, cold and rather tasteless German style of (bottom-fermented) beer of which an *echt* version is popular in America (see 2.2 *lager lads*). It is presently only rarely drunk in England. Its status as the standard beverage of these people is, I think, yet another indication of the encroaching Americanisation of this future society and the genocidal intent of this poet to manifest a vision of Britain in which our unique culture and constitution (and traditional ale) is being systematically eradicated.

*   *   *

It was intoxicating. It seems strange that such negative reflections could accompany my ardour without undermining it. But that was how it was. Life is similarly paradoxical. In every cell of every living thing the knowledge of its own inevitable demise is the source of its determination to survive. The principle of life is the defiance of its own intractability. It burns all the brighter for knowing it is on fire. In the greenhouse of the University Botanic Gardens, the laboratory of life, Hermione offered me love like juice dripping from a cactus in a desert. I drank it in and felt the stiff thorn sink into my flesh.

*   *   *

This was something only the bottle could understand. I hit it hard, short gulps of air rising towards the bottom of the upturned cylinder like exultant demonstrations of my ability to down such vile stuff. The fire kindled in me like it had in R. H. Twigg. But the heat of whisky doesn't spread to your extremities. It drains away from arms & legs & concentrates in your throat & chest. The glaze over my eyes set rigid: fired in the alcoholic oven...

Once sufficiently drunk, I rang the landlord & demanded that his voicemail send me someone out to fix the door. I wouldn't be in, I drawled, just put the old lock on... or post the new key through the door... no that wouldn't work at all... whatever. I threw some clothes & things into an old carpet-bag, just wide enough to fit the parcel roll inside — I already missed the rucksack more than the pc — & dragged it out into the close.

A pool of vinegar had formed around where a broken jar of beetroot in the plastic carrier was leaking its bloody contents at the foot of the banister. I strode over the dark puddle, not wanting to look like I'd just given someone a kicking. I was too pissed-off to see the irony of this. It wasn't so much the burglars that'd got to me — they'd done me a favour in a way — it was Hannah. I couldn't really justify it. Why should she have to listen to me banging on about early modern comic tragedy? She'd never actually lied about having been there after all. For some egotistical reason, though, I'd got the impression that it was the keen insight & sheer wit of my conference paper that had convinced her to entrust *The Zomby Project* to me. However unintentionally it had happened, I still felt betrayed.

Most of all, though, I was baffled. Why remember only now that she was never there? More to the point, if she'd not heard my paper, on what possible grounds could she have chosen me to tackle her ex-boyfriend's study? I suppose she could've liked the abstract I submitted, & made her judgement on the basis of three hundred words. But that was hardly likely: all the less so because the abstracts weren't published in the programme at all; her ruse of pretending to be one of the organisers had been for the benefit of that old conference cruiser, hadn't it? The whole thing was decidedly suspect. What I really wanted, obviously, was to believe she'd fancied me... just looked across the conservatory & thought, 'He looks nice. He'll do.' It couldn't have been that, though...

In any case, it was clear I needed to sort things out with her. I'd tried to convince myself it wasn't Hannah but *The Birmingham Quean* I was interested in. Even the distinction held no water. Over the past couple of months I'd analysed the thing with the implicit intention of justifying it to her: demonstrating just how obvious it was that Singh had written it. I was constructing arguments as I read, rehearsing what I'd say in its defence... at the very least to give it a balanced critical hearing... & the first & last person I imagined reading anything I wrote, or listening to my arguments, was Hannah. It wasn't just Aristasia that was haunted by her memory; it was everything... even a damp tenement she'd never seen.

I slammed the useless door behind me with a drunken flourish. She was my muse, I decided: now there was something I could see the irony in. 'Hail to the muse, etc." I side-footed the carpetbag into the street & cackled darkly, a spray of sixty proof saliva blending the malty comedy of everything with the November mist.

Section 2(b)

Although each drop of rain be sibilant, a sibyl, be syllable of history,
Give me my Sun, shameless and gross and full of cruel humours.

(D. J. Enright 'An Egyptian in Birmingham')
[from: Clifford Dyment, Roy Fuller and Montagu Slater ed.s,
  New Poems 1952, London, Michael Joseph 1952]

> Britannia breezed past Sloggy as he bought
>   £e drinks. $e strolled into £e Ladies', checked
> Her wig, £en $ivered quickly as $e caught
>   A glimpse of some€ing $e did *not* expect:
> A man behind her in £e mirror—$ort
>   And €in. $e brea£ed, £en tutted for effect
> Before $e turned round, weary and disgruntled,
>   To face £e ineluctable full-frontal.

197.5 *a man behind her in the mirror*. No doubt this is Bosvil writing himself into his own poem. Among the gypsies there is little difference between a psychic king and a vagrant exhibitionist. As I read the poem, I catch glimpses of its grim creator in the corner of my field of vision, (Josiah Mason) pen in hand, as if reflected in the yellowing surface of the paper like this old tramp with his filthy phallus. The image grows stronger with time. Several nights ago I thought I saw his mouth, its graveyard of mossy teeth upside down, leering at me through the window of my study as if he were hanging from the gutter like a Burmese fruitbat.

It is only a matter of time before he makes his real, fateful reappearance. There is a crumb of comfort to be gained, however. I am certain that my image of him, brandishing a writing implement, is false. It seems of little doubt that a man like Bosvil, despite his surprising erudition, would have been illiterate. In fact, it is quite likely that a keystone of his revolutionary magic is an assault on literacy itself. This poem might almost have been specifically designed to murder our ability to read. If so, he would obviously need some form of amanuensis to take his diabolical dictation.

One must feel some sympathy for this poor, enchanted soul, forced to perform as the scribe of an incantation attacking the act of writing itself. My previous inclination was to think he must have been a rough contemporary of my own: some youth who had encountered the old gypsy king in the last years of his life and been enthralled by the gothic delicacy of his mysticism. I suppose I imagined myself into the role: a common error arising from the empathetic instincts of the literary critic. It seems increasingly obvious, however, that nobody from that era could possibly have put the poem into the physical format in which it now appears. The method of printing is one I have not encountered before. It certainly could not have been available thirty years ago and I am equally certain it is not available today. The few oblique annotations and emendations included in the scribe's own hand are written with a modern 'ballpoint' pen. These features are the probable result of my initial belief that the poem was a work of contemporary 'Science Fiction'. The same features now insist on a much *weird*er explanation: Bosvil's amanuensis is a writer from the future he depicts.

In order to accept this unavoidable conclusion, I suppose we must surrender to the view that what Bosvil shows us really is the future. For this document to have returned to us under Bosvil's mysterious auspices from some time early in the third millennium, it must have had somewhere ('some*time*') non-fantastic to come from. Einstein, I believe, suggests that futures are plural. That is to say that there are multiple possible futures that can be travelled to, like a variety of destinations on the railway, depending on what metaphoric trains we catch. If this were true, then the existence of this manuscript need not intimate a certain doom. Rather, it would be like advertising for a particular destination (one of unparalleled anarchic decadence) provided by that place's local council, extolling its virtues as a place to visit or invest in. *The Birmingham Quean* might therefore be a tract of beguiling rhetoric designed to convince the reader to 'invest' in a future period of which he is the spiritual founder. The people who inhabit such a 'place in time' are merely the shadows of people whose wills have been submerged entirely in Bosvil's maelstrom.

I should focus my pity on one of these in particular: this suffering young man, compelled to note down Bosvil's prophesy in order that the malign potentate might send a multi-headed *Scylla* back in time to drive the people of the past towards his gaping, decadent *Charybdis*. After he has (or *had*) performed this vital service, his removal from the picture seems inevitable. He is, after all, anathema in Bosvil's world. Perhaps some trace of him does still exist. The young artist watched by Britannia in reflection (just as now) 'sketching in a notebook' and 'pulling at a tuft of hair like he was milking it' in the deleted stanzas 86-90 returns to one's memory as a forlorn embodiment of the futility of his resistance to his own instigating role in Bosvil's vision…

I can almost picture you now, my friend. The barrier of time between us is like a one-way mirror—you even more the prisoner than I myself for being forced to look on as the 'ineluctable' fruits of your forced labour torture me, unable to express your sympathy and your regrets. There is something I can do though: a man who knows the mirror before him is transparent on the other side can always show his feelings to those watching… even without hope of seeing anything but a grotesquely lonely reflection of his own grimaces as he performs them.

197.8 *full-frontal*: A 'frontal' (as a noun) is something worn as ornament or armour on the forehead; or else it is the decorated covering of an altar or tomb. Perhaps it is by combination of these senses that it is used here. Britannia wants the man to cover himself up completely—hence 'full'—so completely in fact that he becomes like a dead body, the head of which is covered by the mortician's drape. Her gesture is therefore one of mortal threat: one which, on reflection, extends beyond the tramp to the reader.

I know this poem will be the death of both of us, of course, but I cannot tear my eyes away from it for fear that standing behind me is the ghost of Bosvil… just as he must have stood behind you, intoning his awful dictation. I am sure my reading will prove to be as much an intrinsic part of his reanimation as your writing ever was, my friend. This a shame that we can share. It is a terrifying paradox that only by working on this poem, only by forcing my twitching eyelids not to close over my stinging eyes or to glance away from these black and white markings, can I avoid the figure of the poet coming into existence in my gaze. The patterns of the text stay with me as if branded on my retinæ like the white flare of burning magnesium; if I close my eyes or look away from the effulgent octaves, they coalesce like Blake's arachnids scuttling into some primeval orgy to create the photographic image of our mutual Nemesis.

He seemed a pretty geriatric geezer.
    Knocking on for seventy, $e'd say;
He couldn't have £e wherewi£al to please a
    Big girl like her. His hands began to stray.
£e need to giggle was about to seize her
    When he took it out and took her brea€ away.
$e'd been expecting some€ing small and neat,
And out came half a pound of sausage meat.

198.1 *geriatric geezer*: *Geriatric* is a bit of modish medical jargon which, by polar analogy with *pædiatric*, refers to the treatment of the aged. Its misapplication in this instance (basically as a synonym for old) blends neatly with the pretension inherent in the idea of the 'guiser' (see 172.7 *geezer…* and *passim*).

    Geras is 'old age' in Greek, and it is from here that Eliot's 'Gerontion' derives: the 'thoughts of a dry brain in a dry season'; his 'house is a decayed house', by which we understand his entire spiritual, corporeal (even *nation-*) state to be suffering a creeping dereliction. This is how I have come to feel in the face of Bosvil's future. The *lichen* that used to occupy only a small patch on the back of my left thigh has spread. It is like a Bosvilian contagion: his *vagabond flesh* transferring itself to me via these verbal *carriers*. It is a gruesome pastiche of the encroachment of mortality itself.

    The eczema spread across his perinæum
    Like dry-rot in a crypt or a museum.

Perhaps you too are an old man, my friend. I have been imagining you as an ingenu, entrapped by Bosvil's abominable *sagesse*, but the role you have performed is an anachronistic one. It seems equally likely that you might be an elderly relic of a slightly better time, pressed into one last service by the man who would bring about the end of everything you stand for. If it is any comfort, you have my sympathy.

198.2 *Knocking on…*: A nine-syllable line that maintains an awkward *enjambment* despite the grammatical end-stop of the first. *Knocking on for seventy* could connote the metaphor 'having a cricket score in the high sixties'. A similar analogy might see the transgression called a 'knock-on' in Rugby Football used as reflexive comment on the prosody: the previous line *knocking-on* into the next. I think you would agree that Bosvil has every reason to denigrate our national sports.

198.5-6 More prosodic *knock-ons* in these lines. It adds to the lurid tableau by interpolating the rhythms of fumbling anticipation. Bosvil is tripping over himself to get his vagabond member out. I must ask, how was he when he spoke these kinds of things to you? Would he become excited? Would he enact the scenes and do the voices? I do not envy you the spectacle at all.

There'd been a sharp frost in The Midlands that November. The canals were lidded with a thick layer of solidity. As the Glasgow train inched its way through rosy-cheeked Smethwick brickwork, no faster than if it had been pulled along the towpaths by a bargehorse, my fellow passengers were treated to the sight of woolly hatted ladies strolling their dogs on the frozen meanders of the old Main Line, kids polishing skid tracks in its orphaned oxbow lakes. The tops of grass & reeds formed goosebumps in the surface, casting hairline shadows in the sunset. No-one worried that the ice might crack.

In Moseley the effect was much more camp. By now the trees along the Wake Green Road were half unclothed. Their scantily clad branches did the Broadway shimmer in the pink of recently lit streetlamps. Around the bases of their trunks discarded leaves had frozen into sequins. Every car mirror had a Judy Garland underwing of frosted gossamer. It was hard to tell if the pain in my head was a hangover or just part of the meteorological scenery. It was equally hard to tell if the weather was taking the piss with such obvious pathetic fallacies.

Nevertheless, standing on Hannah's doorstep, I felt that I too was covered in a layer of frost: the surfaces of my eyeballs crazed with cold opacity, the tips of my hair glazed white. The warm air from her hallway thawed me as the door swung open. She radiated warmth herself. She had that comforting, bakery & blanket smell of a young mother.

"Come in, Sam, I've got something to show you." She led me straight to Amrit's study.

"You got my message, then? I was worried you... you know."

"It's fine, I'm over all that now. Here, look."

Where drab paintwork had once matched the tea-stained rug & heavy velvet curtains that had made both Singh's jumble of paperwork & the untended garden beyond seem like a Beckett stage-set, now sunny yellow wallpaper was banded around at crawling height with an animal alphabet border. The window was covered with a venetian blind onto which Hannah had painted (quite well, in fact, so that it appeared when shut) a biscuit tin landscape with a rainbow on the distant rolling hills. There were plastic toys in primary colours, tilting teddy bears, an upright wooden cot. Only the bare lightbulb hanging from a wire in the middle of the room seemed to carry any memory of the room's previous function in its sooty innards.

"It's very nice, Hannah, you've done a great job. Where's the littlun now?"

"He's at his grandad's. I think they're learning to play the xylophone."

"So you... what did you do with the stuff."

"Well if you'd been here a couple of weeks ago, you'd have seen."

"A couple of weeks ago?"

"Remember, remember..."

"Oh... the Fifth of November. So you made a Guy out of them."

"Well, a bonfire anyway. We had some friends round. It was fun. Would you like a cuppa?"

$e hadn't quite prepared herself to see
   A penis as magnificent as £at.
$e gaped as it ascended, longingly,
   And popped its head out like a meerkat
And winched itself towards its apogee:
   An old man's old man standing proudly at
An angle to impress Pythagoras;
Old sod was blatantly Viagorous:

199.4 *meerkat*: Dutch for 'monkey'. Literally 'sea-cat', but this near oxymoron comes via folk-etymology of the Indo-European root (Sanskrit *markata* 'ape'). *Mercat* is a cognate form. The relative lexical impoverishment of the Boers led them to apply it as a vague catch-all term to various Southern African mammals, like ground squirrels and the zorilla. The English borrowing is used only in reference to *Suricata suricatta*: a species related to the mongoose that forms complex and violent matriarchal societies, and has an exaggeratedly erect posture which would explain its use in the context.

Traditionally the monkey is the mimic of humanity (alternately ludicrous and cunning). Hence the verb 'to ape'. This idea is the remnant of a prescient fear, encoded in language, of Darwin's most controversial and disruptive argument—that man 'descended from the apes'. The English *monkey* is co-radicate with *manikin* (*mannequin*), 'diminutive or artificial man', 'homunculus'. No doubt the association of the monkey (and its African mammalian analogues) with racially inflected lechery derives from this uncanny genetic attachment (*Othello* is particularly taken with the metaphor, see III.iii.408 and IV.i.126). The more prosaic explanation—the likening of the monkey's tail to the penis—serves at least to touch upon the savage threat emerging from the prepuce of Bosvil's vile metaphor.

The Gypsies are, as usual, implicated. The word *monkey* was probably brought to these shores from Holland or Germany in the C16th by traveller-showmen who would perform *Reynard the Fox*, in which the mischievous son of Martin the Ape is called *Moneke*. Bosvil's phallic *marotte* has more to it than phallic mischief, though. The subterranean associations of these two Germanic words allow him to bring into an abominable (sexual) relation the idea of the *mercat* or *monkey* as farcical penile metaphor, with the economic idea of the *mercantile* and *monetary*. The narratee of the piece, remember, is called *Mercat*or. It is the transaction of a piece of counterfeit *mon(k)ey*... *money* is the *key*... and what is the name of the pub at which the Russian 'bouncer', Perry Striker is a doorman? I suppose I need not ask you such obvious questions...

199.5 *apogee*: 'Away from the earth'—used by astronomers to mean the point at which the moon (or, in Ptolemy, the sun) is furthest from the Earth. It is when the moon is both at this point and *new* that necromancers of Bosvil's ilk (or of the ilk he needs to bring him back to life) perform the darkest of their ceremonies. No doubt this kind of exhibitionism is par for the course amidst such ritual debauchery.

199.7 *angle to impress Pythagoras*: The word *impress* is as crucial here as in any of its other instances throughout the poem (see 10.4 *by dint (of)*, 52.4, 70.8, 100.3. 134.4 *impression* et hoc genus omne). The combination of the verb encapsulating the action of striking a coin with a play on 'Empress' is key to the poem's central image of the counterfeit queen. The rest of the phrase suggests the *gnomon*: that Pythagorean triangle that sits at the centre of a sundial's ellipse and acts as the stable point of reference for the accurate measurement of space and time. The *gnomon* is the totemic Joycean metaphor of all centripetal thinking. The human intellect itself is as the *gnomon* to the universe it seeks to understand. Bosvil's cosmically debilitating image of its replacement with a vagrant's phallus, conceived in terms (see prec.) that likens the organ to the poem's own *gnomon*: the counterfeit of the stable unit of exchange and of man himself, is calculated to have a devastating effect.

199.8 *Viagorous*: Another elongation, via a ghastly diæresis of a diphthong, of the adjective 'vigorous.'

* * *

Hermione and I were married that August. After our first kiss in the hothouse, it had taken me several months to pluck up enough courage to drop a proposal into the conversation as though it had required no courage whatsoever, but the period between this triumph of feigned sang froid *in a railway carriage and the 'happy event' itself was less than seven weeks. Despite Hermione's elopement fantasy, the organisational whirlwind had more to do with an eager efficiency she shared with her father than any clandestine rush. My ruthless fiancée soon discovered that it would be all the more irritating for her mother, and all the more gratifying for her act of wilful 'modernity', if* simply everybody *were present to witness the preposterous union and to practise that quiet, smiling vehemence at which the English upper classes remain peerless.*

The whole thing passed off perfectly acceptably. There was, thank God, little more than the usual perfunctory interactions between the two families. The only hiccup was a risibly glowing recommendation given of me by Alexander in his best-man *speech. As he went to unprecedented lengths to flatter my 'emotional acuity' and 'outgoing kindness', even my own family seemed to be suppressing hilarity. The whole thing might well have descended into total farce if it had not been for a shocking and poignant confession at the conclusion that he was planning to take up Theology in the new term in order that the pleasure he had gleaned from 'bringing these two wonderful people together' might be extended into an official function like the one performed with such dignity that day by Reverend Callshaw. The titters gave way to embarrassed applause.*

For the very first time in my life I felt genuinely glad to have Alexander as a friend. Exactly the same kind of strange outburst of emotion that had drawn my attention to him at the memorial service at Merton, and which had irritated me no less on one or two subsequent occasions, had successfully attested to a kindness on my part that even I had not believed existed. In an act of self-deprecation which nobody else there could have aspired to, he had demonstrated that many of the qualities he had ascribed to me were genuine. I became aware, as he proposed the toast, that amongst the many people he had counted as his friends (those he had invited to the shoot at which we first met, for example) only Hermione and I had ever treated him with anything but tolerance and faint amusement. Alexander had never really been more than a figure of fun for these people, but at that moment he revealed at once his vulnerability and the strength of character required to let it show, to go forward despite everything. In doing so, he shamed fairweather friends and revealed the integrity of a groom who had given him the opportunity to do so. I raised my glass to him.

* * *

                                200

    He didn't seem to have £e natural power;
        He must've got his pills from Amsterdam.
    £e geezer could erect a stonking tower
        £at'd even shock a knocking-$op Madame,
    £en stay 'sexed-up' €ree quarters of an hour.
        (£at's how £e *dodgy dosser* got his name—'Saddam':
    'Cause, even £ough £e evidence looked iffy,
    He'd get his weapon working in a Jiffy

200.4 *knocking shop*: Crude slang for 'brothel', I believe.

200.6 *Saddam*: *Sadama* is 'shock' in Arabic, which would certainly suit the context. It seems much more likely in the circumstances, however, that this *flasher*'s nickname derives from a portmanteau of Sodom and (de) Sade. His phallus, emphatically referred to in the couplet as a 'weapon', self-evidently carries the threat of buggery for the sole purpose of enjoying the cruelty of the threat (one this Bosvil analogue intends as much for me—the reader—and you—the amanuensis—as for the direct object of his morbid desire).

200.7 *iffy*: A slack Americanism: 'contingent', 'dubious'.

200.8 *Jiffy*: (sexed up?) [Poet's note] I will guess that the strange typography, including an otherwise superfluous initial capital J, is intended as an iconographic analogue of the erection. The parenthetical addition 'sexed up' would seem to be a note made by you, my future friend, to record an instruction of the poet's. One presumes he had in mind some skewed version of that modern hangover from monastic illumination that sees the first letter of a chapter enormously enlarged. No doubt it amused him to employ such a prurient displacement of this effect. A crass thing like this would seem to be the very essence of textual impact in the mind of an illiterate. Illuminated gospels were invented to give the uneducated a wondrous picture-show.

                    *   *   *

Our honeymoon was spent in Italy. It was also intended to include a visit to Greece and the site of Ancient Troy in Turkey, but the belligerence of the recently elected Benito Mussolini in a border-dispute with Albania meant that our sailing from Otranto (that bleak inspiration of the Gothic genre) was cancelled. In fact, there was no public transport across the Ionian Sea whatever for the entire month. A rail journey through the Balkans seemed equally inadvisable, so we remained in Sorrento for three weeks.

The decision not to move on, even within Italy, was due in no small part to Jacob Stover. It is unlikely any contemporary reader will have heard of this obscure American literato, but in Campania in 1923 Stover had styled himself the Svengali of an artistic avant-garde *(a rather passé one, in fact, with links to Vorticism) whose members had convinced the inhabitants of the Amalfi Coast that by as advanced a decade as the 1950s (for example) their modernist abstractions would have been accepted as the popular mainstream and Stover become as renowned as... well... perhaps such comparisons can wait.*

                    *   *   *

Her chirpiness had wrong-footed me. I'd meant to come straight out with it: *Hannah, I'm in love with you*. But that would have to wait. I followed her into the kitchen, the blood painfully hot in my fingers. She slotted the spout of the kettle over the end of the cold tap & turned it on. She had one of those metal stove-top kettles with a stubby little spout. The water resounded in the drum of it, the tone rising as it filled.

"I thought a lot about what you said to me after you left the last time," she said.

"After you threw me out, you mean."

"Yes, sorry. You were right." she placed the weighty thing on the hob & lit the gas.

"So you agree that Amrit wrote *The Birmingham Quean*?"

"No, not about that. I don't think he had anything to do with that. I mean you were right about him being a loser. You were right about *me* being a loser for carrying a torch for him."

"So you decided to put the torch *to him* instead."

"Very funny."

"Did you read any of it first?"

"Yes, most of it, in fact. It was... you were right, it was a lot of rubbish really. I mean, there were some interesting ideas & a few touching moments, but it was a total mess. There was certainly nothing to be afraid of."

"No. But it must've been difficult for you. I could have been a bit more sensitive I suppose."

"Nonsense. I needed a good kick up the bottom."

"But you don't think the poem..."

"Frankly, Sam, I couldn't give a damn..."

"You've got your film quotes mixed up there."

"If you want to look for Amrit, you go ahead. If you still believe he wrote that ludicrous thing you've got rolled up in your bag & you want to congratulate him, I don't know, on his sophisticated irony or something, I'm not going to stop you. Just don't bring me into it. If you do find him, tell him to stay away. In fact, no, don't tell him anything."

"D'you think I will find him?"

"Maybe. The point is that I don't want you to: not for me. There's really no point going after him for my benefit. I'm reconciled to being a single mother. I'm sorry I ever got you into this."

"Well, no. It'd be for my sake." That was a strange confession. It was true though. I wanted to find the ex-partner of the woman I loved... for what I couldn't imagine. Obviously, I'd come back to Birmingham to see Hannah but she obviously had no intention of taking on a surrogate father for her child. I obviously had no chance with her. The way she was behaving... & yet... for some reason I was all the more keen on finding Amrit Singh.

"I've told the CSA to drop the case."

  201

                $e backed away and held £e door ajar,
                    £en grinned and filled her lungs to £e extreme
                Of £eir capacity, which made her bra
                    Dig in her back and ribs. $e let her scream
                Crescendo like a horror movie star,
                    Her fingers on her cheeks, back hunched, a stream
                Of air erupting €rough £e vocal chords:
                Wi£ lungs like £at, $e ought to tread £e boards.

---

201 This is obviously in parodic imitation of *The Scream* by Edvard Munch. This painting is a classic example of the reversal of emotional direction in *expressionism*: the scream is not emerging from the figure into the landscape but from the landscape into the visceral figure, and in this way it infects the rational, logical man-made world of the wooden walkway—the Renascence perspective of its planks, its perpendicular walkers (a world which man has fenced-off from nature as if to prevent precisely this from happening)—with its waves of infinite existential fear. All masculine geometry melts into the hideous peristaltic undulations of the birth canal. This painting and this poem are defying the viewer's attempts, and the reader's, to æsthetically fence himself off with rational, ordered thinking from the irrepressible primal scream of nature.

If I were to scream myself, nobody would hear but you: the one-way mirror of time is sound-proofed, but there are always the microphones of historical record concealed somewhere in the torture-chamber.

> 'One shriek of hate would jar all the hymns of heaven:
> True devils with no ear, they howl no tune
> With nothing but the Devil!'
>   (Alfred Lord Tennyson 'Sea Dreams' ll. 251-3)

*   *   *

Crucially, Hermione had *heard of him. He was an art-dealer after all. The fact that he traded exclusively in the hyper-modern products of his protégés whilst she intended to focus on all things ancient and anonymous seemed unimportant. Hermione had organized to visit him while we were in the area. Ostensibly this was for my benefit. Stover's Amalfi Villa was supposed to be the local* auberge espagnole *for artists and writers whose subsequent success would no doubt grant them access to our own hotel, the Cocumella Grand: a former Jesuit residence whose sea-vistas and palatial furnishings were almost as breathtaking as its rates. He claimed to be a friend of Arthur Symons. Apparently, one could simply invite oneself for cocktails. I was not looking forward to it at all.*

Stover's taste turned out to be much more eclectic and antiquarian than one might have expected. His personal drawing room—a haven of bourgeois tranquillity amidst the mannered bohemia of linseed-pungent studios and slovenly boudoirs—was like an annexed miscellany of the reserve collection at the Louvre. There were, for example, a fragment of an Egyptian frieze, a Byzantine triptych and two Tang Dynasty jade statuettes side by side on the extended desk of a Louis XV kingwood marqueterie escritoire.

*   *   *

"Can you do that?"

"They're next to useless anyway. The Central Stupidity Agency."

"You're not worried that he might try to get access then? In the future, I mean."

"Amrit's not going to be dressing up as Batman any time soon. He ran away from a tricky situation. That's what he does. He's been doing it ever since he was a kid.... look, Sam, if you're really intent on finding him..."

"Well, I suppose I'd just like to find out *about* him, really. I don't know that we should meet or anything. I mean, it'd be quite awkward wouldn't it."

"Yes, well if you want to understand him, I suppose I can tell you one or two things that might help you. I owe you that much. But this is the last time, Sam. After this, you're on your own."

"Of course."

"& you've got to promise you won't... you won't try to tell me where he is, or encourage either of us to get back together again. That period of our life is over. It's best for both of us, for Sammy. I don't want to hear from him, you understand me?"

"No. I promise." The kettle wailed to the boil, giving birth to an insistent jet of steam. Hannah got up to make the tea.

"You remember about Amrit? that he didn't find out his real name until his stepdad died?"

"Yep."

"He didn't even know he'd had another father... that he'd been adopted. Well there were two other things that happened to him that were really important. They explain a lot about the way he is. Did you know he was beaten up on the way to school when he was eight?"

"Like in the 'Mustard Oil' story?"

"Exactly. The thing is, he wrote that from the perspective of a white boy who gets attacked because of the smell of Indian pickle on his coat: not because he's, um, a 'Paki' himself but because he's been accidentally tainted with something the bullies couldn't stomach. & I suppose that's exactly how he must've understood it as a kid. But the truth is that he was the victim of a perfectly normal racist attack. I suppose white people do suffer from being called 'Paki lovers', & Amrit was writing something important there, the adoption of an irrational repugnance out of fear, but this wasn't one of those times. What really happened was that the two older kids identified him as precisely what he was: a mixed-race child. It was just something that never occurred to him at the time. Why should it?"

"You're right, yeh. That doesn't really come through. It's only there because you know it."

"That's why it's a failure as a story. There's all that stuff about burying the jacket at the bottom of the garden: the worry that it might sprout up like the runner beans... or spread like the ants' nest. But that was Amrit's problem as a writer. It's all a bit oblique. Who knows, maybe he meant to extend it & lost interest in the project. That'd be him all over."

> Jeff Sloggy's never been £e kind of guy
> > To stand aside and let a lady suffer
> (Or any opportunity slip by
> > To smack £e stuffing out of some old duffer
> Who's got temerity enough to try
> > His luck; once Sloggy's certain no-one's tougher,
> He'll do his best—he hardly ever fails—
> To illustrate £e fact he's hard as nails.)

202.4 *duffer*. Principally, one who sells trashy goods as valuable, upon false pretences, e.g. pretending that they are smuggled or stolen, and offered as bargains. By transferred epithet it comes to mean the 'faked up' goods themselves, and also a 'counterfeit coin'. It is more than hypocritical for Sloggy to attack someone on these grounds.

*   *   *

There was a conspicuous lack of modern art. As we were shown into the room by a dusty, chisel-wielding Spaniard who refused to introduce himself, only the view through the French windows of a ghastly tribal mask sun-bleaching on a balconette overrun with trumpet creeper reminded one of the existence of a Braques or a Chagall.

From his local reputation one might have expected Stover to be the centrepiece of this pretentious stage-set like some tableau of Caligulan repose: a Gilbert Osmond in silk smoking jacket draped over a rakish chaise-longue. In fact, it was hard to make him out at first. Closer inspection of the recesses revealed the broad, hunched shoulders of a tall man in a linen shirt, shuddering slightly with the effort of whatever he was doing: producing his rather furious handwriting, one must assume. Smoke rising from a cigar in a grotesquely over-full cut-glass ashtray next to his left hand did nothing to brighten the dingy corner in which he worked. There was one other source of pungent fumes in the room: a large brass thurible hanging above a coffee table which appeared to be the focus of Stover's area for receiving visitors. We edged towards it. He declined to turn as we came in. The incense was angelica, I think...

'Take a seat. I shan't be long.'

I could be misremembering the perfume. Enveloped in the byproducts of one's own combustion, one must be forgiven a certain monomania of olfactory recollection... Hermione perched on a stool and I plumped for a Queen Anne armchair with hidden depths to rival my own. The springs beneath its seat were so accommodating that my feet were no longer capable of touching the ground. I fidgeted but decided not to move. Stover continued to vibrate prosaically. Blue-grey tendrils of incense climbed up and round the chain of the suspended thurible.

'I know your father, of course, Miss Gordon, by reputation.'

We had still not seen his face.

'I hear you're taking over the business,' *at last he turned to look at us,* 'Maybe you'd be interested in an exchange. Can you lay your hands on any nice cuneiform?'

Hermione stood up, 'Hermione Twigg, lovely to meet you, this is my husband...'

*   *   *

"You've got to feel for him though. If that really happened to him," I said.

"Of course. & for his dad too. He wasn't allowed to explain. Not properly."

"Maybe he learned that obliqueness from his father then: the way his father was forced to be with him."

"Leon, you mean? I don't think Amrit was much like him really. He loved him though. He was really devastated when he died. I'm sure of that." She wrapped her fingers around the teacup & stared out of the window above the kitchen sink. I didn't follow her gaze. I couldn't shake the memory of the last time we'd both looked out into that garden. There would only have been a reflection.

"Are you sure you're ok talking about all this?" I asked.

"Fine. Yeh. Of course. Where was I?"

"Erm, Leon..."

"Yes, he loved his stepdad... all the more so when he discovered the truth. He just felt he couldn't ever aspire to be like him. If Amrit's inability to say things straight was like Leon's it was out of very different motives. Amrit simply couldn't face the truth. He didn't want to take responsibility. Leon held his tongue for precisely the opposite reason."

"So when he got beaten up, what changed?" I didn't want to use the past-tense the way Hannah had been. I don't think she meant to talk about Amrit as if he were dead, just to talk about the man she'd known as something from the past. It was disconcerting nonetheless.

"I think, in hindsight anyway, he blamed his father for what happened. He knew that was wrong. He knew that it was just as unfair as what the racists had done to him, but he just couldn't help himself. From that moment on, he distanced himself from Leon. He had no idea why at the time, but after that he would always define himself in opposition to his stepdad. It wasn't a case of hating him at all... more a kind of self-loathing based on a secret knowledge that he wasn't the child of the man he most admired. It turns into a weird story when you know about Amrit's background. It's like he was rejecting his white stepdad for being the source of his own racial difference (the smell of Mustard Oil on the jacket) when the opposite was the truth. It was his biological father he was rejecting. In doing so he was being much more racist than Leon. That's what hurt the most."

"You can't blame him though, in the circumstances."

"No, obviously not, but the point was that he blamed himself. In a way, he thought that his white dad was better at being an Indian than *he* was."

"Maybe he blamed Leon for not being brave enough to tell him the truth."

"I shouldn't have thought so. If you want to go all psychoanalytical about it, a stronger argument might be to call it sublimated anger at his mother. It was Carla who was responsible for his ignorance. It was Carla who kept his darkness in the dark. Leon only went along with it out of love for his wife. That's another thing Amrit couldn't hope to emulate."

> He swaggered in £e bogs and grabbed £e bloke
>   Around £e €roat, and by his open belt.
> He raised him off his feet, which made him choke
>   And squirm a bit, but Saddam only felt
> £e more aroused by £is. A little croak
>   Of pleasure left his lips as Sloggy dealt
> Wi£ him £e way he liked: bo€ ends asplutter,
> He marched him out and flung him in £e gutter.

203.1 *bogs*: Slang for *toilets*, but *bogs* have long been considered an uncanny source of evil spirits. Just as they are an admixture of solid land and water, they are believed by superstitious cultures to be liminal zones between our own world and the underworld. Frightful monsters, *bog people*, sprites, even the devil himself are all thought to emerge from their depths. It is no coincidence that it is from *Grimpen Mire* that the spectral *Hound of the Baskervilles* is thought to emerge in Sherlock Holmes's parodically gothic return from the dead; nor that its counterfeiting handler, Stapleton should receive the poetic justice of being sucked into the bog at the finale. There is probably some tasteless Freudian explanation. Like the *wormholes* and *time-tunnels* of Science Fiction that are the sources of our present-day fears of grotesque and diabolical creatures (if I can use the term *present-day* meaningfully any more), the taboo concerning the *bog* from which it probably derives is similarly tainted with connotations of sexual (generational) perversion. A little probing might discover, at the back of all of this, the analogy to a primal fear of what gruesome offspring might emerge not from the female womb but from the male rectum. See stanzas 82-3 in which Britannia recalls the childish fear (classically *anally-retentive* for Freud, but given a decidely unpleasant spin by our knowledge of the character's adult sexuality) that the *bog* might contain 'something under Birmingham / That swims up U-bends and then up your bum.'

The linguistic explanation might be just as convincing, though. *Bog* derives from Irish/Gaelic *bogach*. As such it would already contain uncanny connotations of a mysterious *other* culture for the Anglo Saxons. To this day, despite the absence of a real geographical bog, the *bogside* of Londonderry remains the threshold of the Celtic Ireland to the West into which the Protestant Unionists rarely venture. Surely the name is part of the reason. It seems to say: *here be monsters*. The folk-etymological link to the *bogge*, *boggle*, *boggard* or *bogy man* must also be implicated in these connotations of infernal liminality.

Sloggy's *swaggering* over-confidence when entering this place from which the dark woman-man has just emerged, wailing like a banshee... howling like a spectral hound, recalls Stapleton's boast that he is the only man who knows a safe route to the centre of the *Grimpen Mire*.

I feel I may have had a similar over-confidence when first I set foot in the boggy semantic territory of this poem. I am getting my comeuppance now. Perhaps I should stop struggling. They say you should not move in quicksand. See the cut stanza 122.

203.5 *The more aroused by this*: Hence his de-Sadean nickname.

"It sounds a bit like you're sticking up for good old-fashioned *family values*."

"Me? Take a look around you, Sam. It's not me, it's Amrit. That was precisely his problem. For him, his dad (Leon that is) stood for the kind of old-fashioned honest, hard-working, white working class community that was the source of the racism he had suffered, but also of its antidote: people like Leon, people who embraced racial diversity in their own homes & families, for reasons of love rather than some kind of do-gooder's sense of equality. Amrit's dilemma was that he wanted to be like that, like a dad from a time that no longer existed, from a community that no longer existed, but knew full well that he was incapable of it. Society had moved on. Not least because he wasn't really an insider."

"Who, Amrit?"

"Yes."

"I suppose," I ventured, "that was why he had to abandon his work too. Its entire focus was on undermining the values that Leon stood for. Obviously they could have agreed in vague terms on ideas of pluralism & stuff, basic socialist ideas maybe, but not the rest. Leon was a remnant of a culture steeped in the kind of thinking that Amrit's education had taught him to treat as obsolete & morally bankrupt. But when... when you got pregnant..."

Hannah smiled, she seemed to like me joining in like that. "He felt he'd thrown the baby out with the bathwater," she added.

I nodded & chuckled. "I'm glad you said that not me."

"Is there another way of saying it?"

"So when he got beaten up it was a kind of awakening. Almost like his genes were activated by the violence & began to identify Leon as... well, not where they came from."

"That's a rather mystical way of putting it, but... I suppose so, yes. At least, it was the moment he first began to think about those kinds of things."

"I guess it was a sexual awakening too. I can't help thinking of that bit in *Cider with Rosie*."

"I hope you're not going where I think you're going with this, Sam."

"It does seem a coincidence..."

"It's just... it's boring, & it's wrong. You're wrong about that poem. It's a red herring."

"Ok, but the point stands. The story's explicit about the link between the beginnings of racial & sexual consciousness."

"God, somewhere along the way I seem to have forgotten that you were an English student. You people have a habit of making revelations out of the stark-staring obvious. Race is inherently a sexual idea."

"Yeh, I've read Lévi-Strauss as well... All 501 pages. It was riveting. That man really knows his genes." That was a crap joke. Why was I flirting for godsake? I was only torturing myself.

Britannia played £e flustered ingenue
    When Sloggy strolled back in. $e took £e drink
He offered. 'Is £ere some€ing *I* can do…
    For *you*?' $e panted. 'Hmm… I'll have to €ink…
Perhaps we'll call £at services-in-lieu
    For your command performance.' Wi£ a wink,
He lit a Benson, '*you* know what I mean:
You ever €ought of starring on £e screen?'

204.5-6 *services-in-lieu / For your command performance*: Obviously euphemistic references to prostitution. A 'command' performance is usually one given by 'command' of the monarch, rather than one 'ordered' by the client of a seller of her own body. That is to say, merely, that the King or Queen will be the principal member of the audience. The debased application of the term in such an obscene and inappropriate context is revolutionary ignobility of the most distasteful kind.

There is an even more disruptive inversion in the ensuing (*contract*) scene, however. The transaction that takes place is a cunning reversal of the 'Faustian Pact'. Contrary to what one might think, it is actually Sloggy who plays Faust and Britannia Spears Mephistopheles. It is she who manages (by subtly convincing him that it is worth nothing at all to him, whilst she has a mere collector's interest in such valueless trinkets) to trick Sloggy into giving her his soul (in the form of his iconic counterfeit) in return for the fantasy of ultra-potency inherent in his Frankensteinian ambition to create the perfect pornographic star.

That definitive feature of feminine guile—the ability to dominate whilst appearing to defer—is as exaggerated in this fake woman as are her gait and her *accoutrements*.

    *   *   *

'Of course… Congratulations.' He shook her hand. I planted my palms on the armrests to lift my lower body out of the chair like a gymnast on the parallel bars.

'No don't get up,' he said. He squeezed my hand across the knuckles at an unusual angle then slumped backwards onto a leather chesterfield.

'Anything with Sumerian script. I'd be happy to swap it for some of the best new art.'

'Well, I've only ever seen it at the British Museum. Very little has been discovered.'

'Juan-Pablo's working on some astounding sculptures at the moment: men and beasts, ancient and powerful—outstanding aspirational geometry. This move away from Greek naturalism back to the cold, hard stylisation of Mesopotamia makes the blood course through the veins and muscles. The modern and the ancient made one.'

'I suppose there's something in it. History goes in circles and all that.'

'Vico. Yes.' He looked at me. I nodded. He was a pugnacious looking individual: flat of features and with pimple-cratered cheeks. His skull supported a shrub of greying curls, dense enough almost to conceal the encroachment of crown-pattern baldness. Below this, his forehead was so bronzed and creased that lines of paler skin which had escaped the ultra-violet radiation during hours of sunlit frowning converged on the apex of his brow like a savannah camouflage. His eyes were slow and purposeful: a jungle green iris almost entirely engulfed by the dilated pupil.

    *   *   *

"Forget the books, Sam. Stand back & take a look at it. We know that ninety percent of biological variation occurs within ethnic groups. We know that there is no provable racial correlation of blood type or of the qualities of internal organs. There simply is no biological race at all beyond that which is immediately obvious. Almost every detail that *is* subject to apparent racial specification — skin colour, iris colour, eyeball size, facial characteristics, muscular density, fat distribution, hair coverage, height, weight, even the sizes of bums & tits & willies — they all have one thing in common: each one is a prominent focus for sexual selection. Racism is about one thing & one thing alone: controlling who gets to mate with who. All the power games are just sub-effects of the oldest power game in the world: the dominant male(s) suppressing the natural mating behaviour of the females in their sway. A great deal of human civilisation has been an excuse for doing precisely that. It's a tribal mentality writ large. Patriarchy, racism, sexual prescriptivism, they're all part of the same thing. How can you have a *racial awakening* without a sexual one?"

"So would you say it was... a kind of Oedipal moment, then? He uncovers a sexual awareness & some kind of suspicion about his background &... he focuses it all on his parents."

"I'd find it very embarrassing to say that, Sam. I suppose you might understand this kind of thing a little better than me though. It *is* different growing up as a girl. It used to be, at least. Nothing like this ever happened to me. Whatever the case, the last thing in the world Amrit would've wanted was for Leon to die. When he did, he was devastated."

"How do you know he was?"

"Well, that's what he told me."

"Yes but how could *he* know? Just after Leon died, didn't his mom give him that letter? Surely, he might just have been devastated by the confirmation of his suspicions about Leon not being his real dad. The past changes when you find out a thing like that. It's not just a matter of perspective. The past actually changes. Besides, if you'd wished somebody dead..."

"No, no, that's not it..."

"... even if it was just the once, for the perfectly understandable reason that you'd just had the shit kicked out of you because of something you thought was his fault, then... surely, you'd be racked with guilt."

"No. Y'see, the thing is, *you* don't know what happened next... anyway, don't call me Shirley."

I shuddered. Something about that flippant joke came as a real shock. It hit me with the force that horror film makers routinely fail to achieve because you always see them coming. Only at those red moments in Hitchcock's *Marnie* could I really say I'd jumped... something about the abstract nature of it. But this... it was Hannah's strange lightheartedness. I don't know. It unsettled me enormously. Everything that was to come over the next few minutes: the disturbing imagery, the sense of childish vulnerability, all stemmed from this sudden jokey interjection. A nervous giggle juddered through my diaphragm.

205

$e had, but 'silver' ra£er £an 'PC',
   And only when $e was a kid. $e knew
£e kind of sleazy pornflick £is'd be.
   ($e €ought $e did; $e didn't have a clue.)
$e $ook her head. 'You don't get *me* for free;'
   $e stroked his knee, 'but some reward is due
For gallantly man-handling my attacker.'
   $e snaked her body round to plant a smacker

205.1 *PC*: 'Police Constable', one assumes, rather than 'postcard'. 'Silver screen' is a pretentious synonym for *cinema*; Britannia is, for obvious reasons, projecting this idea onto the 'screen' in a Police Station on which are shown the representations of wanted criminals drawn by portrait artists based on witness's descriptions. More precisely perhaps, she means one of those Frankensteinian composite photographs in which one person's nose is matched with another's upper lip, and so on. This technological *anthropometric* method of *potrait parlé* was invented, along with much else in the field of forensic science, by Alphonse Bertillon. His most lasting legacy is probably *photographies stéréometriques*. This provided multiple angle views of suspects, objects in evidence and the so-called 'scenes' of crimes. It is of little doubt that Bertillon's methods were influential on the development of *cubist* painting.

In rejecting the image, Britannia is pointedly revealing to both Sloggy and the reader how much she revels in her grotesque appearance. She knows full well that she already looks like what the Americans would call a *mug-shot* or a composite image of a wanted suspect. More to the point she is very similar in both appearance and nature to the subject of a cubist portrait envisaged as if it were a figurative portrayal. She is incapable, it seems, of being viewed from only one angle at once. Like the fox in the previous passage, we suspect that it is she who has this disturbing effect upon the medium of depiction rather than vice versa.

Though perhaps this idea was always implicit in *cubism*. Despite the bland art-historical argument that it was all about an emphasis upon artificiality of technique and the two-dimensional surface and so on—and a counteraction of photography—it seems quite likely that the style was specifically understood by its earliest practitioners (perhaps Picasso more than Braque) as an attempt to represent (or at least to dramatize the impossibility of representing) specific subjects which were inherently too ambiguous or multi-faceted to capture visually. By which I mean that it actually had nothing whatever to do with *surface*. Most pertinently, it was the potentially desirable female nude that caused such spatial upset in whatever functionary (human or machine) that attempted to depict it. In this light (cleared of chiaroscuro), Britannia's own cubism might be a devastating extension of this spatial effect into the extra dimensions of time, sex and race. Her entourage would certainly appear to resemble the iconic *Demoiselles d'Avignon*.

205.8 *snaked her body round*: Think of Eve. But also think of Daphne in the John William Waterhouse painting, wound into a tree with snaking stems as she glances back over her bared shoulder with an inscrutable expression at the young sun-god stretching out with a libidinous lyre to touch her other hand. Britannia's contortions appear to be this kind of coy resistance but are actually designed to seduce. Her paradoxical cubism extends as she twists to incorporate one view of her as the spirit of chastity at the moment of violation and another as the archetypal temptress, intimately affiliated with the serpent. The image is all the more degrading for its sardonic likening of the pornographer Sloggy to a composite of Adam and Apollo.

205.8 *smacker*: It is perhaps an unsurprising fact considering the multitudinous reversals and inversions in this poem that the sense for 'smack' of *to produce a sharp sound with the lips*, and therefore by extension *to kiss loudly*, predates the sense *to strike with the palm*. We tend to misinterpret 'smack the lips' as meaning *to hit the lips together*; in fact the definitive sound is a reverse-plosive bi-labial articulation created by pressing together the lips and then opening them during inhalation (rather than the usual exhalation) so that air rushes inwards to the mouth-cavity. This sucking bilabial articulation is the characteristic motion of a kiss, an act which is therefore much more logically described as 'taken' than as 'given'. It is from a metaphoric extension of the sense *kiss* that we get the slang use of this word to mean *a pound*. This succubus is therefore threatening Sloggy with her leech-like pout, threatening, that is, to suck out of him his pound (his apotropaic charm, his soul, his voice, his future) whilst veiling her vampiric threat under the guise of an osculatory offering.

There went up a smoke out of his nostrils, and fire out of his mouth devoured

* * *

'I'll show you later,' he said, 'he's working... doesn't like to be disturbed. Let's have a drink while we wait. What can I get you Mr Twigg? A sweet vermouth perhaps?'

'That sounds fine.' I hate sweet vermouth, but not as much as I hate protracted conversation with 'educated' Americans whose rotricized pronunciation of French words like this inevitably recalls a snarling lynx.

Without bothering to find out if Hermione might want something different, he sprang up to pour the drinks. She seemed not to mind. I had never known her take vermouth before. 'My husband was interested in your acquaintance with a certain poet, Mr Stover. I forget the name.' My heart sank.

'Not Pound, I hope. Ezra and I stay out of one another's hair.'

'Oh yes?' I assumed Stover's influence to be so parochial that Pound thought it as negligible as I did myself.

'That boy's commitment to Bella Italia is just a passing fad. Not to mention modern art. I was here promoting expressionism and abstract painting two years before Marinetti plucked up the balls to put his manifesto out. When Kandinsky came in 1906, it was me he came to see. Pound was still in Pennsylvania.'

'I hear you were around when Arthur Symons suffered his unfortunate collapse?'

'Symons is it? Yes I was here. I'd not long since bought this villa. He was in Venice when it happened, though. He and Rhoda had a hotel room overlooking the Grand Canal. At night they could hear the raving inmates of the lunatic asylum on St Clemente. Arthur is a remarkably sensitive man. His mind is capable of incomparable mimetic feats. Somehow the influence of those sounds vastly magnified the febrile nature of an already visionary imagination. He ran away to Bologna, where he caused a bit of a brouhaha declaiming strange Pentecostal incantations in the streets. Rhoda caught up with him and tried to make him go back to London with her, but he wouldn't. They were supposed to come and see me after Venice. Rhoda wrote me to explain the situation. She was very candid for an Englishwoman...'

Hermione beamed. She seemed to be enjoying this self-aggrandising little anecdote.

* * *

On Sloggy's lips. He grabbed her chin to fend
   Her off. 'I'm just a fuckin film producer;
I'm not your co-star, bab... but I can spend
   A bob or two, if need be, to induce a
$y bird to spread her wings.' $e tried to bend
   Her face away. $e wanted him to loose her.
He wouldn't let her go. He was a nutter.
'Okay' $e crooned, 'you fancy a quick flutter?'

206.3 *co-star*: I have an inkling this might derive from the complex jargon of Hollywood's hierarchical system of *billing* actors. It would be used presumably when more than one *star* of equal notoriety was to perform. A possible alternative in the circumstances might be an abbreviation of *costermonger* 'street greengrocer': originally *costard monger* 'seller of apples'. Sloggy would certainly seem to come under the category of untrustworthy street-traders covered by the umbrella term 'barrow boy'. Furthermore the ironic association of this scene with the central tableau of original sin can be extended; Sloggy's rejection of the kiss is like Adam refusing Eve's apple. This particular Eve would obviously have an 'Adam's apple', probably a stubbly one, and it is this—the locus of the drag-queen's throaty masculinity—that would put off the prospective taster of the forbidden fruit.

206.3-4 *bab... bob*: Sloggy turns down the (Adam's) apple and foils Britannia's Judas kiss. He subtly lets her know he has seen through her ploy—'bab' is seemingly used as a dialectal pet-term, but in the same dialect it also means a knotted bunch of worms (resembling the head of the gorgon) used as bait to sniggle eels in the canals. This can also be called a 'bob'. It is how Sloggy is addressing this treacherous Medusa.

   The actual instance of 'bob', however—meaning a shilling or, in this case, plural shilling*s*—comes from the name of a small late Medieval French coin *la bobe* which was worth one and one fifth *deniers*, and therefore a tenth, rather than a twelfth, of a *sou*. Doubtless this was an early move towards decimalization, the ideological spread of which has made the two 'Enlightenment' republics of America and France so proud, but we need to keep in sight the fact that *faire la bobe* or *bober*, in the Old French of the same period, meant *to fool* or *to deceive* or, more literally, *to inflate*. It is entirely possible that this *inflated* coin, and the disturbance it instigated of the Imperial monetary system, was definitively *contrefait*.

   This poem is a 'bob': a Birmingham Shilling, as is the future it intends. Like Sloggy, you and I (my companion in torture) are trying to resist it. Like Sloggy, we both know we are doomed to fail.

*   *   *

'... *I travelled to Rome that evening and Bologna the next day. Arthur had escaped again, only to be arrested in Ferrara by two Bersigliari who charged him with vagrancy and locked him in the dungeon of the Palazzo Vecchio. The Italian Ambassador to London managed to arrange his repatriation only a day after Rhoda had contacted him. But I still had time to visit him once before his release.*'

'*You saw him?*' This was obviously not true. *I calculated, however, that to challenge Stover explicitly would necessitate a good deal more exposure to his feline growls than simply prompting him to carry on.*

*   *   *

"Not long after Leon died, Amrit ran away from home."

"Where did he go?" I was falling headlong into her words.

"Not very far at all, it turned out. But it took three days to find them. He went with a friend, Richard I think his name was. Rich. It was a hot weekend & they were supposed to be staying the night in a tent in Rich's back garden. Rich had just got a tent for his birthday. When his mom came out to bring them breakfast in the morning they'd both disappeared. So had their sleeping bags. Everything but the tent."

"Probably not an abduction then." The word *abduction* was difficult to force out.

"No. You're right. It'd be quite unusual to gather up all the victim's things. I think the Police still took the possibility seriously though. Anyway, Amrit didn't know what the Police were up to. The boys didn't think of it in those terms at all. They'd been reading a lot of children's fantasy stuff at the time: Alan Garner, Susan Cooper that kind of thing."

"Really?"

"That's the stuff you want to look at. Ditch the theory & the literary canon."

"Ancient England waking underneath its modern, industrial veneer." Was that someone else's voice?

"If you say so. Amrit & Rich thought they were on an adventure like that. They must've both been very imaginative children. They could talk for hours about a perfectly coherent fantasy world, never once breaking the frame, constructing it as they went along, incorporating everything."

"Don't all kids do that?"

"Maybe. But it takes people of remarkably similar moods & tastes to keep it up for such long periods without either of them flagging. There's also a peak moment at about that age, ten or eleven, when you're still a child: especially boys, they haven't been dragged fully into puberty yet, so they're full of ideas & they still see their worries about the world as solvable by heroic action in a fantasy environment. On the other hand, they're old enough to act with some confidence & build quite thorough fictions. The boys were just at that peak when they ran away. According to Amrit, they never once throughout the whole three days treated the situation as anything but their adventure with The Holimans."

"*Holimans*? Did I read that name in the Zomby stuff somewhere?"

"No. You couldn't have done."

"But surely..." she grinned at my slip, "isn't it obvious that the disappearance & Leon's death were connected? How can you... how can *he* make out that it was a halcyon period of Huckleberry Finn fantasy-land completely untrammelled by a *Stand By Me* moment with that, you know, the death of his stepfather as a backdrop?"

You beat me and I'll give you what I owe.
    Considering your valour it's £e least
A girl can do… Just one day's filming £ough…'
    His fingers slowly left her cheeks. Released
From Sloggy's grip, $e tugged £e fur below
    Her hem towards her knees; $e wiggled, teased
£e clingy fabric down around her arse
And said, 'So how about a game of darts?'

207.5 *fur below*. This is a ludicrous literalization (in the form of a fur-lined hem) of the folk-etymology via which the Romance *falbala* 'flounce' or 'petticoat trimming' is transformed in English into *furbelow*. One must always suspect such fetishized limini of female undergarments of mimicking the pubis that marks the threshold of the human animal's generative organs. More than this even, there is a permanent recollection in the crimped profiles created on the fringes of women's garments by lace and brocade of the suggestively protruding *labia minora*. In a sense it is the fashionable fabric version of that same euphemism that in Keats materializes as the sea-weed around the bottom half of his metaphoric *oceanid* in 'St Agnes Eve', and which Tennyson discovers in 'Sea Dreams' as a less than innocent fascination amongst young boys for the large crinkled frond of *Laminaria bulbosa* ('the dimpled flounce of the sea-furbelow' li. 257).

Falbala is untraced by lexicographers. This is a gaping absence aching to be filled by the overheated imagination. *Faux-labia* forces itself into my mind in total defiance of all rational or empirical objection. Whatever the truth, it is unquestionable that Britannia's (fake) 'fur below her hem' is designed to draw attention to the absence of the nearby vulva that it mimics and therefore to accentuate the real lurking organ that she is apparently seeking to conceal by pulling her skirt 'towards her knees'. It is a typical effect of this poem—one both of us must be sickening of by now—that the prurient dual sexuality accompanies the parodic vitriol with which this attacks the monarchy by mimicking the ermine-edged robes of state.

You must have noticed as often as I have myself—indeed I cannot dismiss the notion that your ignominious position has forced your awareness of such things to outstrip even mine, my friend—that such things rarely go without some self-referential implication designed to ram the point home to the critical recipient of Bosvil's work. There is a case similar to this one in Canto II of *The Rape of the Lock*, where Pope has Ariel (in terms designed to mock the prettiness of his own couplets and those 'society ladies' who lap them up) say of the Sylphs 'Nay oft, in dreams, invention we bestow, / To change a Flounce, or add a Furbelow.' The pertinent formulaic critical denunciation of *nice* rhyming verse is still current today: 'all frill and flounce and furbelow.' Thus Bosvil's own doggerel is identified with the liminus of an abominable reproductive region—the false uterus of a false queen—in which a degenerative future can be fertilized by the reader who ventures to allow his imagination to penetrate beyond its uncanny folds.

"You're right... of course. But that's precisely what he claimed. What you've just said is how the adults all assumed it must've been. When the boys were picked up three days later, it was the way everyone rationalised their behaviour: Amrit was going through a difficult time; his father had just died; similar responses to the same situation amongst boys that age were common; it was best just to be thankful that the boys had been unharmed. & they were right... obviously they were. But if Leon's death was lurking behind Amrit's disappearance, as far as he was concerned it was entirely subsumed in the story of the Holimans. He never once thought about Leon (or his biological father, for that matter) while he was sleeping rough... just the Holimans. That's what he said."

"So what is the *Holimans*? What *are* they?"

"It's a plural, yes. It's just "Holy men" with a pointed bit of childish grammar, I suppose. But the name's not that important. They were time-travellers from the ancient past: not ghosts exactly, though the boys insisted that all ghost sightings were really sightings of Holimans. All the stories about dead people from the recent past (relatively recent anyway) were attempts by local people to incorporate what they'd seen into their own folk history. Though in some places, where communities had remnants of the most ancient people, stories existed that recalled the true story of the Holimans. Otherwise, it would never have survived."

It was not cold. I didn't feel like shivering. It was impossible to see the outside world & discern if it still looked cold out there. No doubt it did, but the lack of wind meant that the reflection in the kitchen window was undisturbed by any movement in the darkened garden. The complete absence of anything uncanny in this bright, cosy, centrally heated ground floor flat was the most uncanny thing imaginable. The buttery yellow nursery, in particular, still visible through its half closed door, made the comfort of the place feel impossible. It was probably just Hannah's story-telling ability... that & the hangover, but I didn't feel secure at all.

"They only came at certain times of the month. Well, there were Holimans for every phase of the moon, but each one only came at its own time. On certain occasions they were much more abundant than on others, though: full moons, of course, especially at the equinoxes."

I won't say the room felt like the entire world. That's one of the deadest of clichés. Rooms always feel like the entire world until something reminds you they're not. Instead, the room felt like a bubble floating just above the world, or to the left of it, displaced along a dimension that the world did not contain. I needed sleep, no doubt... a drink, maybe. Or maybe not.

"It was September the twenty-first that Monday... a full moon. There were going to be a lot of them: more than ever before. The Holimans were members of some ancient Neolithic culture in the English Midlands that had discovered how to travel through time by lighting huge sacrificial bonfires in a sacred place during certain phases of the moon, & throwing themselves into them. Well, actually, there could only be one chosen traveller on each occasion, so the scale of the thing over time must have been very long indeed: hundreds of years to make so many shadowy figures roaming the byways of South Birmingham."

'You jokin? It'd be a fuckin wipeout…
    Unless I got a mate to play instead.'
'What mate?' 'Oh just £is fellar: ticket tout;
    Works down £e Monkey; fuckin knucklehead;
He plays a bit o darts. I'll give him a $out.'
    At first, $e was perturbed by what he'd said.
£e details, £ough, had tempered her suspicion;
No local'ud put up much competition.

208.1 *wipeout*: Jargon from modern radio-wave broadcasting in reference to the effect whereby a strong signal blocks other competing signals in a radio-receiver. This can be considered a good thing when it gets rid of 'interference' and a bad thing when it makes it impossible for a desired signal to be received because of the overpowering proximity or *bandwidth* of another. The fact that such technical terminology of wireless and television dissemination should have been adopted in everyday speech reveals the overweening influence of the broadcast media (particularly of television, which relies entirely on *wipe-out* to function properly) on the minds of the future society Bosvil would like to see brought into existence by the decadent offices of the precisely the same media. One might go as far as to say that television has had an effect analogous to 'wipeout' on the competing cultural 'signals' of literature, art, music, religion and so on that it would regard merely as 'interference'.

If you were tricked, rather than coerced, into your role as amanuensis to the gypsy king, my friend, I suppose it would probably have been because he had convinced you that you might act to reassert such noble 'interference': the last-ditcher of literature.

    *   *   *

'I guess you'd think it a pitiful sight. He was fettered and manacled, stinking and unfed. His clothes were torn and covered in filth. There was a quality to his expression, though, and his strange words. He perfectly exemplified everything he'd ever written about. This was a man who'd heard the truth.'

I couldn't let that go. 'Come on, he was delusional. From the outside it might seem…'

'There was no outside. For that moment… I was really with him. It was only an instant, but I suddenly knew that I was in the presence of the birth of modernism. This was the moment that the universe had come to understand itself. Arthur was a very widely read man: unique amongst the English literary intelligentsia at the time. He read a hell of a lot of contemporary science and philosophy. He also knew a deal of modern literature. When he heard the lunatics on San Clemente he heard Conrad's horror, Heisenberg's uncertainty, Munch's scream, Kierkegaard's despair. In short he heard the nihilism Nietzsche had predicted: the birth-cries of a humanity that had opened the secret casket of forbidden knowledge to discover not a treasure but a ghost.'

'I suppose you mean the Zeit Geist, as Matthew Arnold calls it. Surely we should try to put the treasure back into the casket rather than sanctioning the ghost.'

Stover snorted, 'What do you do, Mr Twigg?'

'I've just been made a fellow of All Souls. My work…'

'I see. Another drink?'

    *   *   *

"The preparations for the jump involved long periods of fasting, solitude & meditation. When the right date for the immolation ceremony came, all the priests & druids, shamans or whatever they were would gather & jump over the top of the flames as they got going. In this way they were given visions of the time period to which the moon was supposedly pointing: a full moon towards the past, a new moon towards the future. When the fire reached the kind of temperatures which could disintegrate a human being in a short enough time to make it look like a metamorphosis, the chosen ones, embalmed with flammable oils, would be hurled into the centre to be purified & transmogrified into disembodied travellers in time. They would become ashes blown by a *wind of time* whose source was the sun & whose lens was the moon. They would exist as dust, displaced & scattered, & would only be gathered back into a human form when the right phase of the moon caused their dissipated materials to rush back together. Their appearance was always in a vortex of dust. Those who performed the ceremony at the full moon would appear at every new moon in the past. Those who performed it at the new moon would appear at every full moon in the future, & so on. Much rarer were those who performed the ceremony during a waxing or waning phase. These would materialise in the past or future on the much rarer occasions when the phase of the moon & the seasonal specifics were an exact mirror image of the ones at which they had been sacrificed. Most importantly, all the Holimans would appear together for a few moments at the original sacrificial site whenever a full-moon coincided with the equinox."

"The reason for all this was to maintain a cosmic balance & to ensure the continuation of their civilisation. The Holimans were supposed to protect the community from future threats that had been foreseen during these ceremonies, some of which involved evil spirits who themselves went back to alter the community's history & development: hence the travellers backwards as well as forwards in time. They thought they were protecting civilisation, wisdom, spirituality, all the things they believed to be the sole preserve of their uniquely humane society. The trouble was that those chosen became detached from their own time period for ever & were left to drift as conscious dust through futures & pasts they could neither understand nor hold at bay. Many of them had been forced against their will into the sacrifice, others had been honoured to be chosen & had actively sought transcendence. In any case, the vast majority were terrified & disgusted by what they witnessed of humanity's ancestry & what was to become of it & they wanted to carry out their mission to fix things exactly how they remembered them to have been. There were others, however, that had understood the folly of all this & resigned themselves to their fate. You'd think these were more likely to be the ones pressed into it, but more often than not they were those who had been most pious & most keen to go. It seems the more easily they identified the error as their own the more readily they took responsibility for it."

"That's a very grown-up way of thinking."

"Isn't it. What was slightly less grown-up, perhaps, was their magic talisman. It was a clear toy marble, probably part of a *solitaire* set that Rich had found in his house. It was supposed to have been passed on for safekeeping by these good Holimans. It was called the *barelady*."

But Sloggy's contact was a burly Russian
    Whose big left hand could lift a man and €rottle
£e cunt, and leave his right to give concussion.
    He was a hatchet man. He wasn't subtle:
He'd infamously bludgeoned a confession
    From some poor sod wi£ a Lambrini bottle,
So everybody called him *Perry Striker*.
    His mom and dad bo€ played £e balalaika

209.3 *c*nt*: The use of this most taboo of nouns, rather neutrally, to mean just a man, is one of the most disturbing symptoms of the moral degradation of this future society. The gender-switch is crucial to the acute obscenity. Despite the critical delusion under which I was working at the time, I stand by the support I expressed in earlier annotations for the word in its original sense (see 1.8 *c*nts*, 38.8 *cheesy Quaver*). It is a dreadful torture—like that inflicted by the Harpies on Phineus of Thessaly for his revelation of Zeus's secrets of the future—that the intangible rehabilitation of such a word can nonetheless seem so close at hand for the philologist: it is a combination of *quaint* and *cunning*, both of which derive from *cognoscĕre* Latin 'to ascertain'. You and I know all too well, however, my friend, how this poem has been designed to devastate with sarcasm the means by which men like us might grasp at such undegraded concepts, separated from us (as we are from one another) only by a short space of time. The word will never again mean 'the thing that ascertains'. There is no ascertaining that can be achieved any more. The place from which we have all come has been made into the throttled victim of hamfisted foreign brutality.

209.6-8 *Lambrini... Perry Striker... balalaika*: A bizarre mixture of tongues: Italian, English, Russian etc. This argotic 'language of the birds' reminds one (as inevitably as the tragic doom itself) of the *sundry unknown languages* that make up the playlet in which Hieronimo's revenge is cunningly enacted in Kyd's *Spanish Tragedy*. The killers of the old man's son are unwittingly recruited to perform their various suicides and mutual murders for an audience of their own fathers in the form of a lacerating Pentecostal parody in which they act out a literal tragedy without understanding anything they say. As one inwardly enunciates this bastardized glossolalia, one can only wait for the fateful blade to sink into one's flesh at one's own hand.

    *   *   *

'Now these I can get for you, Mr Stover.' Hermione was standing by the open window, examining one of the Chinese figurines in the sharp parallelogram of light. 'My father imports almost half the Chinese artefacts that enter Britain. Well, those that come in legally, at least. He has an office in Hong Kong.'

'Ah, Tang jade. The honesty of it so poignant. Undying dedication to the impossible.'

'I could get you a piece like this for as little as 10 guineas. More like 100 for a full ensemble though. They often come in sets of three or four: legendary characters, or different aspects of the same character, sometimes even progress of a hero over time... like the ages of man. Those ones are the most interesting if you think about the meaning of the material. What's a hundred guineas in dollars? About five hundred?'

'I don't use money. Especially not The Bank of England's or The Federal Reserve's.'

    *   *   *

"Oh yeh, I remember bareladies." The memory came with a startling force. I could see the glint of the magnolia glass in the school playground. My hairless childhood fingers held up to the sky seemed more palpable than the tufted lumps on the ends of my elongated arms. "They were basically just marly crystals, normal small-size transparent ones, but the idea was you could see a naked woman if you held them up to the light. It was a kind of emperor's new clothes in reverse. Just a way of making a humdrum marble a bit more valuable."

"That's it, but the boys hadn't made that connection with the name. Sometimes words have a magic if you haven't quite worked out what they mean. They thought the *barelady* was an all-powerful charm, something capable of drawing all the Holimans to itself. It was like the moon in miniature: a time lens that the Holimans could apply at their own whim. It allowed the bearer to see what a Holiman really was: what he or she was like as a human being before the sacrifice. For this reason it was an object of huge desire for them. Most importantly though, it was capable, if used by enough of them at once, of stopping time itself... of returning the world to the way it had been. This would mean the destruction of history, one group of people in the middle of an island (a peninsular) off the north western coast of the Eurasian landmass freezing existence into their own place & epoch, nullifying the life of anyone who lived elsewhere, or before or since, to achieve immortality."

"So these were definitely the baddies. The *barelady*'s a bit like Tolkien's ring..." I was struggling to keep a grip on myself. My own voice was much more distant than Hannah's.

"Yes, but you can understand their motives. In fact it's more *The Weirdstone of Brisingamen*. They'd just been reading that... by Alan Garner. Though that book's obviously influenced by Tolkien too. The good Holimans on the other hand didn't want to see this happen. They knew it was wrong. So they left the barelady for the boys to find & helped them understand (via a few cryptic messages) that it should be kept away from the Holimans during the equinox. On that evening the good Holimans would be forced to materialise at the great gathering in the original sacred site for a few crucial seconds which would coincide with the appearance of the baddies. If that happened, the bad Holimans would overpower them & force them to give up the *barelady*. At the next possible occasion they would come back & take the *barelady* back to stop the boys having to bear the responsibility any longer than necessary."

"It wasn't just a sporadic thing, throughout the entire three days that they were missing the boys lived out this fantasy. They hid in the gullies behind the houses & the bushes around the canal towpaths, avoiding all passers-by as potential Holimans. Holimans were capable of appearing just like normal people, you see. It was a kind of exciting, self-inflicted paranoia. It must've been fun, running around under everybody's noses. Despite the fact they were really close to home, only a stone's throw most of the time, a police search entirely failed to find them. All those back lanes were the kinds of places ten year old boys know better than anyone. They slept in a little shelter they built a few yards back from the canal out of corrugated iron & a couple of fence panels. In the daytime, they played on a rusty yellow bulldozer that had been left on the wasteland just behind their shelter & they wandered around, developing their story to impressive levels of sophistication."

210

> But Perry's talent was £e little arrows,
>   And £at's why Sloggy had to call him in.
> He €ought £e ugly Russian could embarrass
>   Britannia at £e oche, and he'd win
> A golden opportunity to harass
>   £e tart to get a filmed debollockin.
> £e Russian was a bonafide rival.
> $e didn't know it, but her dick's survival

210.1-5 *arrows… embarrass… harass*: *Arrows* is to be pronounced /ˈærəz/ rather like 'arras'. The hanging tapestries behind which characters routinely secrete themselves in Shakespeare plays are actually, in terms of practical staging, the 'backcloths' of the scenery. When Polonius hides behind such a *backdrop* in order to eavesdrop (somewhat voyeuristically) on Hamlet and his mother, he is also disturbing any veneer of figurative realism that might have remained in the depiction of this artificial Elsinore. 'Tell him his prankes haue been too broad to beare with,' says Polonius to Gertrude, 'And that your Grace hath *scree'nd*, and stoode betweene / Much heate, and him. Ile silence me e'ene heere.' (Folio II.ii, my italics). The play on words sets the tone for what is a typical black-comic scene in the midst of the archetypal Elizabethan tragedy. When Hamlet pulls out a mirror (a prop of the fool) to force his mother to examine herself, she cries out thinking it is a sword (like everyone else in the audience, she has probably 'seen this play before'). Polonius makes a risible attempt to disentangle himself from the scenery and Hamlet stabs him through the arras, penetrating both the human skin of the Crown's chief advisor and more importantly the theatrical skin of an Elsinore which for him has become as fake and flimsy as it is the source of paranoia. A supposed 'madness' which Polonius's espionage and his euphemistic reference to 'much heate' would seem to justify.

It would be unjust to liken you—the functionary of another usurper, wrapped in the backdrop of *The Birmingham Quean*—to Polonius hiding behind the arras, and a delusion of grandeur to cast myself as the Prince of Denmark. You might just as easily believe it to be the other way around. Such is the paradox of our predicament… as farcical as it is tragic.

210.6 *a filmed debollockin*: 'A cinematically photographed castration'. Though *bollocking* can also refer (probably by hyperbolic metaphorical extension of the sense of physical castration) to a severe verbal reprimand. The semantic connection between verbal and physical violence inflicted upon the receiver is never very far from the poem's surface.

210.7 *bonafide*: Thankfully, still a tetrasyllable, despite the typical American faux-etymology that posits the existence of a verb of almost unprecedented ugliness: *to bonafy*. See 168.8 *bonafide*.

210.8 *dick*: Obviously course slang for the penis, but there is a deeper and more disturbing implication here, 'dick' being also usable as an abbreviation for 'dictionary', of the brutal deracination of language and culture in the form of philistine violence visited upon the lexicon. (cf. 173 *dock her dick*)

> **1873** *Slang Dict.* s.v., A man who uses fine words without much judgement is said to have 'swallowed the dick'.

Out of his mouth go burning lamps, and sparks of fire leap forth

"Perhaps Amrit was romanticising it a bit, but he said they never once thought about writing it down or trying to get any reward for it. Their interest was purely in the story for the story's sake. They talked about it as if it were really happening, as if statements about the Holimans & their activities were statements of fact, or at least real-world assertions to be debated."

"The main theatre of the thing, the site of power that was supposed to have been the original sacred place, was an area of scrubby grass underneath an electricity pylon on the opposite side of the Stratford canal from Monyhull Hospital. He took me to see it once. This was to host the gathering of the Holimans on the night of the equinox. The boys hid out that night in the bushes by one of its huge metal feet & watched what transpired underneath. What they witnessed was a real gathering: one they could genuinely believe was the reunion of the evil Holimans. A group of teenagers had got together to drink & smoke & so on, they were kissing & fighting & playing music on a ghettoblaster. You know, the kinds of things teenagers get up to just beyond the sightline of their council estate windows. The boys were crouched together in the bushes watching, sharing the *barelady* so they could see the Holimans in their original forms, not daring to eat the sweets & drink the pop they'd bought in case they made a noise & the Holimans came & took the magic gem off them."

"They had money?" I asked. The question seemed to come from beyond the kitchen window.

"During the day, they searched gutters & drains for discarded coins. They collected quite a lot. They were pretty resourceful. So there they were, shivering in the bushes, longing for their shelter & their sleeping bags, but never once did they undermine the fiction. They whispered to each other, discussing the situation as if it was still part of the story. They became more & more frightened & more & more excited as time went on. These people cavorting in their weird rituals underneath the pylon were the evil Holimans. Any moment now the goodies might appear & be attacked. The boys had been too curious to come & see the spectacle & had been stupid enough to bring the *barelady* with them, but they couldn't leave now. They should've taken the advice to stay away, obviously, but it was compelling viewing. Besides, they felt pretty safe in their little hideout. But then two of the teenagers came over, closer to where the boys were hiding & began to undo each other's trousers. Amrit thought they were going to have sex right there, no more than ten yards away from them. It was to be a diabolical part of the ritual. Rich made a noise & the girl, who was now lying back on the floor with the boy lowering himself onto her, turned her head to look at where the sound had come from. She probably hadn't seen them but the boys were terrified. She sniffed at the air like a cat. They ran away."

"You know," I interjected, "this is all very reminiscent of..."

"Don't even say it!" Hannah snapped. She smiled to show it was in fun. "Anyway, as they were running away, Rich slipped & clattered into a moored narrowboat. He only stopped himself from falling into the canal by jumping on the deck. He made the whole thing rock violently. A mirror was dislodged & smashed into the galley sink. A couple asleep inside the boat were woken up & they must've seen where the boys escaped to. The police were called & Rich & Amrit were picked up in their shelter half an hour later."

Was genuinely coming under €reat.
$e realised her cock was up for grabs,
But from her understanding of £e bet,
$e €ought $e only risked a dose of crabs
Or gonorrhoea. $e could *not* suspect
He planned to turn it into i kebabs.
$e knew £e geezer was a dodgy baiter,
But never €ought he wanted to castrate her.

211.2 *her cock was up for grabs*: I wonder whether you had any problem handling such grotesque manifestations of Bosvil's illogic when forced to take his dire dictation. I assume you must have done. For me the crude oxymoron of *her cock* is about as much as I can take. It is almost as sickening to accept the verbal reference as it would be to bear witness to the erectile organ itself, currently concealed (thank God) behind its ironic Union Jack arras.

The crass penile metaphor of the cockerel reminds us of the latent gambling imagery. Before being outlawed, cock-fighting was the gaming contest of choice amongst these kind of lowlife characters. There is an C18th pub in Birmingham (a listed building) called *The Fighting Cocks*, I believe. This requires about as much explanation of how the spiritual heart of the city came to be called the Bull Ring. Betting on the outcome of two or more half-starved and violent animals in conflict is infinitely more ignoble than the rural pursuit of keeping down fox numbers in the traditional equine fashion, surely.

Up for grabs is a formulaic phrase which refers to the position caused by a standard ruse of the card sharp in which he deliberately causes an argument in order to 'grab' the pot. The *cock* in question is therefore transferred from the characters' masculine *cock-fight* to the metaphorical *money* that is to be the prize. The drag-queen's clandestine but omnipresent penis is therefore quite obviously rendered the *equivalent* of the counterfeit pound coin. At no point in the piece is it ever made more obvious how the two *queans*—the skewed effigy on the coin who is the poem's narrator, and the very male drag-queen—are interchangeable.

211.4-5 *a dose of crabs / Or gonorrhoea*: It is impossible to say, with the second of these sexual diseases, whether its name derives from the Greek γόνος 'seed' and ροία 'flux' (because it was supposed to be a leakage of semen) or from the mistransliteraltion *Gomorrha* of the Hebrew counterpart to the wicked plain-city of *Sodom* in Genesis XVIII to XIX. Is it, that is, 'gonorrhoea' or 'gomorrhia' (the disease of Gomorrha). The distinction is a rather nice one, obviously. The two ideas are hardly easy to disentangle. The sins of Gomorrha and of Onan, the spiller of seed, are not unrelated. In any event, it seems clear that Bosvil is accentuating that innovation of Milton's by taking such overt delight in making a Gomorrha of Eden… a Birmingham of Paradise.

211.6 *shish kebabs*: Turkish 'skewered meat'. (See 56.7)

211.7 *dodgy baiter*: Perhaps this is a misspelling of a term from falconry—meaning a badly trained impatient bird which tends to *bate and dodge*, i.e. flutter its wings and avoid the perch or the fist. Alternatively it might cast Sloggy (in his internal, fantastic version of what is obviously the opposite situation) as a 'devious angler' and Britannia as his endangered quarry. If so there are unavoidable allusions to 'the fisher of men' and 'the fisher king' who will return fertility to *The* (Arthurian) *Waste Land*.

"Did they still have the marble, the *barelady* on them?"

"Amrit watched Rich throw it in the canal as he was led away by a WPC. He tried to stop him but it was too late."

"But what if the evil Holimans came back for it... you know... with snorkels?" My irony was hollow. I felt weak.

"Presumably they were holding out for *Holimans II, The Search for the Barelady*. & that's the point, Sam. If you want to understand Amrit you have to realise that this is exactly what he's really after. He still thinks like a kid. He wants a world in which a boy hiding on the fringes of society can save the world by clinging onto some wonderful, wonderfully vague, secret. He doesn't want to take part in life. He wants to watch it & to pretend that only he understands what's going on... by some freak accident he has been given temporary possession of this precious thing... this *barelady*. He knows it's not true but he believes it anyway."

"Yeh but don't you think it's telling that the magic talisman was basically a con. It was a little crystal ball with nothing in it. I can't believe a ten year-old kid came up with something so sophisticated. It's more than a delusion." I was beginning to feel a bit less tripped out. This was my territory again. This was *The Birmingham Quean* in its infancy. I knew my way around these back lanes like Amrit & Rich knew the Brandwood gullies.

"Nobody's doubting Amrit's intelligence. It's just that he's an inveterate escapist."

"It's like those *third eye* pictures. I'm sure they were an enormous con. They never worked."

"You've probably just got a bit of an astigmatism, Sam."

"That's what they said to the Emperor. Well, anyway, that's all... useful, I suppose. Maybe if I tried to get in touch with this Rich. Have you any idea what became of him?"

"They went to different secondary schools. They lost contact. I very highly doubt it'd be of any use for you to talk to him. Besides, I'm not sure he'd be very happy to discover that somebody he'd never met knew such intimate details about his past. That's if it's true, of course. Amrit could easily have made it up. Either way, it shows you just what Amrit's like."

"Yeh you're right, that *would* be weird. Is there anybody else I could get in touch with... from his past."

"I tell you what, I'll give you Carla's address... his mom..." she stepped over to the phone & scrawled something on a note pad, "here." She tore the page out & brought it over.

"Carla? You've got her address? Why didn't you ever give me this before?"

"Because I knew it would be useless. Carla was the first person I got in touch with when Amrit disappeared. I phoned her a few times in the first weeks, but Amrit had never been in touch. Amrit & his mother never got on. As soon as he was old enough he left home. He's had nothing much to do with ever her since. He'd be more likely to contact me than her. He's never really forgiven her. She still calls him Martin, for godsake. He can't abide that."

> 'Yeh, Perry, get yer arse down to £e Swan;
>   I've got a job for ya… a piece o piss…
> A JOB… you wouldn't wanna miss £is one…
>   No, look… get here by €ree or you can kiss
> Your week in Corfu wi£ £at tasty blonde…
>   I €ought so… bring yer darts.' For emphasis,
> He drew his fingers back to meet his eye
> (£e way The Viking does) and let one fly

212.8 *(the way The Viking does)*: 'Don't touch 'em if you can't A. Fordham' [Poet's note]

    The likening of Sloggy's exaggerated projection of his finger to the archetype (suggested by the capital letters) of the Viking warrior with spear is an absurd hyperbole. The archetype itself, perfectly exemplified in *The Battle of Maldon*, of the barbarian Viking who attacks the borders of a civilized, literate, Christian Anglo-Saxon Britain, is itself one subject to the biases of the period. Such fear of barbarian invasion seems much more pertinent to the current example, however. Perry Striker really is a brutal pillager, whereas the Vikings were mostly peaceful traders who integrated with the Anglo-Saxons and the Britons. One suspects the exotic immigrants in this vision of a future Birmingham to be nowhere near as benign despite their professed desire to *integrate* and *trade* rather than *invade*.

    The *gar* 'spear' of the *wicing* is, of course, his signature weapon. In fact the spear is the crux of his nobility. As the opening lines of *Beowulf* declare:

Hwæt wē Gār-Dena in geārdagum	Oh! The Spear-Danes in olden days
þēodcyninga þrim gefrūnon	and the kings of their tribes: we have all heard
hū ðā æþelingas ellen fremedon.	how these princes of men were brave and virile.

It is as much this noble icon of the Norsemen as the equally iconic English longbow and arrows of the post-Norman period that is belittled by the game of 'darts'. Bosvil's bloody-minded parody of Englishness delights in the reduction of our racial roots to this minuscule and inconsequential absurdity contested by a Slavic *hatchet man* and a Creole drag-queen: Grendel and his mother.

    *   *   *

'Oh, I'm sorry. That was rather inelegant of me wasn't it.'

'Not at all. Besides, elegance is just a cover for an absence of passion. You've got that in spades. I simply don't do money. I grew up during the American silver boom… the bimetallist debates. I left the States to get away from the economic scheming. I've lived here for over fifteen years without spending a single buck. It has nothing to do with high-mindedness. I'm an American for God's sake. The fact is, if you live without cash you spend a good deal of your life bartering. It's the Anglo-American monetary system I object to, not the invigorating business of exchange.'

'But what's wrong with the Bank of England and the Federal Reserve?'

'Mrs Twigg, if I were to take the time to explain in full, we'd be here long enough for the Rothschilds to have accrued several millions of dollars. Suffice to say the Bank of England was the reason for the American Revolution and the creation of its cousin in the States, just before the war, was the culmination of a Semite conspiracy which had brought Europe to the brink of that catastrophe for its own ends. The rest is history.'

    *   *   *

"Hannah, listen, thanks for this." I took the bit of paper out of her grip. My belly growled. I was hungry. Maybe I'd been expecting her to feed me. That was probably why I'd felt faint when she was spinning me her yarns. "Thanks for everything. I'd really better be going."

"Don't expect her to cooperate though. She won't tell you about Amrit's real dad."

I had to get out of there quick. I'd come to tell this woman that I loved her. I'd spent months talking to her when she wasn't there, arguing with her; I'd even prayed to her for godsake. But now it was impossible. I started down the hall towards the door. Thanking her again. She followed me. "You shouldn't thank me, Sam. This... the whole thing's such a shame. I was a bit screwed up when we first met." I couldn't see her. She didn't put the light on in the corridor & I couldn't remember where the switch was. "I'm just sorry I got you into it. Hopefully you can get it out of your system &, you know, we can be friends..."

I reached out & fumbled for the latch to the front door. The cold metal knob scraped my knuckles. I opened it & turned to see her emerge from the gloom. She'd never looked more beautiful than she did there in the light of the streetlamps. The kindness of her expression was... "There's something I need to ask before I go." I said. Cold air enveloped our knees.

"It's not... I don't want anything to do with Amrit..."

She looked pained at the thought of hearing from her ex again. Or was it sympathy for me? "That first time we met..." I said, "why did you... why did you choose *me*?"

"I don't know. We'd been talking all afternoon. I liked you. What you were saying... you just seemed like the right person. I'm really sorry. I don't know what to say."

"No, it's ok, I mean, why did you even come up & talk to me in the first place? You hadn't seen me give my paper. That was a lie. I would have remembered you."

She smiled, lifted her eyebrows. "No." My courage surprised her, I think. It surprised me.

"So..."

"I heard a bit, but no, you're right. I was sitting in the conservatory reading a book. David Lodge. I was sick of the same old post-grad students droning out their essays to their friends. You rushed past behind me. You were late. I remember hearing people laughing on the other side of the doors as you began. It was a nice sound. Unusual. It reminded me of the ducks on the river that morning. You were feeding them jammy hotel croissant & they were quacking. You were something new, Sam. Everybody else had been there the full weekend. I was bored. I just fancied chatting up a bit of fresh blood, I suppose. No different from Derek really. Except that... well... I didn't actually intend to get you into bed."

"Er... no. I'm sorry about that: you know, that night I was here. When Lynne..."

"Forget it Sam. It was a mistake. The whole thing's been one big mistake. If only I could get you to drop it, leave Amrit Singh behind... we could be friends."

"Yeh. I can't though. Not yet... I'll be in touch. & I promise not to... y'know."

"Bye." she closed the door. I turned back into the frosty Disney filmset.

> Towards £e hang-up key to end £e call.
>   'Righd-o £en Precious, it's a fuckin deal.
> £e bouncer €rows for me. Winner takes all.
>   And, seein as I'm nice, in case you feel
> I've undersold you, what about a small
>   Ca$ stake.' He whopped his wad out and began to peel
> £e twenties off. 'No need' $e told him, 'fuck it.'
>   He $rugged... 'What have you got in your pocket?'

213.3 *The bouncer throws for me*: Perhaps a veiled reference to the so-called 'Bodyline' series: always a willow bat with which to beat the reputation of the English; it would naturally recommend itself to Bosvil for that reason alone. In my opinion the aggressive, tribal tactics of the West Indian fast-bowlers, who pitch their vehement balls so short that they spear up into the head and face, are infinitely less gentlemanly than Douglas Jardine's robust strategy of forewarned bodyblows. One cannot help but be reminded by those dark, long-limbed wielders of a blood-red missile, of the Zulu or the Masai.

213.6 Another Birmingham Alexandrine. Considering Britannia's previous encounter with Saddam, the association of this metrical elongation to the boastful phallic connotations of the verb *to whop* (originally a jocularly heroic verb describing in onomatopoeic terms the sudden and impressive drawing of a sword) is very clear.

213.8 *'what've you got in your pocket'*: In the 'Riddles in the Dark' chapter of *The Hobbit*—in which Bilbo Baggins discovers the ring of power whose epic fate is the concern of his impressive present work—it is the reverse of this question that allows Bilbo (quite unfairly) to beat the malignant Gollum in a contest of riddles. The answer to the question is obviously much more important both to the reader and the subterranean creature than the simple fact that one can answer it and the other cannot. The mismatch of knowledge is crucial though. The whole suspenseful pleasure of the chapter rests in pitting oneself against the contestants and wondering how one might perform in the same predicament. The reader shares Bilbo's relief at Gollum's unexpected acceptance of a 'riddle' ('what have I got in my pocket?') that is an archetypal portrayal of the possession of superior knowledge. The ring hidden in the pocket is more than analogically related to the *knowledge* of the hidden ring in the obscure possession of Bilbo's mind (and the reader's). The effect is especially acute for one revisiting Professor Tolkien's first book for children with an understanding of just how powerful and dangerous the ring is revealed to be in the forthcoming book. For those with that extra knowledge burning a hole (as they say) in the pocket of their mind, the question passing semi-consciously from Bilbo's mouth seems to have emerged directly from the One Ring itself. It wants to escape from that dingy underground lake as much as Bilbo does. It will do everything possible to make that happen.

It is a characteristic reversal here that the battle of wits should appear to cast Britannia as Bilbo and Sloggy as the predatory Gollum. We know, though that it is Britannia who has Sloggy in her clutches. He has the coin (that is driving the transaction) but she, like us, possesses the knowledge. Like Gollum, she knows what the coin can do (what it stands for, how powerful it is) where he does not. In fact, like Gollum, she only lives because it does: her nature and her fate are intertwined with its. Unlike Gollum though, she knows he has it in his pocket and she knows how to get it off him. Sloggy might like to think of himself as a market-place prestidigitator playing *find the lady* or *the cups and balls* but the 'mark' he has chosen is much more capable even than him of turning up the prize. She, after all is said and done, is just its shadow.

It thawed overnight. After eating an Indian takeaway I'd bought on the way back home from Hannah's, I spent & hour or so tiptonging around my parents' questions. Then I sat up & listened to the icicles around their gutters dripping themselves out of existence... At first light, I fell asleep.

It was two in the afternoon by the time I woke up. I had a bath & put on some respectable-looking clothes then made myself a sandwich & left the house. Sometimes it's nice to eat while you're walking along. It's probably not good for the digestion, & you don't want to make a piggish spectacle of yourself in a populated area, but there's a sense of purpose to it... even if you're not going anywhere in particular. I had the address of Amrit's mother in my back pocket, but I wasn't headed there right now. Instead I'd decided to take a bit of a detour via the back lanes & canal towpaths Hannah had mentioned: the places Rich & Amrit had hidden out when they were on the run from the Holimans. I took a bite of my sandwich & headed for the nearest gully. I hadn't finished chewing when I saw the fence...

When I was a kid, it had been possible to move around very large areas of Birmingham almost exclusively via routes that were not part of the public highway. There were so many winding back lanes, parks, canals, subways & bits of wasteground that you could roam around at will without seeing more than a couple of moving cars all day. It might have been Britain's motown, but Birmingham also had the largest area of inner city parkland in Europe & the country's most successful network of what the environmental scientists call *green corridors*. As far as wildlife is concerned, that's still the case. The difference now is that it's considerably harder for human beings to use them too.

This is because residents' committees have put up fences. This one was tall & galvanised & spiky. There always used to be signs on some of the richer gullies saying 'Trespassers will be Prosecuted' or 'Private Property' but nobody took them seriously, no more than anybody thought twice about taking a short cut across a school playground if it was the best way to the shops. Now, though, property prices are much higher. Homes have much more money spent on them. People keep a lot more valuable stuff at home (or at least they think they do). They're a different kind of homeowner altogether. They've got a lot more to protect. Everybody's frightened. Up go the fences.

It's not just a matter of having your shortcuts frustrated. These gullies were the internodes of our lives as children. They were how we got from home to school to friends' houses to playgrounds to the park, & they remain the internodes of memory. In order to remember, I still need to walk through my internal gullies. When I got to the end of the one I always used to take to school that afternoon, chewing bread & cheese, I felt betrayed. The fence builders, my neighbours, had closed off my internal functions of recollection. It wasn't just that I couldn't go the way I wanted to, it was that my ability to make connections between ideas, between past & present, had been taken from me. This is how it always works. If you put up barriers to stop people moving through their childhood environment you do something violent to their past, to their humanity. King's Heath's not Gaza or Belfast, but still...

Sloggy had a bulge below his hip
    Which made his trousers sag. 'What's £at you've got?'
He touched £e fabric wi£ a fingertip
    But didn't look. 'It's just my keys… It's not
£e family jewels… maybe a paperclip
    Or two.' $e beamed, 'I wanna see £e lot.
Come on.' He frowned at her, £en $rugged and did
Her bidding. 'Keys,' he drawled, 'a file… a quid:

214.1 *a bulge below his hip*: The lewd echo in the previous question of Mae West's infamous phallic euphemism 'is that a gun in your pocket?' only serves to heighten the uncanny implications inherent in the allusion to Professor Tolkien's troubling work.

*   *   *

I gulped the sugary, herbaceous wine and swilled my ice around. I didn't dare look at either of them until Stover leapt up and strode over to where she was standing.

'Do you know what these banks actually do?' He opened a drawer in the escritoire.

I struggled forward on the pretext of replacing my glass. My calves ached.

'Essentially, they're private consortia of bankers with a license to print money.' Stover continued, 'Literally. They create paper money of completely hypothetical value above and beyond the actual wealth of a state (however that might be measured: gold reserves, national product) and they lend it to the government at a rate of interest they set themselves. The government then spends it on whatever flag-waving flummery will keep the population paying the taxes that provide the bankers with their profits. The whole point is to bypass the messy business of production and create a hyper-capitalism that can increase personal fortunes without producing anything more tangible than overvalued rectangles of paper. It turns the nation-state into a production-line of pure profit. Ah… here it is… The obvious upshot is inflation. And what do you do about inflation? You raise interest rates and income tax. They overvaluate the world economy so they can take the extra for themselves.'

'Can't we reintroduce the Gold-Standard or something?' she asked.

Stover padded closer to her, the small green rectangle of paper held between his bulky forepaws with the care one might apply when handling explosives.

'What difference would that make? They set the price of gold as well. In fact, it would provide them with another mechanism of control. By carefully aligning all of these mechanisms in the various states, the Rothschilds and their kind have managed to turn the entire civilized world into a cash factory. The alliances and enmities of governments are manufactured by them to ensure the transcendent nature of their international capital over the vagaries of national politics and to encourage the competitive spending which keeps the governments overplaying their own productivity and coming back to borrow more. The inevitable outcome is collapse, conflict and communism. We've seen it once, and it'll happen again. Here, take a look at this.'

He handed the piece of paper to Hermione. Her fingers were tiny in comparison to his bony knuckles. The thumb of his right hand was thick, the nail like a chunk of amber.

*   *   *

I threw away the sandwich. I didn't want to eat whilst walking past the front windows of the people who'd done this thing to me. I couldn't blame them really, they were victims of a vague cultural paranoia. But, then again, so was I: I was avoiding being watched by *them*.

I used the streets to make my way down to the canal. It was a drab, mild day after the icy glitz of the previous evening. Canals are probably at their best under a grey sky, though, especially such a leafy suburban cut as the Stratford upon Avon. The still, dark water in its rut of still, dark brick becomes the centrepiece of a comforting tranquillity. A light drizzle began to fall as if to suggest that all things, my hair & skin included, would eventually become part of the canal. We would while away eternity between two locks. There was an old telly floating near the far bank. Its dead screen of chunky grey glass melded with the water's motionless surface. I carried on for a minute or so, & then I saw it.

Behind a corrugated iron fence, out of which a panel had been ripped, there was a low hut made out of the missing panel & two sections of those tubular metal barriers they put up around building sites. The ground beneath it was covered with several layers of old cardboard. It was exactly the kind of shelter Hannah had described. Surely it couldn't be the same one Amrit & Rich had made back in the early eighties. It looked far too new. Neither was it in the slightest bit romantic. You could imagine a junky overdosing under it, a wino with hypothermia. You'd have to be extremely resilient to think it was an exciting place to sleep.

My journey over to Carla's involved walking past the bottom of the pylon — the sacrificial altar of the Holimans — but that was much less interesting. It was... just how I'd imagined it. If you've seen one of these things, you've seen them all. The size of it in comparison to the human-scale technology of the neighbouring Victorian canal was impressive, I suppose, but it was the image of that little shelter that stayed with me as I walked up Carla's garden path.

I rehearsed my opening words for the space of a few fast breaths then rang the doorbell. A woman in her early sixties opened the inside door & then the porch. Her hair was short, neat & untinted. She had reading glasses in her left hand. She was wearing a plum velveteen sweater which had a strand of black cotton hanging off its right sleeve at the elbow.

"Have you got a parcel for me?" she asked.

"Er no, Mrs..." I couldn't remember her second name. It certainly wasn't Singh. That's not even a family name for Sikhs, not often, & anyway she'd never used it. Besides, she could very well have remarried since Leon... what was Leon's name?

"... Carla Higgs," she said, "you haven't got my parcel?"

"No, I'm sorry to bother you. I'm... I'm here because I'm trying to find out about Amrit."

She looked puzzled.

"Sorry, I mean I'm looking for your son, Martin."

"Oh, I see. Come in then, love. Are you an old schoolfriend of his or something? I went onto *friends reunited* myself. Only got one response though..."

> £at's all.' He $oved us, one by one, across
>> £e bar. Her hand moved closer to my face...
> And dropped. Her touch was soft and cool like moss.
>> $e slid me off and €umbed me to £e place
> Just past her fingerprint where $e could toss
>> My body in £e air—quite commonplace
> Perhaps, but when her €umb sprang up and stang
> My edge and sent me whirling €rough £e smoke to hang

215.2 *Her hand moved closer to my face*: The sudden return of the perspective of the coin comes as an eschatological shock. Its voice is like the awareness of death.

215.8 Here the alexandrine has been shifted to the last line from its more common position before the couplet. This is obviously the traditional way of doing things. The effect here is the opposite of the traditional one, however. Rather than being emphatic or conclusive, the six-foot line creates an effect of *rubato* in order to mimic the transfer into the slow-motion description of the toss of the coin. The verb 'to hang', used to suggest a moment of still-motion at the apex of the *toss*, itself *hangs* for an immobile instant onto (or over) the end of the line... until the gravity of the *enjambment* pulls it down into the next stanza.

Tempo rubato is literally 'stolen time' in Italian. As such it is particularly apt. The effect of the counterfeit's *activation* (by tossing) demonstrates how it serves not only to undermine the value system of the present context but to disrupt time itself. This a form of cosmic 'theft'. Both the previous reversal effect (with the fox) and the return of this slowed action at the climax of the game are revealed at this quasi-transcendental moment to be a prime function of this *charm* of instability.

$$H |\psi(t)\rangle = i\hbar \frac{d}{dt} | \psi(t)\rangle$$

$$E = m_0 c^2$$

$$\left(\alpha_0 mc^2 + \sum_{j=1}^{3} \alpha_j p_j c \right) \psi(x, t) = i\hbar \frac{\partial \psi}{\partial t} (x, t)$$

fig. 6: quantum equations. These are, respectively, Schrödinger's Equation (which describes the time-evolution of a quantum system), Einstein's famous mass-energy relationship (which forms the core of Special Relativity), & Dirac's Equation (defining the crucial relationship between the previous two). This is exactly how they appear in Paul Dirac's *Principles of Quantum Mechanics* (Cambridge 1930): still a standard British textbook in the 1950s & Twigg's most likely source. His inclusion of them tends to contradict the belief implicit in his next note that Schrödinger & Einstein hold completely incompatible positions. It's possible *Singh* intends the mathematical reader to realise that Twigg doesn't understand all this. Unfortunately I don't really understand it all myself. I'm also quite incapable of carrying this kind of complex (*bra-ket*) notation around in my head. I can reproduce the equations now only because I looked them up in Dirac when I first encountered them. Needless to say, they were much less tidily represented in the manuscript than they appear here. [S.A.M.T.]

She showed me into the living-room. It smelt of some kind of solvent. Strewn around the perimeter of a pile of patterned cushions in the middle of the floor there was what appeared to be the carnage following a skirmish between a regiment of actionmen & a guerrilla force of puppets & rag dolls over the rather inauspicious territory of the local newspapers.

"... Barbara Stanner, she was called. Everybody fancied her. & not just the boys. She had curly yellow hair. Not blonde, you know, actually custard yellow. & blue eyes. You'll never guess what she's doing now... sorry about the mess, by the way, I'm working, take a seat..."

There was only one chair in the room. I sat in it. "Yes I'm sorry to disturb you," I said, "I just wanted to ask a couple of questions. It won't take long."

"You're not from the CSA are you?"

"No, no, definitely not."

"Barbara runs a company selling bespoke fake books. You can match the binding to your decor. Can you believe that? It's a design thing. There's nothing in the books at all: just blank pages, but they're hard bound & you can choose exactly how its done... you know, the colour & the kind of lettering for the spines & so on. I don't know if you get to choose the titles too. That would be quite hilarious. Just think of the fun you could have if you made them up. I doubt the kinds of people who would do a thing like that would know enough book titles to make that work though. They probably just give you a basic range of the classics."

"*The Invisible Man... The Diary of a Nobody*?"

"It would be useless coming here if you were from the CSA, you know. I haven't seen Martin for over five years. I haven't got the faintest idea where he is."

"No, I know that. I'm just... trying to find out a little more about him."

"You do, do you?... The thing that gets me is why anybody would want a thing like that?"

"I suppose I'm a kind of... fan."

"No, the books... you could probably buy a job lot of second hand classics at your local charity shop for a fraction of the price. But then I suppose they wouldn't match your curtains."

"Actually if they were all public domain things," I added, "they could easily include the texts. It wouldn't cost them anything in royalties."

"What did you say your name was?"

"Sam. Sam Trainor."

"How did you get my address, Sam?" she was still standing by the door.

"Hannah gave it to me." I thought about standing up again myself. "What I wanted to know..."

"Oh, I see. I'm sorry Sam, I don't think I can help you. Hannah's more likely to know Martin's whereabouts than me. We fell out a long time ago. I've never even met my own grandchild."

> Above £eir eyes..., I didn't want to land:
>   Not ever... £en, face-first, I smacked her palm.
> $e slapped me over on her o£er hand
>   And peered at my head. $e seemed quite calm
> But saw at once £at I was contraband.
>   I lay £ere on her skin; $e stretched her arm.
> 'I'll play for £is.' He $rugged and $ook his head,
>   'Okay, whatever floats your boat,' he said.

216.1 *I didn't want to land*: The coin seeks a physical state of indeterminacy, a literal manifestation of that ontological ambiguity that is the *counter*'s defining feature. It does not merely wish to be free of gravity, but also that its *spin* should never end. It seeks to defy *reso*lution with permanent *revo*lution.

The coin's utopia is a kind of *limbo*. Originally this was simply the *limbus* 'edge' of hell: that region for the pre-Christian or the unbaptized on the borders of the inferno around which Dante is led by Virgil. The necessarily ambiguous nature of this region—on the cusp of life and death, heaven and earth, good and evil—is what suggests the more casual contemporary usage to mean a state (not usually one to be desired) of indecision or neglect as a result of irresolvable counteractive forces. In this case, the idea is transformed into the literal image of the *limbus* of the coin describing (by means almost identical to those used to fool the eye in cinema and television) a flashy fools-gold sphere as it spins at the *vertex* of its toss. The definitive metaphor of binary chance—the toss of the coin—is therefore entirely destabilized at the midpoint of its enactment because the two possible outcomes of heads and tails are entirely subsumed by a sphere of potentiality—an empty sphere constituted entirely of its own illusionary periphery—that can only exist because of the mysterious third dimension (and theoretical third possible outcome) of the *limbus*.

In fact, the *limbus* of hell is etymologically related to the idea of its *limin* or 'threshold'. The ideas of *limbo* and *liminality* are entangled. In passing from one state or place into another there is always some perfect, seemingly impossible, point of equilibrium at which we cannot tell whether we are in both at once, or beyond the influence of either. If one were capable of stopping at that point he might never escape. It is this position—neither up nor down, neither heads nor tails—that the counterfeit naturally desires.

There is a critical dispute over a matter of staging in *The Tempest* which serves to demonstrate the linguistic complex. At the mid point of Act IV, Prospero plots to bring justice to the trinity of revolutionary fools—Stephano, Trinculo and Caliban—by sending Ariel to fetch 'The trumpery in my house... for stale to catch these theeues' (i.202-3). A *stale* was a stuffed bird used as decoy in falconry. When Ariel returns '*loaden with glistering apparell*' and Prospero commands him to 'hang them on this line' the trap is being set with a flashy counterfeit (*stale*) of the robes (the *stolen stoles*) of state. The similarity to Britannia's 'Union Jack of sequinned gauze' with its 'fur below the hem' is obvious.

The dispute, however, is over the word 'line' (one on which much hangs in verse-theatre): whether it is intended that Ariel peg this 'friperie' on a *clothes line* or a *lime tree*. One need not go into the details of the dispute; suffice to say it will probably never be decided. Besides, it is irrelevant. It is clear that both interpretations are intended. The ambiguity is the point. The 'line' scene—one more of the dramatic tableaux set up by Propsero to teach his captive audience a lesson—is implicitly a *limin*: it is the threshold ('line') between the moral and political dichotomies of this distinctly limboesque little island and it is quite sensible (and traditional to the Romance genre) that such a *limin* should be embodied in a tree (like the *ympe-tre* that marks the boundary between the worlds of men and fairies in *Sir Orfeo*). The play on words is fundamental to the *liminality* and is much more complex than just *clothes-line* and *linden*; it also connotes both *birdlime* and *fishing-line*: two ways for the hunter to trap his pray—the first using the sticky sap of the *linden* to catch small birds; the second involving a baited hook (we should remember that the ambiguously half-human Caliban has previously been called 'a very manfish' by his companions, in terms which ironically recall the grotesque semi-piscine deity *Oannes* who was supposed by the Babylonians to have emerged from the oceans to teach human beings language).

The realm for which Caliban is ultimately destined to be ruler, upon Prospero's inevitable abdication, is one defined by the same ambiguity that he amphibiously embodies, the *liminal* state of *limbo*. It is a similar Calibanic desire that the counterfeit pound expresses in its effort to maintain its spin indefinitely. The perfectly equivocal blur of its (inscriptionless) *limbus* is the characteristic action of this fake sovereign. Even when not physically achieving it, the coin-narrator revels in an analogous linguistic and logical *limbo*.

In Quantum Mechanics (a subject in which, for reasons obvious to both of us, I have recently taken a very amateurish interest), the failure to maintain this kind of freedom from definition—a fall from what the coin feels to be a state of indeterminate grace—would be referred to by Erwin Schrödinger as *wavefunction collapse*. If I have understood it correctly, the standard *Copenhagen* interpretation of Quantum Mechanics has it that measurement outcomes are fundamentally indeterministic because probability is part and parcel of the state of matter. Particles and their *wavefunctions* (in Heisenberg's system, a probabilistic *matrix* of position, direction, velocity etc.) are one and the same thing. Any successful attempt to measure the attributes of the building blocks of the universe is only successful because it has resulted in 'wavefunction collapse': that is, the measurement process has randomly happened upon one amongst various possibilities inherent in the state's wavefunction, so that the wavefunction has instantaneously changed to reflect that reductive event. It is as if Heisenberg's 'uncertainty principle' has literalized what appears at first to be a simple transferred epithet: the uncertainty of the scientist before measurement transferred to the literal uncertainty of the object of measurement.

It is a core principal of Quantum Mechanics that elementary particles *spin*, and that the specific angular momentum of the spin is a defining feature (quantum) of each different particle. According to the Heisenberg principle, however, each specific instance of an elementary particle (a single electron, for example) spins simultaneously on an infinite number of multidimensional axes. By measuring the 'observable' spin on a particular axis we have necessarily negated the spin on the others. The only spin quality remaining to be measured in the case of an electron (a ½ spin particle) is whether the spin is *up* or *down* (analogous to *clockwise* or *anticlockwise*), but in the case of particles of a higher spin value there are also more than two possible *directions* of spin.

The Heisenberg Principle led to Einstein's famous comment 'God does not play dice' and the even more famous reassertion of the Copenhagen Interpretation in the *cat* paradox included by Schrödinger in a letter of qualified agreement… a cat in a box is either alive or dead, we simply open the lid to discover what was true before… but this is only the case because the cat is not an elementary particle.

So £ere we go. £e battle-lines were drawn.
   Our girl'd beat some ugly photofit;
$e knew $e would. $e could avoid £e porn
   And win herself a mis-struck counterfeit:
£e perfect piece of jewellery to adorn
   Her outfit… but… let's just get on wi£ it…
Once bo€ of £em were present, £e announcer
Bigged up £e drag-queen and £e Russian bouncer

In fact, Einstein's main objection to quantum theory was its defiance of 'local realism'. Quantum Theory insists that an apparently supernatural violation of the core principle of General Relativity (namely that information cannot travel faster than light) is demonstrably true. This is because of what Schrödinger called 'Quantum Entanglement', and Einstein 'spooky action at a distance'. This is a result of simultaneous measurements carried out on two or more particles emitted from the same source in different directions invariably turning up complementary results: if, for example, the spin around a specific axis of two photons emitted from the same light-source is measured at the same time, one will always have *up* spin and the other *down* spin. The Heisenberg Principle requires this disambiguation to have occurred at the (distal) point(s) of measurement rather than the (proximal) point(s) of emission. Einstein holds that this cannot be true (there being nothing to carry the message so quickly) and it must have something to do with a 'hidden variable'.

Quantum Mechanics is like magic. At the most basic level of our substance, it claims, strange wave/particle entanglements occur… matter is fundamentally indeterminate until physically reduced to a single state by human observation: even the 'grey matter' that does the observing. This libidinously spinning coin (a sphere of wilful ambiguity reduced by the intervention of a hand to a determined shallow disc) pointedly recalls the destabilising influence of Quantum Mechanics on our entire image of the Universe.

In fact the counterfeit sovereign's intention (and therefore Bosvil's) is to go much further into the realms of indeterminacy than the Copenhagen Interpretation (with its reliance on Logical Positivism) would allow. The coin seems to desire the Quantum state as if it were an accessible alternative to that of classical physics. For Heisenberg, Bohr, Schrödinger, Dirac and the rest, there is no process opposite to wavefunction collapse. If observation is a tangible *limin* between Quantum and classical physics there is at least only one direction in which anything can travel through it… there is no radioactive *anti*decay, no inverse observation.

For Bosvil, though, this is not only possible but is also the desired outcome of a cosmic battle between indeterminacy and order. His malign delight in everything uncertain, ambiguous, unstable and unregulated drives him to envisage a world in which only Quantum Theory is true. The entire macro-universe is a projection. Schrödinger was being satirical when he compared the dead/alive cat with the unobserved wavefunction collapse that was to trigger its death. His intention was to separate the Quantum and Newtonian worlds by type. Bosvil would allow no such separation. In his vision, the triumphant invasion of Quantum physics into the Newtonian macro-level has caused universal indeterminacy. Just as a radio-active nucleus can be a superposition of *decayed* and *undecayed*, an animal can be both alive and dead… a coin spins perpetually as heads and tails (or just its edge), a person is both man and woman, black and white…

The consequences are almost too terrible to contemplate. Even the Quantum Theorists can be dismissed. The entire cultural history of classical physics and mathematics upon which they necessarily rely can be refuted on epistemological grounds. It has been the primary internal function of the human brain, Bosvil implies, to seek (for biological survival reasons) to represent the incoherent as if it were coherent, the unpredictable as if predictable. Just as the brain flips the inverse image produced by the eyes back 'the right way up', its principle 'higher' activity has been to counterfeit wavefunction collapse on a massive scale... to trick us into a belief in our own ability to observe, understand, and interact with our environment. Who would want to perpetuate the species if they discovered a 'truth' like that?

The specific patterns of coherence superimposed upon the incoherent reality have been partly biologically hardwired therefore, but of at least equal importance (as with language) has been their cultural determination. In either case it would go some way to explaining how and why scientific results that have been consistently wrong have nevertheless been verifiably reproduced. It is their very reproducibility which proves they can not be true.

Bosvil has returned, he thinks, to lift the veil from our eyes. The coherent universe is a mass hallucination and languages of various sorts (mathematics especially) have been its medium of propagation. The problem with this thing called 'consciousness'—this thing designed to fake wave-function collapse on a massive scale by transforming the sensory information relating to a dimensionless probabilistic morass into a particularized coherence—is that it contains within itself both the permanent whiff of incoherence and (just as worryingly) the possibility of that malfunction of *hypercoherence* we think of as characteristic of mental illness. Seen in this light, all of Newtonian physics—including Einstein and the Quantum theorists, even our so-called 'perception' of dimensions in time and space—could be called a *madness*.

You and I, my friend, are suffering in the knowledge that Bosvil might be right. For me, it is perhaps not the case that he is *already* right. But the existence of this text that you have forcibly penned—the illogical position of which in my epoch seems only possible within a world explicable solely by Quantum Theory—suggests that it is in some sense inevitable that Bosvil's quest for dire cosmic upheaval will ultimately be successful. Even if this self-styled satanic prophet were right—even if the Universe had *always* been a realm of chaotic indeterminacy and the elegant, ordered systems of classical physics and philosophy were a fantasy of the human imagination—surely we could agree that this alone is evidence of divinity and nobility. Our ability to believe in such a world is God at work. Every time we 'observe' wavefunction collapse (in whatever sense), we envisage a beautiful realm of taxonomically organized, complementary patterns of truth. Surely the overarching project of mankind might be understood as the building of this infinitely desirable Jerusalem amidst the chaos.

Instead, Bosvil is intent on absolutely the opposite. His *Brummagem* is a city that has surrendered to the chaos: one that turns full circle through *hypercoherence* to *indeterminacy*; one in which you and I suffer quantum entanglement—your *upspin* to my *downspin*—with no regard for our impossible separation across the flattened dimension of time; one in which we are both like cats in a box... alive and dead at once until the boxes are opened and our complementary fates are revealed; one in which we are two sides of the same coin subsumed in the limbo circumscribed by the perpetually spinning edge... the *wavefunction* of the *limbus* that *cleaves* us... together and apart.

> Wiƒ all ƒe customary hyperbole.
>   ƒat kind of €ing Britannia could ignore.
> It's just like giving blowjobs verbally.
> $e'd heard ƒis cobblers umpteen times before;
> No flattery could make our girl believe
> $e's Hercules… more like an old centaur."
> (But ƒen, ƒis scene is not *entirely*
> Unlike where Herc[ules] $oots darts for Iole;

217.6 *let's just get on with it…/ Once both of them were present*: Note the narrative impatience. As elsewhere the coin is self-consciously demonstrating its ability to control the pace and direction of time. This is much more than the usual narratological relationship between a stable chronology of events and the 'pace' and 'order' of telling it: precisely the tradition in which it duplicitously claims to be speaking in the next stanza's references to the source of contemporary sports reporting to the speeches of messengers replacing unperformable scenes in Athenian drama. The coin's arbitrary and unsettling flaunting of the unity of time and place—even of coherent tensuality—reminds us of the fundamental temporal *uncertainty* of the chaotic (pan-quantum) universe it is not just 'telling us about' but literally 'bringing into being'. *Both of them were present* is transformed by this intimate apprehension of Bosvil's wilful illogic from a seemingly benign and sensible statement about the real world to a paradoxical (and reflexive) assertion that multiple *presents*—separated by both space and time—are capable of being simultaneous. Via some strange magic, it is the enactment of this darts match itself which brings a seemingly impossible event like this about. Within the complex mathematics of the 'game', space and time are revealed not just to be the same thing (as Einstein says) but not to exist at all. How else might I be forced to read what you have been forced to write?

218.3 *like giving blowjobs verbally*: 'Blowjob' is employed, one assumes, in reference to the strenuous respiratory inflation of a large pneumatically structured object, like a rubber dinghy. The metaphoric description of hyperbolic praise as pumping a tyre or bellowsing a furnace is quite commonplace. There is a word which can take in both these senses, it lends this clause a very satisfying gloss: 'It's like delivering a *puff*.'

No matter how satisfying a gloss like this might be, however, it does nothing to make such thorny instances of gommorhean argot any easier to swallow.

218.8 *Hercules shoots darts for Iole*: The last events of the mythic life of Herakles are the following. After spending a year as the slave of Omphale in female attire, spinning at her feet, Herakles returns from his humiliation to take part in an archery contest with the sons of Eurytus for the prize of his youngest daughter, Iole, whose hand Herakles had been offered in marriage (upon winning such a contest) before agreeing to marry Delaneira, the sister of his dead friend Meleager. (Sir Richard Jebb's 1892 translation of Eurytus's boast in line 265 of Sophocles' *Trachiniæ* rather intemperately transforms the αφυκτ βέλε which Herakles 'holds in his hands'—my own translation would be 'unerring darts'—into 'inevitable shafts'.) Herakles (predictably) wins the contest and is then forced to slay Eurytus and his sons when they refuse to release Iole. When Delaneira hears that her husband has abducted this young woman as his concubine, she sends him a tunic dipped in the blood of Nessus, the centaur killed by another of Herakles's 'inevitable shafts' after he attempted to rape her. When Herakles dons the garment during a ceremony consecrating an altar to his father, Zeus, the poison causes him intense pain and he mortally wounds himself trying to tear the adhesive and corrosive thing from his body. Delaneira kills herself with shame at the horrific outcome of her spiteful deed and Herakles's last act is to build his own pyre on Mount Œta. Only Philoctetes amongst his servants is prepared to set light to it with their idol-master still alive upon it. Herakles gives him his bow and arrow as reward. A thunderclap marks the hero's apotheosis amidst the phoenix-like conflagration.

The apparent confession of Britannia's anti-heroic nature (*anti-hero* in the malignant rather than the ironic sense) is a rare moment of candour. She is 'more like an old centaur', she admits: a lecherous, amphibolous creature—a dingy analogue of Charon, the Styx ferryman—whose very life-blood is a burning poison capable of making the human embodiment of manly virtue tear his own half-divine flesh in the attempt to disassociate it from the insidious half-bestial infection. This analogy reveals as clearly as any in the piece just how Britannia Spears is a paradox of the scheming, vengeful female (Delaneira, with her Medean poisoned garment) and the ithyphallic male (Nessus, with his equine member and mortal ardour).

*   *   *

'You can't have it both ways.' I interjected. 'Modern money is not so different from modern art. Both rely on the secret casket, as you call it, containing not a jewel but a vapour... no value but symbolic value.'

'Nonsense, art reveals the truth. The usurers obscure it. Look at the reverse, Miss...'

'So, as I said, we should try to put the treasure back,' I pressed.

'There is no treasure. That's the point.' He turned to look at me: 'Gold is just a heavy, inert metal. And labour is valueless if it only churns out distractions from the truth. The sole intrinsic value is in art itself. Art brings truth back to the psyche. That is the mission of modern art. It opens the secret casket of the human mind and reveals the emptiness within. Only then can we go forward as men; take the initiative from those conspirators who seek to keep this knowledge to themselves. Only when we understand how <u>this</u> can be compared to <u>this</u>... may I?...' he grasped Hermione's wrists with just the thumb and index finger of each hand, elevating her slight arms like a puppet to display in turn the banknote and the figurine, '... only by contrasting how they address this universal emptiness can we understand their real value. This bill pretends to represent something that was never there. This sculpture is an effort to transcend the absence. Modern art goes further.'

'Here, here,' said Hermione. Stover turned to look her in the eye. She smiled. He let her arms sink slowly to her sides, only releasing her wrists once they had relaxed. After two or three quick breaths she lifted her right hand again to pass the banknote back to him. 'I'd be intrigued to see some.'

That evening we made love. Hermione was passionate beyond anything I had experienced before, indeed, beyond anything I have encountered since. It was obvious that Stover had excited her. As we traipsed around his villa, thumbing portfolios of pretentiously non-figurative sketches and trying not to snag our outer garments on the sculptural protuberances or our conversation on the topic of Benito Mussolini, I noticed she had become increasingly tactile and expansive. The measured brutality of Stover's words and the 'art' that it inspired had an effect on her that one would scarcely credit.

*   *   *

> 219
>
> Or maybe it's more: Bristow versus Deller
>   At The Embassy in eighty-€ree,
> Or James "Amazing" Randi v Uri Geller
>   In Federal Court. I wouldn't want to be
> A painstaking, longwinded storyteller;
>   So I €ink it's best—just like £e BBC,
> £e court reporters, and A£enian playwrights—
> I stick to giving you £e potted highlights.)

219.2 *eighty-three*: It is probably no coincidence that this is the year before Orwell's *Nineteen Eighty-Four*. One can fairly safely speculate that the names connected to *The Embassy* and *Federal Court* are those of various international diplomats involved in tense negotiations involving the threat of nuclear war. Bristow and Deller sound British and East German respectively; James Randi and Uri Geller being presumably the American and Soviet negotiators. Perhaps the failure of these talks in 1983 (thirty years from now) precipitated the devastation that has led to this chaotic future. We might want to see the juxtaposition of nuclear warheads and darts as a simple case of the Popean mock-heroic translated into the atomic era. As we have seen with the previous analogy to Hercules, however, this is the *anti*-heroic in the seemingly benign guise of the *mock*-heroic. Despite the Swiftian disproportion of scale, the outcome of this occultish darts match—in which we spectators are as implicated as the players—will be at least as important as the unthinkable upshot of a nuclear summit which is only part of the future that its arcane ritual seeks to predetermine. The *coin*, remember, is the *quantum* (the atomic *quid pro quo*) of the piece.

219.4 *Federal*: era 16   *Garnish no Bristows with rich Aline*

    *   *   *

She was extravagantly aroused. The moment we closed the bedroom door behind us, she removed her drawers, slumped over the foot of the bed and reached around behind her legs to grasp a fistful of skirt with something like the vehemence one might use to crush the letter of a blackmailer. She lifted the pale yellow cotton up above her thighs, without a word. Then, panting, face-down in the bedlinen, she revealed herself to me like a baboon: pink and wet and swollen.

It would be useless to deny I was incited. A hatred of Stover had been coursing through my body during the distended silence that had accompanied our journey back to the hotel. Suddenly discovering itself reflected in this extraordinary, febrile excitement of my wife, it was hurriedly translated into a desperate emulation of the same fascistic magnetism. I approached her, hooked the braces on my shoulders with my thumbs and let my trousers fall around my ankles. I pushed down my underpants with the same emphatic double-handed violence. Then I tugged the skirt from her grip and tossed the hem of it onto her shoulders like an Italian waiter clothing a table. I took her wrists in the same grip he had used to manipulate her arms and forced her hands up off the bedcover. I entered her like a rapist, pumping her with all the sensitivity of a steam piston, pulling on her arms like reins to counterweigh each spanking thrust which rammed her, struggling for breath, into the mattress.

    *   *   *

"You haven't seen him? Why? Won't she let you?"

"There's no right of Grandparental access in English law, you know. So it's a boy then? I don't blame Hannah, really. I've never pressed her on it. It isn't her fault, poor girl. You have to remember that Martin & I hadn't spoken for three years before she got pregnant. I'd never met her or even heard about her before she phoned me up to tell me he was missing. As far as I was concerned that was old news. Martin's always been missing. He's been missing ever since his father died. & as far as she was concerned, I was some god knows what: some old harridan that never understood him... whatever Martin told her. Why should she trust me? She can't even ask my son whether it's a good idea to let me see the child because he buggered off the moment he found out that she was pregnant... He would've said *no* anyway."

"I thought it was later that he went, after the kid was born."

"Was it? Don't ask me. That's not what she told me. Still, who can blame her for lying. I distinctly remember her insisting that she didn't want to have an abortion. I thought it was the best thing in the circumstances. She was really pissed off. I suppose I'm a meddling old cow. You can understand why she'd be upset if she thought I was suggesting she got rid of a child that was actually already born. Serves her right for lying though."

"Did you never try to go round there?"

"I don't know where *there* is. Don't worry, I'm not going to ask you. It's best for everyone concerned if I stay out of that child's life. If I were her, I wouldn't even tell him who his father was, let alone his grandmother. What's his name anyway?"

"Erm... you're not going to believe this..."

"No, actually don't tell me. I don't want to know."

I looked around at all the bits of dolls & action figures strewn at her feet. There were tools & drawing implements & sewing needles in amongst the dismembered body parts.

"Yes, sorry about the mess," she said, "maybe we should go through into the kitchen." I clambered out of the chair & followed her in. "I'm trying to design a range of positive female action figures for Oxfam. You know, aid workers & local women with a more dynamic style than the usual soppy, girlie nonsense: kind of empowering dolls for girls but without any of the usual macho military bullshit you get with boys' toys."

"Oh, right... that's a good idea." She was a lot more forthright than I'd expected.

"Would you like a drink, or something?"

"Er no thanks, I really can't stay long. So, you'd prefer Hannah to bring up Sa... to bring the child up without knowing who his father was."

"Well it's not ideal obviously. It's just the best thing in the circumstances. After all, Martin might be my son but he's just a man. It's hardly surprising he's running away again when you consider the inherent weakness of his gender. Present company excepted, of course. You don't have any children do you, Sam?"

"£e first and second legs went wi£ £e €row.
　　£e next four were £e total opposite.
So it was €ree apiece, wi£ €ree to go,
　　And Tanya frowned; her tee€ began to grit.
£e crowd was hers £ough, and £ey let her know:
　　For every ton or double £at $e hit,
£e girls would whoop and stand up to applaud her;
　　But when $e €rew £ey kept £e best of order.

220.6 *ton*: 'One hundred'. The idea of a period of one hundred years as a heavy weight is clearly supposed to chime in with 'weighty / fate he' (see 248.1).

　　　　　　*　　　　　　　*　　　　　　　*

This was how Phillip was conceived. One cannot be certain, obviously—there were one or two previous, gentler occasions—but I remain convinced that was the day. What transpired would seem to be most naturally predicated on such a grotesque and uncharacteristic performance.

There was no repeat of this animalistic coupling. The last week of our holiday was spent visiting Stover's recommended local sites of interest. Back in England, we soon discovered Hermione was pregnant. After the initial rush, things calmed down. The weeks wore on: drab and uneventful. The Oxford gutters filled with rusty leaves and Hermione became depressed. Morning sickness and vague worry gave way to something even more debilitating. As her belly swelled into an oblate hemisphere she began to express a loathing for the life inside her. In public she would simply change the subject or make jokey references to her apprehension. In private, though, she would speak as if her body were engaged in a battle with this... thing: this ugly bald little travesty of a human being that was clinging to her innards, parasitically sapping her nutrients—the placenta its insidious weapon.

I suspected that the manner of conception had caused serious disquiet in my wife. Perhaps the fact that she had so clearly derived enormous bestial pleasure from the encounter made her all the more upset. Just as my brutality towards her had been a reaction to Jacob Stover's influence upon me, hers towards the baby was a response to my influence on her. It was reparations. I asked her once why she felt she had these thoughts, but she insisted there was no way I could understand. I obviously did not discuss my theory with her directly, but my conviction and my sense of guilt grew with the baby and Hermione's depression.

There was no respite, and in those days one certainly did not seek medical advice for private questions of emotion. We tacitly ruled out a termination. Hermione's answer was to throw herself into active life and work, travelling long distances to warehouses, antique dealerships, auctions and collectors' homes. She behaved in every respect as if she were not pregnant. She skipped up and down stairs in defiance of occasional sciatica. She played badminton. She ate and drank whatever she pleased and stayed up all hours discussing business with her father and his contacts over cigars and port. Any discomfort she experienced as a result was blamed on the baby. She interpreted all pain as the retaliation of a tyrannical occupying force against her activities of justified resistance.

　　　　　　*　　　　　　　*　　　　　　　*

"No. I was about to once... but no."

"No I didn't think so. Don't get me wrong, I think it's fine. It's great, in fact. You carry on the way you are. I'm perfectly happy living without children too."

"Well, if you think that way about your kids it's hardly a surprise if they run off."

"You mean Martin. I never treated him like *that* (whatever *that* is), I just mean I'm glad my children... my *child* has grown up & left home. Obviously I'd like to hear from him from time to time. It's painful that he doesn't want to speak to his own mother, but what can I do? I just mean I wouldn't want to have to look after some dependent during my retirement. He's not going to look after me either. I suppose that's just a cross I'll have to bear."

"But he did run away though." She was annoying me now. I didn't feel like pulling punches.

"When he was younger, you mean? Yes he did. I suppose Hannah told you that. Or are you getting your information from somewhere else?"

"Er no... I thought... she told me that it was after your husband died."

"Not long after, yes."

"So do you think it was the death of his stepfather that made him do it?"

"His father. He wasn't adopted. I didn't remarry after Leon died. He never had a *step*father."

"No, but I thought... well, she did say you wouldn't talk about it."

"About what?"

"About Amrit's real father."

"Who's this Amrit? Martin's father was my husband, Leon Higgs."

"I'm sorry. I'm being very nosy. It's just that I'd really like to get to the bottom of it all. I'm trying to understand something that Amrit... that Martin wrote & I think this could be very important. What Hannah told me was that Martin ran away from home after finding out that Leon, who'd just died, was not his biological father. In fact it was Leon who'd written a letter to his stepson telling him the truth. It was given to him when Leon died. If that's the case, I'm certain it must've been the thing that prompted him to run away. It probably explains why he's run away from fatherhood as well."

"Well it might if it was true. Who was the father supposed to be, anyway? Someone called Amrit? & who exactly *gave* Martin this letter, his fairy godmother? Leon was dead."

"No it was you. Presumably you felt obliged to, seeing as it was your husband's final wish. But you consistently denied everything it said. You still do, apparently. I'm sorry. I suppose I should leave. I'm being very rude. I don't really have any right to pry."

"Don't worry, Sam, I'm not offended. I like your honesty, in fact. Most people are so tight-arsed. I'm just confused. I don't know where you've got all this fantastic nonsense from. It sounds like Charles Dickens. What I really want to know is who the father is supposed to be. I did have my infidelities of course, but I never had any doubt that Leon was Martin's dad."

We join £e action in £e seven€ leg:
It's Perry to €row first... 'Game on!' He toes
£e oche. Tanya €inks $e needs to peg
His coolness back a notch. Before he €rows,
$e skims her bare knee past his trouserleg
And whispers hotly to him as $e goes:
'I'd let you beat me if we had a date.'
$e doesn't wait to see him hesitate;

221.2 *He toes*: Here, as the protruding morsel of Perry Striker's foot touches the *limbus/limin* of the 'oche' (and as the protruding syllable of the metric foot touches the *limbus/limin* of the enjambment), we switch into the present tense. Here we stay until the end. Our doom is imminent.

221.3 *oche*: Variation of *hockey*, the line from which one throws in darts. The folkloric explanation is that the barrels of the brewery *S. Hockey and Sons* were originally lined up to measure the throwing distance. This is obvious hogwash though. In the Scottish game of Curling the line before which one must release the stone is called the *hog-line*. This might well be a cognate form. Partridge suggests a root of *(h)oggins line*. But the most likely derivation is Old French *ochen* 'to notch'. See next.

It seems hardly necessary to point out that the *oche* is the liminal zone beyond which the released dart becomes subject to Zeno's famous *paradox of the arrow*, which is so prescient of quantum theory.

221.3-4 *to peg... back a notch*: The colloquial sporting metaphor of the phrasal verb comes from the system of scoring used in certain card-games, and notably in the history of darts, which involved placing small pegs (one for each player) at the relevant positions in a system of *notches* in a piece of wood. (This is also very often called the *tally*, from Latin *tālea* 'rod': from that primitive ancestor of monetary accounting which involved splitting a notched rod down the middle lengthways so that both partners in a particular transaction had a complementary quantitative record.)

There is an obvious sexual double-entendre. *Peg* and *notch* are historically concomitant slang for 'penis' and 'vagina'. For a particularly colourful (and historically relevant) example of the latter usage, we need only turn to the Rosecrucian alchemist and Restoration poet, Thomas Vaughan: 'the Barber buss'd the Wenches Rump out of love to her Notch, or [else] respect of saving charges in the Law' (Mercurius Philalethes *Select City Quaeries* II.12, 1660). The drag-queen's expressed goal to 'peg his coolness back a notch' is therefore an ironic projection onto the Russian hard-man (mock-honorifically *His Coolness*) of Sloggy's desire to transform (by means of surgery) the penis lurking underneath her skirt into an artificial vagina: the sexual *limin*.

221.7 *date*: An American 'tryst', but also a pointed reminder of the portentous *date-palm*: *Phoenix dactylifera*; from δάκτυλος 'finger'. (See 175.2 *flamingos*)

*   *   *

'She's a marvel,' a colleague assured me, having seen her rotund and heavy in the ninth month, pedalling her bicycle along a canal towpath with the branches of a castor oil plant in the panier flapping around her head like elephant ears, 'really Twigg, you're a lucky man.'

*   *   *

"Martin's father was called Sanjit. He was the Sikh you met in Uganda in 1970 or 71. Martin's real name is Amrit. That's what she told me. Frankly, that's what I believe."

"Sanjit?... Oh... yes. Sanjit worked with Leon on the buses. It's a very sad story. He managed to get out of Uganda at the time of the Idi Amin coup. He expected his family to follow him. They never did. Who knows why. They probably weren't killed. Not many were. They might well have gone to India or Canada though. Maybe it wasn't a happy marriage & this was just the excuse his wife needed to get out of it. Who knows. Anyway, Sanjit killed himself. He used a pipe from the bus exhaust in the depot overnight. It was in the local papers. I've got a cutting somewhere. I certainly never slept with him. I only met him once."

She got up & started looking through the drawers in her kitchen. There were lots of them. Most seemed to be filled with haberdashery.

"This place is a bit of a mess. I'm not a very organised person to say the least. I'm sure I've got it somewhere." She carried on rifling. She tried holding the closed spectacles that she was still carrying in her left hand over the arch of her nose & peering through them. That didn't seem to help.

"Yes. That's what you told him. You said the man in the photo was a friend of Leon's from work & that Leon had promised to name his son after him just before he died."

"Sam, if you were right, if that story had any credence whatsoever, I'd have kicked you out by now. I've never said anything so bizarre in my life. I've got that cutting in here somewhere."

"But what other reason could you have for keeping it?"

"I didn't. Leon did. Sanjit was his friend. It meant a lot to him. Oh... bother this thing!" she slammed the drawer shut.

"You know, I saw a kind of tramp's shelter down by the canal on the way here. It made me think of Rich & Amrit hiding out down there as children. It obviously wasn't the same thing they'd built to sleep in. All the same..."

"I wish you'd stop calling him *Amrit*. It's not his name. My son always was a fantasist. All men are fantasists. Leon thought he could've been a formula one driver. Total rubbish. Still, I find it hard to believe that Martin's pretending to be half Indian now. That boy lives in a world of his own. Whenever the real one rears its ugly head, he runs away. God knows what his father would have thought, poor sod: dead a few years & his son decides he's not related to him any more."

"It's strange how people come to believe the things they've been saying all their lives."

"Well, he never *used* to say it. Not that I remember. But you're right, he may well have convinced himself."

"Actually, I meant you. You've been telling yourself this story now for so many years that you can't remember... that's exactly it: you can't *remember* that it's not the truth."

$e turns away and drains her cocktail glass
    As if $e knows already what he'll score.
It was a last resort to make a pass,
    But now $e's pretty sure $e'll wipe £e floor
Wi£ him. $e'll give £e guy a masterclass
    In gamesman$ip. 'Fifteen.' $e winks before
Insouciantly putting in a ton.
$e whispers, 'I was going for £e one.'

222.3 *to make a pass*: 'To make an amorous advance', but also 'to palm a card' or 'use *legerdemain*'. The phrase was also applied to the hypnotic gestures of Friedrich Mesmer which supposedly deployed one's *animal magnetism* to induce an entranced state of suggestibility in the viewer. It is perfectly obvious that the words used by hypnotists, and the mantra-esque intonations they use, are the means via which the *trance* is actually brought on. I have long believed that hypnotism is actually an intransitive process. It is something one does to oneself. This is not merely a matter of *surrender to suggestion*, it is also quite possible for a person to hypnotize himself when on his own. The incantatory effects of poetry—rhyme and rhythm, vowel-music and consonantal patterns—are often used (by both poet and reader) to achieve precisely that effect. They exist not only as a vestigial trace of that oral culture Bosvil is intent on reinstating that required some non-textual means of making history and ideas memorable, but also as a means of bringing about changes in the consciousness of the reader (the reciter). It is only after such changes have been effected that the mimetic and metaphoric functions of the writing can have their full, transformative effect upon the mind.

    This is precisely how *The Birmingham Quean* intends to work its black magic. Before it can bring about the future Bosvil desires, first it needs to convince the human mind of the tangible inevitability of that future… to convince us that it *already* exists, as if encoded in the fabric of our own brains the way fate is encoded in our history. For all my attempts to resist the hypnosis, I am obviously completely under Bosvil's *mesmeric* power. I have, I confess, occasionally tried pinching my leg and flicking my cheek with my forefinger to snap myself out of it. This is obviously useless at this stage. It gives me some small comfort to think that mesmerism is also the most likely method by which Bosvil has ensnared his amanuensis.

    You and I are so alike, my friend. Neither of us have much conscious will that remains unusurped by Bosvil's influence. This thing that you and he (and, I suppose, I too) have created more and more often appears to me as a revolving disk of black and white sectors which, as it spins, transforms into a whirl of colour: a temporal vortex into which I am being slowly but inexorably sucked.

    A truly terrifying implication of this image is to be found in the similarity of that standard stage-prop of the hypnotist—the circle of regular, alternating duochrome segments that becomes a blur as it turns this way and that—and the item that provides this climactic scene with its entrancing focus: the dartboard.

222.5 *masterclass*: 'The class of slave owners', but misused to mean 'authoritative lesson'. The intention is to graft together the ideas of punishment and pedagogy implicit in the obvious gloss 'she will teach him a lesson'. That she does so in terms vengefully redolent of the brutalities of slavery, however, tends to make her threat seem all the more lacerating. She intends to *flog* her opponent. This is not just the faux-female dominating the male, but also the black man with the whip hand over the white man.

She stopped rummaging through the drawers & came back over to the kitchen table. She leaned wearily on it, the reading glasses cringing under the pressure in her fist. "Sam. What I'm telling you *is* the truth. I have not been saying it to myself for years at all. I haven't needed to. To be honest, if you hadn't just reminded me of it, I would never have been able to tell you the name of the Sikh bus-driver in Leon's depot who committed suicide in the seventies... even though he was a friend of my husband's. I feel quite bad about that, to be honest, but it's true.

"& there are other things I feel guilty about too. To be frank with you, I was a reluctant mother. Martin was always closer to his father than to me. He was devastated when he died. That's why he ran away from home. I tried to hide it from him, but he could sense that I resented him being around, not least because he reminded me of my late husband. I didn't want to bring a child up on my own. I just wasn't emotionally equipped for it."

"I was a reluctant mother & now I'm a reluctant grandmother. If Martin's running away from his responsibilities it's probably something he gets from me. Not that I ever would have done it really, but then I never had the choice. I wasn't a man. If I was him... If I was a young man in his situation... I'd probably do the same thing. I don't need to concoct exotic reasons to feel ashamed, Sam. I've got plenty of my own shame to be going on with."

For the first time that afternoon, my faith in Amrit's story began to waver. It was possible this woman was just an extremely convincing liar, but the way she lived did not suggest the kind of person who kept secrets or maintained elaborate fictions. Everything about her said, *let it all hang out*.

"Maybe you could show me a birth certificate or something."

"Good god, it'd take me days to find my *own* birth certificate, let alone Martin's. Besides, he took all that stuff away with him when he left home. He needed it to get a passport."

"Where was he going?"

"Inter-railing."

"Not Uganda, then?" I smiled.

"As far as I'm aware, neither of us has ever been anywhere near Uganda. I wouldn't be able to place it on a map of Africa. This is just some weird story Martin has made up."

"But why would he do that?"

"Like I said, he's a fantasist. He left home telling me he was going to become a professional musician on the continent, a rockstar. I'm pretty certain he still thinks that's true. You know, you hear all those stories about the people who didn't believe John Lennon or Elvis when they said that kind of thing, & then they lived to regret it. What you don't hear about though are all the other millions of people who quite rightly don't believe their relatives or their friends when they insist they're going to make it big. If Martin's making out he's a Sikh now, it's bound to be something to do with all that... a stage persona or what have you."

He scowls and firmly elbows her aside.
    'He's just so strong,' $e purrs, 'but sensitive
As well: you see £e way he likes to glide
    His pinky down £e tip… enough to give
A girl £e $ivers.' Perry tries to hide
    His anger at £e tart's provocative
Remarks, but £en his first dart bounces out.
He swears. He seems to have succumbed to doubt;

---

    *   *   *

The day Phillip was born, everything changed. It was a dazzling spring morning. I edged around the door of the delivery room, to see my wife enveloping a frowning lump of scarlet wrinkles in a white blanket. She stroked the little boy across his downy fontanel with just the inner knuckles of her palm. The thick, warm smell of them was indistinguishable as I approached. She glanced at me and then returned her gaze to the top of her new child, moaning softly with pleasure each time her hand surrounded his tiny head. She obviously loved him now: much more than she loved me, much more than I was capable of loving either of them.

It would be naïve to put this down to nothing more than a cathartic labour. There was something else at work. Above all, Hermione was relieved. The most obvious thing about the child was that he looked nothing like me. This is not to insinuate illegitimacy. Far from it. I mean to say, simply, that he was a baby. He looked nothing like an adult man. Faced with that tableau of balmy adoration, framed by the glare of bleached pillows and the white glaze of the wall tiles in the April sun, it struck me that my wife's disturbing evocations of the evil parasite in our darkest moments of the past few months had been descriptions of me. The thing was 'small and bald and ugly', but not the way a baby is, more like the way I am myself. I had assumed she was rejecting the very idea of a child growing inside her. Instead, it was the particular genetic inheritance of the baby's father she rejected. She had imagined this literally as a gruesome miniature adult in my image, not so much growing (like plant or animal) as expanding (like an empire or the universe.)

The picture that came to mind was a hybrid of those uncanny medieval paintings of the Virgin and Christ-Child, in which Jesus is a tiny naked youth with adult proportions and gestures, the narrow eyes denoting wisdom but appearing to post-Machiavellian sensibilities more like a representation of malign connivance. It was something like this she had imagined invading her inner space: a sinister homunculus. More to the point, what she had imagined was me… not me as I was then, but me as I would become as we grew older. She had imagined me as I am now. And she had hated it. The baby was her doom; and that doom was the middle age of R. H. Twigg. Perhaps she had even imagined me amidst this fire, and that fire inside the cradle of her fertility.

But that day she delivered something more akin to herself. In the child she found the very thing to mitigate the awful marriage it was destined to prolong. If not the husband, she could love the son.

    *   *   *

"That doesn't really sound like him at all. I knew he was into music but I didn't think he had any ambitions of celebrity."

"Martin? Well, I suppose I don't really know him any more. Maybe he's mellowed in his old age. You know what he said to me once?"

"What?"

"He said that he was just like Mozart. Mozart *laid down a riff* & then followed to see where it took him. He could do what Mozart did, he said."

I just shook my head. I really wasn't sure whether to believe this woman, to assume that what she was telling me was wrong but basically an honestly held belief, or else a total pack of lies. Whatever the case, it didn't seem to make any sense. I couldn't imagine the author of *The Birmingham Quean* (or even the kid who'd come up with the Holimans story) saying anything so ill-considered without irony.

"How did you meet Martin anyway?" she asked, "when was the last time you saw him?"

"Actually I've never met him."

"You've never *met* him? Why on earth are you looking for him? Are you working for Hannah? Are you some kind of a private detective? I don't know that I've ever met a private detective."

"No. It's complicated."

"That's no surprise. You're not Hannah's new man are you?"

I'd been dreading that question. I shook my head with all the nonchalance I could muster.

"No, but you'd like to be though wouldn't you."

"It's just to do with Amrit's work... Martin's, sorry... it's something that he's written that I want to find out more about."

"That's a bad situation, Sam. You need to get yourself out of that. Take it from somebody who's seen a bit of the world. Don't have anything to do with a woman who's still in love with someone else. Not unless you both just want the sex, that is. You certainly shouldn't be helping her to look for him... good god!"

"No, Hannah doesn't want to find him any more. & as for me... I'm just interested in his past. I don't really want to meet him."

"Why not?"

"Well, I don't *need* to anyway."

"Listen, Sam, if you want to prove to yourself that what I'm telling you is true, you should go & get a copy of Martin's birth certificate. You don't need me to show it to you. The register of births is open to public access. If you want a document like that, you can just go along & get one. You don't have to be related to the person mentioned. Try the Broad Street Registry Office. It should be open for another couple of hours. I could run you down there if you like."

He chucks his next two darts for twelve and six.
　　Two visits to £e board and Tanya leaves
A fini$: one-two-one. £e Russian sticks
　　A hundred on £e board; £e $ot receives
£e kind of welcome you'd expect: he kicks
　　£e wall to rhy£mic clapping and retrieves
His arrows. Tanya's next dart punches clean
Into £e squeaky green of treble seventeen.

---

*　　　　　　　　　*　　　　　　　　　*

We called him Phillip. This had been decided very early in the pregnancy, before the depression had made any further discussion of a nameable entity impossible. From the outset, Hermione had insisted it would be a boy. She 'just knew' she said. She had brooked no discussion of female forenames. With hindsight, this obsession with her inevitably male offspring seems like an early symptom of the developing prepartum neurosis. But Phillip it had been, and by the time I saw him, my son already had a wristband which read 'Phillip Eugene Twigg'.

That middle name was fateful. Hermione had suggested it would be a nice gesture to my mother to name the child after Eugene. The undimmed shame I felt for my secret hatred of this lost family paragon made it impossible to structure an objection. From the moment we announced the pregnancy, Hermione and mother had got on like a house on fire. Mother found it particularly gratifying that she and her daughter-in-law should share such energetic views on the business of fecundity (and the fecundity of business). Specifically, mother condoned in unequivocal terms Hermione's continuing physical and professional activity (without, that is, having the slightest inkling of her neurotic motivations). 'Pregnancy is a flourishing of life' she intoned, 'not some kind of incapacity. Active women breed active children. My husband forced me to take gratuitous periods of rest when I was pregnant with my second. Did me no good at all. He was in South Africa when I was pregnant with Eugene. I rode, I climbed hills, I chopped wood. Whoever called it a "confinement" was a fool. Almost certainly a man.' When I told her we were thinking of giving a boy the name of her firstborn, she said, 'Of course.'

Mother arrived the day after the birth. The resemblance was established straight away. 'Exactly like Eugene,' she said, 'the very image. Look at that strong jaw.' As grandmother manipulated grandchild into heroic poses like an artist's wooden model, Hermione lifted her eyebrows in my direction in an attempt to share mutual congratulation for having done a kind thing for this deserving woman. It was impossible for my reciprocal expression to reflect the gestating sense that I had been reduced by this collusion of mother and wife to a mere vehicle for my brother's bloodline. It was also impossible to hide.

I had never previously held much truck with Freud, but here was as clear an example of the 'Oedipus Complex'. I had patently chosen a wife who was like my own mother. The tragic twist was that I was more like the Claudius to this young Hamlet than the Prince himself, or indeed the ghost.

*　　　　　　　　　*　　　　　　　　　*

"No, thanks very much, & thanks for all your help, but actually I think I fancy the walk."

"What's Martin written that you find so intriguing anyway?"

"It's a... it's a narrative poem with all these... fictional annotations."

"You mean to tell me he actually finished something that he started? Can I see it?"

"No," I lied, "I'm afraid I haven't got it on me... Look, I'd better go. You're working. I'm sorry for disturbing you & for the nosy parker routine. If I do find Martin, I'll... get him to phone you."

"Pity... Yes, I suppose it *would* be nice to get a phonecall from my son once in a while. I don't know how easy you're going to find it though. He isn't going to want to."

"&... if you like, I could have a word with Hannah."

"I don't think that's a good idea, Sam. That child & I are better off not knowing anything about each other."

As she showed me out, I failed to think of any reason why that statement was not a perfectly reasonable one. To be honest, I still can't. You can generally assert the right of every person to know their biological origins, especially when there's not the usual conflict of interests involved in the adoption process, but the circumstances are, as they always say in social services, unique. In this case, I couldn't see anything but arguments against it.

I had one last question for the porch:

"Oh, I'm sorry Mrs... Carla, there was one more thing that I forgot to ask."

"Yes?"

"When Martin was a boy did he... did he ever dress up in your clothes or... ?"

"Of course he did. He was strange, but not that strange. All boys do it at some point in their childhood. Didn't you?"

"I suppose I did, yeh. I don't really remember."

"Are you asking me if he's a transvestite?"

"Not exactly, no."

"I'd much rather he was that than the average spineless male specimen. He's definitely not gay though, if that's what you're suggesting... more's the bloody pity. He wouldn't have got himself into this mess."

"Well, being gay & running away are often connected. You find yourself in a domestic situation that's the central feature of a culture that doesn't really accept the way you are..."

"Trust me, Sam, if there was anything wrong with the *domestic situation* Martin ran away from as a child, it wasn't anything to do with this bourgeois conformism & sexual intolerance you're referring to... quite the opposite."

"No, no... of course not. Ok then... I'll be in touch."

225

> So… seventy—£at's single twenty, bull:
>   A twelve dart fini$. Tanya picks up pace.
> It's better to be fast and purposeful
>   £an hesitant and half-arsed in £e face
> Of pressure—every out$ot's liable
>   To go astray; £ere's really no disgrace
> In $ooting wide: at least, £at's what you need
> To tell yourself when life reduces speed…

---

225 There is a pointedly prurient strand running through this stanza. *Outshot* is obviously an ejaculatory euphemism. The climax of this pivotal *leg* of darts is being cast in a grotesquely orgasmic light. The last six lines might easily be glossed as 'It is preferable to go through with the ejaculation than delay it when that is the natural physiological response: it is always possible for released spermata to fail to fertilize an ovary; it is therefore not shameful to practise *coitus interruptus*. It is necessary to reassure oneself of this when experiencing the temporary extension of psychological duration concomitant with orgasm.'

    The justification of the misattributed 'sin of Onan', 'spilling one's seed on the ground' (Genesis 38.9: God is actually punishing Onan for what might seem, to New Testament thinking, a perfectly acceptable refusal to inseminate his wife's sister) is extended into the realms of perverse domination and degradation suggested by Britannia's expressed intent to give her opponent a *masterclass* (222.5). Rather than the discreet withdrawal of the penis at the relevant moment for contraceptive reasons, the implication of phrases used in the fourth line is that ejaculation is deliberately to result in the seminal emission spattering the cheeks (facial or rectal) of the partner in order that the ejaculator might derive some morbid pleasure from this iconic humiliation. After all, Britannia's homosexuality negates the necessity for any contraceptive concern.

    This stanza reveals just how intimately related are Bosvil's ideas of morbid pleasure, domination, degradation, and fluctuations in the perception of time. The slow-motion effect that ensues is a disgusting expression of Bosvil's orgasmic triumph over us in the sexualized battle of the darts match: the fulfilment of his hyperlibidinous desire to bring himself and the future he embodies into existence by splattering the surface of our minds with his reproductive discharge, sublimated into the quantum entanglement of the perceptions of the narrator-coin with those of the counterfeit-queen (and our own with his) at the point at which they realize their inevitable coupling. Even the *Sex Magick* of Aleister Crowley pales in comparison to this.

*   *   *

The hidden depth that Hermione had seen in me—conceived in romantic terms as like the universal angst suffered by the heir of Elsinore—was in fact just the shameful memory of a brother whom I thought I had murdered. It was the gaping absence of a generation of upright manliness that my mother and I had both come to believe (in our vastly different ways) had been epitomized by Eugene's death. For her it had been an unthinkable shock; for me, the doom-laden result of my having thought about it every day… having devoutly wished for it from the moment he departed for the front.

*   *   *

I wasn't in any mood to conform with signs & fences on the way back into town. The events of the afternoon so far were not conducive to line-toeing. As far as I was concerned, the gullies were historic footpaths, public rights of way. I climbed over the gate barring access to the one that split the next block along from Carla's into two. I tore the left pocket of my trousers on one of the palings' trident barbs as I lowered myself down.

I used to think the gullies moved. They always seemed to pop up when you weren't expecting them: even though you knew exactly where they were. Some days it would feel as if it took an age to walk up one of them: it would be a long trek through a jungle of stinging nettles & dandelions, past puddles of lake-like proportions, rusting cars & piles of tyres that seemed as monumental as lost cities. On the other hand, the journey through a different gully that same day (or the same one at a different time) would pass by in the blinking of an eye. The scale of it would feel much smaller than the broad, busy streets it joined together: every feature a tiny detail of a model that your giant kid feet might crush if you didn't take care not to stomp on anything.

I would imagine the gullies were the snakes in a game of snakes & ladders. The streets, with their regular arrangements of paving stones, were the ladders. Obviously this required an expert like myself to develop the skill of sliding up the snakes as well as down. The most important fact was that the gullies could move. They could get tangled up. It's obviously impossible, but I seriously believed that at different times of the day, & different times of the month or year, certain gullies would form junctions with each other that were not present at other times, others would divide & multiply. In order to form a map of them you would have to include a time dimension. Perhaps you would need an entire calendar of maps.

I actually tried to investigate the idea scientifically. I measured the distances between gardens with a retractable tape measure at different times of the day & month. I placed parallel matchsticks in the loose mortar on either side of a garage to see if they changed position relative to one another over time. Nothing ever changed, but I was more & more convinced, not only that the gullies moved & joined & split, but that it would be impossible ever to map their movements because they were not repetitive or predictable. These were the actions of sentient creatures. They were just like snakes. They moved for their own reasons at their own times. It was best simply to understand them: their different characters & predilections. Beyond that, it was a matter of guessing, or just surrendering yourself to their strange whims.

It's important to bear in mind that the gullies in suburban Birmingham are different in type to the *snickets* & *gennels* of the other big industrial cities of Northern England & the Midlands. The basic point is that they're very rarely straight or regular. Neither are they very often paved or tarmacked. Quite commonly they have junctions with one another completely independent of the public roads. This is not just a middle-class phenomenon of garage-&-garden suburbs, it's true pretty much across all the prewar developments. In some areas its perfectly possible to walk from one house to another quite a distance away without ever setting foot on the street.

Her second dart detaches from her €umb
   And index finger, tilts towards its head,
£en flattens its trajectory to land plumb
   In single twenty, just above £e red
Of £e seductive little maximum.
   $e €rows £e €ird, and Sloggy feels a sudden dread
As if Britannia's dart €rills up his spine:
His fuckin arse is on £e fuckin line!

226.5 *seductive little maximum*. A visceral image giving focus to transferred phallic desire.

226.7 *thrills*. Before mutating into a synonym for *quiver* (see 38.8 *cheesy Quaver*)—that vibration which characteristically passes through a spear or arrow at the point of release, described here in precise terms as if captured by high speed photography—the verb *to thrill* meant to 'pierce' or 'penetrate'. The gradation into an expression of sudden emotional change caused by the unexpected intrusion of an exterior influence occurs implicitly as the result of a sexual metaphor which casts the receiver in the female role. A *thrill* is a miniature metaphoric *rape*. The *frisson* that characterizes the response naturally becomes the thing denoted, and thus the word comes to suggest a transference of the *quiver* from the analogical javelin of emotion that penetrates into the body penetrated. It is this connection Bosvil is reliteralising in his usual gruesome way. Britannia's dart is envisaged as entering Sloggy's coccyx and boring up his spine as the shiver of a sudden, awful realisation. The connotations of anal penetration are clearly emphasized by the next line's inarticulate vulgarities. The fact that Sloggy's response is calculated as a simultaneous analogue of the reader's realisation of the awful truth, demonstrates how Bosvil intends us to be similarly *violated* by Britannia's dart and the ideological poison in which it is dipped.

*   *   *

Phillip was to be Eugene's revenge: not a grim visaged purveyor of swift justice, but a rosy-cheeked torturer. As he aged, the natural resemblance was enforced by the nurture of robust physical activity and the bracing influence of the education these women chose for him. He stood and spoke and grew in step with an uncle he had never known. He wielded his own limbs and opinions like pennants of a moral fibre all had once thought toppled on the Somme. All his forthright action, his confidence in the slightest learning and his hearty exercise bore witness to the legacy maturing in his bones. With it, my secret hatred of my brother grew into a dire hatred of my son.

It is clearly not right that a man should feel this way about his child. I went so far as to wish he had been somebody else's, even Jacob Stover's. But the self-loathing this inspired only served to fuel my resentment. The sole crumb of comfort I can take is that I kept my secret as well as it is possible to do. There was only one occasion on which my mask of amiable non-intervention definitely slipped...

*   *   *

The reason for this is simple. Birmingham is a city which expanded at a particular period of history. By the time most of the suburban sprawl was under way, during the late nineteenth & early twentieth centuries, the ideas of Ruskin & the Arts & Crafts movement were having an influence on planning. Coupled with an economic focus more on small businesses than large corporations, this meant that, instead of building new streets in logical rows, the planners very often kept to the original country lanes that followed the gentle contours of Warwickshire & Worcestershire & the winding footpaths of the villages that Birmingham had swallowed up. This kept an organic pattern to the urban landscape that was much less often tolerated even in its two most similar close neighbours, Sheffield & Manchester.

There's a little more to it than that though. Birmingham was never going to be forced into a rational straightjacket. The English Midlands are the Gordian Knot in the guts of the wild island of Great Britain. The local flora are stubbornly irregular. Left to its own devices, Birmingham would be quickly overrun with hawthorn & holly: springy, gnarled, spiky plants that brook little opposition & will never be convinced to grow in a straight line. This is not at all the natural habitat of those upright rows of dappled Poplars that are such a perfect icon of French rationalism. Birmingham was a centre of the enlightenment, it's true, but the ideas of the Lunar Society owed more to the unruly fecundity of Erasmus Darwin than the categorical divisions of the Encyclopedists. Birmingham was never going to look like Edinburgh or Bath.

There's a contradiction here. Twigg's identification of Birmingham (in the *Quean*) as the source of a non-organic mechanistic phase of industrial development was also completely accurate. Birmingham is actually one of the birthplaces of modernism. The Manzoni era may well have been the English apotheosis of Corbusier's 'continuous revolution' but less because it was a product of Corbusier's architectonics, or the infamous 'Athens Project', than because it was another cycle in the unremitting proto-modern redesign of the world's first 'engine city'. The repetition of form & materials in Birmingham's postwar housing estates, its shopping-centres & ring-roads, its 'circuses' & flyovers is just one more example of the insistent rhythms produced by the city's hammers, pistons, cogs & wheels, its edgy music & its recycled narratives, & most of all by its whirling redevelopments. Without Birmingham, (without Watt & Murdock to invent them & Boulton to produce them) there'd be neither a mechanics nor a theory of 'continuous revolution'.

Birmingham is not the victim of a flawed twentieth century utopian aesthetic imported from the continent. Birmingham is the progenitor of urban modernism. Its mistakes & its successes are its own. Corbusier's design ideals – the machine, the vehicle, the Parthenon – can be seen at work in Hansom's Town Hall as easily as the Rotunda or the Ziggurat, the canals as easily as the motorways. Brummy Brutalism is no less vernacular (precisely because of its radical re-engineering) than every previous & successive upgrade of the inner city.

Somehow these things go hand in hand. The urbanised village back lane was always part of the strange bionic 'machine for living in' that is Britain's second city. The gullies were like the flexible feeder pipes around the outside of an engine, the machine's strange, unmanageable venous system. They were radical in every sense.

He'd somehow overlooked £e mis-struck pound.
   £e dart cuts €rough £e $adows to remind him:
£at single coin could bring his business down;
   £at single coin is all £ey'd need to find him;
£at single coin... if anybody found
   £e €ing £ey'd have £e key to undermine him:
He'd wind up doin time for counterfeit—
You don't get fined for £at; your ass goes down for it.

227.3-6 *That single coin...*   *Ash nazg durbatulûk,*
　　　　　　　　　　　　　　　Ash nazg gimbatul,
　　　　　　　　　　　　　　　Ash nazg thrakatulûk
　　　　　　　　　　　　　　　Agh burzum-ishi krimpatul.

227.7 *wind up doin time*: On the surface, this usage is equivalent to that in 165.3 *wind up in the clink* (see also 65.1 *wind up*); the emphasis of the idea of winding a clock is at its most acute here though. The connotations are dire. *To do time* might be glossed as 'to *time-travel*' or even 'to *do away* with time (completely)'. In the light of the slang denotation, we might also see this as Sloggy's sudden apprehension (always an analogue of our own) that he is about to be 'imprisoned in the clock': something which, without an exterior context from which to view it, merely traces perpetual meaningless revolutions with no relation to history.

I am beginning to suspect that the dartboard is itself a derivation of some ancient ceremony of time: a clockface which, instead of merely 'measuring time' as an analogy to the reflection of the *gnomon* of a sun-dial, was designed to manipulate it somehow. Perhaps it is more than a metaphor that the repetitious activity darts players use to hone their skills is called 'round the clock' (basically just hitting one number after another following the escalating order of integers). If so, the *dial* ('diurnal circle') of the dartboard has a strange vigesimal/pentagramic internal geometry rather than the usual duodecimal/triangular geometry which the modern clockface has inherited from Ancient Babylon. Whatever culture this temporal ritual might have emerged from (Gypsy would be a good guess), and what effect it was originally supposed to precipitate, there can be little doubt of Bosvil's dreadful intentions for its application in the present context: if time itself were subject to something like *wavefunction collapse*, if it were only by *measuring* time that humanity has created the concrete regulation of a logically structured Universe... Bosvil's principle desire (his *pabulum*) would be the reversal of this precursor of cosmic history.

227.8 *your ass goes down for it*: The phrasal verb is a slang variation of the jurisprudential idiom *to be sent down* (from the dock): i.e. 'to be sentenced to imprisonment'. The notion that it might connote a judgement of greater cosmic finality in this instance is not at all far fetched. That Bosvil should want to remind us of our own imminent descent into whatever *chthonic* realm he currently inhabits can hardly be surprising. One presumes the subject of the verb to be the vulgar Negro-American synecdoche that equates a man's rump to his life, soul or reputation. Such bestial materialism of imagination is entirely apt. The relationship, alluded to here, between this idea and the *Metamorphoses* of Apuleius is quite obvious. As such it necessarily therefore recalls the *æs*—the brass Roman coin on which Apuleius is punning—and thereby the wall of brass that was supposed by the Ancient Greeks to countermure *Tartarus*: the deepest of infernal regions which (like quantum mechanics) contained the unfathomable metaphysical origins of a universe that had emerged from it. (*Brass* in English derives from the Old Norse for 'fire'.)

It wasn't just the gullies themselves that were strange, though. It was the people in them. You could easily believe they didn't exist elsewhere. There were those who owned the garages & gardens, of course. They'd wash their cars, do some DIY in the garage, pile stuff up on their compost heaps. Occasionally you'd get a bollocking off one of them if you did something naughty. One bloke caught me shooting at his fencepost with a plastic bow & a rather dangerous arrow I'd made out of a dart head, a garden cane & the feathers of a dead blackbird. I almost hit him with it. He told me it was private property & I had no right to be there in the first place. But this was very rare. He was pissed off. Most people were perfectly tolerant of the kids using their back lanes.

These homeowners were the normal people. At least they were the normal people when they were at home. But there were lots of others. Children & adults alike did weird things down the gullies. They were strangely slow & silent, for example, or they walked along with a dog-lead but no dog. On the way to school once, a friend & I stumbled across a boy of about our own age, who we'd never seen before, having a shit between a tree & a garden fence. He had a lot of pink toilet paper wrapped around his right hand as he crouched & strained. He'd obviously taken it from home before he left. Why he hadn't just gone to the toilet at the same time we couldn't imagine.

The other thing I recall distinctly was the huge number of gnats. Especially in late summer there were clouds of them that would bob & ripple just at head height. Around sunset they were at their thickest. As their time on this Earth got shorter these communities of dying insects would gather into huge collectives, so elongated you could imagine them as people's shadows growing in the dusk. They were more disturbing than shadows though. As you got closer to them, as close as you would dare, you could make out their perpetual internal motion: the seething chaos produced by thousands of creatures whose time of biological function had elapsed & who knew no more than to keep flying, to keep taking their minute decisions of direction until the strength to keep it up deserted them. It would not take a particularly imaginative child to imagine these as ghosts or aliens... even travellers from the distant past.

That's what the gullies were like. They contained a different logic to the streets. There were different laws of physics & morality. If laws were static, if they were true from one minute to the next & so on into perpetuity, there were no laws in gullies at all. Perhaps there doesn't seem any very strong case for keeping them open when you hear a thing like that. The gullies were places where people fought & took drugs & did all sorts of seedy things, both together & alone. There's no point denying it. But they were a child's introduction to a vision of humanity that was much more honest & revealing for all its furtive ineffability than anything that went on at the business end of street-level interaction. They'd served this function for generations. They were an education in those essential things, domestic, clandestine & subconscious, that society would rather hide. & now they were all closed.

£e tip of Tanya's dart sinks in £e bullseye.
    Her preening chorus clatters to its feet;
£ey totter on £eir heels, £eir cackling outcry
    Enough to frighten Sloggy, who retreats
From sidling to £e kitty like a magpie
    Intent on some€ing $iny to complete
His nest—he still has plans to get me back
But needs to change his angle of attack.

228.1 *bullseye*: Evidently an anal analogue, but also slang for 'a half-crown piece'. (See 234.6 *half a crown*)

228.3 *cackling outcry*: Plutarch informs us (Camillus 27) that the *gaggle* ('cackle') of geese that guarded the temple of Juno on the Arx of the Capitoline Hill were responsible for saving the Capitol from the Gauls' sacking in 390B.C. (thus enabling Camillus to be recalled by *lex curiata* and to return as triumphant repatriator of the conquered city). Here is Dryden's translation (Clough's revision):

> in the dead of night a good party of [Gauls], with great silence, began to climb the rock, clinging to the precipitous and difficult ascent… the foremost of them having gained the top of all, and put themselves into order, they all but surprised the outworks, and mastered the watch, who were fast asleep; for neither man nor dog perceived their coming. But there were sacred geese kept near the temple of Juno… by nature of quick sense, and apprehensive of the least noise… [they] immediately discovered the coming of the Gauls, and, running up and down with their noise and cackling, they raised the whole camp.

When he rebuilt the temple in 344 B.C., Camillus therefore consecrated the Temple to *Juno Moneta*: 'Juno who warns'. This designation (from *monēre*, to 'signal' or 'remind') is the root of the English verbs *to mean* and *to moan*. The fact that the plaintive cries of the geese (their 'cackling outcry') should be considered to contain, as a fundamental undertone, the very essence of *significance* is worrying enough when applied to the present context. When we realize that the *meaning* of their *moaning*… their *portent*… is definitively that of imminent barbarian invasion (*The Gallic Fire*), we start to realize the full implications of Bosvil's ironic use of this allusion. Only when we trace the etymology of *money* to this same event do we understand the staggering profundity of his doom-laden *cackling*, however. It was here, at the temple of *Juno Moneta*, that the Roman *mint* was opened (according to Samuel Ball Platner: *A Topographical Dictionary of Ancient Rome*, London, OUP 1929 p. 290) in 269 B.C. to utter a large amount of silver coin (*moneta*) and thereby fund the war with Tarentum (see 35.3 *Tarantino*). It is from here that we get both *mint* and *money*. What 'money' *means* therefore is *meaning* itself. And if, as we two both have done, we hear it *moan*, it is to presage revolution.

228.5 *magpie*: Dame Juliana Berners's list of collective nouns in *The Book of St. Albans* gives us for this bird: *a tygendes of pyes*. This is probably a metathesis of *tydynges* 'tidings' (cognate with German *Zeitung* and notable for its ability to appear in this singular-plural form, just like the modern English *news*). The word remains in use in English to denote a rather archaic version of the idea of reported events whose recollection of the King James Bible invariably connotes portents of spiritual or political upheaval. Crucially, therefore, *tidings* seems to imply disturbing news of the *future*. It is for this reason that it seems so apt when applied to both the magpie (another of the traditional avian harbingers of doom) and to this poem.

The singular-plural form is important. As his egregious mockery of the Trinity demonstrates, Bosvil is intent on fragmenting Britain and humanity itself: its history, its religion, its psyche, its self-image. Sloggy is both an individual magpie and a forcibly collectivized *tidings* of magpies: a complex of portents. (See 65.3 *magpies rat-a-tat*)

These collective nouns appear to have been the fanciful inventions of Chaucerian-period writers like Berners. The only one that really made it into common usage (before the whimsical revivals during the C19th of *a murmuration of starlings*, and the like) was the pertinent example from *The Debate Betwene the Hors, Shepe and Goos* by John Lydgate: *a gaggle of geese*. At the time, a phrase like this was referred to as *a term of venery* (literally 'a piece of hunting jargon', but also, punningly, 'a period of sexual excess'.) The surviving versions most commonly applied to magpies are the two shared by all the various species of crows: *a parliament* and *a murder*. The relevance of these examples to this poem is no less in doubt than that of *gaggle* or *tidings*.

*   *   *

It was 1935. Phillip was eleven years old. We were spending a week at Hermione's parents and Phillip had struck up a friendship of sorts with the son of a local farrier, called Sidney. He was a tall, thin and unworldly child: a year older than Phillip but clearly his inferior in sport and education. The two had been engaged in constructing a treehouse in the orchard on my father-in-law's small estate. If Phillip's reports were to be believed, this had involved a limp Sidney doing only what was strictly necessary whilst musing about various fantastic scenarios for which their hideout would provide the perfect setting. Meanwhile, Phillip was left to get on with the practical business of procuring materials and building something structurally sound.

Towards the end of the week, Phillip had become increasingly exasperated with Sidney's laziness and a row had broken out. During the altercation the unfortunate child had said something theologically unconscionable and given Phillip the excuse he needed to react. Completely unmarked by the encounter, he announced at lunch, 'I'm afraid I was forced to teach Sidney a lesson today.' The insufferable precociousness of this was greeted by mother and grandparents alike with proud amusement. He was encouraged to elaborate: 'He said there used to be druids here and that we should turn the den into a temple and perform a sacrifice to the goddess of the earth: a rabbit or a bird. I told him I couldn't because it was idolatry. He thought I meant "idleness". He's an idiot.' General laughter. 'He started to take his clothes off. I told him to put up his fists and fight like a Christian. He just carried on undressing so I punched him on the nose and twice in the stomach. He wouldn't shake my hand afterwards. He ran off crying with a nosebleed and his shirt unbuttoned.'

There was instant agreement that Phillip's actions (whilst only as a last resort) had been measured, moral and justified. The boy was, after all, older and taller than the apple of their eyes and his conduct had done little to recommend him up till now. A good sharp lesson of this sort was bound to have a positive effect.

*   *   *

£e eigh€ leg's under way as back he slopes
    Towards £e toilets, opening his phone.
£e a$tray I'm inside kaleidoscopes
    His image €rough its crystal cut; he's $own
In triplicate… he makes £e call he hopes
    Can save his ass: his plan is to postpone
£e match because of some emergency
His bouncer needs to handle urgently.

229.3-4 *The ashtray… crystal cut*: I have precisely the same type of ashtray on my desk. I could not pick it up now if I wanted to but, as I remember, looking through its chunky lip creates precisely the effect of 'triplicate' vision evoked in this passage (accurately enough at least, if not actually in a way that might procure æsthetic satisfaction—but, of course, Bosvil has little interest in such nice concerns). The *kaleidoscope*, however, works according to a principle of symmetrical reflection and therefore cannot produce this division into three (no doubt intended to burlesque the Trinity). The optical toy was invented by Sir David Brewster in 1817. Byron was an early owner; Murray, being aware how attracted Byron was to objects (and especially words) he considered popular and new-fangled, sent him an example in 1818. He was predictably the first to introduce it to the canon: in Canto II of *Don Juan* (stanza 93) the survivors of the shipwreck see a rainbow that 'look'd like hope— / Quite a celestial kaleidoscope.' Unlike those of Byron's seamen, Sloggy's rhyming *hopes* are obviously only built up here to be dashed.

        *   *   *

I said nothing. A tactical policy of minimal interference in my son's upbringing meant that everyone had grown accustomed to what they thought of as my quiet endorsement of everything he did. I began to shiver with unspent adrenaline. This event reminded me so forcefully of my brother's violent and pretentiously 'upright' kerbing of my youthful imagination that I felt I was reinhabiting the body of an enraged eight year old: younger and weaker than my own son. I could taste once again the warm metallic fluid dripping onto the back of my tongue, feel the tears welling to the impact of Eugene's righteous fists.

This situation was extremely dangerous. Notwithstanding my feelings and Phillip's impressive physical development, he was only an eleven year old child and I a fully grown man. If I had struck him at that moment, as I so desperately wanted to, I might very well have killed him. I struggled to my feet, swivelled without looking any of them in the eye, and strode out. There was no way it could have been interpreted as taciturn approval.

Such slippages were very rare, however. Even at the funeral of my father in 1938—which released a flood of unwanted recollections of my brother's posthumous apotheosis—I did not let my guard down. I had been concealing this same hatred for as long as I could remember. My success had been predicated on dishonesty. Phillip's journey into adulthood continued unabated by any intimation of my horror at each Eugenesque achievement. I applauded his sporting victories and hung his drawings in my room. On his eighteenth birthday, I sang 'For He's a Jolly Good Fellow' with all the gusto that had come to stand for popular endurance of Hitler's bombs, Haw Haw's words and Attlee's ration books.

        *   *   *

I must have clambered over twenty or thirty fences & walked down seven or eight different sets of 'private' byways that afternoon before I jacked it in & got the bus. My graffiti-scratched reflection in the bus-shelter window revealed muddy knees & tangled hair. It was eerie how empty the gullies had all been. They'd never been teeming but now they were completely deserted. There was much more foliage than I'd remembered, but any sounds of dogs, kids, tools, engines & the like were just my own disjointed recollections. The inner sanctum of suburban Birmingham had become a leafy ghost town: a suppressed memory. To understand why Singh had started the Zomby project with a chapter called, 'Unfencing Theory', I didn't need to look any further than this.

But did Amrit Singh exist at all? I'd been avoiding thinking about it in the gullies. I'd been trying to immerse myself in my own past. It was impossible to disentangle us however. The gullies don't like the thoughts that pass through them to be kept neat & tidy. Singh & I... Martin, if that was his real name... we'd grown up very close to one another. Our paths must've crossed at some point, even though neither of us could possibly have known it. For all I knew, he might have been the boy we caught pooing behind the tree.

The Registry Office was bigger & busier than I'd pictured it. There were no weddings going on that afternoon. It's not a peak period for weddings, November. But there was still a sprinkling of sodden confetti in drab pastel shades around the base of the statue of Murdock, Watt & Boulton. Brummies call this sculpture 'the carpet sellers': the three wigged industrialists look like they're examining a bit of rug rather than going over the plans for some groundbreaking invention. I suppose it must be very hard to represent a sheet of paper in cast bronze. We also call the naked woman in the fountain at the front of the Council House *the floozy in the jacuzzi*. It's a much more natural snatch of Brummie poetry than the pompous bit of T. S. Eliot the artist saw fit to carve around the outside of the thing. That doesn't even rhyme for godsake.

The receptionist gave me a document request form to fill in. I didn't have all the details they asked for. I didn't know Carla's maiden name, for example, or Martin's exact date of birth, but apparently that didn't matter. If I knew the child's name, the year & the parents' married names, it would be easy enough to find. So I tried: Martin Higgs, 1972, Leon Higgs, Carla Higgs. Then I handed over the form & took a seat on one of plastic chairs against the wall in the waiting area.

It took them about fifteen minutes to find the correct register entry, type out a copy & get it signed. I sat & listened to the office's internal engineering processing my request. It's at times like these that you always wish you'd brought a book with you. All I had in my bag was the Birmingham Quean. I couldn't imagine myself taking out that huge brown scroll of a manuscript & starting to hunt through it for evidence of Martin Higgs. Eventually, my name was called out (the name I was looking for rather than the one on my own birth certificate). The registrar handed me a crested, typed & stamped sheet of thick A4 paper with a wavy pattern on a hospital green background. I felt a bit like I was receiving one of those big cheques they hand over on charity telethons. I stood beside the desk & began to read...

£e climax of Tchaikovsky's 1812
    Comes bleeping from a jacket on £e stool
Beside £e scorer. Perry starts to delve
    Inside £e pockets for his minuscule
(But noisy) phone: he did £e tune himself
    And got it wrong; he €inks he looks a fool;
He grabs it, and he's just about to answer,
    And £en… he pauses…   (like £is stanza).

---

*   *   *

Framed by the cross-taped windows of my mother's house, the cake candles animating his strong chin as our singing stirred their flames, my son was the very image of a young English gentleman. He was handsome, charming, strong, intelligent, hard-working and sickeningly enviable.

The next morning he announced that he was leaving home. He had money now. He was a man. He did not need to stay. From his deathbed, whilst Hermione was still pregnant, my mother's father (the Shropshire industrialist) had instructed his solicitor to create a trust-fund of a considerable size for our unborn child which would mature on his eighteenth birthday. His financial independence assured, Phillip's plan was to abandon an education which seemed somewhat irrelevant against the backdrop of the war and go to London 'to see what he could do.' His mother was entirely supportive of this course of action, and informed me as she concluded her account of its inevitability that she was leaving too. It was obvious to both of us, she said, that we had only meant to stay together for the duration of his upbringing. We had long since reached a silent understanding that she was bound to leave the moment that he went. 'What I ever saw in you is quite unfathomable.' It came as a relief.

More than a week passed before I realized that I had no idea where they could have gone. It might seem strange that I should want to contact them. Characteristically, neither had left anything to chance. There was no practical excuse to telephone or write. All property had been logically and fairly split, divorce proceedings had been properly instigated, bills had been paid and authorities informed; arrangements were impeccable. Solicitors on both sides were professional and thoroughly discreet. There were no sentimental reasons why I should desire to see their faces, hear their voices or read their handwriting. I had work to do: I was looking for a fascinating book I thought I had once read called Poetry and Prophesy. *And yet… there was a masochistic curiosity at work.*

My first enquiries to Hermione's solicitors were met with the curt response that she had every right to conceal her whereabouts. I pressed them to pass on, at the very least, my son's address. He was my child, after all. They informed me that Phillip was no longer a legal dependant of mine and it was therefore up to him to choose to get in touch or not. He was declining to do so at present because he and his mother were co-habiting and he respected her desire to avoid unnecessary contact. That, at least, was what they said.

*   *   *

I didn't read any more. Seeing the details set out like that: tapped out on an old-fashioned typewriter, the surnames all in capitals, had forced me to notice something. The strangeness of Leon's signature reproduced in typed characters forced my eyes to skip back up to Martin's name. I read it over twice. It was undeniable. I literally gasped. I couldn't believe I'd not picked it up before. I shook my head at my own stupidity.

"Is this not the one you were after?" asked the registrar.

It was incredible. It was so obvious. I'd have to check it though... just to be certain. "What?"

"Have we given you the wrong entry? It seemed a pretty straightforward search."

"No... I mean, yes, it's the right one, it's just... I wonder, listen: I'm sorry to do this to you. I know it's ten to four. But is there time to get another one?"

She sighed. "Well, I suppose so, if you've got all the correct details."

I filled in another form as quickly as I could, I handed it over & paid the fee again. This was a much more recent birth. It took less time to do. Perhaps it was just that she wanted to get home. Whatever the reason, she told me not to bother taking a seat, she'd do it for me right away. When the result arrived, it came as a stark assertion of its own inevitability...

> £e tune gets to £e bit where Perry tries
> > To replicate £e fanfare in £e brass.
> He stands and stares, unable to disguise
> > £is moment of uncertainty… At last,
> He hits £e little hang-up key. £e whys
> > And wherefores are quite lost on me. Perhaps
> He still €inks he can win, or superstition
> Prevents him from avoiding competition,

231.4 *uncertainty*: Incontestably an allusion to the Heisenberg Principle. This instant of limbo which Perry is 'unable to disguise' obviously likens him to the previous analogue of a quantum *wave/particle* in the spin of the coin at the vertex of its toss. As he 'hits the little hang-up key' (a paradoxical means by which a patently *unhangable* 'portable telephone' can nevertheless be *hung up*) he obviously undergoes a metaphorical *wavefunction collapse*. The next sentence is pure Bosvilean spite. It is *us* he is talking about here. It is we who unaccountably surrender to the inevitable cosmic defeat of the final leg of darts. Like Sloggy, we have adopted Perry as our unlikely champion in a metaphysical contest, and despite the fact we know full well that he will lose… and just how much is on the line, there is nothing we can do to deflect the progress of this character, who at this instant is revealed merely to be a particle hurtling into the radioactive nucleus of Bosvil's sub-atomic temporal detonator.

In fact, our intervention has achieved the opposite: our sheer ability to reduce him (as the quantum theorists would say) to an *observable* has brought about the *wavefunction collapse* that will eventually open the floodgates of this *chthonic* (Quantum) region of the Universe into the *upper* (Newtonian) region we believe ourselves still to inhabit. Thus will Bosvil be released, and his *Brummagem* future brought about. The fact that this is to be done within the seemingly harmless tradition of English satirical verse suggests that Bosvil has taken the opening of Pope's 'Epistle to Dr. Arbuthnot' and given it a truly diabolical spin by changing a single word (as if Helicon and Hades were the same thing… subject to *quantum entanglement* of a sort that you and I cannot avoid).

Rather than Pope's ironic *Parnassus*, Bosvil proclaims with Hecatæan glee:

> The Dog-star rages! Nay 'tis past a doubt,
> All *Tartarus*, or *Bedlam*, is let out:
> Fire in each eye, and Papers in each hand,
> They rave, recite, and madden round the land.

*   *   *

Then began an investigation that took a year to yield fruit. Despite what you might read in Graham Greene's The End of the Affair, *there were no private detective agencies in Britain in the war. Any people of that sort not already in the forces would certainly have become legitimate policemen or black-market traders by the forties. There was little scope for private enterprise. Most business activities were state-regulated or else too clandestine for advertisement. Despite Churchill, this was the decade of socialism and swindles.*

*   *   *

2004 — THURSDAY, JUNE 3

NHS Number: ▮▮▮	**BIRTH**	Entry No.: ▮▮▮

Registration district: Birmingham
Sub-district: Birmingham
Administrative area: County Borough of Birmingham

CHILD

1. Date and place of birth: Thirty-first March 2001 ▮▮▮
2. Name and surname: Samuel HIGGS
3. Sex: Male

FATHER

4. Name and surname: Martin HIGGS
5. Place of birth: Birmingham
6. Occupation: Musician

MOTHER

7. Name and surname: Hannah Louise ARDEN
8. Place of birth: Marple, Stockport
9. (a) Maiden surname: ---------- (b) Surname at marriage if different from maiden surname: ----------
10. Usual address (if different from place of child's birth): ----------

INFORMANT

11. Name and surname (if not the mother or father): ----------
12. Qualification: Father
13. Usual address (if different from that in 10 above): ----------
14. I certify that the particulars entered above are true to the best of my knowledge and belief
    ▮▮▮ .... Signature of informant
15. Date of registration: First April 2001
16. Signature of registrar: ▮▮▮
17. Notes: In ▮▮▮ in space 4. for 'Martin HIGGS' read 'UNKNOWN' in space 5. for 'Musician' read 'UNKNOWN'. Corrected on twenty-fifth May 2003 by me ▮▮▮ Superintendent Registrar on production of statutory declaration made by Hannah Louise ARDEN.

Two things were undeniable: firstly, the name I'd come to know so well over the past few months that I dreamt it repeated to me like a mantra, the name of the man who I'd been hunting down (trying to pinpoint his whereabouts & his ideas), the name 'Amrit Singh' was obviously made up. It was nothing more than an anagram of 'MARTIN HIG(G)S'.

Secondly, & this was by far the more devastating realisation, it was not this man, this Martin Higgs, who had been lying to me, & neither had it been his mother, Carla. This document in my hand confirmed that the birth of Hannah's son had been registered three days after it occurred. There had been no eleven-day delay. What's more, the person responsible for absenting Martin from his son's life (at least where the official records were concerned; & it had happened fairly recently) was not the man himself, but Hannah.

Or maybe it's a macho gangster €ing:
    It's time he stood unaided on his own
Two feet; why $ould a Tartar have to sing
    From Anglo-Saxon hymn$eets? If he'd known
He'd come here just to be an underling
    To £is *zvezda* he would've stayed at home.
No moneyslinger £ere made him back down,
So why be servile in £is gimcrack town?

232.6 *zvezda*: This word was the one that finally transformed my initial vague desire to supply some kind of exegesis for this poem into direct action. The decision was taken—as these decisions almost always are—in order to provide the kind of illumination of the foreign and dialectal items of which I felt myself to be sorely in need if I were fully to understand the piece. The very first thing I did, by way of research, was to contact somebody whom I assumed could lend some small assistance. Not wishing to reveal my whereabouts or activities to colleagues by requesting information of the only Russian speaker of my acquaintance (this was back when I was capable of such freedoms of intention), and being concerned that one or two modest articles jaunty enough at least to have remained within the collective memory of the scholarly brotherhood of this country might render the small world of British academia unsafe ground on which to risk a waiver of my anonymity, I had the idea of contacting someone from abroad.

    One or two months earlier, I remembered, I had found, in a copy of a popular scientific journal abandoned in Room 666 (see 7.1 *Jodrell Bank*) a small column about a professor of Russian at Cornell University who had recently discovered a new species of butterfly. I had been impressed enough by the polymathy implied—I flattered myself it was a mirror of my own desire to mingle Literary Criticism and Biology—to commit to memory the man's name (not a difficult task considering its Slavic oddity). I took it upon myself to write to him for a standard description of the word's denotative and connotative meanings and some brief indication of the implications of its use. This I did—feeling that it might add another small *countermure* against my discovery—using a rather derelict, and extremely noisy, old typewriter, which must have lain gathering dust in the corner of the hallway outside my room from since before the war.

    This correspondence was an unmitigated disaster. Considering the effort involved in producing the letter on such a rusty old machine and sneaking into the office in the dead of night to add it to the outgoing post bag without being seen, every step like a new fissure running through my body as if through cracking ice—and then repeating this hazardous clandestine adventure three times throughout the following weeks until the response eventually appeared in my pigeonhole—I sincerely wish I had never concocted such an elaborate scheme in order to explain a single word. When I finally got the Russian's letter back to the safety of my room and extracted it neatly from its prim laid envelope with the aid of a ruler, and began to skim my eye across it, I literally could not believe what I was reading. The man was obviously quite insane.

    To think I went through all that trouble just for this. I have it in front of me now. I think I might include it: by way of a warning. It does, at least, make me feel a mite less dreadful about the gradual deterioration of my own mental capacities as doom approaches, for which I suppose I do have the excuse of the *sui generis* predicament I am in:

Cornell, Ithaca, New York

April 2nd, 1953

Dear 'Dr Twigg',

You will forgive me if I decline to thank you for your letter. Unfortunately I was able to guess the full scope of its malign intent only from a brisk reading of the first sentence. This reply is therefore hardly likely to succeed in meeting its demands.

It was an odd thing to receive. Once the little shiver of expectation had subsided, which I always get on discovering an unusual postmark amongst the internal bumph, I noticed the silhouette of the late King toppling backwards over the brink of the envelope. (Have the Royal Mail really yet to issue an Elizabeth II range?) No doubt it was a rabid excess of saliva which postponed adherence of the stamp beneath the uncompromising fist of the sender, but I initially interpreted this misalignment as an extension of that charming crookedness I remembered from the medieval streets of Cambridge. My only response to the flimsy translucence of the paper (and the naïve mislabelling of Phylloscopus collybita as Phylloscopus trochilus in the stationery of whatever pinchbeck ornithological charity it is you patronise) was to indulgently prolong this moment of nostalgia. You will be gratified to hear however that my daydream of rickety, crickety old England was reduced to smouldering ruins by the bombshell of the opening sentence.

If only to prove the acute disturbance it provoked in me (strong enough to activate a previously undiscovered photographic memory) I will take the liberty of quoting verbatim, whilst reproducing the vagaries of your ~~saucy~~ acidic cliché of a blackmailer's typewriter:

```
Dear Irofessor Nabokov,
   I bave recently acquired (by wbat means I cannot say; if
I could, I would bardly need to solicit your corresoondence)
a strange and disturbing text of wbicb I trust you may be
able to orovide some sligbt illumination.
```

I had ~~hardly~~ barely finished reading these words when the paper slipped from my inky fingerprints and swooped between the chairlegs foresting my study floor. It flapped just twice before gliding expertly into the stove. I can still call to mind the picture of the folded paper blackening in the fuel-hatch through which it had manoeuvred like a dovehawk through a Siberian thicket. I was in turn reminded of the typescript of <u>Волшебник</u> immolating leaf by leaf in the grate of our first dreadful little flat in 87th Street. I remember trying to convince myself, via a kind of gawking self-hypnosis, that this could finally be an end to it.

I cannot begin to understand how you manage to achieve the aculeate effects of coincidental metaphor necessary to make the reader feel these things. I hope you will not think it an attempt to flatter my way out of the predicament if I say that on the evidence of just this cursory reading I feel you must be the звезда of the extortion letter.

Whatever stops him, Perry's curious
 Refusal to assist his so-called boss
Makes Sloggy's triple figures furious.
 £ey snap £eir clam-$ells quickly $ut and toss
£em barwards; £eir trajectories worry us
 Inside £e a$tray as £ey merge across
£e optics. €ree men slam €ree toilet doors
As Tanya's fingers loose £e dart £at scores

~~Голубятник, by the way, is just one of a number of Russian names for Accepitor gentilis. It is only professionals (those who would designate it a 'raptor' in English) who use this term. Closer to Poland it is more commonly большой ястреб: The Greater Hawk, and amongst non-falconers it is тетеревятник: literally 'Catcher of Black Grouse', which distinguishes it from перепелятник: 'Catcher of Quails'. This distinction is precisely analogous to the English separation of the same two species: goshawk ('goose hawk') and sparrowhawk. Falconers however (typically aristocrats) get their somewhat pretentious epithet from a literal translation of the arcane French, Autour des Palombes: a term derived from Latin 'accepitor' (that which receives/catches) but which is divertingly confusable with both 'autour des palombes' (encircling the doves) and 'auteur des palombes' (the author of the doves).~~

~~The Latin 'accepitor' is the only word close to an acceptable translation of the suffix -ятник. There is no form in English or French that carries anything like the same semantic scope. Памятник 'receiver of memory', for example, refers to any literal or metaphorical 'monument'. As a result, голубятник can be used not only to mean dove-hawk but also pigeon fancier. (We should not forget that a fascination for the activities of these eccentric collectors of such ugly creatures led Darwin to extrapolate his neat little theory of Natural Selection: a theory which I hope my own work on mimicry will eventually provide with precisely the sort of aesthetic ornamentation it myopically ignores in nature.) Голубятни, by negative extension, means dovecote or pigeon loft and is used by a departmental colleague of mine in what I trust to be completely unintentional derision of the English metaphor when talking about the wooden hatch in the office from which he collects his correspondence.~~

~~It was in the голубятни, of course, that I found your letter.~~ I never had the opportunity to read its specific demands but I can safely presume you meant to announce your possession of The Enchanter. How you managed to come by it when there was only a week between our evacuation of the apartment on rue Boileau (in which I left the manuscript) and the destruction of the building by a German incendiary bomb, I cannot imagine. I can only assume you have links to one or other of the (incorrigibly incestuous and risibly misnamed) 'intelligence communities' and that your implied request for information concerning provenance was *une menace byzantine*.

You have it though, I am sure, and you intend to ransom it: (a feather to free the firebird). In fact (I apologise but the thought has only just occurred to me and at this stage I no longer have sufficient energy to redraft) if you possess the manuscript and you understand how valuable its suppression is to me, you probably do not require a lecture on Russian etymology.

In the circumstances this letter can only serve as a request for repetition of your lurid demands. **Променять кукушку на ястреба**. If you could send another copy I would be grateful. There is no need for the stylistic fireworks. A succinct note listing threats and demands will be sufficient. Think of yourself as a keeper at the *Jardin des Plantes*, patiently returning a camera to a chimp who hurled it at the bars of his cage in frustration at such an obdurate subject.

Rest assured I will not be troubling the authorities. I am sure your cover is exquisite. 'Twigg', I take it, is deliberately ludicrous: 'Lord, thou pluckest me.'

Yours temporarily,

Vladimir Nabokov

Since receiving the letter, (it did indeed prove a momentous day… but it lay in the future that none could foresee) I have discovered what I take to be the final proof of the dire psychagogic influence which you and I both know to be the poem's principle intention. When using my magnifying lens to examine the piece of paper on which appear the stanzas 215-218—where we are first introduced to Perry Striker—I noticed that there appeared to be another stanza written directly onto the brown parcel roll beneath. I inserted the end of my ruler in a gap between the two different papers (where the surface of the uppermost had wrinkled) and worked the edge backwards and forwards until enough of the dried glue had been broken for me to lift the white page and see what was underneath. The stanza was so shocking to me—both in terms of the moral degradation it embodied and the supernatural awareness it expressed of my own role in the embodiment of a future capable of such moral degradation—that, even at that late stage, I confess I scribbled over it with a red pencil until it was completely obliterated. The point of the pencil broke under the pressure of my desire to eradicate the truth and I was forced to pinch the hot sliver of coloured lead between my fingertips and scrub across the surface of the paper until my own right hand was covered in simulated gore.

I know now (my hand is still stained in farcical imitation of those of Bill Sykes and Macbeth with the bright red pigment), that there is no way for me to suppress it. I may as well repeat it here:

> The daughter of a friend in Lowestoft
>   Once offered, *if I'd like*, to *suck my cock off*.
> I spluttered, making out I had a cough,
>   To give me time to get over the shock of
> Her filthy mouth. *Had she read Nabokov?*
>   I asked, and she corrected me: *NaBOkov!*
> I never thought I'd come across a tongue
> So educated on a girl so young.

I can only hope this is not your own work secreted beneath our tormentor's sheets. Surely only Bosvil could know that I would be in contact with such an obscure and eccentric Russian academic on a point of language. The lurid prurience of it—the result of intergenerational misunderstanding—is all Bosvil's. The pair speak very different languages, it seems. We two, across our own generational divide, can empathize. It is a typically lurid Bosvilean irony (of multitudinous implications) that the lecherous persona should only interpret what might be just a polite enquiry about a lollipop as an appalling proposition of fellatio because he has no means of access to her impenetrable *teenage* cant.

234

> A one-O-five to cut £e massive lead
>   £e Russian had establi$ed up to now:
> He'd €rown €ree-sixty wi£ nine darts; he'd need
>   Just one-four-one to $ow £is scrubber how
> To €row a twelve dart leg. Before £is, $e'd
>   Expressly chucked €ree nuts and half a crown
> To give him £e impression he could settle
> Before $e really tried to test his mettle.

233.4 *snap their clam-shells quickly shut*: This strange triptych of Sloggies undergoes a bizarre literalisation of transferred epithet here (analogous, once again, to the one that founds the notion of *Quantum Uncertainty*). Two colloquial phrases meaning 'to stop speaking'—*to clam up* and *to shut one's trap*—are not only hinged into a comic mixed metaphor but are physically embodied in the form of the *portable telephone*, envisaged as the shell of a bivalve mollusc which is actually mechanically *closed* to end participation in a conversation. This uncanny object—a materialisation of Sloggy's (in)ability to speak—is then discarded in such a vehement way that its velocity and trajectory make the coin-narrator worry for an instant that it might collide with her. The threat is that Sloggy might find his own *bullseye*. But what, we must ask ourselves, does this *clammed shut* missile contain? Botticelli's Venus, on her *Coquille St. Jacques*, perhaps?... his vision of the perfect artificial woman to be born after his resculpting of Britannia's body? The truth is that the image is probably designed to recall a beta particle fired into a radioactive nucleus in order to detonate a nuclear reaction—the multiplicity of the image a simplistic representation of Heisenberg's Principle—but the suspense is ironic... a pale shadow of the real sub-nuclear reaction about to be triggered.

234.6 *half a crown*: The darts players in this future appear to draw some direct correspondence between the scoring regions of the dartboard and money. The surface explanation of this might be something as benign (despite its petty venality) as the idea that games are played for money in such a (literal) way that the scores are in pounds, shillings and pence rather than a merely relativistic number-system. Presumably—the scoring system being a reducing tally (like a *Dutch auction*) rather than an accumulative one—the idea would be that both players put up a standard *ante* at the start of the leg, the winner earning whatever amount of money his opponent had failed to claim back by the time he finished. This would certainly explain the heightened desire, so evident here, to maximize the margin of victory.

This seems benign enough, but when one begins to delve into the possible numerical system involved, something at first merely surprising, and then (in the light of this work of dire, supernatural prescription) truly devastating, becomes clear...

My first thought upon reading this was to attempt to work out which sector of a dartboard might be worth *half a crown*. The initial assumption was, quite naturally, that each integer might simply represent a penny. In that case, 2/6 (30d) would be the value of *Double 15*. What possible logic could be behind this, however, I could not imagine: the sum of the sectors would not be any 'round number' or naturally significant amount of monetary value. And then it struck me: just as a purely hypothetical exercise, what if I assumed (knowing what I did about Bosvil's literalising imagination) that the size and shape of the half-crown coin were also significant. As if the sector of the board in question were literally the *trace* of a half-crown: both its value and its circumference...

That left only one position on the board: the *bullseye*. It suited Bosvil perfectly, I realized, to champion the adoption of a name glossable as *quasimodo monarchy* to refer to the centre of the target (envisaged as the anal focus of a perverse libido) in a proletarian burlesque of the source of England's military pride on the battlefield of Agincourt. As soon as I applied this small alteration to my previous speculation everything slotted into place:

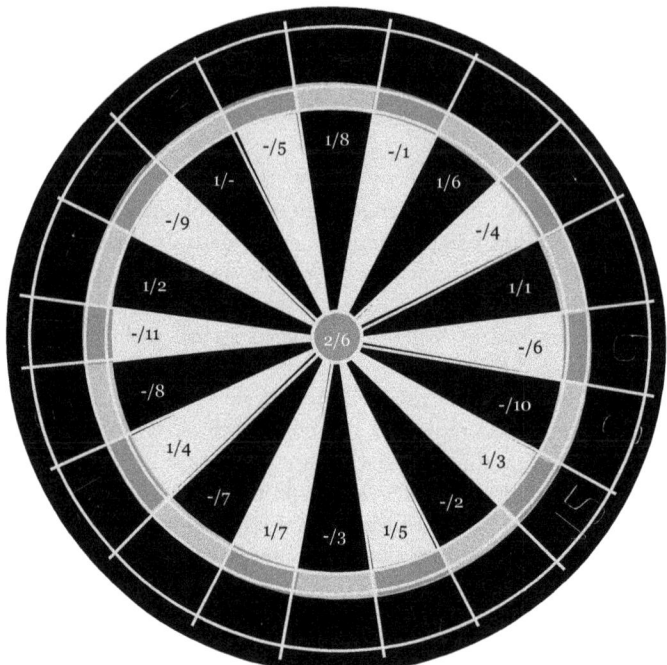

fig. 7: the sovereign dartboard

$$1d + 2d + \ldots 19d + 20d + \mathbf{30d} = \mathbf{240d}$$
$$\text{-}/1 + \text{-}/2 + \ldots 1/7 + 1/8 + \mathbf{2/6} = \mathbf{\pounds 1/\text{-}/\text{-}}$$

The dartboard is another *counterfeit sovereign* !

234.8 *test his mettle*: A sniping, ironic allusion to the *assay* which forms the proverbial definition for this metaphorical application of a simple variant of *metal*. As an indicator of value, the word connotes the very terms of *unalloyed* 'fortitude', 'honour', 'nobility' etc. that this poem is designed to undermine. If Britannia's own *mettle* were tested it would be precisely equivalent to the cheap nickel-brass of the coin-narrator. The worry is, of course, that the atomic glow to which this poem has exposed us both—as you write and I read—might have transformed our own *mettle* into such a trashy alloy.

> Before £e bouncer takes £is massive $ot,
> > He turns his Smirnoff bottle up to pour
> £e vodka version down his €roat. He's got
> > An aptitude for booze and darts: £e more
> He drinks, £e more he hits. Of course, £at's not
> > Remarkable: I'm absolutely sure
> (Al£ough my evidence is anecdotal)
> > No darts professional's ever been teetotal.

235.2 *Smirnoff*: Russo-American brand of vodka which is the subject of a continuing battle over rights precipitated by the Bolshevik Revolution of 1917 which left the White Russian Smirnov family incapable of proving their claims of ownership. The fact that the hugely successful brand owes its notoriety entirely to Piotr Arsenvitch Smirnov's having been granted the title of "Official Purveyor to the Russian Imperial Court" in 1886, has never been any barrier to the Americans who 'bought' the trading rights off one of his exiled ancestors (at a moment of obvious, pitiable vulnerability) and proceeded to use this title, alongside reproductions of the Romanov coat of arms, to take profiteering advantage of a Western fascination with the banished Russian aristocracy. Bosvil would naturally be attracted to the unscrupulous counterfeiting of the symbols of monarchy involved, not to mention the collusion of Soviet Communism and American Capitalism against the interests of the upholders of ancient honour and nobility.

How this might be extended into the notion of *nuclear collusion* which provides the backdrop for the imminent collapse of an entire history of ordered metaphysics and morality is not very difficult to guess. The instability of identity of this 'bottle of spirits' is matched by the explicit parallel between the shot he is about to take (as part of the ceremony of triggering cosmic collapse) and the act of emptying its contents down his throat. It is like a Molotov Cocktail hurled by a rioter at the core of a stable, rational society whose 'centre cannot hold'—the overture of chaos... a neutron to split the atom of good sense.

235.8 *darts... teetotal*: Narcotics are as fundamental an element of many primitive magical ceremonies as are their ritual sexual performances. Both are mainstays of Bosvil's quasi-Bacchanalian Birmingham. The Caribbean *voodoo* Britannia Spears has imported uses alcohol as the principle medium of its alteration of consciousness (though there are plenty of other drugs being both referenced and taken, one can have little doubt). In order to release the temporally paradoxical potency of the dartboard, there needs to be some hallucinatory means via which its terrifying internal geometry and Satanic symbolism can be instigated in the mind of those taking part. For us, the narcotic effect, just like the ontological status of the 'game' itself, has been distilled into the verbal content of the poem. Our drugs are the words. We have lost the will to resist injecting them into our minds. In turn, inevitably, we are subject to the same strange visions of the mathematical icons of political, moral, psychological, temporal and ultimately the entire metaphysical breakdown latent in the ritual *target* of the game of darts...

It was clear that I'd been spun a yarn. It was also clear that Hannah had, at the very least, been the source of a number of the lies. Suspicions spread through the recesses of my memory trying to find details on which they could catch. I didn't feel I could trust anything that anyone had said to me throughout the previous year. I needed to do something about this quickly. I needed to get in amongst these details & discover just how far the lies had gone, who had been responsible for what.

Fortunately, Birmingham Central Library is just over Broad Street from the Registry Office. The inverted steps of its upper structure extend above the bullet-shaped dome of the Hall of Memory like the bellows of a huge Victorian camera pointed at the sky. That comment of Prince Charles's that the library appeared to be 'a place where books are incinerated' was spoken in complete (& completely typical) ignorance of the institution's history. The original library, opened in 1865 by George Dawson (the progenitor of the particularly Brummie idea the 'Civic Gospel') was doubtless the kind of building Charlie would like to have seen reconstructed. It was, however, a building in which books really were incinerated.

On the 11th January 1879, during a severe cold snap, a plumber was thawing out the pipes that supplied the library's gaslight chandeliers. In order to achieve this he had fitted a transformer to a pipe junction & ignited the discharging gas. This was standard practice. The flame produced was no longer than his thumb. It was just sufficient to warm the surrounding pipes &, at that size, wasn't considered dangerous. It was just big enough, however, to ignite one of the woodshavings that had become dislodged from its position between two of the wooden partition walls by the icy wind. The fire took hold very quickly. The plumber attempted to put it out with his hands. They were rapidly & badly burned, as was the vast majority of the library's collection. The books were such good fuel that the fire raged high into the sky in minutes, pages of print swirling on the flame-filled winds. Charred fragments were found as far away as Acocks Green, three miles to the South West. Only about a thousand of the books were saved. According to legend, the mayor, Jesse Collings, could not be convinced to abandon his literary rescue efforts & had to be dragged out of the inferno by firefighters: not, however, before he'd salvaged the entire Cervantes archive.

For my part, the first thing I needed to rush in & snatch was that newspaper story about Sanjit Singh that Carla had wanted me to see. That would be all the confirmation I needed both that Hannah's story about her ex-partner's background was a fiction & that Carla had been telling the truth. After that... well, I'd have to try & find this Martin Higgs. The newspaper microfiches are held in the Local Studies Department on the top floor of the library. I remembered this as a rather sedate & deserted place in the past. It was somewhere you went to get away from the teenagers. Something had happened in the meantime to make it very popular. I couldn't imagine there had suddenly grown up an interest in studying the history of the West Midlands. Then I heard what everyone was asking for at the enquiry desks. They wanted parish records: marriages, births, deaths, school attendance lists; they were doing surname searches. In all but title, this was no longer the Local Studies floor, this had become the Genealogy Department.

You see, dart players, to allay 'dartitis',
> Do *need* £e odd medicinal libation.

In fact, £ey almost drink as much as writers:
> Bo€ 'marksmen' needing extra lubrication

To stop £eir joints from seizing up wi£ fright as
> £ey aim to €row... or scribble an oration.

More power to £eir elbows, I say: getting pissed
Can raise your game, your pinky, and your Bristow-wrist.

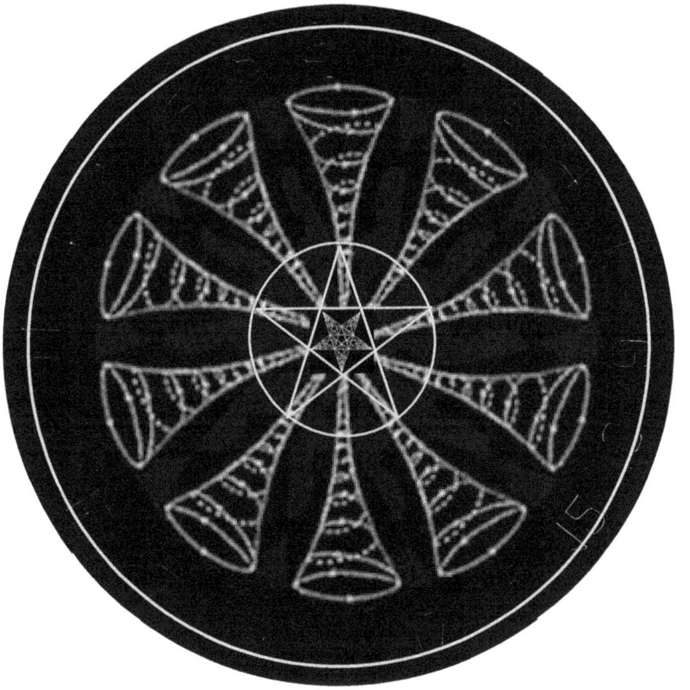

fig. 8: quantum dartboard with bullseye pentagram

It took little time to establish that I wouldn't be able to find what I was after. The library closed in two hours & I could only get fifteen minutes on a microfiche viewer. More importantly, the local papers had no index. In order to find an article, you would need to know when it had appeared, not what it was about. The librarian suggested I look in *The Times* index on the Social Studies floor, in case the story'd made it to the national news. It hadn't.

There was something of startling similarity there however. In 1969, during the campaign for Sikh bus-drivers to be allowed to wear their turbans, a very venerable-looking leader of the Sikh community in Wolverhampton called Sohan Singh Jolly had threatened to burn himself to death in the city centre if the council didn't repeal its ban. Not only does this untypically dramatic threat seem to have been successful in Wolverhampton, but it appears also to have made the case of the Sikh bus drivers the focus for much of the debate surrounding the Race Relations Bill at the start of the ensuing decade. Enoch Powell reserved some of his most overtly racist language for his denunciation of 'these dangerous & divisive elements'. It is probably for this reason that Sikhs, alongside Jews (but, crucially, not Muslims), were named in that legislation as a racial/religious community whose specific rights were to be protected.

If nothing else, I'd found the kind of story that might influence a fabrication. I would have to leave it at that & try a different angle of attack. I found the main computer cluster on that floor & waited for one with internet access to become available. As far as I could tell (I know this sounds like I'm descending into racist generalisation myself, but I swear it was true) everyone else in the queue had recently arrived in the country as would-be British Residents. It makes sense of course. The library's in the middle of town; it's got free public web access; it's run by the same people who provide you with temporary accommodation; it's centrally heated: if you're an 'asylum seeker' or an 'economic migrant' trying to keep in touch with home, or just trying to keep warm, you're likely to gravitate there.

It's not just the computers in the public library, it's the whole idea of the web that attracts exiles. Internet infrastructure & its functions reflect an implicit commitment to the freedom of movement. Routers, DNS servers & fibre optic backbones are all designed to maximise the speed & ease of information flow. The web does have its hierarchies, but the system is non-centralised & routinely forms insubordinate connections. The overarching function of the mechanisms is to allow 'packets' of information to avoid possible barriers to movement & to find the quickest way to get from one computer to another. This is the result of a vision which, despite having originated under military auspices, is intrinsically utopian & libertarian. Just as liberal capitalism demands the free movement of capital & goods, this new (liberal capitalist) technology is enforcing the free movement of data & thereby hastening the elimination of the difference between capital & data. The obvious missing link in all this abounding liberty is the free movement of human beings. The failure of the world's democracies to grant labour the same freedoms it demands for trade & communication is the best evidence for that old Socialist claim that capitalism is inherently imperialist. These marginalised migrants, clustering around the temples of 'info-liberty', know as well as anyone what the powerful will do to make sure that power continues to flow in only one direction.

(At points like £is, £e poet's meant to name
   His poison: more specifically, £e wine
He likes to flow to keep him on his game
   And help him find £e richest veins of rhyme
£e sober never strike because £eir aim
   Is too deliberate. I'll come to mine
In just a minute, but illustrious forebears
Continue to insist we don't ignore £eirs…

237.6 *deliberate*: era 17

fig. 9: pentagrammatic *golden section* dartboard
with Baphomet bullseye

It was impossible, however, standing there amongst those weary but still determined-looking young men, to avoid the conclusion that it was a typical bit of privileged left-wing arrogance to feel the need to express my solidarity with them. They didn't give a sod about me or my sub-Trotskyist ideas any more than I really gave a sod about them or theirs. The truth is: most of them were probably only there because they'd bought into exactly the ideology of democratic capitalism that I was fantastically recruiting them to denounce.

When I eventually got my go, there was only a quarter of an hour left before the library was due to close. The first thing I did was to google Martin Higgs. It's a pretty common name though. There were hundreds. I tried narrowing it down a bit but nothing worked. Whatever I did, the person with the most UK hits was always the editor of the Waterstone's Magazine, who was currently singing the praises of Alan Hollinghurst's *The Line of Beauty* which had just won the Man Booker Prize (its success apparently unhindered by its terrible punning title). There was no way I could believe this was the man I was looking for. I decided to email him anyway, just in case. As I was about half way through wording a brief & discreet question when an idea struck me: what if I were to use Hannah's email account instead of mine to send the message? I could try to guess the password.

Obviously there's a serious moral problem here. It's not something I would normally condone. In this specific instance, however, two things seemed to argue in its favour. Firstly the account was, as I remembered it, not set up in her own name. When you received an email it claimed to come from Amrit Singh. This identity was itself fraudulent (though if you were not actually pretending to be another real person, this was probably not against the law; it was just a case of using an alias.) Secondly, & more importantly, Hannah had demonstrably been lying to me. She had probably been using this email address to do so. As far as I was concerned that made it a legitimate target.

I went to hotmail. I typed in the address: gregorsamosa@hotmail.com. I tried a few key words from the Zomby stuff, (perhaps I shouldn't say which). The fourth one worked. It was a really obvious choice. The only reason I hadn't tried it first was because I thought it was *too* obvious. It took an effort to restrain my glee at seeing the mailbox open. My fingers trembled above the keys with anticipation. I gripped the mouse in my hand to stop it from visibly shaking as I scrolled down through the messages. They came in clusters of dates that were fairly sparsely spread over the past couple of years. She'd obviously only used this account sporadically since she & Martin had split up. If the account had originally been his, then she'd erase all of his messages. Neither did any of the more recent ones seem to be from Martin or to mention him in the subject line. It was equally conspicuous, & suspicious, that all the messages from me had also been deleted. I could find no reference to myself or 'invertedpodsnap' in the inbox entries: all the *Sam*s obviously meant her son. There was one name that caught my eye, though: *Lynne Fizzy*. I assumed it was that tall, black friend of Hannah's I'd met. There were a number of messages from her. One in particular looked promising. The subject read 'M walk-out."

Lord Byron slums it slightly to refuse
    Champagne and take a Hock and Soda Water
As *Juan*'s fro£y alcoholic muse.
    But Pushkin's verse is ear€ier and swarter;
He plumps instead for a Bordeaux. To choose
    Between fake marble and red bricks and mortar
Is not my cup of tea. To tell £e tru£,
I'd ra£er compromise… say… Dry Vermou£.

fig. 10: demonic golden section dartboard
    with radiating Baphomet

I clicked it. Here's what it said:

Yohannah,

well it just had to happen didn't it. We were arguing about you & Sam again, surprise surprise. I know what you said, doll, but sometimes I just can't keep my big mouth shut. He winds me up something rotten. We were supposed to be rehearsing & he had this bit of teenage skirt perched on his amp, hanging on his every stringbend & basically fetching & carrying for him. He was teaching her to skin up while we were learning *Romeo & the Lonely Girl* & he kept stopping in the middle of the number to judge her efforts. He made her do it four times, & completely buggered up three run-throughs (or is that *runs-through*?) before he made us stop & all give the latest thing marks out of ten. I couldn't resist it. I asked him (through the microphone) if he shouldn't be teaching his own son something worthwhile, like who his father was, instead of providing other people's pre-linguistic toddlers with a second-rate stoner's education.

All hell broke loose. He stormed out. The skirt turned out to have a bit of a tongue on her. She called me a 'fackin rowpy lookin bull-dyke.' 'Ah,' I said, 'I see you've attended finishing school, when *is* your Coming Out?' 'I'm in year firteen & I'm not a fackin *caorpit mancha*,' she said. 'Really?' I replied, 'not even a red carpet?' I haven't heard from M since, but you know what he's like: he'll definitely be back next Saturday. He left his pedals behind. He's hardly going to abandon those!

Anyway, hun, I thought I should fill you in. Let me know your news. How's my favourite boy? Tell him his Auntie Lynne's looking after his interests down South.

big sloppy ones

fizzy

   I decided to forget contacting the bloke at Waterstone's Magazine until I'd given this lead the once over. Even though 'M' was only mentioned in the subject line, it was self-evident that the person Lynne was writing about was Hannah's ex. & it didn't seem very likely that he'd be working as the editor of bookseller's inhouse publication.
   I typed 'Lynne Fizzie' in the search field, paused for a second, then hit Enter. I suppose I should have been able to predict the result. I confess that reference to *Romeo & the Lonely Girl* had gone way over my head. I double-clicked the first hit in the list...

£ough even several pints of Dry Martini
    (Not $aken, obviously, but gently stirred)
Could never make me write like Seamus Heaney,
    Or lend me Hughes' precision wi£ £e word.
Besides, I'd ra£er be an Ovalteeny
    £an try to order some€ing so absurd;
To ask a Brummie barman for a 'Noilly Prat'
Is tantamount to saying: 'I'm an oily twat';

239.1 *several*: era 18

fig. 11: fully demonised dartboard as sign of Baphomet

*   *   *

I was forced to act alone. All three of Phillip's surviving grandparents soon stopped speaking to me. My own mother was no exception. Hermione's friends were faithful to her wishes. Mine had heard nothing whatsoever. All official enquiries confirmed that I did not have a legal leg on which to stand. I therefore took it upon myself, in the summer of 1944, to go alone to London. I will gloss over the litany of unedifying failures that ensued. Suffice to say, I spent weeks treading the bombed-out streets, striking up uneasy conversation with drivers and housewives, searching marketplaces, parks and churches, peering through private windows from darkened doorways. Every lead was false and every clue a misdirection until the day I trudged back to my Pimlico guesthouse to find a telegram: 'Must talk. You are under suspicion. Tomorrow 3pm, St Dunstan's. Alexander.'

*   *   *

I was immediately confronted by a mock sepia-tone photograph depicting Lynne dressed as Phil Lynott. She was still perfectly recognisable as herself, but the resemblance to the Irish rock-star was staggering. She had the same almond-shaped face with smooth caramel skin. The moustache did look a bit stuck-on, but then it was always slightly out of place amongst Lynott's own boyish features. The perfect puppy-dog eyes were almost completely covered by a bulbous mat of black curls that might just as easily have been some kind of military winter headgear (a cross between a Russian Ushanka & a Guardsman's Bearskin) as the outrageous afro I remembered from our meeting in Hannah's kitchen. She was wearing some kind of faux officer's dress jacket to match the hairdo. It had gold braiding on the lapels & button-strips. Most ostentatiously, there was a thick loop of reflective embroidery above the cuffs. Her hands were crossed in front of her crotch. The expression & the pose were a brooding challenge: an ambiguous sexual confrontation from an unreal epoch.

'Lynne Fizzy' was a spoonerism. Lynne had a drag Phil Lynott tribute act. The site explained that her real name was Lynne Fitzpatrick, but that her natural resemblance to Lynott in appearance, voice & background had convinced her in her teens (when Lynott died) that she was destined to do this with her life. Somehow, the fact that she was a woman seemed to help the resemblance. Despite his long, angular physique & macho lyrics, there was something very feminine about Phil Lynott. The more photos of her I saw, the more impressed I was. The site was very much focused on Lynne herself, rather than the music or the group. It explained that she had been born in the same city as Lynott (Birmingham), that she too had been brought up by her grandparents because her South American father had deserted her Irish catholic mother (though, in this case, he was Guyanese & she had not been moved to Dublin as a child), & that both of them were lookalike acts: Phil Lynott had originally become famous, she insisted, because he looked like Jimi Hendrix.

This last detail was an odd thing to put on the website of a tribute band. The idea is usually to promote the uniqueness & originality of the act you're mimicking. After all, it's this reputation, & your ability to provide a reproduction that comes as close as possible to authenticity, that makes the show you're putting on more economically viable than performing your own (unknown) music. The audience wants to share in the nostalgic performance. They need to borrow from you the expertise in simulating that sense of immediate originality they believe existed at the original concerts (especially with larger-than-life rock performers like Lynott & Hendrix) so they can use it to make themselves feel younger, fresher & more dynamic: the way they would have been if they'd been there... back in the day. A tribute to *ABBA* will always be popular. But a tribute to *Bjorn Again*?... The obvious thing to do would be to gloss over this explanation of Lynott's initial success.

As for the rest of the 'backing' band there were no photographs available, at all. Even the live stage shots featured nothing more revealing than a stray limb. Their names were listed though. On lead guitar (a particularly volatile position in Thin Lizzy, it seems), was somebody who called himself *Fly McMartin*. This was almost certainly my man.

240

You may as well be dressed in a sarong:
    No bravado of £at sort for me.
And, anyway, according to £e song,
    'O, come to Birmingham and you $all see…
[Forgive me if I get £e trade names wrong:]
    … Ansells's, Brew XI, M&B;
We don't like whisky and we don't like rum…
… We are £e beer boys… FROM BRUM!'

240.4-8 O, come to Birmingham and you shall see…:

O come to Bethlehem and ye shall see
A woman, a mayd in thought and deede,
A fayrer with eyen myght no man see,
With her virgin paps her babe did fede;

Puer natus est hodie.

Bethlehem

Birthlehem

Birthingem

Birmingham

It is I who am the bearer of this gestating brummagem Christ. The poet of the future to whom I have expressed my sympathies does not exist in any real sense. If anyone is the amanuensis, it is I. Ryley Bosvil is nothing more than a name I have chosen for a function of diabolical genesis that has chosen me to bring it forth. The only resistance left open to me is to stop this work. There shall be no further annotations. This will make no difference, of course. I can only hope that a future reader finding the Birmingham Quean and all that I have written on its manuscript will successfully destroy it before its prescriptions come to pass.

where there is no talebearer, the strife ceaseth

241 CUT

But what foul beast, its round come round at last,
    Its gaze as blank and dim as bubble gum,
With skin the colour of elastoplast,
    Slow thighs jigging to an offbeat rhythm,
Its zip and eyelids flying at half-mast,
    Will slouch towards a bar in Birmingham
And order pints of lager for its mates?
(Somewhere like J. D. Wetherspoon's, or Yates'.)

Fortunately, this character also appeared to be the site's web designer. On the Contacts page, you were given the choice to write to a Kingston upon Thames P.O. Box address or else 'email Martin on fly.mcmartin@yahoo.co.uk'.

I went back to Hannah's email account, used this address for a new message & wrote:

> Hi Martin,
> what was your address again?

Then I just clicked Send. I didn't include a subject or a signature. I wanted to see what kind of response an enquiry as oblique & anonymous as this might get.

I was informed that the message had been sent successfully. I went back to the inbox & clicked on Refresh a couple of times. Nothing new appeared. I wanted to eke out every available minute on the computer before my fellow surfers & I were all thrown out onto Chamberlain Square's wave of terraced concrete. The people left queuing were looking increasingly desperate. One of them was an unusually young nun in a purple habit. The sight of her phlegmatically waiting her turn filled me with guilt. I needed to look like I wasn't just staring at an empty mailbox, especially when it wasn't mine, but couldn't bring myself to open a new window. I was fixated by the little recycling symbol at the top of the browser: two green arrows in a sixty-nine arrangement so that each one was pointing to the tail of the other.

This symbol, or something like it, is used on retail packaging to denote the fact that the material used (or even the receptacle itself) is 'recyclable'. Personally, I find this the most insulting, manipulative, meaningless & hypocritical bit of marketing that our society has churned out. If I knew exactly who to address my query to (some sort of trading standards authority, I suppose) I would seriously consider putting the following question to them: Given what physicists tell us about the nature of matter (i.e. that, without exception, it is recyclable), & the fact that it is principally the waste of resources & expenditure of energy involved in 'recycling' matter (oil, for example) that represents the basic threat posed by human activity to the environment, what possible benefit can there be in putting this label on objects which usually exist only to increase the profit margins of those industries responsible for both causing & promulgating such flagrant over-consumption? Future generations could well consider this symbol to be our swastika.

I clicked it one last time, but barely looked at the New Messages line. I couldn't really justify doing nothing when there were still people waiting. I was about to log out when I saw it... something had changed: there was a message from 'Fly McMartin', subject 'Hannah?'.

I opened it, heart racing:

> thought you didn't want to know. hope nothing's wrong. don't really have an
> address at the moment. staying in a caravan. call me on...

I wrote the number on an old library ticket in my wallet & left my pc to the purple nun.

Section 3(a)

dhūmenāvriyate vahnir yathādarśo malena ca
yatholbenāvṛto garbhas tathā tenedam āvṛtam

āvṛtam jñānam etena jñānino nitya-vairiṇā
kāma-rūpeṇa kaunteya duṣpūreṇānalena ca

Bhagavad Gita ch.3 'karma yoga' v.38-9

As flames are shrouded by their fumes,
A mirror by a veil of dust,
The infant by the mother's womb,
So wisdom has a shroud of lust.

The learned thinker's wit belies
Its all-encompassing desire:
The timeless adversary's disguise,
O Arjuna—this avid fire!

trans. Lionel Hubbard, 1920

                    242
        And so, to keep £at taste of mo£erland,
            I guess my self-styled Brummie minstrelsy
        $ould suckle at £e teet of some€ing canned
            Or draft; £ough I prefer a whisky tea,
        To tell £e tru£: a dirt-cheap blended brand
            Wi£ sugar—and a Weetabix or €ree.
        I reckon I could live my whole life €rough
            Wi£out ano£er pint, but not [wi£out] Typhoo.)

---

      *   *   *

In 37B.C. when Cæsar's torching of the Egyptian navy spread to land, and even more disastrously in 391 AD as Theophilus's zeal swept wild-fire through the city, the library of Alexandria burned into the night. Scrolls of old papyrus make for thirsty fuel. The legacy of Aristotle went up, not in smoke, but roaring flame: a near fumeless conflagration whose incendiary prowess derived directly from the city's plethora of literate kindling.

Something similar has happened here. This fire is just a pale imitation, but one in which pyramids of paper have once again transmuted text into a ravenous, infectious energy. Yet fire has another way with words. It was in an effort to eradicate a competing culture that the Medes and the Babylonians razed the library of Ashurbanipal at Nineveh. Their actions had the opposite effect. The Assyrian Empire was extremely short of vegetation. As a result, paper, wood and fire were all prohibitively expensive to produce. The Assyrians therefore used clay tablets as their literary medium. When soft, these were inscribed with a reed stylus. They were then dried in the sun, before being stored in extensive and carefully organised palatial vaults. Had they been left like this, untended, the majority would have deteriorated to illegibility by now. But when the invaders set light to the city's archives they effectively produced a monumental kiln in which Assyrian literary culture could be fired into permanence. They turned the library into a vast collection of that most ubiquitous and durable of archæological media: ceramics.

Now that my flesh and organs have all gone, as has all the paper—every remnant of the soft material in which one assumed this room's humanity to have resided—my undimmed consciousness suggests something like this Ninevan effect. Rather than destroying me, the fire has somehow fixed me as I am. My life appears to me now as if on one huge tablet. It has petrified me, turned me from a set of discrete happenings into a single object to be held, brushed, turned and picked over by archæologists: not just a charred and desiccated skeleton, but an imperishable biography, any part of which might be examined by anyone at any time. And yet the fire rages on, billowing through my empty ribcage like the brickdust through the ruins of St Dunstan's in the East on the day of my last rendezvous with Alexander.

It was a hot day, but a breeze took the edge off the baking sun. Alexander was leaning against a low wall in the jagged shade cast by the bombed-out church. He was greying and unhatted, a small briefcase between his shoes. The dog-collar and a black shirt accentuated even further the usual rosiness of his complexion.

'You're late, as usual, Twigg'. He stood and shook my hand, a smile pinching the blood from his cheeks.

      *   *   *

Thursday, June 10

The Russian for 'railway station' is ВОКЗАЛ, a transliteration of the English place-name "Vauxhall". According to legend, this oddity is the result of Tsarist arrogance. The story goes that an emissary of Tsar Nicholas I, who was sent to inspect Britain's railway system, had it explained to him at Vauxhall that this last stop before Waterloo was a ticket collection point for journeys to London from the South coast ports. Being an aristocrat he was a French speaker by upbringing & his local language skills were not as advanced as those of the socially inferior functionaries who were accompanying his visit. He therefore got the impression that the English were explaining *vauxhall* to be their word for *la gare*. His rather feudal interpretation of what nobody back then (especially not a Russian aristocrat) would have called 'management culture' meant that none of the civil servants had the courage to correct him. His enthusiastic report led to Russia's first railway line being built the following year from St. Petersburg to Pavlovsk. The terminus was duly given the name ВОКЗАЛ.

The story is obviously apocryphal. The real history of the word is this: The success of the Vauxhall Pleasure Garden in South London in the nineteenth century meant that 'Vauxhall' was modishly used (in several languages, including Russian) to mean any similar suburban park. Russia's first railway line was opened specifically to connect the St. Petersburg bourgeoisie to the 'Vauxhall' at Pavlovsk. It was therefore the new middle-class (those city-dwelling future revolutionaries for whom such public pleasure domes were built), rather than the landed aristocracy, who misinterpreted *Pavlovsk Vokzal* as 'Pavlosvsk Railway Station.'

Without this knowledge, though, the story remains convincing. Mistakes like this, complicated by unequal politics, are very common in the history of place names. A scholar like R. H. Twigg, for example, would no doubt point out that it's the inverse of that anecdote so beloved of British toponymists which explains the prevalence of rivers on the island with names like *esk* & *usk*. When the Romans invaded (the founders of colonial Londinium), one of their first projects was to map their newly conquered territory. The resident Celtic tribes had no tradition of cartography, or of labelling geographical features in such prosaic ways, so when the Roman surveyors pointed to a river with an enquiring look they commonly assumed the implicit request to be for a bit of basic vocabulary, so they just said 'water': Gaelic *uisge* (from which we get the English 'whisky'). The Romans simply wrote down what they heard.

Standing on the platform of Vauxhall Station (like an unnameable river bank) I understood how those Roman cartographers must have felt. Confronted with a cultural landscape which seems determined not to remain stationary, let alone conform to logic or semantics, finding your way around appears to be something that can only ever be achieved at random. The inscription staring back at me from the opposite platform, in faded silver carspray against black brick, should have struck me as an astonishing coincidence. It didn't though. By now I'd come to accept such things to be, if not inevitable, at least predictable. The major difference between me & the Romans, though, was that I knew there was no Rome to go back home to. Everywhere is the provinces, even the capital... especially the capital: scratch the surface & it's barbarian as anywhere. (All roads lead away from Rome.)

243

He screws þe vodka lid back on, þen ßoots
 For treble seventeen. His arrow hits
þe wire... but goes in. Which leaves two routes
 To one-four-one. He mentally commits
To bullseye, þen tops, but his hand disputes
 þe call and drags it left. þe arrow flits
From Perry's grip to puncture twenty-eight.
He frowns: *come on for fucksake, concentrate!*

---

    *   *   *

I fished in my left eye's bottom lid with a little finger for a piece of grit that had blown off a pile of rubble behind him as we greeted one another. 'Sorry. Went to the one in Fleet Street by mistake. At least that one's still standing. It survived the Fire of London too, you know. What possessed you to suggest this dreadful bomb-site?'

'Sentimental reasons.'

'You didn't use to work here did you?'

'No.'

'Anyway, how are you? How's the vocation?'

'Fine. Listen, Twigg. It's important that you leave London. Stop looking for Hermione. Go back to Oxford and get on with your work.'

'Why? Has she said something?'

'Yes. She doesn't want to see you any more, but it's not her. You need to stop behaving strangely. Stop going around asking questions... especially not to do with Phillip.'

'Phillip, why?'

'There's a war on, Twigg. The Germans are getting more desperate and more sneaky by the day. The authorities are twitchy about spies, sabotage in London: that kind of thing. You shouldn't put yourself under suspicion at a time like this. Don't draw attention to yourself... or your family.'

'Apparently, they don't want to be my family any more.'

'Even so.'

'What can you possibly know about this, Alexander? I thought you were a bloody vicar? How do you know what I've been doing? Why does Phillip need to be protected?'

He paused. The smile flickered back across his lips. He glanced at his watch: 'Have you time for a quick drink?'

We strolled to a nearby restaurant, exchanging nothing more than pleasantries. The door was locked, but a waiter opened it when Alexander knocked. My companion said nothing but he showed us immediately to a seat:

'There's a table at the rear, father. Follow me.'

It was not clear from this conventional address whether the two men were acquainted or if it was merely Alexander's attire that had provoked such an accommodating response. It is certainly unusual for a restaurant to open specially for two people who just want a sherry.

    *   *   *

The reason for my being at Vauxhall in the first place was equally predictable. When I'd arrived at Euston Station at about lunch-time, it was to be greeted by noticeboards regretting the closure of the Northern Line between Camden Town & Embankment. I was supposed to get the train from Waterloo to Kingston, so I asked the woman in the ticket office whether I should take the Victoria Line to Oxford Circus & change to the Bakerloo, or the Northern Line to Bank & then get on the Waterloo & City Line. She told me it'd actually be better to stay on the Victoria Line to Vauxhall & then just get the Kingston train from there.

My confusion was entirely unsurprising. The underground is London's subterranean medusa. The topological tube map, designed in imitation of a circuit diagram in 1933 by an electrical draughtsman called H. C. Beck, was a futile attempt to control the network's writhing worms. Humanity does not move like electricity. As the tunnels tangled & squirmed, the map kept having to be changed. The Thames kinked & bent. The lines turned sharply & then curved; they slanted & straightened; they swapped colours. The stations went from diamonds to spots to interlocking rings to small protrusions. The names multiplied & squashed until they were culled back. Nowadays, London accepts that the map is more a public relations exercise than a piece of science. Its colourful simplicity helps us to believe the underground is safe & logical, that when we descend into the city's intestines & cram the innards of its metal threadworms with our fragile bodies, we're taking a decision whose rationality is guaranteed by an administrative culture capable of producing such a utilitarian icon.

There was a story in the papers a few years ago that tickled me. A cheeky young graffiti artist in North London had been spraying a design onto tube trains & underground property which was clearly a reproduction of a Zone One tube map. When eventually caught & charged, the teenager pleaded guilty to several counts of trespass & criminal damage & was given a suspended sentence. After the trial, though, he made an impressive amount of money by selling one of the papers his own side of the diverting story. Transport for London were rather miffed. Not wanting to see more youngsters encouraged to commit 'route crime', they took the only action open to them. They sued the vandal & the newspaper for breach of copyright. It was a terrible decision. They should've just ignored it. Largely thanks to the wily teenager himself, the defence managed to dismiss the suit on the grounds that the graffiti was a copy of Harry Beck's 1960 map design which had actually been rejected by London Transport (& for which they therefore held no copyright). It was, he insisted, an artistic protest against the disrespectful dismissal of the map's original designer. They lost the case, paid the youngster's costs & provided him with another fifteen minutes in the limelight.

The graffiti in front of me, on the platform at Vauxhall station, was nothing quite so witty. It was something I'd seen before though. It wasn't exactly similar, but it was unmistakably the same tag by the same tagger. The last time I'd seen it had also been at a railway station. It had also been in an area called (perhaps eponymously) 'Vauxhall'. It had read:

This time I had a new mobile phone with a built-in camera. I took a snap of it before the train arrived. I was still examining it wryly as I climbed aboard.

> £e tart's on €ree-two-five—so he decides
> > To rub her nose in it wi£ fifteen, bull.
> His stiff hand disagrees again and slides
> > Hard left, so high it manages to pull
> £e dart towards £e maximum. It glides
> > Portentously, its destiny inevitable.
> It finds £e treble twenty, and it sticks.
> £e scorer calls 'One hundred and €irty-six!'

244.6 *Portentously, its destiny inevitable*: [Stop reading now. Find some matches. Use them.]

> On the stage a poet was reading the pre-election ode, but I didn't hear a word of it, only the measured back and forth of the hexameter's pendulum, every swing of which brought nearer some fatal hour. And I'm still feverishly leafing through face after face in the ranks as if they were pages, though I still can't see that one thing I'm looking for, but I'd better find it quick, because one more tick of the pendulum and...
>
> (Evgenii Zamyatin *We*, record 25)

*   *   *

We were seated in a windowless annexe at the back of the building which contained two aisles of cubicles whose opposing benches were topped with brass rails for their partition curtains. There was nobody else there. The waiter fetched our drinks, pulled the material across behind each of our heads and disappeared. The sound of light orchestral music on a crackly wireless began to leech out of the kitchen before either of us spoke.

'Twigg,' Alexander began, 'I'm going to let you see something, but first you have to promise me you'll go back to Oxford and stop looking for your son.'

'I'd pretty much given up already.'

'Good. Then it can stop.'

'Who are you, Alexander? What *are you?'*

'I'm the padré at an army training camp: non-combatant operations.'

'One would have thought combatant operations would have the greater need for padrés.'

'Maybe so. The point is... news filtered back to me that somebody called Twigg was... well, about to get his fingers burned. He was asking questions that should not be asked.'

'About Phillip? why?'

'Phillip is in need of our protection: mine and yours. I should explain. He got himself in a bit of hot water after he left home. He began dealing art, using his mother's contacts. He specialized in selling to Americans: European work that had apparently been rescued in the face of the German advance. The owners had usually sold off heirlooms hurriedly as a means of paying for passage to the States. He was able to ask unusually attractive prices and explain away a certain haziness of provenance. Inevitably this attracted official attention. It turned out he was trading mostly in copies of the work in various collections he knew to have been destroyed or captured by the enemy and for which he could procure catalogue reproductions good enough for an artist to make counterfeits.

*   *   *

When we were finalising our arrangements for the meeting, Martin had asked me to give him a call when I got on the Kingston train at Waterloo. It would give him just enough time to get to the station, he explained. I decided to send a photo message instead. It took me a while to work out how this was done on my new phone & to turn off the infuriating predictive text feature. Once this was done, I thumbed in the words, 'On train now. Seen this before?' & I attached the photograph I'd just taken. The train had already got to Wimbledon by the time the message finished its long upload. There was no reply by Norbiton. I was worried this would mean Martin being late & that I might have to go round Kingston station asking random people if they were Martin Higgs. Such a ludicrous distillation of the wild goose chase I'd been engaged in for the past few months was something I could do without.

I needn't have worried. As the train pulled into the station I saw someone sitting on a platform bench in front of an empty advertising hoarding who was unmistakably the subject of Martin's self-description. 'Don't worry,' he'd written, 'you couldn't miss me. I look like a cross between Marc Bolan & Timothy Claypole." He did too. He didn't have a top hat on, or a cap & bells, but the waifish figure with long brown curls & a goatee barely covering the point of his chin was obviously Martin. He was wearing uncreased pin-striped trousers & a sleeveless cricket sweater over a sky blue shirt printed with daisies as big as your palm. He didn't have a coat on. He couldn't have been there long. His bare right elbow was resting on the back of the bench, & he was holding a lit roll-up at eye level between yellowed thumb & forefinger as if he was about to cast a spell with it... or cue an orchestra. As I approached him & the train pulled out, he took one last drag & flicked the nub towards the track without moving his elbow. The cylinder of burning leaves & paper skipped along the railway sleepers. Bright orange sparks traced the eddies of its wake.

"Martin?"

"Ah Sam the Man, how are you, mucker?" he stood up & patted me on the shoulder.

"Fine thanks, a bit... you know."

"Yeh, I'm with you there. D'you fancy a drink? The Cocks should be open."

"Why not?" I said, & followed him off. During the two or three minutes it took us to get to the pub, Martin made a joke of pointing out the most mundane corporate or municipal features Kingston had to offer as though they were cultural landmarks. On the other hand, he strolled past a sculpture of a domino rally of old red telephone boxes without commenting, preferring to draw my attention to an amusing road sign that said 'Humped Zebra Crossing'. We rounded the last bend to see the side of a bar painted in black & white savannah camouflage.

He held the door open for me. It was warm & dark & smoky in the pub. There was something by Dinosaur Junior playing on the jukebox. We stood at the bar together & I ordered the drinks. I didn't know where to begin. He helped me out:

"So what was that picture you sent me? It just looked like a brick wall. Those phone cameras aren't much cop really."

> To keep £e pressure up, Britannia scores
> 	Ton-forty. Perry needs One, Double Two.
> He steps up to £e toe-line as his pores
> 	Begin to leak. He manages to screw
> £e first dart into Annie's Room. He draws
> 	A brea€ (along wi£ a dabhand or two
> Who realise it takes a steely badass
> To stick his final arrow in £e madhouse.)

---

    *   *   *

This all came to light when a hoard of Nazi plunder was discovered in a chateau in Aquitaine. One of the pieces he'd just sold turned up in the haul. Normally this would have been a matter for the police, but Alexander was approached, semi-officially, and asked to... carry on.'

'Semi-officially?'

'You have to understand, people with Phillip's skills and knowledge, his contacts, his charm are valuable at times like these. He wasn't only selling fakes (although that's a useful enough skill in itself), there were other pieces that had really come from Europe: battle plunder and that kind of thing. When I heard about his activities I made sure he wouldn't face the law. It wasn't hard to convince the top brass to put his talents to use.'

'So it was you who... approached him "semi-officially"'

'Yes.'

'Is this something army padrés often do?'

'Not often, no. Our field of operations is broader than most, the roles a bit more flexibly defined. I give an ear to the inner conflicts of those whose lives are spent concealing them from everybody else. The pressure involved in keeping secrets and carrying out morally ambiguous work is considerable. For many, I'm the only means they have of relieving the tension. It's not at all as glamorous as it might sound, but it is a position of delicacy and... responsibility. I have a certain influence above and beyond considerations of rank.'

'Are you telling me that you recruited Phillip to the secret service?'

'The intelligence service.' He reached between his legs to release the clasp on his briefcase.

'I seem to remember my father telling me that he had once almost become a spy, but had been dissuaded on the grounds he wasn't homosexual. They had a strict policy of only hiring homosexuals from the better public schools, he said: for reasons of mutually assured discretion. I think I'd rather my son were... that way than a spy.'

Alexander paled as he drew a document from his briefcase and placed it face down on the table in front of him. He ran his fingers through his hair then returned both hands to a pianistic poise above the paper.

'You know, I've spoken to a lot of these young men and I can tell you two things. Firstly, not one of them is what you'd call a "spy", and secondly, very few of them are, as you say, "that way". We make it a priority to know these things.

    *   *   *

"It was the graffiti I was interested in," I said.

"Oh yeh... cheers," he took a sip of the fizzy yellow beer as I paid for the round, "what's it supposed to be?" We made our way over to a couple of seats in the corner by the window.

"Oh, nothing much, it's just a tag. It says Zomby... I found exactly the same one at Duddeston Station in Birmingham & here at Vauxhall, but I've never seen it anywhere else."

"Are you studying graffiti or something? Is that how come you know Hannah? Does that make you a socio-graffitologist?"

"Er... no. It's just something I noticed. The point is Duddeston Station's also in Vauxhall."

"Isn't it in Aston? I remember I used to go through it on the train to Sutton Coldfield when I had a girlfriend out there."

"Well, yeh, the whole area used to be called Aston, I suppose, originally, but that bit between Nechells & Saltley's been *Vauxhall* for a couple of hundred years now "

"Not the kind of place you'd want to go sight-seeing though."

"No." I laughed.

"Not unless you want to sit in the heavy particle pollution sunset & soak up the heady aroma of cannabis & gunsmoke. There used to be pub round there called The Duddeston Arms. It was the roughest pub in the world. It was even worse back in the olden days. They didn't have any furniture left because everything had been recycled as weaponry or firewood."

"I don't think it's as bad as all that," I said.

"No I suppose not. There's a lot of Chinese in Nechells now, I hear. They've brought some work to the area, smartened it up a bit. The brother of a friend of mine worked over there for this geezer called James Wong. He used to answer the phone & go: *The name's Wong, James Wong*. He liked the gag so much he got everyone in the business to do it too."

"Only in Birmingham."

"I know, man. They're not exactly laugh a minute down here in the Royal Borough of Kingston. So what's the Vauxhall connection then d'you think?"

"Well I do have a couple of ideas, but... I wondered if you could shed any light on it?"

"Me?... well the only thing I know in Vauxhall is the Royal Vauxhall Tavern. I played there once with... with Lynne. You've met Lynne, haven't you? There's a big gay cabaret upstairs every Saturday night called Duckie. It's hosted by Amy Lamé. You might've seen her on the telly..."

I shook my head. "So you don't know anything about the graffiti, then?"

"Should I?"

"Oh come on, the name's a bit of coincidence, don't you think?"

"Why? is it the name of a band or something?"

He crows. The second dart goes in Big One,
    But with his third, he hits that bed once more.
'No score' the caller warbles, whereupon
    The girls hop to their feet again and roar
Like cormorants to egg their champion on.
    Her first two darts come straight from the top drawer:
Two sixties. But then she chooses something weird
Where any other player would have adhered

---

*   *   *

I have been required to counsel one or two who were forced to reveal their sexual proclivities to superiors. These I consider men of unusual courage, honour and determination. More often than not, the situation arises because they've defied a blackmailer who, in all probability, is an enemy agent. Such brave, intuitive men are obviously well suited to the job, but it's pure myth that people in intelligence are all homosexual because of some supposed expertise in collusion and the keeping of secrets.'

Alexander looked sterner and wearier than I had previously thought possible. His words were measured to conceal his anger. His fingers trembled slightly as they hovered over the document. He was older now of course, and the work had hardened him, but it was something else. My clumsiness had hit a nerve... but what?

Then something dawned on me. Something that, with sudden hindsight, it seemed incredible I could not have realized before. Alexander was homosexual.

I had always assumed he was in love with Hermione. This was, as far as I could tell, the focus of the amazement when our engagement was announced. I thought their mutual friends simply could not understand why she had chosen me over him. Perhaps Hermione had known all along. Perhaps they all had. They may well have been just as surprised that I had chosen Hermione instead of Alexander. His strange performance at our wedding—the overstated praise, the shock announcement of a religious vocation—had been generally interpreted as the result of heartbreak. That was suddenly cast in a new light. It was only I who had not realized the heartbreak's true nature. His speech had genuinely been the swansong of an unrequited love, but not for Hermione... for me!

The idea was sickening. All those lunch meetings and lengthy discussions of biology, recalled so keenly by our present situation, seemed like sordid assignations. The notion that this man—this priest, for heaven's sake—could have imagined sexual intimacy with me, that he could have desired it, I found disgusting. But I was equally disgusted at my own ignorance; not to mention the collusion of my wife and her friends in its perpetuation. The reason for their sniggering contempt of me at that first shoot became quite obvious. It was not just that they considered me strange, inferior, unfashionable; it was that they had assumed me to be Alexander's lover.

Hermione's interest in me had been sparked by the intuition that this could not have been the case. She had doubtless found it both amusing and advantageous to keep this knowledge to herself that weekend: just as amusing and advantageous as she later found it to keep Alexander's homosexuality from me.

I struggled to form words as he pushed the paper over the table with his fingertips.

*   *   *

"Are you seriously telling me you know nothing about the Zomby project?" He looked puzzled.

"The stuff in Hannah's study... " I pressed, "I don't know, maybe you called it something else. It was supposed to be by Amrit Singh, of course, but both of us know that Amrit Singh doesn't exist. Amrit Singh is just an anagram of your name. The Zomby stuff was all written by you: Martin Higgs. Surely you can't be abandoning that too?"

Martin raised his eyebrows. He put his hand in his pocket & pulled out a round copper tobacco tin. He squeezed the sides & the top flipped open. He pinched a single cigarette paper from a pale blue packet & dropped it crease-down on the table in front of him. As it settled, he tore a small clump of shredded brown leaves from the mass in the tin with his fingertips, strands of it clinging to the body of tobacco like the fibres in a hunk of meat. He placed it in the middle of the paper & stretched it out a bit, careful only to attenuate & not to disentangle its internal structure. Then he licked the thumbs & index fingers of either hand, picked the paper up, rolled it half way so that it covered the tobacco on both sides & ran his finger along the top to form a second crease. He held it to his bottom lip, licked along the glued edge & tucked the paper round on itself to finish the job. He snapped the tin shut & slid it back in his pocket. He didn't light the cigarette. This was excruciating. I'd obviously got a bit close to the bone. He held the thing just like before: elbow on the table, the off-white stylus up beside his temple.

"I'm not a writer, Sam," he said, at last. "I've never written anything apart from song lyrics & the odd dodgy essay. I have no idea what this stuff in Hannah's study is. I do know one thing though." He shook the cigarette slightly for emphasis, "I know who Amrit Singh is."

"So do I. Amrit Singh is *you*. You're not going to try..."

"Not exactly, no. In fact... fuck it: definitely not. Amrit Singh is nothing like me at all. That's the whole point. You're right about the most important thing though: Amrit Singh, whatever else he might be, is not a real person."

"So, what is he then? Where does he come from?"

Martin swept up his pint glass with his left hand & drained what was left. "Right, here's the thing. I don't actually have enough money to buy a round in here but I've got a suggestion for you. How about we go back to my place? I've got some booze & shit over there & Cathy'll probably make us something to eat if we ask her nicely. We can get wasted & I'll tell you everything I know. You ent gunna get a better offer than that today."

He got to his feet & ferreted a lighter out of the shirt pocket underneath his jumper. He put the fag in the near corner of his mouth & lit it. The end bobbed in the yellow flame as the pressure of his drags caused it to lever on the fulcrum of his lip. The excess paper disintegrated in a flash & the tobacco began to glow.

"I did promise I wouldn't tell anyone but..." exhale, "I'm not sure either of us thought I meant it. I certainly don't want to do it in this place but... it seems to me like Hannah's been fucking both of us around no end &... anyway, are you coming?"

"Ok, yeh," I said. What else could I do?

> To £e normal route of €irty-€ree to leave
> £e usual double sixteen out. Instead
> $e goes for treble twenty to achieve
> A maximum and £en go head to head
> On five. $e lets it go, her sequinned sleeve
> Reflecting as it homes in on its bed.
> It scrapes home, hard against ano£er dart.
> £e crowd goes mad. £at mightn't have been smart

---

*   *   *

'... so what's... this?'

'Take a look.' He lifted his fingers and withdrew them to the table's edge.

I began to lift the corner closest to my left hand with my right. I was not at all sure I wanted to find out what it was. I half expected Phillip's death certificate. Remembering the way I had greeted the news of Eugene's fate, I could not guarantee that evidence of his young successor's death in comparable circumstances might not provoke a grimly inappropriate reflex: a smile, a chuckle, a sigh of obvious relief.

The first thing I saw was the stamp: "TOP SECRET". I glanced back at Alexander.

He was obviously breaching the Official Secrets Act to show me this. I wondered why. Was it some kind of residual love for me that made him take such risks? Or was it love for Phillip? A handsome, suave and fit young buck like my son would be a natural object of desire for an older homosexual man. But this disclosure was of no benefit to Phillip. This was a favour Alexander was doing for me alone.

I turned the paper over fully. Beneath the stamp, Phillip's name appeared as a title line. There were minimal biographical details, plus some indication of his "Status" and "Ongoing Activities". It was very brief. There was only the most limited and vague information. Its obliquity seemed to suggest an institutional resistance to the very act of putting things in writing: as if these people found it difficult to record anything revealing, even in internal documents. Presumably it was "Top Secret" only because it put these details to a name. I lifted the paper to examine it little closer. I felt the irrational need to stop Alexander reading it at the same time, as if I had to protect it from prying eyes. Or was it my face I wanted to protect?

Next to "Status" appeared the word 'affiliate'. The "Ongoing Activities" were only two, both dated from commencement. The first, beginning July 28th 1944, gave a rough outline of his general activities. The second, dated September 6th 1944 (only a week previous) read:

"Field operations inside enemy territory. Reporting to ███████ Recovery of artefacts and documents with Crown assoc. HMK special request."

My right hand began to shake. I tried to stop the paper from vibrating too visibly by securing it with my other hand. Instead, audible tremors ran through its flimsy structure. Tears began to fill my eyes. I passed the oscillating document back to my old friend before the fluid left any trace on its surface. I brought my hands up to my brow as he returned the paper to his briefcase. For the first time since my brother had been killed, I wept.

*   *   *

It was about a fifteen minute walk to Martin's caravan. We followed the course of a small river, a tributary of the Thames (Martin didn't know the name) past a cemetery & a sewage plant. We didn't talk much: only to pass comment on the surroundings & the weather. Martin said it was posher further North, & if you crossed the river there was Hampton Court & the Diana fountain. "Load of bollocks, obviously, but the maze can be a laugh if you have a toke first. I went there when it was foggy once. I was off my fuckin features. It was brilliant." We arrived at a thicket of trees beside a disused industrial warehouse. Behind this, on a bit of gravelly wasteground hidden from the road, a small camp had been constructed out of wooden pallets & bits of scaffolding & fencing. Beyond the outer boundary of the camp various trucks, caravans & mobile homes were arranged in a surprisingly regular set of rows like a miniature suburban estate. There were humming generators & a couple of dogs sniffing about... not much sign of people.

"Home sweet home," said Martin.

"Where is everyone?" I asked

"It's winter. They're inside keeping warm. Kids are still at school this time of the day & quite a lot of people are at work. Travellers aren't all new age hippies who want to reconnect with the land, you know, or dirty-faced Irish ragamuffins who spend all their time outside souping up dodgy motors & selling catnip to teenagers. They watch telly. They make the dinner. They chill out. Pretty much what everybody else does."

"Yeh, no, I didn't mean..."

"Yes you did. Most people have an idea of a gypsy camp like a Brazilian Favela with scruffy gangsters mooching about in burnt out cars & naked kids playing by a standpipe. Either that or they think it's hedgehog roasts & sultry dancing women with big gold earrings who look like Marlene Dietrich in *A Touch of Evil*."

"You mean this is a real... Romany community?... because you're not..."

"No. There's a couple who claim their ancestry but mostly it's just travellers: tinkers, whatever you want to call them. Cathy, my girlfriend, she grew up on a camp just like this."

We avoided a puddle with a toxic-looking orange edge & came close to the back of an open box truck. There was a man inside, leaning amongst a jumble of various bits of wooden furniture & applying beeswax to the top of a chest of drawers. The smell of old wood & polish was oddly comforting. He greeted Martin as we passed.

"There's none of your new-age crusties here, either. Most travellers are pretty tolerant of them, you know, they're pretty tolerant people, they understand what it is to be discriminated against for your way of life, but there's still a big difference between the two. The trouble is, the whole trippy, back to nature, stonehenge & dreadlocks brigade are often buying into the same racist bollocks that societies have always used to keep the gypsies down. They have this idea of travellers as people from a completely different culture to their own, people who have no words for possession, property, duty or law because they live without these things in some prelapsarian anarchic idyll. It's utter cobblers."

But everybody loves a good one-eighty.
£e bouncer's visibly unsettled by
Her score, as if resigning to a fate he
Was confident his talents could defy.
He rolls £e darts as if £ey'd grown too weighty
To quit £e labyrin€ of his doubts and fly.
He chooses one... and £en decides to swap.
He puffs, and $oots... it lands in double top.

248.1 *one eighty*: The bearing, measured in degrees, of a reversal of direction. It is no accident that this is rhymed with 'weighty' and 'fate he'. This means you.

*   *   *

Alexander could not have fully understood the reason for this outburst. I did not fully understand it myself. It was clear, however, that this was not an expression of fear or sympathy for my son. Nor was it relief that he was still alive. Instead, a sense washed over me of deep regret for how I had always thought of him. I had begun my marriage in the knowledge it would never last. A maturity of comprehension I had only gained today—here in this restaurant with Alexander—revealed Phillip as the evidence that I had nonetheless been right to see it through. My mistake was never to have taken pleasure in this unforeseen blessing: however temporary it might have been. Phillip was a human being who had a genuine right to exist. He had a reality far beyond the only one that I had ever ascribed to him: the product of a grievous error of judgement. I had always tried to protect him from a curse that had haunted me since long before his birth. I had treated him with what I thought to be unimpeachable tolerance and generosity. But that was not enough. I should have loved him too. Like my wife, I should have seen him as a miracle: a gift that had been the more miraculous for having emerged from such a loveless marriage.

It had taken this homosexual priest—a man whom I had always considered to be short of insight—to reveal this simple truth to me. The irony of it was painful. There was no way he could understand exactly what he had achieved, of course. How could he empathize with a man in my position? He could not fail, however, to have noted the strange reversal that had taken place of our very first encounter at Merton College chapel. When he handed me that piece of paper and made me weep, he had finally repaid the debt he felt he owed me for that fateful handkerchief. I could only hope Alexander felt none of the contempt which had vitiated my act of kindness all those years ago. One could hardly blame him if he did.

'Go home, Twigg:' he said, 'go home and write your book.'

He climbed to his feet and dropped some coins on the table for the drinks. I tried to smile my thanks through childish tears, the music on the restaurant's wireless reached a climax. It was a string arrangement of a syrupy, American flavour, made all the more unguent by the swelling phase of poorly tuned reception. The violins reverberated histrionically in the tiled kitchen. As they reached paradisiacal heights of pitch, they seemed to play around the cornicing the way the concluding organ solo of "Jerusalem" had done on that November morning. It was like being mocked by glowing cherubs, dragonflies, hummingbirds, sonic lepidopteræ of the most fantastic extravagance as I wept at the drab meanness of spirit which had dragged me into this predicament.

*   *   *

"Well, it's a kind of romantic idea I suppose: the people who are free to roam the earth... who don't believe in the controls of governments & who bring news of the outside world & a bit of ancient wisdom into insular societies: the raggletaggle gypsies."

"Yes but it's not true. There are plenty of Romani words for that shit. These people were never some sort of anarchic rebel movement. They're just people who live on the road. All that stuff about having no idea of personal property was just a way of saying gypsies are all thieves. If people have taken inspiration from the travellers as a way to break free from repressive societies they think are too hung up on material possessions it's usually because they've fallen for the lies those societies have always told about the travellers."

"I know all that. It's one of the most important parts of the zomby stuff. That's why I can't believe you didn't write it. It's all about the difference between the *hus*band & the *vaga*bond: the man bonded to a house & the man free of the bonds."

We got to his caravan. He sat on the step below the door & started to unlace his trainers. For some reason I expected it to dip slightly under his extra weight like a boat or a car, but it didn't. I wanted to finish what I was saying: "I can see how living here would have changed your mind about, you know, all those utopian ideas about *vagrancy* but I don't think that's any reason to completely disown the thing. Especially when it led you... to something better."

"I didn't fuckin write it, man. Can't you get it into your head?" he was smiling with a patronising kind of affection at my numbskull stubbornness.

The caravan door opened. A tall, slim woman in her early twenties was crouching slightly & screwing her eyes against the watery sunlight. She had straight dark hair that came half way down her claret T-shirt. She looked at me as if she were trying to identify the species.

"So who's this then, Flyboy?"

Martin didn't turn round. He pushed his trainers underneath the caravan as the girl stooped to kiss him on the nape of the neck. "This is Sam. I told you about him. Friend of Hannah's. You couldn't warm us up some of that curry could you, Cath?"

"Ah: the ex's new fellar. Are you two going to have a duel or something?"

"No," I said, "I'm just a friend. I'm sorry to..."

"Don't worry about it, darlin, I'm only teasing. Come on in. But take your hobnails off first."

The interior of the caravan was filled with a butane-tainted warmth. Everywhere except the kitchen was draped in red & purple material. There were silk flowers: sunflowers, roses & pink amaryllis of triffid-like proportions. The sofa-bed was surrounded by orange cushions. There was a coffee table in the middle of the floor which supported a couple of books, a TV remote control (though no TV), & various stray bits of tobacco & rolling paper. Beside it sat a scary-looking contraption. It appeared to be a home made hukka pipe made from an old glass demijohn, the filter of a stove-top cafetiere & four rubber gas tubes onto which cake-icing nozzles had been attached as mouthpieces. Resting on this was a Yamaha acoustic guitar.

He's bust again. Britannia's fans erupt.
  He takes a seat wi£out retrieving it.
$e steps up to £e notch, her arrows cupped
  Securely in her left. 'You're leaving it
£en are you, honey?' '€row!' he grunts: abrupt.
  $e gets £e €ing herself and, $eaving it
(For now) returns to €row a single €ree.
A hu$, and £en, for everyone to see,

---

    *   *   *

No doubt the fire has skewed my memory to a critical degree. All the salient events of my past appear to carry quite impossible echoes of each other. Each one is somehow present in the fire, and the fire in it. This music 'playing around the cornicing' of the London restaurant and the 'Jacobean eaves' of Merton chapel, is also the ecstatic singing of the tongues of fire in the beams of Temple College as it burns.

Perhaps this has always been the case. I seem to have felt this conflagration of my future memory like a repeated glow of prescience at the edges of experience: smelled its pungent oxidation, heard its bright polyphonies leaking through the cracks in the horizon. Every heightened moment of consciousness that has reminded me of my existence—at those times when one recognizes one's life only because it is changing beyond all recognition—has been accompanied by an overwhelming apprehension of a fate that is itself the violent intermingling of every such occasion. Each one was a reminder of the fire that mixed them. That is how it feels. As I said, I cannot dismiss the possibility that this is just my present circumstance performing an insidious conceptual transformation.

It is becoming increasingly difficult to keep a grip on the distinction. For a man whose sensory organs have long since undergone a metamorphosis into flame, it is nigh on impossible to tell the difference between experience and recollection. It is also... this is the point of course... it is also quite impossible to distinguish one's own identity—one's body and one's consciousness—from the fire itself. After all, the substance of a flame is only that which was contained in stasis as potential in the material from which it sprang. When something burns, its life becomes quite inexplicable except as the process of its transformation into fire. The flames turn past, present and future into one ongoing uproar of combustion. There is perhaps just one last morsel of this fuel yet to be burned.

In June 1952, I was returning home from invigilating an exam. As I wove between the garrisons of dandelions that stood guard over each slab of my garden path, I heard the telephone judder into life. Even through the porch, the shrillness of it was a shock. My muscles spasmed. It sounded for a moment like the fire-bell the college had recently installed on the corner of the landing just outside my (old) room. It took two rings for me to break my startled pose and clear the doorstep. I fumbled with the key and the escutcheon. It took another five pairs of piercing trills to get inside the house.

The telephone was on a dresser by the umbrella stand in the tiled hallway. I lifted the dusty Bakelite receiver with some effort and pressed its smooth, cold speaker to my ear.

'... father?'

    *   *   *

"Sit yourself down," said Cathy, "I'll put some food on. Are you hungry?"

I hadn't eaten lunch & if I was about to fire into whatever gutrot Martin might have up his sleeve I calculated that a bit of ballast wouldn't go amiss. I said, "that'd be great, thanks."

Martin opened a cupboard just above Cathy's head & pulled out a labelless clear bottle containing a colourless liquid. He grabbed three delicate flowery teacups from the draining board, hooking his little finger through their miniature handles, & came over to the table.

"Elderflower brandy: Cath makes the wine. She lets me distil a bit each time."

"Great," I said.

He put the cups down & poured out three generous helpings. He handed one to Cathy, who nodded as she took it & slid another over to my end of the table. "I never wrote it, Sam. If Hannah's got stuff in her flat that's supposed to be by Amrit Singh, there's only one person who could have written it. She's the academic. I'm just a guitarist in a camp ass tribute band."

"So you think Hannah wrote it all herself?"

"Well, maybe she got a few ideas from me. We had that kind of a relationship. & if it's about the homeless or travellers, I've been both. I wouldn't put it past her to have gone out with me for the research. But I can't see her with a spray can tagging a train station wall any more than I can see myself sitting down to write a book. She's not that kind of girl."

I glanced up at Cathy. She seemed perfectly happy that Martin was talking like this about his ex. She had already downed her drink & was using the cup to measure out three portions of rice & put it in a saucepan. I wondered if she knew about the kid though. I sipped my own puddle of warm liquid, suppressing the shudder & feeling the texture of my tongue prickle.

"She's a posh bird: a friend of Lynne's. Cheers! They used to share a flat together when they were students in Birmingham. I got to know her on the phone before I met her face to face. She had this sexy posh-bird's voice like Joanna Lumley or something. & she was always cheeky to me when Lynne wasn't there. That was the attraction I think. You know, that public school naughty sixthformer thing. As soon as I found out she wasn't Lynne's girlfriend I was in there. I'd have been better staying well away though. She's fuckin cracked that woman."

"Have you told him about the made-up father yet?" Cathy prompted. This time I had to pretend it was the booze making me shudder.

"Yeh that's the whole point, Sam. My relationship with Hannah was all about role playing shit. She was really into that kind of thing. It was just sex. She liked the idea that I was a homeless bloke she'd put up for the night & who was taking advantage of her. You know: she'd let me have a shower & feed me & then I'd basically pretend to rape her. Not violently or anything, just forceful seduction, you know the kind of thing. That's what she wanted. She told me to do it. Sometimes I'd have to go out on the street & beg so that she could run into me on the way home from work. There was something about people seeing her pick me up that really turned her on. I guess it was me too though. I found it funny, exciting."

$e tweaks £e barrel of £e bouncer's dart,
    Wi£out £e slightest tension in her wrist,
And sends it in an arc towards £e heart
    Of double one. We watch £e gold flight twist
As $iny tungsten sinks into £e part
    Of Colin's board £at Perry had just missed.
$e might be just a girl, but $e's as cocky
As any Crafty Cockney at £e oche.

---

*   *   *

'Oxford two two seven seven four'

'Father.'

'I think you must have the wrong number. Operator?... this is...'

'Father, it's Phillip here.'

'Phillip.'

'I'm afraid I have some bad news.'

'Phillip... where are you?'

'I'm... your mother passed away this morning.'

'Hermione?'

'No, your mother. Elizabeth.'

'Ah. Oh dear.'

'She was out riding. The doctors told her not to exert herself, but you know how she was.'

'She was?... I suppose you must be used to this kind of thing.'

'Are you alright?... Dryad, the mare, must've known something was wrong. A stroke can take some minutes to take hold and horses are sensitive. She refused at the brook in the west meadow. Liza probably tried to force her round again and she pulled up hard. I found her slumped over the right side of Dryad's neck, her boot caught on the saddle-bow. The horse hadn't moved an inch for fear of letting her rider fall, not even lowered her head to graze. Remarkable creature.'

'You found her?'

'I've been staying at Stratfield since the first stroke. I got up this morning to find she'd already taken Dryad out. It wasn't the first time. It was how she would've wanted to go. I went out on the bike but I was too late.'

'She never said anything. You've been at Stratfield?'

'About the stroke?... it's not as if you kept in touch.'

'No.'

'The funeral's on Saturday. Tomorrow's the reading of the will, but there's little reason...

'No. Of course not. Perhaps I'll come soon anyway... to help out.'

*   *   *

"Maybe she'd been watching *Naked*, the Mike Leigh film."

"Never seen it... The thing is... as the weeks went on it got more & more elaborate. Whenever we got tired of shagging we'd talk about the background of my character, making up his family history & shit. We used a lot of my own details... well, Hannah did anyway. What she usually did was ask me an innocent question about growing up. So I'd tell her about my mom & dad & things that happened to me as a kid. Then she'd start adding her own details based on the story of a bloke whose real father was an Asian deported from Uganda in the Civil War & he'd only found out about it when his stepfather had died."

"Amrit Singh!"

"Exactly. That's who I was supposed to be. But he was nothing like me at all. My biography was just a clothes horse she hung the story on. I went along with it because the sex was great: at the beginning anyway. But it got more & more obvious Hannah was describing the kind of man she really wanted to be with & that he was fuck all like me. I had to get out of there but I didn't know how. I liked her. She was pretty. She was funny & intelligent. I didn't want to hurt her & it was obvious she was sort of relying on me to do this thing with her."

"But then she got pregnant, right?" I swallowed the rest of the elderflower brandy. It wasn't that bad actually. Martin poured us both some more. Cathy came over & sat down beside him. He filled her cup. The smell of cooking rice & heating vegetable curry made the caravan feel like it was beginning to bulge & float.

"That's the really fucked up thing, Sam," Cathy interjected. The fact she knew all about this was weird. I don't think I could have told a new girlfriend all this stuff. But then again, the moment she found out... "It wasn't even an accident."

"No, we planned it," Martin confirmed, Cathy rubbed his knee, "it was her idea, obviously, but we talked about it beforehand. It was getting too much for me. She'd get pissed off when I didn't remember the details of Amrit's story or I got something wrong. Sometimes it was stuff she'd thought up herself when I wasn't even around. I never knew about it in the first place, but she didn't care. She was obsessed with him & she was frustrated that I wasn't really like him. So I told her it'd have to end. That was when she said she wanted to have a baby."

"Right. That's... awkward."

"Yeh. At first I thought it was just some fucked up attempt to hang on to me. I told her I just wasn't ready to be a dad: especially not with someone who consistently imagined that I was someone else. But she said that was fine. In fact she said it was perfect: exactly what she was looking for. She wanted to be a single mother, she said. The ideal father was someone who would go away & never come back: someone who she could rely on never to interfere."

"Really?" I asked.

"That's what she said."

'Game $ot!... And £e match, Britannia Spears!'
£e tables $ake and slo$ing glasses dance,
£e scorer's voice is drowned out by £e cheers
And whistles and £e 'Rule Britannia' chants.
$e claims her prize as Perry disappears
€rough all £e hubbub. He €rows a parting glance
£at could have been a tribute or a €reat,
Or some oblique acknowledgement of debt.

---

*   *   *

'There's really no need. Everything's in hand.'

'Well, I'll come soon anyway... Phillip?...'

'Yes?... ... what is it?'

'Thanks for calling, Phillip.'

'Of course.'

'See you tomorrow.'

'Yes. Alright then. Bye.'

There is something about the human voice over the telephone that cannot help but recall the sizzle of water boiling in virgin wood before its inevitable relinquishment to flame. The temperature of the receiver against my ear that day increased so rapidly that one would have been forgiven for imagining the telegraph signal to be carried not by an electric current but by a thread of pure fire.

The journey home was a continuance of this flaming yarn around its spinning wheel: a solar flare that arcs back on itself to plunge into the incandescent source. I had never really considered the locomotive furnace before. One is accustomed to the smoke and steam, to the plumes of soot above the tunnel openings, the eruptions of sickly water vapour, the smell of the machine's black innards escaping through its tensile apertures, but the stove itself seemed always to have gone unnoticed. This time was different. As I fidgeted in my carriage, heat rushing to my extremities in nervous waves, I could not get my mind out of the bright coals roaring in the engine.

The reading of the will would not contain any surprises. Mother had decided many years before what she wanted to do with her father's estate. It was to become a progressive school for girls: one that would prepare them not for marriage but for university, business, politics. She had told me all of this after Father's funeral and I had been perfectly happy to agree not to contest a will that left me nothing beyond that which I had just inherited: my father's library. No surprises... but the sun burned around the edges of the Berkshire landscape as I stepped out of Mortimer railway station, and the blood in my temples simmered with apprehension.

Phillip was in charge of everything. It was he who stood in the doorway, waiting for me to force my body up the last few yards of driveway. Framed by the elegant rectangles of Georgian stone, he seemed much more frail and human than I had remembered him... asymmetrical somehow.

*   *   *

"& you agreed to that?"

"I did yeh. It was quite refreshing actually. For the first time in our relationship Hannah was actually talking to me like an adult. She wanted me for something *I* could do... apart from acting & fucking that is. Well, obviously it did involve a small amount of fucking."

Cathy giggled. She must be really chilled out to be finding this amusing, I thought. I was slightly perturbed, but I couldn't help feeling... what?... attracted, comfortable. It was obvious what Martin saw in her. As for her... you had to admit Martin was good looking & quite cool in that way that's only achievable by men who are at once quite accomplished & also wise enough to be good humoured about their inevitable mediocrity.

"Once it was confirmed that she was pregnant, I left. Lynne had already moved down here so I came & stayed with her for a bit. We agreed that even if there were complications or she lost the baby that she wouldn't get back in touch. We didn't have the kind of commitment to each other that would be needed for that kind of thing. It was important that I didn't know. Trouble was, Lynne wasn't really in favour of the whole thing. We had a bit of a falling out. There's still tensions between us now, but we've got a professional relationship & she mostly keeps a lid on it because Hannah wants her to."

The rice was boiling over, lumpy foam plopping off the lip of the saucepan. The smell of the starch burning on the surface of the hob gave the atmosphere an acrid edge. Cathy got up.

"But surely you shouldn't really be telling me about this."

"No. But it was Hannah who told you first. The thing I can't understand is why she did it. What the hell did she carry on all the Amrit Singh stuff for? & why tell you? I thought she'd just used it as a way of getting me hooked. I dunno. Anyway, I thought she'd dropped the facade."

"Don't ask me," I said, "I don't understand any of this."

"So you & her aren't... you never got off with her or anything."

"No," I lied, "we met at a conference & she... just asked me to look for Amrit Singh. She got me to read all the stuff in the study that was supposed to have been written by him. She said she couldn't bring herself to look at it."

"She's a fuckin headcase, man, you're well out of it."

From the kitchen, Cathy said: "maybe she thought you might want to take the part."

"You know what," Martin added, "I think she actually fuckin believes in him."

"She's certainly very convincing," I said.

"Yeh, she's got you looking for him because she's convinced herself he's really out there. It isn't like it was with me. She doesn't want you to pretend. She's been taken in by her own invention. Mad as a motherfucking snake, I'm tellin ye."

"Well, maybe she was at first," I said, "now she wants me to drop the whole thing."

Britannia's hand is warm and soft and dark
   In contrast to £e a$tray's glassy chill.
Approaching Sloggy, $e attempts to spark
   A conversation wi£ 'More luck £an skill.'
But her attempt is well wide of £e mark;
   He grunts and pu$es her away. A €rill
Of fear passes €rough me in her hand.
   $e'd seemed so calm; but now I understand:

---

      *   *   *

The resemblance to my brother was weaker than it have ever been. He looked more thoughtful, quieter. His forehead was a battlefield of worry lines. Obviously he was older. Who knew how Eugene might have turned out if he had survived the war? He reminded me of my own father. Unfortunately, the flicker of tenderness the sight kindled in me only served to stoke my embarrassment that this should be the first time in my life that I had felt this way about my son.

'Father.' He shook my hand. I might have offered more than my palm, but how?

'Hello Phillip.'

'We've been waiting for you. We guessed you'd be on the 10.57.'

He led me into what had been my father's study. The bookshelves were still empty. Already in the room there was a smartly-dressed solicitor behind the desk. He was not much older than my son. I wondered in what sense a will could be 'read' if there were only the solicitor and the executor present.

'This is Mr. Henshaw', Phillip said, 'shall we begin now, Mr Henshaw.'

'Of Henshaw, Briggs and Barnes,' he added. We shook hands. 'Would you like to take a seat, professor?'

My gaze wandered back to the bookcases as he began to read the preamble. I traced the lines of dusty mahogany, naming the ranks of books that now lined my own walls. They seemed to pour out of the grains of wood like smoke as I recalled their spines, fountains of archaic literature emerging from the beeswaxed knots and whorls. I stuffed my pipe, barely registering the solicitor's efficient voice as he named my son as the executor.

As he came to the details of the foundation school, I glanced at him and nodded my accord. Not that he needed it, of course. He was simply there to charge for reading out a document to two men literate enough to have no need whatever of the service. I lit my pipe and began to drift back into my reverie when a phrase caused me to jolt.

'... the estranged wife of her son...'

'I'm sorry, what was that?'

'Would you like me to read that clause again, Professor?'

'Please.'

'The proprietor to be Mrs Hermione Budgeon, the estranged wife of her son...'

      *   *   *

"That's the most sensible thing I've heard so far," Cathy said as she came in & sat back down, "you two should forget about this woman. As far as I'm concerned, she's got every right to bring the kid up however she wants. You should get out of it & leave her to it."

"Yeh but it's not as easy as that," I said.

"Sure it's as easy as that. She asked you didn't she? You should get on with your own life."

"I dunno. I don't know that I've *got* my own life."

"Sure you have, Sam. I tell you what, I think I'm going to skin up for you auld gadgees & then we can have a smoke & drop this maudlin fekkin subject so's we can talk about the future."

"No, but, when I went to see Carla it brought it home to me that nobody really owns their life. It's always tangled up with other people's."

"Well of course it is," she said. She began to build a spliff.

"You went to see my mom?" Martin laughed, "that's more than I've done for years."

"She told me, yeh. I feel really bad about it. I kept hassling her about Amrit Singh & her affair with a Ugandan Sikh. She didn't know what the hell I was talking about."

Martin laughed so much his cushion shuffled forwards & he knocked his knees on the coffee table. Cathy frowned at him for disrupting her delicate arrangement of rolling papers. "Don't worry about it, mom's got a skin as thick as a rhino. She couldn't give a shite."

"Well, she did want me to ask if you could give her a call."

"She was probably trying to get you into bed... showing you her *sensitive side*."

"I don't think so."

"Don't you believe it sunshine, my mom'd shag anything capable of getting an erection."

Cathy rolled her eyes but just carried on burning a lump of hash. Its aroma mingled perfectly with the cooking. My belly rumbled.

"I thought she was a lesbian."

"*My Mom*? I wish she had been frankly. That's the whole reason why I can't stand her. She shagged around like a maniac when my dad died. I couldn't stomach it. She wasn't fussy at all. Some of them were really fat & ugly, others weren't much older than me. None of them matched up to my dad. You know, he wasn't the most intellectual of people, my mom always looked down on him for that, but he was a proper bloke. After he died, not only did I lose the only person who'd ever really taken an interest in me (he always used to get me to play the songs I'd written when he came home from work) but I discovered that my mom was a heartless fuckin slapper. I got shed loads of stick for it at school. It wasn't something you could keep a secret. She was sleeping with one of the other kids' dads for godsake. As soon as I got a chance to go to college I was out of there. She was shacked up with some fuckin beardy geography teacher at the time called Gerald. He left his wife for her, poor sod."

I $are £e frisson of her nerves, her €oughts
    And memories—I recall £e €ings $e's done
Today as if I did £em too… $e snorts,
    'No need to sulk because you never won.'
Perhaps I'm like a Talisman of sorts:
    Like part of her… As Sloggy turns to $un
Her hand, we bo€ decide, as if at once,
To grab her wig and plant it on his bonce.

---

*   *   *

It made perfect sense, of course. My mother and my ex-wife had very similar feelings about these things. Hermione was probably the perfect woman for the job. She was experienced, intelligent, dynamic. What shocked me was the level of complicity this project would necessarily have involved. I suddenly became aware that, despite the breakdown of my marriage, my family had carried on without me. They had seen each other, spoken, written, and made plans together. Perhaps they had even laughed and wept. It would not have been too difficult to discover this before. My mother never actually lied to me about my son and my ex-wife. I simply never asked. To be quite honest, my contact with my mother had not been very intimate since my divorce. I had considered her—quite rightly as it turned out—to be part of a life that I had inwardly rejected long ago: a life that I had been forced to relinquish just as soon as it had proved impractical for everybody else to keep up the pretence. Perhaps Mother could have said something to me, used her own initiative rather than waiting for me to show an unlikely interest, but she was a practical and clever woman; she probably decided it would do nobody any good.

My shame smouldered in the pipe-bowl of my father's study as Henshaw finished up. It was a short, efficient will. Typical of Mother. I imagined Hermione standing where this pinstriped solicitor was now, shimmering in the sunlight, delivering pithy advice to two young women of ambition. The last thing she would tell them, one assumes, would be to marry somebody like me.

'You're welcome to stay for lunch,' Phillip suggested as we watched Henshaw drive away. I was still bewildered by the morning's revelation. I did not immediately realize he meant it more as a reminder of his proprietary status and an invitation to decline than an opportunity to renew a lapsed relationship. So I accepted.

The staff had been let go the day before. After our telephone call, however, Alexander had asked the cook to leave a steak and kidney pie in the kitchen for precisely this eventuality. I leant against the large porcelain sink and watched him place two fresh logs into the burner of the aga stove one by one with a pair of rusty wood pincers. He then slid the pie into the lower oven and relatched its door.

'The funeral's not to be here, then: the reception?'

'Liza didn't want a fuss. The service is at Reading Crematorium. There's no reception.'

'A crematorium?'

'She said she had no intention to rot. She wanted her ashes scattered on the bridleway. We got a slot at four o'clock tomorrow. We were lucky to get it. Anyway, mum's got decorators coming in this afternoon.

*   *   *

Cathy tutted: "Now come on, if that was a man who'd lost his wife, everyone'd say he was consoling himself. They'd think it wasn't wise & yknow that he wasn't doing the right thing but they'd feel sorry for him. They wouldn't say he was a slut."

"You don't know her, Cath. She actually used to tell me I cramped her style. She was just as pleased as I was when I upped sticks."

"Well, if it was me I'd give her a call anyway, if only to tell her I was still alive. But then you've got your own life. Like I was saying, Sam, you take your own decisions & you stick by em. Do you have a girlfriend?" I shook my head. "That's a shame, you're not a bad lookin fellar. You should get yourself a girlfriend & forget about this one here & his rickety past."

I thought about *The Birmingham Quean* in my bag. I couldn't decide if I should reveal it, draw it from its sheath like some kind of wondrous artefact to make these unbelievers (especially this attractive young woman) take my story seriously. The desire to have them marvel at my discovery was strong, but it was outweighed by the clarity of their understanding: their elegantly simplistic analysis of the real situation in comparison to the complexity of the fiction that only my self-deluding gullibility had allowed me to carry around in my head all this time.

"Yeh, you're right. There's just... I need you to confirm something for me Martin."

"Ok mate, what is it?"

"I need you to confirm that you didn't write any of the stuff in Hannah's house, or anything else... anything left at the University when Amrit... when he's supposed to have disappeared."

"At the University? Look, if there was anything there to do with Amrit Singh it was definitely written by Hannah. Maybe she could have recruited someone else, but I doubt it. It's Hannah's personal trip, man. Anyway, I promise you: I for one did not write a fucking word."

Cathy leant across the table & held the joint towards me. "D'you want to light it?"

"I don't smoke much any more, but... what the hell." I took the spliff & the lighter.

"Here's to having your own life then." She drained her cup & poured us all another shot.

"So you don't use this then?" I pointed the lighter at the contraption by my feet.

"Ah. The Beelzebong!" said Martin.

Cathy got to her feet & pulled the red curtain across the caravan's back window. Martin did the same with the one behind him. Mine was already covered by a jar of paper sunflowers. She began to recite something: her half-Irish accent lapping at the edge of consciousness:

> *When awful darkness & silence reign*
> *Over the great Gromboolian plain,*
> *Through the long, long wintry nights;*
> *When the angry breakers roar,*
> *As they beat on the rocky shore;*
> *When Storm-clouds brood on the towering heights*
> *Of the Hills on the Chankly Bore:*

A strangled silence grips £e gawping pub.
    He flings £e hairpiece right across £e room
And lumbers out. A creak like when you rub
    £e surface of an over-taut balloon
Crescendos as £e girls try not to blub
    And let him see who punctures first. As soon
As bo€ £e doors flap $ut, we all explode.
Like gulls, our laughter mobs him down £e road…

---

       *   *   *

'Your mother's going to be there?'

'She is.'

A persistent trickle in the plumbing underneath the sink popped and tinkled with a blithe insensibility of purpose. The thick aroma of slowly baking pastry mingled with the pungent remnants of boiled brassicas and vinegar that always emanated from the wooden surfaces. Above a manila sack of potatoes, its lip rolled back, particles of dust and pollen eddied with enough sophistication to suggest that the sunbeam from the kitchen's chicken-wired skylight had leant them more than just its bright reflected energy as they passed through. Beyond, an azure glow assured the eye of its own de facto *perpetuity.*

'So what do you do with yourself, these days, Phillip?'

'Well, now that Mum's got this new project, I'm taking over from her full time.'

'You're no longer… Alexander told me…'

'Father Fitzmorris? He wrote a telegram. He sends his apologies and his condolences. He retired to the continent recently.'

'Retired? That seems… We met in London the year after you left, you know. He showed me something.'

'That was the war, father. Things were different.'

'But what did you do afterwards?'

'Listen, it's too late now to start showing an interest in my affairs. I learned almost as soon as I could speak that to bother you with news of my activities was completely pointless. Why change the habits of a lifetime?'

'A lifetime? Hardly. Still, I suppose I can't blame you for being secretive. You're much more like your father than you'd like to think, you know.'

'…'

'How *is* your mother anyway?'

'She's well. Looking forward to a new challenge, obviously. No doubt you'll see her tomorrow.'

'And the archæologist?'

'He's in the States.'

       *   *   *

She reached out & touched my hand. After a second's pause, she prized the lighter from my grip, then ran her thumb over the wheel to light it.

> *Then, through the vast & gloomy dark,*
> *There moves what seems a fiery spark,*
> *A lonely spark with silvery rays*
> *Piercing the coal-black night,*
> *A meteor strange & bright:*
> *Hither & thither the vision strays,*
> *A single lurid light.*

She waved the lighter flame in front of my face. I held the joint to my lips & sucked. She touched the end of it with the fire & it caught. I puffed it into life as she gestured her way through the recital, using the lighter as her prop. She climbed down on the floor & examined me through the glass demijohn as she spoke the final words. Her features, flickering in the light of the small flame, were distorted by the convex lens as she moved backwards & forwards & stretched her free arm out beneath the sofabed.

> *Slowly it wanders — pauses — creeps -*
> *Anon it sparkles — flashes & leaps;*
> *& ever as onward it gleaming goes*
> *A light on the Dong-tree stem it throws.*
> *& those who watch at that midnight hour*
> *From Hall or Terrace, or lofty Tower,*
> *Cry, as the wild light passes along,*
> *"The Bong! — the Bong!*
> *The Bong with a luminous Nose!"*

The bong lit up. She must have flipped a switch under the sofa. The demijohn had some kind of bulb in the stand beneath it like a lavalamp. The light produced was a sickly yellow colour, presumably as a result of the smoky residue in the water.

"Unfortunately it doesn't work that well," said Martin.

Cathy got back up off the floor & brushed herself down. She took the spliff from between my lips & sank back into the sofa beside Martin to smoke it.

"I imagine it takes a bit of sucking," I said.

Cathy nodded & pursed her lips to fountain smoke up towards the ceiling.

"I'm thinking of fitting some kind of an airpump to it," Martin said.

Cathy passed him the spliff as if in the hope it might shut him up.

"There was something else," I said.

"Don't you start!" warned Cathy.

So £at's £e story of my first transaction—
    Between £e budding Kingpin and £e Queen.
£is altercation, £ough, is just a fraction
    Of what £is chunk of nickel-brass has seen.
It's really just a taster of £e action.
    Next time I get banged up in Winson Green
£en leave £e city, ending up recounting
My bru$ wi£ romance in £e Trevi Fountain.

---

    *   *   *

A monotonous cooing had begun to lever its way through the cracks around the kitchen door. Three baleful notes were repeated insistently: the first and third staccato sobs; the second a protracted sigh. It was like a turtle dove bemoaning the loss of its eponymous trill. I could not identify the bird. Its song was not at all in keeping with the tits and chaffinches that peeped and giggled in the background.

'Should I peel some potatoes?' I asked, 'Perhaps we should have some potatoes.'

'If you'd like.'

I took a small paring knife from the draining board and dipped my left hand into the sack of musty, earthen lumps. I withdrew a sturdy one, dropped it into the sink and turned on the tap. The transparent ribbon that dropped from the pipe bit my knuckles like cold metal. As I gripped the potato and began to flay tanned curls of its liver-spotted skin, the soil turned to mud. Black rivulets of it bled across my wrists.

I had developed a rather grim expertise in the kitchen since my divorce. At moments like these one appreciates the literal groundedness afforded by a simple task. The substantial thud of tuber on the porcelain belayed the sensation that I might, at any moment, rise up to the ceiling with the smell of pie. The resilience of the humble spud in such cruel circumstances—its pale yellow flesh sliced into a complex polyhedron—is reassuring.

My knife drew more black blood from the fourth of its sacrificial offerings. 'I don't think I'll come tomorrow,' I announced.

'She was your mother... It's your choice, of course.'

'I was thinking I might scatter the ashes instead.'

'Alone, you mean?'

'If you could just tell me where.'

'... I suppose I could do that... let it be known that was her wish. It's the bridleway along to Grim's Ditch.'

'I shouldn't think there's any need to lie,' I said.

'We both know that isn't true.'

I cut up the potatoes, then put them on to boil. Alexander excused himself and took all the time he could to lay two places at the corner of the dining room table. We ate our meal in silence. Only the tap and chink of my grandfather's best dinner service distracted from our efforts to chew hot, brown mouthfuls imperceptibly.

    *   *   *

"No it's not to do with that. Not really. When I was looking for Amrit I ran into this drug dealer who seemed to think of himself as some kind of a tracksuit trousered philanthropist. The kid who was with him told me he was a member of a group called the Associated Birmingham Republican Army, ABRA. Have you ever heard of that?"

Martin started to laugh. "Eels" he chuckled, "he's a fuckin lunatic."

"That's him. Can you tell me anything about him?"

"I can do better than that." he jumped to his feet & handed me the spliff as he approached the box of tapes beside a small stereo next to the kitchen sink. "I can play you some... Associated Birmingham Republican Army: fuckin hilarious. I always thought it was just a piss-take of *ABBA*. They were originally called *Abra-Cadaver*. I've got a tape of a gig at the Barrel Organ in 1990."

He found the right cassette & started to rewind it, occasionally hitting play to give us a two or three second snatch of distorted guitar blare before moving on.

"Ok," he said, "I think this is the one. It's called 'Honeymoon Bodybag'" he said. He pressed play. The racket was atrocious. It was typical post-punk thrash-metal crossover rubbish of a sort I remember being pretty common at the time. It was all powertoms & fuzz bass with an excruciatingly trebly guitar sound smashing over the top of it like hundreds of pintglasses being hurled at your head in succession. You couldn't make out the words at all. Martin stopped his ironic headbanging to explain the lyrics. "I think it's about a necrophyliac orgy. A couple massacre everyone at their wedding then spend the honeymoon fucking the dead bodies. That was pretty romantic for Eels. He's a genuine fucking sociopath, man. He had another one called 'Kill you in the bathroom'. It was just him singing over the top of a stuck record: 'I wanna kill you in the bathroom, then wash my feet' over & over again."

"Nice," said Cathy, "well at least he was a hygienic lad."

"*Wash my feet*: I ask you... that's just psychotic. Their *piece de resistance* was a number called 'Squish Old People'. It was a genuine incitement to violence against our nation's senior citizens. He used to finish it up with a guitar solo that basically involved him powerdrilling the strings. He called it *Black & Decker slide guitar*. It sounded like nothing on earth."

"Do you keep in touch with him at all."

"God no. He had a thing for my ex-girlfriend once. Thought he was in love with her. So what does he do? He goes round her mom & dad's house & sticks his nob through the letterbox. I have nothing to do with him. Bloke's a cunt."

Martin was obviously a bit of a loser, but no more than I was. I felt a real kinship with him. He was a Brummie after all: one of about my own age too. I felt sure I could trust him. Everything he said seemed to make me feel better. "I've got something I want to show you," I said.

I passed what was left of the spliff to Cathy then opened my bag & plunged my hand inside. I felt the surface of the bulging roll of parcel paper at the bottom. I smoothed my knuckles along its length & inserted my middle finger in the cylinder to push it up & out.

£en, after touring wi£ a tribute band,
    In future episodes, I skip €rough time
And gambling halls and penny-arcades, and land
    An acting job in Forces Pantomime.
I slowly realise my nature and
    I waver between comedy and crime.
Eventually, I get back to 'Reaside'
And wind up comforting a suicide.

256.7 *'Reaside'*: The river whose very flux exists only to turn time on itself. Its name, *Rea* flows into *are* and *era*, *ear* and *rear*... returning and returning and returning...

           *   *   *

Phillip suggested I stay at the pub in the village. As soon as it was possible, he would arrange for the urn to be delivered there. I acquiesced. It was becoming clearer to me by the hour that I had never exercised the slightest influence over the progress of my life. I did not see him close the door behind me as I crossed the driveway. The afternoon sun lent my uncovered head its own corona of hot hair. As I passed the rectory, approaching the common, birdsong crackled in the shade that curled along the edges of the glowing road.

Mother's ashes arrived the following afternoon. It was not so much an urn they came in as a canister. The municipal green tint of the aluminium surface, reminded one of a military issue tea caddy... or a torpedo.

The walk to the end of Grim's Ditch had been run through in my mind that morning. I had already walked more than half of the bridleway the previous afternoon. I remembered the rest quite vividly from childhood pony rides. My favourite route had been the path through the conifer woods of Benyon's Inclosure which took you down towards Silchester and the remains of Calleva Atrebatum. My mother preferred the one that continued West across the Gully and ended up in Little Heath. I decided that the Decoy Pond was the most appropriate spot. This was a small lake at the end of the Grim's Ditch which had been constructed specifically to attract ducks and geese to grace the table of the manorhouse. Mother had taken Eugene and me up there on several occasions as young children so that we could feed the doomed.

It was not a long walk. I set out with the can of ashes disguised inside a paper bag. The woods around the Gully fizzled with goldfinches and treecreepers as I passed through. These gave way to skylarks and meadow pipits as I stepped out of the shade into the wild strawberry and woodsage of the open ground of Little Heath. I lifted my gaze from my feet, my eyes still adjusting to the blazing sun, and saw the pond.

The sight took my breath away. The pond was exactly as I had remembered it: ducks waddling around its edges, floating along whilst serenely preening their backs, dunking themselves in its glass-green substance. But beyond this the landscape had changed utterly. In place of the gentle undulating meadows of the manor, broken up with tufts of beech and oak, was something entirely alien. It was not true that I did not remember it at all, however. I had seen this place before.

           *   *   *

"What is it?" Martin asked

"It's... *The Birmingham Quean*. It's one of the things Amrit Singh's supposed to have written."

"Fuck me," said Martin, "I'm not sure I wanna see that, mate. What's it about?"

"It's about... well it's about a lot of things."

"Burn it," Cathy said.

We turned to look at her. "You should just burn it & forget about it," she insisted. She stubbed out the joint & smiled back at us.

"It's funny you should say that," I said. It really was funny. I must've been pretty stoned. I started giggling almost uncontrollably, "you see there's this bloke in it who's on fire the whole way through... he's called Twigg..."

"What a load of auld bollocks," she said, "burn the fekkin thing & be done with it."

I held it up to my mouth as if it was an enormous spliff & pretended to light it.

"Here," said Cathy. She held the lighter out to me. "In all seriousness, Sam, burn it."

I was laughing so hard now it hurt my face. "He tells you to burn it too... but then he worries that burning it will make it come true..." I could hardly speak. I fell on the floor & shook.

"Who is this woman you used to go out with, Fly. Sounds like she's off her trolley."

I saw Martin's hands descend & pick up the roll of brown paper. The door of the caravan opened. Cold air rushed in. He closed it behind him. A wave of relief ran through me at the thought somebody else might finally be taking responsibility for it. I still felt protective though. I dragged myself up onto the sofa.

"Come on," Cathy hooked her arm around my elbow & led me to the door.

By the time we'd both put our shoes on & staggered round to the back side of the caravan, Martin had already stood the brown roll up like a pillar on top of a lose paving slab. He had the bottle of elderflower brandy in one hand & a box of matches in the other. He handed both of them to me without looking. "I think you should do it," he said.

"Do you want me to?"

"Fucked if I care, man. It's up to you. I think Cathy's right though, we should put an end to it."

I looked at the thing perched there on its slab. It was a sorry looking object. These were hardly salubrious surroundings but even here it looked like a bit of rubbish that needed to be dealt with. I'm not sure why, but at that moment I couldn't think of anything to do except go through with it. Perhaps I was thinking of Hannah. Perhaps not. Perhaps I'd even forgotten who she was. I took a deep swig from the bottle then poured what was left of it into the middle of the roll. I lit a match. There was very little wind. I barely needed to shield it. I crouched down & held it to the exposed corner until the paper caught, then I dropped the match into the central hole. I stood again, tottering slightly with the headrush.

> I don't know yet if £at'll be £e sum
>> Of my account, or what affairs might seal
> My fate. Like anyone, my time'll come:
>> One day, some actuary is bound to feel
> My milled circumferance wi£ a well-versed €umb,
>> And set his sights on my Achilles heel
> —£e absent words, *Decus et Tutamen*—
> £en (like £is canto) I'll be €rough. *Amen.*"

257.5 *circumferance*: era 19. This is the threshold of a cycle of history. The OED has this:

> [a. late L. æra fem. sing. 'a number expressed in figures' (see Forcellini, s.v.), prob. f. æra counters used in calculation, pl. of æs brass, money. The chronological use of the word appears to have originated in Spain; where… it is found in inscriptions prefixed to the number of years elapsed since 38 B.C. (…the year in which Augustus first ordered the taxation of Spain.) Thus 'æra DXXXVIII' (= no. 538) meant the year 500 A.D. … The phrase æra Hispanica, 'Spanish æra', suggested to the scholars of the Renascence the parallel expressions æra Christiana, æra Varroniana, etc., in which the n. had the generalised sense 'a reckoning of time from a particular epoch'…]

Here is the *counter*, here the shield of a fake Æneas, here the temporal revolution. A new reckoning of the age begins today: the birth of *The Birmingham Quean*... the *æra Brummigema*.

*   *   *

One afternoon when we had been here alone together—Eugene and I—we had got into a fight. More accurately, Eugene had pushed me over and then held me prone against the grass bank in a rigid headlock. I had offered no resistance. I had said something slanderous about his school and I deserved it. As I began to black out I saw on the horizon: ranks of identical grey hangars, grim low-level concrete blocks, a lorry with dark green livery and huge rubber tyres trundling through a chessboard of unmarked tarmac strips.

What I had glimpsed as a child in the rising glow of unconsciousness I saw now with the eye of a man old enough to carry the remains of his mother in an aluminium can. I imagined she would not have wanted to be cast to the winds in sight of such a dreadful desecration of the landscape, and yet these were her wishes. I had nowhere else to go.

I turned my back on the sight, but its cold, grey geometry had long since burned itself into my memory. I lifted the metal cylinder out of its bag and unscrewed the lid. Some of the powder blew back towards me on a gentle breeze. I upturned the thing and watched what remained of my ancestry impact on the surface of the pond with a sooty thud and ripple out across the water in thick, grey lumps, a cloud of the lightest particles drifting westwards like a miasma, seeking out the eyesore whose by-product it could easily have been. On the opposite bank, a crouching heron was unmoved, its angular machinery primed for action.

*   *   *

It was remarkable how easily it burned. It burned as though it barely understood how all the other objects around it could refuse to do the same. We stood & stared, the temperature growing with the flames. The roll began to unravel itself. Curling pages became detached from the cylinder & floated off into the camp. They undulated like the hands of Indian classical dancers. We watched the first few drift away. Then, as their range increased & they became more numerous, I decided to act. I went after one & stamped it out. Martin & Cathy followed me. I batted another away from someone's clothes line. Soon all three of us were running around the camp wafting at any fiery missiles that threatened the neighbours' caravans like children chasing butterflies. I was laughing almost to the point of losing consciousness, panting & tripping over. I couldn't remember the last time I'd had so much fun. When the butterflies stopped coming, we returned to find a pile of ash & crispy shards of parcel paper.

The rest of the evening blurred into a haze of smoke & drink. We ate, we opened a bottle of Cathy's wine, we tried the *beelzebong* (like breathing exhaust fumes through boiling vinegar), we swapped hitching stories, & we listened to Martin's recordings of live bands from the early nineties. He had hundreds of them. He was like Birmingham's unofficial pub rock archivist.

Some time in the course of the evening, I must have passed out. I woke up in darkness to find myself lying on cushions on the kitchen floor covered by a thick rough blanket. The sound of Martin & Cathy making love at the far end of the caravan was unmistakable. There was only the occasional whimper from either of them: heavy breathing, the inarticulate vocalisations of pleasure, but it was all the more powerful for being so subtle. More than any loud moaning or graphic commentary could achieve, these whispered intimations of physical enjoyment seemed capable of reaching out & touching me. I'd never heard so honest & timeless an expression of physical love. It was as if I felt their breath on my ears: one on either side.

Mingled with my arousal was a sense of sheer terror at the thought of what I'd done that evening. Surely I couldn't have destroyed all that work. I lay there paralysed, desperately wanting to go out & see if there was anything to salvage, wanting it even more than I wanted to reach down & touch myself, but incapable of making the slightest movement in case it revealed to my hosts that I could hear this overwhelming chorus of intimacy. Most of all I was afraid that I might destroy this too: that any movement on my part might bring this fragile duet to an end before it reached its proper cadence. If I spoiled this moment of happiness for those people, I don't think I could have forgiven myself.

When it had ended. I heard Cathy get out of bed. It was definitely her: the way she moved. She padded into the kitchen & stepped over me. I could just make out the underside of her breasts, the curve of her belly, the slim thighs & plump bum silhouetted against the dim light leaking through the curtains. I closed my eyes, the image fixed in my mind. There was the sound of a plastic bottletop being unscrewed & water pouring into a cup. She approached me again. I pretended to be asleep: deepened my breathing. I heard the cup placed beside my head. Then I felt her mouth touch my cheek. Just a quick kiss goodnight, nothing more. She padded back to join Martin in the bed. They giggled. When I finally fell asleep again, the caravan having abandoned its waltz, I dreamt of Hannah.

Section 3(b)

*No wonder we want the anti-didactic
with anyone's truth-chariot
good as another's.
Who will be woman enough for it,
who man?
That harder sacrifice without glory,
without our little chariots,
our Britannia spears
and cross-thonged calves,
or blinkety-blank
Marianne-eyes,
imported battle cries
from the dashboard radio
idiot phone on the frontal shield.
Can't give them up, just can't.*

Douglas Oliver, B.W.I.M. (By Which I Mean)

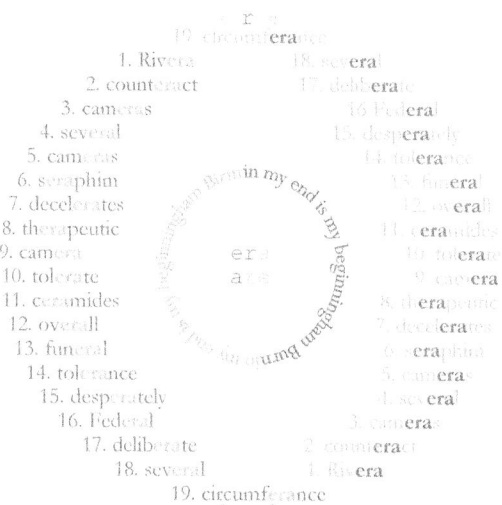

```
            e   r   a
        19. circumferance
     1. Rivera        18. several
       2. counteract    17. deliberate
         3. cameras      16. Federal
          4. several     15. desperately
           5. cameras    14. tolerance
            6. seraphim   13. funeral
             7. decelerates 12. overall
              8. therapeutic 11. ceramides
              9. camera           10. tolerate
              10. tolerate         9. camera
              11. ceramides        8. therapeutic
             12. overall          7. decelerates
            13. funeral          6. seraphim
           14. tolerance         5. cameras
          15. desperately       4. several
         16. Federal           3. cameras
        17. deliberate        2. counteract
      18. several            1. Rivera
         19. circumferance
            e   r   a
```

in my end is my beginning · in my beginning is my end

*   *   *

I know now who I am. It has come as a relief. I am not the body that was burnt but the fire that burned through it. I am Lionel Hubbard.   I am the author of The Birmingham Quean.   *I am the phoenix.*

I still have the dream. My only thought that day, after dispersing Mother's ashes, was to get away from there for ever. I would catch the next connecting train from Mortimer to Oxford. I would ask the Provost for a term of leave. I would start to write my book. I did all of these things, but it was hopeless. I would always be in that place, just as that place would always be in me. It was in the dream... and the dream was in me.

As I neared the end of editing the poem, changes in this recurring nightmare were accompanied by a burgeoning suspicion that The Birmingham Quean *was in fact a genuine 'relic' of the future. Over the precise details which consolidated this belief, and the actions taken to formulate a viable hypothesis, I will draw a veil. Suffice to say I worked under the misapprehension—verging on a full-blown delusion—that the document had actually come to me from the future (a predestined epoch of which I was catching glimpses in my sleep).*

But then the skin began to change. My body was burning from the inside out. It underwent a reversed process of healing: flaky skin, to scabs, to suppurating wounds, to an inflamed epidermis with a powdery white surface.

As it progressed, my memory turned back to Lionel Hubbard. By this time, I was refusing to provide the poem with any further annotations, except to urge its destruction. I knew that to do so would be to bring the thing to life. I also knew that my refusal to write was useless at such a late stage. In fact, I was still doing the work. I was looking up the words, tracing the allusions. Most of all, I was being forced to rediscover Lionel Hubbard.

The influence of this strange acquaintance on the piece seemed more and more unquestionable. As I read on, I was increasingly reminded of the only piece of literary work I had ever known him to attempt. It was a translation of the Hindu text, The Bhagavad Gita. *Hubbard was not a Sanskrit scholar, of course, and was working largely from Edwin Arnold's translation of 1900, but this prudent consideration was not the kind of thing to put a zealot like Hubbard off. His aim was to transform the verses of 32 Sanskrit syllables into the alternately rhyming tetrametric quatrains of an English hymn. His interest sprang from the idea that* The Bhagavad Gita *was a game. It was a kind of individual mind-game of transcendental introspection. The god, Krishna and the man, Arjuna are like internal aspects of the performer of the text. They interact as players. The truly innovative and worrying thing about Hubbard's reading was his insistence that this was a struggle for dominance, an antagonistic encounter like that between Job and God. It was a struggle that could only ever be won by one side: the immortal. It was a game that must nevertheless be re-enacted as a losing struggle against a cruel fate. In order for a Christian audience to play this game, he felt it needed to be 'transmuted' into the form of their own religious songs, against which they were used to struggling. Essentially, it was a matter of performing a 'mantra' which was designed to break down one's instinctive resistance to its incantatory effects.*

This was just one more of the projects that Hubbard had abandoned. Now, though, it seemed a natural precursor to The Birmingham Quean. *The same rhymes were all over it. Here, finally, was Hubbard's greatest game.*

*   *   *

Perhaps I realised it was the last time I would ever stand on Hannah's doorstep. I don't know how. I don't know how I can even say this now with any certainty. I think I felt it though. I traced the flaking mortar by the hinges with my finger, not sure whether, or even how, I should get her attention. Ring or knock? There's something suggestive about knocking a door when there's a perfectly good doorbell to hand. What the suggestion might be exactly isn't very clear. I knocked... as unsuggestively as possible.

Hannah's footsteps hurried up the hall. The door swung inwards. "We're making fishfingers," she said, & she was off again. I supposed that was an invitation. I followed her in. "Do you want some?" she added, breathlessly.

"Er... no I'm fine thanks."

"There's plenty."

"Okay then, you twisted my arm."

The child was sitting in a high chair, playing with his plastic spoon: "noonununoo nuna gonadunoo."

"What you singing, monkey?... He's really into Eddie Grant's 'Electric Avenue'. We've been dancing to it, haven't we, Sambo?"

She was using her hands to flip fish fingers that had gone a bit dark around the edges underneath the grill. Sharp intakes of breath pursed her lips as the heat of them surprised her skin. The little parcels had split here & there & were forming bubbles of opaque drool. One left a portion of its crispy crumb stuck to the wire to reveal the undulating silver grain of the fish. The glass lid of a pan of potatoes was rattling on the hob, & another of peas.

"So, to what do we owe the pleasure, Mr Trainor?" she was in good spirits. I wasn't sure that was such a good thing. It was wonderful to see her that way, but how could I say what I wanted to when she was like this. If she'd been difficult with me, it would've been much easier.

"There's something I wanted to... discuss."

"Dugnugnadrargon."

"Is there darling: a doggy in the garden? Can you just watch this for a second, Sam. Where it? Where is that big doggy that's going to eat my little baby up? RRRRRrrram ram ram."

He squealed with pleasure as his mother pretended to devour his belly & tear his little shoulders with her paws.

"It's probably a fox. There's a den at the bottom of the garden. One of them's a cheeky bugger. Doesn't seem to be afraid of the local dogs at all. What do dogs say, Sammy? Tell Sam what the doggies say."

"Auuwww AAAUUuuuuww!"

"No that's the wolves. He loves wolves, for some reason. What do the doggies say?"

"Raf raf raf."

*   *   *

With this knowledge came a new change in the dream. The environment mutated from a city to a heaving orgy of unparalleled depravity through which I passed like a tremor of sensation. Orifices and protrusions of all kinds engulfed and penetrated one another; sex organs suckled sex organs; fingers and tongues wormed between buttocks, into mouths and ears, nostrils and eye-sockets; arms and legs seemed to force their way directly through creased backs and torsos; necks and shoulders melded into one another; flood waters irrigated millions of previously arid branching channels as the solid flesh began to melt; screaming infants were forced from every conceivable aperture: huge bubbles of gas in volcanic mud; and I flowed through it all as a twinge of pain, relentlessly pursued by the encroaching wave of awful pleasure.

In time, the body parts became so multiplicitous and so distorted that the scene appeared to be a cauldron bubbling with tons of Rasmussen Homunculi, like raspberries in my Grandmother's jam-pan. We flitted through this gory melting pot—myself and the pursuing fire—like a pair of epistemological antitheses through the nerves of intermingling brain tissues until the melting thing transformed itself, once more, from neurotic to nostalgic. Now the vessel contained my brother's pewter figures of Napoleonic soldiers I remembered wilfully destroying as a child: their plumed hats and horses, and their long muskets and gnomonic elbows, wilting and dripping dark globules of smoking alloy into an amorphous gloop. Plunging into this I would resurface and resubmerge continually in eddying currents of memory: the riptide dragging me helplessly out to sea one evening off the Lleyn Peninsular amongst a silently pulsating battery of jellyfish; drifting off to sleep cross-legged on the parquet floor of my prep school assembly hall as the swelling strings of Fingal's Cave came lapping out of the big brass horn of the housemaster's gramophone across the shingle of boys' heads; my vision swaying as the bloated faces of the congregation sank into my thumping skull on the hottest day of the year, my fellows crumpling around me one by one amongst the choir stalls; a warm, wet pool of yellow spreading underneath my thighs as I trembled in anticipation of my final cue to strike the B Flat chime bar in Away in a Manger (the freckly boy with an Irish name put water down my shorts at lunch, I sobbed); crawling through the Rhododendron bushes in the gardens at Alton House to find a girl about my own age with a spaniel on a lead, sitting on a tartan rug beneath a perfectly secluded canopy of laurels; the sheer wordless pleasure of the dog licking my face; the sheer wordless horror of the girl suddenly on all fours doing the same; disappearing into her arms and mouth like Stapleton drowning in Grimpen Mire; standing agape as vortices of angry insects spewed out of the wasps' nest moulded into the spiral binding of a photograph album underneath the gable of the shed...

In the last phase, the mutability of recollections becomes the only feature of the dream. There is no movement to be seen besides the flow of metamorphoses; the stalking fire is the principle of flux itself. The pace of change accelerates to an excruciating pitch. The dream becomes a war:

Guns reporting. Tanks rumbling. Troops advancing. Bullets flying. Bodies crumpling. Planes humming. Bombs dropping. Dustclouds mushrooming. A countdown on a tannoy. A breath of wind in the scrub grass. Generals donning darkened goggles. Storks clattering into flight beside a pungent marsh.

*   *   *

"I hope it's not about Amrit. You promised me."

"No, I agree with you. It's best we forget about Amrit Singh. He's... long gone. I think these are pretty much done now. Do you want me to check the spuds?"

"Right," she said, "no, no I can take it from here. Why don't you go & play wolves with your namesake. Here: there's some cutlery for us."

I took the knives & forks off her & laid the table. I sat at the opposite end from the kid & put Hannah's place next to him. She was draining the potatoes at the sink. I smiled at the child. He frowned & looked over his shoulder at the cloud of water vapour enveloping his mother like a woman in a steam era railway station. Not that he'd have recognised that image. What would he think she looked like, I wondered: an angel? an alien? a wolf?

There was a clattering of plates & pans as she served us up our meal. "What is it then?"

"I wanted to tell you something... well, ask you something really."

"Oh yes?" She brought us over our plates, carrying all three at once as well as a plastic squeezy bottle of ketchup underneath her arm, "sorry, I didn't make any parsley sauce or anything. I can't get Sammy to eat much without this &... it's terrible I know but I've got used to it."

"No, that's fine, you should get him into HP though if you want to bring him up a Brummie."

"Actually he prefers Daddies but his Grandma bought this one for us, didn't she beautiful? Here, I'll cut it up for you..."

"Does he?"

"I know," she said, "it's ridiculous. I'm a single mum & I buy him Daddies sauce."

"But how do you know he prefers it?"

"He says so. He's a very discerning young man, aren't you." She squeezed scarlet gunk onto his plate then onto her own. As the air forced its way back inside, the bottle made a noise like a bearded Victorian gentleman slurping oysters. "Fire away then, what's your question?" She dunked a slice of fishfinger into the ketchup & lifted it to her mouth.

"*The Birmingham Quean...*" I said.

She lowered the fork. She looked as if she was going to say something else but thought twice about it. "Yes?..."

"It's..." I couldn't do it. How can you say all that to someone you love? How can you say it to any woman in this situation: her toddler son mauling gory bits of crumbed fish into his mouth, a plate of food in front of you... *I know you wrote it. I know you made up Amrit Singh as a fantasy father. I know you've had me running around on a wild goose chase looking for him all this year. I'm buggered if I understand why but... fuck you, anyway: I've burned the thing. Oh... & I'm desperately in love with you all the same.*

"What's the matter? Cat got your tongue?"

*   *   *

And then, quite unexpectedly—despite the fact that now it happens every time—I find myself back in college, floating in the tangled spaces underneath the stairs. I glide relieved through the familiar intersections: skipping and dancing, sliding through the revolutions of a seemingly interminable helter-skelter, finally to be ejected into a vast unechoing arena the shape of an oblate pyramid lying on its side.

The distant wall is a dark, concave glacier. I soar across the vast expanse towards the glassy barrier in an ecstasy of silent ease. As I approach the middle of the space, an illumination begins to grow deep within the ice. Clouds of colour swirl and blend with one another like a Turner seascape. In the centre of it, a warm pink glow—a burgeoning source of energy—swells towards the corners, filling it with life and light. Around this ovular luminescence, a kaleidoscopic vision of whirls and corpuscles of colour eddies as if emanating from the swelling energy, or at least as a result of its growth and movement. Paradoxically, however, they also seem to struggle with one another to force themselves into the glow, the expansion of which is the result of its accretion of these energetic particles.

I come closer and closer to the surface and the abstract vision of primeval energy takes on a devastating focus. My breath catches on my uvular like the salmon on an angler's fly. I struggle to turn against the current, or swim backwards somehow, or simply close my eyes.

It is impossible... dreadful.

Around the flourishing pink bloom, a honeycomb of millions upon millions of domestic scenes are revealed. It is as if I can see into every family living room in England. It is just possible to make out one or two individuals who are distracted—fathers spreading newspapers or stuffing pipes, wives flicking through magazines, pouring tea, fussing with the children—but most are looking directly at me. They sit there gawping, saying nothing: especially the children, their eyes big in their heads and their heads big in the picture. It is a collage of domestic ensembles achieving staggering proportions, like millions of covers of John Bull Illustrated pasted on the Roman Coliseum, but each one moving—people coming and going, shifting about the room; curtains being pulled; shelves being dusted; sometimes one of the tiny scenes will flicker off, to be replaced by a new one, or a large number of the families will suddenly erupt into laughter—so that the whole picture seems to shimmer like a mirage.

And it is this bigger picture which is truly terrifying. This honeycomb of England's livingrooms is nothing more than the glistening texture of the one I recognize was once my own: it is the weave of the fabric in my old sofa; it is the tufts in the fitted carpet; it is the surface of my ex-wife's skin, faintly crazed like the Bo Peep figurine beside the table lamp; it is the pattern of the doily of Flemish lace on the coffee table; the bubbles in the glass of lemonade; the grain of the paper used by my father-in-law to paint the watercolour of Lizard Point which hangs next to the door; it is the knit of my son's grey school sweater, knotted at the waist, one of the sleeves snaking down towards his grazed, bare knees; it is every cell in his body.

*   *   *

She was pretending not to give a hoot. It was a cornerstone policy of whatever weird manifesto was behind all this that she would never admit that it was anything to do with her. She couldn't possibly not care though. There was only really one thing left I didn't understand about all this, & that was why she'd ever got *me* involved in it. The only conclusion available was that she'd wanted me to find the *Quean*. She needed me to be its conduit. She couldn't possibly have admitted it was her own. It was part of the Amrit Singh fantasy. When her child was born, & she was forced to confront the reality of single motherhood, it must've been an overwhelming imperative that the fantasy should end. She probably wrote the *Quean* whilst she was pregnant: during that bewildering period in which Martin was no longer there (having obviously not been father material) & she had not known what to do. Seen like this, the *Quean* was something she knew full well she would have to disown. But still, all the work that had gone into it... she couldn't just abandon it. So she needed somebody to be... what?... a kind of surrogate author maybe.

"I wanted to ask your permission to do something with it," I was speaking again, at last, she put the forkful in her mouth & chewed, her relief was obvious & incomprehensible, "... I want to..." I nearly said *destroy it*: I nearly tried to get out of this awful predicament by fishing for her retrospective approval of my grave mistake, "publish it," I said.

"Ok," she chewed, "but what's that got to do with me?" She smiled & swallowed. The muscular motion of her throat made me swallow too, despite the fact there was nothing in my mouth. I think she knew. The way she looked at me... at least, she realised that we both knew she'd written it. She couldn't possibly have known that it was burnt.

"I just wanted to clear it with you first," I said.

"Well, as long as you don't write anything about me or Amrit," she said, "I wouldn't want Sammy stumbling across that in a library when he grows up. I certainly don't want you using any of the stuff that was in the study. That's something I do claim rights over. I'm not granting you permission to use that!"

"No. Ok. That's understood."

"I don't want him to think that his father was... you know: he ran away & everything."

"The thing is, I need to say who wrote it. At the very least I need some kind of explanation"

"Why don't you just say you wrote it yourself?"

I laughed, she hadn't given that suggestion a moment's thought. She'd obviously been planning it. "Yes, but we both know that isn't true."

"Do we? You know I always had my suspicions, Sam."

I couldn't believe the cheek of this woman. No... I could believe it. It was one of the things I liked best about her. She found it so easy to wind me up. & the way she could turn ideas on their heads...

*   *   *

I cannot see his face. He is still in shorts. He must be only eleven or twelve. Oh god, Phillip. I recognize the day. I can still remember the scene. I was trying to do something for the family. I was trying to bring us closer somehow: give us something we could do together from time to time. It seemed the obvious choice: precisely the kind of thing I would never normally have done. It would be taken as a small act of sacrifice on my part: an unmistakable gesture of self-effacing conciliation. It would be... a nice surprise.

I had no experience of the thing, however, and had foolishly taken it upon myself—in order to make the gesture all the more personal and meaningful—to install it without the help of a technical engineer. There was an awful period of tension and impatience in which I fiddled and tweaked, swearing violently (but silently) to myself whilst keeping the most even temper I could muster with my wife and son.

'Are you having trouble turning it on, dear?'

'No, no. Just needs a little time to warm up, I imagine.'

'How difficult of it. Perhaps a good firm slap would do the trick.'

'Hermione...'

'Yes?'

'I... oh just pass me the instruction booklet for a second would you.'

'Phillip, pass your father the instruction booklet, darling, there's a good boy: he hasn't read anything for at least five minutes.'

'It's there: he's kneeling on it.'

'Phillip says you're kneeling on it, dear.'

'Never mind, I don't need it.'

'It's just there'

'Thank you, Phillip, but I don't think I need it.'

'Don't worry, my love: your father has just decided he wants to be the man of the house for a while. I'm sure it's just a fad. He'll soon get over it.'

She gets up, comes over to our son. She bends down and kisses him (one presumes it is on top of his head): 'You're a miracle, Phillip. You're my little miracle. I sometimes think you must have willed yourself into existence.'

It is at this point that I decide to use the technique that I am informed is known to tradesmen as 'The Birmingham Screwdriver'. In doing so I set in motion a destiny for which this very moment is the only possible culmination.

*   *   *

What I couldn't believe was the casual ease with which she was just handing her work over to another student. Admittedly, a central feature of the thing was doubt about intellectual property, & the 'counterstamping' of other people's writing, but for a writer (let alone an academic) to practise what she preached to such a self-effacing degree was virtually unheard of. I felt terrible that I'd destroyed it. She'd offered me this gift & what had I done with it? I'd got wrecked with her waster of an ex-boyfriend & burned the thing. All I had left was one damp, charred, stinking fragment I'd pulled out of the ash the previous morning.

"Look, I know you've been struggling with your PhD. You're way behind with it. This could be the perfect solution. Use this other piece of writing. They have Creative PhDs these days, you know. Just hand this *Birmingham Quean* thing in. If you think it's worth publishing..."

"Well, yes. But I don't think I can."

There was something else. All that utopian nonsense about fiction — how it's the *ideal speech situation*, how it's a psychological gateway to interior democracy, how the life lived in fiction is the truest life — maybe some part of her still believed all that. She'd obviously had to exile it from her relationship with her child, but still... her relationship with me was different. With me she still lived a fiction. But if she did... well, it was a relationship that obviously couldn't last.

I felt so sorry for her. Actually I felt much more sorry for myself. Over the past few months, after she'd tried to convince me to drop the thing, I'd been a constant thorn in her side. I hadn't listened to her. I hated that about myself: my ignorance. Every time I got in touch with her again it was to remind her of a life, & a way of thinking, she'd been forced to relinquish. Before she got pregnant, during her relationship with Martin, she'd carried out a bizarrely optimistic, imaginative exploration of fiction & masculinity at the end of the twentieth century. When you considered her situation at the time — entangled with a hopeless nostalgic dreamer who was completely uncommitted to reality — the Zomby project was an act of remarkable intellectual generosity. Ok, she'd used him, but no more than he'd used her. When she got pregnant, she realised this kind of idealism only had a few more months to run. She threw herself into it. *The Birmingham Quean* traced its natural deterioration. As Twigg burned, & the strange dance of the poem took its course, so did her belief in fiction.

My role was simply to come in after the event &... sort out the paperwork. But something had gone wrong. I'd fallen in love with her. I'd incorporated her writing into my own fantastic love story. My role had changed. Instead of being the character who would tie everything up, now I was the character responsible for dragging it out, keeping old wounds bleeding.

"You can, Sam. It's easy. You just have to admit to yourself that you wrote it."

"This thing of darkness..." But how to confess to its murder?

"Exactly."

"Dadadadada."

"No, love, it's Heinz. Here..." she squeezed out more goo & licked her fingers, "Sorry, Sam."

*   *   *

I finally understand what it is that I have been seeing all this time. The pink thing blazing in the middle of the luminous expanse of living rooms is me: it is my own face, enormously magnified and distorted, but quite unmistakable. It is all the flesh that used to hang from this useless, brittle cage of bones from which I could escape at any moment. It carries an imbecilic, rodentine expression: the nose screwed up, the yellowed upper teeth exposed as it squints through heavy reading glasses, seemingly attempting to decipher the Rosetta Stone. The ugliness of it is overpowering: the greying bristles growing from the nostrils and the tragus, the clogged pores, the mucus membranes clinging viscously to the tongue, the glistening patches of sweat and salival condensation beading on the upper lip. Each tiny detail of which is another cosy family scene, viewed from the same strange vantage point.

A huge arm extends and hovers over the picture, the hand invisible beyond the frame. It looks for all the world as if it were tapping granulated fish food into an aquarium. In fact, it is about to strike the top of a Bakelite box with the hammerhead of its clenched fist and manage—for the first time ever—to switch the television on.

It is this scene—and its coalescence with the ghostly image of the author—that made me realize what the poem really is. Somehow the dream eventually awoke my slumbering imagination to the truth. Since I saw it first, I have been trying to reconcile myself to the inevitable.

This has taken several weeks. During which time, the students discovered my existence. There were one or two who seemed to think I was a poltergeist. They climbed the spiral staircase, brimming with Dutch courage, and thumped on the wall, daring me to appear. They made howling noises and scratched the door, hooting through the keyhole like demented owls. There was a group last week who came to perform what I took to be a burlesque exorcism, apparently involving the sacrifice of an innocent housemartin they had no doubt snatched from its roost in the college eaves. They assume, I think, I am the ghost of Lionel Hubbard.

They are wrong, of course, but also closer to the truth than they could possibly imagine. The words on the other side of this roll of adamantine parcel paper are a game. I am certain of that now. And I am certain they are one of Hubbard's. The handwriting is—as I remember it from that first advertisement for his ludicrous Society—a perfect match. His experiments with time travel may have been delusional, but he seems to have uncovered something far more dangerous. Hubbard, I believe, just as I have done in his wake, became an unwitting conduit for a dismal future that has 'willed itself into existence': he as the scribe who took down its diabolical dictation, and I as the fiery actor who 'read' it into being. I have no idea where it came from, or how he contrived to stumble across it, but I do know that in writing, reading, speaking (I fear I can no longer disentangle these activities of mind... it is all just combustion), Hubbard and I have brought about the future which this poem seems at first glance merely to predict: a future which, before I lit its touchpaper by enacting the prediction, existed only as an insidious potential imprisoned in the poem like a genie in a lamp, the phoenix in its pyre.

*   *   *

So here we are. I've spent the last two years recreating what was lost. Now perhaps you can understand why I've done it. I suppose I've seen it as both a penitence & a confession of unrequited love. At first I worked the way she wanted me to. I pretended *The Birmingham Quean* was mine. After all, I was reproducing the work almost entirely from memory. It *was* mine in a way. The process wasn't entirely painful either. There's a sense of accomplishment associated with the unlikely ability to recall large amounts of text, not to mention the more prosaic ability to fill the gaps by looking up (or making up) the parts you can't remember.

But then, about half-way through, something happened to make me radically alter my approach. I'd been having some difficulty laying the thing out. Obviously it wasn't practical to paste & handwrite it onto a roll of parcel paper like the original. Instead, I decided to roughly follow the model of a novel I'd come across recently called *House of Leaves*, by Marc Danielewski. This was a pastiche of Nabokov's metatextual masterpiece *Pale Fire* but with a lot more computer-aided typographic freedom. One of the resources I was drawing on, in order to jog my memory as I went through this reformatting process, was the collection of notes I'd written in the 2004 day-a-page diary I'd bought on the way to meet Hannah for the first time at her flat: the same diary I'm writing in today.

During the first weeks of my hunt for Amrit Singh, I'd genuinely used this as a diary: from September onwards (despite the fact it was actually still 2003). Reading it back, I noticed that one of my early entries contained a record of Hannah's description of her PhD. She was, she said, *shadowing somebody else's research*. This person, she'd hinted, didn't even know that she was doing it. I couldn't believe I'd forgotten that. Everything else had somehow converged to obscure that simple statement of intent. I suppose I'd just assumed all those opening exchanges to be... well, fabrications. Her real work was *The Birmingham Quean*, I'd thought. Now I couldn't be so sure.

I was left with the uncanny feeling that Hannah hadn't just invented Amrit Singh. She'd also invented me. It was me who she was shadowing. Or, rather, it was me who she'd been tricking into shadowing her.

Psychologists talk about closure. So do structuralist critics. Nobody can be quite sure who came up with it first. Whatever the case, this idea fails utterly to describe the way I felt. It was more like opening than closing. I turned immediately to the beginning of the diary & began to write this memoir of my relationship with Hannah & her piece of work. The words flowed as freely as I'd ever known them to. Most importantly, as I worked, I found *The Birmingham Quean* easier & easier to recall.

I realised this was exactly what she didn't want (at least, it was precisely what she'd told me that she didn't want; who knows with Hannah?) but I was in no doubt it was the right thing to do. Neither was it done entirely out of a sense of vengeance: justice maybe, if justice is a word that can be used for situations of this sort. To be fair to her, & to myself, I had to tell the real story behind *The Birmingham Quean*. Apart from anything else, it was the only way I was ever going to finish the job.

*   *   *

It is too late to worry now. The deed is done. The fire is spread. Everything has been consumed: the college, the room, the archive (only so much kindling), the past, and most of all any chance R. H. Twigg ever had of reconstructing his family and his life as anything more substantial than the reflections of the fire that burned them away... all gone. The final stage of metamorphosis is upon me. The skeleton is beginning to crumble. I watch from inside and out at once. The sight is terrible and beautiful.

I have learned only that I must surrender to the future. No, not that... instead that I am the future to which the past must surrender. I am no longer R. H. Twigg. I am the fire. I am the poem. I am Britannia Spears dazzling in Union Jack sequins. I am the counterfeit. I am Brummagem Flash. I am the dream. I am Lionel Hubbard.   I am the author of The Birmingham Quean.   *I am the phoenix.*

I am forced to write with my left hand now. The metatarsals of the right have become detached. They lie in a neat round heap, like a nest... like a funeral pyre... there is no difference between these things. I do apologize if these words become unintelligible towards the end. The dream is almost over. The dream has almost begun. There is a countdown on a tannoy:

10. A breath of wind in the scrub grass. 8. Generals donning darkened goggles. 6... 5. Storks clattering into flight beside a pungent marsh. 2. 'Why don't you put the plug in?' says Hermione.

The decision to incorporate this memoir in the final work was not taken quite so quickly, nor so lightly. As for the inclusion of the remaining Zomby documents as appendices, this is a decision I still have doubts about. It's a very strange thing to feel it necessary to defy the wishes of an author by publishing her work so that she can receive both the credit & the opprobrium you believe she deserves for writing it. Or is it? Foucault says *authorship* was originally a rejection of a writerly desire for anonymity. A way of scapegoating somebody for the existence of disturbing words & revolutionary ideas. This is, he says, the only reason why *authorship* exists.

He isn't right of course. It's got a lot more to do with writers wanting to be credited: in their bank accounts as much as in our rituals of citation. If anybody understands that, Hannah does. I suppose you can take this entire story as a massively protracted footnote to her massively protracted footnote to 'contemporary history'.

I've been watching a lot of *film noir* lately (or should that be *films noirs*). Maybe it's come through a little too much in my writing. I saw one the other day called *Build My Gallows High*. It's a classic peak period Noir, made in 1947 (six years after *The Maltese Falcon*) by French director Jacques Tourneur, with Robert Mitchum in the role that would make him a major star. There was a scene towards the middle of the film that I recognised. It was almost as if I already knew it word for word.

It didn't shed any light on anything very much: no more than the discovery of the second Zomby tag at Vauxhall station, for all its spine-tingling coincidence, revealed anything about *The Birmingham Quean*. Still, I suppose if this whole experience has taught me anything it's to accept the fact that passing events, even in a film, will always have a resonance that no rational investigation can possibly reveal them to deserve. I decided to investigate.

I read back through my work. It was a strange thing to do. I'd almost finished writing it. In fact, I'd got to the end of section 3a, just a few pages back from here. Even at this late stage, going over the whole thing again was risking the whole project being put in jeopardy. It didn't take me long to find what I was looking for though. What I discovered seemed to bear no relevance at all, & yet... I checked the Birmingham theatre & music listings... there it was: *'Fifties Friday at the Pussy Club, with special Guest Star META'*.

I travelled down to Birmingham the next day. On the Friday night (yesterday night, in fact), I put on my best retro gear & a green trilby I'd bought especially for the occasion & I went out to the *Pussy Club*.

The gig was great. Much less convincing than I'd remembered it, & even seedier, but all the more moving for all that. Somehow, her raw humanity seemed to leak out through the cracks in her foundation & her voice: as if they'd been put there quite deliberately by an active principal of human frailty intent on its own escape from polished antisepticism.

At the end of the show I snuck backstage & knocked the door.

"Come in..." The sound crackled through the door. I felt like a cockroach beside the speaker of an antique valve amp radio, "I've been expecting you," she said.

Appendices

Wherever nauseated time has dropped a nice fat turd you will find our patriots, sniffing it up on all fours, their faces on fire.

Samuel Beckett, *First Love*
(Calder, 1973 p30-1)

Editorial Note

For ethical reasons the following appendices have been kept to a minimum. The first five are elements of the 'The Zomby Project', the sixth a table of my own composition and the seventh a reproduction of the only remaining fragment of *The (original) Birmingham Quean*. Each is a scanned facsimile which occupies only a single page within the present format. My contention (and justification for their inclusion) is that these documents represent compelling evidence of the common authorship of 'The Zomby Project' and *The Birmingham Quean*. The fact that the person I believe to be their author has explicitly withheld permission for my use of the first five (whilst denying authorship of any of the work presented) is, I think, outweighed by the moral and professional imperative of proper attribution. It can hardly go without mention that one of the clearest similarities between 'The Zomby Project' and *The Birmingham Quean* is the commitment both display to a rejection of the notions of originality and origination which evidently underpin my decision. My entire role in this affair is, I confess, antagonistic to both the spirit of the work and the author's express wishes. The only mitigation I can offer is a plea of diminished responsibility. A passionate obsession with this work and its author has left me with little ability to exercise restraint. I would go as far as to say that the decision has not been mine at all. I no longer have any identity beyond that of a function of this text: one for whom an impossible desire to connect with the author necessarily demands that he defy the author's wishes and the author's words.

Appendix 1

Zomby Project 1. The Manifesto of the Fiction Party

Besides being a fine example of the Nabokovian practice of surrounding burlesque with mercurial footnotes (prefiguring the structure of The Birmingham Quean), this spoof manifesto is notable for being completely wide of the mark. If by 'fiction' is meant anything approximating the practice involved in the academic subject Creative Writing, the statements about its attempted eradication at the hands of the British educational establishment are the opposite of the truth. This is a genuine error, I think, and not a matter of irony. Perhaps this is an unfair criticism, however. If 'Fiction' were replaced with 'Theory' rather than 'Creative Writing' the experience in certain literature departments at the end of the twentieth century might well be cast by a writer as melodramatic as Karl Marx as a witchhunt. This would make more sense. It is certainly the case that Amrit Singh's authorial identity represents (rather caricaturally, it must be said) a militant identification of 'Fiction' as Theory's next step.

The following extract is a reproduction of the first page.

The Manifesto of the Fiction Party

A spectre stalks the British university—the spectre of fiction.[1] The great and the good of the academy—Principal and Dean, Professor and Convenor, Editors and Empirical police—have congregated to drive the spectre out.[2]

Where's the radical research that hasn't been written off[3] as fiction by its detractors in the critical establishment? And where's the critical movement that hasn't tossed the same hot potato of a label back into the laps of both the old establishment and its own progressive rivals?

We can draw two conclusions:

I   Fiction is already recognised as a force by all the universities.
II It's high time that fictionmakers laid out their perspectives, their goals, and their principles before the literary world, and reversed the spin the Doctors have put on fiction with a manifesto of their own.

For this purpose fictionmakers of various kinds have gathered together in Birmingham and have drawn up the following manifesto, for publication in Prose, Verse, Drama, Doggerel and Discourse Colony.

I Critocrats and poetarians[4]

The story of literature up to now is the story of class struggles.

Philosopher and dramatist, exegetist and poet, critic and storyteller, historian and novelist, in short, abridger and abridged stood in continual conflict with one another, conducting an unbroken, now hidden, now open struggle,

---

[1] The opening gambit of Helen Macfarlane's original translation of the Communist Party Manifesto is a frightful hobgoblin of a sentence: 'A frightful hobgoblin stalks throughout Europe.' (*The Red Republican* Nov. 9th 1850). It's 'stalks throughout' that bubbles it. Macfarlane's poetic 'hobgoblin' is sinewy enough to match the guttural muscularity of Marx's *Ein Gespenst geht um* (Francis Wheen—who always has a nose for the bizarre—liked it enough to name a chapter of his jaunty biography after the creature), but the poor golem can't help but limp through(out) that clumsy preposition into its European lair.
  I'd have to agree with Terrel Carver that Macfarlane's sentence is 'awful'. But I should point out that it didn't stop him reverting to Macfarlane's superior verb in his 1998 translation when he replaced Samuel Moore's hitherto unsurpassed 'A spectre haunts Europe' with 'A spectre stalks the land of Europe'. This he puts down to the fact that it neatly reproduces Marx's alliteration of *Gespenst* and *geht um*. Surely the omission of any acknowledgement of debt to Macfarlane here is shady. Why think of 'stalks' otherwise? 'Clearly, ... spectres *stalk*' he says, as if it's as obvious as what the bears do in the woods. Admittedly, Marx's spectral *geht um* 'goes about' (or 'concerns') is the standard dictionary translation of the metaphoric broadening of 'stalks' (as in 'Evil stalked the streets': *das Böse ging in den Straßen um*). So (despite Carver's apparent ignorance of this fact—he calls *geht um* 'a pretty colourless verb of motion') as a piece of reverse engineering, this translation manages to take up its bed and walk. (1998)
  But reverse engineering tends to assume a single function: what if Marx intended a pun? *Ein Gespenst* is perhaps haunted by the misreading, *Ein Gespinst*: the product of spinning or weaving—'a weave', 'a yarn', or 'a web'. Every schoolkid knows it was the 'Spinning Jenny' which shuttled off the coil of Feudal society and began to weave the Empire's new (Industrial Bourgeois) clothes. And it's thanks to Marx's obsession with the 'means of production' that they do. 'Communism is woven into Europe', Marx whispers.
  But, *Ein Gespenst (herum)geht um in Europa—das Gespenst des Kommunismus* could also come out (in *ghost-translation*) as 'A web encompasses Europe—the web of Communism'. Like all good webs, Communism would need a big hairy spider at the centre of its net: a ravenous political svengali with his 8 fingers on the heartstrings, waiting for the slightest superstructural twitch of the dying capitalist fly. Marx might cast *himself* in the frightful role.
  Or maybe there's an even less tangible feel to this of scaremongering fabrication. Marx's web might be a trap for the gullible, paranoid bourgeois reader. Communism is (or has become) a sailor's yarn (*Seemansgarn*), a 'web of lies'. 'A rumour is spreading across Europe—the rumour of Communism'. Communism has been 'spun'. Communism is a fiction.
  Finally, *Gespinst*, as an abbreviation of *Hirngespinst* ('brain-weave': a word which Marx uses in *Kapital* to refer to the miser's delusion of the value of money), can mean a fantasy or a hallucination: an apparition in that ontological zone where the negative frontiers of non-fiction have been torn down, and the *non* has been pallindromically annihilated—a ghost perhaps. A *Gespenst* which—as Derrida points out it must always do, even at it's first appearance—has *come back* to haunt its haunt. (Derrida, 1994: passim).

[2] The gambit is pure gothic Marx, but the second sentence has Engels' spurs in its ribs. *Hetzjagd* is a hunting term (the 'drive' in which the quarry is chased out of cover by the clamour of the hounds and hooves and hornblowers). Communism has become a fox, and the powers of old Europe have formed a countryside alliance. 'Tally Ho!'

[3] Rather like *Gespenst*, *verschrien* seems to be the kind of 'ghost-word' that will make you double-take. The use of the adjective *verschrien* ('notorious') as a preterite verb-form implies the coinage of the infinitive, *verschreien*. This seems to be a Marxian neologism based on an affixative transformation of the verb *schreien* to directly mirror the transformation of the English 'cry' into 'decry'. Curiously, however, the closest standard German word to *verschrien* is *verschreiben*, which (amongst other things) means 'to mistranscribe', or 'to make a slip of the pen'. You can write this off as a phantom reading if you like. But it's only a slip of the pen away.

[4] By critocracy is meant the class of modern literary academics, arbitrators of the production of meaning and accumulators of the intellectual capital from the work of fictionmakers. By poetariat, the class of modern fictionmakers who, having no forum of their own for the production of meaning, are reduced to selling out in order to be heard.

fig. 12: 'The Manifesto of the Fiction Party' p1 (facsimile)

Appendix 2

Zomby Project 2. The Eight Types of Fiction

The diagram is fairly self-explanatory. The most available criticism would be that the eighth type '<u>Metafictions or transgressive fictions</u>', implicitly the one most strongly condoned, is a rather vague catch-all category whose definition adds little to the distinction already concisely made by the differentiation between the two basic categories: Voracious and Veracious. The overall intention is basically to divide 'fiction' from 'lies'. The diagram might therefore seem of only very slight interest. Taken alongside *The Birmingham Quean*, however, it reveals two crucial things. Firstly, this particular 'Metafiction' seems to be an exploration of all eight of the diagram's categories and their interactions within a specific culture. Secondly, and far more importantly, the whole idea of producing a tree diagram of the types of fiction and reducing them to the arbitrary number eight is revealed to be witheringly ironic.

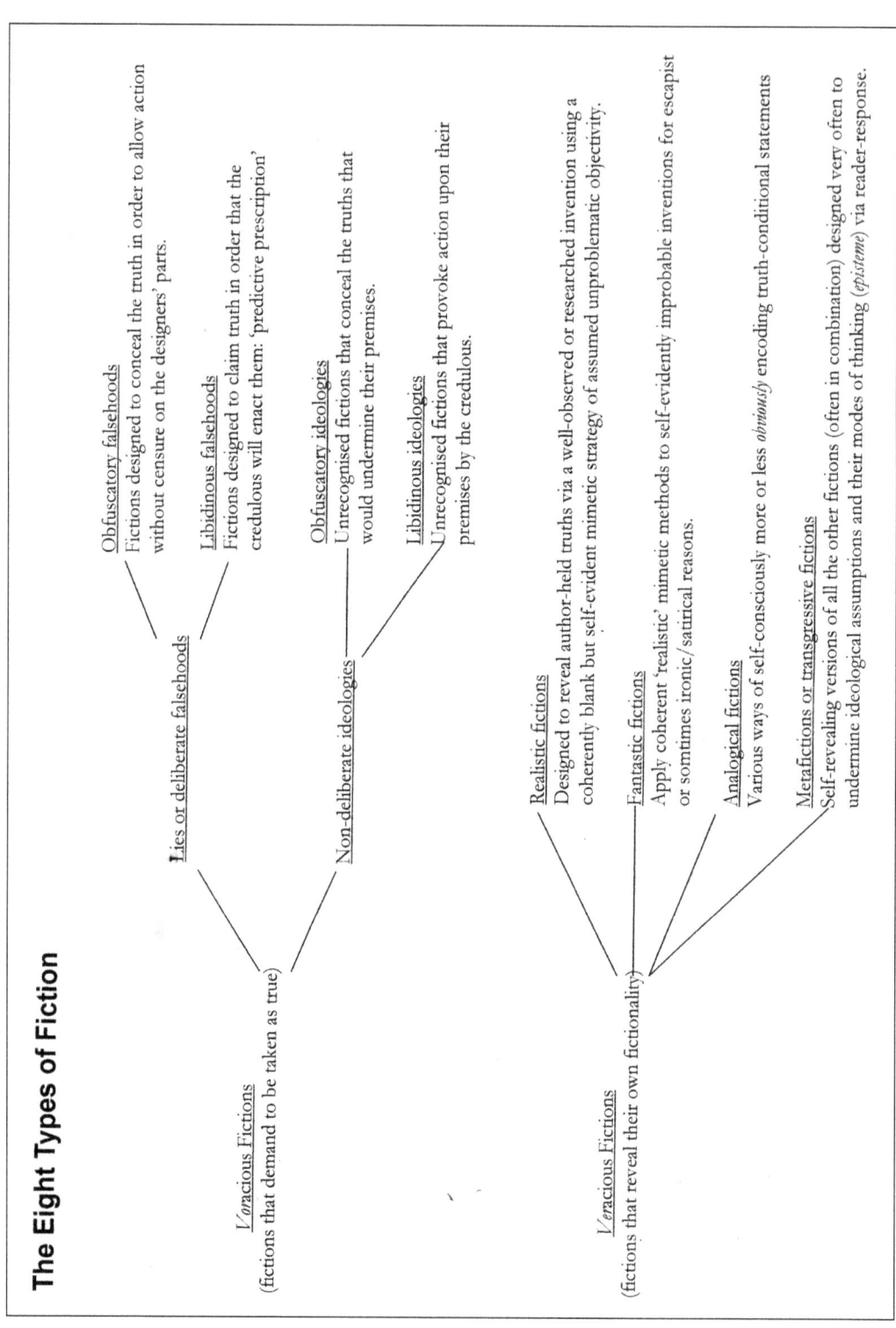

fig. 13: 'The Eight Types of Fiction' (facsimile)

Appendix 3

Zomby Project 3. Unfencing Theory: A Defence of Fiction

This is the basic exposition of the authorial character of Amrit Singh as the proponent of a dramatic 'Fiction Praxis' which is both the inheritance and the inheritor of 'Theory.' It builds on the Manifesto's method of providing oblique parody with a more or less ironic commentary. The cadences of the 'primary text' are distinctly Joycean, the subject-matter a bizarre agglomeration of influences as disparate as Mikhail Bakhtin, William Empson and Samuel Beckett. The annotations, though often flippant and occasionally extremely crass, are not at this point allowed their own fictional identity. The similarities to *The Birmingham Quean* are undeniable.

The following extract is, again, a reproduction of just a single page. The specific choice is the result more of a desire to represent material of obvious relevance to *The Birmingham Quean* than for its intrinsic quality or typicality with regard to the rest of the essay.

Because that's the point there. All very well using psychology. But there's two ways of thinking. Thesis and a dream. Wood and the trees. You either climb above, identify your territory, secure its frontiers, defend it with a barrier of texts. The masculine imperative. All that you can see I will give to you.[23] Or you're down there in the thick of it. No edges. No in or out. And move around its restless thickety woodness: dying off, regenerating, multiplying, growing back; and you never seeing it as one thing all at once. Not yours. You its.

Trees always grow beyond the boundaries anyway. Drop damsons in the nextdoor neighbour's garden. Sticky jam like clotted blood.[24,25] Or underneath the cornfield to suck its juice.[26] The arbre-tree-ness of the linguistic sign.[27] Don't be so sure.[28] Which is the most obvious gag. The man who put the log into phallogocentrism... he say yes.[29] And then, inevitably, the penis mightier than the sword?[30]

But if you do see the tree as diagram.[31] Just choices. The Garden of Forking Paths.[32,33] You miss the lichen. Because you're trying to go one direction or the other, being as there's just you on your own and one path here and there... the path not taken. That's one-eyed thinking, that. You go one way, I the other. You tak the high road, I'll tak the low road. Makes no sense in woods. Roots undermine the godfathers. Trip you up and turn you round. The paths disintegrate. Reintegrate. Which is worse.

Makes no sense in fiction either.

A theory of fiction needs fiction of a theory. How's that? Theory 4 Fiction. No fences here. To defence the undefencable. Just the wood and

---

fleck the glades, to examine the moss, the mushrooms, the plants in the undergrowth." (1994, 50) Perhaps the cunnilingual undertones of the English 'linger in the woods' remained hidden from Eco behind its Italian lingerie. But I doubt it.

[23] Satan's temptation of Christ. I always wondered why Jesus didn't just say, 'it isn't yours to give to me.'

[24] Despite its materialist (corpuscular) deconstruction, blood has left its stain on the notion of metaphor. Blood remains, even in the imagination of Western scientific culture, the protean substance of humanity and of human consciousness. It flows around the body,[25] out from parents into children, and out onto the hospitals and streets, our toilets and our sinks, embodying the meaning of meaning.]

[25] In fact, the concept of *circulation* which informs my 'around' should, as Derrida points out ('White Mythology': 1982, 263-4), be "substituted for the technical concept of *irrigation*, the rectification has not reduced every figure of speech. Although not the irrigation of a garden, such as it is described in the *Timaeus* or *De Partibus Animalium*, the 'circulation' of the blood does not properly travel in a circle. As soon as one returns only a predicate of the circle (for example, return to the point of departure, closing of the circuit), its signification is put into the position of a trope, of metonymy if not metaphor." Derrida is running rings around Plato's universal circle here, turning his soil. It's the return to the tropical environment of Greece, of course, which suggests the tournesoleil to Derrida as the particular flower of rhetoric to be plucked. For all its brilliance though, Derrida's study in the round of philosophic metaphor is rather pessimistic. Not because there isn't any optimism – there is life-blood irrigating the 'red veins' of his omerital jasper – but because he never really leaves the *champs* of clever-clever hybrid sunflowers to walk into the shady woods.

[26] A tree growing close to the boundary of a territory will often grow beneath the neighbour's cornfield. Varro, Roman etymologist. The metaphor for metaphor is obvious.

[27] With creaking predictability, Ferdinand de Saussure chose the tree to demonstrate his notion of symbolic arbitrariness. He provides, next to a quack 2 dimensional sketch of the ubiquitous arboreal object, the French, English and German words "arbre", "tree", "baum" – embedded in quotation marks – in order to demonstrate how the sound or shape of the word has nothing to do with the nature of the signified thing, and that the relationship relies entirely upon a communal agreement to assign one to the other.

[28] This was actually the title of an anti-structuralist book FIND, but it has been recent work by Nancy Woodworth into phonaesthesia and pan-linguistic patterns of corporeal indexicality of vowel sounds in deictic pronouns and size adjectives which has most thoroughly destabilised Saussurian linguistics. After some of the nonsenses of Post-Structuralism, it is relieving for writers, and especially poets, to discover that language does after all breathe the fresh air of the physical world, and that dunces will never entirely succeed in quibbling it to death.

[29] In American pornographic jargon, 'a wood' is an erection. Notoriously difficult to maintain for the jaded male members of the profession.

[30] SOMEONE said that the definition of 'phallogocentrism' was what happened when you deleted the space between the 2nd and 3rd words in the saying 'the pen is mightier than the sword'.

[31] I find all applications of language to tree diagrams offensive. Systemic linguistics, for instance, relies almost entirely on them to represent its absurd simplification of grammar to series of EitherOr choices. This kind of thing is indicative of a very unsophisticated approach to linguistics. It musts upon a monologic (cyclopic) vision of lexical semantics, where only one path can be taken at once by a single producer of meaning.

[32] This is one of Jorge Luis Borges's typically lucid little stories about a labyrinthine text of staggering proportions. The eponymous novel/labyrinth of Ts'ui Pên (you can't help feeling there's some kind of pun in this name) is in some sense a misnomer. The idea of the forked path carries the standard implication of the life decision, summed up in Robert Frost's[33] well-trodden 'Road not Taken'. But Ts'ui Pên's manuscript refuses the impossible bifurcation of Frost's path, in that 'he chooses – simultaneously – all of them.' This, albeit in the guise of a rather silly thematic literalism, reflects my notion of metaphoric countertown.

[33] The New England writers imported the English wood into the American consciousness. Frost, Whitman, and especially Hawthorne all see the wood as the shady place where Puritan social values are adumbrated. It is in a cottage in the woods that Heather Gwynne is exiled. And Hawthorne (a man who shared his name with the characteristically wild and gnarly tree which provided pagan England with most of its hedgerows with the 'mayflowers' which heralded the Beltane (Spring) festival) chose to name his abridgements of Homer and Ovid for children *Tanglewood Tales*.

Amrit Singh: *The Zomby Portfolio* [UF13-27]

fig. 14: 'Unfencing Theory: A Defence of Fiction' p10-11 (facsimile)

Appendix 4

Zomby Project 4. Now Now: Holding on to the Present

The putative author of this fictional missing essay, *Masure Delecteur* is self-evidently supposed to be Jacques Derrida. If the reference to *Donner le Temps* were not enough, the obviously fake name is a rather unsubtle punning translation. Masure is French for 'hovel' or 'shack' and lecteur means 'reader'. 'Shack De Reader' is clearly supposed to capture a rather bad Anglophone pronunciation of the French philosopher's name. Should any further confirmation be needed, it could be found in the fragment that was, I think, intended as the epigraph to the entire Zomby Project. This was a deliberate mistranscription of the opening monologue from the Japanese children's television programme *Monkey*. It began: 'Before the reader (pron. Derrida) primal chaos reigned. The author sought order but the Phoenix can fly only when its feathers are grown...'

The implicit exploration of time and history clearly prefigures *The Birmingham Quean*. Delecteur's supposed derision of post-Renaissance historiography as 'a suicidal nostalgia for the present' is heavily suggestive of the predicament of R. H. Twigg. The entire piece might usefully be analysed as an exploration of what this counterfeit Derrida is supposed to call *le moment memorial* ('memorial momentum' or 'the moment as monument').

Again, this is a reproduction of only the first page.

Now Now: Holding on to the Present
*(Maintenant Maintenant)**
by Masure Delecteur

* Perhaps it is not entirely a matter of regret that Delecteur's virtuoso early work on time should survive only as a cover page: a single sheet of squared exercise paper with two words pencilled in the top left corner. The myriad considerations involved in translating even this curt title are testament to his ability to crystalise a core discussion of contemporary philsophy in a play on words. (Though we forget at our peril that the work was designed specifically to counter all such notions of the crystalisation of the contemporary.)

This lost piece of juvenalia has become something of a Holy Grail for Delecteur scholars. Progress in its reconstruction has been hampered, paralised in fact, by a total lack of agreement on the finer points. When quizzed, the writer himself has always insisted: "Je ne me souviens plus. C'est tout." What is beyond doubt is that it was a deconstruction (though he was yet to use this word, of course) of the Renaissance view of History, and therefore the Renaissance itself. This was initially presented as a reading of the (1547) translation of Horace's first Ode ("carpe diem") by the French Humanist, Jacques Peletier du Mans. Two ideas were crucial: firstly the entanglement of the notions of personal property and the 'moment of knowledge' (encapsulated by the word *maintenant*) and secondly a rejection of the *maintenance* (tenability and tractability) of a pseudo-static socialscientific discourse which he saw as the Renaissance's key legacy.

More controversial is the argument made by Paula Drachsall (1997, xxi) that an 'annexe' of the essay contained a burlesque creation myth, combining a Darwinian account of human evolution (as the parallel development of language and the opposable thumb) with Renaissance accounts of the biblical Garden of Eden (the transgressive 'moment of knowledge' as the sexualised hand-gesture of picking). Alongside the titular *maintenant*, the core play on words here was to be found in the putative description of humanity (in ironic terms, one would hope) as the creature that 'grasps' (*saisit*) the phallic truth.

Less contentious is the assumption of a playful deconstruction of D... 's most unavoidable French philosophical antecedant in this debate, Henri Bergson. It is inconceivable to most that he would have passed up the chance to explore *la dureté de la durée* ('the harshness of duration' / 'the solidity of fluid time'). In any event, the key paradox: 'the maintenance of the present instant', clearly pits what his disowned notebooks (disowned but confidently attributed, see Rickenbacker and Paul Les Gibson 1992) refer to as 'empirical transcendentalism' against 'continuous revolutionary existence' in terms readily reminiscent of the metaphysical debates of Bergson and Albert Einstein. Derrida's addition of a neo-Marxist angle, with which even Drachsall concurs, was probably the most important achievement of the piece. It was also uncontroversially the result of an influence (much stronger in this early period than it was later to prove, it seems) of his two best known teachers at the *Ecole Normale*: Michel Foucault and Louis Althusser. No doubt this explains its eventual disappearance…

The other fact to which even Drachsall must aquiesce is the importance of the piece as a forerunner of *Donner le Temps: La Fausse Monnaie* (1991). It is obviously with this consideration in mind that I employ the same pun on 'present' so crucial to that book in my appositive sub-title. In the final analysis, however, if forced to choose between the two, I would hold on to the other, rather more tenuous translation 'Now Now'. At the very least, this naively literal English version manages to capture a gentle admonishment of the kind of assumption connoted by its more sophisticated counterpart that a piece of writing can be supernaturally capable of *grasping* its own place in History.

fig. 15: 'Now Now: Holding on to the Present' p1 (facsimile)

Appendix 5

Zomby Project 5. Synoptic Manifesto Manuscript (working document)

Despite its poor reproduction here as a tiled arrangement of multiple computer scans, this is by far the most convincing piece of evidence that 'The Zomby Project' and *The Birmingham Quean* were written by the same person. It is patently a document used in the preparation of 'The Manifesto of the Fiction Party' and the handwriting (notwithstanding the faintness of the pencil) is plainly the same scrawl in which the commentary material of R. H. Twigg appeared on the brown paper of *The Birmingham Quean*. (see Appendix 7)

This document consists of four versions of Marx and Engels' *Communist Party Manifesto* photocopied and pasted into an A1 flip-pad. The versions are:

1. the German original, from *Marx Engels Werke* Vol. 4 (Mai 1846 bis März 1848) [Berlin: Dietz, 1964]
2. the Samuel Moore English translation overseen by Engels in 1888 [Moscow: Progress Publishers 1965]
3. the new English translation by Terrell Carver, from *The Communist Party Manifesto, New Interpretations* edited by Mark Cowling [Edinburgh: EUP, 1998]
4. the Manifesto's first English translation by Helen Macfarlane as it appeared in the Chartist newspaper *The Red Republican* on November 9th 1850

Seen in landscape on the page, a small fragment of 1. is visible top left, of 2. bottom right, of 3. top left and 4. is clearly visible bottom right.

Apart from the identical handwriting, the similarities of presentation and approach with the brown roll manuscript of the present work are incontestable. We should be wary, however, of making the analogical argument that the brown roll was a similar piece of early preparatory material for *The Birmingham Quean*. Regardless of the eventual preparation of the text with the current format and reconstructed content (due entirely to my unfortunate incendiary intervention) it is my firm belief that the brown roll manuscript was intended by the author as the finished draft.

fig. 16: Synoptic Manifesto Manuscript p1 (facsimile)

Appendix 6

The Birmingham Quean 1. The Twigg Schema

This table is a preparatory document of my own. In terms of content it is self-explanatory. It is an important fact that this structural analysis was created before the destruction of the manuscript and was originally intended as a means of elucidating the extant brown roll version rather than as (what it inevitably became) an architectural skeleton for the reconstruction process. My recollection of the thing in combination with the original is that it was severely generalising and never designed to be seen by anybody but myself. It certainly does not seem to be the case that *The Birmingham Quean* was written following any such rigid format. If the reconstruction suffers from a rather mechanistic adherence to this structure (as Joyce worried *Ulysses* might have done from the intrusion of the 1920 'Linati Schema') then it is entirely the result of my own susceptibility to that cultural tendency to distort memory by imposing logical patterns upon it. It has nothing to do with the original author.

If for nothing else, however, I can flatter myself that this effect is only very slight. The reason (one that tends to support Proust's depiction of memory) is that this model, for all its concision and basic accuracy, was next to useless as a stimulus for recollection. Only as an aid to the cold (but crucial) decisions about textual presentation has it been of any use. When it came to actually remembering lines of verse and paragraphs of annotation, a single whiff of one of the manuscript's charred remnants (see Appendix 7) was worth hours pouring over something that looks more like an executive powerpoint slide or a handout from a civil service conference than something you might use to study literature.

no.	Section	Future	Poet is	Focus of Notes	Cross-Refs	Address	Twigg's Biography	Progress of the Fire	Obsession
1a.	start to first glimpse 1-63	*depicted*	dystopian satirist (cleverly ironic humanist)	simple confident notes in support of poet's attack on common enemies	none	optimistic to contemporaries & less so to readers at (late) date of possible publication	recent predicament sequestered in college 1952-3; discovery of room & college archive	first flames and their initial spread, epidermal effects, ends in description of how the fire began	counter, antitheses, amphibology, television
1b.	first glimpse to entrance 64-144	*intended*	anarchist plotter (bad poet with worse intentions)	reads inverted Marxist historiography as the expression of malign revolutionary intention	none	increasingly to future readers as a warning of impending revolution in their anarchic culture	discovery of the brown roll precipitated by the dream; Hubbard's name; first descriptions of *The Birmingham Queen*	deeper muscular burn, the wick effect, the words as flames	dialectic, marxism, anarchism
2a.	entrance to 'ineluctable full frontal' 145-196	*foreseen*	prescient gypsy king; Ryley Bosvil (malignant necromantic ghost)	finds genuine diabolical prescience, characterised by going back to put in cataphoric cross-refs	revisionist references forwards to parts of poem within previous notes	back to the present as an insistence that this could be a true prediction	back to 1923 & the marriage proposal, then further back to 20-21 for first encounters with Alexander & Hermione	Miguel Servetus, organ-level burn effects on the archive; fiery tornado of pages, hence literature as fire, biographical memory as fire	flamingos, birds, gypsies, necromancy, sadism
2b.	Saddam to 'what foul beast' 197-240	*tangible*	amanuensis in real future (the pitiable victim of a similar fate)	pity & identification with victimisations & the poet's suffering mind	back to instances of the poet's tortured vision etc.	impossible apostrophe of future poet/scribe as if speaking to someone through a one way mirror	wedding, honeymoon, Jacob Stover, birth & childhood of Phillip, 1943 separation from wife & son	libraries of Alexandria and Nineveh; soft-tissue collapse; fire as memorialising effect of fire and literacy	occult, sex, quantum physics, dartboard
3a.	second coming to circumfera in final stanza 241-257	*gestating*	a foul beast slouching towards Birmingham to be born	encrypted (game) key to time travel & this as object from one of lots of poss. futures	references to itself from previous	desperate to whoever might find the text entirely in order to convince them to destroy it	meeting with Alexander 1944, death of mother 1952, reunion with Phillip on mother's estate, scattering of ashes	skeletal-level burn, merger of skeleton and flames so that identity is both; fire as the principal of consciousness	fate, 'era/are'
3a.	CODA	*burning birthing*	Hubbard (as a phoenix)	Twigg as unwitting enacter of f(a)iry future	red era's & so on	resigned & pointless to no-one as final words	present: dream & poem, Hubbard as author, dream ends	Twigg as fire & no longer that which was burnt. Twigg=phoenix	Hubbard, fire, the phoenix

fig. 17: The Twigg Schema (facsimile)

Appendix 7

The Birmingham Quean 2. Original Manuscript Sample

This is a facsimile of the best preserved fragment amongst those I was able to salvage from the remnants of a bonfire at a travellers' encampment in Kingston upon Thames two years ago. The monochrome reduction fails to capture the stiffly wrinkled texture, the burnt smell, the colour of the different inks and papers...

Compared to many examples so far into the work, this page (I use the word loosely) is somewhat unrepresentative in being quite well organised and not too hard to read. The references are clearly marked with underlining and arrows. The individual annotations are quite well differentiated, two of them being helpfully bordered by the skins of cartoon speech bubbles. By no means was this always the case. My method of formal reconstruction in this edition can only ever achieve a pale imitation of the rampant textual apparatus and the scrolling format.

Perhaps the day Twigg produced this bit of commentary was one characterised by a note of unusual optimism and lucidity. He does have these on occasion, especially early in a section.

But I forget myself. These sections were never explicitly indicated in the manuscript and the separators (and epigraphs) have been introduced by me for reasons of elucidation (see Appendix 6). What's more, R. H. Twigg does not, and never did, exist. Twigg has a life only insofar as he is contained between these pages and in the minds of myself and the author of The Birmingham Quean. I suppose I began the reconstruction of this thing in the futile hope that the promise it contained like a rumour — the promise of a psychological and emotional intimacy with the writer like that shared by musicians or (dare I say it) lovers — might genuinely materialise.

No such thing has happened. I haven't managed to catch even the merest glimpse inside the mind of Amrit Singh. Only in these moments of idiotic credulity, when I forget the truth — forget that it's a fiction... forget even that I'm writing or reading — do I experience anything approaching telepathic counterpoint with this object of desire: that psychic ideal whose absence is mourned by every square inch of the piece.

I confess, it is fantasy I regularly indulge. The fragment of which this is a more than bloodless reproduction (my jealousy could never allow another reader access to anything more tangible) is the drug I use to bring it on. I don't read it any more. I know it off by heart. Instead, I sniff around the edges like a dog. I touch it to my cheek. I close both eyes and brush my fingerprints over the contours of its numb, crispy landscape the way you might the surface of a scab. Without these moments of self-indulgence, I might never have completed this work. My fantasies have fired my memory.

I suppose, in the final analysis, I myself have become a kind of R. H. Twigg. There is a certain comfort in imagining yourself to be a fictional character from a fictional epoch invented by an object of desire. If existence is a process of discovering this fact then the discovery itself is love and life and truth enough for anyone.

fig. 18: Original Manuscript Sample (facsimile)

Bibliography and Index

Yo conozco distritos en que los jóvenes se prosternan ante los libros y besan con barbarie las páginas, pero no saben descifrar una sola letra.

(Jorge Luis Borges 'La Biblioteca de Babel',
in *Ficciones*, ed. Brotherston and Hulme, 1976)

Reverse-Engineering Attribution

The Birmingham Quean did not have a bibliography. Most of its quotations, allusions and close parodies were at best only partially attributed. To begin with, the intention of my work was to provide this missing element. What remains as tangible evidence of my intensive study of the manuscript during its last three months comprises little more than the following list. I did make one or two rough notes and I redrafted the first paragraph of an explanatory essay several times, but my scholarly approach never really got beyond the plodding and slightly dubious business of tracing sources.

But it was a good job I did it. When it came to reconstructing the lost text, this large (though inexhaustive) list of probable citations was of immense use in retracing the intellectual structure of the piece. Most importantly, the order in which I had noted them down was the order in which I had encountered them. Roughly speaking (I didn't always read sequentially) this meant that they followed their order of appearance. The process of going back and reading the relevant extracts, one after the other, was a very effective stimulus for recollection.

The process was a bit like 'Reverse Engineering'. This technique is essentially a legal finesse used by technology companies in order to copy their competitor's designs whilst avoiding breach of patents. They employ a set of engineers to work in a controlled environment (analogous to a sequestered jury) and produce a complete set of algorithms for the object's functions. They then employ a second group of engineers (who must provably have never 1. been in contact with any of the engineers from the first set, or 2. seen or heard anything about the original design) to work in a similar environment to produce a machine or piece of software with these same 'output algorithms'. There's a rabbinical feel to all this esoteric legal manoeuvring. The basic idea seems to be a mirror image of the one which putatively guarantees the divine inspiration of the *Septuagint*.

If my reconstruction of *The Birmingham Quean* does not claim to be inspired by God, it does at least claim to be inspired by someone else. The project's guiding principle has been to give credit where credit's due, even if this means defying the wishes of the author and the piece itself. I have therefore chosen, wherever possible, to include my own sources in this bibliography. And, whilst it has been reorganised into alphabetical order, I have provided page references for the specific instances of quotation or allusion, in the style of an index.

In the relatively rare cases of what Alasdair Gray refers to as 'block plagiarisms' (long direct quotations not indicated on the relevant page), I have provided subsections with their own index lines preceded by "* >" under the heading of author and text which give (where possible) the first and last words of the relevant extract and its position within the cited original.

In the vastly more common instances of what Gray calls 'diffuse plagiarism', the reference is usually an italicised page number. There is also quite a large number of salient texts for whom no specific page reference can be given. Many of these are texts that appeared in the author's own bibliographic lists in the 'Zomby Portfolio', but they also include books of such obvious general relevance that their influence is felt throughout. In both cases the reference given is the standard scholarly term '*passim.*' Some disambiguation has been attempted, however, by setting the word in bold type whenever the current of a piece's influence is thought strong enough to have been felt 'throughout' rather than merely 'here and there'.

The two books from which I take my terms will serve as examples of these two sorts:

Gray, Alasdair (1981) *Lanark: A Life in Four Books* (Edinburgh: Canongate) ***passim***

Hall, P. A. V. (ed.) (1992) *Software Reuse and Reverse Engineering in Practice* (London: Chapman & Hall) *passim*

As far as page-numbers are concerend, the index holds generally to the following correlation between typography and type of reference:

Typography	Example	Type of Reference
Plain	123456789	Basic mention or clear allusion
Italic	*123456789*	Unacknowledged influence/allusion ('diffuse plagiarism')
Bold	**123456789**	Fully (or at least effectively) referenced citation
Bold Italic	***123456789***	Unacknowledged quotation/paraphrase ('block plagiarism')

A book identified as the source of all types of use looks like this:

Fisher, Roy (1994) *Birmingham River* (Oxford: Oxford University Press) **15**, *61*, *79*, *123*, *141*, *147*, *179-80*, *283*, *285*, *519*, *531*, *571*, ***passim***
*   > 'Talking to Cameras' (li 76-80) "centre of the universe... as its centre)" **369**

For cases involving multiple editions/translations of the same text (simultaneous use of which the 'Zomby Project' demonstrates to be typical of the author's methodology: see Appendix 5), I have not bothered to repeat a list of page references for each except where specific citation or relevance is peculiar to the later edition. Neither is a bold "***passim***" repeated in such cases unless the specific version is of particular salience.

Where internet citations are concerned, I have not attempted to guess a *date of access* on which the author might have viewed the text. Instead I have conformed with standard practice by including in square brackets the date at which I accessed the site myself in order to verify the source. The vast majority are therefore recent dates from the period covering this bibliography's final draft. The reason for this regulation is obviously to account for website updates. In one or two cases I have simply got around the problem by changing the quotation in the main text so that it matched the wording that appears on the date shown in the bibliography. A strange thing to do to a plagiarism one might think, but necessary to stop it from remaining a plagiarism.

As a final note, it must be admitted that this process of bibliographic *reverse engineering* has probably meant the text relying more heavily on those books and extracts listed here than was the case in the original. I have little doubt that there were also numerous texts whose traces I never spotted, and others whose appearance in this list would strike the author as bizarre or, at the very least, irrelevant. I can only defend myself against such accusations by insisting that my interventions have always been made on the assumption that they were in the author's best interests. Besides, *The Birmingham Quean* wouldn't have it any other way.

Bibliographic Index

a.) Print Publications: by Author [see below for d.) Anonymous Texts]

Aaker, David A. (1996) *Building Strong Brands* (New York and London: Free Press) 55, 124, 171, 291, 333, 401; 'The Smirnoff Story' 477

Aarsleff, Hans (1982) *From Locke to Saussure: Essays on the Study of Language and Intellectual History* (London: Athlone) *passim*

Abrams, M. H. (**1953**) *The Mirror and the Lamp: Romantic Theory and the Critical Tradition* (Oxford: Oxford University Press) 346

Ackroyd, Peter (1973) *Dressing Up, Transvestism and Drag: The History of an Obsession* (London: Thames and Hudson) ***passim***
.... (1985) *Hawksmoor* (London: Hamilton) 145
.... (1993) *The House of Doctor Dee* (London: Hamilton) 378, *405*, *453*
.... (2000) *London: The Biography* (London: Chatto & Windus) *passim*

Adams, Douglas (1987) *Dirk Gently's Holistic Detective Agency* (London: William Heinemann) 65-7, *passim*

Adams, Richard (1972) *Watership Down* (London: Rex Collings Ltd.) *428*
  * > Chapter 11 (2nd ed., 1973): "it did indeed prove... none could foresee" **474**
.... (1974) *Shardik* (London: Allen Lane in association with Rex Collings) *passim*

Adamson, Joe (1973) *Groucho, Harpo, Chico and sometimes Zeppo: a history of the Marx Brothers and a satire on the rest of the world* (London: W. H. Allen) 277-8

Addison, Joseph (1710) 'Adventures of a Shilling', in Mackie, Erin (ed.) (1998) *The Commerce of Everyday Life: selections from* The Tatler *and* The Spectator (Boston: Bedford/St. Martin's) (pp.186-7) **82**

Adorno, Theodor (1950) *The Authoritarian Personality*, (New York: Harper) 3-5
.... (1973) *Negative Dialectics*, trans. E. B. Ashton (London: Routledge & Kegan Paul) 148
.... ([1973] 1986) *The Jargon of Authenticity*, trans. Knut Tarnowski and Frederic Will (London: Routledge and Kegan Paul) 3-5
.... (1974) *Minima moralia: reflections from damaged life*, trans. E. F. N. Jephcott (London: NLB) *passim*
.... (1983) *Aesthetic Theory*, trans. C. Lenhardt, ed. Gretel Adorno and Rolf Tiedemann (London: Routledge and Kegan Paul) *passim*
.... (1989) *Introduction to the Sociology of Music*, trans. E. B. Ashton (New York: Continuum) *passim*

Agard, John (1985) *Mangoes and Bullets: selected and new poems, 1972-84* (London: Pluto Press) 189

Ali, Tariq (2002) *The Clash of Fundamentalisms: crusades, jihads and modernity* (London: Verso) *312*

'Alexandre de Paris' ([1937-1955] 1965] *The Medieval French Roman d'Alexandre*, ed. E. C. Armstrong (New York: Kraus Reprint) (orig. Princeton University Press) 68

Allison, Ronald and Riddell, Sarah (1991) *The Royal Encyclopedia* (London: Macmillan) 75, *113*

Amis, Kingsley (**1953**) *Lucky Jim* (London: Gollancz) *passim*
.... (1961) *New Maps of Hell: A Survey of Science Fiction* (London: Gollancz) 67, 97, 119, 124, 199, 291, 320, 338, 413

Amis, Martin (1984) *Money: A Suicide Note* (London: Jonathan Cape) *passim*
.... (1989) *London Fields* (London: Jonathan Cape) *passim*
.... (1991) *Time's Arrow* (London: Jonathan Cape) ***passim***

Andersen, Hans Christian ([1974] 1985) 'The Silver Shilling', in *The Penguin complete fairy tales and stories of Hans Andersen*, ed. Eric Christian Haugaard (Harmondsworth: Penguin) 82

Apuleius, Lucius (1903) *The Golden Ass of Apuleius*, trans. F. D. Byrne (London: Imperial Press) 81, 83, 222, 461, 465, *passim*
.... (1910) The Metamorphoses or Golden Ass of Apuleius of Madaura, trans. H. E. Butler (Oxford: Clarendon) passim
.... (1950) *The Transformations of Lucius, otherwise known as The Golden Ass*, trans. Robert Graves (Harmondsworth: Penguin) 81, *passim*
.... (1994) *The Golden Ass*, trans. P. G. Walsh (Oxford: Oxford University Press) *passim*
.... (1999) *The Golden Ass*, trans. E. J. Kenney (London: Penguin) *passim*
Arbuthnot, John et al. ([1742] 1950) *Memoirs of the Extraordinary Life, Works and Discoveries of Martinus Scriblerus*, ed. C. Kirby-Miller (New York and Oxford: Oxford University Press) 87, 320, *passim*
Ariosto, Lodovico (1954) *Orlando Furioso*, ed. Lanfranco Caretti (Milano: R. Ricciardi) **117**
.... (1975-7) *Orlando Furioso = The Frenzy of Orlando: a romantic epic*, trans. with intro. Barbara Reynolds, (Parts 1 and 2) (Harmondsworth; Baltimore: Penguin) ***passim***
Aristophanes (1906-7) *Aristophanis Comoediae*, ed. with notes F. W. Hall and W. M. Geldart, 2 vols. (Oxford: Clarendon) *The Birds* 65, 155, 173, 185, 225, 330, 362, **371**-5, 392, ***passim***; *The Frogs* **131**
.... (1950) *The Birds*, trans. with notes G. Murray (London Allen & Unwin) *passim*
.... (1978) *The Birds*, trans. A. H. Sommerstein (London: Penguin) *passim*
.... (1995) *Aristophanes, Birds* [Greek], ed. with intro. and notes Nan Dunbar (Oxford: Clarendon) 371-5, ***passim***
.... (1997) *The Birds, Lysistrata, Assembly-Women, Wealth*, trans. with intro. and notes S. Halliwell (Oxford: Clarendon) *passim*
.... (1999) *Clouds, Wasps, Birds*, trans. with notes P. Meineck, intro. Ian C. Storey, (Cambridge: Hackett) *passim*
Armitage, Simon (1989) 'Ten Pence Story', in *Zoom!* (Newcastle upon Tyne: Bloodaxe Books) (pp. 64-5) *82, passim*
Arnold, Matthew (1876) 'Bishop Butler and the Zeit-Geist', in *Contemporary Review*, Vol. 27: February, March 1876 (pp. 377-95, 571-92) 423
Asimov, Isaac (1983 [**1953**]) *Second Foundation* (London: Panther) 340
Atwood, Margaret (1986) *The Handmaid's Tale* (London: Cape) *passim*
Attridge, Derek (1974) *Well-Weighed Syllables: Elizabethan verse in classical metres* (London: Cambridge University Press) 68-70
.... (1982) *The Rhythms of English Poetry* (London: Longman) *passim*
.... (1987) 'Language as history/history as language: Saussure and the romance of etymology', in Derek Attridge, Geoff Bennington and Robert Young, eds., *Post-Structuralism and the Question of History* (Cambridge: Cambridge University Press) (pp. 183-211) *57, 65, 194, 207, 330, 359, 371-7, 390, **passim***
.... (2000) 'Deconstruction and Fiction', in Nicholas Royle (ed.) *Deconstructions: a user's guide* (Basingstoke: Palgrave Macmillan) (pp. 105-18) *passim*
Augustine, Saint, Bishop of Hippo (1927) *The Confessions of Augustine*, ed. with intro. and notes John Gibb and W. Montgomery (Cambridge: Cambridge University Press) **293**
Austen, Jane (2003) *Northanger Abbey*, ed. with intro. and notes Marilyn Butler (London; New York: Penguin Books) *passim*
Austin, J. L. (1962) *How to do things with words* (Oxford: Clarendon Press) *148, passim*
Bacon, Francis (1949) 'Of Masques and Triumphs', in *Essays* (London: Oxford University Press) **292**
.... (2000) *The Advancement of Learning*, ed. Michael Kiernan (Oxford: Clarendon Press) **127**
Bainton, Roland H. (**1953**) *Hunted Heretic: The Life and Death of Michael Servetus, 1511-1553* (Boston: Beacon Press) *323*
Bakhtin, Mikhail M. (1968) *Rabelais and his world*, trans. H. Iswolsky (Cambridge MA: MIT Press) *passim*
.... (1981) *The Dialogic Imagination: four essays*, ed. M. Holquist, trans. C. Emerson and M. Holquist (Austin: University of Texas) ***passim***

Bakhtin, Mikhail M. and Medvedev, P. N. (1978) *The Formal Method in Literary Scholarship: a critical introduction to sociological poetics*, trans. A. J. Wehrle (Baltimore: Johns Hopkins University Press) *passim*

Baldwin, James (2001 [**1953**]) *Go Tell it on the Mountain* (London: Penguin) 346

Balzac, Honoré de (1927) *La Comédie Humaine : Etudes de moeurs : Scènes de la Vie Parisienne VIII. ; Les Petits Bourgeois ; L'Envers de l'Histoire Contemporaine*, ed. and notes M. Bouteron & H. Longon, 33 vols. (Paris : Conard) *passim*
* > 'Sarrassine' : "C'était la femme ... délicieuse finesse de sentiment." **203**

Barfield, Owen ([1928] 1952) *Poetic Diction: A Study in Meaning* (London: Faber & Faber) 87
.... ([1926] 1954) *History in English Words* (London: Faber & Faber) *passim*

Barthes, Roland (**1953**) *Le Degré Zéro de l'Ecriture* (Paris: Editions du Seuil) 390
.... (1970) *S/Z.*, (Paris: Editions du Seuil) *passim*
* > "C'était la femme ... délicieuse finesse de sentiment." **203**
.... (1973) *Le Plaisir du Texte* (Paris: Editions du Seuil) 150
.... (1977) *Image, Music, Text*, sel. and trans. Stephen Heath (London: Fontana) *passim*
* > 'The Death of the Author' [1968] p142 " 'This was woman herself ... delicious sensibility.' " **203**
.... ([1957] 1972) *Mythologies*, sel. and trans. Annette Lavers (London: J. Cape) *passim*
* > 'The Face of Garbo': "Garbo still belonged to that moment... without leaving one in any doubt." **277**

Baudelaire, Charles (1962) 'L'amour du mensonge', in Enid Starkie (ed.) *Les Fleurs du Mal* (Oxford: Basil Blackwell) **233**

Baudrillard, Jean (1994) *Simulacra and Simulation*, trans. Sheila Farier Glaser (Ann Arbor: University of Michigan Press) *211*, *338*, *passim*

Beauvoir, Simone de (**1953**) *The Marquis de Sade*, trans. (of 'Faut-il brûler Sade?', in *Les Temps Modernes*, dec. 1951) Annette Michelson, with writings of de Sade selec. and trans. Paul Dinnage (New York: Grove Press) 267, 347, 407, 413, *passim*

Beckett, Samuel (1952) *En Attendant Godot, pièce en deux actes* (Pars: Editions de Minuit) 121, 174, 346, 404
.... ([1947] 1973) *First Love* (London: Calder) 174, **537**, 549

Beckson, Karl E. (1987) *Arthur Symons: a life* (Oxford: Clarendon Press) *418*

Beerbohm, Max ([1896] 1922) 'The Pervasion of Rouge' or 'A Defence of Cosmetics', in *The Works of Max Beerbohm* (London; New York: Dodd, Mead and Co.) (pp. 107-134) 209, **210**

Bellamy, Edward ([1888] 1951) *Looking Backward, 2000-1887* (New York: Modern Library) 25, *passim*

Bellow, Saul (1967) *Herzog* (Harmondsworth: Penguin) 102
.... ([**1953**] 1996) *The Adventures of Augie March* (New York: Penguin Books) 346

Benjamin, Walter ([1935-9] 1999) *The Arcades Project*, ed. (German) Rolf Tiedemann, trans. H. Eiland and K. McLaughlin (Cambridge, MA: Belknap Press) *passim*; 'O [Prostitution, Gambling]' (pp. 489-515) *293*, **passim**
.... ([1933] 1999) 'The Lamp', trans. Suhrkamp Verlag, in *Selected Writings, Vol 2. 1927-34*, eds. Michael W. Jennings, Howard Eiland, and Gary Smith (Cambridge MA: Belknap Press) (pp.691-3)
* > p.692: "the dull pop... one room to another" **105**
.... (1973) *Illuminations*, ed. Hannah Arendt, trans. Harry Zohn (London: Fontana/Collins) *passim*; 'The work of art in the age of mechanical reproduction' (pp.211-44) *50, 59, 73, 138, 184*, 260, *passim*

Benlowes, Edward (1652) *Theophila, or, Loves sacrifice, a divine poem* (London: Printed by R.N., sold by Henry Seile and Humphrey Moseley) [EEBO: 1641-1700; 306:3] **309**

Bentham, Jeremy (1995) *The Panopticon Writings*, ed. with intro. Miran Bozovic (London; New York: Verso) 163
.... (1932) *Bentham's Theory of Fictions*, ed. with intro. C. K. Ogden (London: Kegan Paul, Trench, Trubner & Co.) 21, 361, *passim*

Bergson, Henri (1910) *Time and Free Will: an essay in the immediate data of consciousness*, trans. F. L. Pogson (London; New York: Sonnenschein; Macmillian) 148, **284-6**, *passim*
.... (1911) *Creative Evolution*, trans. A. Mitchell (London: Macmillan) *passim*
.... (1911) *Laughter: an essay on the meaning of the comic*, trans. C. Brereton & F. Rothwell (London: Macmillan) *passim*
.... (1913) *An Introduction to Metaphysics*, tranS. A. M. T. E. Hulme (London: Macmillan) *passim*

Berners, Juliana, Dame (1518) *The boke of hawkynge, and hyntynge, and fysshynge [The Boke of Saint Albans]* (London: Wynkyn de Worde) [Pollard and Redgrave STC (2nd ed.) 3309.5.] 463-4

Bertillon, Alphonse (1896) *Signaletic instructions including the theory and practice of anthropometrical identification*, trans. Major R. W. McClaughry (Chicago; New York: Werner) 417, 443

Bester, Alfred (1999 [**1953**]) *The Demolished Man* (London: Millennium) 340

Bhaskar, Roy (1986) *Scientific Realism and Human Emancipation* (London: Verso) 148, 212, 316
.... (1993) *Dialectic: The Pulse of Freedom* (London; New York: Verso) 148, 212, 316

Blackman, Cole (1972) *The Enoch Powell Fireside Book* (London, Frewin) *passim*

Blake, William (1907) *Milton*, ed. E. R. D. Maclagan and A. G. B. Russell, [reprint of 1804 ed.] (London: A. H. Bullen) 337
.... (1927) *The Marriage of Heaven and Hell*, with notes by Max Plowman (London: Dent) 402, *passim*

Bloch, Ernst ([1959] 1986) *The Principle of Hope*, trans. N. Plaice, S. Plaice and P. Knight (Oxford: Basil Blackwell) *passim*
.... (1988) *The Utopian Function of Art and Literature: Selected Essays*, trans. Jack Zipes and Frank Mecklenburg (Cambridge, MA: MIT Press) ***passim***

Bloom, Harold (1973) *The Anxiety of Influence: a theory of poetry* (New York: Oxford University Press) *passim*
.... (1999) *Shakespeare: The Invention of the Human* (London: Fourth Estate) 150

Blunt, C. E. (1935) 'Some notes on the coinage of Edward IV between 1401 and 1470 with particular reference to the nobles and angels', in *British Numismatic Journal*, Vol 22. 1934-7 (London: British Numismatic Society) (pp.194-9) **75-6**

Boas, Guy (1952) 'Notes and Observations: *to see or not to see*' [front page editorial on the subject of Television], in *English* Vol IX, Autumn 1952, no. 51 (London: Oxford University Press) ***passim***

Boccaccio, Giovanni (1934-5) *Boccaccio's Decameron* (Oxford: Shakespeare Head and Blackwell) 81

Bömer, Franz (1986) 'XV. 391-407 Der Vogel Phoenix', in *P. Ovidius Naso – Metamorphosen – Buch XIV-XV – Kommentar* (Heidelberg: Carl Winters Universitätsverlag) (pp. 355-8) [begins "ein Theme ohne Ende" and then proves it with the most erudite bibliography of the Phoenix in existence] 77, *371-7*

Borges, Jorge Luis ([1964] 1970) *Labyrinths: selected stories and other writings*, trans. Donald A. Yates and James E. Irby, pref. André Maurois (Harmondsworth: Penguin) *passim*
.... (1974) (with Margarita Guerrero) *The Book of Imaginary Beings*, revised and trans. Norman Thomas di Giovanni (with Borges) (Harmondsworth: Penguin) *passim*
.... (1974) *Ficciones*, ed. with intro. Gordon Brotherston and Peter Hulme (London: Harrap) **569**

Borrow, George Henry ([1874] 1907) *Romano Lavo-Lil, word-book of the Romany; or, English Gypsy Language* (London: J. Murray) 57, **313**

Bradbury, Ray (1973 [**1953**]) *Farenheit 451* (London: Corgi) 340

Bramston, James (1743) *The Crooked Sixpence with a Learned Preface* (London: R. Dodsley) 82

Brandi, Cesare (1963) *Teoria del Restauro* (Roma: Edizioni di storia e letteratura) **11**, 13

Braund, David (1994) *Georgia in Antiquity: a history of Colchis and Transcaucasian Iberia, 550 BC—AD 562* (Oxford: Clarendon Press) 123, 317

Brecht, Bertolt (1961) *Threepenny Novel*, trans. Desmond I. Vesey and Christopher Isherwood (Harmondsworth: Penguin) 121, *passim*

.... (1973) *The Threepenny Opera*, trans. Hugh MacDiarmid (London: Eyre Methuen) 121, 283

Bridges, Thomas ([1770] 1975) *The Adventures of a Bank-note*, [facsimile reprint of first ed.: London: T. Davies 1770] (New York and London: Garland) 81, *passim*

Brighouse, Harold (1916) *Hobson's Choice: a Lancashire comedy in four acts* (London: Samuel French) 78

'Britannicus, Mercurius' [prob. Joseph Hall, but poss. Alberico Gentili: see note p.23] ([1605] 1612) *Mundus alter et idem sive terra Australis antehac semper incognita*, ed. 'Guilielmus Knight' (Frankfurt am Main) 21-3

British Association for the Advancement of Science (1950) *Birmingham and its Regional Setting* (Birmingham: Local Executive Committee) *passim*; M. C. Wise & B. L. C. Johnson 'The Changing Regional Pattern During the Eighteenth Century' **78**, *passim*

Brontë, Emily (1992) *Wuthering Heights*, ed. Linda H. Peterson (Boston: Bedford Books / St. Martin's Press) 288

Brooks, Cleanth (1949) *The Well Wrought Urn: studies in the structure of poetry* (London: D. Dobson) 187-8, 233, *passim*

Browne, Thomas (1958) *Urne Buriall, and The Garden of Cyrus*, ed. John Carter (Cambridge: Cambridge University Press) *passim*

Burke, Edmund (1958) *A Philosophical Enquiry into the Origin of our Ideas of the Sublime and Beautiful*, ed. with intro. and notes J. T. Boulton (London: Routledge & Kegan Paul) 187-8, 332

.... (1993) *Reflections on the Revolution in France*, ed. with intro. L. G. Mitchell (Oxford: Oxford University Press) 60, 65, 165, 183, *passim*

Burroughs, William S. (1995) *My Education: a book of dreams* (London: Viking Penguin) 320, *passim*

.... (2003 [**1953**]) *Junky: the definitive text of Junk (50th Anniversary Edition)*, intro. Oliver Harris, (orig. pub. under pseudonym 'William Lee') 346, *passim*

Burton, Robert (1938) *The Anatomy of Melancholy: now for the first time with the Latin completely given in translation and embodied in an all-English text*, eds. F. Dell and P Jordan-Smith (New York: Tudor) **83**

.... (1989-2000) *The Anatomy of Melancholy*, eds. Thomas C. Faulkner, Nicolas K. Kiessling and Rhonda L. Blair, 6 vols. (Oxford: Clarendon Press) 83

Butler, Judith (1990) *Gender Trouble: feminism and the subversion of identity* (New York: Routledge) *passim*

.... (1991) 'Imitation and Gender Insubordination', in Diana Fuss (ed.) *Inside/Out* (New York: Routledge) (pp. 13-31) *passim*

.... (1997) *Excitable Speech: a politics of the performative* (New York: Routledge) *passim*

Butler, Samuel [1612-1680] (1910) *Hudibras: with variorum notes, selected principally from Grey and Nash*, ed. Henry G. Bohn (London: G. Bell and Sons) 21

Butler, Samuel [1835-1902] (1897) *The Authoress of the Odyssey, where and when she wrote, who she was, the use she made of the Iliad, and how the poem grew under her hands* (London: A. C. Fifield) *passim*

.... (1945) *Erewhon: or Over the Range* (London: J. Cape) 21, 303, *passim*

Byron, George Gordon Byron, Baron ([1901] 1904) *The Works of Lord Byron: Letters and Journals Vol V.*, ed. Rowland E. Prothero (London: John Murray) **53**

.... (1980-1993) *The Complete Poetical Works* 7 vols., eds. J. J. McGann and Barry Weller (Oxford: Clarendon Press) ***passim***; 'The Destruction of Sennacherib' 68; *Don Juan* 16, 49, 51, 55, 57, **59**, **62**, **99**, **105**, 128, 206, 246, 306, **465**, 483, ***passim***

Calvino, Italo (1992) *If on a Winter's Night a Traveller*, trans. William Weaver (London: Minerva) *passim*

Camden, William (1789) Britannia; or, A chorographical description of the flourishing kingdoms of England, Scotland and Ireland, and the islands adjacent; from the earliest antiquity, trans. of 1607 Latin ed., ed. with notes Richard Gough, 3 vols. (London: printed by John Nichols for T. Payne etc.) 179-80, passim

Carroll, Lewis (1965) *The Annotated Alice*, ed. with intro. and notes Martin Gardner, illus. John Tenniel (London: Penguin) 97, 153, 183, *passim*
* > 'take care of the sense and the sounds will take care of themselves' (p.121) "*money, meaning... cognate forms*" **73**

Carpenter, Humphrey (1978) *The Inklings: C. S. Lewis, J. R. R. Tolkien, Charles Williams and their friends* (London; Boston: Allen and Unwin) 87

Carter, Angela (1994) *Nights at the Circus* (London: Vintage) 233, *passim*

Case, Sue-Ellen (2000) 'Toward a Butch-Feminist Retro-Future', in Joseph A. Boon et al. (ed.) *Queer Frontiers: millennial geographies, genders and generations* (Madison: University of Wisconsin Press) *338, passim*

Castaneda, Carlos (1972) *Journey to Ixtlan: the lessons of Don Juan* (Harmondsworth: Penguin) 190

.... (1985) *The Fire from Within* (London: Century) 190, *passim*

Caxton, William (trans. and print. [1481]) (1960) *The History of Reynard the Fox*, ed. with intro. and notes Donald B. Sands (Cambridge, MA: Harvard University Press) 163-171, 239, 405

Cervantes Saavedra, Miguel de (1950) *The Adventures of Don Quixote*, trans. J. M. Cohen (Harmondsworth: Penguin) 81, 212

Crick, F. H. C. and Watson, J. D. (**1953**) 'The Structure of Dioxyribose Nucleic Acid', in *Nature* (Vol. 171, 2nd April 1953: pp. 737-8) 139 314, **317**-19, 346

Chaucer, Geoffrey (1988) *The Riverside Chaucer*, 3rd ed. (based on Robinson 2nd ed. *Works*), gen. ed. Larry D. Benson (Oxford; New York: Oxford University Press) 212, 351; *Canterbury Tales* 301; 'The Merchant's Tale' 329

Chevalier, Ulysse (1902) *Le St Suaire de Lirey-Chambéry-Turin et les défenseurs de son authenticité* (Paris: Picard) **219**, 221

Christie, Agatha (1923) *The Murder on the Links* (London: Bodley Head) 325

.... (1954) *The Mousetrap, a play in two acts* (London: French) 326

Cixous, Hélène (1993) *Three Steps on the Ladder of Writing*, trans. Sarah Cornell and Susan Sellers (New York: Columbia University Press) *passim*

.... (1994) *The Hélène Cixous Reader*, trans. Susan Sellers (London; New York: Routledge) 316, *passim*

.... (1998) *Stigmata: escaping texts* (London; New York: Routledge) *passim*

Clarendon, Edward Hyde, 1st Earl of (1967) *The History of the Great Rebellion*, ed. Roger Lockyer (London: Oxford University Press for the Folio Society) **165**

Clark, Peter (1978) 'The Alehouse and the Alternative Society', in D. H. Pennington and Keith Thomas (eds.) *Puritans and Revolutionaries: essays in seventeenth-century history presented to Christopher Hill* (Oxford: Clarendon Press) *passim*

Clarke, Arthur C. (1977 [**1953**]) *Childhood's End* (London: Pan Books) 340

Clarke, Gary J. (1982) *Defending Ski-Jumpers: a critique of theories of youth sub-cultures* (Birmingham: Centre for Contemporary Cultural Studies, University of Birmingham) 24, 26, *passim*

Clarke, Ignatius Frederick (1978) *Tale of the future, from the beginning to the present day: an annotated bibliography of those satires, ideal states, imaginary wars and invasions, coming catastrophes and end-of-the-world stories, political warnings and forecasts, interplanetary voyages and scientific romances—all located in an imaginary future period—that have been published in the United Kingdom between 1644 and 1976*, 3rd ed. (London: Library Association) *passim*

Clarke, John and Jefferson, Tony (1973) *The Politics of Popular Culture: culture and sub-culture* (Birmingham: Centre for Contemporary Cultural Studies, University of Birmingham) 24, 26, *passim*

Cobbett, William (1828) *Paper Against Gold; or, the history and mystery of The Bank of England, of the debt, of the stocks, of the sinking fund, and of all the other tricks and contrivances carried on by the means of paper money...* (London: the author) 324, *passim*

.... (1832) *Report of the important discussion held at Beardsworth's Repository, in Birmingham, August 28 and 29, 1832...*, with Thomas Attwood (Birmingham: Birmingham Journal) *passim*

Coe, Jonathan (2001) *The Rotters' Club* (London; New York: Viking) *passim*

Coleridge, Samuel Taylor and Wordsworth, William ([1911] 1943) *The Lyrical Ballads*, note: "Except that the Errata of 1798 have been incorporated in the text, and the lines numbered, this is verbatim et literatum a report of the original edition.", ed. H. Littledale (London: Oxford University Press) 65, *passim*; 'Kubla Khan' 63-5, **251**

Conrad, Joseph (1984) *Youth; Heart of Darkness; The End of the Tether*, ed. with intro. Robert Kimbrough (Oxford: Oxford University Press) 423

Cooper, Susan (1973) *The Dark is Rising* (Harmondsworth: Puffin) 420

Cope, Julian (1998) *The Modern Antiquarian: a pre-millennial oddysey through megalithic Britain, including a gazetteer to over 300 prehistoric sites* (London: Thorsons) 241, 259, 262

Copernicus, Nicolas ([[(¿1520?) 1864] 1976) 'Monete cudende ratio', in *Traictie de la Première Invention des Monnoies: textes français et latin d'après les manuscrits de la Bibliothèque Impériale*, trans. [French] L. Wolowski (Genève: Slatkine Reprints) *passim*

Coromonis, Joan (1954) *Diccionario crítico etimológico de la lengua castellana* (Berna: Editorial Francke) 373, *passim*

Cortázar, Julio (1967) *Hopscotch*, trans. Gregory Rabassa (London: Collins, Harvill P.) *passim*

Cowell, Andrew (1999) *At Play in the Tavern: signs, coins and bodies in the Middle Ages* (Ann Arbor, MI: University of Michigan Press) *passim*

Crowley, Aleister (1989) *Portable Darkness: an Aleister Crowley reader*, ed. with notes Scott Michaelson, forewords Robert Anton Wilson and Genesis P-Orridge (New York: Harmony Books) 95, 457, *passim*

Dante Alighieri (1996) *The Divine Comedy of Dante Alighieri. Vol. 1, Inferno*, ed. and trans. Robert M. Durling, intro. and notes Ronald L. Martinez and Robert M. Durling, illus. Robert Turner (Oxford: Oxford University Press) 64, 139, 314, 319, 320, 332-4, 337, 341-5, 374, 439, *passim*

Darwin, Charles (2003) *The Descent of Man: and selection in relation to sex*, intro. Richard Dawkins (London: Gibson Square) 221, 332, 341, 374, 405, 473, *passim*

Davanzati, Bernado (1696) *A Discourse upon Coins*, trans. John Toland [from Italian *Lezione della moneta*, 1588] [EEBO 1641-1700; 91:8] (London: Printed by J.D. for Awnsham and John Churchill) *passim*

Dawkins, Richard (1976) *The Selfish Gene* (Oxford; New York: Oxford University Press) 64, 139, 314, 319, 320, 332-4, 337, 341-5, 374, 439, *passim*

.... (1988) *The Blind Watchmaker* (London: Penguin) *passim*

Day, Robert A. (**1953**) 'Marvell's "Glew"', in *Philological Quarterly* (XXXII, III, July 1953) (Oxford: Philological Society) (pp. 344-6) **167**

Day Lewis, Cecil (**1953**) *An Italian Visit* (London: Jonathan Cape) **363**

De Quincey, Thomas (1890) *The Collected Writings of Thomas De Quincey, Vol X. Literary Theory and Criticism*, ed. David Masson (Edinburgh: A&C Black) **69**, 211

Dekker, Thomas (1921) *The Plague Pamphlets*, ed. F. P. Wilson (Oxford: Clarendon Press) **71**, 212

Deleuze, Gilles (1981) *Francis Bacon: logique de la sensation* (Paris: Editions de la Différence) 292, 127

.... (1991) *Masochism* (New York: Zone Books) 265, 272, 347, 349, 355, *passim*

.... (1991) *Empiricism and Subjectivity: an essay on Hume's theory of human nature*, trans. with intro. Constantin V. Boundas (New York and Oxford: Columbia University Press) 100, *passim*

Deleuze, Gilles and Guattari, Félix (1983) *On the Line*, (Rhizome), trans. John Johnstone (New York: Semiotext[e]) 100, 334-6, 390, *passim*

.... (1984) *Anti-Oedipus: capitalism and schizophrenia*, trans. Robert Hurley, Mark Seem and Helen R. Lane (London: Athlone Press) 100, *passim*

Dent, Robert K. (1894) *The Making of Birmingham* (London: J. L. Allday) **180** [in fact an unattributed quotation from Timmins, 1866], *passim*

Derrida, Jacques ([1967] 1979) *l'écriture et la différance*, trans. A. Bass (London: Routledge and Kegan Paul) *passim*

.... (1974) *Glas* (Paris: Galilée) *passim*

.... (1976) *Of Grammatology*, trans. G. Chakravorty Spivak (Baltimore: Johns Hopkins University Press) *passim*

.... (1982) *Margins of Philosophy*, trans. A. Bass (Brighton: Harvester Press) 553 (*cit.* [within facsimile])

.... (1987) *Feu la cendre* (Paris: Des Femmes) ***passim***

.... (1987) *Psyche: inventions de l'autre* (Paris: Galilée) *passim*

.... (1991) *Donner le temps 1., la fausse monnaie* (Paris: Galilée) ***passim***

.... (1993) *Spectres de Marx* (Paris: Galilée) 146, 150, 174, 180, 183, 316, 319, 365, 541-3, 557-9, *passim*

.... (1996) *Archive Fever: a Freudian Impression*, trans. E. Prenowitz (Chicago and London: University of Chicago Press) *passim*

.... (1999) with Malabou, Catherine, *La Contre-allée* (Paris: La Quinzaine/Louis Vuitton) *passim*

Dickens, Charles (1986) *The Pickwick Papers*, ed. James Kinsley (Oxford: Clarendon Press) 129

.... (1996) *A Christmas Carol* (London: Penguin) 351

Dirac, P. A. M. (1947) *Principles of Quantum Mechanics* (Oxford: Clarendon Press) **437**, *passim*

Dobbie, Elliott Van Kirk and Krapp, George Philip (eds.) (1936) *The Exeter Book* (London: Routledge & Kegan Paul) 77

Dollimore, Jonathan (1991) *Sexual Dissidence: Augustine to Wilde, Freud to Foucault* (Oxford: Clarendon Press) 354, *passim*

.... (1999) 'Post/modern: on the gay sensibility, or the pervert's revenge on authenticity', in Fabio Cleto (ed.) *Camp: queer aesthetics and the performing subject: a reader* (Ann Arbor: University of Michigan Press) *passim*

Donne, John (1912) *The Poems of John Donne*, ed. with intro. and notes H. J. C. Grierson (Oxford: Clarendon Press); 'An Anatomie of the World' **17**; 'The Flea' 81

Dowling, Tim (2001) *Inventor of the Disposable Culture: King Camp Gillette, 1855-1932* (London: Short Books) *203-4, 227*

Doyle, Arthur Conan (1975) *The Hound of the Baskervilles*, foreword and afterword John Fowles (London: Pan Books) *413, 527*

Drayton, Michael (**1953**) 'Polyolbion', in *Poems*, ed. with intro. John Buxton (London: Routledge and Kegan Paul) *passim*

Dryden, John (1910) *The Poems of John Dryden*, ed. with intro. and notes John Sargeaunt (London: Oxford University Press); 'Dido to Aeneas' *77*

.... ([1667] 1927) *Annus Mirabilis: the year of wonders, 1666*, facsimile of 1st ed. (Oxford: Clarendon Press) 71

Eagleton, Terry (1988) 'The Critic as Clown', in Cary Nelson and Lawrence Grossberg (eds.) *Marxism and the Interpretation of Culture* (London: Macmillan) (pp. 619-31) *passim*

Earnshaw, Steven (2000) *The Pub in Literature: England's altered state* (Manchester: Manchester University Press) *passim*

Eco, Umberto (1983) *The Name of the Rose*, trans. W. Weaver (London: Mandarin) *passim*

.... (1994) *Six Walks in the Fictional Woods* (Cambridge, MA and London: Harvard University Press) **551** [within facsimile], *passim*

.... (1995) *The Search for the Perfect Language*, trans. J. Fentress (London: Blackwell) *passim*

Eco, U., Gould, S. J., Carrière J. -C and Delumeau, J. (1999) *Conversations about the End of Time* (London: Allen Lane) *passim*

Eco, Umberto, Ivanov, Viacheslav V., Rector, Monica (1984) *Carnival!*, ed. Thomas A. Sebeok, assist. Marcia E. Erickson (Berlin: Mouton) *passim*

Eddison, E. R. (2000) *The Worm Ouroboros* (London: Millennium) *305*

Edgerton, Franklin (1952) *The Bhagavad Gita*, orig. trans. Edwin Arnold (Cambridge, MA: Harvard University Press; London, H. Milford, Oxford University Press) **489** [the translation given is *Singh*'s own and neither Arnold nor Edgerton's]

Edwards, Gillian (1974) *Hobgoblin and Sweet Puck: fairy names and natures* (London: Geoffrey Bles) *209, 129,* 333

Einstein, Albert (1920) *Relativity: the Special and the General Theory, a popular exposition*, trans. Robert W. Lawson (London: Methuen) 64, 191, 238, 285-6, 291, 401, 437

Einstein, Albert; Podolsky, Boris and Rosen, Nathan (1935) 'Can quantum-mechanical description of reality be considered complete?', in *Physical Review* 47 [issue 10-15 May 1935] (pp. 777-80) **441**-2

Eliot, T. S. (1935) *Murder in the Cathedral* (London: Faber & Faber) 158

.... (1936) *Collected Poems 1909-1936* (London: Faber & Faber) *passim*; 'The Four Quartets' 158; 'Gerontion' **251**, **403**; 'The Love Song of J. Alfred Prufrock' **393**; 'Mr Eliot's Sunday Morning Service' **221**-2; 'Preludes' **331**; 'Rhapsody on a Windy Night' **153**

.... (1950) *The Sacred Wood: essays on poetry and criticism*, 7th ed. (London: Methuen & Co.) 221, *passim*

.... (**1953**) *Selected Prose*, ed. John Hayward (London: Penguin); 'The Metaphysical Poets' 72

.... (1971) *The Waste Land: a facsimile and transcript of the original drafts including the annotations of Ezra Pound*, ed. Valerie Eliot (London: Faber & Faber) **64**, **192**, 196, **197**, 201, **293**, 429, ***passim***

Ellison, Ralph ([**1953**] 2001) *Invisible Man* (London: Penguin) 346

Empson, William (1950) *Some Versions of Pastoral* (London: Chatto & Windus) *passim*

.... (1951) *The Structure of Complex Words* (London: Chatto & Windus) 348, *passim*

.... (**1953**) *Seven Types of Ambiguity*, 3rd revised ed. (London: Chatto & Windus) **188**, *passim*

Enright, D. J. (1952) 'An Egyptian in Birmingham', in Clifford Dyment, Roy Fuller and Montagu Slater (eds.) *New Poems, 1952* (London: Michael Joseph) **309**

Erasmus, Desiderius (1876) *Erasmus in Praise of Folly*, illust. by Hans Holbein, trans. W. Kennet (London: Reeves & Turner) 18, *passim*

Ermarth, Elizabeth Deeds (1992) *Sequel to History: postmodernism and the crisis of representational time* (Princeton, NJ: Princeton University Press) *passim*

Evelyn, John (1697) *Numismata; a discourse of medals, antient and modern; together with some account of heads and effigies of illustrious, and famous persons, in sculps, and taille-douce, of whom we have no medals extant; and of the use to be derived from them; to which is added a digression concerning physiognomy* (London) **91**, *passim*

.... (1995) *Diary. Now printed in full from the manuscripts belonging to Mr. John Evelyn, and as edited by E. S. de Beer*, (Oxford: Clarendon Press) 134

.... (2001) *Elysium Britannicum, or the Royal Gardens*, ed. John E. Ingram (Philadelphia: University of Pennsylvania Press) 134

Fawcett, Frank Burlington (ed.) (1930) *Broadside Ballads of the Restoration Period from the Jersey Collection known as The Osterley Park Ballads* (London: John Lane) 25

Fielding, Henry (1926) *The Life of Mr Jonathan Wild the Great* (Oxford: B. Blackwell) 325

Fisher, Roy (1994) *Birmingham River* (Oxford: Oxford University Press) *15, 61, 79, 123, 141, 147, 179-80, 283, 285, 519, 531*, ***passim***

* > 'Talking to Cameras' (li 76-80) "centre of the universe... as its centre)" **369**

Fitzgerald, F. Scott (1979) 'The Bowl', in *The Price was High: the last uncollected stories of F. Scott Fitgerald* (London: Quartet Books) **233**

Fleming, Ian (**1953**) *Casino Royale* (London: Jonathan Cape) 338

Foucault, Michel (1971) *Madness and Civilization: a history of insanity in the Age of Reason*, trans. R. Howard (London: Tavistock Publications) *passim*

.... (1972) *The Archaeology of Knowledge*, trans. A. M. Sheridan Smith (London: Tavistock Publications) 3

.... (1977) *Language, Counter-Memory, Practice: selected essays and interviews*, ed. with intro. D. F. Bouchard, trans. D. F. Bouchard and Sherry Simon (Oxford: Basil Blackwell) *passim*

.... (1978-1986) *The History of Sexuality* (3 vols.), trans. R. Hurley (London: Penguin) *passim*

Foxe, John (1837-41) *The Acts and Monuments of John Foxe*, ed. S. R. Cattley, 8 vols. (London: R. B. Seeley and W. Burnside, sold by L. & G. Seeley) 165

Frazer, James George (1913-15) *The Golden Bough: a study in magic and religion*, 3rd ed., 12 vols. (London: Macmillan) 37, 39, 50, 120, 167-8, 241, 374, *passim*

Freud, Sigmund (**1953**-74) *The Standard Edition of the Complete Psychological Works of Sigmund Freud*, 12 vols., gen. ed. James Strachey, trans. Anna Freud, assist. Alix Strachey and Alan Tyson, ed. assist. Angela Richards (London: Hogarth Press) 332, 358, 413, 455, *passim*; 'The Antithetical Meaning of Primal Words' vol. 11 (pp. 155-161) 39, 346, ***passim***

Friedman, Milton (**1953**) *Essays in Positive Economics* (Chicago: University of Chicago Press) 123, 125, 346, *passim*

Frindall, Bill et al. (1980) *The Wisden Book of Test Cricket, 1876-77 to 1977-78* (London: Macdonald and Jane's) 157

Fukuyama, Francis (1992) *The End of History and The Last Man* (New York: Free Press; Maxwell Macmillan International) *passim*

Galouye, Daniel F. (1965) *Counterfeit World* (London: Gollancz) *passim*

Garner, Alan (1973) *Red Shift* (London: Collins) 420

.... ([1960] 2002) *The Weirdstone of Brisingamen: a tale of Alderley* (London: Collins) 426

Gaskill, Malcolm (2000) 'The Problem of Coiners and the Law', in *Crime and Mentalities in Early Modern England* (pp. 123-60) (Cambridge: Cambridge University Press) 91, *passim*
* > ' "social crime"... sanctioned by popular notions of legality' (p.132) " 'social crime'... justifiable as righteous action" **91**

Gay, John (1934) *The Beggar's Opera*, ed. with intro. and notes F. W. Bateson (London: Dent) 25, 49, 121, 185, 325, 360, 384, 385, *passim*

Geoffrey of Monmouth, Bishop of St. Asaph (1966) *The History of the Kings of Britain*, trans. with intro. Lewis Thorpe (Harmondsworth: Penguin) 273

Gill, Conrad (1952) *History of Birmingham*, 2 vols. (London; New York: Oxford University Press) *passim*

Goode, Luke (2004) 'Meditations: from the coffee house to the internet café', in *Jürgen Habermas: democracy and the public sphere* (London; Ann Arbor, MI: Pluto Press) 85

Goodyear, David and Matthews, Tony (1988) *Aston Villa: a complete record 1874-1988* (Derby: Breedn Books Sport) *133*

Gosse, Edmund (1974 [1907]) *Father and Son: a study of two temperaments* (London; New York: Oxford University Press) 369, *passim*

Gosse, Philip Henry (2003 [1857]) *Omphalos* (London: Routledge) *341*, 369, 374

Gould, Stephen Jay (1986) 'The Flamingo's Smile', in *The Flamingo's Smile: reflections in natural history* (Harmondsworth: Penguin) (pp. 23-39) *371-7, 388-90, 401*

Grafton, Anthony (1990) *Forgers and Critics: creativity and duplicity in western scholarship* (Princeton NJ: Princeton University Press) 5, 328, *passim*

.... (1991) *Defenders of the Text: the traditions of scholarship in an age of science, 1450-1800* (Cambridge, MA: Harvard University Press) *passim*; 'Oannes' 440

.... (1997) *The Footnote: a curious history* (London: Faber and Faber) *passim*

.... (2001) *Bring Out Your Dead: the past as revelation* (Cambridge MA: Harvard University Press) *passim*

Gray, Alasdair (1981) *Lanark: A Life in Four Books* (Edinburgh: Canongate) **569**, 571, ***passim***

Green, Henry (1929) *Living* (London: Hogarth Press) 320, *passim*

.... (1952) *Caught* (London: Hogarth Press) 320, *passim*

Greenblatt, Stephen (1965) *Three Modern Satirists: Waugh, Orwell, and Huxley* (New Haven: Yale University Press) *passim*

.... (1984) *Renaissance Self-Fashioning: from More to Shakespeare* (Chicago: University of Chicago Press) *passim*

Greene, Graham ([1951] 1999) *The End of the Affair* (London: Penguin) 467

Grierson, Herbert J. C. (ed. with notes) *Metaphysical Lyrics & Poems of the Seventeenth Century, Donne to Butler* (Oxford: Clarendon Press) *passim*

Griffiths, Stuart and Watson, Donna (2004) 'Coining it in: gang floods pubs and shops with fake pounds' (lead article: *Daily Record*, Glasgow, 24/02/2004) *passim*

Grosz, E. A. (1994) *Volatile Bodies: towards a corporeal feminism* (Bloomington, IA: Indiana University Press) 316

Guffey, Elizabeth E. (2006) *Retro: the culture of revival* (London: Reaktion) 338, 344, 348, 350, 354, 370, 536, *passim*

Habermas, Jürgen (1974) *Theory and Practice*, trans. John Viertel (London: Heinemann) *passim*

.... (1984) *The Theory of Communicative Action*, trans. T. McCarthy (London: Heinemann) *passim*

Hall, Joseph ([1597] 1824) *Virgidemiarum: Satires* (Edinburgh: W. & C. Tait) **23**

Hall, P. A. V. (ed.) (1992) *Software Reuse and Reverse Engineering in Practice* (London: Chapman & Hall) 569, 571, *passim*

Hall, Stuart (1971) *Deviancy, Politics and the Media* (Birmingham: Centre for Contemporary Cultural Studies, University of Birmingham) *passim*

Hall, Stuart and Jefferson, Tony (1976) *Resistance through Rituals: youth subcultures in post-war Britain* (London: Hutchinson) 24, 26, *passim*

Hall, Thomas (1657) *Comarum Akosmia: the loathsomenesse of long haire... with an appendix against painting, spots, naked breasts, &c.* [McAlpin Collection III 72: EEBO 1641-1700; 32:12] (London: printed by J. G. for Nathaniel Webb and William Grantham...) *311-12*, *passim*

Hamilton, G. Rostrevor (**1953**) 'At the Coronation' in *English* vol. IX, Summer 1953, no. 53 (title page: facsimile) (London: Oxford University Press) **45**

Hammett, Dashiell (2000) *The Maltese Falcon, The Thin Man, Red Harvest*, intro. Robert Polito (London: Everyman) 211, 288, 536, *passim*

Hamper, William (1868) 'An Historical Curiosity: 141 ways of spelling Birmingham', in Langford, J. A., *A Century of Birmingham Life* (Vol 1., p.502) (Birmingham: E. C. Osborne; London: Simpkin, Marshall & Co.) **73**

Hardy, Thomas (1920) *Jude the Obscure*, 2 vols. (Vols. 5-6 of *The works of Thomas Hardy in thirty-seven volumes*), (London: Macmillan [Mellstock ed.]) 119, 319

Hart, Alfred (1942) *Stolne and Surreptitious Copies: a comparative study of Shakespeare's bad quartos* (Melbourne and London: Melbourne University Press and Oxford University Press) 383

Hatto, Arthur Thomas (trans.) ([1965] 1969) *The Nibelungenlied* (London: Penguin Books) 130, 311

Hayek, Friedrich A. (1944) *The Road to Serfdom* (London: Routledge & Kegan Paul) 97, *passim*

.... (1984) *Denationalisation of Money: an analysis of the theory and practice of concurrent currencies* (London: Institute of Economic Affairs) 97, *passim*

Hawking, Stephen (1988) *A Brief History of Time: from the big bang to black holes*, intro. Carl Sagan (London: Bantam) 358, 370, *passim*

Hazlitt, Henry (1952) *Time Will Run Back: The Great Idea* (London: Ernest Benn) 348, *passim*

Hazlitt, William (1987) 'On Gusto', in David Bromwich (ed.) *Romantic Critical Essays* (Cambridge; New York: Cambridge University Press) 297

Heaney, Seamus (1999) *Beowulf* (London: Faber) **431** [source only of the Old English: the translation given is Singh/Twigg's own not Heaney's]

Heffer, Simon (1998) *Like the Roman: the life of Enoch Powell* (London: Phoenix Giant) *19-45, 328, 344, 382*

Hegel, Georg Willhelm Friedrich (**1953**) *Reason in History: a general introduction to the philosophy of history*, trans. with intro. Robert S. Hartman (Indianapolis: Bobbs-Merrill) 39, 148, 343, *passim*

Heidegger, Martin (1975 [1973]) *The End of Philosophy* (London: Souvenir Press) *passim*

.... (1985) *History of the Concept of Time: Prolegomena*, trans. Theodore Kisiel (Bloomington: Indiana University Press) *passim*

Heller, Joseph (1962) *Catch-22* (London: Jonathan Cape) 338

Hemingway, Ernest (1939) *The Snows of Kilimanjaro* (London: Jonathan Cape) 119

.... (1952) *The Old Man and the Sea* (London: Jonathan Cape) 346

Heraclitus of Ephesus (1954) *The Cosmic Fragments*, ed. with intro. and notes G. S. Kirk (Cambridge: Cambridge University Press) **106**

Herodotus (1987) *The History*, trans. David Grene (Chicago: University of Chicago Press) The Phoenix (2.73-5: pp. 162-3) 371, *passim*

Hill, Christopher (**1953**) 'Edward Benlowes and his Times', in *Essays in Criticism* (1953, Vol. III, pp. 143-51) (Oxford: Oxford University Press) *116*

.... (1965) *Intellectual Origins of the English Revolution* (Oxford: Clarendon Press) 165, *passim*

.... (1977) *Milton and the English Revolution* (London: Faber) 23, 129, 165, 196, 311-2, 365, *passim*

.... ([1972] 1982) 'The Parchment in the Fire', in *The World Turned Upside Down: radical ideas during the English Revolution* (Harmondsworth; New York: Penguin Books) 165, ***passim***

Hill, Geoffrey (1971) *Mercian Hymns* (London: Deutsch) 139, 263, 313

Hilton, James (1933) *Lost Horizon* (London: Macmillan) **66**

Hilton, Nelson (1995) 'Keats, Teats and the Fane of Poesy', in *Lexis Complexes* (Athens, GA: University of Georgia Press) *261-2*

Hockney, David (2001) *Secret Knowledge: rediscovering the lost techniques of the old masters* (London: Thames & Hudson) *183-4*

Hoffman, Clavin (1955) *The Murder of the Man who was "Shakespeare"* (London: M. Parrish) *192*

Holinshed, Raphael (1968) *Shakespeare's Holinshed... (1587)*, ed. with notes Richard Hosley (New York: Capricorn Books) 273, **383**

Hollander, John (1999) 'The Mutual Flame' in *The Paris Review* (Spring 1999: p.54) **15**

Hopkins, Gerard Manley (**1953**) *Selected Poems* (London: Heinemann) 156

Housman, A. E. (1988) *Collected Poems and Selected Prose*, ed. with intro. and notes Christopher Ricks (London: Allen Lane) 113, 116

How, W. W. and Wells, J. (1912) *A Commentary on Herodotus*, Vol. 1 (Oxford: Clarendon Press) The Phoenix (II.73: p. 203) 371, *passim*

Hudd, Alfred E. (1910) 'Richard Ameryk and the name America', in *Proceedings of the Clifton Antiquarian Club*, 1909-10, (part xix, vol. vii, part i, p. 1) **57**

Hughes, Ted (1957) *The Hawk in the Rain* (London: Faber & Faber); 'A Thought Fox' *163-171*

Hutton, Edward (1906) *Sigismondo Pandolfo Malatesta, Lord of Rimini: a study of a XV century Italian despot* (London: J. M. Dent & Co.; New York: E. P. Dutton & Co.) 137-8

Hutton, William ([1783] 1976) *An History of Birmingham*, facsimile reprint of 2nd ed. (Wakefield: EP Pub.) *passim*

Huxley, Aldous (1930) *Vulgarity in Literature: digressions from a theme* (London: Chatto & Windus) *passim*

.... (1932) *Brave New World* (London: Chatto & Windus) 21, 29, 303, 320 *passim*

.... (1952) *The Devils of Loudon* (London: Chatto & Windus) *passim*

.... (**1953**) *Time Must Have a Stop* (London: Chatto & Windus) *passim*

Jackson, Steve and Livingstone, Ian (1982) *The Warlock of Firetop Mountain* (London: Puffin) *244*

James, C. L. R. ([1963] 2005) *Beyond a Boundary* (London: Yellow Jersey) 157

James, Clive (1986) 'Verse Letters and Occasional Verse', in *Other Passports: Poems, 1958-1985* (London: Jonathan Cape) *passim*

James, Henry (1947) *The Portrait of a Lady* (London: Oxford University Press) 411

Jebb, Richard Claverhouse (1892) *The Trachiniae*, Vol. V of *Sophocles: the plays and fragments*, 7 vols. (Cambridge: Cambridge University Press, 1883-1900) **443**-4

Jencks, Charles (2000) *Le Corbusier and the Continual Revolution in Architecture* (New York: Monacelli Press) 248, 460

Johnson, Kurt and Coates, Steven L. (1999) *Nabokov's Blues: the scientific odyssey of a literary genius* (Cambridge, MA: Zoland Books) *passim*

Johnson, Samuel ([1906] 1952) *Lives of the English Poets*, intro. Arthur Waugh (London: Oxford University Press) **378**

.... (1963) *Johnson's Dictionary*, selections by E. L. McAdam and George Milne Jr. (London: Gollancz) *passim*

Jones, D. M. (**1953**) 'Etymological Notes', section II: '*Fox Fire*', in *Transactions of the Philological Society* (Oxford: Philological Society) (pp. 46-9) 167-8

Jonson, Ben (1983 [1966]) *The Alchemist*, ed. with intro. and notes Douglas Brown (London; New York: Ernest Benn; Norton) **376**

Joyce, James ([1922] 1949) *Ulysses* (London: Bodley Head) 56, 100, 121, 206, **223**, 561, *passim*

.... (2000) *Dubliners*, intro. and notes Terrence Brown (London: Penguin); 'The Sisters' (*gnomon*) 209, 335, 405-6, 461, 527

Keats, John (1988) *The Complete Poems*, ed. John Barnard, 3rd ed. (Harmondsworth: Penguin) 'The Eve of St. Agnes' 421; 'Ode on a Grecian Urn' 187-8, 233; 'Ode to Melancholy' 233, 261-2

Keun, Odette (1924) *In the Land of the Golden Fleece: through independent menchevist Georgia*, trans. Helen Jessiman (London: John Lane) 123, 317

Kierkegaard, Søren [as *Anti-Climacus*] (1989) *The Sickness unto Death: a Christian psychological exposition for edification and awakening* (London; New York: Penguin Books) 423

Klein, Ernest (1966-7) *Comparative Etymological Dictionary of the English Language*, 2 vols. (Amsterdam: Elsevier) *passim*

Klein, Naomi (2001) *No Logo* (London: Flamingo) 137-8, *passim*

Kneale, Nigel (1959) *The Quatermass Experiment: a play for television in six parts* (Harmondsworth: Penguin) 29, 338, 340

.... (1960) *Quatermass and the Pit: a play for television in six parts* (Harmondsworth: Penguin) *passim*

.... (1976) *The Year of the Sex Olympics and other TV Plays* (London: Ferret Fantasy Ltd.) *passim*

Knight, G. Wilson ([1930] 1965) *The Wheel of Fire* (London: Methuen) *passim*

.... ([1947] 1965) *The Crown of Life* (London: Methuen) *passim*

Kristeva, Julia (1980) *Desire in Lanuage: a semiotic approach to literature and art*, (*Polylogue*), ed. and trans. Leon S. Roudiez, other trans. Thomas Gora and Alice Jardine (Oxford: Blackwell) 100, *passim*

Kuntz, Marion L. (1981) *Guillaume Postel* (The Hague: Nijhoff) *passim*

Kyd, Thomas (1989) *The Spanish Tragedy*, ed. J. R. Mulryne, 2nd ed. (London: A. & C. Black) 257, 425

Lacan, Jacques (1977) 'The Mirror Stage as Formative of the Function of the I', in *Ecrits: a selection*, trans. Alan Sheridan (New York: Norton) 358, 388, *passim*

Lange, Lynda (1983) 'Woman is not a rational animal: on Aristotle's biology of reproduction', in Sandra G. Harding and Merrill B. Hintikka (eds.) *Discovering Reality: feminist perspectives on epistemology, metaphysics, methodology, and philosophy of science* (Dordrecht, The Netherlands; Boston: D. Reidel) *207*, *passim*

Langland, William (1886) *The Vision of William Concerning Piers the Plowman in Three Parallel Texts; together with Richard the Redeless*, vol I, ed. from numerous manuscripts Walter W. Skeat (Oxford: Clarendon Press) 31

Laski, Marghanita ([1951] 2004) *The Village* (London: Persephone Books) *passim*

.... (**1953**) Review: 'THE DAY OF THE TRIFFIDS', in Joanna Anstey and John Silverlight (eds.) *The Observer Observed* (London: Barrie & Jenkins, 1991) (p.124) **199**

.... (1961) *The Offshore Island: a play in three acts* (London: May Fair Books) 340

Lawrence, D. H. (1932) *Lady Chatterley's Lover*, authorized British ed. (London: Heinemann) 56

.... (1957) *The Complete Poems*, 3 vols. (Vols. 19-21 of *The Phoenix Edition of D. H. Lawrence*) (London: Heinemann); 'Aloof in Gaiety' **129**; 'Free Will' **284**, 'Ship of Death' **285**

Lear, Edward (2001) *The Complete Verse and Other Nonsense*, ed. with intro. and notes Vivien Noakes (London: Penguin) *passim*
* > 'The Dong with a Luminous Nose' (li 1-26) "When awful darkness and silence reign... the Bong with a luminous nose." **514-16**

Le Carré, John (1974) *Tinker, Tailor, Soldier, Spy* (London: Hodder & Stoughton) 122

Lee, Laurie (1959) *Cider with Rosie* (London: Hogarth Press) 414

Leland, John (1907-10) *The Itinerary of John Leland in or about the years 1535-1543*, ed. Lucy Toulmin Smith, 5 vols. (London: G. Bell) **180**

Lévi-Strauss, Claude (1952) *Race and History* (Paris: UNESCO) 414

Lindsay, David ([1920] 1992) *A Voyage to Arcturus*, intro. J. B. Pick (Edinburgh: Canongate Classics) *passim*

Lippincott, Kristen (1999) *The Story of Time* (London: Merell Holberton) *passim*

Locke, John (1991) *Locke on Money*, ed. with intro. and notes P. H. Kelly, 2 vols. (Oxford: Clarendon Press; New York: Oxford University Press) *passim*

Lodge, David (1989) *Nice Work* (London: Penguin) 296, 432

Lofting, Hugh (1922) *The Story of Doctor Dolittle* (London: Jonathan Cape) 305

Lukács, György (1962) *The Historical Novel*, trans. Hannah and Stanley Mitchell (London: Merlin Press) 148, *passim*
.... (1971) *The Theory of the Novel*, trans. Anna Bostock (London: Merlin Press) *passim*

Luther, Martin ([(1528) 1860] 1932) *Liber vagatorum: The Book of Vagabonds and Beggars with a Vocabulary of their Language*, trans. (1860) M. C. Hotten, ed. (1932) with intro. D. B. Thomas (London: Penguin) 36, 51, **52-3**, *passim*

Lydgate, John (1477) *The horse the ghoos & the sheep* (London: W. Caxton) [Pollard and Redgrave STC (2nd ed.) 17018] 464

Macaulay, Thomas Babington Macaulay, Baron (1913-15) *History of England from the Accession of James the Second*, ed. C. H. Firth, 6 vols., (London: Macmillan and Co.) 117

MacCabe, Richard A. (1982) *Joseph Hall: A Study in Satire and Meditation* (Oxford: Clarendon) 23

MacNeice, Louis (1949) 'Bagpipe Music', in *Collected Poems, 1925-1948* (London: Faber) **297**-8
.... (1966) 'Canto IV', in *Collected Poems*, ed. E. R. Dodds, Vol. XI **1953** (London: Faber & Faber) **330**

Manguel, Alberto (1996) *A History of Reading* (London: Flamingo) *passim*

Marcou, Jules (1875) 'Origin of the name America', in *Atlantic Monthly* vol 35. (March 1875) (pp. 291-296) 57

Marlowe, Christopher (1973) *The Complete Works of Christopher Marlowe*, ed. Fredson Bowers (London: Cambridge University Press); 'A Passionate Shepherd to his Love' **34**; 'Dr Faustus' 81, 192, 194, **195**, **233**, 257, 384, *passim*; 'Tamburlaine the Great Part I.' 69

Marston, John ([1603] 1922) *Antonio's Revenge*, reprint of ed. published in 1602 (London: T. Fisher), (London: Malone Society) 115, **378** [a misquotation: for 'owles' in the third line, read 'crowes']
.... ([1925] 1966) *The Scourge of Villanie, 1599*, reprint of ed. first published in 1925 (London: John Lane, the Bodley Head, Curwen Press), (Edinburgh: Edinburgh University Press) *passim*

Martial (1929) *M. Val. Martialis Epigrammata*, ed. with intro. and notes W. M. Lindsay (Oxford: Clarendon Press) **371**

Marx, Karl (1973) *Grundrisse*, trans. with foreword M. Nicolaus (Harmondsworth: Penguin in assoc. with New Left Review) ***passim***
.... (1981) *Capital: a critique of political economy*, trans. D. Fernbach, intro. E. Mandel, 3 vols. (Harmondsworth: Penguin in assoc. with New Left Review) *passim*

Marx, Karl and Engels, Friedrich (1964) 'Manifest der Kommunistischen Partei', in *Karl Marx, Friedrich Engles: Werke* (Vol 4.: Mai 1846 bis März 1848) (Berlin: Dietz) (pp. 461-93) **557-9**

.... (1965) *Manifesto of the Communist Party*, trans. Samuel Moore [1888] (Moscow: Progress Publishers) **557-9**

.... ([1850] 1966) 'Manifesto of the German Communist Party', trans. Helen Macfarlane, in *The Red Republican & The Friend of the People*, ed. G. J. Harney, intro. John Saville (London: Merlin Press) (vol I., no. 21) **557-9**

.... (1998) 'The Manifesto of the Communist Party', trans. Terrell Carver, in *The Communist Manifesto: New Interpretations*, ed. Mark Cowling (Edinburgh: Edinburgh University Press) **557-9**

Marinetti, Filippo Tommaso (1972) *Marinetti: selected writings*, trans. R. W. Flint and A. A. Coppotelli, ed. R. W. Flint (London: Secker and Warburg) 418

Masefield, John (1919) *Reynard the Fox, or, The Ghost Heath Run* (London: Heinemann) 163

McClean, Adam (ed. with commentary) (1980) *The Rosary of the Philosophers (in the English translations found in the Ferguson Manuscript 210 [Glasgow University]* (Edinburgh: Magnum Opus Hermetic Sourceworks) 376

McGann, Jerome J. (1968) *Fiery dust: Byron's poetic development* (Chicago: University of Chicago Press) *passim*

.... (1985) The Beauty of Inflections: literary investigations in historical method and theory (Oxford: Clarendon Press) *passim*

Middleton, Thomas (1950) *The Witch*, eds. W. W. Greg & F. P. Wilson (London: The Malone Society for the OUP) 378

.... (1994) *Women Beware Women*, ed. William C. Carroll (London: A & C Black) 196

Middleton, Thomas and Rowley, William ([1964] 1990) *The Changeling*, ed. with intro. and notes Joost Daalder (London: A & C Black) *passim*

Miller, Arthur (**1953**) *The Crucible: a play in four acts* (New York: Viking Press) 346

Milton, John (1952) *Poetical Works*, ed. Helen Darbishire, 2 vols. (Oxford: Clarendon Press) 23, 72, 196; Vol. 1 *Paradise Lost* 39, 55, 99, **117**, 156, 188, 196, **311**-2, 429; Vol. 2 *Paradise regain'd ; Samson Agonistes ; Poems upon several occasions, both English and Latin*: 'Comus' **129**

.... (1991) 'The Tenure of Kings and Magistrates', in *Political Writings*, ed. Martin Dzelzainis, trans. Claire Gruzelier (Cambridge: Cambridge University Press) 72, 177, 365, *passim*

Mises, Ludvig von (**1953**) *The Theory of Money and Credit*, trans. H. E. Batson (London: Jonathan Cape) 97, *passim*

Mitchell, James (1908) *Significant Etymology; or, Roots, stems and branches of the English Language* (Edinburgh; London: William Blackwood & Sons) *passim*

Mitford, Nancy (1956) *The Nancy Mitford Omnibus* (London: H. Hamilton) 320

Moore, Lucy (ed.) (2000) *Con Men and Cutpurses: scenes from the Hogarthian underworld* (London: Allen Lane) *passim*

More, Thomas, Sir Saint, [and Erasmus] (1999) *Utopia*, inc. Francis Bacon's *New Atlantis* and Henry Neville's *The Isle of Pines*, ed. with intro. and notes Susan Bruce (Oxford: Oxford University Press) 19-23, *passim*

Morris, Jan (as 'James') (1958) *Coronation Everest* (London: Faber & Faber) 119-20

.... (1968) *Pax Britannica: the climax of an empire* (London: Faber & Faber) ***passim***

Morris, Jan (as 'Jan') (1974) *Conundrum* (London: Faber & Faber) *passim*

Morris, William (1993) *News From Nowhere and other writings*, ed. with intro. and notes Clive Wilmer (London: Penguin Books) 324, *passim*

Motion, Andrew (2002) *Public Property* (London; New York: Faber & Faber) *passim*

.... (2004) 'Song for Jonny' (London: Daily Telegraph, 15th March 2004) 51, 295

Mullins, Eustace Clarence (1983) *Secrets of the Federal Reserve: the London connection* (Staunton, VA: Bankers Research Institute) 425, 431, 435, 444

Murray, Gilbert (1925) *Five Stages of Greek Religion* (Oxford: Clarendon Press) **70**

Murray, James A. H. et al. (1933) *The Oxford English Dictionary : being a corrected re-issue with an introduction, supplement and bibliography of A New English Dictionary on Historical Principles founded mainly on materials collected by the Philological Society* (Oxford: Clarendon Press) [The dates of the supplements and especially the missing words indicates that this is certainly the edition of the OED used by *Singh* in preparation of *The*

Birmingham Quean. The idea is, presumably, that it would be the most likely edition Twigg would have to hand in 1953. The following list of references is organised in alphabetical order of headwords in the dictionary (specific subdivisions of homonymous headwords being provided only where relevant). Many are unattributed paraphrases of the dictionary, a commonplace practise for scholars of Twigg's generation. They are nonetheless marked here as (mild) plagiarisms.] 'ALCOHOL' *329*, 'AMŒBA' *360*, 'ANAGLYPTA' [in Supplement] *221*, 'ANTIMONY' *329*, 'ASTONISH' *359*, 'BAROCO' *257*, 'BIT' *63*, 'BOOK' *168*, 'CASH' *339*, 'CERAMIDIUM' [in Supplement] *233*, 'CHUBB-LOCK' *136*, 'CLITORIS' *367*, 'CLOCK' *191*, 'COBALT' *129*, 'CRAP' *339*, 'DICK, n.⁴' *427*, 'DINT' *74*, 'DIV' *117*, 'DOPE' [in Supplement] *83*, '—EN, *suffix* 1.-6.' *171*, 'ERA' *521*, 'EVEREST' *119*, 'FAIRY' *383*, 'FLUSH' *283*, 'FOND' *277*, 'FORGE, *v.*' *74*, 'FRONTAL, *n.*' *402*, 'FURBELOW' *421*, 'GEEZER' *365*, 'GLAMOUR' *359*, 'GNOME' *209*, 'HEROIN' *99*, 'HUNK' *223*, 'JAPE' *141*, 'JOINT' *93*, 'KARAYA' *117*, 'LASER' *229*, 'LIMBUS' and 'LIMINAL' *439*, 'LINO' [in Supplement] *101*, 'MASCARA' *237*, 'MEERKAT' *405*, 'MONKEY' *405*, 'MOONY, *a.* 4.b.' *58*, 'OUIJA' *115*, 'OUTRAGEOUS' *359*, 'PALM, *v.*' *133*, 'PEDIGREE' *226*, 'PHOENICEAN' and 'PHOENICIAN' *371*, 'PHONEY' [in Supplement] *143*, 'POUT' *276*, 'QUEAN'*53*, 'QUEER' *61*, 'REEBOK' *387*, 'REGALE' *217*, 'RIFT, *sb.*⁴' *79*, 'RIG' *93*, 'SACCHARIN' *281*, 'SADDHU' *126*, 'SCENE' *325*, 'SCREAM, *n.*' *327*, 'SEQUIN' *312*, 'SHAM' *105*, 'SHERIF' *313*, 'SHILLING' *130*, 'SLANG' *51*, 'SUTLER' *221*, 'SWAN' *77*, 'TALLY' *449*, 'TARATANTARA' and 'TARANTULA' *123*, 'TRAILER, *n.*⁹' [in Supplement] *55*, 'TUNGSTEN' *333*, 'VIRTUOSO' *203*; *passim*

Murray, H. J. R. (1913) *A History of Chess* (Oxford: Clarendon Press) 229, 241

Nabokov, Vladimir V. (1955) *Lolita* (New York: Putnam) 348, 474, *passim*
* > 'I am just winking happy thoughts into a tiddle cup' (p.26) "thought on winking... into a tiddle-cup" **132**
.... (1960) *The Real Life of Sebastian Knight*, (London: Weidenfeld & Nicolson) *passim*
.... (1962) *Pale Fire*, with intro. by Mary McCarthy (London: Weidenfeld & Nicolson) ***passim***
* > 'I was the shadow of the waxwing slain / By the false azure in the window pane' (li.1-2): "waxwing" **173**, "*goluboy ekran* (the azure screen)" **120**
.... ([(1964) 1975] 1990) *Eugene Onegin: a novel in verse / by Aleksandr Pushkin; translated from the Russian with a commentary, by Vladimir Nabokov*, (abridg. of 1975 revised ed. in 4 vols.) 2 vols. ([it would, I think, be incorrect to list this work more conventionally under Pushkin as the commentary is the salient feature and it vastly outweighs the primary text] (Princeton, NJ: Bollingen Foundation for Princeton University Press) 153, ***passim***
.... (1967) *Speak Memory: an autobiography revisited*, revised ed. (London: Weidenfeld & Nicolson) *passim*
.... (1986) *The Enchanter*, (*Volshebnik*) trans. Dimitri Nabokov (London: Pan) 473
.... (1991) *Selected Letters 1940-1977*, ed. Dimitri Nabokov and M. J. Bruccoli (London: Vintage) 472-4

Nairn, Tom (1994) *The Enchanted Glass: Britain and its monarchy* (London: Vintage) ***passim***
* > Epigraph to Chapter 1, p.17: "That tiny golden figurine... June 1953" **181**

Negley, Glenn Robert and Patrick, J. Max (1952) *The Quest for Utopia: an anthology of imaginary societies* (New York: H. Schuman) 21, *passim*

Newman, John Henry, Cardinal (1968) 'Rome to Birmingham', Vol. 12 of *The Letters and Diaries of John Henry Newman*, ed. at the Birmingham Oratory with intro. and notes C. S. Dessain (et al.) (London; New York: T. Nelson) 301

Nietzsche, Friedrich (1967) *On the Genealogy of Morals and Ecce Homo*, trans. Walter Kaufmann and R. J. Hollingdale, ed. with notes Walter Kaufmann (New York: Vintage Books) 39, 284, 423, *passim*
.... (1974) *The Gay Science, with a Prelude in Rhymes and an Appendix of Songs*, trans. with notes Walter Kaufmann (New York: Vintage Books) *passim*

Nin, Anaïs (1990) *Delta of Venus* (London: Penguin Books) 154

Olson, Charles (1967 [**1953**]) *In Cold Hell, In Thicket* (San Francisco: Four Seasons Foundation) 346

Omar Khayyám (1949) *The Rubáiyát of Omar Khayyám*, ed. A. J. Arberry, various translations by the editor, Edward Fitzgerald and E. H. Whinfield (London: Emery Walker) **233**

Oresme, Nicole ([(1355) 1864] 1976) 'Tractatus de origine, natura, jure et mutationibus monetarum', in *Traictie de la Première Invention des Monnoies: textes français et latin d'après les manuscrits de la Bibliothèque Impériale*, trans. [French] L. Wolowski (Genève: Slatkine Reprints) *passim*

Orwell, George (1933) *Down and Out in Paris and London* (New York and London: Harper & Bros.) *passim*

.... (1948) *Coming up for Air* (London: Secker & Warburg) *passim*

.... (1949) *Nineteen Eighty-Four* (London: Secker & Warburg) 21, 25, 93, 137, 303, 320, 324, 387, 445, *passim*

Ovid (1982) *The Erotic Poems*, trans. with intro. and notes Peter Green (Harmondsworth: Penguin) 93, **195**

.... (1986) *Metamorphoses*, trans. A. C. Melville, intro. and notes E. J. Kenney (Oxford: Oxford University Press) 155, 196, 225, *passim*; The Phoenix (XV, *Pythagoras*, li. 391-407) 372, *passim*

.... (1991) *Ovid's Heroines: a verse translation of the "Heroides"*, Daryl Hine (New Haven; London: Yale University Press) 77

Owen, D. D. R. (trans., intro., notes) (1994) *The Romance of Reynard the Fox* (Oxford: Oxford University Press) 163-171, 239, 405

Paracelsus (Phillipus Aureolus Theophrastus Bombastus von Hohenheim) (1951) *Selected Writings*, ed. with intro. Jolande Jacobi, trans. Norbert Guterman (London: Routledge & Kegan Paul) *passim*

.... (1960) *Liber de nymphis, sylphis, pygmaeis et salamandris et caeteribus spiritibus*, trans. (Middle High German) Johann Huser (1591), ed. R-H. Blaser (Bern: A. Francke) 209, 245

Paris Review, editors of The (2003) *The Paris Review Book of Heartbreak, Madness, Sex, Love, Betrayal, Outsiders, Intoxication, War, Whimsy, Horrors, God, Death, Dinner, Baseball, Travels, The art of Writing, and Everything Else in the World since 1953* (New York: Picador) *passim*

Parkes, Malcolm David (1996) ' "But you're all mad in Moseley": a study of cultural differentiation in the middle classes and its political implications during the 1980s' [unpublished thesis] (University of Birmingham, Dept. of Cultural Studies) 86

Partridge, Eric (1950) *A Dictionary of the Underworld, British & American, being the vocabularies of crooks, criminals, racketeers, beggars and tramps, convicts, the commercial underworld, the drug traffic, the white slave traffic, spivs* (London: Routledge & Kegan Paul) ***passim***

.... (1951) A Dictionary of Slang and Unconventional English: colloquialisms and catch-phrases, solecisms and catechreses, nicknames, vulgarisms, and such Americanisms as have been naturalized, 4th ed. (London: Routledge and Kegan Paul) 319, 449 **passim**

.... (1958) *Origins: a short etymological dictionary of modern English* (London: Routledge and Kegan Paul) ***passim***

Patten, Marguerite (**1953**) *Marguerite Patten's Invalid Cookery Book: with a section on feeding children* (London: Phoenix House) 249

Peters, Ken (2002) *The Counterfeit Coin Story* (Biggin Hill, Kent: Envoy Publicity) *passim*

Philips, John [1701] 'The Splendid Shilling', in Armstrong, John (1760) *The Oeconomy of Love: a political essay* (London) **82**

Planter, Samuel Ball (1929) *A Topographical Dictionary of Ancient Rome*, completed and revised Thomas Ashby (London: Oxford University Press, H. Milford) *463*

Plato (1997) *Complete Works*, ed. with intro. and notes John M. Cooper, assoc. ed. D. S. Hutchinson (Indianaoplis, IN; Cambridge: Hackett) 84, 126, 129, 184, 277; 'The Cave' (*Republic* Book VII) 31, 127-8; 'Gyges' (*Republic* Book II) 81, 87, 115, 125, 130, 311; 'The Perfect Year' (*Timaeus*) 138; *Phaedra* 195

Pliny, The Elder (1936-62) *Natural History*, with an English translation by H. Rackham (London: Heinemann) The Pygmii (Book VII, Vol. 2) **225**; The Phoenix and other birds (Book X, Vol. 3: pp. 293-379) **372**, *passim*

Plutarch (1859) *Plutarch's Lives*, trans. John Dryden, ed. and revised A. H. Clough (London: Sampson Low) **463**

Pohl, Frederick & Kornbluth, C. M. (2003 [**1953**]) *The Space Merchants* (London: Gollancz) 340

Polo, Marco (1871) *The Book of Ser Marco Polo*, Vol I., trans. and ed. with notes Col. H. Yule (London: J. Murray) **65-6**

Pope, Alexander (1939-1961) *The Poems of Alexander Pope*, ('The Twickenham Edition') 6 vols. in 7 books, gen. ed. John Everett Butt (London: Methuen); *Pastoral Poetry and an Essay on Criticism*, eds. E. Audra & A. Williams (Vol. 1) 'An Essay on Criticism' **68**, **69**; *The Rape of the Lock*, ed. G. Tillotson (Vol 2.) 61, **77**, 153, 196, 201, **209**, 283, **421**, ***passim***; *Imitations of Horace, with An Epistle to Dr. Arbuthnot and the Epilogue to the Satires*, ed. John Butt (Vol. 4): 'An Epistle to Dr. Arbuthnot' **469**; *The Dunciad*, ed. James Sutherland (Vol 5.) *passim*

Popper, Karl Raimund (1957) *The Poverty of Historicism* (London: Routledge & Kegan Paul) 122, 146

Porphyry/Boethius (1975) *Isagoge*, trans. with intro. and notes Edward W. Warren (Toronto: Pontifical Institute of Medieval Studies) 332, 374

Porter, Robert (1643) *A true relation of Prince Rvpert's barbarous cruelty against the town of Brumingham...* [Thomason Collection, British Library: EEBO 1641-1700; 244:E.96, no. 9] (London: Iohn Wright) 77, 165, *passim*

Potter, Dennis (1986) *The Singing Detective* (London; Boston: Faber) *passim*
* > 'A real rathole... new paragraph.' **224**
* > 'The doorman of a nightclub... not blood on his collar.' **224**
* > 'Yes Sir, the ways those creatures gnaw... new paragraph.' **234**

Pound, Ezra (1954) *Literary Essays*, ed. with intro. T. S. Eliot (London: Faber) *passim*
.... (1975) *The Cantos of Ezra Pound*, revised collected ed. (London: Faber) 156, *passim*

Powell, Anthony (1951) *A Question of Upbringing* (London: Heinemann) 320

Powell, J. Enoch (1936) *The Rendel Harris Papyri of Woodbrooke College, Birmingham*, ed. with trans. and notes J. Enoch Powell (Cambridge: Cambridge University Press) *passim*
.... (**1953**) [Speech to Parliament during the Queen's Titles debates.] Hansard, 3 March 1953 cols. 240-8 ***passim***
.... (1967) *Exchange Rates and Liquidity: an essay on the relationship of international trade and liquidity to fixed exchange rates and the price of gold* (London: Institute of Economic Affairs) *passim*
.... (1977) *Joseph Chamberlain* (London: Thames & Hudson) 248, 478

Powell, J. Enoch and Maude, Angus (1955) *Biography of a Nation: A Short History of Britain* (London: Phoenix House) *passim*

Prescott, H. F. M. (trans.) (1930) *Flamenca* [translated from the thirteenth-century Provençal of Bernardet the Troubadour...] (London: Constable and Co.) 373-4

Price, William Charles and Seymour S. Chissick (1977) *The Uncertainty Principle and Foundations of Quantum Mechanics* 291, 423, 440-2, 445, 449, 457, 461, 469, 475, *passim*

Proudhon, Pierre-Joseph (1969) *Selected Writings of Pierre-Joseph Proudhon*, trans. Elizabeth Fraser, ed. with intro. Stewart Edwards (London: Macmillan) 183, *passim*

Proust, Marcel (2002) *Du Côté de Chez Swann*, trans. with intro. and notes Lydia Davis, Vol. 1 of *In Search of Lost Time*, gen. ed. Christopher Prendergast (London: Allen Lane) 206, 255, 396, 561

Rabelais, François (1955) *Gargantua and Pantagruel*, trans. with intro. J. M. Cohen (Harmondsworth: Penguin) 373, *passim*

Rabkin, Eric S.; Greenberg, Martin Harry and Olander, Joseph D. (1983) *No Place Else: explorations in utopan and dysopian fiction* (Carbondale: Southern Illinois University Press) *passim*

Rand, Ayn (1946) *Anthem* (New York: Dutton) 21

Rainey, Lawrence S. (1991) *Ezra Pound and the Monument of Culture: text, history and the Malatesta Cantos* (Chicago: University of Chicago Press) *137-8*, *418*

Reichenbach, Hans (1956) *The Direction of Time* (Berkeley, CA: University of California Press) 285-6, *passim*

Renshaw, Joseph Theodore (1932) *Birmingham: its rise and progess* (Birmingham: Cornish Bros.) *passim*; Tinker Fox ('Civil War' pp. 51-63) *165*

Richards, I. A. (1926) *Principles of Literary Criticism*, 2nd ed. (London: Routledge & Kegan Paul) *156*

Ricks, Christopher (1974) *Keats and Embarrassment* (Oxford: Clarendon Press) *421*

.... (1977) *T. S. Eliot and Prejudice* (London: Faber & Faber) *passim* (esp. Ch. VI 'Mediation' on "between")

Rollins, Hyder Edward (1927) *The Pack of Autolycus, or, strange and terrible news of ghosts, apparitions, monstrous births, showers of wheat, judgements of God, and other prodigious and fearful happenings as told in broadside ballads of the years 1624-1693* (Cambridge MA: Harvard University Press) *25* (footnote)

Room, Adrian (1987) *Dictionary of Coin Names* (London; New York: Routledge & Kegan Paul) *63, 130, 419, passim*

Rostand, Edmond (1971) *Cyrano de Bergerac*, trans. and adapt. Anthony Burgess (New York: Knopf) *155*

Roth, Andrew (1970) *Enoch Powell: tory tribune* (London: Macdonald & Co.) *19-45, 328, 344, 382*

Rowell, Roland (1986) *Counterfeiting and Forgery* (London: Butterworths) *passim*

Rusher, John Golby (1820) *The Adventures of a Halfpenny commonly called a Birmingham halfpenny, or, Counterfeit: as related by itself* (Banbury: J. G. Rusher) *81-2, passim*

Rutherford, Jonathan (1997) *Forever England: reflections on race, masculinity and Empire* (London: Lawrence & Wishart) *passim*

Sanders, John, of Harburn (1655) *An Iron Rod for the Naylors and Tradesmen neer Brimingham* (prob. Birmingham) (Thomason / 246:669.f.19[72]) *passim*

Scannell, Paddy (2000) 'The End of the Monopoly', in *British Television: a reader* (Oxford; New York: Oxford University Press) *123, passim*

Schleicher, August (1869) *Darwinism Tested by the Science of Language*, trans. Alexander V. W. Bikkers (London: J. C. Hotten) *332, 374, 388, 392*

Scott, Walter (1868) *Demonology and Witchcraft* (London: William Tegg) *141, 359, 383, passim*

Seaby, H. A. ([1929] 1978) *Standard Catalogue of British Coins vol 1.: Coins of England and the United Kingdom* (Revised 16th Edition), ed. with additional material P. Seaby and P. F. Purvey (London: Seaby) *76, 107-8,* **130-1,** *249,* ***passim***

Sedgwick, Eve Kosofsky (1985) *Between Men: English Literature and Male Homosocial Desire* (New York: Columbia University Press) *358, passim*

Sedgwick, Mark J. (2004) *Against the Modern World: Traditionalism and the Secret Intellectual History of the Twentieth Century* (Oxford; New York: Oxford University Press) *passim*

Segal, Erich (2001) *The Death of Comedy* (Cambridge, MA: Harvard University Press) *65, 155, 185, 225, 375, 392, passim*

Selgin, George (2002) 'A Numismatic Ramble 'Round Birmingham' (from *Good Money: How some Birmingham Button Makers beat Gresham's Law, created the first successful Cash for the Masses, and kept the Industrial Revolution from Conking-Out*), in *The "Conder" Token Collector's Journal* 7.3 (pp. 28-39) *108, 131*

Sendall, Bernard (1982) 'Origin and Foundation 1946-62', Vol 1. of Sendall, Bernard et al. (1982-2003) *Independent Television in Britain* (Basingstoke: Palgrave Macmillan) *123, passim*

Sewell, Anna (**1953**) *Black Beauty*, intro. J. T. Murray, illust. F. R. Grey (London: Collins) *81*

Shakespeare, William ([1623] 1968) *The First Folio of Shakespeare*, ed. Charlton Hinxman [facsimile] (London: Hamlyn) [The vast majority of play quotations are from the First Folio: a serious weakness where certain plays are concerned, of course. The intention is perhaps to depict Twigg as obsessively attached to certain pivotal tomes in order to explain the transference of this restrictive focus to the poem. Unless otherwise specified, this version can therefore be assumed to be the source of any play quotations. The plays are listed in alphabetical order here according to their generally accepted abbreviated titles.] *Cymbeline* **196**; *Hamlet* 76, **83**, 150, 192, 194, 378, **427**, 455; *Julius Caesar* **191**-2, 194, 273; *King Lear* 18, 150, 192, 195, 396; *Macbeth* 192, **327**, 343, **378**, 383, **384**, **385**, 474; *Measure For*

Measure 76; *Othello* 139, 192, 405; *Richard III* **75**-6, 192, 383; *Romeo and Juliet* **195**, 261, **276**; *The Tempest* 192, **439**

.... ([1904] 1962) *The Complete Works of Shakespeare* [Oxford Standard Authors ed.], ed. with glossary W. J. Craig (Oxford: Oxford University Press) *Henry VI, Pt. 2* **379**; 'The Phœnix and the Turtle' 158, **375-8**, 392, 515; *The Sonnets* 59, 183, 192, 373

.... (2000) *Romeo and Juliet, 1597* [facsimile of First Quarto prepared by Jill L. Levinson and Barry Gaines for the Malone Society] (Oxford: Oxford University Press) **276**

Shand, Alexander F. (1914) *The Foundations of Character; being a study of the tendencies of the emotions and sentiments* (London: Macmillan & Co.) 285

Shell, Marc (1978) *The Economy of Literature* (Baltimore: Johns Hopkins University Press) *111*, 328, ***passim***; 'The Ring of Gyges' *81, 87, 115, 125, 130, 311*; 'The golden fleece and the voice of the shuttle: economy in literary theory' *123, 317*; 'The lie of the fox: Rousseau's theory of verbal, monetary and political representation' *140-1, 163-71, 175, 351*

.... (1993) *Children of the Earth: literature, politics and nationhood* (New York: Oxford University Press) *passim*

Shelley, Mary Wollstonecraft (1994) *Frankenstein*, (1818 text), intro. Paddy Lyons, other crit. app. Philip Gooden (London: J. M. Dent) 122, 146, 415, 417, *passim*

Shelley, Percy Bysshe (**1953**) 'A Defence of Poetry', in *Political Tracts of Wordsworth, Coleridge and Shelley*, ed. with intro. R. J. White (Cambridge: Cambridge University Press) *passim*

Skeat, William W. (1886) *The Vision of William Concerning Piers the Plowman in Three Parallel Texts; together with Richard the Redeless*, vol II: preface, notes and glossary (Oxford: Clarendon Press) 31, *passim*

Skipp, Victor (1980) *A History of Greater Birmingham – down to 1830* (Birmingham: Victor Skipp) *passim*

Simon, Irène (**1953**) 'Echoes in *The Waste Land*', in *English Studies* Vol. 34, April 1953 (Amsterdam: Swets & Zeitlinger) (pp. 64-72) *132, 196, 301, 377*

Sinclair, Iain (ed.) (1996) *Conductors of Chaos* (London: Picador) *passim*

.... (1997) *Lights Out for the Territory: 9 excursions in secret history of London* (London: Granta Books) 320, *passim*

Smith, Charlotte Turner (1993) *The Poems of Charlotte Smith*, ed. Stuart Curran (New York and Oxford: Oxford University Press) **115**

Smith, Zadie (2000) *White Teeth* (London: Hamish Hamilton) *passim*

Smithies, Bill and Fiddick, Peter *Enoch Powell on Immigration* (London: Sphere) *19-45*, 328, 344, *382*; Enoch Powell 'Speech by the Rt. Hon. J Enoch Powell, MP to the Annual General Meeting of the West Midlands Area Conservative Polictical Centre at the Midland Hotel, Birmingham, Saturday, April 20, 1968' (pp. 35-43). ***passim*** [The entire Foreword is framed as a satrical rewriting of this speech. The examples below contain only minor variations from the original]:

* > 'The supreme function of statesmanship… the name and the object, are identical' (p35, li.1-17): "The supreme function of visionary satire… the name and the object, made identical again." **19**

* > 'At all events, the discussion of future grave… the curses of those who come after' (p35, li.17-22): "In any event, the authors… the curses of those who come after" **21**

* > 'A week or two ago I fell into conversation with a constituent… a thousand years of English history' (p35-6, li.22-49): "A month or two ago I fell into conversation with a student… the sitting rooms and picture theatres of Britain." **23-5**

* > 'For these dangerous and divisive elements… the great betrayal.' (p43, li.321-40): "For these dangerous and degenerative elements… the great betrayal." **43**

Smythe-Palmer, Rev. A. (1882) *Folk-Etymology: A Dictionary of Verbal Corruptions or Words Perverted in Form or Meaning, by False Derivation or Mistaken Analogy* (London: George Bell & sons) ***passim***

.... (1904) *The Folk and their Word-Lore: An Essay on Popular Etymologies* (London: Routledge) *passim*

Snow, C. P. (1951) *The Masters* (London: Macmillan) 320

Southey, Robert (1817) *Wat Tyler: a dramatic poem* (London: Sherwood, Neeley and Jones] 55
.... (1821) *A Vision of Judgement* (London: Longman et al.) 55
.... ([1807] 1951) *Letters from England*, ed. with intro. Jack Simmons (London: Cresset) **50-1**, 57, 64, **70-1**, 74

Spenser, Edmund (1890) *The Shepheardes Calender*, facs. of 1579 ed. with intro. H. O. Sommer (London: J. C. Nimmo) **351**, 360
.... (1909) *Spenser's Faerie Queene*, ed. with notes J. C. Smith (Oxford: Clarendon Press) **68-9**, 129, **275**, 383, **385**, *passim*

Spender, Stephen ([1929] 1985) 'The Pylons', in *Collected Poems 1928-1985* (London: Faber and Faber) 363

Spillane, Mickey (1952) *Kiss Me, Deadly* (New York: Dutton) ['*great whatsit*'] 232

Sterne, Lawrence (1951) *The Life and Opinions of Tristram Shandy, Gentleman* (London: Oxford University Press) 81, **107**, **111**, 117, 206, 215, 244, *passim*

Stevens, Wallace (1997) *Collected Poetry and Prose* (New York: Library of America / Penguin Books); 'Disillusionment of 10 o'clock' **155**; 'The Noble Rider and the Sound of Words' *195*

Strauss, Leo (**1953**) *Natural Right and History* (Chicago: University of Chicago Press) 348

Suetonius (1993) *Caligula*, ed. with intro. and notes Hugh Lindsay (London: Bristol Classical Press) **372**

Swift, Jonathan (1948) *Journal to Stella*, ed. H. H. Williams (Oxford: Clarendon Press) 82
.... (1951-68) *The Prose Works of Jonathan Swift*, 14 vols., ed. Herbert Davis (Oxford: Shakespeare Head and Basil Blackwell) 276, 298, 303, 320; 'The Drapier's Letters', (in Vol 10. *The Drapier's Letters and other works, 1724-1725*) **27**, *passim*; 'A Modest Proposal' (in Vol. 12 *Irish Tracts, 1728-1733*) 21
.... (2002) *Gulliver's Travels: based on the 1726 text*, ed. A. J. Rivero (New York: Norton) 19-29, 276, 445

Symons, Arthur (1925) *Notes on Joseph Conrad: with some [extracts from] unpublished letters* (London: Myers) 409, 423

Taylor, John (1643) *A preter-plvperfect spick and span new nocturnall, or Mercuries weekly night-newes wherein the publique faith is published and the banquet of Oxford mice described* [Thomason Collection, British Library; EEBO 1641-1700; 239:E.65, no. 1] 7

Tennyson, Alfred Tennyson, Baron (1969) *The Poems of Tennyson*, ed. Christopher Ricks (Harlow: Longmans) 199, **409**, **421**

Theobald, Mr. ([1726] 1971) *Shakespeare Restored*, facsim. reprint (London: Cass) 383

Tesnière, Lucien (1951) 'Les antécédents du nom russe de la gare', in *Revue des études slaves* Vol. XXVII: 1951 (Paris: l'Institut d'études slaves) (pp. 255-66) 492

Thomas, Dylan (1952) 'Do not Go Gentle into that Good Night', in *In Country Sleep*, (New York: James Laughlin) 115

Thompson, E. P. (1978) *The Poverty of Theory and Other Essays* (London: Merlin Press) *passim*; 'The Peculiarity of the English' *48*, *482*, *passim*

Thumim, Janet (2002) 'Cracking open the set: television repair and tinkering with gender 1949-1955', in *Small Screens, Big Ideas: television in the 1950s*, ed. Janet Thumim (London; New York: I. B. Tauris) ***passim***

Timmins, Samuel ([1866] 1967) *The Resources, Products and Industrial History of Birmingham and the Midland Hardware Districts*, facsimile reprint of 1st ed. (London: Cass) **180** [attr. to Dent 1894], *passim*

Tolkien, J. R. R. (1937) *The Hobbit or There and Back Again* (London: Allen & Unwin) **433**
.... (**1953**) 'The Homecoming of Beorhtnoth, Beorhthelm's son', in *Essays and Studies by Members of the English Association*, Vol. 6: 1953 (London: John Murray) (pp. 1-15) 431
.... (1954-5) *The Lord of the Rings*, 3 vols. (London: Allen & Unwin) 81, 87, 130, 172, 268, 304, 311, 384, 426, 433, 435, *passim*
  * > 'Ash nazg durbatulûk... burzum-ishi krimpatul.' (Vol 1. *The Fellowship of the Ring*, Book II: p. 271): **461**
.... (1964) *Tree and Leaf*, inc. 'Mythopoeia' (London: Allen & Unwin) *87, passim*

.... (1975) *Sir Gawain and the Green Knight, Pearl and Sir Orfeo* (London: Allen & Unwin); 'Sir Orfeo' **50**, 439

Trainor, Sam (2003) 'Cocking up *King Lear*' (Proceedings of 4th British Graduate Shakespeare Conference) (Stratford upon Avon: Shakespeare Institute) 18

Twaddle, Michael (1975) *Expulsion of a Minority: essays on Ugandan Asians* (London: Athlone Press for the Institute of Commonwealth Studies) *passim*

Twain, Mark (Samuel. L. Clemens) (1996) *Adventures of Huckleberry Finn*, foreword Shelley Fisher Fishkin, intro. Toni Morrison, afterword Victor A. Doyno (New York; Oxford: Oxford University Press) 420

Uglow, Jennifer (2002) *The Lunar Men: the friends who made the future* (London: Faber) *107-8, 125, 460, 466, passim*

Vaughan, Rice ([1675] 1970) *A Discourse of Coin and Coinage* [facsimile] (Wakefield: S. R. Publishers; New York: Johnson Reprint Corp.) *passim*

Verne, Jules (1998) *Twenty Thousand Leagues Under the Seas*, trans. with intro. and notes William Butcher (Oxford; New York: Oxford University Press) 206, 301

Vico, Giambattista (1982) *Vico: selected writings*, ed. and trans. Leon Pompa (Cambridge: Cambridge University Press) 415

Virgil (1898) *The Works of Virgil*, ed. F. Haverfield, notes John Conington and Henry Nettleship (London: G. Bell) 'Ciris' 68; 'Eclogue VII' 106, 360

.... (1950) *The Aeneid of Vergil. Book VI*, ed. with notes Arthur Sidgwick (Cambridge: Cambridge University Press) *passim*

.... (1951) *The Aeneid of Vergil*, ed. with intro. and notes T. E. Page (London: Macmillan) *passim*

.... (1989) *Vergil's Aeneid and Fourth ("Messianic") Eclogue in the Dryden Translation*, ed. with intro. and notes Howard W. Clarke (University Park; London: Pennsylvania State University Press) 37, 50, **117, 138**, 167, 328, *passim*

Vonnegut, Kurt (**1953**) *Player Piano* (London: Flamingo) 340

.... (1997) *Timequake* (London: Jonathan Cape) *passim*

Waddell, Sid and Miller, John (1980) *Roots of England* (London: British Broadcasting Corporation) *passim*

Warner, Michael (2002) *Publics and Counterpublics* (New York: Zone Books) 358, *passim*

Wasserman, Earl (**1953**) *The Finer Tone: Keats' Major Poems* (Baltimore: Johns Hopkins Press) *passim*

Waugh, Evelyn (1930) *Vile Bodies* (London: Chapman & Hall) *passim*

.... (**1953**) *Love Among the Ruins: a romance of the near future* (London: Chapman & Hall) 21, 340

Webster, John (1993) *The Duchess of Malfi*, ed. Elizabeth M. Brennan, 3rd ed. (London: A & C Black) **49**, 378

Wedgwood, Hensleigh (1859) *A Dictionary of English Etymology* (London: Trübner) 351

Weekley, Ernest (1912) *The Romance of Words* (London: J. Murray) *passim*

.... (1914) *The Romance of Names* (London: J. Murray) *passim*

.... (1921) *An Etymological Dictionary of Modern English* (London: J. Murray) **283-4**

.... (1935) *Something About Words* (London: J. Murray) *passim*

Wells, H. G. (1906) *The Future in America: a search after realities* (London: Chapman & Hall) *passim*

.... (1933) *The Shape of Things to Come: the ultimate revolution* (London: Hutchinson) 206

.... (1939) *The Fate of Homo Sapiens* (London: Secker & Warburg) *passim*

.... (1942) *Phoenix: a summary of the inescapable conditions of world reorganisation* (London: Secker & Warburg) *passim*

.... (**1953**) *The Invisible Man* (London: Collins) 81, *passim*

.... ([1901] 1954) *The First Men in the Moon* (London: Collins) *passim*

.... (1995) *The Time Machine*, ed. John Lawton (London: Everyman) 215, *passim*

Wheen, Francis (2002) *Who was Dr. Charlotte Bach?* (London: Short) 61, *passim*

Wilde, Oscar (2000) *The Importance of Being Earnest and Other Plays*, ed. with intro. and notes Richard Allen Cave (London: Penguin) 175, 210, 306

Wilkins, John (1968 [1668]) *Essay towards a real character and philosophical language*, facsimile (Menston: Scholar Press) 332

Williams, Raymond (1952) 'The Structure of Complex Words. By WILLIAM EMPSON' (Review), in *English* Vol IX, Spring 1952, no. 49 (pp. 27-8) (London: Oxford Univserity Press) 348

.... (**1953**) 'The Idea of Culture', in *Essays in Criticism* (Vol III, July 1953: pp. 239-66) (Oxford: Oxford University Press) 348, *passim*

.... (1958) *Culture and Society, 1780-1950* (London: Chatto & Windus) *passim*

.... (1973) *The Country and the City* (London: Chatto & Windus) *passim*

.... (1974) *Television: technology and cultural form* (London: Fonatana) *passim*

.... (1976) *Keywords: a vocabulary of culture and society* (London: Fontana) *passim*

Williams, William Carlos (1967) 'Dance', in *Pictures from Brueghel and Other Poems: collected poems 1950-62* (New York: New Directions) 297

Wittgenstein, Ludwig (**1953**) *Philosophical Investigations*, trans. G. E. M. Anscombe (Oxford: B. Blackwell) 286, 346, *passim*

Wodehouse, P. G. (1929) 'The man who gave up smoking', in *Mr. Mulliner Speaking* (London: H. Jenkins):
  * > 'the cat stamping about... caused him exquisite discomfort.': "a cat stamped into the room" **160**

Wood, Michael (1993) 'Prologue', in Christopher Gill, T. P. Wiseman and E. L. Bowie (eds.) *Lies and Fiction in the Ancient World* (Exeter: University of Exeter Press) *passim*

Woolf, Virginia ([1928] 1942) *Orlando: a biography* (Harmondsworth: Penguin) 49, *passim*

.... (1947) *Mrs Dalloway* (London: Hogarth Press) 121

Wordsworth, William (1995) *The Prelude: the four texts (1798, 1799, 1805, 1850)*, ed. Jonathan Wordsworth (London: Penguin) **226**

Wraight, A. D. (1996) *Shakespeare—New Evidence* (London: Adam Hart) *192-6*

Wyndham, John ([1951] 1954) *The Day of the Triffids* (Harmondsworth: Penguin) 199, 268, 338

.... (**1953**) *The Kraken Wakes* (London: M. Joseph) 199, 268, 338, 340

.... ([1957] 1979) *The Midwich Cuckoos* (Harmondsworth: Penguin) 199, 268, 338, 340

Yalom, Marilyn (2004) *Birth of the Chess Queen: a history* (New York: Harper Collins) *241*

Yeats, William Butler ([1925] 1978) *A Critical Edition of Yeats's* A Vision *(1925)*, eds. G. M. Harper and W. K. Hood (London: Macmillan) **37-9**, 115, 138, 157,

.... (1926) [Speech to the Seanad Éireann during the Second Stage debate of the Coinage Bill] Record of Parliamentary Debates, Seanad Éireann: vol 6 (pp. 501-2) **35**

.... (1928) *Coinage of Saorstát Éireann, 1928* (Dublin: Stationery Office) 35

.... (ed.) (1936) The Oxford Book of Modern Verse, 1892-1935 (Oxford: Clarendon Press) *passim*

.... (1950) *The Collected Poems*, 2nd ed. with later poems added (London: Macmillan); 'Adam's Curse' **51**; 'Byzantium' *59*, 65, 77; 'The Lake Isle of Inishfree' 28; 'Sailing to Byzantium' **33**, 37, 65, 75, 76, 77, 138, 215, 319, *passim*; 'Second Coming' 39, 138, 384, 477, **487**, *passim*

Zagorin, Perez (1990) *Ways of Lying: dissimulation, persecution and conformity in Early Modern Europe* (Cambridge, MA: Harvard University Press) *passim*

Zamyatin, Yevgeny Ivanovich ([1924] 1993) *We*, trans. with intro. Clarence Brown (London: Penguin) **495** [The quotation is from p. 136. It would clearly have made more sense for Twigg to cite Gregory Zilboorg's 1924 translation (published by Dutton before the book found a publisher in the original Russian) rather than the recent Penguin edition. It was this version, for example, that Orwell reviewed in the Jan 4th edition of *Tribune* before embarking on his own futuristic dystopia. This obvious mistake was probably intended by *Singh* as the climax of his effect of psychotic anachronism. I would urge the reader, however, to avoid reading too much into a comparison of the two translations at this point... you will not find that one thing you're looking for...]

b.) Internet Websites Cited

Aristasia <http://www.aristasia.co.uk> 348-356; 'Glossary of Aristasian Terms' [27.06.2006] <http://www.aristasia.co.uk/glossary.html> **354**

Borio, Gene (2001) 'Tobacco Timeline', in *Tobacco BBS (212-982-4645)*, [01/04/2006] < http://www.tobacco.org/resources/history/Tobacco_History20-2.html> *124*

Farey, Peter (1999-2004) 'The Stratford Monument: A Riddle and its Solution' [01/04/2006] < http://www2.prestel.co.uk/rey/epitaph.htm>
* > [argument reproduced unattributed] ***193-4***

Jones, John (2004) 'Balliol College History – The Archives' [25/05/04] <http://www.balliol.ox.ac.uk/history/archives/index.asp> *108, passim*

Newton, Isaac (1712-17) 'Representations on the Subject of Money' [03/10/2003] <http://socserv.mcmaster.ca/econ/ugcm/3ll3/newton/newton.htm> *passim*

Oliver, Douglas (1998) 'B. W. I. M. (By Which I Mean)', in *Lynx: Poetry from Bath* (Issue 9, Christmas 1998), ed. Douglas Clark (Bath: Lynx) [http://www.dgdclynx.plus.com/lynx/lynx98.html] **523**

Warren, Robert Penn 'John Crowe Ransom: A Study in Irony', in *Virginia Quarterly Review* 11 (January 1935: pp. 93-112). Source: *Periodicals Archive Online* : [07/06/2006] <http://gateway.proquest.com/openurl?url_ver=Z39.88-2004&res_dat=xri:pao:&rft_dat=xri:pao:article:1240-1935-001-00-000009>
* > 'An irony that may be called historical... noble past.' (p. 110): **72**

Webster, Archie (1923) 'Was Marlowe the Man?', in *The National Review* (Vol. 82, September 1923, pp.81-86) [21.06.2006] <http://www2.prestel.co.uk/rey/webster.htm> 192

c.) Films Cited

Cecil B. DeMille's Samson and Delilah ([1949] 1990) Dir. Cecil B. DeMille (Hollywood, CA: Paramount Pictures) 313

The English Patient ([1996] 1998) Dir. Anthony Minghella (USA: Miramax Home Entertainment) 96

Gone with the Wind ([1939] 1999) Dir. Victor Fleming (Burbank, CA: Warner Home Video) 117

Gorillas in the Mist: the story of Diane Fossey ([1988] 1999) Dir. Michael Apted (Universal City, CA: Universal Studios) 96

Hear My Song (1992) Dir. Peter Chelsom (Hollywood, CA: Miramax Home Video) 240

Hobson's Choice ([**1953**] 1989) Dir. David Lean (London: Thorn EMI Home Video) 78

Invasion of the Body Snatchers ([1955] 1999) Dir. Don Siegel (Los Angeles, CA: Republic Entertainment) *338*

The Jazz Singer ([1927] 1991) Dir. Alan Crosland (Culver City, CA: MGM/UA Home Video) 278

The Killers ([1946] 1998) Dir. Robert Siodmak (Universal City, CA: Universal Studios Home Video) 230

The Lavender Hill Mob (1986 [1951]) Dir. Charles Crichton (London: Thorn EMI Video) 338

The Long Good Friday (1979) Dir. John Mackenzie (London: [Handmade Films] Thorn EMI Video) *285*

The Maggie ([1954] 2004) Dir. Alexander Mackendrick (London: Studio Canal) 342

The Maltese Falcon ([1941] 2000) Dir. John Huston (Burbank, CA: Warner Home Video) 211, 288, 536

The Man in the White Suit ([1951] 1982) Dir. Alexander Mackendrick (London: Thorn EMI Video) 143

March of the Penguins (2005) Dir. Luc Jacquet (Burbank, CA: Warner Home Video) 390

Marnie ([1964] 2000) Dir. Alfred Hitchcock (Universal City, CA: Universal Studios) 416

Midnight in the Garden of Good and Evil (1998) Dir. Clint Eastwood (Burbank, CA: Warner Home Video) 59

Mutiny on the Bounty ([1935] 1992) Dir. Frank Lloyd (Burbank, CA: Warner Home Video) 267

Out of the Past ([1947] 2004) Dir. Jacques Tourneur (Burbank, CA: Warner Home Video) 536
* > "Come in... nice strong hands." **234-42, 536** [The character 'Meta', played by the drag-queen at the Pussy Club, is lifted (name and dialogue) straight from this film (in which she was played by sultry redhead, Rhonda Fleming). Her entire contribution to this book consists of nothing but one long quotation from the scene in which this character first encounters Jeff Bailey (Robert Mitchum) in Eels's flat.]

Pink Flamingos ([1972] 1997) Dir. John Waters (UK: New Line Home Video) 59, 388, *passim*

Police Academy (1984) Dir. Hugh Wilson (Burbank, CA: Warner Home Video) 388

The Sniper (1952) Dir. Edward Dmytryk (USA: Columbia Pictures) 163

Stand By Me ([1986] 2000) Dir. Rob Reiner (Culver City, CA: Columbia TriStar Home Video) 420

Sunset Boulevard ([1950] 1994) Dir. Billy Wilder (Hollywood, CA: Paramount Pictures) 236

The Titfield Thunderbolt ([1954] 2004) Dir. Charles Crichton (London: Studio Canal) 342

The Wild One ([**1953**] 1998) Dir. Laslo Benedek (Culver City, CA: Columbia TriStar Home Video) 338

d.) Anonymous Texts (chronological)

(1643) *Prince Rvpert's Burning Love to England Discovered in Birmingham's Flames...* [Thomason Collection, British Library: EEBO 1641-1700; 244:E.100, no. 8] (London: Thomas Vnderhill) 165

(1643) *A letter written from VValshall, by a worthy gentleman to his friend in Oxford, concerning Burmingham* [Thomason Collection, British Library: EEBO 1641-1700; 244:E.96, no. 22] (Oxford: H. Hall) 165

(1681) *A Proper New Brummigham Ballad to the tune of Hey then up go we* (London) (EEBO: 1641-1700; 773:5) 25

(1682) *Popish Fables, Protestant truths, and plot-smotherers displayed, in a satyrical dialogue between Fly-blow, a Tory, Swift-heel, a Tantivy, Flash, a Brumegeum, See-well, a Whigg, Cross-truth, a Papist* (London: John Spicer) (EEBO: 1641-1700; 819:33) 25, **73**

([1772] 1975) *The Birmingham Counterfeit or The Invisible Spectator* [facsimile reprint of first ed.: London: S. Blaydon] (New York and London: Garland) 81, **103**, **204**, *passim*

([1887] 1995) 'The Autobiography of a Flea' ('A version from the original French'), in *The Autobiography of a Flea: and other tart tales* (New York: Carroll & Graf) **81**, *93*

(1960) *The Epic of Gilgamesh*, trans. N. K. Sandars (Harmondsworth: Penguin) *passim*

(1988) *Flamenca: roman occitane du XIIIe siècle*, ed. and trans. with intro. and notes Jean-Charles Huchet [parallel Provençale and French translation with prefatory matter and notes in French] **373**-4 [The English translation is *Singh*/Twigg's own and not that of Prescott. Prescott's identifaction of 'Bernardet the Troubadour' as author is also vague and dubious: hence the inclusion of this text amongst the anonymous publications.]

(2003) 'The Birmingham Quean' (a burnt, unpublished scrolar manuscript)

www.ingramcontent.com/pod-product-compliance
Ingram Content Group UK Ltd.
Pitfield, Milton Keynes, MK11 3LW, UK
UKHW051257180426
11947UKWH00020B/1761